Affinities

Affinities

A Short Story Anthology

1976 Impression with Headnotes

edited by John Tytell

QUEENS COLLEGE OF THE CITY UNIVERSITY OF NEW YORK

and Harold Jaffe

SOUTHAMPTON COLLEGE

THOMAS Y. CROWELL COMPANY
NEW YORK
ESTABLISHED 1834

L. C. Card: 77-107309
ISBN: 0-690-05248-0

Fifth Printing, July 1976

Designed by Barbara Kohn Isaac

Manufactured in the United States of America

ACKNOWLEDGMENTS

Acknowledgment is gratefully made as follows (pages iv–vi) for permission to reprint material in copyright:

CONRAD AIKEN, "Mr. Arcularis," from *The Collected Short Stories of Conrad Aiken* (New York: The World Publishing Company, 1960), copyright © 1931, 1959, 1960 by Conrad Aiken, reprinted by permission of the publisher.

SHERWOOD ANDERSON, "I Want to Know Why," from *Triumph of the Egg* (New York: The Viking Press, Inc., 1921), copyright © 1921 by B. W. Huebsch, renewed 1948 by Eleanor Copenhaver Anderson, reprinted by permission of Harold Ober Associates Incorporated.

JAMES BALDWIN, "Notes of a Native Son," from *Notes of a Native Son* (Boston: Beacon Press, 1957), copyright © 1955 by James Baldwin, reprinted by permission of the publisher.

ANTON CHEKHOV, "At Sea: A Sailor's Story," from *Anton Chekhov: Selected Stories*, trans. Ann Dunnigan (New York: The New American Library, Inc., 1960), copyright © 1960 by Ann Dunnigan, reprinted by permission of the publisher.

Preface

Anthologists are fond of saying that the successful short story must, first of all, give pleasure to the reader. Yet why do so many college students still approach the "fine" story with the mistrust and trepidation we like to believe they reserve only for more "academic" subjects? Is it the story itself? In a few instances it undoubtedly is. Often, however, enjoyment is hindered by an unfamiliarity with what might be called the fictional terrain. The reader encounters, in any collection of stories, a variety of experiences that seem foreign to him; he is, consequently, at a disadvantage when asked to perceive how a story functions technically or "artistically."

Anthologists who attempt to aid the reader's perception too frequently emphasize process rather than pleasure. There is the inevitable "critical" apparatus which is designed to promote understanding, and usually includes, at the very least, a preface before, and study questions after, each section. Story and student are surrounded by the editor's terms, and learning is unfortunately equated with the application of these terms to a given story. While it is important to grasp certain theoretical aspects of the short story, surely it is detrimental to impose these from outside; to succeed they must emanate from within, directly from story to reader.

Our aim in designing the present anthology is to encourage the reader into a close and pleasurable reading of even the most difficult stories through the guides and signs existing in the stories themselves. *Affinities* consists of pairs of stories (we have occasionally added a third story to a pair) which are comparable in theme, setting, plot, point of view, symbol, etc. Indeed, every pair depends upon more than one significant affinity. The stories are themselves, we feel, all excellent, and include some that have been rarely or never anthologized. *Affinities* will, we hope, increase the reader's ability to discriminate by revealing how similar details, attitudes, and incidents may be used for different ends; or how similar ends may develop out of different details, attitudes, and incidents. The reader will confront questions of theme, setting, point of view, and so on, but these questions will evolve out of the experience of reading, not from the judgments of the editor. In addition, we have chosen to be flexible in our design so that broader affinities exist outside of our pairings: for example, "The Sailor-Boy's Tale" may readily be compared with "Bright and Morning Star," "First Confession" with "I Want to Know Why," and "Mr. Arcularis" with "In Dreams Begin Responsibilities."

The first pairing is generally representative of the affinities included in this anthology. We have found two versions of a universal experience: the delicate relationship of trust existing between a physician and his patient. Ivan Turgenev's "The Country Doctor" is a nineteenth-century realistic depiction of this experience, while Franz Kafka's "A Country Doctor" may be read as a twentieth-century surrealistic transformation of a quite similar experience. As the reader becomes involved in the two stories, he cannot help being attracted to the uncanny resemblances of detail, of the doctors' attitudes toward their predicaments, despite the obvious differences in style and method. We think that the similarities generated from these stories will enable the student to identify those aspects of each story that contribute to a given effect: the manner in which Kafka, for example, will twist a detail in Turgenev's story to create a different attitude; or the function of secondary characters in either story; or perhaps the effectiveness of the setting in contributing to the mood of each story. We have added a third story to this pairing, William Carlos Williams's "The Use of Force," which presents still another variation of the physician-patient relationship, with results which resemble those of the two earlier writers—and yet which in other ways are strikingly different.

Affinities, then, is organized according to this principle of the pair or triad, each story reinforcing or modifying another, so that the reader can determine through comparison how the different stories "work." In the first nine pairings, we have linked stories from the nineteenth and twentieth centuries in which there are significant bases of comparison functioning beyond the element of time. The last six pairings are all of twentieth-century stories, and in the last three pairings we have aligned similar stories by black and white authors. The final pairing, that of James Baldwin's "Notes of a Native Son" with Robert Lowell's "91 Revere Street," might seem anomalous, since both are technically autobiographical essays; still they have the density and suggestiveness of superior fiction in addition to the veracity of autobiography.

Contents

1

The Country Doctor

by Ivan Turgenev

A Country Doctor

by Franz Kafka

The Use of Force

by William Carlos Williams

IVAN TURGENEV *Turgenev used a realistic style to describe the closed class society of nineteenth century Russia—from the common injustices of serfdom to the superfluity of artists struggling to envisage the new. Turgenev was a traditionalist in technique, but his later years, spent in the cosmopolitan presence of writers like Flaubert and James, broadened his sense of the possibilities of fiction. When Turgenev remarked to Henry James that the future function of the novelist would be to sever the umbilical cord between writer and reader, he offered a prophecy for the evolution of narrative technique. His major works are* A Sportsman's Sketchbook *and* Fathers and Children.

FRANZ KAFKA *Kafka's fiction is our clearest mirror of what the poet W. H. Auden once termed the "Age of Anxiety." Raised in Prague by a middle class Jewish family, Kafka received his doctorate in law in 1906, but chose to work as a clerk for the workmen's compensation bureau of the Austrian government. His art was as paradoxical as his life: a bizarre, nightmarish vision of the terrors haunting the mind in the twentieth century. In* The Trial *and* The Castle, *Kafka captured the suffering of a victim trapped by his own guilt and a bureaucratic labyrinth.*

WILLIAM CARLOS WILLIAMS *Williams is a major American poet, but he once declared that his proudest achievement was the delivery of over two thousand babies as an obstetrician in New Jersey. Williams relied on his medical practice to connect him to the natural speech and organic rhythms he perfected in poems like* Paterson.

*The Country Doctor**

Ivan Turgenev (*Russian, 1818–1883*)

One autumn, on the way back from an outlying property, I caught a heavy chill. Luckily I was in the local market-town, at the inn, when the fever came on. I sent for the doctor. After half an hour he appeared, a shortish, thinnish man, with black hair. He prescribed the usual sudorific, ordered a mustard-plaster to be applied, deftly tucked my five-rouble note away up his sleeve—meanwhile coughing loudly, it is true, and averting his gaze—and was on the point of going home, when somehow or other he got talking and stayed on. I was oppressed by my fever; I foresaw a sleepless night and was glad to have the chance of a talk with the good man. We had tea served. My friend the doctor let himself go. The little fellow was no fool. He had a lively and rather amusing way of expressing himself. It's strange how things happen in life: you live with someone for a long time, you are on the best of terms, yet you never once speak to them frankly and from the heart; with someone else, you've hardly even got acquainted—and there you are: as if at confession, one or other of you is blurting out all his most intimate secrets. I do not know what I did to deserve the confidence of my new friend—anyway, for no particular reason, he got going, as they say, and told me a rather remarkable story, which I will relate here for the benefit of my courteous reader. I will try to express myself in the doctor's own words.

"You don't happen to know," he began, in a voice that had grown suddenly faint and trembling (such is the effect of unadulterated "birch" snuff), "you don't happen to know our local judge, Pavel

* Translation by Charles and Natasha Hepburn.

Lukich Mylov? You don't? . . . Well, it doesn't matter." He cleared his throat and wiped his eyes. "Anyway, this is the story. Let me see, now—to be exact, it was in Lent, at the time of the thaw. I was sitting at the judge's, playing Preference. Our judge is a capital fellow and a great hand at Preference. Suddenly"—this was a word that the doctor often used—"a message comes that someone is asking for me. I say, 'What does he want?' 'He's brought a note' —doubtless from a patient. 'Give me the note,' I say. Yes: it's from a patient. . . . Well, all right—you know, it's our daily bread. . . . The note is from a landowner's widow; she says: 'My daughter is dying, for God's sake come, I've sent horses to fetch you.' Well, that's all right . . . but the lady lives twenty versts from town, and night's upon us, and the roads are in such a state, my word! and the lady herself is not so well off as she was; two silver roubles is the most you can expect, and even that is doubtful. Perhaps all that I shall get out of it will be a piece of linen and a little flour. . . . However, duty first, you know: someone's dying. At once I pass my hand to Councillor Kalliopin and return home. I see a small cart standing outside my porch; real peasant's horses—enormous pot bellies, and woolly hair as thick as felt; and a coachman sitting bareheaded, as a sign of respect. Well, my friend, I think, it's plain that *your* masters don't eat off gold plate. . . . You, sir, may well smile, but I tell you: we are poor men in our profession and we have to notice all these things. . . . If the coachman sits up like a prince and doesn't take off his cap, if he sniggers at you in his beard and toys with his whip—you can rely on a couple of five-rouble notes. But this turn-out here is a very different pair of shoes. Well, I think, it can't be helped: duty first. I grab the essential medicines, and off I go. Believe me, it was all we could do to get there. The road was hellish: streams, snow, mud, ravines, then, suddenly, a burst dam. Chaos! At last I'm there. A little house with a thatched roof. The windows are lit up: they must be waiting for me. A dignified little old lady in a cap comes to meet me. 'Save her,' she says, 'she is dying.' I say: 'Pray calm yourself. . . . Where is the patient?' 'Here, please come this way.' I see a small, clean room, an oil lamp in the corner, on the bed a girl of about twenty, unconscious, heat fairly blazing from her, breathing heavily: a high fever. There are two other girls there, too, her sisters—badly scared, and in tears. 'Yesterday,' they say, 'she was perfectly well and had a good appetite; this morning she complained of a headache, then suddenly in the evening she became like this.' I repeat again, 'Pray calm yourselves'—it's part of the doctor's job, you know—and I set to work.

I bleed her, I order mustard-plasters, I prescribe a mixture. Meanwhile I look at her. I look and look; my goodness, never have I seen such a face before . . . an absolute beauty! I feel so sorry for the girl, it fairly tears me to pieces. Such lovely features, such eyes. . . . At last, thank God, she gets more comfortable; she begins to sweat, partly recovers consciousness; looks round, smiles, passes her hand over her face. . . . The sisters bend over her and ask: 'What's the matter?' 'Nothing,' she says, and turns her head away. . . . I look—she's dropped off to sleep. 'Well,' I say, 'now we must leave the patient in peace.' We all tiptoe out; only the maid stays behind in case of emergencies. In the sitting-room the samovar's on the table and a bottle of rum beside it: in our job we can't get along without it. They gave me tea; they asked me to stay the night. I accepted: where else could I go at that hour! The old lady keeps up a steady groaning. 'What's the matter?' I ask. 'She'll live; calm yourself and go to bed: it's two o'clock.' 'You'll have me woken up if anything happens?' 'Of course I will.' The old lady retired and the girls went to their room; a bed was put up for me in the drawing room. I lay down—but couldn't get to sleep, strangely enough. You'd have thought that I'd worried my head enough already. I couldn't get my patient out of my head. Finally I could stand it no longer and all of a sudden I got up; I thought I'd just go and see how she was. Her bedroom adjoined the drawing-room. Well, I got up, and quietly opened the door, and my heart was fairly beating away. I saw the maid asleep, with her mouth open, snoring away like an animal, and the patient lying with her face towards me, her arms moving restlessly, poor girl! I went up to her . . . and suddenly she opened her eyes and stared at me. 'Who are you?' I felt awkward. 'Don't be afraid,' I said; 'I am the doctor; I've come to see how you feel.' 'You're the doctor?' 'Yes, I am . . . your mother sent for me from town; we've bled you, and now, please, you must rest, and in two days, with God's help, we shall have you up and about.' 'Oh, yes, yes, doctor, don't let me die . . . please, please.' 'Good Heavens, whatever next!' But, I thought to myself, the fever is on her again; I felt her pulse: yes, I was right. She looked at me—and suddenly she took me by the hand. 'I'll tell you why I don't want to die, I'll tell you . . . now that we're alone: only not a word, please . . . listen. . . .' I bent over her; her lips moved right against my ear, her hair touched my cheek—I admit, my head went round in circles—and she began to whisper. . . . I didn't understand a word. . . . Oh, of course, she must be delirious. She whispered and whispered, but so quickly, as if in a foreign language, and when she had done she shuddered, dropped her head on the pillow and raised a finger at me. 'Listen, doctor, not a word.' . . . Somehow or other I calmed her, gave her a drink, woke the maid and went out."

The doctor took another violent pinch of snuff and sat stock-still for a moment.

"Anyhow," he continued, "next day, contrary to my expectations, the patient was no better. I thought and thought and suddenly decided to stay on, although I had other patients waiting for me. . . . You know, one shouldn't neglect them: it's bad for one's practice. But, in the first place, the girl was really desperately ill; and secondly, to tell the truth, I felt myself strongly attracted to her. Besides, I liked the whole family. Although they were very hard up, they were extraordinarily cultivated people. . . . The father had been a scholar, a writer; he died a poor man, of course, but he'd managed to give his children an excellent education; he left them a lot of books, too. Whether it was because I put my whole heart into looking after the patient, or whether there were other reasons, anyway, I'd go so far as to say that they came to love me in that house like one of the family. . . . Meanwhile the thaw got worse and worse: communications were completely broken, I could hardly even get medicines sent out from town. . . . The girl got no better . . . day after day, day after day . . . but then . . . well. . . ." The doctor paused. "The truth is that I don't know how to explain to you. . . ." He took another pinch of snuff, sneezed, and swallowed a gulp of tea. . . . "I'll tell you straight out, my patient . . . how shall I put it? . . . fell in love with me, I suppose . . . or rather, she wasn't exactly in love . . . but anyway . . . it's certainly. . . ." The doctor looked down and blushed.

"No," he continued with some animation, "'Love' is the wrong word. One must see oneself at one's own worth, after all. She was a cultivated, intelligent, well-read girl, and I, well, I'd even forgotten my Latin, more or less completely. My figure, too"—and the doctor looked at himself with a smile—"is nothing to boast about, I think. But God didn't make me a fool either: I don't call white black; I've got a mind that works at times. For instance, I understood very well that what Alexandra Andreyevna—that was her name—felt towards me was not love, but affection, so to speak, regard, or what not. Although she herself probably misread her feelings towards me, her condition was such, as you can imagine. . . . Anyhow," added the doctor, who had uttered all these disjointed statements without drawing breath, and with obvious embarrassment, "I think I've let my tongue run away with me . . .

and the result is that you won't understand what happened . . . so I'll tell you the story in its proper order."

He finished his glass of tea and resumed in a calmer voice.

"This is how it was. My patient continued to get worse and worse. You, my good sir, are not a doctor; you have no idea of what goes on inside a doctor's head, especially in his early days, when it dawns on him that a patient's illness is defeating him. All his self-assurance vanishes into thin air. I can't tell you how scared he gets. It seems to him that he's forgotten everything he ever knew, that his patient has no confidence in him, that other people are beginning to notice that he's out of his depth, and don't want to describe the patient's symptoms, that they are looking at him strangely, and whispering . . . oh, it's terrible! He feels there must be some way of treating the case if only it could be found. Perhaps this is it? He tries—no, wrong after all. He leaves no time for the treatment to take its proper effect. . . . He snatches first at one method, then at another. He takes up his book of prescriptions . . . here it is, he thinks, this is it! To be quite honest, sometimes he opens the book at random: this, he thinks, must be the hand of fate. . . . Meanwhile there is someone dying; someone whom another doctor would have saved. I must have another opinion, you think; I won't take the whole responsibility myself. But what a fool you look on such occasions! Well, as time goes on, you get used to it, you say to yourself: never mind. The patient has died—it's not your fault; you only followed the rules. But what disturbs you still more is this: when other people have blind confidence in yourself, and all the time you know that you're helpless. It was exactly such confidence that all Alexandra Andreyevna's family felt towards me; they no longer even thought of her as in danger. And I, on my side, was assuring them that there was nothing to worry about, but really my heart was in my boots. To make things even worse, the thaw became so bad that the coachman spent whole days fetching medicines. Meanwhile I never left the patient's room; I simply couldn't tear myself away. I told her all sorts of funny stories; I played cards with her; I spent the nights at her bedside. The old lady would thank me with tears in her eyes; but I thought to myself: I don't deserve your gratitude. I confess to you frankly—there is no reason why I should conceal it now—I was in love with my patient. And Alexandra Andreyevna grew fonder and fonder of me: she would allow no one into her room except me. We would get talking; she would ask me where I studied, what sort of life I led, and about my parents and my friends. And I felt that we shouldn't be talking, but to stop her, stop her really firmly, was more than I could do. I would bury my head in my hands: what are you doing, scoundrel? . . . And then she would take my hand and hold it, look at me for a long, long time, turn away, sigh and say: 'How good you are!' Her hands were so feverish, her eyes so big and languid. 'Yes,' she would say. 'You're a good, kind man. You're not like our neighbors . . . you're quite, quite different. . . . To think that I never knew you until now!' 'Alexandra Andreyevna, calm yourself,' I'd say. 'Believe me, I appreciate it; I don't know what I've done to . . . only calm yourself, for Heaven's sake, calm yourself . . . everything will be all right; you'll get quite well again.' By the way, I must tell you," added the doctor, leaning forward and lifting his eyebrows, "they had little to do with their neighbors, because the smaller people weren't up to them, and they were too proud to get to know the richer ones. I tell you, it was an extraordinarily cultivated family; so that, for me, it was quite flattering. Alexandra would only take her medicine from my hands . . . the poor girl would lift herself up, with my help, swallow the medicine and gaze at me . . . and my heart would fairly turn over. But all the time she was getting worse and worse: she will die, I thought, she will surely die. Believe me or not, I would gladly have lain in the coffin instead of her; but there were her mother and sisters watching me, looking into my eyes, and I could feel their confidence on the wane. 'Well, how is she?' 'Nothing to worry about, nothing at all'—but what did I mean, 'nothing at all'? My head was in a daze. There I was, one night, alone, as usual, sitting at the bedside. The maid was sitting in the room too, snoring for all she was worth . . . well, one couldn't find fault with the poor girl, she too was quite exhausted. Alexandra had been feeling very bad the whole evening; the fever gave her no rest. Right up to midnight she had been tossing away; at last she seemed to fall asleep; at any rate she stopped moving and lay still. The oil lamp was burning in the corner in front of the icon. I sat there, my head dropped forward, you know, and I too dozed off. Suddenly it was as if someone had given me a push in the ribs; I looked round . . . God Almighty! Alexandra was staring at me wide-eyed . . . her lips parted, her cheeks aflame. 'What is it?' 'Doctor, am I going to die?' 'For Heaven's sake!' 'No, please, doctor, please, don't tell me that I'm going to live . . . don't tell me that . . . if only you knew . . . listen, for God's sake don't try to hide my condition from me.' I noticed how quickly she was breathing. 'If I can know for sure that I am going to die . . . then I can tell you everything I have to say.' 'Alexandra Andreyevna, for mercy's sake!' 'Listen, I haven't slept a wink, I've been looking and looking at you . . . for God's sake . . . I trust you, you're kind, you're honest, I implore you by everything that's holy on earth—tell me the truth! If only you knew how much it matters to me. . . . Doctor, tell me, for God's sake, am I in danger?' 'What *can* I tell you, Alexandra Andreyevna?' 'For God's sake, I beseech you to tell me.' 'Alexandra Andreyevna, I can't hide the truth from you—you *are* in danger, but God is merciful. . . .' 'I'm going to die, I'm going to die. . . .' And it was as if she was overjoyed at the thought, her face lit up so; I was fairly terrified. 'Never fear, never fear, death has no terror for me.' All of a sudden she raised herself on one elbow. 'Now . . . well, now I can tell you that I'm grateful to you from all my heart; that you're good and kind; that I love you.' . . . I looked at her like a man possessed; I can tell you, I had quite a creepy feeling. . . . 'Listen to me. I love you.' 'Alexandra Andreyevna, what have I done to deserve this?' 'No, no, you don't understand me, my dear one. . . .' And suddenly she reached out, took my head in her hands and kissed me. Believe me or not, it was all I could do not to cry out loud. . . . I fell on my knees and hid my head in the pillow. She said nothing; her fingers trembled on my hair; I could hear her crying. I began to comfort her, to assure her. . . . I really don't know what I said to her. 'You'll wake the maid . . . believe me when I say . . . how grateful I am . . . and calm yourself.' 'Don't . . . don't,' she kept repeating. 'Never mind any of them, let them wake, let them come—it doesn't signify: I'm dying anyway. . . . Why are you so shy and timid? Lift your head. . . . Or can it be that you don't love me, that I was mistaken? . . . If that is so, please forgive me.' 'What are you saying? . . . I love you, Alexandra Andreyevna.' She gazed at me, straight in the eyes, and opened her arms. 'Then, put your arms around me.' . . . I tell you honestly: I don't understand how I got through that night without going out of my mind. I knew that my patient was killing herself; I saw that she was half delirious; I also understood that if she had not believed herself on the point of death, she would never have given me a thought; but, say what you like, there must be something appalling about dying at twenty-five without ever having loved; that was the thought that tormented her, that was why, in despair, she seized on me. Now do you see it all? She still held me tightly in her arms. 'Have pity on me, Alexandra Andreyevna, have pity on us both,' I said. 'Why?' she answered, 'what is there to pity? Don't you understand that I've got to die?' She kept on repeating this phrase. 'If I knew that I was going to live and turn into a well-brought-up young lady again, I should be ashamed, yes, ashamed . . . but, as it is? . . .' 'And who told you that you were going to die?' 'Oh, no, enough of that, you can't deceive me, you don't know how to lie, just look at yourself.' 'You will live, Alexandra Andreyevna; I will cure you; we will ask your mother for her blessing . . . nothing will part us; we shall be happy.' 'No, no, I have your word that I must die . . . you promised me . . . you told me I must. . . .' It was a bitter moment for me, bitter for many reasons. You know, sometimes small things can happen: they amount to nothing, but they hurt all the same. It occurred to her to ask me my name, my Christian name, I mean. Of course it would be my ill-luck to be called Trifon.[1] Yes, sir; Trifon, Trifon Ivanich. In the house, all the family called me doctor. Well, there was nothing for it, so I answered: 'Trifon.' She screwed her eyes up, shook her head and whispered something in French—oh, it was something unflattering, and she laughed unkindly, too. Well, like this, I spent almost the whole night with her. At dawn I went out, like one possessed; it was midday when I returned to her room, after taking tea. God Almighty! You couldn't recognize her: I've seen prettier sights laid out in the coffin. Upon my word, I don't know to this day, I simply don't know how I stood the ordeal. For three days and three nights my patient's life still flickered on . . . and what nights they were! What things she told me! . . . On the last night of the three—just fancy—I was sitting beside her, praying now for one thing only: O, God, take her quickly, and take me as well . . . when suddenly the old lady, her mother, burst into the room. . . . I had already told her the day before that there was little hope, that things were bad, and that it would be as well to send for the priest. As soon as she saw her mother, the sick girl said: 'I'm glad that you've come . . . look at us, we love each other, we are pledged to each other.' 'What's she saying, doctor, what's she saying?' I went pale as death. 'She's delirious,' I said, 'it's the fever.' But then, from Alexandra: 'Enough of that, just now you spoke to me quite differently and accepted my ring. . . . Why pretend? My mother is kind, she will forgive, she will understand, but I am dying—why should I lie? Give me your hand.' I jumped up and ran from the room. Of course, the old lady guessed the whole story.

"Anyway, I won't attempt to bore you further, and, what's more, to tell you the truth, it hurts me to remember. The following day my patient passed away. May God rest her soul!" added the doctor

[1] "Trifon" is roughly the equivalent of "Cuthbert".—*Translators.*

hurriedly, with a sigh. "Before she died, she asked that everyone should go out and leave me alone with her. 'Forgive me,' she said. 'Perhaps I've acted wrongly towards you . . . it's my illness . . . but, believe me, I've never loved anyone more than you . . . don't forget me . . . treasure my ring. . . .'"

The doctor turned away; I seized him by the hand.

"Och!" he said, "let's talk about something else, or perhaps you'd like a little game of Preference for low stakes? You know, in our profession we should never give way to such exalted sentiments. In our profession all we should think about is how to stop the children from yelling and the wife from nagging. For, since then, I have gone in for holy matrimony, as they call it . . . with a vengeance . . . I married a merchant's daughter: seven thousand roubles dowry. Her name is Akulina; it's on a par with Trifon. A spiteful hag, I must say, but luckily she sleeps all day. . . . What about that game of Preference?"

We got down to Preference for copeck stakes. Trifon Ivanich won two and a half roubles from me—and went home late, very pleased with his victory.

*A Country Doctor**

Franz Kafka (*German, 1883–1924*)

I was in great perplexity; I had to start on an urgent journey; a seriously ill patient was waiting for me in a village ten miles off; a thick blizzard of snow filled all the wide spaces between him and me; I had a gig, a light gig with big wheels, exactly right for our country roads; muffled in furs, my bag of instruments in my hand, I was in the courtyard all ready for the journey; but there was no horse to be had, no horse. My own horse had died in the night, worn out by the fatigues of this icy winter; my servant girl was now running round the village trying to borrow a horse; but it was hopeless, I knew it, and I stood there forlornly, with the snow gathering more and more thickly upon me, more and more unable to move. In the gateway the girl appeared, alone, and waved the lantern; of course, who would lend a horse at this time for such a journey? I strode through the courtyard once more; I could see no way out; in my confused distress I kicked at the dilapidated door of the yearlong uninhabited pigsty. It flew open and flapped to and fro on its hinges. A steam and smell as of horses came out from it. A dim stable lantern was swinging inside from a rope. A man, crouching on his hams in that low space, showed an open blue-eyed face. "Shall I yoke up?" he asked, crawling out on all fours. I did not know what to say and merely stooped down to see what else was in the sty. The servant girl standing beside me. "You never know what you're going to find in your own house," she said, and we both laughed. "Hey there, Brother, hey there, Sister!" called the groom, and two horses, enormous creatures with powerful flanks, one after the

* Translated by Willa and Edwin Muir.

other, their legs tucked close to their bodies, each well-shaped head lowered like a camel's, by sheer strength of buttocking squeezed out through the door hole which they filled entirely. But at once they were standing up, their legs long and their bodies steaming thickly. "Give him a hand," I said, and the willing girl hurried to help the groom with the harnessing. Yet hardly was she beside him when the groom clipped hold of her and pushed his face against hers. She screamed and fled back to me; on her cheek stood out in red the marks of two rows of teeth. "You brute," I yelled in fury, "do you want a whipping?" but in the same moment reflected that the man was a stranger; that I did not know where he came from, and that of his own free will he was helping me out when everyone else had failed me. As if he knew my thoughts he took no offense at my threat but, still busied with the horses, only turned round once towards me. "Get in," he said then, and indeed: everything was ready. A magnificent pair of horses, I observed, such as I had never sat behind, and I climbed in happily. "But I'll drive, you don't know the way," I said. "Of course," said he, "I'm not coming with you anyway, I'm staying with Rose." "No," shrieked Rose, fleeing into the house with a justified presentiment that her fate was inescapable; I heard the door chain rattle as she put it up; I heard the key turn in the lock; I could see, moreover, how she put out the lights in the entrance hall and in further flight all through the rooms to keep herself from being discovered. "You're coming with me," I said to the groom, "or I won't go, urgent as my journey is. I'm not thinking of paying for it by handing the girl over to you." "Gee up!" he said; clapped his hands; the gig whirled off like a log in a freshet; I could just hear the door of my house splitting and bursting as the groom charged at it and then I was deafened and blinded by a storming rush that steadily buffeted all my senses. But this only for a moment, since, as if my patient's farmyard had opened out just before my courtyard gate, I was already there; the horses had come quietly to a standstill; the blizzard had stopped; moonlight all around; my patient's parents hurried out of the house, his sister behind them; I was almost lifted out of the gig; from their confused ejaculations I gathered not a word; in the sickroom the air was almost unbreathable; the neglected stove was smoking; I wanted to push open a window; but first I had to look at my patient. Gaunt, without any fever, not cold, not warm, with vacant eyes, without a shirt, the youngster heaved himself up from under the feather bedding, threw his arms around my neck, and whispered in my ear: "Doctor, let me die."

I glanced round the room; no one had heard it; the parents were leaning forward in silence waiting for my verdict; the sister had set a chair for my handbag; I opened the bag and hunted among my instruments; the boy kept clutching at me from his bed to remind me of his entreaty; I picked up a pair of tweezers, examined them in the candlelight and laid them down again. "Yes," I thought blasphemously, "in cases like this the gods are helpful, send the missing horse, add to it a second because of the urgency, and to crown everything bestow even a groom—." And only now did I remember Rose again; what was I to do, how could I rescue her, how could I pull her away from under that groom at ten miles' distance, with a team of horses I couldn't control. These horses, now, they had somehow slipped the reins loose, pushed the window open from the outside, I did not know how; each of them had stuck a head in at a window and, quite unmoved by the startled cries of the family, stood eyeing the patient. "Better go back at once," I thought, as if the horses were summoning me to the return journey, yet I permitted the patient's sister, who fancied that I was dazed by the heat, to take my fur coat from me. A glass of rum was poured out for me, the old man clapped me on the shoulder, a familiarity justified by this offer of his treasure. I shook my head; in the narrow confines of the old man's thoughts I felt ill; that was my only reason for refusing the drink. The mother stood by the bedside and cajoled me towards it. I yielded, and, while one of the horses whinnied loudly to the ceiling, laid my head to the boy's breast, which shivered under my wet beard. I confirmed what I already knew; the boy was quite sound, something a little wrong with his circulation, saturated with coffee by his solicitous mother, but sound and best turned out of bed with one shove. I am no world reformer and so I let him lie. I was the district doctor and did my duty to the uttermost, to the point where it became almost too much. I was badly paid and yet generous and helpful to the poor. I had still to see that Rose was all right, and then the boy might have his way and I wanted to die too. What was I doing there in that endless winter! My horse was dead, and not a single person in the village would lend me another. I had to get my team out of the pigsty; if they hadn't chanced to be horses I should have had to travel with swine. That was how it was. And I nodded to the family. They knew nothing about it, and, had they known, would not have believed it. To write prescriptions is easy, but to come to an understanding with people is hard. Well, this should be the end of my visit, I had once more been called out needlessly, I was used to that, the whole district made my life a torment with my night bell, but that I should have to sacrifice Rose this time as well, the pretty girl who had lived in my house for years almost without my noticing her—that sacrifice was too much to ask, and I had somehow to get it reasoned out in my head with the help of what craft I could muster, in order not to let fly at this family, which with the best will in the world could not restore Rose to me. But as I shut my bag and put an arm out for my fur coat, the family meanwhile standing together, the father sniffing at the glass of rum in his hand, the mother, apparently disappointed in me—why, what do people expect?—biting her lips with tears in her eyes, the sister fluttering a blood-soaked towel, I was somehow ready to admit conditionally that the boy might be ill after all. I went towards him, he welcomed me smiling as if I were bringing him the most nourishing invalid broth—ah, now both horses were whinnying together; the noise, I suppose, was ordained by heaven to assist my examination of the patient—and this time I discovered that the boy was indeed ill. In his right side, near the hip, was an open wound as big as the palm of my hand. Rose-red, in many variations of shade, dark in the hollows, lighter at the edges, softly granulated, with irregular clots of blood, open as a surface mine to the daylight. That was how it looked from a distance. But on a closer inspection there was another complication. I could not help a low whistle of surprise. Worms, as thick and as long as my little finger, themselves rose-red and blood-spotted as well, were wriggling from their fastness in the interior of the wound towards the light, with small white heads and many little legs. Poor boy, you were past helping. I had discovered your great wound; this blossom in your side was destroying you. The family was pleased; they saw me busying myself; the sister told the mother, the mother the father, the father told several guests who were coming in, through the moonlight at the open door, walking on tiptoe, keeping their balance with outstretched arms. "Will you save me?" whispered the boy with a sob, quite blinded by the life within his wound. That is what people are like in my district. Always expecting the impossible from the doctor. They have lost their ancient beliefs; the parson sits at home and unravels his vestments, one after another; but the doctor is supposed to be omnipotent with his merciful surgeon's hand. Well, as it pleases them; I have not thrust my services on them; if they misuse me for sacred ends, I let that happen to me too; what better do I want, old country doctor that I am, bereft of my servant girl! And so they came, the family and the village elders, and stripped my clothes off me; a school choir with the teacher at the head of it stood before the house and sang these words to an utterly simple tune:

Strip his clothes off, then he'll heal us,
If he doesn't, kill him dead!
Only a doctor, only a doctor.

Then my clothes were off and I looked at the people quietly, my fingers in my beard and my head cocked to one side. I was altogether composed and equal to the situation and remained so, although it was no help to me, since they now took me by the head and feet and carried me to the bed. They laid me down in it next to the wall, on the side of the wound. Then they all left the room; the door was shut; the singing stopped; clouds covered the moon; the bedding was warm around me; the horses' heads in the open windows wavered like shadows. "Do you know," said a voice in my ear, "I have very little confidence in you. Why, you were only blown in here, you didn't come on your own feet. Instead of helping me, you're cramping me on my death bed. What I'd like best is to scratch your eyes out." "Right," I said, "it is a shame. And yet I am a doctor. What am I to do? Believe me, it is not too easy for me either." "Am I supposed to be content with this apology? Oh, I must be, I can't help it. I always have to put up with things. A fine wound is all I brought into the world; that was my sole endowment." "My young friend," said I, "your mistake is: you have not a wide enough view. I have been in all the sickrooms, far and wide, and I tell you: your wound is not so bad. Done in a tight corner with two strokes of the ax. Many a one proffers his side and can hardly hear the ax in the forest, far less that it is coming nearer to him." "Is that really so, or are you deluding me in my fever?" "It is really so, take the word of honor of an official doctor." And he took it and lay still. But now it was time for me to think of escaping. The horses were still standing faithfully in their places. My clothes, my fur coat, my bag were quickly collected; I didn't want to waste time dressing; if the horses raced home as they had come, I should only be springing, as it were, out of this bed into my own. Obediently a horse backed away from the window; I threw my bundle into the gig; the fur coat missed its mark and was caught on a hook only by the sleeve. Good enough. I swung myself on to the horse. With the reins loosely trailing, one horse barely fastened to the other, the gig swaying behind, my fur coat last of all in the snow. "Gee-up!" I said, but there was no galloping; slowly, like old men, we crawled through the snowy wastes; a long time echoed behind us the new but faulty song of the children:

O be joyful, all you patients,
The doctor's laid in bed beside you!

Never shall I reach home at this rate; my flourishing practice is done for; my successor is robbing me, but in vain, for he cannot take my place; in my house the disgusting groom is raging; Rose is his victim; I do not want to think about it any more. Naked, exposed to the frost of this most unhappy of ages, with an earthly vehicle, unearthly horses, old man that I am, I wander astray. My fur coat is hanging from the back of the gig, but I cannot reach it, and none of my limber pack of patients lifts a finger. Betrayed! Betrayed! A false alarm on the night bell once answered—it cannot be made good, not ever.

The Use of Force

William Carlos Williams (*American, 1883–1963*)

They were new patients to me, all I had was the name, Olson. Please come down as soon as you can, my daughter is very sick.

When I arrived I was met by the mother, a big startled looking woman, very clean and apologetic who merely said, Is this the doctor? and let me in. In the back, she added. You must excuse us, doctor, we have her in the kitchen where it is warm. It is very damp here sometimes.

The child was fully dressed and sitting on her father's lap near the kitchen table. He tried to get up, but I motioned for him not to bother, took off my overcoat and started to look things over. I could see that they were all very nervous, eyeing me up and down distrustfully. As often, in such cases, they weren't telling me more than they had to, it was up to me to tell them; that's why they were spending three dollars on me.

The child was fairly eating me up with her cold, steady eyes, and no expression to her face whatever. She did not move and seemed, inwardly, quiet; an unusually attractive little thing, and as strong as a heifer in appearance. But her face was flushed, she was breathing rapidly, and I realized that she had a high fever. She had magnificent blonde hair, in profusion. One of those picture children often reproduced in advertising leaflets and the photogravure sections of the Sunday papers.

She's had a fever for three days, began the father and we don't know what it comes from. My wife has given her things, you know, like people do, but it don't do no good. And there's been a lot of sickness around. So we tho't you'd better look her over and tell us what is the matter.

As doctors often do I took a trial shot at it as a point of departure. Has she had a sore throat?

Both parents answered me together, No . . . No, she says her throat don't hurt her.

Does your throat hurt you? added the mother to the child. But the little girl's expression didn't change nor did she move her eyes from my face.

Have you looked?

I tried to, said the mother, but I couldn't see.

As it happens we had been having a number of cases of diphtheria in the school to which this child went during that month and we were all, quite apparently, thinking of that, though no one had as yet spoken of the thing.

Well, I said, suppose we take a look at the throat first. I smiled in my best professional manner and asking for the child's first name I said, come on, Mathilda, open your mouth and let's take a look at your throat.

Nothing doing.

Aw, come on, I coaxed, just open your mouth wide and let me take a look. Look, I said opening both hands wide, I haven't anything in my hands. Just open up and let me see.

Such a nice man, put in the mother. Look how kind he is to you. Come on, do what he tells you to. He won't hurt you.

At that I ground my teeth in disgust. If only they wouldn't use the word "hurt" I might be able to get somewhere. But I did not allow myself to be hurried or disturbed but speaking quietly and slowly I approached the child again.

As I moved my chair a little nearer suddenly with one cat-like movement both her hands clawed instinctively for my eyes and she almost reached them too. In fact she knocked my glasses flying and they fell, though unbroken, several feet away from me on the kitchen floor.

Both the mother and father almost turned themselves inside out in embarrassment and apology. You bad girl, said the mother, taking her and shaking her by one arm. Look what you've done. The nice man . . .

For heaven's sake, I broke in. Don't call me a nice man to her. I'm here to look at her throat on the chance that she might have diphtheria and possibly die of it. But that's nothing to her. Look here, I said to the child, we're going to look at your throat. You're old enough to understand what I'm saying. Will you open it now by yourself or shall we have to open it for you?

Not a move. Even her expression hadn't changed. Her breaths however were coming faster and faster. Then the battle began. I had to do it. I had to have a throat culture for her own protection. But first I told the parents that it was entirely up to them. I explained the danger but said that I would not insist on a throat examination so long as they would take the responsibility.

If you don't do what the doctor says you'll have to go to the hospital, the mother admonished her severely.

Oh yeah? I had to smile to myself. After all, I had already fallen in love with the savage brat, the parents were contemptible to me. In the ensuing struggle they grew more and more abject, crushed, exhausted while she surely rose to magnificent heights of insane fury of effort bred of her terror of me.

The father tried his best, and he was a big man but the fact that she was his daughter, his shame at her behavior and his dread of hurting her made him release her just at the critical moment several times when I had almost achieved success, till I wanted to kill him. But his dread also that she might have diphtheria made him tell me to go on, go on though he himself was almost fainting, while the mother moved back and forth behind us raising and lowering her hands in an agony of apprehension.

Put her in front of you on your lap, I ordered, and hold both her wrists.

But as soon as he did the child let out a scream. Don't, you're hurting me. Let go of my hands. Let them go I tell you. Then she shrieked terrifyingly, hysterically. Stop it! Stop it! You're killing me!

Do you think she can stand it, doctor! said the mother.

You get out, said the husband to his wife. Do you want her to die of diphtheria?

Come on now, hold her, I said.

Then I grasped the child's head with my left hand and tried to get the wooden tongue depressor between her teeth. She fought, with clenched teeth, desperately! But now I also had grown furious —at a child. I tried to hold myself down but I couldn't. I know how to expose a throat for inspection. And I did my best. When finally I got the wooden spatula behind the last teeth and just the point of it into the mouth cavity, she opened up for an instant but before I could see anything she came down again and gripping the wooden blade between her molars she reduced it to splinters before I could get it out again.

Aren't you ashamed, the mother yelled at her. Aren't you ashamed to act like that in front of the doctor?

Get me a smooth-handled spoon of some sort, I told the mother. We're going through with this. The child's mouth was already bleeding. Her tongue was cut and she was screaming in wild hysterical shrieks. Perhaps I should have desisted and come back in an hour or more. No doubt it would have been better. But I have seen at least two children lying dead in bed of neglect in such cases, and feeling that I must get a diagnosis now or never I went at it again. But the worst of it was that I too had got beyond reason. I could have torn the child apart in my own fury and enjoyed it. It was a pleasure to attack her. My face was burning with it.

The damned little brat must be protected against her own idiocy, one says to one's self at such times. Others must be protected against her. It is social necessity. And all these things are true. But a blind fury, a feeling of adult shame, bred of a longing for muscular release are the operatives. One goes on to the end.

In a final unreasoning assault I overpowered the child's neck and jaws. I forced the heavy silver spoon back of her teeth and down her throat till she gagged. And there it was—both tonsils covered with membrane. She had fought valiantly to keep me from knowing her secret. She had been hiding that sore throat for three days at least and lying to her parents in order to escape just such an outcome as this.

Now truly she *was* furious. She had been on the defensive before but now she attacked. Tried to get off her father's lap and fly at me while tears of defeat blinded her eyes.

2

A Passion in the Desert

by Honoré de Balzac

Love of Life

by Jack London

HONORÉ DE BALZAC *In 1845, Balzac wrote that his public would one day realize that he was more of an historian than a novelist; and through his own boisterous quarrel with his age he recorded the first half of the nineteenth century in France with a graphic eye. In his cycle of novels,* The Human Comedy, *Balzac capably investigated such diverse fields as philosophy and physiology, and documented a concern for environmental cause and social consequence that makes him a precursor of Naturalism. The best account of his unorthodox involvements is by Andre Maurois in* Prometheus: The Life of Balzac, *1965.*

JACK LONDON *London's personal adventures are as remarkable as his literary activity (which though considerable, was uneven): childhood poverty in San Francisco, shipping out to the Far East as a teenager, later struggling with alcoholism, being jailed as a vagrant, going to the Alaskan gold rush at twenty-one to discover the subjects for his first accepted stories. In later years, London vigorously identified himself with socialist causes, but in his writing he tended to dramatize the lives of Nietzchean supermen more often than the class struggle. His best works are* Martin Eden *and* The Sea Wolf.

A Passion in the Desert

Honoré de Balzac (*French, 1799–1850*)

"The whole show is dreadful," she cried, coming out of the menagerie of M. Martin. She had just been looking at that daring speculator "working with his hyena"—to speak in the style of the program.

"By what means," she continued, "can we have tamed these animals to such a point as to be certain of their affection for—."

"What seems to you a problem," said I, interrupting, "is really quite natural."

"Oh!" she cried, letting an incredulous smile wander over her lips.

"You think that beasts are wholly without passions?" I asked her. "Quite the reverse; we can communicate to them all the vices arising in our own state of civilization."

She looked at me with an air of astonishment.

"Nevertheless," I continued, "the first time I saw M. Martin, I admit, like you, I did give vent to an exclamation of surprise. I found myself next to an old soldier with the right leg amputated, who had come in with me. His face had struck me. He had one of those intrepid heads, stamped with the seal of warfare, and on which the battles of Napoleon are written. Besides, he had that frank good-humored expression which always impresses me favorably. He was without doubt one of those troopers who are surprised at nothing, who find matter for laughter in the contortions of a dying comrade, who bury or plunder him quite light-heartedly, who stand intrepidly in the way of bullets; in fact, one of those men who waste no time in deliberation, and would not hesitate to make friends with the devil himself. After looking very attentively at the proprietor of the menagerie getting out of his box, my companion pursed up his lips with an air of mockery and contempt, with that peculiar and expressive twist which superior people assume to show they are not taken in. Then when I was expatiating on the courage of M. Martin, he smiled, shook his head knowingly, and said, 'Well known.'

"How 'well known'?" I said. "If you would only explain to me the mystery I should be vastly obliged."

"After a few minutes, during which we made acquaintance, we went to dine at the first *restaurateur's* whose shop caught our eye. At dessert a bottle of champagne completely refreshed and brightened up the memories of this odd old soldier. He told me his story and I said he had every reason to exclaim, 'Well known.'"

When she got home, she teased me to that extent and made so many promises, that I consented to communicate to her the old soldier's confidences. Next day she received the following episode of an epic which one might call "The Frenchman in Egypt."

During the expedition in Upper Egypt under General Desaix, a Provençal soldier fell into the hands of the Mangrabins, and was taken by these Arabs into the deserts beyond the falls of the Nile.

In order to place a sufficient distance between themselves and the French army, the Mangrabins made forced marches, and only rested during the night. They camped round a well overshadowed by palm trees under which they had previously concealed a store of provisions. Not surmising that the notion of flight would occur to their prisoner, they contented themselves with binding his hands, and after eating a few dates, and giving provender to their horses, went to sleep.

When the brave Provençal saw that his enemies were no longer watching him, he made use of his teeth to steal a scimitar, fixed the blade between his knees, and cut the cords which prevented using his hands; in a moment he was free. He at once seized a rifle and dagger, then taking the precaution to provide himself with a sack of dried dates, oats, and powder and shot, and to fasten a scimitar to his waist, he leaped onto a horse, and spurred on vigorously in the direction where he thought to find the French army. So impatient was he to see a bivouac again that he pressed on the already tired courser at such speed that its flanks were lacerated with his spurs, and at last the poor animal died, leaving the Frenchman alone in the desert. After walking some time in the sand with all the courage of an escaped convict, the soldier was obliged to stop, as the day had already ended. In spite of the beauty of an oriental sky at night, he felt he had not strength enough to go on. Fortunately he had been able to find a small hill, on the summit of which a few palm trees shot up into the air; it was their verdure seen from afar which had brought hope and consolation to his heart. His fatigue was so great that he lay down upon a rock of granite, capriciously cut out like a camp-bed; there he fell asleep without taking any precaution to defend himself while he slept. He had made the sacrifice of his life. His last thought was one of regret. He repented having left the Mangrabins, whose nomad life seemed to smile on him now that he was afar from them and without help. He was awakened by the sun, whose pitiless rays fell with all their force on the granite and produced an intolerable heat—for he had had the stupidity to place himself inversely to the shadow thrown by the verdant majestic heads of the palm trees. He looked at the solitary trees and shuddered—they reminded him of the graceful shafts crowned with foliage which characterize the Saracen columns in the cathedral of Aries.

But when, after counting the palm trees, he cast his eye around him, the most horrible despair was infused into his soul. Before him stretched an ocean without limit. The dark sand of the desert spread farther than sight could reach in every direction, and glittered like steel struck with a bright light. It might have been a sea of looking-glass, or lakes melted together in a mirror. A fiery vapor carried up in streaks made a perpetual whirlwind over the quivering land. The sky was lit with an oriental splendor of insupportable purity, leaving naught for the imagination to desire. Heaven and earth were on fire.

The silence was awful in its wild and terrible majesty. Infinity, immensity, closed in upon the soul from every side. Not a cloud in the sky, not a breath in the air, not a flaw on the bosom of the sand, ever moving in diminutive waves; the horizon ended as at sea on a clear day, with one line of light, definite as the cut of a sword.

The Provençal threw his arms around the trunk of one of the palm trees, as though it were the body of a friend, and then in the shelter of the thin straight shadow that the palm cast upon the granite, he wept. Then sitting down he remained as he was, contemplating with profound sadness the implacable scene, which was all he had to look upon. He cried aloud, to measure the solitude.

His voice, lost in the hollows of the hill, sounded faintly, and aroused no echo—the echo was in his own heart. The Provençal was twenty-two years old;—he loaded his carbine.

"There'll be time enough," he said to himself, laying on the ground the weapon which alone could bring him deliverance.

Looking by turns at the black expanse and the blue expanse, the soldier dreamed of France—he smelt with delight the gutters of Paris—he remembered the towns through which he had passed, the faces of his fellow-soldiers, the most minute details of his life. His southern fancy soon showed him the stones of his beloved Provence, in the play of the heat which waved over the spread sheet of the desert. Fearing the danger of this cruel mirage, he went down the opposite side of the hill to that by which he had come up the day before. The remains of a rug showed that this place of refuge had at one time been inhabited; at a short distance he saw some palm trees full of dates. Then the instinct which binds us to life awoke again in his heart. He hoped to live long enough to await the passing of some Arabs, or perhaps he might hear the sound of cannon; for at this time Bonaparte was traversing Egypt.

This thought gave him new life. The palm tree seemed to bend with the weight of the ripe fruit. He shook some of it down. When he tasted this unhoped-for manna, he felt sure that the palms had been cultivated by a former inhabitant—the savory, fresh meat of the dates was proof of the care of his predecessor. He passed suddenly from dark despair to an almost insane joy. He went up again to the top of the hill, and spent the rest of the day in cutting down one of the sterile palm trees, which the night before had served him for shelter. A vague memory made him think of the animals of the desert; and in case they might come to drink at the spring, visible from the base of the rocks but lost farther down, he resolved to guard himself from their visits by placing a barrier at the entrance of his hermitage.

In spite of his diligence, and the strength which the fear of being devoured asleep gave him, he was unable to cut the palm in pieces, though he succeeded in cutting it down. At eventide the king of the desert fell; the sound of its fall resounded far and wide, like a sign in the solitude; the soldier shuddered as though he had heard some voice predicting woe.

But like an heir who does not long bewail a deceased parent, he tore off from this beautiful tree the tall broad green leaves which are its poetic adornment, and used them to mend the mat on which he was to sleep.

Fatigued by the heat and his work, he fell asleep under the red curtains of his wet cave.

In the middle of the night his sleep was troubled by an extraordinary noise; he sat up, and the deep silence around him allowed him to distinguish the alternative accents of a respiration whose savage energy could not belong to a human creature.

A profound terror, increased still further by the darkness, the silence, and his waking images, froze his heart within him. He almost felt his hair stand on end, when by straining his eyes to their utmost he perceived through the shadows two faint yellow lights. At first he attributed these lights to the reflection of his own pupils, but soon the vivid brilliance of the night aided him gradually to distinguish the objects around him in the cave, and he beheld a huge animal lying but two steps from him. Was it a lion, a tiger, or a crocodile?

The Provençal was not educated enough to know under what species his enemy ought to be classed; but his fright was all the greater, as his ignorance led him to imagine all terrors at once; he endured a cruel torture, noting every variation of the breathing close to him without daring to make the slightest movement. An odor, pungent like that of a fox, but more penetrating, profounder—so to speak—filled the cave, and when the Provençal became sensible of this, his terror reached its height, for he could not longer doubt the proximity of a terrible companion, whose royal dwelling served him for shelter.

Presently the reflection of the moon, descending on the horizon, lit up the den, rendering gradually visible and resplendent the spotted skin of a panther.

The lion of Egypt slept, curled up like a big dog, the peaceful possessor of a sumptuous niche at the gate of an hotel; its eyes opened for a moment and closed again; its face was turned toward the man. A thousand confused thoughts passed through the Frenchman's mind; first he thought of killing it with a bullet from his gun, but he saw there was not enough distance between them for him to take proper aim—the shot would miss the mark. And if it were to wake!—the thought made his limbs rigid. He listened to his own heart beating in the midst of the silence, and cursed the too violent pulsations which the flow of blood brought on, fearing to disturb that sleep which allowed him time to think of some means of escape.

Twice he placed his hand on his scimitar, intending to cut off the head of his enemy; but the difficulty of cutting the stiff, short hair compelled him to abandon this daring project. To miss would be to die for *certain,* he thought; he preferred the chances of fair fight, and made up his mind to wait till morning; the morning did not leave him long to wait.

He could now examine the panther at ease; its muzzle was smeared with blood.

"She's had a good dinner," he thought, without troubling himself as to whether her feast might have been on human flesh. "She won't be hungry when she gets up."

It was a female. The fur on her belly and flanks was glistening white; many small marks like velvet formed beautiful bracelets round her feet; her sinuous tail was also white, ending with black rings; the overpart of her dress, yellow like unburnished gold, very lissom and soft, had the characteristic blotches in the form of rosettes, which distinguish the panther from every other feline species.

This tranquil and formidable hostess snored in an attitude as graceful as that of a cat lying on a cushion. Her blood-stained paws, nervous and well-armed, were stretched out before her face, which rested upon them and from which radiated her straight, slender whiskers, like threads of silver.

If she had been like that in a cage, the Provençal would doubtless have admired the grace of the animal, and the vigorous contrasts of vivid color which gave her robe an imperial splendor; but just then his sight was troubled by her sinister appearance.

The presence of the panther, even asleep, could not fail to produce the effect which the magnetic eyes of the serpent are said to have on the nightingale.

For a moment the courage of the soldier began to fail before this danger, though no doubt it would have risen at the mouth of a cannon charged with shell. Nevertheless, a bold thought brought daylight to his soul and sealed up the source of the cold sweat which sprang forth on his brow. Like men driven to bay who defy death and offer their body to the smiter, so he, seeing in this merely a tragic episode, resolved to play his part with honor to the last.

"The day before yesterday the Arabs would have killed me perhaps," he said; so considering himself as good as dead already, he waited bravely, with excited curiosity, his enemy's awakening.

When the sun appeared, the panther suddenly opened her eyes; then she put out her paws with energy, as if to stretch them and get rid of cramp. At last she yawned, showing the formidable apparatus of her teeth and pointed tongue, rough as a file.

"A regular *petite maîtresse,*" thought the Frenchman, seeing her roll herself about so softly and coquettishly. She licked off the blood which stained her paws and muzzle, and scratched her head with reiterated gestures full of prettiness. "All right, make a little toilet," the Frenchman said to himself, beginning to recover his gaiety with his courage; "we'll say good morning to each other presently," and he seized the small, short dagger which he had taken from the Mangrabins. At this moment the panther turned her head toward the man and looked at him fixedly without moving.

The rigidity of her metallic eyes and their insupportable luster made him shudder, especially when the animal walked toward him. But he looked at her caressingly, staring into her eyes in order to magnetize her, and let her come quite close to him; then with a movement both gentle and amorous, as though he were caressing the most beautiful of women, he passed his hand over her whole body, from the head to the tail, scratching the flexible vertebrae which divided the panther's yellow back. The animal waved her tail voluptuously, and her eyes grew gentle; and when for the third time the Frenchman accomplished this interesting flattery, she gave forth one of those purrings by which our cats express their pleasure; but this murmur issued from a throat so powerful and so deep, that it resounded through the cave like the last vibrations of an organ in a church. The man, understanding the importance of his caresses, redoubled them in such a way as to surprise and stupefy his imperious courtesan. When he felt sure of having extinguished the ferocity of his capricious companion, whose hunger had so fortunately been satisfied the day before, he got up to go out of the cave; the panther let him go out, but when he had reached the summit of the hill she sprang with the lightness of a sparrow hopping from twig to twig, and rubbed herself against his legs, putting up her back after the manner of all the race of cats. Then regarding her guest with eyes whose glare had softened a little, she gave vent to that wild cry which naturalists compare to the grating of a saw.

"She is exacting," said the Frenchman, smilingly.

He was bold enough to play with her ears; he caressed her belly and scratched her head as hard as he could.

When he saw that he was successful, he tickled her skull with the point of his dagger, watching for the right moment to kill her, but the hardness of her bones made him tremble for his success.

The sultana of the desert showed herself gracious to her slave; she lifted her head, stretched out her neck, and manifested her delight by the tranquillity of her attitude. It suddenly occurred to the soldier that to kill this savage princess with one blow he must poignard her in the throat.

He raised the blade, when the panther, satisfied no doubt, laid herself gracefully at his feet, and cast up at him glances in which, in spite of their natural fierceness, was mingled confusedly a kind of good-will. The poor Provençal ate his dates, leaning against one of the palm trees, and casting his eyes alternately on the desert in quest of some liberator and on his terrible companion to watch her uncertain clemency.

The panther looked at the place where the date stones fell, and every time that he threw one down her eyes expressed an incredible mistrust.

She examined the man with an almost commercial prudence. However, this examination was favorable to him, for when he had finished his meager meal she licked his boots with her powerful rough tongue, brushing off with marvellous skill the dust gathered in the creases.

"Ah, but when she's really hungry!" thought the Frenchman. In spite of the shudder this thought caused him, the soldier began to measure curiously the proportions of the panther, certainly one of the most splendid specimens of its race. She was three feet high and four feet long without counting her tail; this powerful weapon, rounded like a cudgel, was nearly three feet long. The head, large as that of a lioness, was distinguished by a rare expression of refinement. The cold cruelty of a tiger was dominant, it was true but there was also a vague resemblance to the face of a sensual woman. Indeed, the face of this solitary queen had something of the gaiety of a drunken Nero: she had satiated herself with blood, and she wanted to play.

The soldier tried if he might walk up and down, and the panther left him free, contenting herself with following him with her eyes, less like a faithful dog than a big Angora cat, observing everything and every movement of her master.

When he looked around, he saw, by the spring, the remains of his horse; the panther had dragged the carcass all that way; about two-thirds of it had been devoured already. The sight reassured him.

It was easy to explain the panther's absence, and the respect she had had for him while he slept. The first piece of good luck emboldened him to tempt the future, and he conceived the wild hope of continuing on good terms with the panther during the entire day, neglecting no means of taming her, and remaining in her good graces.

He returned to her, and had the unspeakable joy of seeing her wag her tail with an almost imperceptible movement at his approach. He sat down then, without fear, by her side, and they began to play together; he took her paws and muzzle, pulled her ears, rolled her over on her back, stroked her warm, delicate flanks. She let him do whatever he liked, and when he began to stroke the hair on her feet she drew her claws in carefully.

The man, keeping the dagger in one hand, thought to plunge it into the belly of the too-confiding panther, but he was afraid that he would be immediately strangled in her last conclusive struggle; besides, he felt in his heart a sort of remorse which bid him respect a creature that had done him no harm. He seemed to have found a friend, in a boundless desert; half unconsciously he thought of his first sweetheart, whom he had nicknamed "Mignonne" by way of contrast, because she was so atrociously jealous that all the time of their love he was in fear of the knife with which she had always threatened him.

This memory of his early days suggested to him the idea of making the young panther answer to this name, now that he began to admire with less terror her swiftness, suppleness, and softness. Toward the end of the day he had familiarized himself with his perilous position; he now almost liked the painfulness of it. At last his companion had got into the habit of looking up at him whenever he cried in a falsetto voice, "Mignonne."

At the setting of the sun Mignonne gave, several times running, a profound melancholy cry. "She's been well brought up," said the light-hearted soldier; "she says her prayers." But this mental joke only occurred to him when he noticed what a pacific attitude his companion remained in. "Come, *ma petite blonde,* I'll let you go to bed first," he said to her, counting on the activity of his own legs to run away as quickly as possible, directly she was asleep, and seek another shelter for the night.

The soldier waited with impatience the hour of his flight, and when it had arrived he walked vigorously in the direction of the Nile; but hardly had he made a quarter of a league in the sand when he heard the panther bounding after him, crying with that saw-like cry more dreadful even than the sound of her leaping.

"Ah!" he said, "then she's taken a fancy to me; she has never met any one before, and it is really quite flattering to have her first love." That instant the man fell into one of those movable quicksands so terrible to travellers and from which it is impossible to save oneself. Feeling himself caught, he gave a shriek of alarm; the panther seized him with her teeth by the collar, and, springing vigorously backward, drew him as if by magic out of the whirling sand.

"Ah, Mignonne!" cried the soldier, caressing her enthusiastically; "we're bound together for life and death—but no jokes, mind!" and he retraced his steps.

From that time the desert seemed inhabited. It contained a being to whom the man could talk, and whose ferocity was rendered gentle by him, though he could not explain to himself the reason for their strange friendship. Great as was the soldier's desire to stay upon guard, he slept.

On awakening he could not find Mignonne; he mounted the hill, and in the distance saw her springing toward him after the habit of these animals, who cannot run on account of the extreme flexibility of the vertebral column. Mignonne arrived, her jaws covered with blood; she received the wonted caress of her companion, showing with much purring how happy it made her. Her eyes, full of languor, turned still more gently than the day before toward the Provençal, who talked to her as one would to a tame animal.

"Ah! Mademoiselle, you are a nice girl, aren't you? Just look at that! so we like to be made much of, don't we? Aren't you ashamed of yourself? So you have been eating some Arab or other, have you? that doesn't matter. They're animals just the same as you are; but don't you take to eating Frenchmen, or I shan't like you any longer."

She played like a dog with its master, letting herself be rolled over, knocked about, and stroked, alternately; sometimes she herself would provoke the soldier, putting up her paw with a soliciting gesture.

Some days passed in this manner. This companionship permitted the Provençal to appreciate the sublime beauty of the desert; now that he had a living thing to think about, alternations of fear and quiet, and plenty to eat, his mind became filled with contrast and his life began to be diversified.

Solitude revealed to him all her secrets, and enveloped him in her delights. He discovered in the rising and setting of the sun sights unknown to the world. He knew what it was to tremble when he heard over his head the hiss of a bird's wing, so rarely did they pass, or when he saw the clouds, changing and many-colored travellers, melt one into another. He studied in the night time the effect of the moon upon the ocean of sand, where the simoom made waves swift of movement and rapid in their change. He lived the life of the Eastern day, marvelling at its wonderful pomp; then, after having revelled in the sight of a hurricane over the plain where the whirling sands made red, dry mists and death-bearing clouds, he would welcome the night with joy, for then fell the healthful freshness of the stars, and he listened to imaginary music in the skies. Then solitude taught him to unroll the treasures of dreams. He passed whole hours in remembering mere nothings, and comparing his present life with his past.

At last he grew passionately fond of the panther; for some sort of affection was a necessity.

Whether it was that his will powerfully projected had modified the character of his companion, or whether, because she found abundant food in her predatory excursions in the desert, she respected the man's life, he began to fear for it no longer, seeing her so well tamed.

He devoted the greater part of his time to sleep, but he was obliged to watch like a spider in its web that the moment of his deliverance might not escape him, if any one should pass the line marked by the horizon. He had sacrificed his shirt to make a flag with, which he hung at the top of a palm tree, whose foliage he had torn off. Taught by necessity, he found the means of keeping it spread out, by fastening it with little sticks; for the wind might not be blowing at the moment when the passing traveller was looking through the desert.

It was during the long hours, when he had abandoned hope, that he amused himself with the panther. He had come to learn the different inflections of her voice, the expressions of her eyes; he had studied the capricious patterns of all the rosettes which marked the gold of her robe. Mignonne was not even angry when he took hold of the tuft at the end of her tail to count her rings, those graceful ornaments which glittered in the sun like jewelry. It gave him pleasure to contemplate the supple, fine outlines of her form, the whiteness of her belly, the graceful pose of her head. But it was especially when she was playing that he felt most pleasure in looking at her; the agility and youthful lightness of her movements were a continual surprise to him; he wondered at the supple way in which she jumped and climbed, washed herself and arranged her fur, crouched down and prepared to spring. However rapid her spring might be, however slippery the stone she was on, she would always stop short at the word "Mignonne."

One day, in a bright mid-day sun, an enormous bird coursed through the air. The man left his panther to look at this new guest; but after waiting a moment the deserted sultana growled deeply.

"My goodness! I do believe she's jealous," he cried, seeing her eyes become hard again; "the soul of Virginie has passed into her body; that's certain."

The eagle disappeared into the air, while the soldier admired the curved contour of the panther.

But there was such youth and grace in her form! she was beautiful as a woman! the blond fur of her robe mingled well with the delicate tints of faint white which marked her flanks.

The profuse light cast down by the sun made this living gold, these russet markings, to burn in a way to give them an indefinable attraction.

The man and the panther looked at one another with a look full of meaning; the coquette quivered when she felt her friend stroke her head; her eyes flashed like lightning—then she shut them tightly.

"She has a soul," he said, looking at the stillness of this queen of the sands, golden like them, white like them, solitary and burning like them.

"Well," she said, "I have read your plea in favor of beasts; but how did two so well adapted to understand each other end?"

"Ah, well! you see, they ended as all great passions do end—by a misunderstanding. For some reason *one* suspects the other of treason; they don't come to an explanation through pride, and quarrel and part from sheer obstinacy."

"Yet sometimes at the best moments a single word or a look is enough—but anyhow go on with your story."

"It's horribly difficult, but you will understand, after what the old villain told me over his champagne.

"He said—'I don't know if I hurt her, but she turned round, as if enraged, and with her sharp teeth caught hold of my leg—gently, I daresay; but I, thinking she would devour me, plunged my dagger into her throat. She rolled over, giving a cry that froze my heart; and I saw her dying, still looking at me without anger. I would have given all the world—my cross even, which I had not got then—to have brought her to life again. It was as though I had murdered a real person; and the soldiers who had seen my flag, and were come to my assistance, found me in tears.'

"'Well sir,' he said, after a moment of silence, 'since then I have been in war in Germany, in Spain, in Russia, in France; I've certainly carried my carcass about a good deal, but never have I seen anything like the desert. Ah! yes, it is very beautiful!'

"'What did you feel there?' I asked him.

"'Oh! that can't be described, young man. Besides, I am not always regretting my palm trees and my panther. I should have to be very melancholy for that. In the desert, you see, there is everything, and nothing.'

"'Yes, but explain—'

"'Well,' he said, with an impatient gesture, 'it is God without mankind.'"

Love of Life

Jack London (*American, 1876–1916*)

'This out of all will remain—
  They have lived and have tossed:
So much of the game will be gain,
  Though the gold of the dice has been lost.'

They limped painfully down the bank, and once the foremost of the two men staggered among the rough-strewn rocks. They were tired and weak, and their faces had the drawn expression of patience which comes of hardship long endured. They were heavily burdened with blanket packs which were strapped to their shoulders. Head-straps, passing across the forehead, helped support these packs. Each man carried a rifle. They walked in a stooped posture, the shoulders well forward, the head still farther forward, the eyes bent upon the ground.

"I wish we had just about two of them cartridges that's layin' in that cache of ourn," said the second man.

His voice was utterly and drearily expressionless. He spoke without enthusiasm; and the first man, limping into the milky stream that foamed over the rocks, vouchsafed no reply.

The other man followed at his heels. They did not remove their foot-gear, though the water was icy cold—so cold that their ankles ached and their feet went numb. In places the water dashed against their knees, and both men staggered for footing.

The man who followed slipped on a smooth boulder, nearly fell, but recovered himself with a violent effort, at the same time uttering a sharp exclamation of pain. He seemed faint and dizzy, and put out his free hand while he reeled, as though seeking support against the air. When he had steadied himself he stepped forward, but reeled again and nearly fell. Then he stood still and looked at the other man, who had never turned his head.

The man stood still for fully a minute, as though debating with himself. Then he called out:

"I say, Bill, I've sprained my ankle."

Bill staggered on through the milky water. He did not look around. The man watched him go, and though his face was expressionless as ever, his eyes were like the eyes of a wounded deer.

The other man limped up the farther bank and continued straight on without looking back. The man in the stream watched him. His lips trembled a little, so that the rough thatch of brown hair which covered them was visibly agitated. His tongue even strayed out to moisten them.

"Bill!" he cried out.

It was the pleading cry of a strong man in distress, but Bill's head did not turn. The man watched him go, limping grotesquely and lurching forward with stammering gait up the slow slope toward the soft sky-line of the low-lying hill. He watched him go until he passed over the crest and disappeared. Then he turned his gaze and slowly took in the circle of the world that remained to him now that Bill was gone.

Near the horizon the sun was smouldering dimly, almost obscured by formless mists and vapours, which gave an impression of mass and density without outline or tangibility. The man pulled out his watch, the while resting his weight on one leg. It was four o'clock, and as the season was near the last of July or first of August —he did not know the precise date within a week or two—he knew that the sun roughly marked the northwest. He looked to the south and knew that somewhere beyond those bleak hills lay the Great Bear Lake; also, he knew that in that direction the Arctic Circle cut its forbidding way across the Canadian Barrens. This stream in which he stood was a feeder to the Coppermine River, which in turn flowed north and emptied into Coronation Gulf and the Arctic Ocean. He had never been there, but he had seen it, once, on a Hudson Bay Company chart.

Again his gaze completed the circle of the world about him. It was not a heartening spectacle. Everywhere was soft sky-line. The hills were all low-lying. There were no trees, no shrubs, no grasses —naught but a tremendous and terrible desolation that sent fear swiftly dawning into his eyes.

"Bill!" he whispered, once and twice; "Bill!"

He cowered in the midst of the milky water, as though the vastness were pressing in upon him with overwhelming force, brutally crushing him with its complacent awfulness. He began to shake as with an ague-fit, till the gun fell from his hand with a splash. This served to rouse him. He fought with his fear and pulled himself together, groping in the water and recovering the weapon. He hitched his pack farther over on his left shoulder, so as to take a portion of its weight from off the injured ankle. Then he proceeded, slowly and carefully, wincing with pain, to the bank.

He did not stop. With a desperation that was madness, unmindful of the pain, he hurried up the slope to the crest of the hill over which his comrade had disappeared—more grotesque and comical by far than that limping, jerking comrade. But at the crest he saw a shallow valley, empty of life. He fought with his fear again, overcame it, hitched the pack still farther over on his left shoulder, and lurched on down the slope.

The bottom of the valley was soggy with water, which the thick moss held, spongelike, close to the surface. This water squirted out from under his feet at every step, and each time he lifted a foot the action culminated in a sucking sound as the wet moss reluctantly released its grip. He picked his way from muskeg to muskeg, and followed the other man's footsteps along and across the rocky ledges which thrust like islets through the sea of moss.

Though alone, he was not lost. Farther on he knew he would come to where dead spruce and fir, very small and weazened, bordered the shore of the little lake, the *titchinnichilie*—in the tongue of the country, the "land of little sticks." And into that lake flowed a small stream, the water of which was not milky. There was rush-grass on that stream—this he remembered well—but no timber, and he would follow it till its first trickle ceased at a divide. He would cross this divide to the first trickle of another stream, flowing to the west, which he would follow until it emptied into the river Dease, and here he would find a cache under an upturned canoe and piled over with many rocks. And in this cache would be ammunition for his empty gun, fish-hooks and lines, a small net—all the utilities for the killing and snaring of food. Also, he would find flour—not much—a piece of bacon, and some beans.

Bill would be waiting for him there, and they would paddle away south down the Dease to the Great Bear Lake. And south across the lake they would go, ever south till they gained the Mackenzie. And south, still south, they would go, while the winter raced vainly after them, and the ice formed in the eddies, and the days grew chill and crisp, south to some warm Hudson Bay Company post, where timber grew tall and generous, and there was grub without end.

These were the thoughts of the man as he strove onward. But hard as he strove with his body, he strove equally hard with his mind, trying to think that Bill had not deserted him, that Bill would surely wait for him at the cache. He was compelled to think this thought, or else there would not be any use to strive, and he would have lain down and died. And as the dim ball of the sun sank slowly into the northwest he covered every inch—and many times—of his and Bill's flight south before the downcoming winter. And he conned the grub of the cache and the grub of the Hudson Bay Company post over and over again. He had not eaten for two days; for a far longer time he had not had all he wanted to eat. Often he stooped and picked pale muskeg berries, put them into his mouth, and chewed and swallowed them. A muskeg berry is a bit of a seed enclosed in a bit of water. In the mouth the water melts away and the seed chews sharp and bitter. The man knew there was no nourishment in the berries, but he chewed them patiently with a hope greater than knowledge and defying experience.

At nine o'clock he stubbed his toe on a rocky ledge, and from sheer weariness and weakness staggered and fell. He lay for some time, without movement, on his side. Then he slipped out of his pack-straps and clumsily dragged himself into a sitting posture. It was not yet dark, and in the lingering twilight he groped about among the ricks for shreds of dry moss. When he had gathered a heap he built a fire—a smouldering, smudgy fire—and put a tin pot of water on to boil.

He unwrapped his pack and the first thing he did was to count his matches. There were sixty-seven. He counted them three times to make sure. He divided them into several portions, wrapping them in oil paper, disposing of one bunch in his empty tobacco pouch, of another bunch in the inside band of his battered hat, of a third bunch under his shirt on the chest. This accomplished, a panic came upon him, and he unwrapped them all and counted them again. There were still sixty-seven.

He dried his wet foot-gear by the fire. The moccasins were in soggy threads. The blanket socks were worn through in places, and his feet were raw and bleeding. His ankle was throbbing, and he gave it an examination. It had swollen to the size of his knee. He tore a long strip from one of his two blankets and bound the ankle tightly. He tore other strips and bound them about his feet to serve for both moccasins and socks. Then he drank the pot of water, steaming hot, wound his watch, and crawled between his blankets.

He slept like a dead man. The brief darkness around midnight came and went. The sun arose in the northeast—at least the day dawned in that quarter, for the sun was hidden by grey clouds.

At six o'clock he awoke, quietly lying on his back. He gazed straight up into the grey sky and knew that he was hungry. As he rolled over on his elbow he was startled by a loud snort, and saw a bull caribou regarding him with alert curiosity. The animal was not more than fifty feet away, and instantly into the man's mind leaped the vision and the savour of a caribou steak sizzling and frying over a fire. Mechanically he reached for the empty gun, drew a bead, and pulled the trigger. The bull snorted and leaped away, his hoofs rattling and clattering as he fled across the ledges.

The man cursed and flung the empty gun from him. He groaned aloud as he started to drag himself to his feet. It was a slow and arduous task. His joints were like rusty hinges. They worked harshly in their sockets, with much friction, and each bending or unbending was accomplished only through a sheer exertion of will. When he finally gained his feet, another minute or so was consumed in straightening up, so that he could stand erect as a man should stand.

He crawled up a small knoll, and surveyed the prospect. There were no trees, no bushes, nothing but a grey sea of moss scarcely diversified by grey rocks, grey lakelets, and grey streamlets. The sky was grey. There was no sun nor hint of sun. He had no idea of north, and he had forgotten the way he had come to this spot the night before. But he was not lost. He knew that. Soon he would come to the land of the little sticks. He felt that it lay off to the left somewhere, not far—possibly just over the next low hill.

He went back to put his pack into shape for travelling. He assured himself of the existence of his three separate parcels of matches, though he did not stop to count them. But he did linger, debating, over a squat moose-hide sack. It was not large. He could hide it under his two hands. He knew that it weighed fifteen pounds—as much as all the rest of the pack—and it worried him. He finally set it to one side and proceeded to roll the pack. He paused to gaze at the squat moose-hide sack. He picked it up hastily with a defiant glance about him, as though the desolation were trying to rob him of it; and when he rose to his feet to stagger on into the day, it was included in the pack on his back.

He bore away to the left, stopping now and again to eat muskeg berries. His ankle had stiffened, his limp was more pronounced, but the pain of it was as nothing compared with the pain of his stomach. The hunger pangs were sharp. They gnawed and gnawed until he could not keep his mind steady on the course he must pursue to gain the land of little sticks. The muskeg berries did not allay this gnawing, while they made his tongue and the roof of his mouth sore with their irritating bite.

He came upon a valley where rock ptarmigan rose on whirring wings from the ledges and muskegs. "Ker—ker—ker" was the cry they made. He threw stones at them, but could not hit them. He placed his pack on the ground and stalked them as a cat stalks a sparrow. The sharp rocks cut through his pants' legs till his knees left a trail of blood; but the hurt was lost in the hurt of his hunger. He squirmed over the wet moss, saturating his clothes and chilling his body; but he was not aware of it, so great was his fever for food. And always the ptarmigan rose, whirring before him, till their "ker—ker—ker" became a mock to him, and he cursed them and cried aloud at them with their own cry.

Once he crawled upon one that must have been asleep. He did not see it till it shot up in his face from its rocky nook. He made a clutch as startled as was the rise of the ptarmigan, and there remained in his hand three tail-feathers. As he watched its flight he hated it, as though it had done him some terrible wrong. Then he returned and shouldered his pack.

As the day wore along he came into valleys or swales where game was more plentiful. A band of caribou passed by, twenty and odd animals, tantalizingly within rifle range. He felt a wild desire to run after them, a certitude that he could run them down. A black fox came toward him, carrying a ptarmigan in his mouth. The man shouted. It was a fearful cry, but the fox, leaping away in fright, did not drop the ptarmigan.

Late in the afternoon he followed a stream, milky with lime, which ran through sparse patches of rush-grass. Grasping these rushes firmly near the root, he pulled up what resembled a young onion-sprout no larger than a shingle-nail. It was tender, and his teeth sank into it with a crunch that promised deliciously of food. But its fibres were tough. It was composed of stringy filaments saturated with water, like the berries, and devoid of nourishment. He threw off his pack and went into the rush-grass on hands and knees, crunching and munching like some bovine creature.

He was very weary and often wished to rest—to lie down and sleep; but he was continually driven on—not so much by his desire to gain the land of little sticks as by his hunger. He searched little ponds for frogs and dug up the earth with his nails for worms, though he knew in spite that neither frogs nor worms existed so far north.

He looked into every pool of water vainly, until as the long twilight came on, he discovered a solitary fish, the size of a minnow, in such a pool. He plunged his arm in up to the shoulder, but it eluded him. He reached for it with both hands and stirred up the milky mud at the bottom. In his excitement he fell in, wetting himself to the waist. Then the water was too muddy to admit of his seeing the fish, and he was compelled to wait until the sediment had settled.

The pursuit was renewed, till the water was again muddied. But he could not wait. He unstrapped the tin bucket and began to bail the pool. He bailed wildly at first, splashing himself and flinging the water so short a distance that it ran back into the pool. He worked more carefully, striving to be cool, though his heart was pounding against his chest and his hands were trembling. At the end of half an hour the pool was nearly dry. Not a cupful of water remained. And there was no fish. He found a hidden crevice among the stones through which it had escaped to the adjoining and larger pool—a pool which he could not empty in a night and a day. Had he known of the crevice, he could have closed it with a rock at the beginning and the fish would have been his.

Thus he thought, and crumpled up and sank down upon the wet earth. At first he cried softly to himself, then he cried loudly to the pitiless desolation that ringed him around, and for a long time after he was shaken by great dry sobs.

He built a fire and warmed himself by drinking quarts of hot water, and made camp on a rocky ledge in the same fashion he had the night before. The last thing he did was to see that his matches were dry and to wind his watch. The blankets were wet and clammy. His ankle pulsed with pain. But he knew only that he was hungry, and through his restless sleep he dreamed of feasts and banquets and of food served and spread in all imaginable ways.

He awoke chilled and sick. There was no sun. The grey of earth and sky had become deeper, more profound. A raw wind was blowing, and the first flurries of snow were whitening the hill-tops. The air about him thickened and grew white while he made a fire and boiled more water. It was wet snow, half rain, and the flakes were large and soggy. At first they melted as soon as they came in contact with the earth, but ever more fell, covering the ground, putting out the fire, spoiling his supply of moss-fuel.

This was a signal for him to strap on his pack and stumble onward, he knew not where. He was not concerned with the land of little sticks, nor with Bill and the cache under the upturned canoe by the river Dease. He was mastered by the verb "to eat." He was hunger-mad. He took no heed of the course he pursued, so long as that course led him through the swale bottoms. He felt his way through the wet snow to the watery muskeg berries, and went by feel as he pulled up the rush-grass by the roots. But it was tasteless stuff and did not satisfy. He found a weed that tasted sour and he ate all he could find of it, which was not much, for it was a creeping growth, easily hidden under the several inches of snow.

He had no fire that night, nor hot water, and crawled under his blanket to sleep the broken hunger-sleep. The snow turned into a cold rain. He awakened many times to feel it falling on his upturned face. Day came—a grey day and no sun. It had ceased raining. The keenness of his hunger had departed. Sensibility, as far as concerned the yearning for food, had been exhausted. There was a dull, heavy ache in his stomach, but it did not bother him so much. He was more rational, and once more he was chiefly interested in the land of little sticks and the cache by the river Dease.

He ripped the remnant of one of his blankets into strips and bound his bleeding feet. Also, he recinched the injured ankle and prepared himself for a day of travel. When he came to his pack, he paused long over the squat moose-hide sack, but in the end it went with him.

The snow had melted under the rain, and only the hill-tops showed white. The sun came out, and he succeeded in locating the points of the compass, though he knew now that he was lost. Perhaps, in his previous days' wanderings, he had edged away too far to the left. He now bore off to the right to counteract the possible deviation from his true course.

Though the hunger pains were no longer so exquisite, he realized that he was weak. He was compelled to pause for frequent rests, when he attacked the muskeg berries and rush-grass patches. His tongue felt dry and large, as though covered with a fine hairy growth, and it tasted bitter in his mouth. His heart gave him a great deal of trouble. When he had travelled a few minutes it would begin a remorseless thump, thump, thump, and then leap up and away in a painful flutter of beats that choked him and made him go faint and dizzy.

In the middle of the day he found two minnows in a large pool. It was impossible to bail it, but he was calmer now and managed to catch them in his tin bucket. They were no longer than his little finger, but he was not particularly hungry. The dull ache in his stomach had been growing duller and fainter. It seemed almost as if his stomach was dozing. He ate the fish raw, masticating with painstaking care, for the eating was an act of pure reason. While he had no desire to eat, he knew that he must eat to live.

In the evening he caught three more minnows, eating two and saving the third for breakfast. The sun had dried stray shreds of moss, and he was able to warm himself with hot water. He had not covered more than ten miles that day; and the next day, travelling whenever his heart permitted him, he covered no more than five miles. But his stomach did not give him the slightest uneasiness. It had gone to sleep. He was in a strange country, too, and the caribou were growing more plentiful, also the wolves. Often their yelps drifted across the desolation, and once he saw three of them slinking away before his path.

Another night; and in the morning, being more rational, he untied the leather string that fastened the squat moose-hide sack. From its open mouth poured a yellow stream of coarse gold-dust and nuggets. He roughly divided the gold in halves, caching one half on a prominent ledge, wrapped in a piece of blanket, and returning the other half to the sack. He also began to use strips of the one remaining blanket for his feet. He still clung to his gun, for there were cartridges in that cache by the river Dease.

This was a day of fog, and this day hunger awoke in him again. He was very weak and was afflicted with a giddiness which at times blinded him. It was no uncommon thing now for him to stumble and fall; and stumbling once, he fell squarely into a ptarmigan nest. There were four newly hatched chicks, a day old—little specks of pulsating life no more than a mouthful; and he ate them ravenously, thrusting them alive into his mouth and crunching them like egg-shells between his teeth. The mother ptarmigan beat about him with great outcry. He used his gun as a club with which to knock her over, but she dodged out of reach. He threw stones at her and with one chance shot broke a wing. Then she fluttered away, running, trailing the broken wing, with him in pursuit.

The little chicks had no more than whetted his appetite. He hopped and bobbed clumsily along on his injured ankle, throwing stones and screaming hoarsely at times; at other times hopping and bobbing silently along, picking himself up grimly and patiently when he fell, or rubbing his eyes with his hand when the giddiness threatened to overpower him.

The chase led him across swampy ground in the bottom of the valley, and he came upon footprints in the soggy moss. They were not his own—he could see that. They must be Bill's. But he could not stop, for the mother ptarmigan was running on. He would catch her first, then he would return and investigate.

He exhausted the mother ptarmigan; but he exhausted himself. She lay panting on her side. He lay panting on his side, a dozen feet away, unable to crawl to her. And as he recovered she recovered, fluttering out of reach as his hungry hand went out to her. The chase was resumed. Night settled down and she escaped. He stumbled from weakness and pitched head foremost on his face, cutting his cheek, his pack upon his back. He did not move for a long while; then he rolled over on his side, wound his watch, and lay there until morning.

Another day of fog. Half of his last blanket had gone into foot-wrappings. He failed to pick up Bill's trail. It did not matter. His hunger was driving him too compellingly—only—only he wondered if Bill, too, were lost. By midday the irk of his pack became too oppressive. Again he divided the gold, this time merely spilling half of it on the ground. In the afternoon he threw the rest of it away, there remaining to him only the half-blanket, the tin bucket, and the rifle.

An hallucination began to trouble him. He felt confident that one cartridge remained to him. It was in the chamber of the rifle and he had overlooked it. On the other hand, he knew all the time that the chamber was empty. But the hallucination persisted. He fought it off for hours, then threw his rifle open and was confronted with emptiness. The disappointment was as bitter as though he had really expected to find the cartridge.

He plodded on for half an hour, when the hallucination arose again. Again he fought it, and still it persisted, till for very relief he opened his rifle to unconvince himself. At times his mind wandered farther afield, and he plodded on, a mere automaton, strange conceits and whimsicalities gnawing at his brain like worms. But these excursions out of the real were of brief duration, for ever the pangs of the hunger-bite called him back. He was jerked back abruptly once from such an excursion by a sight that nearly caused him to faint. He reeled and swayed, doddering like a drunken man to keep from falling. Before him stood a horse. A horse! He could not believe his eyes. A thick mist was in them, intershot with sparkling points of light. He rubbed his eyes savagely to clear his vision, and beheld, not a horse, but a great brown bear. The animal was studying him with bellicose curiosity.

The man had brought his gun half-way to his shoulder before he realized. He lowered it and drew his hunting-knife from its beaded sheath at his hip. Before him was meat and life. He ran his thumb along the edge of his knife. It was sharp. The point was sharp. He would fling himself upon the bear and kill it. But his heart began its warning thump, thump, thump. Then followed the wild upward leap and tattoo of flutters, the pressing as of an iron band about his forehead, the creeping of the dizziness into his brain.

His desperate courage was evicted by a great surge of fear. In his weakness, what if the animal attacked him. He drew himself up to his most imposing stature, gripping the knife and staring hard at the bear. The bear advanced clumsily a couple of steps, reared up, and gave vent to a tentative growl. If the man ran, he would run after him; but the man did not run. He was animated now with the courage of fear. He, too, growled, savagely, terribly, voicing the fear that is to life germane and that lies twisted about life's deepest roots.

The bear edged away to one side, growling menacingly, himself appalled by this mysterious creature that appeared upright and unafraid. But the man did not move. He stood like a statue till the danger was past, when he yielded to a fit of trembling and sank down into the wet moss.

He pulled himself together and went on, afraid now in a new way. It was not the fear that he should die passively from lack of food, but that he should be destroyed violently before starvation had exhausted the last particle of the endeavour in him that made toward surviving. There were the wolves. Back and forth across the desolation drifted their howls, weaving the very air into a fabric of menace that was so tangible that he found himself, arms in the air, pressing it back from him as it might be the walls of a wind-blown tent.

Now and again the wolves, in packs of two and three, crossed his path. But they steered clear of him. They were not in sufficient numbers, and besides they were hunting the caribou, which did not battle, while this strange creature that walked erect might scratch and bite.

In the late afternoon he came upon scattered bones where the wolves had made a kill. The debris had been a caribou calf an hour before, squawking and running and very much alive. He contemplated the bones, clean-picked and polished, pink with the cell-life in them which had not yet died. Could it possibly be that he might be that ere the day was done! Such was life, eh? A vain and fleeting thing. It was only life that pained. There was no hurt in death. To die was to sleep. It meant cessation, rest. Then why was he not content to die?

But he did not moralize long. He was squatting in the moss, a bone in his mouth, sucking at the shreds of life that still dyed it faintly pink. The sweet meaty taste, thin and elusive almost as a memory, maddened him. He closed his jaws on the bones and crunched. Sometimes it was the bone that broke, sometimes his teeth. Then he crushed the bones between rocks, pounded them to a pulp, and swallowed them. He pounded his fingers, too, in his haste, and yet found a moment in which to feel surprise at the fact that his fingers did not hurt much when caught under the descending rock.

Came frightful days of snow and rain. He did not know when he made camp, when he broke camp. He travelled in the night as much as in the day. He rested wherever he fell, crawled on whenever the dying life in him flickered up and burned less dimly. He, as a man, no longer strove. It was the life in him, unwilling to die, that drove him on. He did not suffer. His nerves had become blunted, numb, while his mind was filled with weird visions and delicious dreams.

But ever he sucked and chewed on the crushed bones of the caribou calf, the least remnants of which he had gathered up and carried with him. He crossed no more hills or divides, but automatically followed a large stream which flowed through a wide and shallow valley. He did not see this stream nor this valley. He saw nothing save visions. Soul and body walked or crawled side by side, yet apart, so slender was the thread that bound them.

He awoke in his right mind, lying on his back on a rocky ledge. The sun was shining bright and warm. Afar off he heard the squawking of caribou calves. He was aware of vague memories of rain and wind and snow, but whether he had been beaten by the storm for two days or two weeks he did not know.

For some time he lay without movement, the genial sunshine pouring upon him and saturating his miserable body with its warmth. A fine day, he thought. Perhaps he could manage to locate himself. By a painful effort he rolled over on his side. Below him flowed a wide and sluggish river. Its unfamiliarity puzzled him. Slowly he followed it with his eyes, winding in wide sweeps among the bleak, bare hills, bleaker and barer and lower-lying than any hills he had yet encountered. Slowly, deliberately, without excitement or more than the most casual interest, he followed the course of the strange stream towards the sky-line and saw it emptying into a bright and shining sea. He was still unexcited. Most unusual, he thought, a vision or a mirage—more likely a vision, a trick of his disordered mind. He was confirmed in this by sight of a ship lying at anchor in the midst of the shining sea. He closed his eyes for a while, then opened them. Strange how the vision persisted! Yet not strange. He knew there were no seas or ships in the heart of the barren lands, just as he had known there was no cartridge in the empty rifle.

He heard a snuffle behind him—a half-choking gasp or cough. Very slowly, because of his exceeding weakness and stiffness, he rolled over on his other side. He could see nothing near at hand, but he waited patiently. Again came the snuffle and cough, and outlined between two jagged rocks not a score of feet away he made out the grey head of a wolf. The sharp ears were not pricked so sharply as he had seen them on other wolves; the eyes were bleared and bloodshot, the head seemed to droop limply and forlornly. The animal blinked continually in the sunshine. It seemed sick. As he looked it snuffled and coughed again.

This, at least, was real, he thought, and turned on the other side so that he might see the reality of the world which had been veiled from him before by the vision. But the sea still shone in the distance and the ship was plainly discernible. Was it reality, after all? He closed his eyes for a long while and thought, and then it came to him. He had been making north by east, away from the Dease divide, and into the Coppermine Valley. This wide and sluggish river was the Coppermine. That shining sea was the Arctic Ocean. That ship was a whaler, strayed east, far east, from the mouth of the Mackenzie, and it was lying at anchor in Coronation Gulf. He remembered the Hudson Bay Company chart he had seen long ago, and it was all clear and reasonable to him.

He sat up and turned his attention to immediate affairs. He had worn through the blanket-wrappings, and his feet were shapeless lumps of raw meat. His last blanket was gone. Rifle and knife were both missing. He had lost his hat somewhere, with the bunch of matches in the band, but the matches against his chest were safe and dry inside the tobacco pouch and oil paper. He looked at his watch. It marked eleven o'clock and was still running. Evidently he had kept it wound.

He was calm and collected. Though extremely weak, he had no sensation of pain. He was not hungry. The thought of food was not even pleasant to him, and whatever he did was done by his reason alone. He ripped off his pants' legs to the knees and bound them about his feet. Somehow he had succeeded in retaining the tin bucket. He would have some hot water before he began what he foresaw was to be a terrible journey to the ship.

His movements were slow. He shook as with a palsy. When he started to collect dry moss, he found he could not rise to his feet. He tried again and again, then contented himself with crawling about on hands and knees. Once he crawled near to the sick wolf. The animal dragged itself reluctantly out of his way, licking its chops with a tongue which seemed hardly to have the strength to curl. The man noticed that the tongue was not the customary healthful red. It was a yellowish brown and seemed coated with a rough and half-dry mucus.

After he had drunk a quart of hot water the man found he was able to stand, and even walk as well as a dying man might be supposed to walk. Every minute or so he was compelled to rest. His steps were feeble and uncertain, just as the wolf's that trailed him were feeble and uncertain; and that night, when the shining sea was blotted out by blackness, he knew he was nearer to it by no more than four miles.

Throughout the night he heard the cough of the sick wolf, and now and then the squawking of the caribou calves. There was life all around him, but it was strong life, very much alive and well, and he knew the sick wolf clung to the sick man's trail, in the hope that the man would die first. In the morning, on opening his eyes, he beheld it regarding him with a wistful and hungry stare. It stood crouched, with tail between its legs, like a miserable and woebegone dog. It shivered in the chill morning wind, and grinned dispiritedly when the man spoke to it in a voice that achieved no more than a hoarse whisper.

The sun rose brightly, and all morning the man tottered and fell forward toward the ship on the shining sea. The weather was perfect. It was the brief Indian Summer of the high latitudes. It might last a week. To-morrow or next day it might be gone.

In the afternoon the man came upon a trail. It was of another man, who did not walk, but who dragged himself on all fours. The man thought it might be Bill, but he thought in a dull, uninterested way. He had no curiosity. In fact, sensation and emotion had left him. He was no longer susceptible to pain. Stomach and nerves had gone to sleep. Yet the life that was in him drove him on. He was very weary, but it refused to die. It was because it refused to die that he still ate muskeg berries and minnows, drank his hot water, and kept a wary eye on the sick wolf.

He followed the trail of the other man who dragged himself along, and soon came to the end of it—a few fresh-picked bones where the soggy moss was marked by the foot-pads of many wolves. He saw a squat moose-hide sack, mate to his own, which had been torn by sharp teeth. He picked it up, though its weight was almost too much for his feeble fingers. Bill had carried it to the last. Ha! ha! He would have the laugh on Bill. He would survive and carry it to the ship on the shining sea. His mirth was hoarse and ghastly, like a raven's croak, and the sick wolf joined him, howling lugubriously. The man ceased suddenly. How could he have the laugh on Bill if that were Bill; if those bones, so pinky-white and clean were Bill.

He turned away. Well, Bill had deserted him; but he would not take the gold, nor would he suck Bill's bones. Bill would have, though, had it been the other way round, he mused as he staggered on.

He came to a pool of water. Stooping over in quest of minnows, he jerked his head back as though he had been stung. He had caught sight of his reflected face. So horrible was it that sensibility awoke long enough to be shocked. There were three minnows in the pool, which was too large to drain; and after several ineffectual attempts to catch them in the tin bucket he forbore. He was afraid, because of his great weakness, that he might fall in and drown. It was for this reason that he did not trust himself to the river astride one of the many drift-logs which lined its sandspits.

That day he decreased the distance between him and the ship by three miles; the next day by two—for he was crawling now as Bill had crawled; and the end of the fifth day found the ship still seven miles away and him unable to make even a mile a day. Still the Indian Summer held on, and he continued to crawl and faint, turn and turn about; and ever the sick wolf coughed and wheezed at his heels. His knees had become raw meat like his feet, and though he padded them with the shirt from his back it was a red track he left behind him on the moss and stones. Once, glancing back, he saw the wolf licking hungrily his bleeding trail, and he saw sharply what his own end might be—unless—unless he could get the wolf. Then began as grim a tragedy of existence as was ever played—a sick man that crawled, a sick wolf that limped, two creatures dragging their dying carcasses across the desolation and hunting each other's lives.

Had it been a well wolf, it would not have mattered so much to the man; but the thought of going to feed the maw of that loathsome and all but dead thing was repugnant to him. He was finicky. His mind had begun to wander again, and to be perplexed by hallucinations, while his lucid intervals grew rarer and shorter.

He was awakened once from a faint by a wheeze close in his ear. The wolf leaped lamely back, losing its footing and falling in its weakness. It was ludicrous, but he was not amused. Nor was he even afraid. He was too far gone for that. But his mind was for the moment clear, and he lay and considered. The ship was no more than four miles away. He could see it quite distinctly when he rubbed the mists out of his eyes, and he could see the white sail of a small boat cutting the water of the shining sea. But he could never crawl those four miles. He knew that, and was very calm in the knowledge. He knew that he could not crawl half a mile. And yet he wanted to live. It was unreasonable that he should die after all he had undergone. Fate asked too much of him. And, dying, he declined to die. It was stark madness, perhaps, but in the very grip of Death he defied Death and refused to die.

He closed his eyes and composed himself with infinite precaution. He steeled himself to keep above the suffocating languor that lapped like a rising tide through all the wells of his being. It was very like a sea, this deadly languor, that rose and rose and drowned his consciousness bit by bit. Sometimes he was all but submerged, swimming through oblivion with a faltering stroke; and again, by some strange alchemy of soul, he would find another shred of will and strike out more strongly.

Without movement he lay on his back, and he could hear, slowly drawing nearer and nearer, the wheezing intake and output of the sick wolf's breath. It drew closer, ever closer, through an infinitude of time, and he did not move. It was at his ear. The harsh dry tongue grated like sandpaper against his cheek. His hands shot out—or at least he willed them to shoot out. The fingers were curved like talons, but they closed on empty air. Swiftness and certitude require strength, and the man had not this strength.

The patience of the wolf was terrible. The man's patience was no less terrible. For half a day he lay motionless, fighting off unconsciousness and waiting for the thing that was to feed upon him and upon which he wished to feed. Sometimes the languid sea rose over him and he dreamed long dreams; but ever through it all, waking and dreaming, he waited for the wheezing breath and the harsh caress of the tongue.

He did not hear the breath, and he slipped slowly from some dream to the feel of the tongue along his hand. He waited. The fangs pressed softly; the pressure increased; the wolf was exerting its last strength in an effort to sink teeth in the food for which it had waited so long. But the man had waited long, and the lacerated hand closed on the jaw. Slowly, while the wolf struggled feebly and the hand clutched feebly, the other hand crept across to a grip. Five minutes later the whole weight of the man's body was on top of the wolf. The hands had not sufficient strength to choke the wolf, but the face of the man was pressed close to the throat of the wolf and the mouth of the man was full of hair. At the end of half an hour the man was aware of a warm trickle in his throat. It was not pleasant. It was like molten lead being forced into his stomach, and it was forced by his will alone. Later on the man rolled over on his back and slept.

There were some members of a scientific expedition on the whale-ship *Bedford*. From the deck they remarked a strange object on the shore. It was moving down the beach toward the water. They were unable to classify it, and, being scientific men, they climbed into the whale-boat alongside and went ashore to see. And they saw something that was alive but which could hardly be called a man. It was blind, unconscious. It squirmed along the ground like some monstrous worm. Most of its efforts were ineffectual, but it was persistent. and it writhed and twisted and went ahead perhaps a score of feet an hour.

Three weeks afterwards the man lay in a bunk on the whale-ship *Bedford,* and with tears streaming down his wasted cheeks told who he was and what he had undergone. He also babbled incoherently of his mother, of sunny Southern California, and a home among the orange groves and flowers.

The days were not many after that when he sat at table with the scientific men and ship's officers. He gloated over the spectacle of so much food, watching it anxiously as it went into the mouths of others. With the disappearance of each mouthful an expression of deep regret came into his eyes. He was quite sane, yet he hated those men at mealtime. He was haunted by a fear that the food would not last. He inquired of the cook, the cabin-boy, the captain, concerning the food stores. They reassured him countless times; but he could not believe them, and pried cunningly about the laz-arette to see with his own eyes.

It was noticed that the man was getting fat. He grew stouter with each day. The scientific men shook their heads and theorized. They limited the man at his meals, but still his girth increased and he swelled prodigiously under his shirt.

The sailors grinned. They knew. And when the scientific men set a watch on the man, they knew too. They saw him slouch for'ard after breakfast, and, like a mendicant, with outstretched palm, accost a sailor. The sailor grinned and passed him a fragment of sea biscuit. He clutched it avariciously, looked at it as a miser looks at gold, and thrust it into his shirt bosom. Similar were the donations from other grinning sailors.

The scientific men were discreet. They let him alone. But they privily examined his bunk. It was lined with hardtack; the mattress was stuffed with hardtack; every nook and cranny was filled with hardtack. Yet he was sane. He was taking precautions against another possible famine—that was all. He would recover from it, the scientific men said; and he did, ere the *Bedford's* anchor rumbled down in San Francisco Bay.

3

Bartleby the Scrivener

by Herman Melville

Of This Time,
Of That Place

by Lionel Trilling

The Mohammedans

by H. J. Kaplan

HERMAN MELVILLE *Widely acknowledged as one of the two or three greatest American fiction writers, Melville was obsessively concerned with human potential in a universe that is at once infinite and limiting. Unlike his peers Whitman, for whom man was essentially holy, and Hawthorne, for whom man was essentially limited, Melville could (in Hawthorne's words) "neither believe nor be happy in his unbelief." The extraordinary tension between these two poles largely accounts for Melville's power.*

Though the work-a-day setting and distinctly unheroic personages of "Bartelby the Scrivener," contrast markedly with Moby Dick *or* Billy Budd, *the moral burden of the story is quintessentially Melville. Bartelby's "I would prefer not to," though in a minor key, is as reverberant as Ahab's "No! in Thunder."*

LIONEL TRILLING *Teacher, writer, critic, philosopher, Lionel Trilling had an exceptionally wide range of interests and brilliant perceptions recalling that other broad-gauge American intellectual: Edmund Wilson. In addition to his work on Freud, Keats, Matthew Arnold, E. M. Forster, Sherwood Anderson, and numerous other figures, Trilling, like Wilson, tried his hand at fiction—and succeeded admirably.* The Middle of the Journey, *1947, is a substantial, lucidly written novel of ideas; and he has written at least two brilliant short stories: "The Other Margaret," and "Of this Time, Of that Place."*

In the latter story, the fluctuating relationship between Dr. Howe and Tertan recalls certain signal aspects of the unnamed lawyer's entanglement with Bartelby in Melville's story.

H. J. KAPLAN *After serving as Paris correspondent for the* Partisan Review *in the early 1940s, Kaplan joined the United States Foreign Service, serving in France and South Vietnam, among other places. Although he has never brought out a volume of his own fiction, Kaplan published an imaginative book-length study of fiction called* The Passive Voice: An Approach to Modern Fiction, *1966.*

Bartleby the Scrivener

A Story of Wall Street

Herman Melville (*American, 1819–1891*)

I am a rather elderly man. The nature of my avocations, for the last thirty years, has brought me into more than ordinary contact with what would seem an interesting and somewhat singular set of men, of whom, as yet, nothing, that I know of, has ever been written—I mean, the law-copyists, or scriveners. I have known very many of them, professionally and privately, and, if I pleased, could relate divers histories, at which good-natured gentlemen might smile, and sentimental souls might weep. But I waive the biographies of all other scriveners, for a few passages in the life of Bartleby, who was a scrivener, the strangest I ever saw, or heard of. While, of other law-copyists, I might write the complete life, of Bartleby nothing of that sort can be done. I believe that no materials exist, for a full and satisfactory biography of this man. It is an irreparable loss to literature. Bartleby was one of those beings of whom nothing is ascertainable, except from the original sources, and, in his case, those are very small. What my own astonished eyes saw of Bartleby, *that* is all I know of him, except, indeed, one vague report, which will appear in the sequel.

Ere introducing the scrivener, as he first appeared to me, it is fit I make some mention of myself, my *employés,* my business, my chambers, and general surroundings; because some such description is indispensable to an adequate understanding of the chief character about to be presented. Imprimis: I am a man who, from his youth upwards, has been filled with a profound conviction that the easiest way of life is the best. Hence, though I belong to a profession proverbially energetic and nervous, even to turbulence, at times, yet nothing of that sort have I ever suffered to invade my peace. I am one of those unambitious lawyers who never addresses a jury, or in any way draws down public applause; but, in the cool tranquillity of a snug retreat, do a snug business among rich men's bonds, and mortgages, and title-deeds. All who know me, consider me an eminently *safe* man. The late John Jacob Astor, a personage little given to poetic enthusiasm, had no hesitation in pronouncing my first grand point to be prudence; my next, method. I do not speak it in vanity, but simply record the fact, that I was not unemployed in my profession by the late John Jacob Astor; a name which, I admit, I love to repeat; for it hath a rounded and orbicular sound to it, and rings like unto bullion. I will freely add, that I was not insensible to the late John Jacob Astor's good opinion.

Some time prior to the period at which this little history begins, my avocations had been largely increased. The good old office, now extinct in the State of New York, of a Master in Chancery, had been conferred upon me. It was not a very arduous office, but very pleasantly remunerative. I seldom lose my temper; much more seldom indulge in dangerous indignation at wrongs and outrages; but I must be permitted to be rash here and declare, that I consider the sudden and violent abrogation of the office of Master in Chancery, by the new Constitution, as a——premature act; inasmuch as I had counted upon a life-lease of the profits, whereas I only received those of a few short years. But this is by the way.

My chambers were up stairs, at No. — Wall Street. At one end, they looked upon the white wall of the interior of a spacious skylight shaft, penetrating the building from top to bottom.

This view might have been considered rather tame than otherwise, deficient in what landscape painters call "life." But, if so, the view from the other end of my chambers offered, at least, a contrast, if nothing more. In that direction, my windows commanded an unobstructed view of a lofty brick wall, black by age and everlasting shade; which wall required no spy-glass to bring out its lurking beauties, but, for the benefit of all near-sighted spectators, was pushed up to within ten feet of my window panes. Owing to the great height of the surrounding buildings, and my chambers being on the second floor, the interval between this wall and mine not a little resembled a huge square cistern.

At the period just preceding the advent of Bartleby, I had two persons as copyists in my employment, and a promising lad as an office-boy. First, Turkey; second, Nippers; third, Ginger Nut. These may seem names, the like of which are not usually found in the Directory. In truth, they were nicknames, mutually conferred upon each other by my three clerks, and were deemed expressive of their respective persons or characters. Turkey was a short, pursy Englishman, of about my age—that is, somewhere not far from sixty. In the morning, one might say, his face was of a fine florid hue, but after twelve o'clock, meridian—his dinner hour—it blazed like a grate full of Christmas coals; and continued blazing—but, as it were, with a gradual wane—till six o'clock, P.M., or thereabouts; after which, I saw no more of the proprietor of the face, which, gaining its meridian with the sun, seemed to set with it, to rise, culminate, and decline the following day, with the like regularity and undiminished glory. There are many singular coincidences I have known in the course of my life, not the least among which was the fact, that, exactly when Turkey displayed his fullest beams from his red and radiant countenance, just then, too, at that critical moment, began the daily period when I considered his business capacities as seriously disturbed for the remainder of the twenty-four hours. Not that he was absolutely idle, or averse to business, then; far from it. The difficulty was, he was apt to be altogether too energetic. There was a strange, inflamed, flurried, flighty recklessness of activity about him. He would be incautious in dipping his pen into his inkstand. All his blots upon my documents were dropped there after twelve o'clock, meridian. Indeed, not only would he be reckless, and sadly given to making blots in the afternoon, but, some days, he went further, and was rather noisy. At such times, too, his face flamed with augmented blazonry, as if cannel coal had been heaped on anthracite. He made an unpleasant racket with his chair; spilled his sand-box; in mending his pens, impatiently split them all to pieces, and threw them on the floor in a sudden passion; stood up, and leaned over his table, boxing his papers about in a most indecorous manner, very sad to behold in an elderly man like him. Nevertheless, as he was in many ways a most valuable person to me, and all the time before twelve o'clock meridian, was the quickest, steadiest creature, too, accomplishing a great deal of work in a style not easily to be matched—for these reasons, I was willing to overlook his eccentricities, though, indeed, occasionally, I remonstrated with him. I did this very gently, however, because, though the civilest, nay, the blandest and most reverential of men in the morning, yet, in the afternoon, he was disposed, upon provocation, to be slightly rash with his tongue—in fact, insolent. Now, valuing his morning services as I did, and resolved not to lose them—yet, at the same time, made uncomfortable by his inflamed ways after twelve o'clock—and being a man of peace, unwilling by my admonitions to call forth unseemly retorts from him, I took upon me, one Saturday noon (he was always worse on Saturdays) to hint to him, very kindly, that, perhaps, now that he was growing old, it might be well to abridge his labors; in short, he need not come to my chambers after twelve o'clock, but, dinner over, had best go home to his lodgings, and rest himself till tea-time. But no; he insisted upon his afternoon devotions. His countenance became intolerably fervid, as he oratorically assured me—gesticulating with a long ruler at the other end of the room—that if his services in the morning were useful, how indispensable, then, in the afternoon?

"With submission, sir," said Turkey, on this occasion, "I consider myself your right-hand man. In the morning I but marshal and deploy my columns; but in the afternoon I put myself at their head, and gallantly charge the foe, thus"—and he made a violent thrust with the ruler.

"But the blots, Turkey," intimated I.

"True; but, with submission, sir, behold these hairs! I am getting old. Surely, sir, a blot or two of a warm afternoon is not to be severely urged against gray hairs. Old age—even if it blot the page—is honorable. With submission, sir, we *both* are getting old."

This appeal to my fellow-feeling was hardly to be resisted. At all events, I saw that go he would not. So, I made up my mind to let him stay, resolving, nevertheless, to see to it that, during the afternoon, he had to do with my less important papers.

Nippers, the second on my list, was a whiskered, sallow, and, upon the whole, rather piratical-looking young man, of about five-and-twenty. I always deemed him the victim of two evil powers—ambition and indigestion. The ambition was evinced by a certain impatience of the duties of a mere copyist, an unwarrantable usurpation of strictly professional affairs, such as the original drawing up of legal documents. The indigestion seemed betokened in an occasional nervous testiness and grinning irritability, causing the teeth to audibly grind together over mistakes committed in copying; unnecessary maledictions, hissed, rather than spoken, in the heat of business; and especially by a continual discontent with the height of the table where he worked. Though of a very ingenious mechanical turn, Nippers could never get this table to suit him. He put chips under it, blocks of various sorts, bits of pasteboard, and at last went so far as to attempt an exquisite adjustment, by final pieces of folded blotting-paper. But no invention would answer. If, for the sake of easing his back, he brought the table-lid at a sharp angle well up towards his chin, and wrote there like a man using the steep roof of a Dutch house for his desk, then he declared that it stopped the circulation in his arms. If now he lowered the table to his waistbands, and stooped over it in writing, then there was a sore aching in his back. In short, the truth of the matter was, Nippers knew not what he wanted. Or, if he wanted anything, it was to be rid of a scrivener's table altogether. Among the manifestations of his diseased ambition was a fondness he had for receiving visits from certain ambiguous-looking fellows in seedy coats, whom he called his clients. Indeed, I was aware that not only was he, at times, considerable of a ward-politician, but he occasionally did a little business at the Justices' courts, and was not unknown on the steps of the Tombs. I have good reason to believe, however, that one individual who called upon him at my chambers, and who, with a grand air, he insisted was his client, was no other than a dun, and the alleged title-deed, a bill. But, with all his failings, and the annoyances he caused me, Nippers, like his compatriot Turkey, was a very useful man to me; wrote a neat, swift hand; and, when he chose, was not deficient in a gentlemanly sort of deportment. Added to this, he always dressed in a gentlemanly sort of way; and so, incidentally, reflected credit upon my chambers. Whereas, with respect to Turkey, I had much ado to keep him from being a reproach to me. His clothes were apt to look oily, and smell of eating-houses. He wore his pantaloons very loose and baggy in summer. His coats were execrable; his hat not to be handled. But while the hat was a thing of indifference to me, inasmuch as his natural civility and deference, as a dependent Englishman, always led him to doff it the moment he entered the room, yet his coat was another matter. Concerning his coats, I reasoned with him; but with no effect. The truth was, I suppose, that a man with so small an income could not afford to sport such a lustrous face and a lustrous coat at one and the same time. As Nippers once observed, Turkey's money went chiefly for red ink. One winter day, I presented Turkey with a highly respectable-looking coat of my own—a padded gray coat, of a most comfortable warmth, and which buttoned straight up from the knee to the neck.

I thought Turkey would appreciate the favor, and abate his rashness and obstreperousness of afternoons. But no; I verily believe that buttoning himself up in so downy and blanket-like a coat had a pernicious effect upon him—upon the same principle that too much oats are bad for horses. In fact, precisely as a rash, restive horse is said to feel his oats, so Turkey felt his coat. It made him insolent. He was a man whom prosperity harmed.

Though, concerning the self-indulgent habits of Turkey, I had my own private surmises, yet, touching Nippers, I was well persuaded that, whatever might be his faults in other respects, he was, at least, a temperate young man. But, indeed, nature herself seemed to have been his vintner, and, at his birth, charged him so thoroughly with an irritable, brandy-like disposition, that all subsequent potations were needless. When I consider how, amid the stillness of my chambers, Nippers would sometimes impatiently rise from his seat, and stooping over his table, spread his arms wide apart, seize the whole desk, and move it, and jerk it, with a grim, grinding motion on the floor, as if the table were a perverse voluntary agent, intent on thwarting and vexing him, I plainly perceive that, for Nippers, brandy-and-water were altogether superfluous.

It was fortunate for me that, owing to its peculiar cause—indigestion—the irritability and consequent nervousness of Nippers were mainly observable in the morning, while in the afternoon he was comparatively mild. So that, Turkey's paroxysms only coming on about twelve o'clock, I never had to do with their eccentricities at one time. Their fits relieved each other, like guards. When Nippers's was on, Turkey's was off; and *vice versa*. This was a good natural arrangement, under the circumstances.

Ginger Nut, the third on my list, was a lad, some twelve years old. His father was a carman, ambitious of seeing his son on the bench instead of a cart, before he died. So he sent him to my office, as student at law, errand-boy, cleaner and sweeper, at the rate of one dollar a week. He had a little desk to himself, but he did not use it much. Upon inspection, the drawer exhibited a great array of the shells of various sorts of nuts. Indeed, to this quick-witted youth, the whole noble science of the law was contained in a nutshell. Not the least among the employments of Ginger Nut, as well as one which he discharged with the most alacrity, was his duty as cake and apple purveyor for Turkey and Nippers. Copying law-papers being proverbially a dry, husky sort of business, my two scriveners were fain to moisten their mouths very often with Spitzenbergs, to be had at the numerous stalls nigh the Custom House and Post Office. Also, they sent Ginger Nut very frequently for that peculiar cake—small, flat, round, and very spicy—after which he had been named by them. Of a cold morning, when business was but dull, Turkey would gobble up scores of these cakes, as if they were mere wafers—indeed, they sell them at the rate of six or eight for a penny—the scrape of his pen blending with the crunching of the crisp particles in his mouth. Rashest of all the fiery afternoon blunders and flurried rashnesses of Turkey, was his once moistening a ginger-cake between his lips, and clapping it on to a mortgage, for a seal. I came within an ace of dismissing him then. But he mollified me by making an oriental bow, and saying—

"With submission, sir, it was generous of me to find you in stationery on my own account."

Now my original business—that of a conveyancer and title hunter, and drawer-up of recondite documents of all sorts—was considerably increased by receiving the master's office. There was now great work for scriveners. Not only must I push the clerks already with me, but I must have additional help.

In answer to my advertisement, a motionless young man one morning stood upon my office threshold, the door being open, for it was summer. I can see that figure now—pallidly neat, pitiably respectable, incurably forlorn! It was Bartleby.

After a few words touching his qualifications, I engaged him, glad to have among my corps of copyists a man of so singularly sedate an aspect, which I thought might operate beneficially upon the flighty temper of Turkey, and the fiery one of Nippers.

I should have stated before that ground-glass folding-doors divided my premises into two parts, one of which was occupied by my scriveners, the other by myself. According to my humor, I threw open these doors, or closed them. I resolved to assign Bartleby a corner by the folding-doors, but on my side of them, so as to have this quiet man within easy call, in case any trifling thing was to be done. I placed his desk close up to a small side-window in that part of the room, a window which originally had afforded a lateral view of certain grimy back-yards and bricks, but which, owing to subsequent erections, commanded at present no view at all, though it gave some light. Within three feet of the panes was a wall, and the light came down from far above, between two lofty buildings, as from a very small opening in a dome. Still further to a satisfactory arrangement, I procured a high green folding screen, which might entirely isolate Bartleby from my sight, though not remove him from my voice. And thus, in a manner, privacy and society were conjoined.

At first, Bartleby did an extraordinary quantity of writing. As if long famishing for something to copy, he seemed to gorge himself on my documents. There was no pause for digestion. He ran a day and night line, copying by sun-light and by candle-light. I should have been quite delighted with his application, had he been cheerfully industrious. But he wrote on silently, palely, mechanically.

It is, of course, an indispensable part of a scrivener's business to verify the accuracy of his copy, word by word. Where there are two or more scriveners in an office, they assist each other in this examination, one reading from the copy, the other holding the original. It is a very dull, wearisome, and lethargic affair. I can readily imagine that, to some sanguine temperaments, it would be altogether intolerable. For example, I cannot credit that the mettlesome poet, Byron, would have contentedly sat down with Bartleby to examine a law document of, say five hundred pages, closely written in a crimpy hand.

Now and then, in the haste of business, it had been my habit to assist in comparing some brief document myself, calling Turkey or Nippers for this purpose. One object I had, in placing Bartleby so handy to me behind the screen, was, to avail myself of his services on such trivial occasions. It was on the third day, I think, of his being with me, and before any necessity had arisen for having his own writing examined, that, being much hurried to complete a small affair I had in hand, I abruptly called to Bartleby. In my haste and natural expectancy of instant compliance, I sat with my head bent over the original on my desk, and my right hand sideways, and somewhat nervously extended with the copy, so that, immediately upon emerging from his retreat, Bartleby might snatch it and proceed to business without the least delay.

In this very attitude did I sit when I called to him, rapidly stating what it was I wanted him to do—namely, to examine a small paper with me. Imagine my surprise, nay, my consternation, when, without moving from his privacy, Bartleby, in a singularly mild, firm voice, replied, "I would prefer not to."

I sat awhile in perfect silence, rallying my stunned faculties. Immediately it occurred to me that my ears had deceived me, or Bartleby had entirely misunderstood my meaning. I repeated my request in the clearest tone I could assume; but in quite as clear a one came the previous reply, "I would prefer not to."

"Prefer not to," echoed I, rising in high excitement, and crossing the room with a stride. "What do you mean? Are you moon-struck? I want you to help me compare this sheet here—take it," and I thrust it towards him.

"I would prefer not to," said he.

I looked at him steadfastly. His face was leanly composed; his gray eye dimly calm. Not a wrinkle of agitation rippled him. Had there been the least uneasiness, anger, impatience or impertinence in his manner; in other words, had there been anything ordinarily human about him, doubtless I should have violently dismissed him from the premises. But as it was, I should have as soon thought of turning my pale plaster-of-paris bust of Cicero out of doors. I stood gazing at him awhile, as he went on with his own writing, and then reseated myself at my desk. This is very strange, thought I. What had one best do? But my business hurried me. I concluded to forget the matter for the present, reserving it for my future leisure. So, calling Nippers from the other room, the paper was speedily examined.

A few days after this, Bartleby concluded four lengthy documents, being quadruplicates of a week's testimony taken before me in my High Court of Chancery. It became necessary to examine them. It was an important suit, and great accuracy was imperative. Having all things arranged, I called Turkey, Nippers and Ginger Nut, from the next room, meaning to place the four copies in the hands of my four clerks, while I should read from the original. Accordingly, Turkey, Nippers and Ginger Nut had taken their seats in a row, each with his document in his hand, when I called to Bartleby to join this interesting group.

"Bartleby! quick, I am waiting."

I heard a slow scrape of his chair legs on the uncarpeted floor, and soon he appeared standing at the entrance of his hermitage.

"What is wanted?" said he, mildly.

"The copies, the copies," said I, hurriedly. "We are going to examine them. There"—and I held towards him the fourth quadruplicate.

"I would prefer not to," he said, and gently disappeared behind the screen.

For a few moments I was turned into a pillar of salt, standing at the head of my seated column of clerks. Recovering myself, I advanced towards the screen, and demanded the reason for such extraordinary conduct.

"*Why* do you refuse?"

"I would prefer not to."

With any other man I should have flown outright into a dreadful passion, scorned all further words, and thrust him ignominiously from my presence. But there was something about Bartleby that not only strangely disarmed me, but, in a wonderful manner, touched and disconcerted me. I began to reason with him.

"These are your own copies we are about to examine. It is labor saving to you, because one examination will answer for your four papers. It is common usage. Every copyist is bound to help examine his copy. Is it not so? Will you not speak? Answer!"

"I prefer not to," he replied in a flute-like tone. It seemed to me that, while I had been addressing him, he carefully revolved every statement that I made; fully comprehended the meaning; could not gainsay the irresistible conclusion; but, at the same time, some paramount consideration prevailed with him to reply as he did.

"You are decided, then, not to comply with my request—a request made according to common usage and common sense?"

He briefly gave me to understand, that on that point my judgment was sound. Yes: his decision was irreversible.

It is not seldom the case that, when a man is browbeaten in some unprecedented and violently unreasonable way, he begins to stagger in his own plainest faith. He begins, as it were, vaguely to surmise that, wonderful as it may be, all the justice and all the reason is on the other side. Accordingly, if any disinterested persons are present, he turns to them for some reinforcement for his own faltering mind.

"Turkey," said I, "what do you think of this? Am I not right?"

"With submission, sir," said Turkey, in his blandest tone, "I think that you are."

"Nippers," said I, "what do *you* think of it?"

"I think I should kick him out of the office."

(The reader of nice perceptions will here perceive that, it being morning, Turkey's answer is couched in polite and tranquil terms, but Nippers replies in ill-tempered ones. Or, to repeat a previous sentence, Nippers's ugly mood was on duty, and Turkey's off.)

"Ginger Nut," said I, willing to enlist the smallest suffrage in my behalf, "what do *you* think of it?"

"I think, sir, he's a little *luny*," replied Ginger Nut, with a grin.

"You hear what they say," said I, turning towards the screen, "come forth and do your duty."

But he vouchsafed no reply. I pondered a moment in sore perplexity. But once more business hurried me. I determined again to postpone the consideration of this dilemma to my future leisure. With a little trouble we made out to examine the papers without Bartleby, though at every page or two Turkey deferentially dropped his opinion, that this proceeding was quite out of the common; while Nippers, twitching in his chair with a dyspeptic nervousness, ground out, between his set teeth, occasional hissing maledictions against the stubborn oaf behind the screen. And for his (Nippers's) part, this was the first and the last time he would do another man's business without pay.

Meanwhile Bartleby sat in his hermitage, oblivious to everything but his own peculiar business there.

Some days passed, the scrivener being employed upon another lengthy work. His late remarkable conduct led me to regard his ways narrowly. I observed that he never went to dinner; indeed, that he never went anywhere. As yet I had never, of my personal knowledge, known him to be outside of my office. He was a perpetual sentry in the corner. At about eleven o'clock though, in the morning, I noticed that Ginger Nut would advance toward the opening in Bartleby's screen, as if silently beckoned thither by a gesture invisible to me where I sat. The boy would then leave the office, jingling a few pence, and reappear with a handful of ginger-nuts, which he delivered in the hermitage, receiving two of the cakes for his trouble.

He lives, then, on ginger-nuts, thought I; never eats a dinner, properly speaking; he must be a vegetarian, then, but no; he never eats even vegetables, he eats nothing but ginger-nuts. My mind then ran on in reveries concerning the probable effects upon the human constitution of living entirely on ginger-nuts. Ginger-nuts are so called, because they contain ginger as one of their peculiar constituents, and the final flavoring one. Now, what was ginger? A hot, spicy thing. Was Bartleby hot and spicy? Not at all. Ginger, then, had no effect upon Bartleby. Probably he preferred it should have none.

Nothing so aggravates an earnest person as a passive resistance. If the individual so resisted be of a not inhumane temper, and the resisting one perfectly harmless in his passivity, then, in the better moods of the former, he will endeavor charitably to construe to his imagination what proves impossible to be solved by his judgment. Even so, for the most part, I regarded Bartleby and his ways. Poor fellow! thought I, he means no mischief; it is plain he intends no insolence; his aspect sufficiently evinces that his eccentricities are involuntary. He is useful to me. I can get along with him. If I turn him away, the chances are he will fall in with some less-indulgent employer, and then he will be rudely treated, and perhaps driven forth miserably to starve. Yes. Here I can cheaply purchase a delicious self-approval. To befriend Bartleby; to humor him in his strange willfulness, will cost me little or nothing, while I lay up in my soul what will eventually prove a sweet morsel for my conscience. But this mood was not invariable with me. The passiveness of Bartleby sometimes irritated me. I felt strangely goaded on to encounter him in new opposition—to elicit some angry spark from him answerable to my own. But, indeed, I might as well have essayed to strike fire with my knuckles against a bit of Windsor soap. But one afternoon the evil impulse in me mastered me, and the following little scene ensued:

"Bartleby," said I, "when those papers are all copied, I will compare them with you."

"I would prefer not to."

"How? Surely you do not mean to persist in that mulish vagary?"

No answer.

I threw open the folding-doors near by, and, turning upon Turkey and Nippers, exclaimed:

"Bartleby a second time says, he won't examine his papers. What do you think of it, Turkey?"

It was afternoon, be it remembered. Turkey sat glowing like a brass boiler; his bald head steaming; his hands reeling among his blotted papers.

"Think of it?" roared Turkey. "I think I'll just step behind his screen, and black his eyes for him!"

So saying, Turkey rose to his feet and threw his arms into a pugilistic position. He was hurrying away to make good his promise, when I detained him, alarmed at the effect of incautiously rousing Turkey's combativeness after dinner.

"Sit down, Turkey," said I, "and hear what Nippers has to say. What do you think of it, Nippers? Would I not be justified in immediately dismissing Bartleby?"

"Excuse me, that is for you to decide, sir. I think his conduct quite unusual, and, indeed, unjust, as regards Turkey and myself. But it may only be a passing whim."

"Ah," exclaimed I, "you have strangely changed your mind, then—you speak very gently of him now."

"All beer," cried Turkey; "gentleness is effects of beer—Nippers and I dined together to-day. You see how gentle *I* am, sir. Shall I go and black his eyes?"

"You refer to Bartleby, I suppose. No, not to-day, Turkey," I replied; "pray, put up your fists."

I closed the doors, and again advanced towards Bartleby. I felt additional incentives tempting me to my fate. I burned to be rebelled against again. I remembered that Bartleby never left the office.

"Bartleby," said I, "Ginger Nut is away; just step around to the post office, won't you?" (it was but a three minutes' walk) "and see if there is anything for me."

"I would prefer not to."

"You *will* not?"

"I *prefer* not."

I staggered to my desk, and sat there in a deep study. My blind inveteracy returned. Was there any other thing in which I could procure myself to be ignominiously repulsed by this lean, penniless wight?—my hired clerk? What added thing is there, perfectly reasonable, that he will be sure to refuse to do?

"Bartleby!"

No answer.

"Bartleby," in a louder tone.

No answer.

"Bartleby," I roared.

Like a very ghost, agreeably to the laws of magical invocation, at the third summons, he appeared at the entrance of his hermitage.

"Go to the next room, and tell Nippers to come to me."

"I prefer not to," he respectfully and slowly said, and mildly disappeared.

"Very good, Bartleby," said I, in a quiet sort of serenely-severe self-possessed tone, intimating the unalterable purpose of some terrible retribution very close at hand. At the moment I half intended something of the kind. But upon the whole, as it was drawing towards my dinner-hour, I thought it best to put on my hat and walk home for the day, suffering much from perplexity and distress of mind.

Shall I acknowledge it? The conclusion of this whole business was, that it soon became a fixed fact of my chambers, that a pale young scrivener, by the name of Bartleby, had a desk there; that he copied for me at the usual rate of four cents a folio (one hundred words); but he was permanently exempt from examining the work done by him, that duty being transferred to Turkey and Nippers, out of compliment, doubtless, to their superior acuteness; moreover, said Bartleby was never, on any account, to be dispatched on the most trivial errand of any sort; and that even if entreated to take upon him such a matter, it was generally understood that he would "prefer not to"—in other words, that he would refuse point-blank.

As days passed on, I became considerably reconciled to Bartleby. His steadiness, his freedom from all dissipation, his incessant industry (except when he chose to throw himself into a standing revery behind his screen), his great stillness, his unalterableness of demeanor under all circumstances, made him a valuable acquisition. One prime thing was this—*he was always there*—first in the morning, continually through the day, and the last at night. I had a singular confidence in his honesty. I felt my most precious papers perfectly safe in his hands. Sometimes, to be sure, I could not, for the very soul of me, avoid falling into sudden spasmodic passions with him. For it was exceeding difficult to bear in mind all the time those strange peculiarities, privileges, and unheard-of exemptions, forming the tacit stipulations on Bartleby's part under which he remained in my office. Now and then, in the eagerness of dispatching pressing business, I would inadvertently summon Bartleby, in a short rapid tone, to put his finger, say, on the incipient tie of a bit of red tape with which I was about compressing some papers. Of course, from behind the screen the usual answer, "I prefer not to," was sure to come; and then, how could a human creature, with the common infirmities of our nature, refrain from bitterly exclaiming upon such perverseness—such unreasonableness? However, every added repulse of this sort which I received only tended to lessen the probability of my repeating the inadvertence.

Here it must be said, that, according to the custom of most legal gentlemen occupying chambers in densely-populated law buildings, there were several keys to my door. One was kept by a woman residing in the attic, which person weekly scrubbed and daily swept and dusted my apartments. Another was kept by Turkey for convenience sake. The third I sometimes carried in my own pocket. The fourth I knew not who had.

Now, one Sunday morning I happened to go to Trinity Church, to hear a celebrated preacher, and finding myself rather early on the ground I thought I would walk round to my chambers for a while. Luckily I had my key with me; but upon applying it to the lock, I found it resisted by something inserted from the inside. Quite surprised, I called out; when to my consternation a key was turned from within; and thrusting his lean visage at me, and holding the door ajar, the apparition of Bartleby appeared, in his shirt sleeves, and otherwise in a strangely tattered *déshabillé*, saying quietly that he was sorry, but he was deeply engaged just then, and—preferred not admitting me at present. In a brief word or two, he moreover added, that perhaps I had better walk round the block two or three times, and by that time he would probably have concluded his affairs.

Now, the utterly unsurmised appearance of Bartleby, tenanting my law-chambers of a Sunday morning, with his cadaverously gentlemanly *nonchalance,* yet withal firm and self-possessed, had such a strange effect upon me, that incontinently I slunk away from my own door, and did as desired. But not without sundry twinges of impotent rebellion against the mild effrontery of this unaccountable scrivener. Indeed, it was his wonderful mildness chiefly, which not only disarmed me, but unmanned me as it were. For I consider that one, for the time, is sort of unmanned when he tranquilly permits his hired clerk to dictate to him, and order him away from his own premises. Furthermore, I was full of uneasiness as to what Bartleby could possibly be doing in my office in his shirt sleeves, and in an otherwise dismantled condition of a Sunday morning. Was anything amiss going on? Nay, that was out of the question. It was not to be thought of for a moment that Bartleby was an immoral person. But what could he be doing there?—copying? Nay again, whatever might be his eccentricities, Bartleby was an eminently decorous person. He would be the last man to sit down to his desk in any state approaching to nudity. Besides, it was Sunday; and there was something about Bartleby that forbade the supposition that he would by any secular occupation violate the proprieties of the day.

Nevertheless, my mind was not pacified; and full of a restless curiosity, at last I returned to the door. Without hindrance I inserted my key, opened it, and entered. Bartleby was not to be seen. I looked round anxiously, peeped behind his screen; but it was very plain that he was gone. Upon more closely examining the place, I surmised that for an indefinite period Bartleby must have eaten, dressed, and slept in my office, and that too without plate, mirror, or bed. The cushioned seat of a rickety old sofa in one corner bore the faint impress of a lean, reclining form. Rolled away under his desk, I found a blanket; under the empty grate, a blacking box and brush; on a chair, a tin basin, with soap and a ragged towel; in a newspaper a few crumbs of ginger-nuts and a morsel of cheese. Yes, thought I, it is evident enough that Bartleby has been making his home here, keeping bachelor's hall all by himself. Immediately then the thought came sweeping across me, what miserable friendlessness and loneliness are here revealed! His poverty is great; but his solitude, how horrible! Think of it. Of a Sunday, Wall Street is deserted as Petra, and every night of every day it is an emptiness. This building, too, which of week-days hums with industry and life, at nightfall echoes with sheer vacancy, and all through Sunday is forlorn. And here Bartleby makes his home; sole spectator of a solitude which he has seen all populous—a sort of innocent and transformed Marius brooding among the ruins of Carthage!

For the first time in my life a feeling of overpowering stinging melancholy seized me. Before, I had never experienced aught but a not unpleasing sadness. The bond of a common humanity now drew me irresistibly to gloom. A fraternal melancholy! For both I and Bartleby were sons of Adam. I remembered the bright silks and sparkling faces I had seen that day, in gala trim, swan-like sailing down the Mississippi of Broadway; and I contrasted them with the pallid copyist, and thought to myself, Ah, happiness courts the light, so we deem the world is gay; but misery hides aloof, so we deem that misery there is none. These sad fancyings—chimeras, doubtless, of a sick and silly brain—led on to other and more special thoughts, concerning the eccentricities of Bartleby. Presentiments of strange discoveries hovered round me. The scrivener's pale form appeared to me laid out, among uncaring strangers, in its shivering winding-sheet.

Suddenly I was attracted by Bartleby's closed desk, the key in open sight left in the lock.

I mean no mischief, seek the gratification of no heartless curiosity, thought I; besides, the desk is mine, and its contents, too, so I will make bold to look within. Everything was methodically arranged, the papers smoothly placed. The pigeon holes were deep, and removing the files of documents, I groped into their recesses. Presently I felt something there, and dragged it out. It was an old bandana handkerchief, heavy and knotted. I opened it, and saw it was a savings's bank.

I now recalled all the quiet mysteries which I had noted in the man. I remembered that he never spoke but to answer; that, though at intervals he had considerable time to himself, yet I had never seen him reading—no, not even a newspaper; that for long periods he would stand looking out, at his pale window behind the screen, upon the dead brick wall; I was quite sure he never visited any refectory or eating house; while his pale face clearly indicated that he never drank beer like Turkey, or tea and coffee even, like other men; that he never went anywhere in particular that I could learn; never went out for a walk, unless, indeed, that was the case at present; that he had declined telling who he was, or whence he came, or whether he had any relatives in the world; that though so thin and pale, he never complained of ill health. And more than all, I remembered a certain unconscious air of pallid—how shall I call it?—of pallid haughtiness, say, or rather an austere reserve about him, which had positively awed me into my tame compliance with his eccentricities, when I had feared to ask him to do the slightest incidental thing for me, even though I might know, from his long-continued motionlessness, that behind his screen he must be standing in one of those dead-wall reveries of his.

Revolving all these things, and coupling them with the recently discovered fact, that he made my office his constant abiding place and home, and not forgetful of his morbid moodiness; revolving all these things, a prudential feeling began to steal over me. My first emotions had been those of pure melancholy and sincerest pity; but just in proportion as the forlornness of Bartleby grew and grew to my imagination, did that same melancholy merge into fear, that pity into repulsion. So true it is, and so terrible, too, that up to a certain point the thought or sight of misery enlists our best affections; but, in certain special cases, beyond that point it does not. They err who would assert that invariably this is owing to the inherent selfishness of the human heart. It rather proceeds from a certain hopelessness of remedying excessive and organic ill. To a sensitive being, pity is not seldom pain. And when at last it is perceived that such pity cannot lead to effectual succor, common sense bids the soul be rid of it. What I saw that morning persuaded me that the scrivener was the victim of innate and incurable disorder. I might give alms to his body; but his body did not pain him; it was his soul that suffered, and his soul I could not reach.

I did not accomplish the purpose of going to Trinity Church that morning. Somehow, the things I had seen disqualified me for the time from church-going. I walked homeward, thinking what I would do with Bartleby. Finally, I resolved upon this—I would put certain calm questions to him the next morning, touching his history, etc., and if he declined to answer them openly and unreservedly (and I supposed he would prefer not), then to give him a twenty dollar bill over and above whatever I might owe him, and tell him his services were no longer required; but that if in any other way I could assist him, I would be happy to do so, especially if he desired to return to his native place, wherever that might be, I would willingly help to defray the expenses. Moreover, if, after reaching home, he found himself at any time in want of aid, a letter from him would be sure of a reply.

The next morning came.

"Bartleby," said I, gently calling to him behind his screen.

No reply.

"Bartleby," said I, in a still gentler tone, "come here; I am not going to ask you to do anything you would prefer not to do—I simply wish to speak to you."

Upon this he noiselessly slid into view.

"Will you tell me, Bartleby, where you were born?"

"I would prefer not to."

"Will you tell me *anything* about yourself?"

"I would prefer not to."

"But what reasonable objection can you have to speak to me? I feel friendly towards you."

He did not look at me while I spoke, but kept his glance fixed upon my bust of Cicero, which, as I then sat, was directly behind me, some six inches above my head.

"What is your answer, Bartleby?" said I, after waiting a considerable time for a reply, during which his countenance remained immovable, only there was the faintest conceivable tremor of the white attenuated mouth.

"At present I prefer to give no answer," he said, and retired into his hermitage.

It was rather weak in me I confess, but his manner, on this occasion, nettled me. Not only did there seem to lurk in it a certain calm disdain, but his perverseness seemed ungrateful, considering the undeniable good usage and indulgence he had received from me.

Again I sat ruminating what I should do. Mortified as I was at his behavior, and resolved as I had been to dismiss him when I entered my office, nevertheless I strangely felt something superstitious knocking at my heart, and forbidding me to carry out my purpose, and denouncing me for a villain if I dared to breathe one bitter word against this forlornest of mankind. At last, familiarly drawing my chair behind his screen, I sat down and said: "Bartleby, never mind, then, about revealing your history; but let me entreat you, as a friend, to comply as far as may be with the usages of this office. Say now, you will help to examine papers to-morrow or next day: in short, say now, that in a day or two you will begin to be a little reasonable:—say so, Bartleby."

"At present I would prefer not to be a little reasonable," was his mildly cadaverous reply.

Just then the folding-doors opened, and Nippers approached. He seemed suffering from an unusually bad night's rest, induced by severer indigestion than common. He overhead those final words of Bartleby.

"*Prefer not,* eh?" gritted Nippers—"I'd *prefer* him, if I were you, sir," addressing me—"I'd *prefer* him; I'd give him preferences, the stubborn mule! What is it, sir, pray, that he *prefers* not to do now?"

Bartleby moved not a limb.

"Mr. Nippers," said I, "I'd prefer that you would withdraw for the present."

Somehow, of late, I had got into the way of involuntarily using this word "prefer" upon all sorts of not exactly suitable occasions. And I trembled to think that my contact with the scrivener had already and seriously affected me in a mental way. And what further and deeper aberration might it not yet produce? This apprehension had not been without efficacy in determining me to summary measures.

As Nippers, looking very sour and sulky, was departing, Turkey blandly and deferentially approached.

"With submission, sir," said he, "yesterday I was thinking about Bartleby here, and I think that if he would but prefer to take a quart of good ale every day, it would do much towards mending him, and enabling him to assist in examining his papers."

"So you have got the word, too," said I, slightly excited.

"With submission, what word, sir?" asked Turkey, respectfully crowding himself into the contracted space behind the screen, and by so doing, making me jostle the scrivener. "What word, sir?"

"I would prefer to be left alone here," said Bartleby, as if offended at being mobbed in his privacy.

"*That's* the word, Turkey," said I—"*that's* it."

"Oh, *prefer*? oh yes—queer word. I never use it myself. But, sir, as I was saying, if he would but prefer—"

"Turkey," interrupted I, "you will please withdraw."

"Oh certainly, sir, if you prefer that I should."

As he opened the folding-doors to retire, Nippers at his desk caught a glimpse of me, and asked whether I would prefer to have a certain paper copied on blue paper or white. He did not in the least roguishly accent the word "prefer." It was plain that it involuntarily rolled from his tongue. I thought to myself, surely I must get rid of a demented man, who already has in some degree turned the tongues, if not the heads of myself and clerks. But I thought it prudent not to break the dismission at once.

The next day I noticed that Bartleby did nothing but stand at his window in his dead-wall revery. Upon asking him why he did not write, he said that he had decided upon doing no more writing.

"Why, how now? what next?" exclaimed I, "do no more writing?"

"No more."

"And what is the reason?"

"Do you not see the reason for yourself?" he indifferently replied.

I looked steadfastly at him, and perceived that his eyes looked dull and glazed. Instantly it occurred to me, that his unexampled diligence in copying by his dim window for the first few weeks of his stay with me might have temporarily impaired his vision.

I was touched. I said something in condolence with him. I hinted that of course he did wisely in abstaining from writing for a while; and urged him to embrace that opportunity of taking wholesome exercise in the open air. This, however, he did not do. A few days after this, my other clerks being absent, and being in a great hurry to dispatch certain letters by the mail, I thought that, having nothing else earthly to do, Bartleby would surely be less inflexible than usual, and carry these letters to the post office. But he blankly declined. So, much to my inconvenience, I went myself.

Still added days went by. Whether Bartleby's eyes improved or not, I could not say. To all appearance, I thought they did. But when I asked him if they did, he vouchsafed no answer. At all events, he would do no copying. At last, in reply to my urgings, he informed me that he had permanently given up copying.

"What!" exclaimed I; "suppose your eyes should get entirely well —better than ever before—would you not copy then?"

"I have given up copying," he answered, and slid aside.

He remained as ever, a fixture in my chamber. Nay—if that were possible—he became still more of a fixture than before. What was to be done? He would do nothing in the office; why should he stay there? In plain fact, he had now become a millstone to me, not only useless as a necklace, but afflictive to bear. Yet I was sorry for him. I speak less than truth when I say that, on his own account, he occasioned me uneasiness. If he would but have named a single relative or friend, I would instantly have written, and urged their taking the poor fellow away to some convenient retreat. But he seemed alone, absolutely alone in the universe. A bit of wreck in the mid Atlantic. At length, necessities connected with my business tyrannized over all other considerations. Decently as I could, I told Bartleby that in six days' time he must unconditionally leave the office. I warned him to take measures, in the interval, for procuring some other abode. I offered to assist him in this endeavor, if he himself would but take the first step towards a removal. "And when you finally quit me, Bartleby," added I, "I shall see that you go not away entirely unprovided. Six days from this hour, remember."

At the expiration of that period, I peeped behind the screen, and lo! Bartleby was there.

I buttoned up my coat, balanced myself; advanced slowly towards him, touched his shoulder, and said, "The time has come; you must quit this place; I am sorry for you; here is money; but you must go."

"I would prefer not," he replied, with his back still towards me.

"You *must*."

He remained silent.

Now I had an unbounded confidence in this man's common honesty. He had frequently restored to me sixpences and shillings carelessly dropped upon the floor, for I am apt to be very reckless in such shirt-button affairs. The proceeding, then, which followed will not be deemed extraordinary.

"Bartleby," said I, "I owe you twelve dollars on account; here are thirty-two; the odd twenty are yours—Will you take it?" and I handed the bills towards him.

But he made no motion.

"I will leave them here, then," putting them under a weight on the table. Then taking my hat and cane and going to the door, I tranquilly turned and added—"After you have removed your things from these offices, Bartleby, you will of course lock the door—since every one is now gone for the day but you—and if you please, slip your key underneath the mat, so that I may have it in the morning. I shall not see you again; so good-by to you. If, hereafter, in your new place of abode, I can be of any service to you, do not fail to advise me by letter. Good-by, Bartleby, and fare you well."

But he answered not a word; like the last column of some ruined temple, he remained standing mute and solitary in the middle of the otherwise deserted room.

As I walked home in a pensive mood, my vanity got the better of my pity. I could not but highly plume myself on my masterly management in getting rid of Bartleby. Masterly I call it, and such it must appear to any dispassionate thinker. The beauty of my procedure seemed to consist in its perfect quietness. There was no vulgar bullying, no bravado of any sort, no choleric hectoring, and striding to and fro across the apartment, jerking out vehement commands for Bartleby to bundle himself off with his beggarly traps. Nothing of the kind. Without loudly bidding Bartleby depart—as an inferior genius might have done—I *assumed* the ground that depart he must; and upon that assumption built all I had to say. The more I thought over my procedure, the more I was charmed with it. Nevertheless, next morning, upon awakening, I had my doubts—I had somehow slept off the fumes of vanity. One of the coolest and wisest hours a man has, is just after he awakes in the morning. My procedure seemed as sagacious as ever—but only in theory. How it would prove in practice—there was the rub. It was truly a beautiful thought to have assumed Bartleby's departure; but, after all, that assumption was simply my own, and none of Bartleby's. The great point was, not whether I had assumed that he would quit me, but whether he would prefer so to do. He was more a man of preferences than assumptions.

After breakfast, I walked down town, arguing the probabilities *pro* and *con*. One moment I thought it would prove a miserable failure, and Bartleby would be found all alive at my office as usual; the next moment it seemed certain that I should find his chair empty. And so I kept veering about. At the corner of Broadway and Canal Street, I saw quite an excited group of people standing in earnest conversation.

"I'll take odds he doesn't," said a voice as I passed.

"Doesn't go?—done!" said I, "put up your money."

I was instinctively putting my hand in my pocket to produce my own, when I remembered that this was an election day. The words I had overheard bore no reference to Bartleby, but to the success or non-success of some candidate for the mayoralty. In my intent frame of mind, I had, as it were, imagined that all Broadway shared in my excitement, and were debating the same question with me. I passed on, very thankful that the uproar of the street screened my momentary absent-mindedness.

As I had intended, I was earlier than usual at my office door. I stood listening for a moment. All was still. He must be gone. I tried the knob. The door was locked. Yes, my procedure had worked to a charm; he indeed must be vanished. Yet a certain melancholy mixed with this: I was almost sorry for my brilliant success. I was fumbling under the door mat for the key, which Bartleby was to have left there for me, when accidentally my knee knocked against a panel, producing a summoning sound, and in response a voice came to me from within—"Not yet; I am occupied."

It was Bartleby.

I was thunderstruck. For an instant I stood like the man who, pipe in mouth, was killed one cloudless afternoon long ago in Virginia, by summer lightning; at his own warm open window he was killed, and remained leaning out there upon the dreamy afternoon, till some one touched him, when he fell.

"Not gone!" I murmured at last. But again obeying that wondrous ascendancy which the inscrutable scrivener had over me, and from which ascendancy, for all my chafing, I could not completely escape, I slowly went down stairs and out into the street, and while walking round the block, considered what I should next do in this unheard-of perplexity. Turn the man out by an actual thrusting I could not; to drive him away by calling him hard names would not do; calling in the police was an unpleasant idea; and yet, permit him to enjoy his cadaverous triumph over me—this, too, I could not think of. What was to be done? or, if nothing could be done, was there anything further that I could *assume* in the matter? Yes, as before I had prospectively assumed that Bartleby would depart, so now I might retrospectively assume that departed he was. In the legitimate carrying out of this assumption, I might enter my office in a great hurry, and pretending not to see Bartleby at all, walk straight against him as if he were air. Such a proceeding would in a singular degree have the appearance of a home-thrust. It was hardly possible that Bartleby could withstand such an application of the doctrine of assumptions. But upon second thoughts the success of the plan seemed rather dubious. I resolved to argue the matter over with him again.

"Bartleby," said I, entering the office, with a quietly severe expression, "I am seriously displeased. I am pained, Bartleby. I had thought better of you. I had imagined you of such a gentlemanly organization, that in any delicate dilemma a slight hint would suffice—in short, an assumption. But it appears I am deceived. Why," I added, unaffectedly starting, "you have not even touched that money yet," pointing to it, just where I had left it the evening previous.

He answered nothing.

"Will you, or will you not, quit me?" I now demanded in a sudden passion, advancing close to him.

"I would prefer *not* to quit you," he replied, gently emphasizing the *not*.

"What earthly right have you to stay here? Do you pay any rent? Do you pay my taxes? Or is this property yours?"

He answered nothing.

"Are you ready to go on and write now? Are your eyes recovered? Could you copy a small paper for me this morning? or help examine a few lines? or step round to the post office? In a word, will you do anything at all, to give a coloring to your refusal to depart the premises?"

He silently retired into his hermitage.

I was now in such a state of nervous resentment that I thought it but prudent to check myself at present from further demonstrations. Bartleby and I were alone. I remembered the tragedy of the unfortunate Adams and the still more unfortunate Colt in the solitary office of the latter; and how poor Colt, being dreadfully incensed by Adams, and imprudently permitting himself to get wildly excited, was at unawares hurried into his fatal act—an act which certainly no man could possibly deplore more than the actor himself. Often it had occurred to me in my ponderings upon the subject that had that altercation taken place in the public street, or at a private residence, it would not have terminated as it did. It was the circumstance of being alone in a solitary office, up stairs, of a building entirely unhallowed by humanizing domestic associations—an uncarpeted office, doubtless, of a dusty, haggard sort of appearance—this it must have been, which greatly helped to enhance the irritable desperation of the hapless Colt.

But when this old Adam of resentment rose in me and tempted me concerning Bartleby, I grappled him and threw him. How? Why, simply by recalling the divine injunction: "A new commandment give I unto you, that ye love one another." Yes, this it was that saved me. Aside from higher considerations, charity often operates as a vastly wise and prudent principle—a great safeguard to its possessor. Men have committed murder for jealousy's sake, and anger's sake, and hatred's sake, and selfishness' sake, and spiritual pride's sake; but no man, that ever I heard of, ever committed a diabolical murder for sweet charity's sake. Mere self-interest, then, if no better motive can be enlisted, should, especially with high-tempered men, prompt all beings to charity and philanthropy. At any rate, upon the occasion in question, I strove to drown my exasperated feelings towards the scrivener by benevolently construing his conduct. Poor fellow, poor fellow! thought I, he don't mean anything; and besides, he has seen hard times, and ought to be indulged.

I endeavored, also, immediately to occupy myself, and at the same time to comfort my despondency. I tried to fancy, that in the course of the morning, at such time as might prove agreeable to him, Bartleby, of his own free accord, would emerge from his hermitage and take up some decided line of march in the direction of the door. But no. Half-past twelve o'clock came; Turkey began to glow in the face, overturn his inkstand, and become generally obstreperous; Nippers abated down into quietude and courtesy; Ginger Nut munched his noon apple; and Bartleby remained standing at his window in one of his profoundest dead-wall reveries. Will it be credited? Ought I to acknowledge it? That afternoon I left the office without saying one further word to him.

Some days now passed, during which, at leisure intervals I looked a little into "Edwards on the Will," and "Priestley on Necessity." Under the circumstances, those books induced a salutary feeling. Gradually I slid into the persuasion that these troubles of mine, touching the scrivener, had been all predestinated from eternity, and Bartleby was billeted upon me for some mysterious purpose of an allwise Providence, which it was not for a mere mortal like me to fathom. Yes, Bartleby, stay there behind your screen, thought I; I shall persecute you no more; you are harmless and noiseless as any of these old chairs; in short, I never feel so private as when I know you are here. At last I see it, I feel it; I penetrate to the predestinated purpose of my life. I am content. Others may have loftier parts to enact; but my mission in this world, Bartleby, is to furnish you with office-room for such period as you may see fit to remain.

I believe that this wise and blessed frame of mind would have continued with me, had it not been for the unsolicited and uncharitable remarks obtruded upon me by my professional friends who visited the rooms. But thus it often is, that the constant friction of illiberal minds wears out at last the best resolves of the more generous. Though to be sure, when I reflected upon it, it was not strange that people entering my office should be struck by the peculiar aspect of the unaccountable Bartleby, and so be tempted to throw out some sinister observations concerning him. Sometimes an attorney, having business with me, and calling at my office, and finding no one but the scrivener there, would undertake to obtain some sort of precise information from him touching my whereabouts; but without heeding his idle talk, Bartleby would remain standing immovable in the middle of the room. So after contemplating him in that position for a time, the attorney would depart, no wiser than he came.

Also, when a reference was going on, and the room full of lawyers and witnesses, and business driving fast, some deeply-occupied legal gentleman present, seeing Bartleby wholly unemployed, would request him to run round to his (the legal gentleman's) office and fetch some papers for him. Thereupon, Bartleby would tranquilly decline, and yet remain idle as before. Then the lawyer would give a great stare, and turn to me. And what could I say? At last I was made aware that all through the circle of my professional acquaintance, a whisper of wonder was running round, having reference to the strange creature I kept at my office. This worried me very much. And as the idea came upon me of his possibly turning out a long-lived man, and keep occupying my chambers, and denying my authority; and perplexing my visitors; and scandalizing my professional reputation; and casting a general gloom over the premises; keeping soul and body together to the last upon his savings (for doubtless he spent but half a dime a day), and in the end perhaps outlive me, and claim possession of my office by right of his perpetual occupancy: as all these dark anticipations crowded upon me more and more, and my friends continually intruded their relentless remarks upon the apparition in my room; a great change was wrought in me. I resolved to gather all my faculties together, and forever rid me of this intolerable incubus.

Ere revolving any complicated project, however, adapted to this end, I first simply suggested to Bartleby the propriety of his permanent departure. In a calm and serious tone, I commended the idea to his careful and mature consideration. But, having taken three days to meditate upon it, he apprised me, that his original determination remained the same; in short, that he still preferred to abide with me.

What shall I do? I now said to myself, buttoning up my coat to the last button. What shall I do? what ought I to do? what does conscience say I *should* do with this man, or, rather, ghost. Rid myself of him, I must; go, he shall. But how? You will not thrust him, the poor, pale, passive mortal—you will not thrust such a helpless creature out of your door? you will not dishonor yourself by such cruelty? No, I will not, I cannot do that. Rather would I let him live and die here, and then mason up his remains in the wall. What, then, will you do? For all your coaxing, he will not budge. Bribes he leaves under your own paperweight on your table; in short, it is quite plain that he prefers to cling to you.

Then something severe, something unusual must be done. What! surely you will not have him collared by a constable, and commit his innocent pallor to the common jail? And upon what ground could you procure such a thing to be done?—a vagrant, is he? What! he a vagrant, a wanderer, who refuses to budge? It is because he will *not* be a vagrant, then, that you seek to count him *as* a vagrant. That is too absurd. No visible means of support: there I have him. Wrong again: for indubitably he *does* support himself, and that is the only unanswerable proof that any man can show of his possessing the means so to do. No more, then. Since he will not quit me, I must quit him. I will change my offices; I will move elsewhere, and give him fair notice, that if I find him on my new premises I will then proceed against him as a common trespasser.

Acting accordingly, next day I thus addressed him: "I find these chambers too far from the City Hall; the air is unwholesome. In a word, I propose to remove my offices next week, and shall no longer require your services. I tell you this now, in order that you may seek another place."

He made no reply, and nothing more was said.

On the appointed day I engaged carts and men, proceeded to my chambers, and, having but little furniture, everything was removed in a few hours. Throughout, the scrivener remained standing behind the screen, which I directed to be removed the last thing. It was withdrawn; and, being folded up like a huge folio, left him the motionless occupant of a naked room. I stood in the entry watching him a moment, while something from within me upbraided me.

I re-entered, with my hand in my pocket—and—and my heart in my mouth.

"Good-by, Bartleby; I am going—good-by, and God some way bless you; and take that," slipping something in his hand. But it dropped upon the floor, and then—strange to say—I tore myself from him whom I had so longed to be rid of.

Established in my new quarters, for a day or two I kept the door locked, and started at every footfall in the passages. When I returned to my rooms, after any little absence, I would pause at the threshold for an instant, and attentively listen, ere applying my key. But these fears were needless. Bartleby never came nigh me.

I thought all was going well, when a perturbed-looking stranger visited me, inquiring whether I was the person who had recently occupied rooms at No.—Wall Street.

Full of forebodings, I replied that I was.

"Then, sir," said the stranger, who proved a lawyer, "you are responsible for the man you left there. He refuses to do any copying; he refuses to do anything; he says he prefers not to; and he refuses to quit the premises."

"I am very sorry, sir," said I, with assumed tranquillity, but an inward tremor, "but, really, the man you allude to is nothing to me —he is no relation or apprentice of mine, that you should hold me responsible for him."

"In mercy's name, who is he?"

"I certainly cannot inform you. I know nothing about him. Formerly I employed him as a copyist; but he has done nothing for me now for some time past."

"I shall settle him, then—good morning, sir."

Several days passed, and I heard nothing more; and, though I often felt a charitable prompting to call at the place and see poor Bartleby, yet a certain squeamishness, of I know not what, withheld me.

All is over with him, by this time, thought I, at last, when, through another week, no further intelligence reached me. But, coming to my room the day after, I found several persons waiting at my door in a high state of nervous excitement.

"That's the man—here he comes," cried the foremost one, whom I recognized as the lawyer who had previously called upon me alone.

"You must take him away, sir, at once," cried a portly person among them, advancing upon me, and whom I knew to be the landlord of No.—Wall Street. "These gentlemen, my tenants, cannot stand it any longer; Mr. B———," pointing to the lawyer, "has turned him out of his room, and he now persists in haunting the building generally, sitting upon the banisters of the stairs by day, and sleeping in the entry by night. Everybody is concerned; clients are leaving the offices; some fears are entertained of a mob; something you must do, and that without delay."

Aghast at this torrent, I fell back before it, and would fain have locked myself in my new quarters. In vain I persisted that Bartleby was nothing to me—no more than to any one else. In vain—I was the last person known to have anything to do with him, and they held me to the terrible account. Fearful, then, of being exposed in the papers (as one person present obscurely threatened), I considered the matter, and, at length, said, that if the lawyer would give me a confidential interview with the scrivener, in his (the lawyer's) own room, I would, that afternoon, strive my best to rid them of the nuisance they complained of.

Going up stairs to my old haunt, there was Bartleby silently sitting upon the banister at the landing.

"What are you doing here, Bartleby?" said I.

"Sitting upon the banister," he mildly replied.

I motioned him into the lawyer's room, who then left us.

"Bartleby," said I, "are you aware that you are the cause of great tribulation to me, by persisting in occupying the entry after being dismissed from the office?"

No answer.

"Now one of two things must take place. Either you must do something, or something must be done to you. Now what sort of business would you like to engage in? Would you like to re-engage in copying for some one?"

"No; I would prefer not to make any change."

"Would you like a clerkship in a dry-goods store?"

"There is too much confinement about that. No, I would not like a clerkship; but I am not particular."

"Too much confinement," I cried, "why, you keep yourself confined all the time!"

"I would prefer not to take a clerkship," he rejoined, as if to settle that little item at once.

"How would a bar-tender's business suit you? There is no trying of the eye-sight in that."

"I would not like it at all; though, as I said before, I am not particular."

His unwonted wordiness inspirited me. I returned to the charge.

"Well, then, would you like to travel through the country collecting bills for the merchants? That would improve your health."

"No, I would prefer to be doing something else."

"How, then, would going as a companion to Europe, to entertain some young gentleman with your conversation—how would that suit you?"

"Not at all. It does not strike me that there is anything definite about that. I like to be stationary. But I am not particular."

"Stationary you shall be, then," I cried, now losing all patience, and, for the first time in all my exasperating connection with him, fairly flying into a passion. "If you do not go away from these premises before night, I shall feel bound—indeed, I *am* bound—to—to—to quit the premises myself!" I rather absurdly concluded, knowing not with what possible threat to try to frighten his immobility into compliance. Despairing of all further efforts, I was precipitately leaving him, when a final thought occurred to me—one which had not been wholly unindulged before.

"Bartleby," said I, in the kindest tone I could assume under such exciting circumstances, "will you go home with me now—not to my office, but my dwelling—and remain there till we can conclude upon some convenient arrangement for you at your leisure? Come, let us start now, right away."

"No: at present I would prefer not to make any change at all."

I answered nothing; but, effectually dodging every one by the suddenness and rapidity of my flight, rushed from the building, ran up Wall Street towards Broadway, and, jumping into the first omnibus, was soon removed from pursuit. As soon as tranquillity returned, I distinctly perceived that I had now done all that I possibly could, both in respect to the demands of the landlord and his tenants, and with regard to my own desire and sense of duty, to benefit Bartleby, and shield him from rude persecution. I now strove to be entirely care-free and quiescent; and my conscience justified me in the attempt; though, indeed, it was not so successful as I could have wished. So fearful was I of being again hunted out by the incensed landlord and his exasperated tenants, that, surrendering my business to Nippers, for a few days, I drove about the upper part of the town and through the suburbs, in my rockaway; crossed over to Jersey City and Hoboken, and paid fugitive visits to Manhattanville and Astoria. In fact, I almost lived in my rockaway for the time.

When again I entered my office, lo, a note from the landlord lay upon the desk. I opened it with trembling hands. It informed me that the writer had sent to the police, and had Bartleby removed to the Tombs as a vagrant. Moreover, since I knew more about him than any one else, he wished me to appear at that place, and make a suitable statement of the facts. These tidings had a conflicting effect upon me. At first I was indignant; but, at last, almost approved. The landlord's energetic, summary disposition, had led him to adopt a procedure which I do not think I would have decided upon myself; and yet, as a last resort, under such peculiar circumstances, it seemed the only plan.

As I afterwards learned, the poor scrivener, when told that he must be conducted to the Tombs, offered not the slightest obstacle, but, in his pale, unmoving way, silently acquiesced.

Some of the compassionate and curious bystanders joined the party; and headed by one of the constables arm-in-arm with Bartleby, the silent procession filed its way through all the noise, and heat, and joy of the roaring thoroughfares at noon.

The same day I received the note, I went to the Tombs, or, to speak more properly, the Halls of Justice. Seeking the right officer, I stated the purpose of my call, and was informed that the individual I described was, indeed, within. I then assured the functionary that Bartleby was a perfectly honest man, and greatly to be compassionated, however unaccountably eccentric. I narrated all I knew, and closed by suggesting the idea of letting him remain in as indulgent confinement as possible, till something less harsh might be done—though, indeed, I hardly knew what. At all events, if nothing else could be decided upon, the alms-house must receive him. I then begged to have an interview.

Being under no disgraceful charge, and quite serene and harmless in all his ways, they had permitted him freely to wander about the prison, and, especially, in the inclosed grass-platted yards thereof. And so I found him there, standing all alone in the quietest of the yards, his face towards a high wall, while all around, from the narrow slits of the jail windows, I thought I saw peering out upon him the eyes of murderers and thieves.

"Bartleby!"

"I know you," he said, without looking round—"and I want nothing to say to you."

"It was not I that brought you here, Bartleby," said I, keenly pained at his implied suspicion. "And to you, this should not be so vile a place. Nothing reproachful attaches to you by being here. And see, it is not so sad a place as one might think. Look, there is the sky, and here is the grass."

"I know where I am," he replied, but would say nothing more, and so I left him.

As I entered the corridor again, a broad meat-like man, in an apron, accosted me, and, jerking his thumb over his shoulder, said —"Is that your friend?"

"Yes."

"Does he want to starve? If he does, let him live on the prison fare, that's all."

"Who are you?" asked I, not knowing what to make of such an unofficially speaking person in such a place.

"I am the grub-man. Such gentlemen as have friends here, hire me to provide them with something good to eat."

"Is this so?" said I, turning to the turnkey.

He said it was.

"Well, then," said I, slipping some silver into the grub-man's hands (for so they called him), "I want you to give particular attention to my friend there; let him have the best dinner you can get. And you must be as polite to him as possible."

"Introduce me, will you?" said the grub-man, looking at me with an expression which seemed to say he was all impatience for an opportunity to give a specimen of his breeding.

Thinking it would prove of benefit to the scrivener, I acquiesced; and, asking the grub-man his name, went up with him to Bartleby.

"Bartleby, this is a friend; you will find him very useful to you."

"Your sarvant, sir, your sarvant," said the grub-man, making a low salutation behind his apron. "Hope you find it pleasant here, sir; nice grounds—cool apartments—hope you'll stay with us some time—try to make it agreeable. What will you have for dinner to-day?"

"I prefer not to dine to-day," said Bartleby, turning away. "It would disagree with me; I am unused to dinners." So saying, he slowly moved to the other side of the inclosure, and took up a position fronting the dead-wall.

"How's this?" said the grub-man, addressing me with a stare of astonishment. "He's odd, ain't he?"

"I think he is a little deranged," said I, sadly.

"Deranged? deranged is it? Well, now, upon my word, I thought that friend of yourn was a gentleman forger; they are always pale and genteel-like, them forgers. I can't help pity 'em—can't help it, sir. Did you know Monroe Edwards?" he added, touchingly, and paused. Then, laying his hand piteously on my shoulder, sighed, "he died of consumption at Sing-Sing. So you weren't acquainted with Monroe?"

"No, I was never socially acquainted with any forgers. But I cannot stop longer. Look to my friend yonder. You will not lose by it. I will see you again."

Some few days after this, I again obtained admission to the Tombs, and went through the corridors in quest of Bartleby; but without finding him.

"I saw him coming from his cell not long ago," said a turnkey, "may be he's gone to loiter in the yards."

So I went in that direction.

"Are you looking for the silent man?" said another turnkey, passing me. "Yonder he lies—sleeping in the yard there. 'Tis not twenty minutes since I saw him lie down."

The yard was entirely quiet. It was not accessible to the common prisoners. The surrounding walls, of amazing thickness, kept off all sounds behind them. The Egyptian character of the masonry weighed upon me with its gloom. But a soft imprisoned turf grew under foot. The heart of the eternal pyramids, it seemed, wherein, by some strange magic, through the clefts, grass-seed, dropped by birds, had sprung.

Strangely huddled at the base of the wall, his knees drawn up, and lying on his side, his head touching the cold stones, I saw the wasted Bartleby. But nothing stirred. I paused; then went close up to him; stooped over, and saw that his dim eyes were open; otherwise he seemed profoundly sleeping. Something prompted me to touch him. I felt his hand, when a tingling shiver ran up my arm and down my spine to my feet.

The round face of the grub-man peered upon me now. "His dinner is ready. Won't he dine to-day, either? Or does he live without dining?"

"Lives without dining," said I, and closed the eyes.

"Eh!—He's asleep, ain't he?"

"With kings and counselors," murmured I.

There would seem little need for proceeding further in this history. Imagination will readily supply the meagre recital of poor Bartleby's interment. But, ere parting with the reader, let me say, that if this little narrative has sufficiently interested him, to awaken curiosity as to who Bartleby was, and what manner of life he led prior to the present narrator's making his acquaintance, I can only reply, that in such curiosity I fully share, but am wholly unable to gratify it. Yet here I hardly know whether I should divulge one little item of rumor, which came to my ear a few months after the scrivener's decease. Upon what basis it rested, I could never ascertain; and hence, how true it is I cannot now tell. But, inasmuch as this vague report has not been without a certain suggestive interest to me, however sad, it may prove the same with some others; and so I will briefly mention it. The report was this: that Bartleby had been a subordinate clerk in the Dead Letter Office at Washington, from which he had been suddenly removed by a change in the administration. When I think over this rumor, hardly can I express the emotions which seize me. Dead letters! does it not sound like dead men? Conceive a man by nature and misfortune prone to a pallid hopelessness, can any business seem more fitted to heighten it than that of continually handling these dead letters, and assorting them for the flames? For by the cartload they are annually burned. Sometimes from out the folded paper the pale clerk takes a ring—the finger it was meant for, perhaps, moulders in the grave; a bank-note sent in swiftest charity—he whom it would relieve, nor eats nor hungers any more; pardon for those who died despairing; hope for those who died unhoping; good tidings for those who died stifled by unrelieved calamities. On errands of life, these letters speed to death.

Ah, Bartleby! Ah, humanity!

Of This Time, Of That Place

Lionel Trilling (*American, 1905–1975*)

It was a fine September day. By noon it would be summer again, but now it was true autumn with a touch of chill in the air. As Joseph Howe stood on the porch of the house in which he lodged, ready to leave for his first class of the year, he thought with pleasure of the long indoor days that were coming. It was a moment when he could feel glad of his profession.

On the lawn the peach tree was still in fruit and young Hilda Aiken was taking a picture of it. She held the camera tight against her chest. She wanted the sun behind her, but she did not want her own long morning shadow in the foreground. She raised the camera, but that did not help, and she lowered it, but that made things worse. She twisted her body to the left, then to the right. In the end she had to step out of the direct line of the sun. At last she snapped the shutter and wound the film with intense care.

Howe, watching her from the porch, waited for her to finish and called good morning. She turned, startled, and almost sullenly lowered her glance. In the year Howe had lived at the Aikens', Hilda had accepted him as one of her family, but since his absence of the summer she had grown shy. Then suddenly she lifted her head and smiled at him, and the humorous smile confirmed his pleasure in the day. She picked up her bookbag and set off for school.

The handsome houses on the streets to the college were not yet fully awake, but they looked very friendly. Howe went by the

Bradby house where he would be a guest this evening at the first dinner party of the year. When he had gone the length of the picket fence, the whitest in town, he turned back. Along the path there was a fine row of asters and he went through the gate and picked one for his buttonhole. The Bradbys would be pleased if they happened to see him invading their lawn and the knowledge of this made him even more comfortable.

He reached the campus as the hour was striking. The students were hurrying to their classes. He himself was in no hurry. He stopped at his dim cubicle of an office and lit a cigarette. The prospect of facing his class had suddenly presented itself to him and his hands were cold; the lawful seizure of power he was about to make seemed momentous. Waiting did not help. He put out his cigarette, picked up a pad of theme paper, and went to his classroom.

As he entered, the rattle of voices ceased, and the twenty-odd freshmen settled themselves and looked at him appraisingly. Their faces seemed gross, his heart sank at their massed impassivity, but he spoke briskly.

"My name is Howe," he said, and turned and wrote it on the blackboard. The carelessness of the scrawl confirmed his authority. He went on, "My office is 412 Slemp Hall, and my office-hours are Monday, Wednesday and Friday from eleven-thirty to twelve-thirty."

He wrote, "M., W., F., 11:30–12:30." He said, "I'll be very glad to see any of you at that time. Or if you can't come then, you can arrange with me for some other time."

He turned again to the blackboard and spoke over his shoulder. "The text for the course is Jarman's *Modern Plays,* revised edition. The Co-op has it in stock." He wrote the name, underlined "revised edition" and waited for it to be taken down in the new notebooks.

When the bent heads were raised again he began his speech of prospectus. "It is hard to explain—" he said, and paused as they composed themselves. "It is hard to explain what a course like this is intended to do. We are going to try to learn something about modern literature and something about prose composition."

As he spoke, his hands warmed and he was able to look directly at the class. Last year on the first day the faces had seemed just as cloddish, but as the term wore on they became gradually alive and quite likable. It did not seem possible that the same thing could happen again.

"I shall not lecture in this course," he continued. "Our work will be carried on by discussion and we will try to learn by an exchange of opinion. But you will soon recognize that my opinion is worth more than anyone else's here."

He remained grave as he said it, but two boys understood and laughed. The rest took permission from them and laughed too. All Howe's private ironies protested the vulgarity of the joke, but the laughter made him feel benign and powerful.

When the little speech was finished, Howe picked up the pad of paper he had brought. He announced that they would write an extemporaneous theme. Its subject was traditional, "Who I am and why I came to Dwight College." By now the class was more at ease and it gave a ritualistic groan of protest. Then there was a stir as fountain pens were brought out and the writing-arms of the chairs were cleared, and the paper was passed about. At last, all the heads bent to work, and the room became still.

Howe sat idly at his desk. The sun shone through the tall clumsy windows. The cool of the morning was already passing. There was a scent of autumn and of varnish and the stillness of the room was deep and oddly touching. Now and then a student's head was raised and scratched in the old, elaborate students' pantomime that calls the teacher to witness honest intellectual effort.

Suddenly a tall boy stood within the frame of the open door. "Is this," he said, and thrust a large nose into a college catalogue, "is this the meeting place of English 1A? The section instructed by Dr. Joseph Howe?"

He stood on the very sill of the door, as if refusing to enter until he was perfectly sure of all his rights. The class looked up from work, found him absurd and gave a low mocking cheer.

The teacher and the new student, with equal pointedness, ignored the disturbance. Howe nodded to the boy, who pushed his head forward and then jerked it back in a wide elaborate arc to clear his brow of a heavy lock of hair. He advanced into the room and halted before Howe, almost at attention. In a loud, clear voice he announced, "I am Tertan, Ferdinand R., reporting at the direction of Head of Department Vincent."

The heraldic formality of this statement brought forth another cheer. Howe looked at the class with a sternness he could not really feel, for there was indeed something ridiculous about this boy. Under his displeased regard the rows of heads dropped to work again. Then he touched Tertan's elbow, led him up to the desk and stood so as to shield their conversation from the class.

"We are writing an extemporaneous theme," he said. "The subject is, 'Who I am and why I came to Dwight College.'"

He stripped a few sheets from the pad and offered them to the boy. Tertan hesitated and then took the paper, but he held it only tentatively. As if with the effort of making something clear, he gulped, and a slow smile fixed itself on his face. It was at once knowing and shy.

"Professor," he said, "to be perfectly fair to my classmates"—he made a large gesture over the room—"and to you"—he inclined his head to Howe—"this would not be for me an extemporaneous subject."

Howe tried to understand. "You mean you've already thought about it—you've heard we always give the same subject? That doesn't matter."

Again the boy ducked his head and gulped. It was the gesture of one who wishes to make a difficult explanation with perfect candor. "Sir," he said, and made the distinction with great care, "the topic I did not expect, but I have given much ratiocination to the subject."

Howe smiled and said, "I don't think that's an unfair advantage. Just go ahead and write."

Tertan narrowed his eyes and glanced sidewise at Howe. His strange mouth smiled. Then in quizzical acceptance, he ducked his head, threw back the heavy, dank lock, dropped into a seat with a great loose noise and began to write rapidly.

The room fell silent again and Howe resumed his idleness. When the bell rang, the students who had groaned when the task had been set now groaned again because they had not finished. Howe took up the papers, and held the class while he made the first assignment. When he dismissed it, Tertan bore down on him, his slack mouth held ready for speech.

"Some professors," he said, "are pedants. They are Dryasdusts. However, some professors are free souls and creative spirits. Kant, Hegel and Nietzsche were all professors." With this pronouncement he paused. "It is my opinion," he continued, "that you occupy the second category."

Howe looked at the boy in surprise and said with good-natured irony, "With Kant, Hegel and Nietzsche?"

Not only Tertan's hand and head but his whole awkward body waved away the stupidity. "It is the kind and not the quantity of the kind," he said sternly.

Rebuked, Howe said as simply and seriously as he could, "It would be nice to think so." He added, "Of course I am not a professor."

This was clearly a disappointment but Tertan met it. "In the French sense," he said with composure. "Generically, a teacher."

Suddenly he bowed. It was such a bow, Howe fancied, as a stage-director might teach an actor playing a medieval student who takes leave of Abelard—stiff, solemn, with elbows close to the body and feet together. Then, quite as suddenly, he turned and left.

A queer fish, and as soon as Howe reached his office, he sifted through the batch of themes and drew out Tertan's. The boy had filled many sheets with his unformed headlong scrawl. "Who am I?" he had begun. "Here, in a mundane, not to say commercialized academe, is asked the question which from time long immemorably out of mind has accreted doubts and thoughts in the psyche of man to pester him as a nuisance. Whether in St. Augustine (or Austin as sometimes called) or Miss Bashkirtsieff or Frederic Amiel or Empedocles, or in less lights of the intellect than these, this posed question has been ineluctable."

Howe took out his pencil. He circled "academe" and wrote "vocab." in the margin. He underlined "time long immemorably out of mind" and wrote "Diction!" But this seemed inadequate for what was wrong. He put down his pencil and read ahead to discover the principle of error in the theme. "Today as ever, in spite of gloomy prophets of the dismal science (economics) the question is uninvalidated. Out of the starry depths of heaven hurtles this spear of query demanding to be caught on the shield of the mind ere it pierces the skull and the limbs be unstrung."

Baffled but quite caught, Howe read on. "Materialism, by which is meant the philosophic concept and not the moral idea, provides no aegis against the question which lies beyond the tangible (metaphysics). Existence without alloy is the question presented. Environment and heredity relegated aside, the rags and old clothes of practical life discarded, the name and the instrumentality of livelihood do not, as the prophets of the dismal science insist on in this connection, give solution to the interrogation which not from the professor merely but veritably from the cosmos is given. I think, therefore I am (cogito etc.) but who am I? Tertan I am, but what is Tertan? Of this time, of that place, of some parentage, what does it matter?"

Existence without alloy: the phrase established itself. Howe put aside Tertan's paper and at random picked up another. "I am Arthur J. Casebeer, Jr.," he read. "My father is Arthur J. Casebeer and my grandfather was Arthur J. Casebeer before him. My mother is Nina Wimble Casebeer. Both of them are college graduates and my father is in insurance. I was born in St. Louis eighteen years ago and we still make our residence there."

Arthur J. Casebeer, who knew who he was, was less interesting than Tertan, but more coherent. Howe picked up Tertan's paper again. It was clear that none of the routine marginal comments, no "sent. str." or "punct." or "vocab." could cope with this torrential rhetoric. He read ahead, contenting himself with underscoring the errors against the time when he should have the necessary "conference" with Tertan.

It was a busy and official day of cards and sheets, arrangements and small decisions, and it gave Howe pleasure. Even when it was time to attend the first of the weekly Convocations he felt the charm of the beginning of things when intention is still innocent and uncorrupted by effort. He sat among the young instructors on the platform, and joined in their humorous complaints at having to assist at the ceremony, but actually he got a clear satisfaction from the ritual of prayer, and prosy speech, and even from wearing his academic gown. And when the Convocation was over the pleasure continued as he crossed the campus, exchanging greetings with men he had not seen since the spring. They were people who did not yet, and perhaps never would, mean much to him, but in a year they had grown amiably to be part of his life. They were his fellow-townsmen.

The day had cooled again at sunset, and there was a bright chill in the September twilight. Howe carried his voluminous gown over his arm, he swung his doctoral hood by its purple neckpiece, and on his head he wore his mortarboard with its heavy gold tassel bobbing just over his eye. These were the weighty and absurd symbols of his new profession and they pleased him. At twenty-six Joseph Howe had discovered that he was neither so well off nor so bohemian as he had once thought. A small income, adequate when supplemented by a sizable cash legacy, was genteel poverty when the cash was all spent. And the literary life—the room at the Lafayette, or the small apartment without a lease, the long summers on the Cape, the long afternoons and the social evenings—began to weary him. His writing filled his mornings, and should perhaps have filled his life, yet it did not. To the amusement of his friends, and with a certain sense that he was betraying his own freedom, he had used the last of his legacy for a year at Harvard. The small but respectable reputation of his two volumes of verse had proved useful

—he continued at Harvard on a fellowship and when he emerged as Doctor Howe he received an excellent appointment, with prospects, at Dwight.

He had his moments of fear when all that had ever been said of the dangers of the academic life had occurred to him. But after a year in which he had tested every possibility of corruption and seduction he was ready to rest easy. His third volume of verse, most of it written in his first years of teaching, was not only ampler but, he thought, better than its predecessors.

There was a clear hour before the Bradby dinner party, and Howe looked forward to it. But he was not to enjoy it, for lying with his mail on the hall table was a copy of this quarter's issue of *Life and Letters,* to which his landlord subscribed. Its severe cover announced that its editor, Frederic Woolley, had this month contributed an essay called "Two Poets," and Howe, picking it up, curious to see who the two poets might be, felt his own name start out at him with cabalistic power—Joseph Howe. As he continued to turn the pages his hand trembled.

Standing in the dark hall, holding the neat little magazine, Howe knew that his literary contempt for Frederic Woolley meant nothing, for he suddenly understood how he respected Woolley in the way of the world. He knew this by the trembling of his hand. And of the little world as well as the great, for although the literary groups of New York might dismiss Woolley, his name carried high authority in the academic world. At Dwight it was even a revered name, for it had been here at the college that Frederic Woolley had made the distinguished scholarly career from which he had gone on to literary journalism. In middle life he had been induced to take the editorship of *Life and Letters,* a literary monthly not widely read but heavily endowed, and in its pages he had carried on the defense of what he sometimes called the older values. He was not without wit, he had great knowledge and considerable taste, and even in the full movement of the "new" literature he had won a certain respect for his refusal to accept it. In France, even in England, he would have been connected with a more robust tradition of conservatism, but America gave him an audience not much better than genteel. It was known in the college that to the subsidy of *Life and Letters* the Bradbys contributed a great part.

As Howe read, he saw that he was involved in nothing less than an event. When the Fifth Series of *Studies in Order and Value* came to be collected, this latest of Frederic Woolley's essays would not be merely another step in the old direction. Clearly and unmistakably, it was a turning point. All his literary life Woolley had been concerned with the relation of literature to morality, religion, and the private and delicate pieties, and he had been unalterably opposed to all that he had called "inhuman humanitarianism." But here, suddenly, dramatically late, he had made an about-face, turning to the public life and to the humanitarian politics he had so long despised. This was the kind of incident the histories of literature make much of. Frederic Woolley was opening for himself a new career and winning a kind of new youth. He contrasted the two poets, Thomas Wormser, who was admirable, Joseph Howe, who was almost dangerous. He spoke of the "precious subjectivism" of Howe's verse. "In times like ours," he wrote, "with millions facing penury and want, one feels that the qualities of the *tour d'ivoire* are well-nigh inhuman, nearly insulting. The *tour d'ivoire* becomes the *tour d'ivresse,* and it is not self-intoxicated poets that our people need." The essay said more: "The problem is one of meaning. I am not ignorant that the creed of the esoteric poets declares that a poem does not and should not *mean* anything, that it *is* something. But poetry is what the poet makes it, and if he is a true poet he makes what his society needs. And what is needed now is the tradition in which Mr. Wormser writes, the true tradition of poetry. The Howes do no harm, but they do no good when positive good is demanded of all responsible men. Or do the Howes indeed do no harm? Perhaps Plato would have said they do, that in some ways theirs is the Phrygian music that turns men's minds from the struggle. Certainly it is true that Thomas Wormser writes in the lucid Dorian mode which sends men into battle with evil."

It was easy to understand why Woolley had chosen to praise Thomas Wormser. The long, lilting lines of *Corn Under Willows* hymned, as Woolley put it, the struggle for wheat in the Iowa fields, and expressed the real lives of real people. But why out of the dozen more notable examples he had chosen Howe's little volume as the example of "precious subjectivism" was hard to guess. In a way it was funny, this multiplication of himself into "the Howes." And yet this becoming the multiform political symbol by whose creation Frederic Woolley gave the sign of a sudden new life, this use of him as a sacrifice whose blood was necessary for the rites of rejuvenation, made him feel oddly unclean.

Nor could Howe get rid of a certain practical resentment. As a poet he had a special and respectable place in the college life. But it might be another thing to be marked as the poet of a willful and selfish obscurity.

As he walked to the Bradbys', Howe was a little tense and defensive. It seemed to him that all the world knew of the "attack" and agreed with it. And, indeed, the Bradbys had read the essay but Professor Bradby, a kind and pretentious man, said, "I see my old friend knocked you about a bit, my boy," and his wife Eugenia looked at Howe with her child-like blue eyes and said, "I shall *scold* Frederic for the untrue things he wrote about you. You aren't the least obscure." They beamed at him. In their genial snobbery they seemed to feel that he had distinguished himself. He was the leader of Howeism. He enjoyed the dinner party as much as he had thought he would.

And in the following days, as he was more preoccupied with his duties, the incident was forgotten. His classes had ceased to be mere groups. Student after student detached himself from the mass and required or claimed a place in Howe's awareness. Of them all it was Tertan who first and most violently signaled his separate existence. A week after classes had begun Howe saw his silhouette on the frosted glass of his office door. It was motionless for a long time, perhaps stopped by the problem of whether or not to knock before entering. Howe called, "Come in!" and Tertan entered with his shambling stride.

He stood beside the desk, silent and at attention. When Howe asked him to sit down, he responded with a gesture of head and hand, as if to say that such amenities were beside the point. Nevertheless, he did take the chair. He put his ragged, crammed briefcase between his legs. His face, which Howe now observed fully for the first time, was confusing, for it was made up of florid curves, the nose arched in the bone and voluted in the nostril, the mouth loose and soft and rather moist. Yet the face was so thin and narrow as to seem the very type of asceticism. Lashes of unusual length veiled the eyes and, indeed, it seemed as if there were a veil over the whole countenance. Before the words actually came, the face screwed itself into an attitude of preparation for them.

"You can confer with me now?" Tertan said.

"Yes, I'd be glad to. There are several things in your two themes I want to talk to you about." Howe reached for the packet of themes on his desk and sought for Tertan's. But the boy was waving them away.

"These are done perforce," he said. "Under the pressure of your requirement. They are not significant; mere duties." Again his great hand flapped vaguely to dismiss his themes. He leaned forward and gazed at his teacher.

"You are," he said, "a man of letters? You are a poet?" It was more declaration than question.

"I should like to think so," Howe said.

At first Tertan accepted the answer with a show of appreciation, as though the understatement made a secret between himself and Howe. Then he chose to misunderstand. With his shrewd and disconcerting control of expression, he presented to Howe a puzzled grimace. "What does that mean?" he said.

Howe retracted the irony. "Yes. I am a poet." It sounded strange to say.

"That," Tertan said, "is a wonder." He corrected himself with his ducking head. "I mean that is wonderful."

Suddenly, he dived at the miserable briefcase between his legs, put it on his knees, and began to fumble with the catch, all intent on the difficulty it presented. Howe noted that his suit was worn thin, his shirt almost unclean. He became aware, even, of a vague and musty odor of garments worn too long in unaired rooms. Tertan conquered the lock and began to concentrate upon a search into the interior. At last he held in his hand what he was after, a torn and crumpled copy of *Life and Letters*.

"I learned it from here," he said, holding it out.

Howe looked at him sharply, his hackles a little up. But the boy's face was not only perfectly innocent, it even shone with a conscious admiration. Apparently nothing of the import of the essay had touched him except the wonderful fact that his teacher was a "man of letters." Yet this seemed too stupid, and Howe, to test it, said, "The man who wrote that doesn't think it's wonderful."

Tertan made a moist hissing sound as he cleared his mouth of saliva. His head, oddly loose on his neck, wove a pattern of contempt in the air. "A critic," he said, "who admits *prima facie* that he does not understand." Then he said grandly, "It is the inevitable fate."

It was absurd, yet Howe was not only aware of the absurdity but of a tension suddenly and wonderfully relaxed. Now that the "attack" was on the table between himself and this strange boy, and subject to the boy's funny and absolutely certain contempt, the hidden force of his feeling was revealed to him in the very moment that it vanished. All unsuspected, there had been a film over the world, a transparent but discoloring haze of danger. But he had no time to stop over the brightened aspect of things. Tertan was going on. "I also am a man of letters. Putative."

"You have written a good deal?" Howe meant to be no more than polite, and he was surprised at the tenderness he heard in his words.

Solemnly the boy nodded, threw back the dank lock, and sucked in a deep, anticipatory breath. "First, a work of homiletics, which is a defense of the principles of religious optimism against the pessimism of Schopenhauer and the humanism of Nietzsche."

"Humanism? Why do you call it humanism?"

"It is my nomenclature for making a deity of man," Tertan replied negligently. "Then three fictional works, novels. And numerous essays in science, combating materialism. Is it your duty to read these if I bring them to you?"

Howe answered simply, "No, it isn't exactly my duty, but I shall be happy to read them."

Tertan stood up and remained silent. He rested his bag on the chair. With a certain compunction—for it did not seem entirely proper that, of two men of letters, one should have the right to blue-pencil the other, to grade him or to question the quality of his "sentence structure"—Howe reached for Tertan's papers. But before he could take them up, the boy suddenly made his bow-to-Abelard, the stiff inclination of the body with the hands seeming to emerge from the scholar's gown. Then he was gone.

But after his departure something was still left of him. The timbre of his curious sentences, the downright finality of so quaint a phrase as "It is the inevitable fate" still rang in the air. Howe gave the warmth of his feeling to the new visitor who stood at the door announcing himself with a genteel clearing of the throat.

"Doctor Howe, I believe?" the student said. A large hand advanced into the room and grasped Howe's hand. "Blackburn, sir, Theodore Blackburn, vice-president of the Student Council. A great pleasure, sir."

Out of a pair of ruddy cheeks a pair of small eyes twinkled good-naturedly. The large face, the large body were not so much fat as beefy and suggested something "typical"—monk, politician or innkeeper.

Blackburn took the seat beside Howe's desk. "I may have seemed to introduce myself in my public capacity, sir," he said. "But it is really as an individual that I came to see you. That is to say, as one of your students to be."

He spoke with an English intonation and he went on, "I was once an English major, sir."

For a moment Howe was startled, for the roast-beef look of the boy and the manner of his speech gave a second's credibility to one sense of his statement. Then the collegiate meaning of the phrase asserted itself, but some perversity made Howe say what was not really in good taste even with so forward a student, "Indeed? What regiment?"

Blackburn stared and then gave a little pouf-pouf of laughter. He waved the misapprehension away. "*Very* good, sir. It certainly is an ambiguous term." He chuckled in appreciation of Howe's joke, then cleared his throat to put it aside. "I look forward to taking your course in the romantic poets, sir," he said earnestly. "To me the romantic poets are the very crown of English literature."

Howe made a dry sound, and the boy, catching some meaning in it, said, "Little as I know them, of course. But even Shakespeare who is so dear to us of the Anglo-Saxon tradition is in a sense but the preparation for Shelley, Keats and Byron. And Wadsworth."

Almost sorry for him, Howe dropped his eyes. With some embarrassment, for the boy was not actually his student, he said softly, "Wordsworth."

"Sir?"

"Wordsworth, not Wadsworth. You said Wadsworth."

"Did I, sir?" Gravely he shook his head to rebuke himself for the error. "Wordsworth, of course—slip of the tongue." Then, quite in command again, he went on. "I have a favor to ask of you, Doctor Howe. You see, I began my college course as an English major,"—he smiled—"as I said."

"Yes?"

"But after my first year I shifted. I shifted to the social sciences. Sociology and government—I find them stimulating and very *real*." He paused, out of respect for reality. "But now I find that perhaps I have neglected the other side."

"The other side?" Howe said.

"Imagination, fancy, culture. A well-rounded man." He trailed off as if there were perfect understanding between them. "And so, sir, I have decided to end my senior year with your course in the romantic poets."

His voice was filled with an indulgence which Howe ignored as he said flatly and gravely, "But that course isn't given until the spring term."

"Yes, sir, and that is where the favor comes in. Would you let me take your romantic prose course? I can't take it for credit, sir, my program is full, but just for background it seems to me that I ought to take it. I do hope," he concluded in a manly way, "that you will consent."

"Well, it's no great favor, Mr. Blackburn. You can come if you wish, though there's not much point in it if you don't do the reading."

The bell rang for the hour and Howe got up.

"May I begin with this class, sir?" Blackburn's smile was candid and boyish.

Howe nodded carelessly and together, silently, they walked to the classroom down the hall. When they reached the door Howe stood back to let his student enter, but Blackburn moved adroitly behind him and grasped him by the arm to urge him over the threshold. They entered together with Blackburn's hand firmly on Howe's biceps, the student inducting the teacher into his own room. Howe felt a surge of temper rise in him and almost violently he disengaged his arm and walked to the desk, while Blackburn found a seat in the front row and smiled at him.

II

The question was, At whose door must the tragedy be laid?

All night the snow had fallen heavily and only now was abating in sparse little flurries. The windows were valanced high with white. It was very quiet; something of the quiet of the world had reached the class, and Howe found that everyone was glad to talk or listen. In the room there was a comfortable sense of pleasure in being human.

Casebeer believed that the blame for the tragedy rested with heredity. Picking up the book he read, "The sins of the fathers are visited on their children." This opinion was received with general favor. Nevertheless, Johnson ventured to say that the fault was all Pastor Manders' because the Pastor had made Mrs. Alving go back to her husband and was always hiding the truth. To this Hibbard objected with logic enough, "Well then, it was really all her husband's fault. He *did* all the bad things." De Witt, his face bright with an impatient idea, said that the fault was all society's. "By society I don't mean upper-crust society," he said. He looked around a little defiantly, taking in any members of the class who might be members of upper-crust society. "Not in that sense. I mean the social unit."

Howe nodded and said, "Yes, of course."

"If the society of the time had progressed far enough in science," De Witt went on, "Then there would be no problem for Mr. Ibsen to write about. Captain Alving plays around a little, gives way to perfectly natural biological urges, and he gets a social disease, a venereal disease. If the disease is cured, no problem. Invent salvarsan and the disease is cured. The problem of heredity disappears and li'l Oswald just doesn't get paresis. No paresis, no problem—no problem, no play."

This was carrying the ark into battle, and the class looked at De Witt with respectful curiosity. It was his usual way and on the whole they were sympathetic with his struggle to prove to Howe that science was better than literature. Still, there was something in his reckless manner that alienated them a little.

"Or take birth-control, for instance," De Witt went on. "If Mrs. Alving had some knowledge of contraception, she wouldn't have had to have li'l Oswald at all. No li'l Oswald, no play."

The class was suddenly quieter. In the back row Stettenhover swung his great football shoulders in a righteous sulking gesture, first to the right, then to the left. He puckered his mouth ostentatiously. Intellect was always ending up by talking dirty.

Tertan's hand went up, and Howe said, "Mr. Tertan." The boy shambled to his feet and began his long characteristic gulp. Howe made a motion with his fingers, as small as possible, and Tertan ducked his head and smiled in apology. He sat down. The class laughed. With more than half the term gone, Tertan had not been able to remember that one did not rise to speak. He seemed unable to carry on the life of the intellect without this mark of respect for it. To Howe the boy's habit of rising seemed to accord with the formal shabbiness of his dress. He never wore the casual sweaters and jackets of his classmates. Into the free and comfortable air of the college classroom he brought the stuffy sordid strictness of some crowded, metropolitan high school.

"Speaking from one sense," Tertan began slowly, "there is no blame ascribable. From the sense of determinism, who can say where the blame lies? The preordained is the preordained and it cannot be said without rebellion against the universe, a palpable absurdity."

In the back row Stettenhover slumped suddenly in his seat, his heels held out before him, making a loud, dry, disgusted sound. His body sank until his neck rested on the back of his chair. He folded his hands across his belly and looked significantly out of the window, exasperated not only with Tertan, but with Howe, with the class, with the whole system designed to encourage this kind of thing. There was a certain insolence in the movement and Howe flushed. As Tertan continued to speak, Howe stalked casually toward the window and placed himself in the line of Stettenhover's vision. He stared at the great fellow, who pretended not to see him. There was so much power in the big body, so much contempt in the Greek-athlete face under the crisp Greek-athlete curls, that Howe felt almost physical fear. But at last Stettenhover admitted him to focus and under his disapproving gaze sat up with slow indifference. His eyebrows raised high in resignation, he began to examine his hands. Howe relaxed and turned his attention back to Tertan.

"Flux of existence," Tertan was saying, "produces all things, so that judgment wavers. Beyond the phenomena, what? But phenomena are adumbrated and to them we are limited."

Howe saw it for a moment as perhaps it existed in the boy's mind —the world of shadows which are cast by a great light upon a hidden reality as in the old myth of the Cave. But the little brush with Stettenhover had tired him, and he said irritably, "But come to the point, Mr. Tertan."

He said it so sharply that some of the class looked at him curiously. For three months he had gently carried Tertan through his verbosities, to the vaguely respectful surprise of the other students, who seemed to conceive that there existed between this strange classmate and their teacher some special understanding from which they were content to be excluded. Tertan looked at him mildly, and at once came brilliantly to the point. "This is the summation of the play," he said and took up his book and read, " 'Your poor father never found any outlet for the overmastering joy of life that was in him. And I brought no holiday into his home, either. Everything seemed to turn upon duty and I am afraid I made your poor father's home unbearable to him, Oswald.' Spoken by Mrs. Alving."

Yes that was surely the "summation" of the play and Tertan had hit it, as he hit, deviously and eventually, the literary point of almost everything. But now, as always, he was wrapping it away from sight. "For most mortals," he said, "there are only joys of biological urgings, gross and crass, such as the sensuous Captain Alving. For certain few there are the transmutations beyond these to a contemplation of the utter whole."

Oh, the boy was mad. And suddenly the word, used in hyperbole, intended almost for the expression of exasperated admiration, became literal. Now that the word was used, it became simply apparent to Howe that Tertan was mad.

It was a monstrous word and stood like a bestial thing in the room. Yet it so completely comprehended everything that had puzzled Howe, it so arranged and explained what for three months had been perplexing him that almost at once its horror became domesticated. With this word Howe was able to understand why he had never been able to communicate to Tertan the value of a single criticism or correction of his wild, verbose themes. Their conferences had been frequent and long but had done nothing to reduce to order the splendid confusion of the boy's ideas. Yet, impossible though its expression was, Tertan's incandescent mind could always strike for a moment into some dark corner of thought.

And now it was suddenly apparent that it was not a faulty rhetoric that Howe had to contend with. With his new knowledge he looked at Tertan's face and wondered how he could have so long deceived himself. Tertan was still talking and the class had lapsed into a kind of patient unconsciousness, a coma of respect for words which, for all that most of them knew, might be profound. Almost with a suffusion of shame, Howe believed that in some dim way the class had long ago had some intimation of Tertan's madness. He reached out as decisively as he could to seize the thread of Tertan's discourse before it should be entangled further.

"Mr. Tertan says that the blame must be put upon whoever kills the joy of living in another. We have been assuming that Captain Alving was a wholly bad man, but what if we assume that he became bad only because Mrs. Alving, when they were first married, acted toward him in the prudish way she says she did?"

It was a ticklish idea to advance to freshmen and perhaps not profitable. Not all of them were following.

"That would put the blame on Mrs. Alving herself, whom most of you admire. And she herself seems to think so." He glanced at his watch. The hour was nearly over. "What do you think, Mr. De Witt?"

De Witt rose to the idea; he wanted to know if society couldn't be blamed for educating Mrs. Alving's temperament in the wrong way. Casebeer was puzzled, Stettenhover continued to look at his hands until the bell rang.

Tertan, his brows louring in thought, was making as always for a private word. Howe gathered his books and papers to leave quickly. At this moment of his discovery and with the knowledge still raw, he could not engage himself with Tertan. Tertan sucked in his breath to prepare for speech and Howe made ready for the pain and confusion. But at that moment Casebeer detached himself from the group with which he had been conferring and which he seemed to represent. His constituency remained at a tactful distance. The mission involved the time of an assigned essay. Casebeer's presentation of the plea—it was based on the freshmen's heavy duties at the fraternities during Carnival Week—cut across Tertan's preparation for speech. "And so some of us fellows thought," Casebeer concluded with heavy solemnity, "that we could do a better job, give our minds to it more, if we had more time."

Tertan regarded Casebeer with mingled curiosity and revulsion. Howe not only said that he would postpone the assignment but went on to talk about the Carnival, and even drew the waiting constituency into the conversation. He was conscious of Tertan's stern and astonished stare, then of his sudden departure.

Now that the fact was clear, Howe knew that he must act on it. His course was simple enough. He must lay the case before the Dean. Yet he hesitated. His feeling for Tertan must now, certainly, be in some way invalidated. Yet could he, because of a word, hurry to assign to official and reasonable solicitude what had been, until this moment, so various and warm? He could at least delay and, by moving slowly, lend a poor grace to the necessary, ugly act of making his report.

It was with some notion of keeping the matter in his own hands that he went to the Dean's office to look up Tertan's records. In the outer office the Dean's secretary greeted him brightly, and at his request brought him the manila folder with the small identifying photograph pasted in the corner. She laughed. "He was looking for the birdie in the wrong place," she said.

Howe leaned over her shoulder to look at the picture. It was as bad as all the Dean's-office photographs were, but it differed from all that Howe had ever seen. Tertan, instead of looking into the camera, as no doubt he had been bidden, had, at the moment of exposure, turned his eyes upward. His mouth, as though conscious of the trick played on the photographer, had the sly superior look that Howe knew.

The secretary was fascinated by the picture. "What a funny boy," she said. "He looks like Tartuffe!"

And so he did, with the absurd piety of the eyes and the conscious slyness of the mouth and the whole face bloated by the bad lens.

"Is he *like* that?" the secretary said.

"Like Tartuffe? No."

From the photograph there was little enough comfort to be had. The records themselves gave no clue to madness, though they suggested sadness enough. Howe read of a father, Stanislaus Tertan, born in Budapest and trained in engineering in Berlin, once employed by the Hercules Chemical Corporation—this was one of the factories that dominated the sound end of the town—but now without employment. He read of a mother Erminie (Youngfellow) Tertan, born in Manchester, educated at a Normal School at Leeds, now housewife by profession. The family lived on Greenbriar Street which Howe knew as a row of once elegant homes near what was now the factory district. The old mansion had long ago been divided into small and primitive apartments. Of Ferdinand himself there was little to learn. He lived with his parents, had attended a Detroit high school and had transferred to the local school in his last year. His rating for intelligence, as expressed in numbers, was high, his scholastic record was remarkable, he held a college scholarship for his tuition.

Howe laid the folder on the secretary's desk. "Did you find what you wanted to know?" she asked.

The phrases from Tertan's momentous first theme came back to him. "Tertan I am, but what is Tertan? Of this time, of that place, of some parentage, what does it matter?"

"No, I didn't find it," he said.

Now that he had consulted the sad, half-meaningless record he knew all the more firmly that he must not give the matter out of his own hands. He must not release Tertan to authority. Not that he anticipated from the Dean anything but the greatest kindness for Tertan. The Dean would have the experience and skill which he himself could not have. One way or another the Dean could answer the question, "What is Tertan?" Yet this was precisely what he feared. He alone could keep alive—not forever but for a somehow important time—the question, "What is Tertan?" He alone could keep it still a question. Some sure instinct told him that he must not surrender the question to a clean official desk in a clear official light to be dealt with, settled and closed.

He heard himself saying, "Is the Dean busy at the moment? I'd like to see him."

His request came thus unbidden, even forbidden, and it was one of the surprising and startling incidents of his life. Later when he reviewed the events, so disconnected in themselves, or so merely odd, of the story that unfolded for him that year, it was over this moment, on its face the least notable, that he paused longest. It was frequently to be with fear and never without a certainty of its meaning in his own knowledge of himself that he would recall this simple, routine request, and the feeling of shame and freedom it gave him as he sent everything down the official chute. In the end, of course, no matter what he did to "protect" Tertan, he would have had to make the same request and lay the matter on the Dean's clean desk. But it would always be a landmark of his life that, at the very moment when he was rejecting the official way, he had been, without will or intention, so gladly drawn to it.

After the storm's last delicate flurry, the sun had come out. Reflected by the new snow, it filled the office with a golden light which was almost musical in the way it made all the commonplace objects of efficiency shine with a sudden sad and noble significance. And the light, now that he noticed it, made the utterance of his perverse and unwanted request even more momentous.

The secretary consulted the engagement pad. "He'll be free any minute. Don't you want to wait in the parlor?"

She threw open the door of the large and pleasant room in which the Dean held his Committee meetings, and in which his visitors waited. It was designed with a homely elegance on the masculine side of the eighteenth-century manner. There was a small coal fire in the grate and the handsome mahogany table was strewn with books and magazines. The large windows gave on the snowy lawn, and there was such a fine width of window that the white casements and walls seemed at this moment but a continuation of the snow, the snow but an extension of casement and walls. The outdoors seemed taken in and made safe, the indoors seemed luxuriously freshened and expanded.

Howe sat down by the fire and lighted a cigarette. The room had its intended effect upon him. He felt comfortable and relaxed, yet nicely organized, some young diplomatic agent of the eighteenth century, the newly fledged Swift carrying out Sir William Temple's business. The rawness of Tertan's case quite vanished. He crossed his legs and reached for a magazine.

It was that famous issue of *Life and Letters* that his idle hand had found and his blood raced as he sifted through it, and the shape of his own name, Joseph Howe, sprang out at him, still cabalistic in its power. He tossed the magazine back on the table as the door of the Dean's office opened and the Dean ushered out Theodore Blackburn.

"Ah, Joseph!" the Dean said.

Blackburn said, "Good morning, Doctor." Howe winced at the title and caught the flicker of amusement over the Dean's face. The

Dean stood with his hand high on the door-jamb and Blackburn, still in the doorway, remained standing almost under the long arm.

Howe nodded briefly to Blackburn, snubbing his eager deference. "Can you give me a few minutes?" he said to the Dean.

"All the time you want. Come in." Before the two men could enter the office, Blackburn claimed their attention with a long full "er." As they turned to him, Blackburn said, "Can *you* give *me* a few minutes, Doctor Howe?" His eyes sparkled at the little audacity he had committed, the slightly impudent play with hierarchy. Of the three of them Blackburn kept himself the lowest, but he reminded Howe of his subaltern relation to the Dean.

"I mean, of course," Blackburn went on easily, "when you've finished with the Dean."

"I'll be in my office shortly," Howe said, turned his back on the ready "Thank you, sir," and followed the Dean into the inner room.

"Energetic boy," said the Dean. "A bit beyond himself but very energetic. Sit down."

The Dean lighted a cigarette, leaned back in his chair, sat easy and silent for a moment, giving Howe no signal to go ahead with business. He was a young Dean, not much beyond forty, a tall handsome man with sad, ambitious eyes. He had been a Rhodes scholar. His friends looked for great things from him, and it was generally said that he had notions of education which he was not yet ready to try to put into practice.

His relaxed silence was meant as a compliment to Howe. He smiled and said, "What's the business, Joseph?"

"Do you know Tertan—Ferdinand Tertan, a freshman?"

The Dean's cigarette was in his mouth and his hands were clasped behind his head. He did not seem to search his memory for the name. He said, "What about him?"

Clearly the Dean knew something, and he was waiting for Howe to tell him more. Howe moved only tentatively. Now that he was doing what he had resolved not to do, he felt more guilty at having been so long deceived by Tertan and more need to be loyal to his error.

"He's a strange fellow," he ventured. He said stubbornly, "In a strange way he's very brilliant." He concluded, "But very strange."

The springs of the Dean's swivel chair creaked as he came out of his sprawl and leaned forward to Howe. "Do you mean he's so strange that it's something you could give a name to?"

Howe looked at him stupidly. "What do you mean?" he said.

"What's his trouble?" the Dean said more neutrally.

"He's very brilliant, in a way. I looked him up and he has a top intelligence rating. But somehow, and it's hard to explain just how, what he says is always on the edge of sense and doesn't quite make it."

The Dean looked at him and Howe flushed up. The Dean had surely read Woolley on the subject of "the Howes" and the *tour d'ivresse*. Was that quick glance ironical?

The Dean picked up some papers from his desk, and Howe could see that they were in Tertan's impatient scrawl. Perhaps the little gleam in the Dean's glance had come only from putting facts together.

"He sent me this yesterday," the Dean said. "After an interview I had with him. I haven't been able to do more than glance at it. When you said what you did, I realized there was something wrong."

Twisting his mouth, the Dean looked over the letter. "You seem to be involved," he said without looking up. "By the way, what did you give him at mid-term?"

Flushing, setting his shoulders, Howe said firmly, "I gave him A-minus."

The Dean chuckled. "Might be a good idea if some of our nicer boys went crazy—just a little." He said, "Well," to conclude the matter and handed the papers to Howe. "See if this is the same thing you've been finding. Then we can go into the matter again."

Before the fire in the parlor, in the chair that Howe had been occupying, sat Blackburn. He sprang to his feet as Howe entered.

"I said my office, Mr. Blackburn." Howe's voice was sharp. Then he was almost sorry for the rebuke, so clearly and naively did Blackburn seem to relish his stay in the parlor, close to authority.

"I'm in a bit of a hurry, sir," he said, "and I did want to be sure to speak to you, sir."

He was really absurd, yet fifteen years from now he would have grown up to himself, to the assurance and mature beefiness. In banks, in consular offices, in brokerage firms, on the bench, more seriously affable, a little sterner, he would make use of his ability to be administered by his job. It was almost reassuring. Now he was exercising his too-great skill on Howe. "I owe you an apology, sir," he said.

Howe knew that he did, but he showed surprise.

"I mean, Doctor, after your having been so kind about letting me attend your class, I stopped coming." He smiled in deprecation. "Extracurricular activities take up so much of my time. I'm afraid

I undertook more than I could perform.

Howe had noticed the absence and had been a little irritated by it after Blackburn's elaborate plea. It was an absence that might be interpreted as a comment on the teacher. But there was only one way for him to answer. "You've no need to apologize," he said. "It's wholly your affair."

Blackburn beamed. "I'm so glad you feel that way about it, sir. I was worried you might think I had stayed away because I was influenced by—" he stopped and lowered his eyes.

Astonished, Howe said, "Influenced by what?"

"Well, by—" Blackburn hesitated and for answer pointed to the table on which lay the copy of *Life and Letters*. Without looking at it, he knew where to direct his hand. "By the unfavorable publicity, sir." He hurried on. "And that brings me to another point, sir. I am secretary of Quill and Scroll, sir, the student literary society, and I wonder if you would address us. You could read your own poetry, sir, and defend your own point of view. It would be very interesting."

It was truly amazing. Howe looked long and cruelly into Blackburn's face, trying to catch the secret of the mind that could have conceived this way of manipulating him, this way so daring and inept—but not entirely inept—with its malice so without malignity. The face did not yield its secret. Howe smiled broadly and said, "Of course I don't think you were influenced by the unfavorable publicity."

"I'm still going to take—regularly, for credit—your romantic poets course next term," Blackburn said.

"Don't worry, my dear fellow, don't worry about it."

Howe started to leave and Blackburn stopped him with, "But about Quill, sir?"

"Suppose we wait until next term? I'll be less busy then."

And Blackburn said, "Very good, sir, and thank you."

In his office the little encounter seemed less funny to Howe, was even in some indeterminate way disturbing. He made an effort to put it from his mind by turning to what was sure to disturb him more, the Tertan letter read in the new interpretation. He found what he had always found, the same florid leaps beyond fact and meaning, the same headlong certainty. But as his eye passed over the familiar scrawl it caught his own name, and for the second time that hour he felt the race of his blood.

"The Paraclete," Tertan had written to the Dean, "from a Greek word meaning to stand in place of, but going beyond the primitive idea to mean traditionally the helper, the one who comforts and assists, cannot without fundamental loss be jettisoned. Even if taken no longer in the supernatural sense, the concept remains deeply in the human consciousness inevitably. Humanitarianism is no reply, for not every man stands in the place of every other man for this other comrade's comfort. But certain are chosen out of the human race to be the consoler of some other. Of these, for example, is Joseph Barker Howe, Ph.D. Of intellects not the first yet of true intellect and lambent instructions, given to that which is intuitive and irrational, not to what is logical in the strict word, what is judged by him is of the heart and not the head. Here is one chosen, in that he chooses himself to stand in the place of another for comfort and consolation. To him more than another I give my gratitude, with all respect to our Dean who reads this, a noble man, but merely dedicated, not consecrated. But not in the aspect of the Paraclete only is Dr. Joseph Barker Howe established, for he must be the Paraclete to another aspect of himself, that which is driven and persecuted by the lack of understanding in the world at large, so that he in himself embodies the full history of man's tribulations and, overflowing upon others, notably the present writer, is the ultimate end."

This was love. There was no escape from it. Try as Howe might to remember that Tertan was mad and all his emotions invalidated, he could not destroy the effect upon him of his student's stern, affectionate regard. He had betrayed not only a power of mind but a power of love. And, however firmly he held before his attention the fact of Tertan's madness, he could do nothing to banish the physical sensation of gratitude he felt. He had never thought of himself as "driven and persecuted" and he did not now. But still he could not make meaningless his sensation of gratitude. The pitiable Tertan sternly pitied him, and comfort came from Tertan's never-to-be-comforted mind.

III

In an academic community, even an efficient one, official matters move slowly. The term drew to a close with no action in the case of Tertan, and Joseph Howe had to confront a curious problem. How should he grade his strange student, Tertan?

Tertan's final examination had been no different from all his other writing, and what did one "give" such a student? De Witt must have his A, that was clear. Johnson would get a B. With Casebeer it was a question of a B-minus or a C-plus, and Stettenhover, who had been crammed by the team tutor to fill half a blue-book with his thin feminine scrawl, would have his C-minus which he would accept with mingled indifference and resentment. But with Tertan it was not so easy.

The boy was still in the college process and his name could not be omitted from the grade sheet. Yet what should a mind under suspicion of madness be graded? Until the medical verdict was given, it was for Howe to continue as Tertan's teacher and to keep his judgment pedagogical. Impossible to give him an F: he had not failed. B was for Johnson's stolid mediocrity. He could not be put on the edge of passing with Stettenhover, for he exactly did not pass. In energy and richness of intellect he was perhaps even De Witt's superior, and Howe toyed grimly with the notion of giving him an A, but that would lower the value of the A De Witt had won with his beautiful and clear, if still arrogant, mind. There was a notation which the Registrar recognized—Inc., for Incomplete, and in the horrible comedy of the situation, Howe considered that. But really only a mark of M for Mad would serve.

In his perplexity, Howe sought the Dean, but the Dean was out of town. In the end he decided to maintain the A-minus he had given Tertan at mid-term. After all, there had been no falling away from that quality. He entered it on the grade sheet with something like bravado.

Academic time moves quickly. A college year is not really a year, lacking as it does three months. And it is endlessly divided into units which, at their beginning, appear larger than they are—terms, half-terms, months, weeks. And the ultimate unit, the hour, is not really an hour, lacking as it does ten minutes. And so the new term advanced rapidly, and one day the fields about the town were all brown, cleared of even the few thin patches of snow which had lingered so long.

Howe, as he lectured on the romantic poets, became conscious of Blackburn emanating wrath. Blackburn did it well, did it with enormous dignity. He did not stir in his seat, he kept his eyes fixed on Howe in perfect attention, but he abstained from using his notebook, there was no mistaking what he proposed to himself as an attitude. His elbow on the writing-wing of the chair, his chin on the curled fingers of his hand, he was the embodiment of intellectual indignation. He was thinking his own thoughts, would give no public offense, yet would claim his due, was not to be intimidated. Howe knew that he would present himself at the end of the hour.

Blackburn entered the office without invitation. He did not smile; there was no cajolery about him. Without invitation he sat down beside Howe's desk. He did not speak until he had taken the blue-book from his pocket. He said, "What does this mean, sir?"

It was a sound and conservative student tactic. Said in the usual way it meant, "How could you have so misunderstood me?" or "What does this mean for my future in the course?" But there were none of the humbler tones in Blackburn's way of saying it.

Howe made the established reply, "I think that's for you to tell me."

Blackburn continued icy. "I'm sure I can't, sir."

There was a silence between them. Both dropped their eyes to the blue-book on the desk. On its cover Howe had penciled: "F. This is very poor work."

Howe picked up the blue-book. There was always the possibility of injustice. The teacher may be bored by the mass of papers and not wholly attentive. A phrase, even the student's handwriting, may irritate him unreasonably. "Well," said Howe, "let's go through it."

He opened the first page. "Now here: you write, In *The Ancient Mariner,* Coleridge lives in and transports us to a honey-sweet world where all is rich and strange, a world of charm to which we can escape from the humdrum existence of our daily lives, the world of romance. Here, in this warm and honey-sweet land of charming dreams we can relax and enjoy ourselves."

Howe lowered the paper and waited with a neutral look for Blackburn to speak. Blackburn returned the look boldly, did not speak, sat stolid and lofty. At last Howe said, speaking gently, "Did you mean that, or were you just at a loss for something to say?"

"You imply that I was just 'bluffing'?" The quotation marks hung palpable in the air about the word.

"I'd like to know. I'd prefer believing that you were bluffing to believing that you really thought this."

Blackburn's eyebrows went up. From the height of a great and firm-based idea he looked at his teacher. He clasped the crags for a moment and then pounced, craftily, suavely. "Do you mean, Doctor Howe, that there aren't two opinions possible?"

It was superbly done in its air of putting all of Howe's intellectual life into the balance. Howe remained patient and simple. "Yes, many opinions are possible, but not this one. Whatever anyone believes of *The Ancient Mariner,* no one can in reason believe that it represents a—a honey-sweet world in which we can relax."

"But that is what I *feel*, sir."

This was well-done, too. Howe said, "Look, Mr. Blackburn. Do you really relax with hunger and thirst, the heat and the sea-serpents, the dead men with staring eyes, Life in Death and the skeletons? Come now, Mr. Blackburn."

Blackburn made no answer, and Howe pressed forward. "Now, you say of Wordsworth, 'Of peasant stock himself, he turned from the effete life of the salons and found in the peasant the hope of a flaming revolution which would sweep away all the old ideas. This is the subject of his best poems.'"

Beaming at his teacher with youthful eagerness, Blackburn said, "Yes, sir, a rebel, a bringer of light to suffering mankind. I see him as a kind of Prothemeus."

"A kind of what?"

"Prothemeus, sir."

"Think, Mr. Blackburn. We were talking about him only today and I mentioned his name a dozen times. You don't mean Prothemeus. You mean—" Howe waited, but there was no response.

"You mean Prometheus."

Blackburn gave no assent, and Howe took the reins. "You've done a bad job here, Mr. Blackburn, about as bad as could be done." He saw Blackburn stiffen and his genial face harden again. "It shows either a lack of preparation or a complete lack of understanding." He saw Blackburn's face begin to go to pieces and he stopped.

"Oh, sir," Blackburn burst out, "I've never had a mark like this before, never anything below a B, never. A thing like this has never happened to me before."

It must be true, it was a statement too easily verified. Could it be that other instructors accepted such flaunting nonsense? Howe wanted to end the interview. "I'll set it down to lack of preparation," he said. "I know you're busy. That's not an excuse, but it's an explanation. Now, suppose you really prepare, and then take another quiz in two weeks. We'll forget this one and count the other."

Blackburn squirmed with pleasure and gratitude. "Thank you, sir. You're really very kind, very kind."

Howe rose to conclude the visit. "All right, then—in two weeks."

It was that day that the Dean imparted to Howe the conclusion of the case of Tertan. It was simple and a little anti-climactic. A physician had been called in, and had said the word, given the name.

"A classic case, he called it," the Dean said. "Not a doubt in the world," he said. His eyes were full of miserable pity, and he clutched at a word. "A classic case, a classic case." To his aid and to Howe's there came the Parthenon and the form of the Greek drama, the Aristotelian logic, Racine and the Well-Tempered Clavichord, the blueness of the Aegean and its clear sky. Classic—that is to say, without a doubt, perfect in its way, a veritable model, and, as the Dean had been told, sure to take a perfectly predictable and inevitable course to a foreknown conclusion.

It was not only pity that stood in the Dean's eyes. For a moment there was fear too. "Terrible," he said, "it is simply terrible."

Then he went on briskly. "Naturally, we've told the boy nothing. And, naturally, we won't. His tuition's paid by his scholarship, and we'll continue him on the rolls until the end of the year. That will be kindest. After that the matter will be out of our control. We'll see, of course, that he gets into the proper hands. I'm told there will be no change, he'll go on like this, be as good as this, for four to six months. And so we'll just go along as usual."

So Tertan continued to sit in Section 5 of English 1A, to his classmates still a figure of curiously dignified fun, symbol to most of them of the respectable but absurd intellectual life. But to his teacher he was now very different. He had not changed—he was still the greyhound casting for the scent of ideas, and Howe could see that he was still the same Tertan, but he could not feel it. What he felt as he looked at the boy sitting in his accustomed place was the hard blank of a fact. The fact itself was formidable and depressing. But what Howe was chiefly aware of was that he had permitted the metamorphosis of Tertan from person to fact.

As much as possible he avoided seeing Tertan's upraised hand and eager eye. But the fact did not know of its mere factuality, it continued its existence as if it were Tertan, hand up and eye questioning, and one day it appeared in Howe's office with a document.

"Even the spirit who lives egregiously, above the herd, must have its relations with the fellowman," Tertan declared. He laid the document on Howe's desk. It was headed "Quill and Scroll Society of Dwight College. Application for Membership."

"In most ways these are crass minds," Tertan said, touching the paper. "Yet as a whole, bound together in their common love of letters, they transcend their intellectual lacks since it is not a paradox that the whole is greater than the sum of its parts."

"When are the elections?" Howe asked.

"They take place tomorrow."

"I certainly hope you will be successful."

"Thank you. Would you wish to implement that hope?" A rather dirty finger pointed to the bottom of the sheet. "A faculty recommender is necessary," Tertan said stiffly, and waited.

"And you wish me to recommend you?"

"It would be an honor."

"You may use my name."

Tertan's finger pointed again. "It must be a written sponsorship, signed by the sponsor." There was a large blank space on the form under the heading, "Opinion of Faculty Sponsor."

This was almost another thing and Howe hesitated. Yet there was nothing else to do and he took out his fountain pen. He wrote, "Mr. Ferdinand Tertan is marked by his intense devotion to letters and by his exceptional love of all things of the mind." To this he signed his name, which looked bold and assertive on the white page. It disturbed him, the strange affirming power of a name. With a businesslike air, Tertan whipped up the paper, folding it with decision, and put it into his pocket. He bowed and took his departure, leaving Howe with the sense of having done something oddly momentous.

And so much now seemed odd and momentous to Howe that should not have seemed so. It was odd and momentous, he felt, when he sat with Blackburn's second quiz before him, and wrote in an excessively firm hand the grade of C-minus. The paper was a clear, an indisputable failure. He was carefully and consciously committing a cowardice. Blackburn had told the truth when he had pleaded his past record. Howe had consulted it in the Dean's office. It showed no grade lower than a B-minus. A canvass of some of Blackburn's previous instructors had brought vague attestations to the adequate powers of a student imperfectly remembered, and sometimes surprise that his abilities could be questioned at all.

As he wrote the grade, Howe told himself that his cowardice sprang from an unwillingness to have more dealings with a student he disliked. He knew it was simpler than that. He knew he feared Blackburn; that was the absurd truth. And cowardice did not solve the matter after all. Blackburn, flushed with a first success, attacked at once. The minimal passing grade had not assuaged his feelings and he sat at Howe's desk and again the blue-book lay between them. Blackburn said nothing. With an enormous impudence, he was waiting for Howe to speak and explain himself.

At last Howe said sharply and rudely, "Well?" His throat was tense and the blood was hammering in his head. His mouth was tight with anger at himself for his disturbance.

Blackburn's glance was almost baleful. "This is impossible, sir."

"But there it is," Howe answered.

"Sir?" Blackburn had not caught the meaning but his tone was still haughty.

Impatiently Howe said, "There it is, plain as day. Are you here to complain again?"

"Indeed I am, sir." There was surprise in Blackburn's voice that Howe should ask the question.

"I shouldn't complain if I were you. You did a thoroughly bad job on your first quiz. This one is a little, only a very little, better." This was not true. If anything, it was worse.

"That might be a matter of opinion, sir."

"It is a matter of opinion. Of my opinion."

"Another opinion might be different, sir."

"You really believe that?" Howe said.

"Yes." The omission of the "sir" was monumental.

"Whose, for example?"

"The Dean's, for example." Then the fleshy jaw came forward a little. "Or a certain literary critic's, for example."

It was colossal and almost too much for Blackburn himself to handle. The solidity of his face almost crumpled under it. But he withstood his own audacity and went on. "And the Dean's opinion might be guided by the knowledge that the person who gave me this mark is the man whom a famous critic, the most eminent judge of literature in this country, called a drunken man. The Dean might think twice about whether such a man is fit to teach Dwight students."

Howe said in quiet admonition, "Blackburn, you're mad," meaning no more than to check the boy's extravagance.

But Blackburn paid no heed. He had another shot in the locker. "And the Dean might be guided by the information, of which I have evidence, documentary evidence,"—he slapped his breast pocket twice—"that this same person personally recommended to the college literary society, the oldest in the country, that he personally recommended a student who is crazy, who threw the meeting into an uproar—a psychiatric case. The Dean might take that into account."

Howe was never to learn the details of that "uproar." He had always to content himself with the dim but passionate picture which at that moment sprang into his mind, of Tertan standing on some abstract height and madly denouncing the multitude of Quill and Scroll who howled him down.

He sat quiet a moment and looked at Blackburn. The ferocity had entirely gone from the student's face. He sat regarding his teacher almost benevolently. He had played a good card and now, scarcely at all unfriendly, he was waiting to see the effect. Howe took up the blue-book and negligently sifted through it. He read a page, closed the book, struck out the C-minus and wrote an F.

"Now you may take the paper to the Dean," he said. "You may tell him that after reconsidering it, I lowered the grade."

The gasp was audible. "Oh, sir!" Blackburn cried. "Please!" His face was agonized. "It means my graduation, my livelihood, my future. Don't do this to me."

"It's done already."

Blackburn stood up. "I spoke rashly, sir, hastily. I had no intention, no real intention, of seeing the Dean. It rests with you—entirely, entirely. I *hope* you will restore the first mark."

"Take the matter to the Dean or not, just as you choose. The grade is what you deserve and it stands."

Blackburn's head dropped. "And will I be failed at mid-term, sir?"

"Of course."

From deep out of Blackburn's great chest rose a cry of anguish. "Oh, sir, if you want me to go down on my knees to you, I will, I will."

Howe looked at him in amazement.

"I will, I will. On my knees, sir. This mustn't, mustn't happen."

He spoke so literally, meaning so very truly that his knees and exactly his knees were involved and seeming to think that he was offering something of tangible value to his teacher, that Howe, whose head had become icy clear in the nonsensical drama, thought, "The boy is mad," and began to speculate fantastically whether something in himself attracted or developed aberration. He could see himself standing absurdly before the Dean and saying, "I've found another. This time it's the vice-president of the Council, the manager of the debating team and secretary of Quill and Scroll."

One more such discovery, he thought, and he himself would be discovered! And there, suddenly, Blackburn was on his knees with a thump, his huge thighs straining his trousers, his hand outstretched in a great gesture of supplication.

With a cry, Howe shoved back his swivel chair and it rolled away on its casters half across the little room. Blackburn knelt for a moment to nothing at all, then got to his feet.

Howe rose abruptly. He said, "Blackburn, you will stop acting like an idiot. Dust your knees off, take your paper and get out. You've behaved like a fool and a malicious person. You have half a term to do a decent job. Keep your silly mouth shut and try to do it. Now get out."

Blackburn's head was low. He raised it and there was a pious light in his eyes. "Will you shake hands, sir?" he said. He thrust out his hand.

"I will not," Howe said.

Head and hand sank together. Blackburn picked up his blue-book and walked to the door. He turned and said, "Thank you, sir." His back, as he departed, was heavy with tragedy and stateliness.

IV

After years of bad luck with the weather, the College had a perfect day for Commencement. It was wonderfully bright, the air so transparent, the wind so brisk that no one could resist talking about it.

As Howe set out for the campus he heard Hilda calling from the back yard. She called, "Professor, professor," and came running to him.

Howe said, "What's this 'professor' business?"

"Mother told me," Hilda said. "You've been promoted. And I want to take your picture."

"Next year," said Howe. "I won't be a professor until next year. And you know better than to call anybody 'professor.'"

"It was just in fun," Hilda said. She seemed disappointed.

"But you can take my picture if you want. I won't look much different next year." Still, it was frightening. It might mean that he was to stay in this town all his life.

Hilda brightened. "Can I take it in this?" she said, and touched the gown he carried over his arm.

Howe laughed. "Yes, you can take it in this."

"I'll get my things and meet you in front of Otis," Hilda said. "I have the background all picked out."

On the campus the Commencement crowd was already large. It stood about in eager, nervous little family groups. As he crossed, Howe was greeted by a student, capped and gowned, glad of the chance to make an event for his parents by introducing one of his teachers. It was while Howe stood there chatting that he saw Tertan.

He had never seen anyone quite so alone, as though a circle had been woven about him to separate him from the gay crowd on the campus. Not that Tertan was not gay, he was the gayest of all. Three weeks had passed since Howe had last seen him, the weeks of examination, the lazy week before Commencement, and this was now a different Tertan. On his head he wore a panama hat, broad-brimmed and fine, of the shape associated with South American planters. He wore a suit of raw silk, luxurious, but yellowed with age and much too tight, and he sported a whangee cane. He walked sedately, the hat tilted at a devastating angle, the stick coming up and down in time to his measured tread. He had, Howe guessed, outfitted himself to greet the day in the clothes of that ruined father whose existence was on record in the Dean's office. Gravely and arrogantly he surveyed the scene—in it, his whole bearing seemed to say, but not of it. With his haughty step, with his flashing eye, Tertan was coming nearer. Howe did not wish to be seen. He shifted his position slightly. When he looked again, Tertan was not in sight.

The chapel clock struck the quarter hour. Howe detached himself from his chat and hurried to Otis Hall at the far end of the campus. Hilda had not yet come. He went up into the high portico and, using the glass of the door for a mirror, put on his gown, adjusted the hood on his shoulders and set the mortarboard on his head. When he came down the steps, Hilda had arrived.

Nothing could have told him more forcibly that a year had passed than the development of Hilda's photographic possessions from the box camera of the previous fall. By a strap about her neck was hung a leather case, so thick and strong, so carefully stitched and so molded to its contents that it could only hold a costly camera. The appearance was deceptive, Howe knew, for he had been present at the Aikens' pre-Christmas conference about its purchase. It was only a fairly good domestic camera. Still, it looked very impressive. Hilda carried another leather case from which she drew a collapsible tripod. Decisively she extended each of its gleaming legs and set it up on the path. She removed the camera from its case and fixed it to the tripod. In its compact efficiency the camera almost had a life of its own, but Hilda treated it with easy familiarity, looked into its eye, glanced casually at its gauges. Then from a pocket she took still another leather case and drew from it a small instrument through which she looked first at Howe, who began to feel inanimate and lost, and then at the sky. She made some adjustment on the instrument, then some adjustment on the camera.

She swept the scene with her eye, found a spot and pointed the camera in its direction. She walked to the spot, stood on it and beckoned to Howe. With each new leather case, with each new instrument, and with each new adjustment she had grown in ease and now she said, "Joe, will you stand here?"

Obediently Howe stood where he was bidden. She had yet another instrument. She took out a tape-measure on a mechanical spool. Kneeling down before Howe, she put the little metal ring of the tape under the tip of his shoe. At her request, Howe pressed it with his toe. When she had measured her distance, she nodded to Howe who released the tape. At a touch, it sprang back into the spool. "You have to be careful if you're going to get what you want," Hilda said. "I don't believe in all this snap-snap-snapping," she remarked loftily. Howe nodded in agreement, although he was beginning to think Hilda's care excessive.

Now at last the moment had come. Hilda squinted into her camera, moved the tripod slightly. She stood to the side, holding the plunger of the shutter-cable. "Ready," she said. "Will you relax, Joseph, please?" Howe realized that he was standing frozen. Hilda stood poised and precise as a setter, one hand holding the little cable, the other extended with curled dainty fingers like a dancer's, as if expressing to her subject the precarious delicacy of the moment. She pressed the plunger and there was the click. At once she stirred to action, got behind the camera, turned a new exposure. "Thank you," she said. "Would you stand under that tree and let me do a character study with light and shade?"

The childish absurdity of the remark restored Howe's ease. He went to the little tree. The pattern the leaves made on his gown was what Hilda was after. He had just taken a satisfactory position when he heard in the unmistakable voice, "Ah, Doctor! Having your picture taken?"

Howe gave up the pose and turned to Blackburn who stood on the walk, his hands behind his back, a little too large for his bachelor's gown. Annoyed that Blackburn should see him posing for a character study in light and shade, Howe said irritably, "Yes, having my picture taken."

Blackburn beamed at Hilda. "And the little photographer?" he said. Hilda fixed her eyes on the ground and stood closer to her brilliant and aggressive camera. Blackburn, teetering on his heels, his hands behind his back, wholly prelatical and benignly patient, was not abashed at the silence. At last Howe said, "If you'll excuse us, Mr. Blackburn, we'll go on with the picture."

"Go right ahead, sir. I'm running along." But he only came closer. "Doctor Howe," he said fervently, "I want to tell you how glad I am that I was able to satisfy your standards at last."

Howe was surprised at the hard, insulting brightness of his own voice, and even Hilda looked up curiously as he said, "Nothing you have ever done has satisfied me, and nothing you could ever do would satisfy me, Blackburn."

With a glance at Hilda, Blackburn made a gesture as if to hush Howe—as though all his former bold malice had taken for granted a kind of understanding between himself and his teacher, a secret which must not be betrayed to a third person. "I only meant, sir," he said, "that I was able to pass your course after all."

Howe said, "You didn't pass my course. I passed you out of my course. I passed you without even reading your paper. I wanted to be sure the college would be rid of you. And when all the grades were in and I did read your paper, I saw I was right not to have read it first."

Blackburn presented a stricken face. "It was very bad, sir?"

But Howe had turned away. The paper had been fantastic. The paper had been, if he wished to see it so, mad. It was at this moment that the Dean came up behind Howe and caught his arm. "Hello, Joseph," he said. "We'd better be getting along, it's almost late."

He was not a familiar man, but when he saw Blackburn, who approached to greet him, he took Blackburn's arm, too. "Hello, Theodore," he said. Leaning forward on Howe's arm and on Blackburn's, he said, "Hello, Hilda dear." Hilda replied quietly, "Hello, Uncle George."

Still clinging to their arms, still linking Howe and Blackburn, the Dean said, "Another year gone, Joe, and we've turned out another crop. After you've been here a few years, you'll find it reasonably upsetting—you wonder how there can be so many graduating classes while you stay the same. But of course, you don't stay the same." Then he said, "Well," sharply, to dismiss the thought. He pulled Blackburn's arm and swung him around to Howe. "Have you heard about Teddy Blackburn?" he asked. "He has a job already, before graduation—the first man of his class to be placed." Expectant of congratulations, Blackburn beamed at Howe. Howe remained silent.

"Isn't that good?" the Dean said. Still Howe did not answer and the Dean, puzzled and put out, turned to Hilda. "That's a very fine-looking camera, Hilda." She touched it with affectionate pride.

"Instruments of precision," said a voice. "Instruments of precision." Of the three with joined arms, Howe was the nearest to Tertan, whose gaze took in all the scene except the smile and the nod which Howe gave him. The boy leaned on his cane. The broad-brimmed hat, canting jauntily over his eye, confused the image of his face that Howe had established, suppressed the rigid lines of the ascetic and brought out the baroque curves. It made an effect of perverse majesty.

"Instruments of precision," said Tertan for the last time, addressing no one, making a casual comment to the universe. And it occurred to Howe that Tertan might not be referring to Hilda's equipment. The sense of the thrice-woven circle of the boy's loneliness smote him fiercely. Tertan stood in majestic jauntiness, superior to all the scene, but his isolation made Howe ache with a pity of which Tertan was more the cause than the object, so general and indiscriminate was it.

Whether in his sorrow he made some unintended movement toward Tertan which the Dean checked, or whether the suddenly tightened grip on his arm was the Dean's own sorrow and fear, he did not know. Tertan watched them in the incurious way people watch a photograph being taken, and suddenly the thought that, to the boy, it must seem that the three were posing for a picture together made Howe detach himself almost rudely from the Dean's grasp.

"I promised Hilda another picture," he announced—needlessly, for Tertan was no longer there, he had vanished in the last sudden flux of visitors who, now that the band had struck up, were rushing nervously to find seats.

"You'd better hurry," the Dean said. "I'll go along, it's getting late for me." He departed and Blackburn walked stately by his side.

Howe again took his position under the little tree which cast its shadow over his face and gown. "Just hurry, Hilda, won't you?" he said. Hilda held the cable at arm's length, her other arm crooked and her fingers crisped. She rose on her toes and said "Ready," and pressed the release. "Thank you," she said gravely and began to dismantle her camera as he hurried off to join the procession.

The Mohammedans

H. J. Kaplan (*American, 1918–*)

It never occurred to any of us that Simon might have been involved in the affair of the Mohammedans. He himself not only avoided any mention of the case, but shut himself up and saw no one until it was over. This indeed might have been construed as a suspicious circumstance, were it not for the fact that when we went to see Simon it was hardly in order to discuss the pitiful local scandals.

His full name was Charles Rodney Simon, and he had an illustrious ancestry among the local robber barons. He was small, middle-aged, very poor, shy, with a vehement, disjointed way of speaking. We were not disappointed to find him bizarre, with an inward irony and exquisite manners: it was just what we had been led to expect of a man who had lived abroad and seen T. S. Eliot plain. But think! A man who could tell uproarious tales about his adventures as Lord of a Manor that was literally tumbling down about his ears. Ambassador of the Ideal in a town whose rapid development was due to the manufacture of fertilizer and the trading of hogs. He never breathed a word. . . . O, Simon, Simon, what a *soirée* you missed!

One evening, late in the summer of 1942, he was sitting alone at the front window of his ancestral mansion, watching the sun go down over the park. Oddly enough, he was thinking of Negroes. Though both streets within his range of vision shook from time to time with the monstrous rumbling of trucks, Simon cocked his ear to catch the faint, boisterous, confused sounds that drifted from the other side of the park. Over there, beyond the iron fence lined with clumps of trees and bushes, beyond the narrow strip of lawn, the streets of the Negro neighborhood glowed already with the garish neons, the bustling and back-slapping and ribald shouts. Simon often walked in that neighborhood, which only the park had prevented from engulfing his house. And he spoke often, with regret, of the Negroes, "creatures of music and dream," who formed a world apart in America. A world of joy and spirit, a City which one might have opposed, as Lorca had opposed his gypsies, to the real world in which they violently and tragically lived. Only they were too numerous and too contemporary, like most things in this country. . . . The dusk was coming down swiftly. For a moment, Simon was distracted by a tiny, two-seater Ford which pulled up to the curb across the street and disgorged, surprisingly, four people—three women and a squat, long-armed man whose head was heavily bandaged.

He looked away, and precisely because the thing was so unlikely allowed himself to hope that these were some of his rich relatives, come to show him off to one of their friends. They would come in, polite, mildly amused, and Simon would be introduced as a poet. How happy they were to introduce him as a poet! How that saved the whole situation! He would carry on a kind of guerrilla war against them. He would turn to the prettiest woman and say: "Perhaps I have sold you a pair of shoes downtown? I am a poet four days of the week. The rest of the time I sell shoes." He would start a political discussion so that, knowing the arguments of their side better than they, he might demonstrate the shallowness of their rather sporty radicalism. Or he would show them his rooms, painted orange-crates and all, letting them understand that he much preferred this to their modern apartments.

Outside, the group crossed the street and stood now on the sidewalk in front of Simon's house—which was, in fact, the only house left on a block long given over to garages and warehouses. For all his myopia, Simon could see now that they were Negroes and that the man wore a sort of terry-cloth towel wrapped about his head. Half-obscured by the weeds of the lawn, they stood there immobile, like a fresco of dancers. What did they want? What were they waiting for? After a while he looked away to the sunset, now merging downward with the glow that rose from the other side of the park. Then a dilapidated truck rattled around the corner and stopped, and Simon realized that these people were moving into his house.

The idea came easily, without shock, as though his first concern was, defensively, to recall that he was a man of the spirit and that *the house was not necessarily his.* The ancestral mansion belonged to an Insurance Company. They would have torn it down long ago—so they had often assured him—were it not for the fact that Simon's father, an old friend of the Company's president, had expressed the desire that his son should live in the house as long as he pleased. Now, doubtless, they were trying to smoke him out with undesirable neighbors. . . . For a moment, Simon sat quite calmly, pulling his lip and considering what attitude he should take. The squat man with the bandaged head—one of his legs was shorter than the other—was hopping about with great agility, helping the truck-driver unload mattresses, bedsprings, ancient dressers and even (Simon peered out through the arched window and caught every detail) some painted orange-crates. But execrably painted, like the canvas wall of a side-show tent. He decided, finally, upon consternation; and he had a moment of bitterness. He was poor, patronized by fools, ignored by his peers. This was indeed the last straw!

He jumped up, ran to his bedroom, seized his old opera cape and the stick he had inherited from his great-grandfather. After a moment's reflection, he also took his black Homburg hat. Thus accoutred, what would he do? Throw himself into the lake? Deliver a denunciation from the porch-steps? He hadn't the vaguest idea. Perhaps, at bottom, he did not really believe that these people were coming to live in his house. He was five feet four inches tall, quite serious, quite consternated. Yet he gave an almost joyful laugh, muttered *sic transit gloria,* and imagined himself describing to his friends what a droll figure he made as he ran to the foyer and opened the door.

He found himself face to face with the Negro. The three women were still choreographically grouped on the sidewalk. The empty truck had driven away. Simon dropped his stick, picked it up, found the man's outstretched hand before him. He shook it.

"My name's Wiley Bey," said the Negro, in a very deep voice.

"Yes, of course."

"Wiley *Bey.*"

There was a moment of silence.

"I'm not moving in here to hide out," said the Negro. "They can't scare me or the Temple with newspaper articles. I told the man, if the government ask where I live, just tell them."

"Yes, of course, I see," muttered Simon again. He was intimidated and confused. Under the spotless, almost delicate order of the terry-cloth turban, the man's ugliness was imposing. His face was fleshy, with an enormous fat glistening nose, large black eyes, thick lips. He was scarcely taller than Simon, but his great chest and broad shoulders gave the impression of size and power. Perhaps, for once, he too was embarrassed or confused, for he stared at Simon with a slow, baleful, pendulum-like movement of his head, until the white man said:

"O yes, how stupid of me. Simon's the name, Charles Rodney Simon."

Wiley Bey nodded gravely.

"The name sounds Jewish, but it's not. My background is Scotch-Norman. In fact it's my personal opinion that Simon was originally not a family but a christian name. It's easy to imagine young Norman nobles named Jean Simon de Monfort, or Robert Simon de la Tour becoming John Simon and Robert Simon. A question of primogeniture, no doubt. On the other hand—"

"Have you got the key?"

"You flatter me!"

"The man at the office said you had the key, in case he didn't get here."

"Why yes, of course! You mean the key to upstairs," cried Simon with a nervous laugh. "Imagine! I rushed out here to help you move in and I forgot the key entirely. . . . But that's nonsense, don't believe a word of it. I was really quite annoyed when I saw you coming in. No one took the trouble to inform me, you know. And yet this house has been in the family for three generations. Ah well, at my back I always hear Time's winged chariot hurrying near. And why didn't he hand you over the key in the first place? He's a fool, that man is, and a moral coward to boot." He drew back a step and cocked his head. "Are you quite determined to move into this place? . . . I find it picturesque, but not very practical."

The Negro stared at him, like an expressionless ebony idol.

"But pay no attention to me," said Simon. "Idiotic! . . . Now let me see. The key."

Wiley Bey turned to the women on the sidewalk and announced, in a tone of dispassionate disgust: "It's a white man!" The women broke their group, each attaching herself to a small piece of furniture and dragging or carrying it to the steps. Simon found the man's black eyes upon him again.

"What the devil could I have done with that key," he muttered, feeling about in his pockets. "Do you know that nobody's been upstairs for years. The floor is liable to collapse. Ha, ha! If it does, then I'm the one to catch it!"

He ran inside, rummaged in a drawer and found the two keys on a silver ring. The separate entrance to the second floor had been installed at the time of his father's wedding; the keyring had belonged to his father; for a moment Simon stared at it unbelievingly and then, still wearing his opera cape and Homburg hat, brought it out to Wiley Bey, who was staggering up the stairs with a mattress slung over his head. Here, Simon stopped and thought: But this is absurd. I'm giving this creature my father's key. Am I or am I not the lord of the manor? But all the humor and reality had gone out of it, and when the Negro popped his head from under the mattress, transfixing him with his extraordinary black eyes, Simon hastened to unlock the door, pushed it back on its rusty hinges and helped the man carry his burden upstairs. And when he went down again it seemed quite natural, indeed necessary, to pick up a bedpost and take it to the woman who stood waiting on the porch. And then to handle one end of a chest of drawers while the Negro, grasping the other end, grunted "Steady now, right, left, now we got it." . . . Simon was unused to physical labor. His muscles soon began to ache unbearably. Moreover, in manoeuvering a rope-bound crate through the doorway, he painfully crushed his fingers against the jamb. Yet he continued feverishly to shuttle between sidewalk and stairs.

Why? He thought of nothing. Once, one of the women, a tall flat-faced creature with her kinky hair braided into pigtails, murmured: "You are very kind." For the rest, the three women maintained their mysterious silence. Wiley Bey thanked him gravely, but after a while seemed to forget that he was there. In fact, were it not for his febrile insistence, Simon would not have been able to help at all. Yet he could not go away: the whole feeling of this strange event was too unclear. On the one hand, intermittently, he was carried away by an unaccustomed elan of generosity and fraternity, a kind of drunkenness. He babbled incessantly, he laughed for little or no reason, and asked pointless questions which no one bothered to answer. Once he launched into a half-serious harangue on the relation of the races, attributing to a "dear but misguided friend" some notions of his own about Negroes, which he now attacked with a curious mixture of subtlety and offensive buffoonery. He ended with an almost ribald joke and was so thunderstruck by Wiley Bey's black look that he fell silent for several minutes. On the other hand, Simon felt a real and profound sadness as the second floor apartment took on the shape and appearance of a home. Something real was ending, something which he had transformed and played with, as he did with all real things—but which, no matter how, had been part of him. His "consternation" became resentment, directed not at Wiley Bey, but at the World and Time which thus buried his chosen, half-serious, secretly cherished past under a pile of ugly and malodorous furniture.

When it had all been brought up and he had stood for a moment, morosely watching these people move busily about, putting clothes away, adjusting chairs and tables, he suddenly clapped his hand to his head and cried:

"But look here! You can't go through with this!"

"What's that?" said Wiley Bey, looking up from a trunk. He had been silent and preoccupied all evening, a man who exuded authority and power. The tall woman, who was lighting some candles on the mantelpiece, turned around. The other two came out of the kitchen and stood in the doorway.

"You don't know what this house means to me," said Simon, his voice breaking. "I was born in this room. There used to be a big armchair in this corner, next to a black walnut bookcase."

"I'm sorry," said Wiley Bey, bending again to his trunk. "Nobody told us anything about that."

There followed a long silence. It became in the end so unbearable that Simon blurted out the first things that came to his mind.

"Forgive my behaving like Banquo's ghost," he said. "Or rather like the spectre at the banquet, or whatever it was. But you must admit, it's all very odd. Not intrinsically odd, perhaps, but the effect is, if you know what I mean. And a Negro no less! An American instance! Do you know, my grandfather owned a slave? Not that he needed one, but just to show he was a copperhead, in 1860. . . . And a Mohammedan to boot, harem and all! Or are these your sisters? Ha, ha, can you fancy me in the role of a eunuch?"

He would have said more, in his delirium, but he had not the time. He felt his throat seized by an enormous hand, and for a terrifying instant looked into the face of Wiley Bey. Then he was spun around, grasped by the collar and the slack of his pants, and half carried, half pushed through the doorway. Stumbling, he turned around drunkenly, and the door slammed shut in his face.

II

Having been thrown out of the Negro's apartment, Simon quite naturally went back. In fact, no sooner had he found himself in the hall, with the door inexorably shut in his face, and his mouth bitter with the taste of insult and humiliation, than he was moved by an impulse to put his eye to the keyhole! Not that his distress and anger were not real, but his childish curiosity was equally real and (as he had learned from long experience) far more enduring. Mastering his impulse with difficulty, he went downstairs and paced the floor of his living-room, savoring the bitter feelings, the rage of the déclassé, the sense of degradation (how ignominiously the seat of his pants had been gathered in that enormous paw!) but nonetheless cocking his ear from time to time lest a significant movement from above should escape him. . . . Later, as he wrote a long account of the Negro's arrival in his journal, he heard the low plucking of a large string instrument, probably a guitar, and faintly the voice of a woman singing some weird oriental song. For a moment, Wiley Bey's deep voice, vibrantly, and then the music (to which Simon had listened open-mouthed, with delight) faded away. He determined to lodge a protest, in fact only physical terror saved him from thumping on the ceiling with the handle of a broom. It was not enough that these people were Negroes, and smelled queerly like all Negroes. They were given to singing in the dead of the night! At the same time, putting the finishing touches to his *pages de journal,* Simon found himself understanding the Negro's wrath, lingering over his fierce aspect—and, with a little smile of satisfaction, appreciating the dramatic quality of the evening's events.

The next morning, he actually went to the office and lodged his protest, but by that time his resentment seemed unimportant, and in any case useless; indeed he realized instantly that he had come only in the hope of learning something about Wiley Bey. He ended by "performing" his indignation, as he sometimes performed for his friends; and by parrying the man's insinuations about the arrears on his rent.

He felt that something was going to happen: something portentous, perhaps decisive. So that, later in the day, when he caught the first rumbling of the "Wiley Bey Case," he was scarcely surprised. A small rumbling it was—a set of insinuations hidden on a back-page of a local newspaper—but Simon, who spent hours exchanging gossip with butchers and barbers, caught it and kept it alive. . . . For two days he waited in ambush for Wiley Bey: to no avail. He sat by his window, mulling over in his mind the ambiguous phrases he had read, the endless possibilities, the moral problem. This astonishing Negro—what was he after, what did he mean?

At last, late in the afternoon of the third day, Simon contrived to meet Wiley Bey on the porch steps. It was very difficult. The Negro smiled and said hello as though nothing had happened: he deprecated nothing, excused nothing, simply broadened his dazzling smile (which seemed to flatten indefinitely the shiny black nose) and invited Simon to continue the conversation upstairs.

There—it all happened so swiftly that Simon had for an instant the feeling that it had been planned in advance (but by whom?)—Wiley Bey arranged his short leg before him and sank into the armchair. It obviously belonged to him. Simon sat rigidly in an ancient loveseat, with his elbow uncomfortably propped on the chipped armrest. In the broad dullness of the afternoon, the apartment swallowed up the few pieces of furniture, the almost invisible pictures. Only Wiley Bey, with his absurd and magnificent turban, seemed fully there, at ease, exhausting the allotted space. He was in a warm mood. He rubbed his enormous blood-red palms and smiled slowly, like a paternal Buddha. Simon stared at the white teeth in the glistening black face, and found nothing to say.

At last, timidly, he hoped that Wiley Bey had straightened out his ah, difficulties with the draft board.

On the contrary, said the Negro. This morning he had received a note, warning him to present his appeal tonight. In general, Wiley Bey did not recognize the right of these people to order him about as they pleased, and in any case such abominably short notice only proved (he smiled blandly and leaned back in his chair) that they were out to get his hide. Everyone in the neighborhood, even the landlords and storekeepers who ran the draft board, knew where *he* would be tonight.

"But I don't understand," said Simon. "Surely with your ah, physical handicap, they don't expect—"

"That has nothing to do with it," said Wiley Bey. "They want me to register as an American citizen."

"They do! And you registered as—?"

"A Moslem, of course."

With that, he winked: a wink such as Simon had never seen before, the most shameless, the most guileless, the most mad!

"O yes, to be sure, as a Moslem!" cried Simon. And, to hide his amazement and because he had nothing better to say, he assumed an air of intense chattiness: "That's very interesting! You must tell me about that! I understand there are several sects?"

Wiley Bey leaned forward and frowned. Solemn, ministerial, he suddenly reminded Simon of a Jew he had seen in Vienna, an old man who had emerged from the rear of his shop, clad in his colorful ritual garments, his eyes still lost in the misty distance of prayer. The old Jew had removed his prayer shawl, rubbed his hands, focussed his eyes and presto! he was a merchant.

"You are lost," intoned Wiley Bey. "You don't know where to turn. . . ."

Withal, he kept his warmth and good humor, his curious mixture of falseness and sincerity, the unsaintly attitude of a political believer: a man capable (as we later discovered) of misusing the funds of his church; and of all sorts of petty calculations. And immensely naïf! He shook his finger under Simon's nose.

"You are one of God's humble creatures," he said, "even though you are white. But like most of my people, you're tortured by the idea that you need dignity."

"That's very true," said Simon voluptuously.

"Dignity! What they mean is *demeanor*—a window-shade to hide their flesh and their sin!"

"Why that's a very good remark," cried Simon. "Excellent! I must remember that! And may I say in passing that you yourself have plenty of demeanor, what with that turban of yours and your solemn air. But of course you don't find that funny, and at bottom I don't mean it to be. When it pops out that way, it sounds insulting. The fact is—I'm an artist." He paused a moment, cocking his head. "I mean I'm a poet, I write poetry."

"Yes?"

"Please believe me—I have the greatest respect for you. I'm excited, and so everything comes out topsy-turvy. In fact, when I'm with you I feel slightly wacky, so to speak, I can't quite decide what tone to take. To begin with, I have an ambiguous feeling towards you. You've at once outraged me, by moving into my house and all that, and you've intrigued me with your turbans and mysteries and air of superior knowledge. Secondly, I'm a poet of the old school. I haven't the faintest idea how to talk to people who don't read poetry and don't give a damn about it."

"It so happens," said Wiley Bey, "that I'm very fond of poetry. For me, the greatest of them all is Ahmed Ali, a Negro who wrote in Alexandria, in the 12th century."

"I flatter myself," Simon went on, "that mine is the fundamentally poetic endowment. I feel everyone's feelings to the point where I have almost none of my own. At the same time, one must live, that is make decisions and have attitudes. It's very difficult. . . . And then there's this country!" Simon rolled his eyes and made a gesture of desperation. "Do you see what I mean?"

At that moment, one of the women—a slatternly sexy-looking girl who seemed to be wearing nothing at all beneath her apron—came into the room and whispered something in Wiley Bey's ear. The Negro turned to Simon:

"Excuse me a moment, do you have any money?"

"Not very much," said Simon apprehensively.

"Do you mind lending me a dollar?"

Simon handed over his dollar. Being very poor and very miserly, this was in the nature of a catastrophe. Yet for a moment he was quite carried away by the simplicity of the Negro in taking the money, the quiet satisfaction at a difficulty conquered, and above all the ease and naturalness with which he, Simon, was counted upon. He stood up briskly, frowning to hide his pleasure:

"But this is no time for me to be babbling about my little problems! My advice to you is to go to the board meeting and straighten the matter out. You were, I take it, born in the Near East?"

"It doesn't matter where I was born," said Wiley Bey. "I was reborn in Islam."

"O, I see," said Simon, pulling his lip. "Well, there's nothing to do but go and explain the matter. I'm sure they'll understand, especially since you're not fit for military service in any case. On the other hand, if you don't go, they can be quite nasty, as you've no doubt heard."

"You seem to have a very poor grasp of principle," replied Wiley Bey, and even as he creased his face in a curious, almost roguish smile, he kept his eyes on Simon's. "One of our basic doctrines is that we live in this country only in the flesh. Spiritually, we live in Islam. How could I abandon my people for a meeting of the draft board?"

"Yes, of course," said Simon, worriedly. "I see your point. Still—."

The Negro got up impatiently, grimacing as he adjusted his leg. In the spacious apartment, the light was failing, shadows creeping out of corners, over the ceiling. From the kitchen came a strong odor of barley soup, and of an unidentifiable meat. For a desperate moment, Simon felt that despite all his efforts, the feeling of communion, born in the transfer of a rumpled dollar bill, was fading away forever. Then he clapped his hands to his head and cried:

"I've got it! I'll go myself!"

"You'll go yourself?"

"Why of course! I've nothing to do tonight, and come to think of it, I may very well have a friend on your draft board. In fact I expect to be called up sooner or later myself. I'm a man for whom the material world exists, as Gautier said. I'll explain the whole thing. I'm sure it will come out all right."

Wiley Bey rubbed his hand over his face: it left the curious grimace of craftiness and purity, a smile. At the same time, he was hungry, so that half-consciously he moved toward the kitchen door as he said:

"As a matter of fact, I think you're right!"

And, in a tone of amused and paternal scorn:

"You will remind them of my leg, of course. . . ." Then he pushed out his right jowl with his tongue and, fantastically, winked. "There's no doubt about it. Between white men, the thing could be arranged!"

Simon, slightly shocked, tilted his head to one side and pursed his lips ironically. Whereupon the Negro burst into an enormous peal of laughter and slapped his back with an extraordinary air of roguishness, unregenerate vitality, an attitude of fearlessness before his own sins. For a moment, Simon expected that he would be invited to dinner. The prospect intrigued and repelled him: *he would never be able to eat that Negro food!* But Wiley Bey was actually showing him out. At the door, they shook hands, rather ceremoniously, as though Simon were going forth to preach to the gentiles; and it was not until he was half-way down the stairs that it occurred to him that this, his rash and doubtful mission, was what Wiley Bey had wanted all along.

In the end the idea pleased him, bearing as it did the promise of some indefinable intimacy with this strange man. Simon paced his floor and imagined grave and electric conversations, in which problems would rise up and dissolve like paper in flame. . . . Yet the ticking of the clock and the onset of evening recalled him to the seriousness of the Negro's situation; and when the time came to leave he was overcome with terror.

He sat on his bed and thought, But this is absurd, what in the world shall I tell them? And what the devil have I to do with the whole business anyway?

Nevertheless, he arose, donned his black cloak and walked across the park. These shaded lawns and bushes were notorious trystingplaces, already alive in the twilight. There were couples on the benches, whispering, stifled cries. Simon, his head cast down, his cloak almost dragging the ground behind him, passed through quickly, like a shadow, and noticed nothing. And so he walked the crowded streets, where kids ran screaming and cheap radios blared from furniture stores and groups of men and women broke to let him pass. He was so absorbed that he missed the sign on the store-window and had to turn back.

Two steps down, the interior of the store was divided by a low barrier, on the far side of which, around a conference table, sat the members of the board. They were absorbed in papers, spoke to each other in whispers. To the right, a few steps from the door, was a desk, behind which sat a young lady.

"Your name?"

"Charles R. Simon."

A banging of file cabinets.

"Are you sure this is your board? We have no record of you."

"O no, I've been dreaming, I beg your pardon! I've come on behalf of my—ah, client."

"I'm sorry," she said crisply. "It's against the law for selectees to be represented by counsel. If he wants to appeal, he'll have to come himself."

A Negro came in and respectfully removed his hat. The young lady made signs of addressing herself to the newcomer.

"Look," said Simon quickly. "To begin with, it's not a question of appealing but of—how shall I say?—explicating. Secondly, Mr. Wiley Bey is not my client in a legal sense, that was only a manner of speaking. I am his advocate but not his lawyer. In fact, I am not a lawyer at all." In the face of her astonishment, Simon was beginning to find a rare self-possession. "Suppose Mr. Wiley Bey were struck by an automobile and were physically incapable of appearing before the board?"

"Just a moment," she said, and walked back to the long table, letting the little door swing smartly behind her. The board members looked up as she began to whisper furiously and quite audibly her account of what Simon had said. An efficient female, thought Simon, and the idea was large and slow like all his ideas at the moment, and amused him disproportionately; buckteeth and sallow skin!

"Understand," he interposed, "I did not state that Mr. Wiley Bey was struck by an automobile. I merely said that he was as effectively prevented from appearing here tonight *as if* he were so struck." He smiled benignly at the bucktoothed girl. "The difference, you will surely grant, is by no means negligible. To begin with, Mr. Wiley Bey did not receive notice of this meeting until today, a procedure which I regard as highly unfair. Further—"

"Hold on," said the white-haired man at the head of the table. The five men put their heads together for a moment:

"Do you mind stepping in here?"

Simon walked through the barrier that blocked off the interior of the store into two parts. He threw off his cloak with a superb and slightly ridiculous gesture, like an undersized comedian playing bullfighter.

"Let's get this straight," said one of the board members. (A heavy man, with blackrimmed glasses and kinky hair, he spoke with a slightly Jewish intonation.) "As far as the board is concerned, this man's name is Wiley, Hadde Wiley. He's a neighborhood character. I remember when he was leader of some fishy pan-asia cult, in the old days, before he became a Turk. Out to save the colored people through Japan and physical culture."

"Mr. Wiley's past associations," said Simon, "do not in the least affect the present circumstances."

"Okay. Have it your way. Officially we're through with him anyway. We told him half a dozen times he's got to comply with the law or take the consequences. The fact of the matter is that I wrote to him myself, the board had nothing to do with it. I figured we could afford to give him a last chance to straighten himself out."

By now, Simon was in an extraordinary state of controlled excitement. With one eye he watched the door as men came in—there were four of them now, sitting on the bench—and with the other he observed the faces of the members of the board. His mind had a curious clear emptiness; above all, he was filled with the sense of his own *eloquence,* and hadn't the slightest notion of what to say!

"Are you finished?" he asked.

"Not yet. You can do us a favor by telling Wiley he's in a bad way. That's no joke. He's been talking his followers into registering like he did. According to the F.B.I., that's *conspiracy.* Do you know what that means?"

Simon waved his hand deprecatingly: the point (with a little smile) was conceded. There was a moment of silence. Then he put his finger tips together and frowned portentously:

"I want it understood," he began, "that I come in no spirit of disruption or chicanery, but simply as an American citizen. Impelled by my desire for fairness and justice. What other connection could there be between this man and me? I am myself a Presbyterian, as was my grandfather, the first mayor of this town. As for the army, I expect to be called at any minute, and when I am, I shall go gladly, you may take my word for it. But what is the issue involved in this case? Surely you do not *want* to see this man arrested? That would only reflect on the patriotism of this neighborhood."

Of the two Negro board members, one was beginning to doze. The other murmured:

"Exactly!"

"Please come to the point," said the chairman.

"Aha!" replied Simon, with a subtle smile. "But what, precisely, is the point? If Mr. Wiley Bey were merely concerned with evading the draft, he'd need only point to his leg, which is lame and makes him unfit for service. As for his followers, the fact that they register as aliens does not absolve them from military service—"

"Aliens have the right to refuse induction," said the chairman.

"May I ask if any of them have?"

"I don't know. . . . Of course not! We didn't accept their registration in the first place. They were all born in this country. They've got to register as American citizens, which they are."

"Now," said Simon, leaning forward with a great sense of insidious mastery. "Now we come to the point! Are they American citizens? Legally, they are. But as Montesquieu so brilliantly showed, and it is from that great thinker that our very legal structure derives, we must concern ourselves with the *spirit* and not simply with the letter of the law. Wiley Bey finds it impossible to be a Moslem and an American at the same time. He chooses to be a Moslem, i.e., an ally rather than a citizen of our country!"

"There are five appeals waiting," said the young lady.

"One moment," put in the blackrimmed glasses. "Even if what you say is true—and I doubt it: Wiley Bey, I mean Wiley himself stood right here in front of this board and told us that this was a white man's war. That's just what he said: a white man's war—but be that as it may, and all the religious stuff aside, he still has to register properly. Agreed?"

"Agreed. And according to his conscience, to register properly is to register as a Mohammedan."

"But," cried the man in exasperation, "he still remains an American citizen! Anyone born in this country is an American citizen. That's the law! If he wants to be a Mohammedan let him go to China and take out his papers. Here he's an American and that's the end of it. A man can't walk out of his obligations by calling himself a Mohammedan!"

"Excuse me," said Simon imperturbably. "It has not yet been proved that Wiley Bey is trying to avoid any obligations. He called this a white man's war. So it is! It is also a war of the dynasts. Fortunately, our dynasts are interested in fighting it, else we should have been defeated long ago. . . . But granting the modern principle of sovereignty, you are no doubt obliged to take a rather legalistic view of the matter. I see your point perfectly."

"In short," said the chairman, "you consider him guilty yourself and have been wasting our time for nothing. Next case."

Simon was suddenly very tired. He stood there, dreamily, as the "next case" shuffled through the swinging door and came to stand beside him. What was all this nonsense about registrations and sovereignty, wars and citizens? He had been *performing* again, like a lawyer!

"One moment," he suddenly cried, his face working strangely. "I beg of you, one moment more! I came to this meeting with no idea of what I was going to say to you—and now I know! Yes, Simon is guilty, I mean Wiley Bey is guilty. We are all guilty!"

He paused, carried away, and pointed his finger at the ceiling.

"Consider for a moment what a chain of guilt must have produced a situation like this! The infinite multitude of mean and grandoise actions without which—without *all* of which—this world we cling to in desperation would not be ours. What Wiley Bey does not sufficiently realize and who can blame him?—is that the Negroes in this country are only one link in the chain. They were dragged here by men who had sold their souls to the devil. They were set free as a matter of expediency, *and that was the only possible way!* Wiley Bey is a powerful man, above all a man of moral earnestness. He is aware of the guilt of a country which gives birth to the slogans we hear and read every day. Buy Blabber's Beer and remember Pearl Harbor! No Negroes need apply! And so he in turn—I tell you, there's no end to it!—commits the sins of despair and pride, chooses to withdraw from a society which is still capable of absorbing his values. To dissolve the City which grew painfully, crookedly, corruptly, and which alone stands between us and the unending jungle!"

Simon paused again. He would have liked a great roll of drums, not for *effect,* but to make them listen. And, alas, he would have liked the words to come less easily, with no oratorical roundness or niceties of style. For Simon was so made that even now he feared that he might be *performing,* once more: his emotion part of the play.

"Surely, I am not myself a man of moral earnestness. Perhaps you are thinking that I am only a foolish buffoon. But I am capable of seeing how we are all responsible for the wrong we inherit and live with, day by day. It is a small vision, and often worse than useless. But believe me, nothing less than this vision can make sense of such a case as Wiley Bey's."

He stopped, and squinted myopically at the faces of the board members. With the exception of a Negro minister, who was dozing, they all looked rather embarrassed.

"Are you finished?" said the chairman, heavily.

Simon, quite suddenly, was embarrassed himself. He smiled awkwardly and made a deep bow:

"*Opus superabat materiam.* Nevertheless, I have spoken."

"Thank you for your inspiring message. Officer, will you please show this man to the door?"

And so he swirled his cloak around his shoulders and walked out, followed by the policeman who had appeared from nowhere to fill his heart with the familiar unreasoning terror. Sweating, he mounted the two steps. O blueclad terror of marginal men! Had he broken a law? Was the hand coming down on his shoulder? . . . The Negroes, who had been sitting open-mouthed on the bench, turned as he passed, and stared. Then they looked back to the members of the board.

Outside, his sudden fright gave way to confusion. His mind instantly filled with what he had meant, the qualifications and nuances, what was implied or should have been, or what he had simply forgotten—all that a shifting jumble soon impossible to distinguish from what he had actually said. Moreover, it occurred to him that the board had neglected to reply, i.e., to pass formally on the fate of Wiley Bey. In fact, since Simon was not repelled but rather tempted by the absurd, he might have popped his head through the door and demanded his word of decision, were it not that the policeman's broad back so thoroughly blocked the doorway. . . . He hovered there for a moment, and at last decided to go home.

But he could not go home. He carried with him through the crowded streets an obscure feeling that this evening was not done. At the corner of State Street he stood looking across at the dark and uninviting park, until a little black boy, hurtling in pursuit of another, almost knocked him over. Gasping for breath, he smiled feebly, patted the boy's head and drew his hand back as though it had been bitten by the strange and kinky hair. Passers-by turned to stare at this odd little figure in a black cloak. Idlers on the corner moved closer. Simon, his eyes wary and apprehensive, turned quickly and walked down State Street, moving—with the bright lights and crowds and blare of sound receding, and the park lying black and brooding across the street—into a different world. As from the brightness and febrile joy of earthly perdition to the swirling darkness of hell. He walked along a number of warehouses, than past a squat, redbrick building—an undertaking establishment—and an alley which was half-blocked by an old dilapidated hearse. He moved out into the street, skirted the car and found himself staring at Wiley Bey's church.

It was a large store, with two show-windows, one of which bore the multicolored legend: FIRST TEMPLE OF MOHAMMED COME TO ISLAM. On the other window there was a cheap, hand-painted sign in black and white: HEAR WILEY BEY!!! I WENT TO WASHINGTON AND WHAT DID I SEE????

Simon went hesitantly to the door, which was open, and looked in. Wiley Bey, his long arm thrashing the air above his turban, was describing the iniquities he had seen in Washington. For a moment, Simon watched him, curiously and distantly, almost without a sense of recognition. Wiley Bey's face was distorted. His speech, which had been simple and even in tone, with at times a touch of pedantry, was now wilfully and exaggeratedly *Negro,* high-pitched, full of special intention. The audience, crowded on all the benches, standing two-deep along the walls, participated in every phrase and intonation.

"N so I done tole dat ole govment clerk, now look heah man . . ."

"Aymen," cried a shrill voice; and another rhythmically, the voice of an ancient hag who squatted in the rear: "Whad you all done tole dat man, son?"

"Why ah done tole the exac same thing ah done tole you!"

"Tell it, son!"

"Aymen, father!"

"*Do,* Pasha Bey!"

"Ah tole um, you kin beat a colud folks down! You kin take his money n take his skin! You kin lynch him n burn him, BUT YOU AINT GONNA GIT HIS SOUL!"

The enthusiasm leaped up to meet him, almost drowning out his final words. *No, they shouted, never; you tell it, father, no, no, no!*

Simon, frowning, looked about the hall with a curious nervousness, less defined but akin to his mad fear of the blue-coat; he looked about the hall, heard the stamping and groaning and chortling, saw the arms fly up and the moist and shining eyes. In some extraordinarily physical way, he was assailed by all this. He blinked and backed out of the doorway, thinking: he's a charlatan, a rapist, no doubt a very great man! Wiley Bey imperiously calmed the crowd and changed his tone, speaking quietly, persuasively. Now he's telling them he's stronger than they, thought Simon, and that it's useless to resist. At that moment, a white man detached himself from the crowd which lined the wall on the right, and walked back toward the door. He was a well-dressed young man, with a knowing tilt to his new grey hat; very tall and—in that mass of rags, bent backs and ravaged faces—almost offensively handsome, strong, self-possessed. He walked through the doorway, unceremoniously hustling Simon as he passed; then he wheeled about, smiling ironically, and expertly hung a cigarette on his lip.

"You've got to hand it to these niggers," he said. "They sure know how to put on a show!"

Simon did not reply. Usually of an almost neurotic politeness, he was annoyed now, by all this supercilious youthfulness and detachment. The young man broadened his smile.

"I suppose you're a Mohammedan too!"

Simon drew himself up haughtily. "In this country," he said, "we're all Mohammedans. When you've lived a little longer and seen something of the world, you'll understand that."

"Well what do you know!"

"These people, to be sure, are a slightly heretical sect."

O this was his evening of eloquence and public action! Smiling slyly, yet with a face ingenuous and persuasive, his two hands palms outward in a gesture of evidence, clarity, simple faith, Simon turned—to find that the young man had disappeared. Astonished, he moved out to the curb and saw him striding swiftly away, in the direction of the bright lights.

Inside the store, there was a great murmur and chatter, a pushing back of benches. The meeting was over, people were crowding around the platform; Wiley Bey was nodding gravely, shaking hands. This was the moment that Simon, all unconsciously, had come for: he would go in, report on his visit to the draft board, clear the matter up. . . . Negroes were beginning to drift out of the store, eyeing him curiously. A fat old lady, very black, planted herself in front of him and, with the most extraordinary insolence, stared him up and down. Simon backed away. Yes, now that he was here, he was anxious to talk to Wiley Bey. They would have a long conversation, *their first,* full of warmth and understanding. He would tell the Negro where he was wrong and where he was right. He would confess his own intimate sins.

Alas! Now the crowd, moving boisterously out of the hall, threatened to engulf him, pushed him back to the street. All at once, the prospect of making his way through that dense Negro mass was too much for him. There would be time enough, he told himself, tomorrow. He hesitated yet a moment, then turned and walked off, past the hearse in the alleyway and the funeral hall; in the direction of the bright lights.

III

Simon's Journal . . .

Tuesday: Saw Wiley Bey in the morning. He was in a hurried and rather grumpy mood. Noticed for the first time that he has a wart on his neck, just below the turban.

I fear I was rather overwhelmed by the humorous possibilities of the draft board affair. (My old way of escaping the absurd: by being sure to see it first.) I remembered all sorts of details—the voice of the secretary, the cat in the corner, the sleepy minister; and *I saw myself,* dancing before those good citizens like a caricature of a lawyer, another good citizen—so that all in all the story took too long, which irritated Wiley Bey, and I failed to impress him with the seriousness of the situation. When finally I began, in a considered and dignified way, to urge my point of view, W. B. had to go off somewhere.

He's recovered his pristine distance.

In the afternoon, sat down to my desk. But I was rather tired and above all preoccupied with the *whole question* of W. B. Aside from all he means to this time and place (how he barged in and destroyed the very sense of my house!) I kept thinking of his strangeness, the pronounced Negro odor that already possesses his apartment, the three women who continue to hover in the background like permeating incarnations of—what? Who had thought we were so superstitious? . . . In the end I gave up trying to work.

Tuesday: After last notation, rather depressed, gave myself up to the melancholy and damnable practice of drinking alone—and finished the bottle of wine. Slept late and was awakened by W. B. who stood about, jovial and unembarrassed, while I dressed. In the course of my ablutions he shouted through the bathroom door an Arab proverb to the effect that nothing is more pleasant than pissing after wine. Asked him to reconcile that with the Koran's well-known ban on alcohol. He insisted that Moslems consider not wine but drunkenness sinful, i.e., anything tending to surrender the individual's ascendency over his own spirit. Point can be checked. W. B. begged my pardon for his brusquerie of yesterday, alluding to difficulties within his movement (schism?!) which apparently were removed by prompt action. No describing him in a happy mood. While waiting, he strode about, ponderously, filling the air with his deep humming: themes from symphonies, especially Beethoven. Voice, chest, power, the shine of his skin—he positively swells the room.

The whole question of W. B. seemed less theoretical, more fraught with anguish, for I kept thinking: What if they should really pounce on a man like this? At the same time there was something provocative about all that force, and perhaps about the scorn with which he handled my books (like childish things he had long ago put away)—so that I found myself largely talking about myself. When he said something (in reply to my notion of religion) about the dishonesty of *inventing* a divine order, particularly if one knew what one was about, I tried to explain. That is, without stopping to adumbrate the extraordinary complexity of the process of believing, and the subtlety (in a business like this) of knowing 'what you were about,' I told him frankly: "What matters to men like us, is not what we are—an endless question!—but what we manage to distil on the clean white paper."

"That is too bad," he answered (only a literary man could be expected to know what I meant). "For if you don't write what you are you write nothing but verses. There's no hope for you at all."

Just then—I was standing at the window—a police car slowed down at the curb, and an officer poked his head out of a window, scrutinizing the house. The automobile did not stop. It was gone in an instant. But its sudden appearance gave me such a shock that I lost all desire to make W. B. see what I meant. I simply said, in guise of transition to a more pressing problem:

"I suppose *you* think we ought to come to Islam?"

He hesitated, frowned and moved to the door, speaking coldly:

"Islam is for men with dark skins."

Something to be worked out: the question of roles. Rich man, poor man, beggerman, thief—at bottom am I attached to nothing? Is one role as good as another, provided one finds the proper style? Worse: nothing is ever *resolved* in our country. The point is important. I sit here and lose the name of action, grumbling about the moral formlessness of it all: everything is slurred over, arranged, or forgotten. No heroism, no grandeur. Whenever a real question arises, it is destroyed precisely by its American particularity, which means that the principle involved is forever distorted by every kind of irrelevance.

Thursday: Sold shoes today, O *supplice!* Came home early (pleading headache) to see W. B., but no one home upstairs. Tried to do some work: too agitated, expecting W. B. at any moment. But I was already in bed when they finally came home and began singing their weird songs. I put on a robe, went upstairs and entered the room, saying: "Wiley Bey, you are guilty of Satanic pride!" This produced a considerable effect, everyone laughed. The women disappeared as usual, and I told W. B. that the great danger was *Gleichschaltung*, the deadly unifying process, the elimination of conflict. The atomization of groups into helpless individuals in face of the monster state. All this aided and abetted by his voluntary withdrawal. Etc. etc. He was affable, offered me wine (!) but obviously not in a mood to dispute or listen. And apparently my presence inexorably banished the women. Besides, I was chilly in my robe and felt a cold coming on. So I took a little wine and went downstairs. . . .

Friday morning, Simon woke up sneezing. He puttered about dismally, making coffee, washing dishes, trying to think what he had intended to do that day. But of course there was only one thing to do. He dressed and went upstairs. This time he stood shivering in the hall, without exaltation, and knocked. One of the women called softly:

"Who dere?"

"It's I. Simon."

The door opened. Wiley Bey was standing at the front window. He looked small, round, impenetrable, at the end of the long expanse of floor. He turned from the window and said:

"Well, here they are."

Simon walked across the floor. He was already frightened. In fact he had been frightened all along, from the very beginning. He wished Wiley Bey would stop grinning in that ghastly unrecognizable way, like some sinister African idol. Downstairs, the police were mounting to the front door. A dark green sedan had drawn up behind the squad car, and some men in plain-clothes were getting out. The bell rang. Simon was suddenly overwhelmed by the Negro odor of this place.

"Do you mind going down?" said Wiley Bey. "The buzzer doesn't work."

Simon went to the hall and descended the steps. Half-way down, he was stopped by the Negro's voice. "Ask them for a warrant," said Wiley Bey, who was standing at the door. "Tell them they can't come breaking into my house without a warrant." Simon was seized with a violent fit of shivering: it was as though he were *dreaming* of shivering. And oddly, he was struck by the illogic of the Negro's attitude. To begin with, it isn't your house, he thought. Moreover, you've repudiated the whole business, warrants and all. . . . His mind moved slowly, in wide irrelevent sweeps. In any case, it didn't matter: when he turned to speak, Wiley Bey had disappeared from the landing.

Simon first opened his own door, and left it ajar. Then he unlocked the front door, saying:

"Mr. Wiley ah, lives on the second floor . . ."

Of course he had no time to mention the warrant. Three policemen shouldered their way past him and mounted the stairs. Two others stood in the doorway and looked ironically at Simon, who retired to his threshold. One of them said:

"Where you going?"

"I live in here," said Simon. "On the first floor."

"Stay right where you are."

"Keep us company," added the other policeman, in a somewhat less threatening tone. But then he turned to the other and, with an air of quiet philosophical inquiry:

"You know, I never been able to figure it out. Where does a white guy come *off,* living in a house with niggers?"

"Hell, that's nothing," said the other. He looked at Simon and spat on the porch. "There's white girls in houses go down on niggers. . . . You know I think I seen this guy somewhere. What's your name?"

"Simon. Charles R. Simon."

"You a friend of this guy Wiley? How'd you know we was looking for *him?*"

"This house," began Simon, with a miserable awkward ingratiating smile, "has been in my family for many generations. I—"

The stairway door opened and one of the policemen appeared. Simon suddenly flushed red, thinking of what he had been about to say. He felt that he had disgraced himself and would disgrace himself again. Before whom? What god or moral law? He knew only the desertion of his courage which left him no humanity, no hope; he had smiled and smiled and he was damned forever.

"That black bastard's a real lawyer," said the policeman at the stairway door. "He won't let us in without a warrant."

"Break in the door and give him the flub-a-dub."

"Well what do you know," said the other. "Wan-ton bru-tality!" He winked broadly at Simon and walked to the plainclothesmen who were standing by their sedan. Simon (alas!) made another, feebler effort to smile. The uniformed man came back and went up the steps again. He was followed by a plainclothesman.

"If you had any self-respect, you woulda got the hell out of here as soon as these boogies come in."

(Upstairs, the policemen blew the lock off the door and advanced on Wiley Bey who retreated slowly, saying: "Just show me that warrant, that's my right!" One of the men in uniform swung suddenly, knocking the Negro down. Wiley Bey arose, jerked his bad leg stiff and crashed his enormous fist into the blueclad chest. The policeman fainted. The other three began to use their clubs on Wiley Bey, keeping him off balance, battering him about the room.)

"That is what comes of not taking a white man's word."

"I suppose you're a Mohammedan too."

(Upstairs, the women began to scream.)

"Of course I'm not," said Simon, with a nervous laugh. "My family has been Presbyterian for six generations."

A second plainclothesman—Simon recognized with terror the young man he had spoken to in front of Wiley Bey's meeting—came to the hall door and shouted up for the men to hurry. (The women had stopped screaming. They were applying cold water to Wiley Bey's face.) One of the men at the door said:

"What do you say, we take this guy with us too, cap?"

"That's right," said the other. "You can see right off he's a dangerous guy."

The plainclothesman looked at Simon with professional boredom and said:

"Leave him alone. He's just a crackpot."

On the second floor, the policemen emerged from the apartment, half-carrying, half-dragging Wiley Bey. The Negro's turban hung down grotesquely over his bloody face. He was conscious; his eyes met Simon's as he passed; he even smiled, with his swollen lips, and said something indistinct. In general (it seemed to Simon) a quite repulsive air of triumph and self-satisfaction.

The policeman who had been knocked out came down last; very pale, he muttered: "That black bastard broke half my ribs." Simon closed his door, went to the front window, and stood watching them get into the cars and drive away. *The house was his again*. The idea kept getting in the way of what he was trying to think. . . . What was it? But there's nothing, he said to himself bitterly, nothing you can make of it. Wiley Bey, for example, imagines he's proved some point or other. And suddenly Simon (who couldn't bear pain of any kind) began to bang his forehead hard against the wooden panelling between the two windows, saying aloud each time:

"But he hasn't, he hasn't, he hasn't!"

4

At Sea: A Sailor's Story

by Anton Chekhov

I Want to Know Why

by Sherwood Anderson

My Old Man

by Ernest Hemingway

ANTON CHEKHOV *Son of a former Russian serf, Chekhov received a degree in medicine in 1884, when he had already begun publishing brief comic sketches to help support his family. Like the plays for which he is renowned, his stories are understated examples of dramatic irony. A mood of desperate obsession with the aimless and futile colors many of them. His best stories can be read in* The Tales of Chekhov, *translated by Constance Garnett.*

SHERWOOD ANDERSON *Anderson had an irregular education in Clyde, Ohio, where his odd jobs as newsboy, as house painter, on farms, and on race tracks and his experience as a businessman were later reflected in the book which established his reputation,* Winesburg, Ohio. *This collection of thematically related stories about grotesque figures groping to articulate their pain while conflicting with a rigid puritanical legacy was to become a landmark for American fiction.*

ERNEST HEMINGWAY *Recipient of the Nobel Prize in 1954, Hemingway may be the most internationally admired modern American writer. His intensely dramatic situations test his protagonists' ability to achieve "grace under pressure." Hemingway's own predilection for action and danger—as a Red Cross ambulance driver in World War I, as a correspondent during the Spanish Civil War, as a big game hunter and deep sea fisherman—fed a craft distinguished by a style stripped of ornament, as bare, hard and stoical as his characters. His finest achievements,* In Our Time, *1925, and* The Sun Also Rises, *1926, exemplify both the withdrawal and hysteria that characterized what Gertrude Stein called "The Lost Generation."*

At Sea

A Sailor's Story*

Anton Chekhov (*Russian, 1860–1904*)

Only the dimming lights of the receding harbor were visible in an ink-black sky. We could feel the heavy storm clouds overhead about to burst into rain, and it was suffocating, in spite of the wind and cold.

Crowded together in the crew's quarters we, the sailors, were casting lots. Loud, drunken laughter filled the air. One of our comrades was playfully crowing like a cock. A slight shiver ran through me from the back of my neck to my heels, as if cold small shot were pouring down my naked body from a hole in the back of my head. I was shivering both from the cold and certain other causes, which I wish to describe.

In my opinion, man is, as a rule, foul; and the sailor can sometimes be the foulest of all the creatures of the earth—fouler than the lowest beast, which has, at least, the excuse of obeying his instincts. It is possible that I may be mistaken, since I do not know life, but it appears to me that a sailor has more occasion than anyone else to despise and curse himself. A man who at any moment may fall headlong from a mast to be forever hidden beneath a wave, a man who may drown, God alone knows when, has need of nothing, and one on dry land feels pity for him. We sailors drink a lot of vodka and are dissolute because we do not know what one needs virtue for at sea. However, I shall continue.

*Translated by Ann Dunnigan.

We were casting lots. There were twenty-two of us who, having stood watch, were now at liberty. Out of this number only two were to have the luck of enjoying a rare spectacle. On this particular night the honeymoon cabin was occupied, but the wall of the cabin had only two holes at our disposal. One of them I myself had made with a fine saw, after boring through with a corkscrew; the other had been cut out with a knife by one of my comrades. We had worked at it for more than a week.

"You got one hole!"

"Who?"

They pointed to me. "Who got the other?"

"Your father."

My father, a humpbacked old sailor with a face like a baked apple, came up to me and clapped me on the back. "Today, my boy, we're lucky!" he said. "Do you hear, boy? Luck came to us both at the same time. That means something." Impatiently he asked the time; it was only eleven o'clock.

I went up on deck, lit my pipe and gazed out to sea. It was dark, but it can be assumed that my eyes reflected what was taking place in my soul, as I made out images on the black background of the night, visualizing what was so lacking in my own still young but already ruined life. . . .

At midnight I walked past the saloon and glanced in at the door. The bridegroom, a young pastor with a handsome blond head, sat at a table holding the Gospels in his hands. He was explaining something to a tall, gaunt Englishwoman. The bride, a very beautiful, shapely young woman, sat at her husband's side with her light blue eyes fixed on him. A tall, plump, elderly Englishman, a banker, with a repulsive red face, paced up and down the saloon. He was the husband of the middle-aged lady to whom the pastor was talking.

"Pastors have a habit of talking for hours," I thought. "He won't finish before morning." At one o'clock my father came to me, pulled me by the sleeve and said: "It's time. They've left the saloon."

In the twinkling of an eye I flew down the companionway and approached the familiar wall. Between this wall and the side of the ship there was a space where soot, water, and rats collected. I soon heard the heavy tread of the old man, my father. He cursed as he stumbled over a mat-sack and some kerosene cans. I felt for the hole in the wall and pulled out the square piece of wood I had so painstakingly sawed. I was looking at a thin, transparent muslin through which penetrated a soft, rosy light. Together with the light, my burning face was caressed by a delightful, sultry fragrance; this, no doubt, was the smell of an aristocratic bedroom. In order to see the room it was necessary to draw aside the muslin with two fingers, which I hastened to do. I saw bronze, velvet, lace, all bathed in a pink glow. About ten feet from my face stood the bed.

"Let me have your place," said my father, impatiently pushing me aside. "I can see better here." I did not answer him. "Your eyes are better than mine, boy, and it makes no difference to you if you look from far or near."

"Be quiet," I said, "they might hear us."

The bride sat on the side of the bed, dangling her little feet in a foot muff. She was staring at the floor. Before her stood her husband, the young pastor. He was telling her something, what I do not know; the noise of the steamer made it impossible for me to hear. He spoke passionately, with gestures, his eyes flashing. She listened and shook her head in refusal.

"The devil!" my father muttered. "A rat bit me!"

I pressed my chest to the wall, as if fearing my heart would jump out. My head was burning.

The bride and groom talked at great length. At last he sank to his knees and held out his arms, imploring her. She shook her head in refusal. He leaped to his feet, crossed the cabin, and from the expression on his face and the movements of his arms I surmised that he was threatening her. The young wife rose and went slowly towards the wall where I was standing. She stopped near the opening and stood motionless in thought. I devoured her face with my eyes. It seemed to me that she was suffering, struggling with herself, not knowing what to do; but at the same time her features expressed anger. I did not understand it.

We continued to stand there face to face for about five minutes, then she moved slowly away and, pausing in the middle of the cabin, nodded to the pastor—a sign of consent, undoubtedly. He smiled happily, kissed her hand and went out.

Within three minutes the door opened and the pastor reentered followed by the tall, plump Englishman whom I mentioned above. The Englishman went over to the bed and asked the beautiful woman a question. Pale, not looking at him, she nodded her head affirmatively. The banker then took out of his pocket a packet of some sort—evidently bank notes—and handed it to the pastor, who examined it, counted it, bowed and went out. The elderly Englishman locked the door after him.

I sprang away from the wall as if I had been stung. I was frightened. It seemed to me the wind was tearing our ship to pieces, that we were going down. My father, that drunken, debauched old man, took me by the arm and said: "Let's go away from here! You shouldn't see that. You're still a boy."

He was hardly able to stand. I carried him up the steep winding stairs. Above an autumn rain had begun to fall.

I Want to Know Why

Sherwood Anderson (*American, 1876–1941*)

We got up at four in the morning, that first day in the east. On the evening before we had climbed off a freight train at the edge of town, and with the true instinct of Kentucky boys had found our way across town and to the racetrack and the stables at once. Then we knew we were all right. Hanley Turner right away found a nigger we knew. It was Bildad Johnson who in the winter works at Ed Becker's livery barn in our home town, Beckersville. Bildad is a good cook as almost all our niggers are and of course he, like everyone in our part of Kentucky who is anyone at all, likes the horses. In the spring Bildad begins to scratch around. A nigger from our country can flatter and wheedle anyone into letting him do most anything he wants. Bildad wheedles the stable men and the trainers from the horse farms in our country around Lexington. The trainers come into town in the evening to stand around and talk and maybe get into a poker game. Bildad gets in with them. He is always doing little favors and telling about things to eat, chicken browned in a pan, and how is the best way to cook sweet potatoes and corn bread. It makes your mouth water to hear him.

When the racing season comes on and the horses go to the races and there is all the talk on the streets in the evenings about the new colts, and everyone says when they are going over to Lexington or to the spring meeting at Churchill Downs or to Latonia, and the horsemen that have been down to New Orleans or maybe at the winter meeting at Havana in Cuba come home to spend a week before they start out again, at such a time when everything talked about in Beckersville is just horses and nothing else and the outfits start out and horse racing is in every breath of air you breathe,

Bildad shows up with a job as cook for some outfit. Often when I think about it, his always going all season to the races and working in the livery barn in the winter where horses are and where men like to come and talk about horses, I wish I was a nigger. It's a foolish thing to say, but that's the way I am about being around horses, just crazy. I can't help it.

Well, I must tell you about what we did and let you in on what I'm talking about. Four of us boys from Beckersville, all whites and sons of men who live in Beckersville regular, made up our minds we were going to the races, not just to Lexington or Louisville, I don't mean, but to the big eastern track we were always hearing our Beckersville men talk about, to Saratoga. We were all pretty young then. I was just turned fifteen and I was the oldest of the four. It was my scheme. I admit that I talked the others into trying it. There was Hanley Turner and Henry Rieback and Tom Tumberton and myself. I had thirty-seven dollars I had earned during the winter working nights and Saturdays in Enoch Myer's grocery. Henry Rieback had eleven dollars and the others, Hanley and Tom, had only a dollar or two each. We fixed it all up and laid low until the Kentucky spring meetings were over and some of our men, the sportiest ones, the ones we envied the most, had cut out—then we cut out too.

I won't tell you the trouble we had beating our way on freights and all. We went through Cleveland and Buffalo and other cities and saw Niagara Falls. We bought things there, souvenirs and spoons and cards and shells with pictures of the Falls on them for our sisters and mothers, but thought we had better not send any of the things home. We didn't want to put the folks on our trail and maybe be nabbed.

We got into Saratoga as I said at night and went to the track. Bildad fed us up. He showed us a place to sleep in hay over a shed and promised to keep still. Niggers are all right about things like that. They won't squeal on you. Often a white man you might meet, when you had run away from home like that, might appear to be all right and give you a quarter or a half dollar or something, and then go right and give you away. White men will do that, but not a nigger. You can trust them. They are squarer with kids. I don't know why.

At the Saratoga meeting that year there were a lot of men from home. Dave Williams and Arthur Mulford and Jerry Myers and others. Then there was a lot from Louisville and Lexington Henry Rieback knew but I didn't. They were professional gamblers and

Henry Rieback's father is one too. He is what is called a sheet writer and goes away most of the year to tracks. In the winter when he is home in Beckersville he don't stay there much but goes away to cities and deals faro. He is a nice man and generous, is always sending Henry presents, a bicycle and a gold watch and a boy scout suit of clothes and things like that.

My own father is a lawyer. He's all right, but don't make much money and can't buy me things and anyway I'm getting so old now I don't expect it. He never said nothing to me against Henry, but Hanley Turner and Tom Tumberton's fathers did. They said to their boys that money so come by is no good and they didn't want their boys brought up to hear gamblers' talk and be thinking about such things and maybe embrace them.

That's all right and I guess the men know what they are talking about, but I don't see what it's got to do with Henry or horses either. That's what I'm writing this story about. I'm puzzled. I'm getting to be a man and want to think straight and be O.K., and there's something I saw at the race meeting at the eastern track I can't figure out.

I can't help it, I'm crazy about thoroughbred horses. I've always been that way. When I was ten years old and saw I was growing to be big and couldn't be a rider I was so sorry I nearly died. Harry Hellinfinger in Beckersville, whose father is Postmaster, is grown up and too lazy to work, but likes to stand around in the street and get up jokes on boys like sending them to a hardware store for a gimlet to bore square holes and other jokes like that. He played one on me. He told me that if I would eat a half a cigar I would be stunted and not grow any more and maybe could be a rider. I did it. When father wasn't looking I took a cigar out of his pocket and gagged it down some way. It made me awful sick and the doctor had to be sent for, and then it did no good. I kept right on growing. It was a joke. When I told what I had done and why most fathers would have whipped me but mine didn't.

Well, I didn't get stunted and didn't die. It serves Harry Hellinfinger right. Then I made up my mind I would like to be a stable boy, but had to give that up too. Mostly niggers do that work and I knew father wouldn't let me go into it. No use to ask him.

If you've never been crazy about thoroughbreds it's because you've never been around where they are much and don't know any better. They're beautiful. There isn't anything so lovely and clean and full of spunk and honest and everything as some race horses. On the big horse farms that are all around our town Beckersville there are tracks and the horses run in the early morning. More than a thousand times I've got out of bed before daylight and walked two or three miles to the tracks. Mother wouldn't of let me go but father always says, "Let him alone." So I got some bread out of the bread box and some butter and jam, gobbled it and lit out.

At the tracks you sit on the fence with men, whites and niggers, and they chew tobacco and talk, and then the colts are brought out. It's early and the grass is covered with shiny dew and in another field a man is plowing and they are frying things in a shed where the track niggers sleep, and you know how a nigger can giggle and laugh and say things that make you laugh. A white man can't do it and some niggers can't but a track nigger can every time.

And so the colts are brought out and some are just galloped by stable boys, but almost every morning on a big track owned by a rich man who lives maybe in New York, there are always, nearly every morning, a few colts and some of the old race horses and geldings and mares that are cut loose.

It brings a lump up into my throat when a horse runs. I don't mean all horses but some. I can pick them nearly every time. It's in my blood like in the blood of race-track niggers and trainers. Even when they just go slop-jogging along with a little nigger on their backs I can tell a winner. If my throat hurts and it's hard for me to swallow, that's him. He'll run like Sam Hill when you let him out. If he don't win every time it'll be a wonder and because they've got him in a pocket behind another or he was pulled or got off bad at the post or something. If I wanted to be a gambler like Henry Rieback's father I could get rich. I know I could and Henry says so too. All I would have to do is to wait 'til that hurt comes when I see a horse and then bet every cent. That's what I would do if I wanted to be a gambler, but I don't.

When you're at the tracks in the morning—not the race tracks but the training tracks around Beckersville—you don't see a horse, the kind I've been talking about, very often, but it's nice anyway. Any thoroughbred, that is sired right and out of a good mare and trained by a man that knows how, can run. If he couldn't what would he be there for and not pulling a plow?

Well, out of the stables they come and the boys are on their backs and it's lovely to be there. You hunch down on top of the fence and itch inside you. Over in the sheds the niggers giggle and sing. Bacon is being fried and coffee made. Everything smells lovely. Nothing smells better than coffee and manure and horses and niggers and bacon frying and pipes being smoked out of doors on a morning like that. It just gets you, that's what it does.

But about Saratoga. We was there six days and not a soul from home seen us and everything came off just as we wanted it to, fine weather and horses and races and all. We beat our way home and Bildad gave us a basket with fried chicken and bread and other eatables in, and I had eighteen dollars when we got back to Beckersville. Mother jawed and cried but Pop didn't say much. I told everything we done except one thing. I did and saw that alone. That's what I'm writing about. It got me upset. I think about it at night. Here it is.

At Saratoga we laid up nights in the hay in the shed Bildad had showed us and ate with the niggers early and at at night when the race people had all gone away. The men from home stayed mostly in the grandstand and betting field, and didn't come out around the places where the horses are kept except to the paddocks just before a race when the horses are saddled. At Saratoga they don't have paddocks under an open shed as at Lexington and Churchill Downs and other tracks down in our country, but saddle the horses right out in an open place under trees on a lawn as smooth and nice as Banker Bohon's front yard here in Beckersville. It's lovely. The horses are sweaty and nervous and shine and the men come out and smoke cigars and look at them and the trainers are there and the owners, and your heart thumps so you can hardly breathe.

Then the bugle blows for post and the boys that ride come running out with their silk clothes on and you run to get a place by the fence with the niggers.

I always am wanting to be a trainer or owner, and at the risk of being seen and caught and sent home I went to the paddocks before every race. The other boys didn't but I did.

We got to Saratoga on a Friday and on Wednesday the next week the big Mullford Handicap was to be run. Middlestride was in it and Sunstreak. The weather was fine and the track fast. I couldn't sleep the night before.

What had happened was that both these horses are the kind it makes my throat hurt to see. Middlestride is long and looks awkward and is a gelding. He belongs to Joe Thompson, a little owner from home who only has a half-dozen horses. The Mullford Handicap is for a mile and Middlestride can't untrack fast. He goes away slow and is always way back at the half, then he begins to run and if the race is a mile and a quarter he'll just eat up everything and get there.

Sunstreak is different. He is a stallion and nervous and belongs on the biggest farm we've got in our country, the Van Riddle place that belongs to Mr. Van Riddle of New York. Sunstreak is like a girl you think about sometimes but never see. He is hard all over and lovely too. When you look at his head you want to kiss him. He is trained by Jerry Tillford who knows me and has been good to me lots of times, lets me walk into a horse's stall to look at him close and other things. There isn't anything as sweet as that horse. He stands at the post quiet and not letting on, but he is just burning up inside. Then when the barrier goes up he is off like his name, Sunstreak. It makes you ache to see him. It hurts you. He just lays down and runs like a bird dog. There can't anything I ever see run like him except Middlestride when he gets untracked and stretches himself.

Gee! I ached to see that race and those two horses run, ached and dreaded it too. I didn't want to see either of our horses beaten. We had never sent a pair like that to the races before. Old men in Beckersville said so and the niggers said so. It was a fact.

Before the race I went over to the paddocks to see. I looked a last look at Middlestride, who isn't such a much standing in a paddock that way, then I went to see Sunstreak.

It was his day. I knew when I seen him. I forgot all about being seen myself and walked right up. All the men from Beckersville were there and no one noticed me except Jerry Tillford. He saw me and something happened. I'll tell you about that.

I was standing looking at that horse and aching. In some way, I can't tell how, I knew just how Sunstreak felt inside. He was quiet and letting the niggers rub his legs and Mr. Van Riddle himself put the saddle on, but he was just a raging torrent inside. He was like the water in the river at Niagara Falls just before it goes plunk down. That horse wasn't thinking about running. He don't have to think about that. He was just thinking about holding himself back 'til the time for the running came. I knew that. I could just in a way see right inside him. He was going to do some awful running and I knew it. He wasn't bragging or letting on much or prancing or making a fuss, but just waiting. I knew it and Jerry Tillford his trainer knew. I looked up and then that man and I looked into each other's eyes. Something happened to me. I guess I loved the man as much as I did the horse because he knew what I knew. Seemed to me there wasn't anything in the world but that man and the horse and me. I cried and Jerry Tillford had a shine in his eyes. Then I came away to the fence to wait for the race.

The horse was better than me, more steadier, and now I know better than Jerry. He was the quietest and he had to do the running.

Sunstreak ran first of course and he busted the world's record for a mile. I've seen that if I never see anything more. Everything came out just as I expected. Middlestride got left at the post and was way back and closed up to be second, just as I knew he would. He'll get a world's record too some day. They can't skin the Beckersville country on horses.

I watched the race calm because I knew what would happen. I was sure. Hanley Turner and Henry Rieback and Tom Tumberton were all more excited than me.

A funny thing had happened to me. I was thinking about Jerry Tillford the trainer and how happy he was all through the race. I liked him that afternoon even more than I ever liked my own father. I almost forgot the horses thinking that way about him. It was because of what I had seen in his eyes as he stood in the paddocks beside Sunstreak before the race started. I knew he had been watching and working with Sunstreak since the horse was a baby colt, had taught him to run and be patient and when to let himself out and not to quit, never. I knew that for him it was like a mother seeing her child do something brave or wonderful. It was the first time I ever felt for a man like that.

After the race that night I cut out from Tom and Hanley and Henry. I wanted to be by myself and I wanted to be near Jerry Tillford if I could work it. Here is what happened.

The track in Saratoga is near the edge of town. It is all polished up, and trees around, the evergreen kind, and grass and everything painted and nice. If you go past the track you get to a hard road made of asphalt for automobiles, and if you go along this for a few miles there is a road turns off to a little rummy-looking farmhouse set in a yard.

That night after the race I went along that road because I had seen Jerry and some other men go that way in an automobile. I didn't expect to find them. I walked for a ways and then sat down by a fence to think. It was the direction they went in. I wanted to be as near Jerry as I could. I felt close to him. Pretty soon I went up the side road—I don't know why—and came to the rummy farmhouse. I was just lonesone to see Jerry, like wanting to see your father at night when you are a young kid. Just then an automobile came along and turned in. Jerry was in it and Henry Rieback's father, and Arthur Bedford from home, and Dave Williams and two other men I didn't know. They got out of the car and went into the house, all but Henry Rieback's father who quarreled with them and said he wouldn't go. It was only about nine o'clock, but they were all drunk and the rummy-looking farmhouse was a place for bad women to stay in. That's what it was. I crept up along a fence and looked through a window and saw.

It's what give me the fantods. I can't make it out. The women in the house were all ugly mean-looking women, not nice to look at or be near. They were homely too, except one who was tall and looked a little like the gelding Middlestride, but not clean like him, but with a hard ugly mouth. She had red hair. I saw everything plain. I got up by an old rosebush by an open window and looked. The women had on loose dresses and sat around in chairs. The men came in and some sat on the women's laps. The place smelled rotten and there was rotten talk, the kind a kid hears around a livery stable in a town like Beckersville in the winter but don't ever expect to hear talked when there are women around. It was rotten. A nigger wouldn't go into such a place.

I looked at Jerry Tillford. I've told you how I had been feeling about him on account of his knowing what was going on inside of Sunstreak in the minute before he went to the post for the race in which he made a world's record.

Jerry bragged in that bad-woman house as I know Sunstreak wouldn't never have bragged. He said that he made that horse, that it was him that won the race and made the record. He lied and bragged like a fool. I never heard such silly talk.

And then, what do you suppose he did! He looked at the woman in there, the one that was lean and hard-mouthed and looked a little like the gelding Middlestride, but not clean like him, and his eyes began to shine just as they did when he looked at me and at Sunstreak in the paddocks at the track in the afternoon. I stood there by the window—gee!—but I wished I hadn't gone away from the tracks, but had stayed with the boys and the niggers and the horses. The tall rotten-looking woman was between us just as Sunstreak was in the paddocks in the afternoon.

Then, all of a sudden, I began to hate that man. I wanted to scream and rush in the room and kill him. I never had such a feeling before. I was so mad clean through that I cried and my fists were doubled up so my fingernails cut my hands.

And Jerry's eyes kept shining and he waved back and forth, and then he went and kissed that woman and I crept away and went back to the tracks and to bed and didn't sleep hardly any, and then next day I got the other kids to start home with me and never told them anything I seen.

I been thinking about it ever since. I can't make it out. Spring has come again and I'm nearly sixteen and go to the tracks mornings same as always, and I see Sunstreak and Middlestride and a new colt named Strident I'll bet will lay them all out, but no one thinks so but me and two or three niggers.

But things are different. At the tracks the air don't taste as good or smell as good. It's because a man like Jerry Tillford, who knows what he does, could see a horse like Sunstreak run, and kiss a woman like that the same day. I can't make it out. Darn him, what did he want to do like that for? I keep thinking about it and it spoils looking at horses and smelling things and hearing niggers laugh and everything. Sometimes I'm so mad about it I want to fight someone. It gives me the fantods. What did he do it for? I want to know why.

My Old Man

Ernest Hemingway (*American, 1899–1961*)

I guess looking at it, now, my old man was cut out for a fat guy, one of those regular little roly fat guys you see around, but he sure never got that way, except a little toward the last, and then it wasn't his fault, he was riding over the jumps only and he could afford to carry plenty of weight then. I remember the way he'd pull on a rubber shirt over a couple of jerseys and a big sweat shirt over that, and get me to run with him in the forenoon in the hot sun. He'd have, maybe, taken a trial trip with one of Razzo's skins early in the morning after just getting in from Torino at four o'clock in the morning and beating it out to the stables in a cab and then with the dew all over everything and the sun just starting to get going, I'd help him pull off his boots and he'd get into a pair of sneakers and all these sweaters and we'd start out.

"Come on, kid," he'd say, stepping up and down on his toes in front of the jocks' dressing room, "let's get moving."

Then we'd start off jogging around the infield once, maybe, with him ahead, running nice, and then turn out the gate and along one of those roads with all the trees along both sides of them that run out from San Siro. I'd go ahead of him when we hit the road and I could run pretty stout and I'd look around and he'd be jogging easy just behind me and after a little while I'd look around again and he'd begun to sweat. Sweating heavy and he'd just be dogging it along with his eyes on my back, but when he'd catch me looking at him he'd grin and say, "Sweating plenty?" When my old man grinned, nobody could help but grin too. We'd keep right on running out toward the mountains and then my old man would yell,

"Hey, Joe!" and I'd look back and he'd be sitting under a tree with a towel he'd had around his waist wrapped around his neck.

I'd come back and sit down beside him and he'd pull a rope out of his pocket and start skipping rope out in the sun with the sweat pouring off his face and him skipping rope out in the white dust with the rope going cloppetty, cloppetty, clop, clop, clop, and the sun hotter, and him working harder up and down a patch of the road. Say, it was a treat to see my old man skip rope, too. He could whirr it fast or lop it slow and fancy. Say, you ought to have seen wops look at us sometimes, when they'd come by, going into town walking along with big white steers hauling the cart. They sure looked as though they thought the old man was nuts. He'd start the rope whirring till they'd stop dead still and watch him, then give the steers a cluck and a poke with the goad and get going again.

When I'd sit watching him working out in the hot sun I sure felt fond of him. He sure was fun and he done his work so hard and he'd finish up with a regular whirring that'd drive the sweat out on his face like water and then sling the rope at the tree and come over and sit down with me and lean back against the tree with the towel and a sweater wrapped around his neck.

"Sure is hell keeping it down, Joe," he'd say and lean back and shut his eyes and breathe long and deep, "it ain't like when you're a kid." Then he'd get up before he started to cool and we'd jog along back to the stables. That's the way it was keeping down to weight. He was worried all the time. Most jocks can just about ride off all they want to. A jock loses about a kilo every time he rides, but my old man was sort of dried out and he couldn't keep down his kilos without all that running.

I remember once at San Siro, Regoli, a little wop, that was riding for Buzoni, came out across the paddock going to the bar for something cool; and flicking his boots with his whip, after he'd just weighed in and my old man had just weighed in too, and came out with the saddle under his arm looking red-faced and tired and too big for his silks and he stood there looking at young Regoli standing up to the outdoors bar, cool and kid-looking, and I says, "What's the matter, Dad?" 'cause I thought maybe Regoli had bumped him or something and he just looked at Regoli and said, "Oh, to hell with it," and went on to the dressing room.

Well, it would have been all right, maybe, if we'd stayed in Milan and ridden at Milan and Torino, 'cause if there ever were any easy courses, it's those two. "Pianola, Joe," my old man said when he dismounted in the winning stall after what the wops thought was a hell of a steeplechase. I asked him once. "This course rides itself. It's the pace you're going at, that makes riding the jumps dangerous, Joe. We ain't going any pace here, and they ain't any really bad jumps either. But it's the pace always—not the jumps that makes the trouble.

San Siro was the swellest course I'd ever seen but the old man said it was a dog's life. Going back and forth between Mirafiore and San Siro and riding just about every day in the week with a train ride every other night.

I was nuts about the horses, too. There's something about it, when they come out and go up the track to the post. Sort of dancy and tight looking with the jock keeping a tight hold on them and maybe easing off a little and letting them run a little going up. Then once they were at the barrier it got me worse than anything. Especially at San Siro with that big green infield and the mountains way off and the fat wop starter with his big whip and the jocks fiddling them around and then the barrier snapping up and that bell going off and them all getting off in a bunch and then commencing to string out. You know the way a bunch of skins gets off. If you're up in the stand with a pair of glasses all you see is them plunging off and then that bell goes off and it seems like it rings for a thousand years and then they come sweeping round the turn. There wasn't ever anything like it for me.

But my old man said one day, in the dressing room, when he was getting into his street clothes, "None of these things are horses, Joe. They'd kill that bunch of skates for their hides and hoofs up at Paris." That was the day he'd won the Premio Commercio with Lantorna shooting her out of the field the last hundred meters like pulling a cork out of a bottle.

It was right after the Premio Commercio that we pulled out and left Italy. My old man and Holbrook and a fat wop in a straw hat that kept wiping his face with a handkerchief were having an argument at a table in the Galleria. They were all talking French and the two of them were after my old man about something. Finally he didn't say anything any more but just sat there and looked at Holbrook, and the two of them kept after him, first one talking and then the other, and the fat wop always butting in on Holbrook.

"You go out and buy me a *Sportsman,* will you, Joe?" my old man said, and handed me a couple of soldi without looking away from Holbrook.

So I went out of the Galleria and walked over to in front of the Scala and bought a paper, and came back and stood a little way away because I didn't want to butt in and my old man was sitting back in his chair looking down at his coffee and fooling with a spoon and Holbrook and the big wop were standing and the big wop was wiping his face and shaking his head. And I came up and my old man acted just as though the two of them weren't standing there and said, "Want an ice, Joe?" Holbrook looked down at my old man and said slow and careful, "You son of a bitch," and he and the fat wop went out through the tables.

My old man sat there and sort of smiled at me, but his face was white and he looked sick as hell and I was scared and felt sick inside because I knew something had happened and I didn't see how anybody could call my old man a son of a bitch and get away with it. My old man opened up the *Sportsman* and studied the handicaps for a while and then he said, "You got to take a lot of things in this world, Joe." And three days later we left Milan for good on the Turin train for Paris, after an auction sale out in front of Turner's stables of everything we couldn't get into a trunk and a suit case.

We got into Paris early in the morning in a long, dirty station the old man told me was the Gare de Lyon. Paris was an awful big town after Milan. Seems like in Milan everybody is going somewhere and all the trams run somewhere and there ain't any sort of a mix-up, but Paris is all balled up and they never do straighten it out. I got to like it, though, part of it, anyway, and say it's got the best race courses in the world. Seems as though that were the thing that keeps it all going and about the only thing you can figure on is that every day the buses will be going out to whatever track they're running at, going right out through everything to the track. I never really got to know Paris well, because I just came in about once or twice a week with the old man from Maisons and he always sat at the Café de la Paix on the Opera side with the rest of the gang from Maisons and I guess that's one of the busiest parts of the town. But, say, it is funny that a big town like Paris wouldn't have a Galleria, isn't it?

Well, we went out to live at Maisons-Lafitte, where just about everybody lives except the gang at Chantilly, with a Mrs. Meyers that runs a boarding house. Maisons is about the swellest place to live I've ever seen in all my life. The town ain't so much, but there's a lake and a swell forest that we used to go off bumming in all day, a couple of us kids, and my old man made me a sling shot and we got a lot of things with it but the best one was a magpie. Young Dick Atkinson shot a rabbit with it one day and we put it under a tree and were sitting around and Dick had some cigarettes and all of a sudden the rabbit jumped up and beat it into the brush and we chased it but we couldn't find it. Gee, we had fun at Maisons. Mrs. Meyers used to give me lunch in the morning and I'd be gone all day. I learned to talk French quick. It's an easy language.

As soon as we got to Maisons, my old man wrote to Milan for his license and he was pretty worried till it came. He used to sit around the Café de Paris in Maisons with the gang, there were lots of guys he'd known when he rode up at Paris, before the war, lived at Maisons, and there's a lot of time to sit around because the work around a racing stable, for the jocks, that is, is all cleaned up by nine o'clock in the morning. They take the first batch of skins out to gallop them at 5:30 in the morning and they work the second lot at 8 o'clock. That means getting up early all right and going to bed early, too. If a jock's riding for somebody too, he can't go boozing around because the trainer always has an eye on him if he's a kid and if he ain't a kid he's always got an eye on himself. So mostly if a jock ain't working he sits around the Café de Paris with the gang and they can all sit around about two or three hours in front of some drink like a vermouth and seltz and they talk and tell stories and shoot pool and it's sort of like a club or the Galleria in Milan. Only it ain't really like the Galleria because there everybody is going by all the time and there's everybody around at the tables.

Well, my old man got his license all right. They sent it through to him without a word and he rode a couple of times. Amiens, up country and that sort of thing, but he didn't seem to get any engagement. Everybody liked him and whenever I'd come in to the Café in the forenoon I'd find somebody drinking with him because my old man wasn't tight like most of these jockeys that have got the first dollar they made riding at the World's Fair in St. Louis in nineteen ought four. That's what my old man would say when he'd kid George Burns. But it seemed like everybody steered clear of giving my old man any mounts.

We went out to wherever they were running every day with the car from Maisons and that was the most fun of all. I was glad when the horses came back from Deauville and the summer. Even though it meant no more bumming in the woods, 'cause then we'd ride to Enghien or Tremblay or St. Cloud and watch them from the trainers' and jockeys' stand. I sure learned about racing from going out with that gang and the fun of it was going every day.

I remember once out at St. Cloud. It was a big two hundred thousand franc race with seven entries and Kzar a big favorite. I went around to the paddock to see the horses with my old man and you never saw such horses. This Kzar is a great big yellow horse that looks like just nothing but run. I never saw such a horse. He was being led around the paddocks with his head down and when he went by me I felt all hollow inside he was so beautiful. There never was such a wonderful, lean, running built horse. And he went around the paddock putting his feet just so and quiet and careful and moving easy like he knew just what he had to do and not jerking and standing up on his legs and getting wild eyed like you see these selling platers with a shot of dope in them. The crowd was so thick I couldn't see him again except just his legs going by and some yellow and my old man started out through the crowd and I followed him over to the jocks' dressing room back in the trees and there was a big crowd around there, too, but the man at the door in a derby nodded to my old man and we got in and everybody was sitting around and getting dressed and pulling shirts over their heads and pulling boots on and it all smelled hot and sweaty and linimenty and outside was the crowd looking in.

The old man went over and sat down beside George Gardner that was getting into his pants and said, "What's the dope, George?" just in an ordinary tone of voice 'cause there ain't any use him feeling around because George either can tell him or he can't tell him.

"He won't win," George says very low, leaning over and buttoning the bottoms of his pants.

"Who will?" my old man says, leaning over close so nobody can hear.

"Kircubbin," George says, "and if he does, save me a couple of tickets."

My old man says something in a regular voice to George and George says, "Don't ever bet on anything, I tell you," kidding like, and we beat it out and through all the crowd that was looking in over to the 100 franc mutuel machine. But I knew something big was up because George is Kzar's jockey. On the way he gets one of the yellow odds-sheets with the starting prices on and Kzar is only paying 5 for 10, Cefisidote is next at 3 to 1 and fifth down the list this Kircubbin at 8 to 1. My old man bets five thousand on Kircubbin to win and puts on a thousand to place and we went around back of the grandstand to go up the stairs and get a place to watch the race.

We were jammed in tight and first a man in a long coat with a gray tall hat and a whip folded up in his hand came out and then one after another the horses, with the jocks up and a stable boy holding the bridle on each side and walking along, followed the old guy. That big yellow horse Kzar came first. He didn't look so big when you first looked at him until you saw the length of his legs and the whole way he's built and the way he moves. Gosh, I never saw such a horse. George Gardner was riding him and they moved along slow, back of the old guy in the gray tall hat that walked along like he was the ring master in a circus. Back of Kzar, moving along smooth and yellow in the sun, was a good looking black with a nice head with Tommy Archibald riding him; and after the black was a string of five more horses all moving along slow in a procession past the grandstand and the pesage. My old man said the black was Kircubbin and I took a good look at him and he was a nice looking horse, all right, but nothing like Kzar.

Everybody cheered Kzar when he went by and he sure was one swell-looking horse. The procession of them went around on the other side past the pelouse and then back up to the near end of the course and the circus master had the stable boys turn them loose one after another so they could gallop by the stands on their way up to the post and let everybody have a good look at them. They weren't at the post hardly any time at all when the gong started and you could see them way off across the infield all in a bunch starting on the first swing like a lot of little toy horses. I was watching them through the glasses and Kzar was running well back, with one of the bays making the pace. They swept down and around and came pounding past and Kzar was way back when they passed us and this Kircubbin horse in front and going smooth. Gee, it's awful when they go by you and then you have to watch them go farther away and get smaller and smaller and then all bunched up on the turns and then come around towards into the stretch and you feel like swearing and goddamming worse and worse. Finally they made the last turn and came into the straightaway with this Kircubbin horse way out in front. Everybody was looking funny and saying "Kzar" in sort of a sick way and them pounding nearer down the stretch, and then something came out of the pack right into my glasses like a horse-headed yellow streak and everybody began to yell "Kzar" as though they were crazy. Kzar came on faster than I'd ever seen anything in my life and pulled up on Kircubbin that was going fast as any black horse could go with the jock flogging hell out of him with the gad and they were right dead neck and neck for a second but Kzar seemed going about twice as fast with those great jumps and that head out—but it was while they were neck and neck that they passed the winning post and when the numbers went up in the slots the first one was 2 and that meant Kircubbin had won.

I felt all trembly and funny inside, and then we were all jammed in with the people going downstairs to stand in front of the board where they'd post what Kircubbin paid. Honest, watching the race I'd forgot how much my old man had bet on Kircubbin. I'd wanted Kzar to win so damned bad. But now it was all over it was swell to know we had the winner.

"Wasn't it a swell race, Dad?" I said to him.

He looked at me sort of funny with his derby on the back of his head. "George Gardner's a swell jockey, all right," he said. "It sure took a great jock to keep that Kzar horse from winning."

Of course I knew it was funny all the time. But my old man saying that right out like that sure took the kick all out of it for me and I didn't get the real kick back again ever, even when they posted the numbers up on the board and the bell rang to pay off and we saw that Kircubbin paid 67.50 for 10. All round people were saying, "Poor Kzar! Poor Kzar!" And I thought, I wish I were a jockey and could have rode him instead of that son of a bitch. And that was funny, thinking of George Gardner as a son of a bitch because I'd always liked him and besides he'd given us the winner, but I guess that's what he is, all right.

My old man had a big lot of money after that race and he took to coming into Paris oftener. If they raced at Tremblay he'd have them drop him in town on their way back to Maisons, and he and I'd sit out in front of the Café de la Paix and watch the people go by. It's funny sitting there. There's streams of people going by and all sorts of guys come up and want to sell you things, and I loved to sit there with my old man. That was when we'd have the most fun. Guys would come by selling funny rabbits that jumped if you squeezed a bulb and they'd come up to us and my old man would kid with them. He could talk French just like English and all those kind of guys knew him 'cause you can always tell a jockey—and then we always sat at the same table and they got used to seeing us there. There were guys selling matrimonial papers and girls selling rubber eggs that when you squeezed them a rooster came out of them and one old wormy-looking guy that went by with post-cards of Paris, showing them to everybody, and, of course, nobody ever bought any, and then he would come back and show the under side of the pack and they would all be smutty post-cards and lots of people would dig down and buy them.

Gee, I remember the funny people that used to go by. Girls around supper time looking for somebody to take them out to eat and they'd speak to my old man and he'd make some joke at them in French and they'd pat me on the head and go on. Once there was an American woman sitting with her kid daughter at the next table to us and they were both eating ices and I kept looking at the girl and she was awfully good looking and I smiled at her and she smiled at me but that was all that ever came of it because I looked for her mother and her every day and I made up ways that I was going to speak to her and I wondered if I got to know her if her mother would let me take her out to Auteuil or Tremblay but I never saw either of them again. Anyway, I guess it wouldn't have been any good, anyway, because looking back on it I remember the way I thought out would be best to speak to her was to say, "Pardon me, but perhaps I can give you a winner at Enghien today?" and, after all, maybe she would have thought I was a tout instead of really trying to give her a winner.

We'd sit at the Café de la Paix, my old man and me, and we had a big drag with the waiter because my old man drank whisky and it cost five francs, and that meant a good tip when the saucers were counted up. My old man was drinking more than I'd ever seen him, but he wasn't riding at all now and besides he said that whisky kept his weight down. But I noticed he was putting it on, all right, just the same. He'd busted away from his old gang out at Maisons and seemed to like just sitting around on the boulevard with me. But he was dropping money every day at the track. He'd feel sort of doleful after the last race, if he'd lost on the day, until we'd get to our table and he'd have his first whisky and then he'd be fine.

He'd be reading the Paris-Sport and he'd look over at me and say, "Where's your girl, Joe?" to kid me on account I had told him about the girl that day at the next table. And I'd get red, but I liked being kidded about her. It gave me a good feeling. "Keep your eye peeled for her, Joe," he'd say, "she'll be back."

He'd ask me questions about things and some of the things I'd say he'd laugh. And then he'd get started talking about things. About riding down in Egypt, or at St. Moritz on the ice before my mother died, and about during the war when they had regular races down in the south of France without any purses or betting or crowd or anything just to keep the breed up. Regular races with the jocks riding hell out of the horses. Gee, I could listen to my old man talk by the hour, especially when he'd had a couple or so of drinks. He'd tell me about when he was a boy in Kentucky and going coon hunting, and the old days in the States before everything went on the bum there. And he'd say, "Joe, when we've got a decent stake, you're going back there to the States and go to school."

"What've I got to go back there to go to school for when everything's on the bum there?" I'd ask him.

"That's different," he'd say and get the waiter over and pay the pile of saucers and we'd get a taxi to the Gare St. Lazare and get on the train out to Maisons.

One day at Auteuil, after a selling steeplechase, my old man bought in the winner for 30,000 francs. He had to bid a little to get him but the stable let the horse go finally and my old man had his permit and his colors in a week. Gee, I felt proud when my old man was an owner. He fixed it up for stable space with Charles Drake and cut out coming in to Paris, and started his running and sweating out again, and him and I were the whole stable gang. Our horse's name was Gilford, he was Irish bred and a nice, sweet jumper. My old man figured that training him and riding him, himself, he was a good investment. I was proud of everything and I thought Gilford was as good a horse as Kzar. He was a good, solid jumper, a bay, with plenty of speed on the flat, if you asked him for it, and he was a nice-looking horse, too.

Gee, I was fond of him. The first time he started with my old man up, he finished third in a 2,500 meter hurdle race and when my old man got off him, all sweating and happy in the place stall, and went in to weigh, I felt as proud of him as though it was the first race he'd ever placed in. You see, when a guy ain't been riding for a long time, you can't make yourself really believe that he has ever rode. The whole thing was different now, 'cause down in Milan, even big races never seemed to make any difference to my old man, if he won he wasn't ever excited or anything, and now it was so I couldn't hardly sleep the night before a race and I knew my old man was excited, too, even if he didn't show it. Riding for yourself makes an awful difference.

Second time Gilford and my old man started, was a rainy Sunday at Auteuil, in the Prix du Marat, a 4,500 meter steeplechase. As soon as he'd gone out I beat it up in the stand with the new glasses my old man had bought for me to watch them. They started way over at the far end of the course and there was some trouble at the barrier. Something with goggle blinders on was making a great fuss and rearing around and busted the barrier once, but I could see my old man in our black jacket, with a white cross and a black cap, sitting up on Gilford, and patting him with his hand. Then they were off in a jump and out of sight behind the trees and the gong going for dear life and the pari-mutuel wickets rattling down. Gosh, I was so excited, I was afraid to look at them, but I fixed the glasses on the place where they would come out back of the trees and then out they came with the old black jacket going third and they all sailing over the jump like birds. Then they went out of sight again and then they came pounding out and down the hill and all going nice and sweet and easy and taking the fence smooth in a bunch, and moving away from us all solid. Looked as though you could walk across on their backs they were all so bunched and going so smooth. Then they bellied over the big double Bullfinch and something came down. I couldn't see who it was, but in a minute the horse was up and galloping free and the field, all bunched still, sweeping around the long left turn into the straightaway. They jumped the stone wall and came jammed down the stretch toward the big water-jump right in front of the stands. I saw them coming and hollered at my old man as he went by, and he was leading by about a length and riding way out, and light as a monkey, and they were racing for the water-jump. They took off over the big hedge of the water-jump in a pack and then there was a crash, and two horses pulled sideways out off it, and kept on going, and three others were piled up. I couldn't see my old man anywhere. One horse kneed himself up and the jock had hold of the bridle and mounted and went slamming on after the place money. The other horse was up and away by himself, jerking his head and galloping with the bridle rein hanging and the jock staggered over to one side of the track against the fence. Then Gilford rolled over to one side off my old man and got up and started to run on three legs with his off hoof dangling and there was my old man laying there on the grass flat out with his face up and blood all over the side of his head. I ran down the stand and bumped into a jam of people and got to the rail and a cop grabbed me and held me and two big stretcher-bearers were going out after my old man and around on the other side of the course I saw three horses, strung way out, coming out of the trees and taking the jump.

My old man was dead when they brought him in and while a doctor was listening to his heart with a thing plugged in his ears, I heard a shot up the track that meant they'd killed Gilford. I lay down beside my old man, when they carried the stretcher into the hospital room, and hung onto the stretcher and cried and cried, and he looked so white and gone and so awfully dead, and I couldn't help feeling that if my old man was dead maybe they didn't need to have shot Gilford. His hoof might have got well. I don't know. I loved my old man so much.

Then a couple of guys came in and one of them patted me on the back and then went over and looked at my old man and then pulled a sheet off the cot and spread it over him; and the other was telephoning in French for them to send the ambulance to take him out to Maisons. And I couldn't stop crying, crying and choking, sort of, and George Gardner came in and sat down beside me on the floor and put his arm around me and says, "Come on, Joe, old boy. Get up and we'll go out and wait for the ambulance."

George and I went out to the gate and I was trying to stop bawling and George wiped off my face with his handkerchief and we were standing back a little ways while the crowd was going out of the gate and a couple of guys stopped near us while we were waiting for the crowd to get through the gate and one of them was counting a bunch of mutuel tickets and he said, "Well, Butler got his, all right."

The other guy said, "I don't give a good goddam if he did, the crook. He had it coming to him on the stuff he's pulled."

"I'll say he had," said the other guy, and tore the bunch of tickets in two.

And George Gardner looked at me to see if I'd heard and I had all right and he said, "Don't you listen to what those bums said, Joe. Your old man was one swell guy."

But I don't know. Seems like when they get started they don't leave a guy nothing.

5

The Fall of the House of Usher

by Edgar Allan Poe

Under a Glass Bell

by Anaïs Nin

EDGAR ALLAN POE *The* poete maudit *of American letters, Poe was a child prodigy who was emotionally abused by his foster father, but who nevertheless was able to publish a book of poems at the age of eighteen. The incidents of his life (like his marriage to his thirteen-year-old cousin) were as strange as the events in his stories, usually about a terrified individual facing catastrophe. Poe had little literary success until the publication of his poem "The Raven" in 1845, and his unknown stories were rediscovered after his death by the French Symbolists, Baudelaire and Mallarmé, who were overwhelmed by the musical qualities of his prose.*

ANAÏS NIN *Nin is a surrealist whose recent prominence was caused by the publication of her* Diaries*—accounts of her battle for acceptance as a writer despite the unconventionality of her imagistic and sometimes enigmatic fictional techniques. Although she was born in Paris and was part of a European community in the 1930s that included friends like Antonin Artaud, Otto Rank, and Henry Miller, she writes in English and considers herself an American.*

The Fall of the House of Usher

Edgar Allan Poe (*American, 1809–1849*)

Son cœur est un luth suspendu;
Sitôt qu'on le touche il résonne.—*De Béranger*

During the whole of a dull, dark, and soundless day in the autumn of the year, when the clouds hung oppressively low in the heavens, I had been passing alone, on horseback, through a singularly dreary tract of country, and at length found myself, as the shades of the evening drew on, within view of the melancholy House of Usher. I know not how it was—but, with the first glimpse of the building, a sense of insufferable gloom pervaded my spirit. I say insufferable; for the feeling was unrelieved by any of that half-pleasurable, because poetic, sentiment with which the mind usually receives even the sternest natural images of the desolate or terrible. I looked upon the scene before me—upon the mere house and the simple landscape features of the domain—upon the bleak walls—upon the vacant eye-like windows—upon a few rank sedges—and upon a few white trunks of decayed trees—with an utter depression of soul which I can compare to no earthly sensation more properly than to the after-dream of the reveller upon opium—the bitter lapse into every-day life—the hideous dropping off of the veil. There was an iciness, a sinking, a sickening of the heart—an unredeemed dreariness of thought which no goading of the imagination could torture into aught of the sublime. What was it—I paused to think—what was it that so unnerved me in the contemplation of the House of

Usher? It was a mystery all insoluble; nor could I grapple with the shadowy fancies that crowded upon me as I pondered. I was forced to fall back upon the unsatisfactory conclusion, that while, beyond doubt, there *are* combinations of very simple natural objects which have the power of thus affecting us, still the analysis of this power lies among considerations beyond our depth. It was possible, I reflected, that a mere different arrangement of the particulars of the scene, of the details of the picture, would be sufficient to modify, or perhaps to annihilate its capacity for sorrowful impression; and, acting upon this idea, I reined my horse to the precipitous brink of a black and lurid tarn that lay in unruffled lustre by the dwelling, and gazed down—but with a shudder even more thrilling than before—upon the remodelled and inverted images of the gray sedge, and the ghastly tree-stems, and the vacant and eye-like windows.

Nevertheless, in this mansion of gloom I now proposed to myself a sojourn of some weeks. Its proprietor, Roderick Usher, had been one of my boon companions in boyhood; but many years had elapsed since our last meeting. A letter, however, had lately reached me in a distant part of the country—a letter from him—which, in its wildly importunate nature, had admitted of no other than a personal reply. The MS. gave evidence of nervous agitation. The writer spoke of acute bodily illness—of a mental disorder which oppressed him—and of an earnest desire to see me, as his best and indeed his only personal friend, with a view of attempting, by the cheerfulness of my society, some alleviation of his malady. It was the manner in which all this, and much more, was said—it was the apparent *heart* that went with his request— which allowed me no room for hesitation; and I accordingly obeyed forthwith what I still considered a very singular summons.

Although, as boys, we had been even intimate associates, yet I really knew little of my friend. His reserve had been always excessive and habitual. I was aware, however, that his very ancient family had been noted, time out of mind, for a peculiar sensibility of temperament, displaying itself, through long ages, in many works of exalted art, and manifested, of late, in repeated deeds of munificent yet unobstrusive charity, as well as in a passionate devotion to the intricacies, perhaps even more than to the orthodox and easily recognizable beauties, of musical science. I had learned, too, the very remarkable fact, that the stem of the Usher race, all time-honored as it was, had put forth, at no period, any enduring branch; in other words, that the entire family lay in the direct line of descent, and had always, with very trifling and very temporary variation, so lain. It was this deficiency, I considered, while running over in thought the perfect keeping of the character of the premises with the accredited character of the people, and while speculating upon the possible influence which the one, in the long lapse of centuries, might have exercised upon the other—it was this deficiency, perhaps, of collateral issue, and the consequent undeviating transmission, from sire to son, of the patrimony with the name, which had, at length, so identified the two as to merge the original title of the estate in the quaint and equivocal appellation of the "House of Usher"—an appellation which seemed to include, in the minds of the peasantry who used it, both the family and the family mansion.

I have said that the sole effect of my somewhat childish experiment—that of looking down within the tarn—had been to deepen the first singular impression. There can be no doubt that the consciousness of the rapid increase of my superstition—for why should I not so term it?—served mainly to accelerate the increase itself. Such, I have long known, is the paradoxical law of all sentiments having terror as a basis. And it might have been for this reason only, that, when I again uplifted my eyes to the house itself, from its image in the pool, there grew in my mind a strange fancy—a fancy so ridiculous, indeed, that I but mention it to show the vivid force of the sensations which oppressed me. I had so worked upon my imagination as really to believe that about the whole mansion and domain there hung an atmosphere peculiar to themselves and their immediate vicinity—an atmosphere which had no affinity with the air of heaven, but which had reeked up from the decayed trees, and the gray wall, and the silent tarn—a pestilent and mystic vapor, dull, sluggish, faintly discernible, and leaden-hued.

Shaking off from my spirit what *must* have been a dream, I scanned more narrowly the real aspect of the building. Its principal feature seemed to be that of an excessive antiquity. The discoloration of ages had been great. Minute fungi overspread the whole exterior, hanging in a fine tangled web-work from the eaves. Yet all this was apart from any extraordinary dilapidation. No portion of the masonry had fallen; and there appeared to be a wild inconsistency between its still perfect adaptation of parts, and the crumbling condition of the individual stones. In this there was much that reminded me of the specious totality of old wood-work which has rotted for long years in some neglected vault, with no disturbance from the breath of the external air. Beyond this indication of extensive decay, however, the fabric gave little token of instability. Perhaps the eye of a scrutinizing observer might have discovered a barely perceptible fissure, which, extending from the roof of the building in front, made its way down the wall in a zigzag direction, until it became lost in the sullen waters of the tarn.

Noticing these things, I rode over a short causeway to the house. A servant in waiting took my horse, and I entered the Gothic archway of the hall. A valet, of stealthy step, thence conducted me, in silence, through many dark and intricate passages in my progress to the *studio* of his master. Much that I encountered on the way contributed, I know not how, to heighten the vague sentiments of which I have already spoken. While the objects around me—while the carvings of the ceilings, the sombre tapestries of the walls, the ebon blackness of the floors, and the phantasmagoric armorial trophies which rattled as I strode, were but matters to which, or to such as which, I had been accustomed from my infancy—while I hesitated not to acknowledge how familiar was all this—I still wondered to find how unfamiliar were the fancies which ordinary images were stirring up. On one of the staircases, I met the physician of the family. His countenance, I thought, wore a mingled expression of low cunning and perplexity. He accosted me with trepidation and passed on. The valet now threw open a door and ushered me into the presence of his master.

The room in which I found myself was very large and lofty. The windows were long, narrow, and pointed, and at so vast a distance from the black oaken floor as to be altogether inaccessible from within. Feeble gleams of encrimsoned light made their way through the trellissed panes, and served to render sufficiently distinct the more prominent objects around; the eye, however, struggled in vain to reach the remoter angles of the chamber, or the recesses of the vaulted and fretted ceiling. Dark draperies hung upon the walls. The general furniture was profuse, comfortless, antique, and tattered. Many books and musical instruments lay scattered about, but failed to give any vitality to the scene. I felt that I breathed an atmosphere of sorrow. An air of stern, deep, and irredeemable gloom hung over and pervaded all.

Upon my entrance, Usher arose from a sofa on which he had been lying at full length, and greeted me with a vivacious warmth which had much in it, I at first thought, of an overdone cordiality—of the constrained effort of the *ennuyé* man of the world. A glance, however, at his countenance convinced me of his perfect sincerity. We sat down; and for some moments, while he spoke not, I gazed upon him with a feeling half of pity, half of awe. Surely, man had never before so terribly altered, in so brief a period, as had Roderick Usher! It was with difficulty that I could bring myself to admit the identity of the wan being before me with the companion of my early boyhood. Yet the character of his face had been at all times remarkable. A cadaverousness of complexion; an eye large, liquid, and luminous beyond comparison; lips somewhat thin and very pallid, but of a surprisingly beautiful curve; a nose of a delicate Hebrew model, but with a breadth of nostril unusual in similar formations; a finely moulded chin, speaking, in its want of prominence, of a want of moral energy; hair of a more than web-like softness and tenuity;—these features, with an inordinate expansion above the regions of the temple, made up altogether a countenance not easily to be forgotten. And now in the mere exaggeration of the prevailing character of these features, and of the expression they were wont to convey, lay so much of change that I doubted to whom I spoke. The now ghastly pallor of the skin, and the now miraculous lustre of the eye, above all things startled and even awed me. The silken hair, too, had been suffered to grow all unheeded, and as, in its wild gossamer texture, it floated rather than fell about the face, I could not, even with effort, connect its Arabesque expression with any idea of simple humanity.

In the manner of my friend I was at once struck with an incoherence—an inconsistency; and I soon found this to arise from a series of feeble and futile struggles to overcome an habitual trepidancy—an excessive nervous agitation. For something of this nature I had indeed been prepared, no less by his letter, than by reminiscences of certain boyish traits, and by conclusions deduced from his peculiar physical conformation and temperament. His action was alternately vivacious and sullen. His voice varied rapidly from a tremulous indecision (when the animal spirits seemed utterly in abeyance) to that species of energetic concision—that abrupt, weighty, unhurried, and hollow-sounding enunciation—that leaden, self-balanced, and perfectly modulated gutteral utterance, which may be observed in the lost drunkard, or the irreclaimable eater of opium, during the periods of his most intense excitement.

It was thus that he spoke of the object of my visit, of his earnest desire to see me, and of the solace he expected me to afford him. He entered, at some length, into what he conceived to be the nature of his malady. It was, he said, a constitutional and a family evil, and one for which he despaired to find a remedy—a mere nervous affection, he immediately added, which would undoubtedly soon pass off. It displayed itself in a host of unnatural sensations. Some of these, as he detailed them, interested and bewildered me; although, perhaps, the terms and the general manner of their narration had their weight. He suffered much from a morbid acuteness of the senses; the most insipid food was alone endurable; he could wear only garments of certain texture; the odors of all flowers were oppressive; his eyes were tortured by even a faint light; and there were but peculiar sounds, and these from stringed instruments, which did not inspire him with horror.

To an anomalous species of terror I found him a bounden slave. "I shall perish," said he, "I *must* perish in this deplorable folly. Thus, thus, and not otherwise, shall I be lost. I dread the events of the future, not in themselves, but in their results. I shudder at the thought of any, even the most trivial, incident, which may operate upon this intolerable agitation of soul. I have, indeed, no abhorrence of danger, except in its absolute effect—in terror. In this unnerved, in this pitiable, condition I feel that the period will sooner or later arrive when I must abandon life and reason together, in some struggle with the grim phantasm, FEAR."

I learned, moreover, at intervals, and through broken and equivocal hints, another singular feature of his mental condition. He was enchained by certain superstitious impressions in regard to the dwelling which he tenanted, and whence, for many years, he had never ventured forth—in regard to an influence whose supposititious force was conveyed in terms too shadowy here to be restated—an influence which some peculiarities in the mere form and substance of his family mansion had, by dint of long sufferance, he said, obtained over his spirit—an effect which the *physique* of the gray walls and turrets, and of the dim tarn into which they all looked down, had, at length, brought about the *morale* of his existence.

He admitted, however, although with hesitation, that much of the peculiar gloom which thus afflicted him could be traced to a more natural and far more palpable origin—to the severe and long-continued illness—indeed to the evidently approaching dissolution—of a tenderly beloved sister, his sole companion for long years, his last and only relative on earth. "Her decease," he said, with a bitterness which I can never forget, "would leave him (him, the hopeless and the frail) the last of the ancient race of the Ushers." While he spoke, the lady Madeline (for so was she called) passed through a remote portion of the apartment, and, without having noticed my presence, disappeared. I regarded her with an utter astonishment not unmingled with dread; and yet I found it impossible to account for such feelings. A sensation of stupor oppressed me as my eyes followed her retreating steps. When a door, at length, closed upon her, my glance sought instinctively and eagerly the countenance of the brother; but he had buried his face in his hands, and I could only perceive that a far more than ordinary wanness had overspread the emaciated fingers through which trickled many passionate tears.

The disease of the lady Madeline had long baffled the skill of her physicians. A settled apathy, a gradual wasting away of the person, and frequent although transient affections of a partially cataleptical character were the unusual diagnosis. Hitherto she had steadily borne up against the pressure of her malady, and had not betaken herself finally to bed; but on the closing in of the evening of my arrival at the house, she succumbed (as her brother told me at night with inexpressible agitation) to the prostrating power of the destroyer; and I learned that the glimpse I had obtained of her person would thus probably be the last I should obtain—that the lady, at least while living, would be seen by me no more.

For several days ensuing, her name was unmentioned by either Usher or myself; and during this period I was busied in earnest endeavors to alleviate the melancholy of my friend. We painted and read together, or I listened, as if in a dream, to the wild improvisations of his speaking guitar. And thus, as a closer and still closer intimacy admitted me more unreservedly into the recesses of his spirit, the more bitterly did I perceive the futility of all attempt at cheering a mind from which darkness, as if an inherent positive quality, poured forth upon all objects of the moral and physical universe in one unceasing radiation of gloom.

I shall ever bear about me a memory of the many solemn hours I thus spent alone with the master of the House of Usher. Yet I should fail in any attempt to convey an idea of the exact character of the studies, or of the occupations, in which he involved me, or led me the way. An excited and highly distempered ideality threw a sulphureous lustre over all. His long improvised dirges will ring forever in my ears. Among other things, I hold painfully in mind a certain singular perversion and amplification of the wild air of the last waltz of Von Weber. From the paintings over which his elaborate fancy brooded, and which grew, touch by touch, into vagueness at which I shuddered the more thrillingly, because I shuddered knowing not why—from these paintings (vivid as their images now are before me) I would in vain endeavor to educe more than a small portion which should lie within the compass of merely written words. By the utter simplicity, by the nakedness of his designs, he arrested and overawed attention. If ever mortal painted an ideal, that mortal was Roderick Usher. For me at least, in the circumstances then surrounding me, there arose out of the pure abstractions which the hypochondriac contrived to throw upon his canvas, an intensity of intolerable awe, no shadow of which felt I ever yet in the contemplation of the certainly glowing yet too concrete reveries of Fuseli.

One of the phantasmagoric conceptions of my friend, partaking not so rigidly of the spirit of abstraction, may be shadowed forth, although feebly, in words. A small picture presented the interior of an immensely long and rectangular vault or tunnel, with low walls, smooth white, and without interruption or device. Certain accessory points of the design served well to convey the idea that this excavation lay at an exceeding depth below the surface of the earth. No outlet was observed in any portion of its vast extent, and no torch or other artificial source of light was discernible; yet a flood of intense rays rolled throughout, and bathed the whole in a ghastly and inappropriate splendor.

I have just spoken of that morbid condition of the auditory nerve which rendered all music intolerable to the sufferer, with the exception of certain effects of stringed instruments. It was, perhaps, the narrow limits to which he thus confined himself upon the guitar which gave birth, in great measure, to the fantastic character of his performances. But the fervid *facility* of his *impromptus* could not be so accounted for. They must have been, and were, in the notes, as well as in the words of his wild fantasias (for he not unfrequently accompanied himself with rhymed verbal improvisations), the result of that intense mental collectedness and concentration to which I have previously alluded as observable only in particular moments of the highest artificial excitement. The words of one of these rhapsodies I have easily remembered. I was, perhaps, the more forcibly impressed with it as he gave it, because, in the under or mystic current of its meaning, I fancied that I perceived, and for the first time, a full consciousness on the part of Usher of the tottering of his lofty reason upon her throne. The verses, which were entitled "The Haunted Palace," ran very nearly, if not accurately, thus:—

I

In the greenest of our valleys,
By good angels tenanted,
Once a fair and stately palace—
Radiant palace—reared its head.
In the monarch Thought's dominion—
It stood there!
Never seraph spread a pinion
Over fabric half so fair.

II

Banners yellow, glorious, golden,
On its roof did float and flow
(This—all this—was in the olden
Time long ago);
And every gentle air that dallied,
In that sweet day,
Along the ramparts plumed and pallid,
A winged odor went away.

III

Wanderers in that happy valley
Through two luminous windows saw
Spirits moved musically
To a lute's well-tunèd law;
Round about a throne, where sitting
(Porphyrogene!)
In state his glory well befitting,
The ruler of the realm was seen.

IV

And all with pearl and ruby glowing
Was the fair palace door,
Through which came flowing, flowing, flowing
And sparkling evermore,
A troop of Echoes whose sweet duty
Was but to sing,
In voices of surpassing beauty,
The wit and wisdom of their king.

V

But evil things, in robes of sorrow,
Assailed the monarch's high estate;
(Ah, let us mourn, for never morrow
Shall dawn upon him, desolate!)
And, round about his home, the glory
That blushed and bloomed

Is but a dim-remembered story
  Of the old time entombed.

VI

And travellers now within that valley,
  Through the red-litten windows see
Vast forms that move fantastically
  To a discordant melody;
While, like a rapid ghastly river,
  Through the pale door;
A hideous throng rush out forever,
  And laugh—but smile no more.

I well remember that suggestions arising from this ballad led us into a train of thought wherein there became manifest an opinion of Usher's which I mention not so much on account of its novelty (for other men[1] have thought thus), as on account of the pertinacity with which he maintained it. This opinion, in its general form, was that of the sentience of all vegetable things. But, in his disordered fancy, the idea had assumed a more daring character, and trespassed, under certain conditions, upon the kingdom of inorganization. I lack words to express the full extent, or the earnest *abandon* of his persuasion. The belief, however, was connected (as I have previously hinted) with the gray stones of the home of his forefathers. The conditions of the sentence had been here, he imagined, fulfilled in the method of collocation of these stones—in order of their arrangement, as well as in that of the many *fungi* which overspread them, and of the decayed trees which stood around—above all, in the long undisturbed endurance of this arrangement, and in its reduplication in the still waters of the tarn. Its evidence—the evidence of the sentience—was to be seen, he said (and I here started as he spoke), in the gradual yet certain condensation of an atmosphere of their own about the waters and the walls. The result was discoverable, he added, in that silent yet importunate and terrible influence which for centuries had moulded the destinies of his family, and which made *him* what I now saw him—what he was. Such opinions need no comment, and I will make none.

Our books—the books which, for years, had formed no small portion of the mental existence of the invalid—were, as might be supposed, in strict keeping with this character of phantasm. We

[1] Watson, Dr. Percival, Spallanzani, and especially the Bishop of Landaff.—See "Chemical Essays," vol. v.

pored together over such works as the "Ververt et Chartreuse" of Gresset; the "Belphegor" of Machiavelli; the "Heaven and Hell" of Swedenborg; the "Subterranean Voyage of Nicholas Klimm" of Holberg; the "Chiromancy" of Robert Flud, of Jean D'Indaginé, and of de la Chambre; the "Journey into the Blue Distance" of Tieck; and the "City of the Sun" of Campanella. One favorite volume was a small octavo edition of the "Directorium Inquisitorium," by the Dominican Eymeric de Gironne; and there were passages in Pomponius Mela, about the old African Satyrs and Ægipans, over which Usher would sit dreaming for hours. His chief delight, however, was found in the perusal of an exceedingly rare and curious book in quarto Gothic—the manual of a forgotten church—the *Vigiliæ Mortuorum secundum Chorum Ecclesiæ Maguntinæ.*

I could not help thinking of the wild ritual of this work, and of its probable influence upon the hypochondriac, when, one evening, having informed me abruptly that the lady Madeline was no more, he stated his intention of preserving her corpse for a fortnight (previously to its final interment), in one of the numerous vaults within the main walls of the building. The wordly reason, however, assigned for this singular proceeding, was one which I did not feel at liberty to dispute. The brother had been led to his resolution (so he told me) by consideration of the unusual character of the malady of the deceased, of certain obtrusive and eager inquiries on the part of her medical men, and of the remote and exposed situation of the burial-ground of the family. I will not deny that when I called to mind the sinister countenance of the person whom I met upon the staircase, on the day of my arrival at the house, I had no desire to oppose what I regarded as at best but a harmless, and by no means an unnatural, precaution.

At the request of Usher, I personally aided him in the arrangements for the temporary entombment. The body having been encoffined, we two alone bore it to its rest. The vault in which we placed it (and which had been so long unopened that our torches, half smothered in its oppressive atmosphere, gave us little opportunity for investigation) was small, damp, and entirely without means of admission for light; lying, at great depth, immediately beneath that portion of the building in which was my own sleeping apartment. It had been used, apparently, in remote feudal times, for the worst purpose of a donjon-keep, and, in later days, as a place of deposit for powder, or some other highly combustible substance, as a portion of its floor, and the whole interior of a long archway through which we reached it, were carefully sheathed with copper. The door, of massive iron, had been, also, similarly protected. Its immense weight caused an unusually sharp, grating sound, as it moved upon its hinges.

Having deposited our mournful burden upon tressels within this region of horror, we partially turned aside the yet unscrewed lid of the coffin, and looked upon the face of the tenant. A striking similitude between the brother and sister now first arrested my attention; and Usher, divining, perhaps, my thoughts, murmured out some few words from which I learned that the deceased and himself had been twins, and that sympathies of a scarcely intelligible nature had always existed between them. Our glances, however, rested not long upon the dead—for we could not regard her unawed. The disease which had thus entombed the lady in the maturity of youth, had left, as usual in all maladies of a strictly cataleptical character, the mockery of a faint blush upon the bosom and the face, and that suspiciously lingering smile upon the lip which is so terrible in death. We replaced and screwed down the lid, and, having secured the door of iron, made our way, with toil, into the scarcely less gloomy apartments of the upper portion of the house.

And now, some days of bitter grief having elapsed, an observable change came over the features of the mental disorder of my friend. His ordinary manner had vanished. His ordinary occupations were neglected or forgotten. He roamed from chamber to chamber with hurried, unequal, and objectless steps. The pallor of his countenance had assumed, if possible, a more ghastly hue—but the luminousness of his eye had utterly gone out. The once occasional huskiness of his tone was heard no more; and a tremulous quaver, as if of extreme terror, habitually characterized his utterance. There were times, indeed, when I thought his unceasingly agitated mind was laboring with some oppressive secret, to divulge which he struggled for the necessary courage. At times, again, I was obliged to resolve all into the mere inexplicable vagaries of madness, for I beheld him gazing upon vacancy for long hours, in an attitude of the profoundest attention, as if listening to some imaginary sound. It was no wonder that his condition terrified—that it infected me. I felt creeping upon me, by slow yet certain degrees, the wildest influences of his own fantastic yet impressive superstitions.

It was, especially, upon retiring to bed late in the night of the seventh or eighth day after the placing of the lady Madeline within the donjon, that I experienced the full power of such feelings.

Sleep came not near my couch—while the hours waned and waned away. I struggled to reason off the nervousness which had dominion over me. I endeavored to believe that much, if not all of what I felt, was due to the bewildering influence of the gloomy furniture of the room—of the dark and tattered draperies, which, tortured into motion by the breath of a rising tempest, swayed fitfully to and fro upon the walls, and rustled uneasily about the decorations of the bed. But my efforts were fruitless. An irrepressible tremor gradually pervaded my frame; and, at length, there sat upon my very heart an incubus of utterly causeless alarm. Shaking this off with a gasp and a struggle, I uplifted myself upon the pillows, and, peering earnestly within the intense darkness of the chamber, hearkened—I know not why, except that an instinctive spirit prompted me—to certain low and indefinite sounds which came, through the pauses of the storm, at long intervals, I knew not whence. Overpowered by an intense sentiment of horror, unaccountable yet unendurable, I threw on my clothes with haste (for I felt that I should sleep no more during the night), and endeavored to arouse myself from the pitiable condition into which I had fallen, by pacing rapidly to and fro through the apartment.

I had taken but few turns in this manner, when a light step on an adjoining staircase arrested my attention. I presently recognized it as that of Usher. In an instant afterward he rapped, with a gentle touch, at my door, and entered, bearing a lamp. His countenance was, as usual, cadaverously wan—but, moreover, there was a species of mad hilarity in his eyes—an evidently restrained *hysteria* in his whole demeanor. His air appalled me—but anything was preferable to the solitude which I had so long endured, and I even welcomed his presence as a relief.

"And you have not seen it?" he said abruptly, after having stared about him for some moments in silence—"you have not then seen it?—but, stay! you shall." Thus speaking, and having carefully shaded his lamp, he hurried to one of the casements, and threw it freely open to the storm.

The impetuous fury of the entering gust nearly lifted us from our feet. It was, indeed, a tempestuous yet sternly beautiful night, and one wildly singular in its terror and its beauty. A whirlwind had apparently collected its force in our vicinity; for there were frequent and violent alterations in the direction of the wind; and the exceeding density of the clouds (which hung so low as to press upon the turrets of the house) did not prevent our perceiving the life-like velocity with which they flew careering from all points against each other, without passing away into the distance. I say that even their exceeding density did not prevent our perceiving this—yet we had no glimpse of the moon or stars, nor was there any flashing forth of the lightning. But the under surfaces of the huge masses of agitated vapor, as well as all terrestrial objects immediately around us, were glowing in the unnatural light of a faintly luminous and distinctly visible gaseous exhalation which hung about and enshrouded the mansion.

"You must not—you shall not behold this!" said I, shuddering, to Usher, as I led him, with a gentle violence, from the window to a seat. "These appearances, which bewilder you, are merely electrical phenomena not uncommon—or it may be that they have their ghastly origin in the rank miasma of the tarn. Let us close this casement;—the air is chilling and dangerous to your frame. Here is one of your favorite romances. I will read, and you shall listen:—and so we will pass away this terrible night together."

The antique volume which I had taken up was the "Mad Trist" of Sir Launcelot Canning; but I had called it a favorite of Usher's more in sad jest than in earnest; for, in truth, there is little in its uncouth and unimaginative prolixity which could have had interest for the lofty and spiritual ideality of my friend. It was, however, the only book immediately at hand; and I indulged a vague hope that the excitement which now agitated the hypochondriac, might find relief (for the history of mental disorder is full of similar anomalies) even in the extremeness of the folly which I should read. Could I have judged, indeed, by the wild overstrained air of vivacity with which he hearkened, or apparently hearkened, to the words of the tale, I might well have congratulated myself upon the success of my design.

I had arrived at that well-known portion of the story where Ethelred, the hero of the Trist, having sought in vain for peaceable admission into the dwelling of the hermit, proceeds to make good an entrance by force. Here, it will be remembered, the words of the narrative run thus:

"And Ethelred, who was by nature of a doughty heart, and who was now mighty withal, on account of the powerfulness of the wine which he had drunken, waited no longer to hold parley with the hermit, who, in sooth, was of an obstinate and maliceful turn, but, feeling the rain upon his shoulders, and fearing the rising of the tempest, uplifted his mace outright, and, with blows, made quickly room in the plankings of the door for his gauntleted hand; and now pulling therewith sturdily, he so cracked, and ripped, and tore all asunder, that the noise of the dry and hollow-sounding wood alarumed and reverberated throughout the forest."

At the termination of this sentence I started and, for a moment, paused; for it appeared to me (although I at once concluded that my excited fancy had deceived me)—it appeared to me that, from some very remote portion of the mansion, there came, indistinctly, to my ears, what might have been, in its exact similarity of character, the echo (but a stifled and dull one certainly) of the very cracking and ripping sound which Sir Launcelot had so particularly described. It was, beyond doubt, the coincidence alone which had arrested my attention; for, amid the rattling of the sashes of the casements, and the ordinary commingled noises of the still increasing storm, the sound, in itself, had nothing, surely, which should have interested or disturbed me. I continued the story:

"But the good champion Ethelred, now entering within the door, was sore enraged and amazed to perceive no signal of the maliceful hermit; but, in the stead thereof, a dragon of a scaly and prodigious demeanor, and of a fiery tongue, which sate in guard before a palace of gold, with a floor of silver; and upon the wall there hung a shield of shining brass with this legend enwritten—

> Who entereth herein, a conqueror hath bin;
> Who slayeth the dragon, the shield he shall win.

And Ethelred uplifted his mace, and struck upon the head of the dragon, which fell before him, and gave up his pesty breath, with a shriek so horrid and harsh, and withal so piercing, that Ethelred had fain to close his ears with his hands against the dreadful noise of it, the like whereof was never before heard."

Here again I paused abruptly, and now with a feeling of wild amazement—for there could be no doubt whatever that, in this instance, I did actually hear (although from what direction it proceeded I found it impossible to say) a low and apparently distant, but harsh, protracted, and most unusual screaming or grating sound—the exact counterpart of what my fancy had already conjured up for the dragon's unnatural shriek as described by the romancer.

Oppressed, as I certainly was, upon the occurrence of this second and most extraordinary coincidence, by a thousand conflicting sensations, in which wonder and extreme terror were predominant, I still retained sufficient presence of mind to avoid exciting, by any observation, the sensitive nervousness of my companion. I was by no means certain that he had noticed the sounds in question; although, assuredly, a strange alteration had, during the last few minutes, taken place in his demeanor. From a position fronting my own, he had gradually brought round his chair, so as to sit with his face to the door of the chamber; and thus I could but partially perceive his features, although I saw that his lips trembled as if he were murmuring inaudibly. His head had dropped upon his breast—yet I knew that he was not asleep, from the wide and rigid opening of the eye as I caught a glance of it in profile. The motion of his body, too, was at variance with this idea—for he rocked from side to side with a gentle yet constant and uniform sway. Having rapidly taken notice of all this, I resumed the narrative of Sir Launcelot, which thus proceeded:

"And now, the champion, having escaped from the terrible fury of the dragon, bethinking himself of the brazen shield, and of the breaking up of the enchantment which was upon it, removed the carcass from out of the way before him, and approached valorously over the silver pavement of the castle to where the shield was upon the wall; which in sooth tarried not for his full coming, but fell down at his feet upon the silver floor, with a mighty great and terrible ringing sound."

No sooner had these syllables passed my lips, than—as if a shield of brass had indeed, at the moment, fallen heavily upon a floor of silver—I became aware of a distinct, hollow, metallic, and clangorous, yet apparently muffled, reverberation. Completely unnerved, I leaped to my feet; but the measured rocking movement of Usher was undisturbed. I rushed to the chair in which he sat. His eyes were bent fixedly before him, and throughout his whole countenance there reigned a stony rigidity. But, as I placed my hand upon his shoulder, there came a strong shudder over his whole person; a sickly smile quivered about his lips; and I saw that he spoke in a low, hurried, and gibbering murmur, as if unconscious of my presence. Bending closely over him, I at length drank in the hideous import of his words.

"Not hear it?—yes, I hear it, and *have* heard it. Long—long—long—many minutes, many hours, many days, have I heard it—yet I dared not—oh, pity me, miserable wretch that I am!—I dared not—I *dared* not speak! *We have put her living in the tomb!* Said I not that my senses were acute? I *now* tell you that I heard her first feeble movements in the hollow coffin. I heard them—many, many days ago—yet I dared not—*I dared not speak!* And now—to-night—Ethelred—ha ha!—the breaking of the hermit's door, and the death-cry of the dragon, and the clangor of the shield—say, rather, the rending of her coffin, and the grating of the iron hinges of her prison, and her struggles within the coppered archway of the vault! Oh! whither shall I fly? Will she not be here anon? Is she not hurrying to upbraid me for my haste? Have I not heard her footstep on the stair? Do I not distinguish that heavy and horrible beating of her heart? Madman!"—here he sprang furiously to his feet, and shrieked out his syllables, as if in the effort he were giving up his soul—"*Madman! I tell you that she now stands without the door!*"

As if in the superhuman energy of his utterance there had been found the potency of a spell, the huge antique panels to which the speaker pointed threw slowly back, upon the instant, their ponderous and ebony jaws. It was the work of the rushing gust—but then without those doors there *did* stand the lofty and enshrouded figure of the lady Madeline of Usher. There was blood upon her white robes, and the evidence of some bitter struggle upon every portion of her emaciated frame. For a moment she remained trembling and reeling to and fro upon the threshold—then, with a low moaning cry, fell heavily inward upon the person of her brother, and in her violent and now final death-agonies, bore him to the floor a corpse, and a victim to the terrors he had anticipated.

From that chamber, and from that mansion, I fled aghast. The storm was still abroad in all its wrath as I found myself crossing the old causeway. Suddenly there shot along the path a wild light, and I turned to see whence a gleam so unusual could have issued; for the vast house and its shadows were alone behind me. The radiance was that of the full, setting, and blood-red moon, which now shone vividly through that once barely discernible fissure, of which I have spoken as extending from the roof of the building, in a zigzag direction, to the base. While I gazed, this fissure rapidly widened—there came a fierce breath of the whirlwind—the entire orb of the satellite burst at once upon my sight—my brain reeled as I saw the mighty walls rushing asunder—there was a long tumultuous shouting sound like the voice of a thousand waters—and the deep and dank tarn at my feet closed sullenly and silently over the fragments of the "*House of Usher.*"

Under a Glass Bell

Anaïs Nin (*French, 1914–*)

It was a stately house where many lives had accumulated and left their essences. It had perfume of rich lives, of heavily impregnated furniture, and the very folds of the curtains contained secrets and sighs. It was also a house that seemed about to vanish. The tip of the labyrinthian stairway leading to the gate lost itself among the potted plants, the turrets dissolved into the overhanging branches of old trees. The glass doors and windows opened without sound, the floors were so highly polished they looked transparent. The ceilings were powdered white, the damask curtains were stiff like mummy costumes. The butlers knew about the fragility: they walked almost invisibly seemingly not touching anything. What they carried back and forth was borne on silver trays with a minuet lightness of step and was to be received with equal delicacy. Wood, silk, and paint had the brittleness of preserved flowers. The curves of the legs of the chairs were full of debonair assertion like those of the ancient men of the family in their white stockings. The lace covers on the backs of the chairs were starched to look like paper and the paper flowers were painted to look like lace. The mirrors were framed with white roses made of sea shells. From the ceiling hung enormous glass chandeliers, blue icicle bushes shedding teardrops of blue glass light on the gold furniture.

On the mantelpiece, the shepherdesses, the angels, the gods and goddesses of porcelain, all seemed to have been caught while in motion by a secret enchantment and put to sleep with a dust of white sleep like those secret enchantments of nature enclosing the drops of water in dark caves and turning them into stalactite torches, candlesticks, hooded figures. That delicacy of design only created in a void, in great silence and great immobility. No violence here, no tears, no great suffering, no shouting, no destruction, no anarchy. The secret silences, the muted pains brought about by great riches, a conspiracy of tranquility to preserve this flowerlike fragility in crystal, wood, and damask. The violins were muted, the hands were gloved, carpets were unrolled forever under the feet, and the gardens cottoned the sound from the world.

The light from the icicle bushes threw a patina over all objects, and turned them into bouquets of still flowers kept under a glass bell. The glass bell covered the flowers, the chairs, the whole room, the panoplied beds, the statues, the butlers, all the people living in the house. The glass bell covered the entire house.

Every day the silence, the peace, the softness, carved with greater delicacy the glass chandeliers, the furniture, the statuettes and laces, then covered them with glass. Under the giant glass bell the colors looked inaccessible, the shapes strongly beautiful as of something that can never be repeated. Everything had the transparency, the fragility of stalactite created in silence and obscurity and breaking when the caves are opened and the breath of man enters.

Jeanne was sitting with her two brothers in the room they used as children. They were sitting in front of an armored fireplace, in three children's chairs.

Her face seemed stemless and drooped listlessly as she monologued endlessly: "Jean, Paul and I . . . nothing exists beyond our alliance. My own children do not mean as much to me as my brothers. I am devoted to my children only because I have given my word, I owe them that, but what I do for my brothers is a great joy. We cannot live without each other. If I am sick they get sick, if they are sick I get sick. All joys and anxieties are tripled. Their opinion of me and mine of them is our only standard. It forces us into a kind of heroic living. If I should ever say to Jean: 'You have done a petty thing,' he would kill himself. We three belong to the Middle Ages. We have this need of heroism, and there is no place for such feelings in modern life. That is our tragedy. Once I wanted to be a saint. It seemed the only absolute act left to do, for what is most powerful in me is the craving for purity, greatness. I am not living on earth. Neither are my brothers. We are dead. We reached such heights in love that it made us want to die altogether with the loved one, and so we died. We are living in another world. Our having bodies is a farce, an anachronism. We were never even born. We have no ordinary sensual life, no contact with reality. My marriage was a farce, my brothers' marriages meaningless. When my children were born I didn't suffer. The births were difficult. I refused to take gas. I was amused. I wanted to see myself bringing children into the world. I worked hard. I felt pain, of course, but I didn't suffer like a human being. I felt pain detachedly, as if it were not happening to my body: I have no body. I have an external envelope which deludes others into thinking I am alive. My brothers and I hate to see each other. What we like is to have long conversations together from room to room, doors open, but not seeing each other. It enrages us to meet and kiss each other in that stupid, ordinary human way, to keep up the great farce of human movements, gestures, etc. when we are dead. And complete death would be so enjoyable, because everything we do together is an enjoyment. I can't bear to see them as bodies, to see them growing old. Once I sat writing letters and the two of them were playing cards. I looked at them and thought what a crime it was our being alive: it was a simulacrum, everything was really finished long ago. We have lived already, we are far away from husbands', wives, and children. I have tried so hard to love others, and I can up to a certain point, and then no further. Beyond that I begin to hate. Not one of us has any human sympathy. Jean does not understand why his wife weeps sometimes. We laugh at her. She is small and human. She weeps and we despise her for it. We never weep. The only thing I feel sometimes is fear, a terrific fear which catches me unaware sometimes like a fit of madness. Sometimes I become deaf in the street. I see automobiles passing and I hear nothing. At other times I seem to go blind. Everything becomes nebulous around me. But that only happens when I am alone. When I am alone I think I go a little mad. Sometimes I say to my husband: 'Do you know, I believe I am supremely intelligent.' He says: 'How vain you are!' But it isn't vanity. It's an intelligence you get when you are dead. Sometimes while he is reading his newspaper I say: 'Wouldn't you like to be an archangel as I am?' He answers me: 'You're a child.' My brothers never say such things. We can describe to each other how it feels to be an archangel. Then when we are finished with that mood my brothers say: 'Let's pass to a new form of exercise.' I am a descendant of Joan of Arc. Only I have no role to play. I have nothing to save. We still sleep in the beds we used as children. My mother was the true Queen of France, she was loved by all the great men of her time. She ruled them. She never took care of us like a mother. She was always in the center of a great passion.

She never kept a love, only while it was a passion. When the passions were over and she lost her beauty she took drugs. She lay all day in her canopied bed, her eyes burning, murmuring broken phrases. She shut her windows and lived by the light of night candles. Her eyes were dilated and saw nothing but her dreams. She ordered a dinner for twenty-five persons and then forgot about it and took a stronger dose of drugs. When I came home the chef and the housekeeper were running through the corridors shouting: 'Madame is raving about Napoleon. What are we going to do with the two dozen lobsters, the kilos and kilos of fruit? What shall we do? Madame is saying: "Bonjour, Napoleon, I must make a speech, and I don't know what to say."' I made the wrong start in life."

A Georgian Prince fell in love with Jeanne, and she tried to love him. But she complained that he uttered such ordinary words, that he could never say the magic phrase which would open her being.

It was Christmas morning and she went out with the Christmas tinsel rolled around her neck, carrying one of the glass birds perched on her little finger. She took a taxi to visit the Prince. When the taxi driver saw her he would not accept payment for the journey. He was a Russian. He may have remembered the Persian prints of a woman carrying a bird on her finger. He would not let Jeanne pay. He may have divined she was going to see the Prince. Jeanne put the tinsel around the taxi driver's neck and sat the bird on the taximeter, smiled and said: "Drive me home, please!"

That night I mailed Jeanne the first Persion print representing the Queen of Bijabur riding on a white steed harnessed with black velvet. It was handed to her on a silver tray with her breakfast. She thought it came from the Prince and again she took a taxi and this time she rang his bell and paid him a visit.

The next day she received a picture of Baz Bakadur and Rupmati riding together by moonlight. She thought the Prince could not articulate his dreams but that he could dream. She paid him another visit.

I sent her a print of Radha waiting for her lover Krishna. That evening they had supper together and, in accordance with the custom of his country, after they had eaten together they threw all the dishes out of the window.

The fourth day I sent her a Lover's Message in a Persian Garden filled with feather flowers. The fifth day I sent her the Prince and Princess riding through a mountainous region, a servant bearing a torch.

Before I exhausted my collection of Persian prints, Jeanne had discovered that Prince Mahreb could not dream at all, and again her face fell listlessly like a stemless plant.

In the garden one afternoon Paul fell asleep and as the sun was setting it projected the outline of his face on the back of the chair. Jeanne came up and kissed this shadow. Among shadows she was at ease.

The enormous house stood behind them, with a thousand eyes looking down at them.

Jeanne walked into the house and entered the room of mirrors. Ceilings of mirrors, floors of mirrors, windows of quicksilver opening on windows of quicksilver. The air was made of gelatine. Around her hair there was a saffron aureole, and her skin was a sea shell, an egg shell. There was a lunar wax light on the rim of her shoulder. Woman imprisoned in the stillness of mirrors washed only by jellied colors.

On her breast grew flowers of dust and no wind came from the earth to disturb them. Flowers of dust hung serenely. Around her waist a crinoline without its cover of lace and satin, a round crinoline like a bird cage. On her throat a brooch without stones, with its little silver hooks clutching emptiness. The fan in her hand was laceless and featherless, open and bare like winter branches. She breathed on the mirror. The dew of her breath on the mirror vanished. The mirror held nothing. She closed her eyes so many times: a tunnel of eyes closing. Countless sulphurous profiles touching each other accompanied by a rim of light. Countless women smiling; four women walking towards four women walking towards four women vanishing. She looked into the mirror until the dew of her anxiety clouded her face.

She wanted to be where she could not see herself. She wanted to be where everything did not happen twice. She walked, following the deep caverns of diminishing light. She touched ice and was bruised. To watch she must pause, and so what she caught was never the truth—the woman panting, dancing, weeping—it was only the woman who paused. The mirror was always one breath too late to catch the breathing.

Quickly, more quickly she turned to catch the face of her soul, but even when she moved at dream speed she saw the face of the actress, the small curtain closing inside of the pupil. She wanted to smash the mirror and be one. There was a joy of unveiling from which no human joy could call one back, there was joy without feet or voice or warmth, but the mirror revealed only the prying.

If she could not catch the ultimate flame of life could she detect death? She bowed nearer to catch the immobility, the death. But the caverns within the pupil of the eye diminish and close at the sight of death. The eye dead could not see the eye dead in the mirror. At death all mirrors are covered, to bury reflection. Death never permitted an echo, death cannot be made visible, or cast the shadow of its presence.

She watched her sorrow. She looked at the tears. The sorrow unveiled and reflected before her ceased to be her own. It was the sorrow of another, with a space between them. She looked at the tears and they froze and died.

She ran out into the somnambulistic garden. Her brother was still asleep like one enchanted. The glass bell which separated them from the world was visible in the light. Would Jeanne see it? Would she smash it and be free? She did not see it. She kissed the shadow of her brother. He awakened. She said: "Let me touch something warm. Save me from reflections. The mirror frightened me."

But her hand was lying on the shadow of her brother and not on him. Then she said: "I am afraid that of the three of us I will be the first one to die. I am the lightest. I saw in the mirror, not my death but the image of myself in the tomb. I was wearing a brooch without stones, a crinoline with all its silk covering eaten away."

Her guitar was lying at her feet. As she said this the string broke.

6

Love: Three Pages from a Sportsman's Book

by Guy de Maupassant

Love

by Jesse Stuart

The Grave

by Katherine Anne Porter

GUY DE MAUPASSANT *Born in Normandy in 1850, Maupassant moved with his mother to a fishing village near Le Havre, where he lived happily through his teens. He had only just entered law school in Paris when the Franco-Prussian war began. Maupassant enlisted, saw action, but soon grew weary of the fighting and evidently convinced another young man to take his place.*

Returning to Paris, Maupassant secured employment as a clerk and began to write fiction. His acknowledged master was Gustave Flaubert, who oversaw the young man's work, and introduced him to writers like Zola, Daudet, and Turgenev. Maupassant's first published story, "Tallow Ball," Flaubert acclaimed a masterpiece. Stories, novels, dramas, and essays followed apace, and although Maupassant died relatively young apparently of paresis, he had already taken his place among the most famous writers in France.

JESSE STUART *For many years, Jesse Stuart has written movingly of the mountain country in Kentucky, where he was born. His first novel,* Trees of Heaven, *was published in 1940; and he has written serious verse and several autobiographical volumes as well. But his earliest and most enduring success has been with short stories, first collected in* Head o' W-Hollow *in 1936.*

KATHERINE ANNE PORTER *Katherine Anne Porter's fame belies her output. She has in fact published comparatively little, though she began writing stories as a child in Indian Creek, Texas, where she was born. Always exceptionally painstaking and meticulous in her craft, she has produced fictions dense and intricate beneath their rich surfaces.*

Flowering Judas, *Miss Porter's first published work, consisting of six short stories, appeared in 1930. With it she established a reputation—at least with the literary establishment. Yet she did not bring out another volume until five years afterwards: an enlarged edition of* Flowering Judas.

Since then, Miss Porter has published one full length novel, Ship of Fools, *1962, and several masterful novelettes, including* Noon Wine *and* Pale Horse, Pale Rider.

Love

Three Pages from a Sportsman's Book

Guy de Maupassant (*French, 1850–1893*)

I have just read among the general news in one of the papers a drama of passion. He killed her and then he killed himself, so he must have loved her. What matters He or She? Their love alone matters to me, and it does not interest me because it moves me or astonishes me or because it softens me or makes me think, but because it recalls to my mind a remembrance of my youth, a strange recollection of a hunting adventure where Love appeared to me, as the Cross appeared to the early Christians, in the midst of the heavens.

I was born with all the instincts and the senses of primitive man, tempered by the arguments and the restraints of a civilized being. I am passionately fond of shooting, yet the sight of the wounded animal, of the blood on its feathers and on my hands, affects my heart so as almost to make it stop.

That year the cold weather set in suddenly toward the end of autumn, and I was invited by one of my cousins, Karl de Rauville, to go with him and shoot ducks on the marshes at daybreak.

My cousin was a jolly fellow of forty with red hair, very stout and bearded, a country gentleman, an amiable semibrute of a happy disposition and endowed with that Gallic wit which makes even mediocrity agreeable. He lived in a house, half farmhouse, half chateau, situated in a broad valley through which a river ran. The hills right and left were covered with woods, old manorial woods where magnificent trees still remained and where the rarest feathered game in that part of France was to be found. Eagles were shot there occasionally, and birds of passage, such as rarely venture into our overpopulated part of the country, invariably lighted amid these giant oaks as if they knew or recognized some little corner of a primeval forest which had remained there to serve them as a shelter during these short nocturnal halts.

In the valley there were large meadows watered by trenches and separated by hedges; then, further on, the river, which up to that point had been kept between banks, expanded into a vast marsh. That marsh was the best shooting ground I ever saw. It was my cousin's chief care, and he kept it as a preserve. Through the rushes that covered it, and made it rustling and rough, narrow passages had been cut, through which the flat-bottomed boats, impelled and steered by poles, passed along silently over dead water, brushing up against the reeds and making the swift fish take refuge in the weeds and the wild fowl, with their pointed black heads, dive suddenly.

I am passionately fond of the water: of the sea, though it is too vast, too full of movement, impossible to hold; of the rivers which are so beautiful but which pass on and flee away; and above all of the marshes, where the whole unknown existence of aquatic animals palpitates. The marsh is an entire world in itself on the world of earth—a different world which has its own life, its settled inhabitants and its passing travelers, its voices, its noises and above all its mystery. Nothing is more impressive, nothing more disquieting, more terrifying occasionally, than a fen. Why should a vague terror hang over these low plains covered with water? Is it the low rustling of the rushes, the strange will-o'-the-wisp lights, the silence which prevails on calm nights, the still mists which hang over the surface like a shroud; or is it the almost inaudible splashing, so slight and so gentle, yet sometimes more terrifying than the cannons of men or the thunders of the skies, which make these marshes resemble countries one has dreamed of, terrible countries holding an unknown and dangerous secret?

No, something else belongs to it—another mystery, perhaps the mystery of the creation itself! For was it not in stagnant and muddy water, amid the heavy humidity of moist land under the heat of the sun, that the first germ of life pulsated and expanded to the day?

I arrived at my cousin's in the evening. It was freezing hard enough to split the stones.

During dinner, in the large room whose sideboards, walls and ceiling were covered with stuffed birds with wings extended or perched on branches to which they were nailed—hawks, herons, owls, nightjars, buzzards, tercels, vultures, falcons—my cousin, who, dressed in a sealskin jacket, himself resembled some strange animal from a cold country, told me what preparations he had made for that same night.

We were to start at half-past three in the morning so as to arrive at the place which he had chosen for our watching place at about half-past four. On that spot a hut had been built of lumps of ice so as to shelter us somewhat from the trying wind which precedes daybreak, a wind so cold as to tear the flesh like a saw, cut it like the blade of a knife, prick it like a poisoned sting, twist it like a pair of pincers, and burn it like fire.

My cousin rubbed his hands. "I have never known such a frost," he said; "it is already twelve degrees below zero at six o'clock in the evening."

I threw myself onto my bed immediately after we had finished our meal and went to sleep by the light of a bright fire burning in the grate.

At three o'clock he woke me. In my turn I put on a sheepskin and found my cousin Karl covered with a bearskin. After having each swallowed two cups of scalding coffee, followed by glasses of liqueur brandy, we started, accompanied by a gamekeeper and our dogs, Plongeon and Pierrot.

From the first moment that I got outside I felt chilled to the very marrow. It was one of those nights on which the earth seems dead with cold. The frozen air becomes resisting and palpable, such pain does it cause; no breath of wind moves it, it is fixed and motionless; it bites you, pierces through you, dries you, kills the trees, the plants, the insects, the small birds themselves, who fall from the branches onto the hard ground and become stiff themselves under the grip of the cold.

The moon, which was in her last quarter and was inclining all to one side, seemed fainting in the midst of space, so weak that she was unable to wane, forced to stay up yonder, seized and paralyzed by the severity of the weather. She shed a cold mournful light over the world, that dying and wan light which she gives us every month at the end of her period.

Karl and I walked side by side, our backs bent, our hands in our pockets and our guns under our arms. Our boots, which were wrapped in wool so that we might be able to walk without slipping on the frozen river, made no sound, and I looked at the white vapor which our dogs' breath made.

We were soon on the edge of the marsh and entered one of the lanes of dry rushes which ran through the low forest.

Our elbows, which touched the long ribbonlike leaves, left a slight noise behind us, and I was seized, as I had never been before, by the powerful and singular emotion which marshes cause in me. This one was dead, dead from cold, since we were walking on it in the middle of its population of dried rushes.

Suddenly, at the turn of one of the lanes, I perceived the ice hut which had been constructed to shelter us. I went in, and as we had nearly an hour to wait before the wandering birds would awake I rolled myself up in my rug in order to try and get warm. Then, lying on my back, I began to look at the misshapen moon, which had four horns through the vaguely transparent walls of this polar house. But the frost of the frozen marshes, the cold of these walls, the cold from the firmament penetrated me so terribly that I began to cough. My cousin Karl became uneasy.

"No matter if we do not kill much today," he said. "I do not want you to catch cold; we will light a fire." And he told the gamekeeper to cut some rushes.

We made a pile in the middle of our hut, which had a hole in the middle of the roof to let out the smoke, and when the red flames rose up to the clear crystal blocks, they began to melt, gently, imperceptibly, as if they were sweating. Karl, who had remained outside, called out to me: "Come and look here!" I went out of the hut and remained struck with astonishment. Our hut, in the shape of a cone, looked like an enormous diamond with a heart of fire which had been suddenly planted there in the midst of the frozen water of the marsh. And inside we saw two fantastic forms, those of our dogs, who were warming themselves at the fire.

But a peculiar cry, a lost, a wandering cry, passed over our heads, and the light from our hearth showed us the wild birds. Nothing moves one so much as the first clamor of a life which one does not see, which passes through the somber air so quickly and so far off, just before the first streak of a winter's day appears on the horizon. It seems to me, at this glacial hour of dawn, as if that passing cry which is carried away by the wings of a bird is the sigh of a soul from the world!

"Put out the fire," said Karl; "it is getting daylight."

The sky was, in fact, beginning to grow pale, and the flights of ducks made long rapid streaks which were soon obliterated on the sky.

A stream of light burst out into the night; Karl had fired, and the two dogs ran forward.

And then nearly every minute now he, now I, aimed rapidly as soon as the shadow of a flying flock appeared above the rushes. And Pierrot and Plongeon, out of breath but happy, retrieved the bleeding birds whose eyes still, occasionally, looked at us.

The sun had risen, and it was a bright day with a blue sky, and we were thinking of taking our departure, when two birds with extended necks and outstretched wings glided rapidly over our heads. I fired, and one of them fell almost at my feet. It was a teal with a silver breast, and then, in the blue space above me, I heard a voice, the voice of a bird. It was a short, repeated heart-rending lament; and the bird, the little animal that had been spared, began to turn round in the blue sky over our heads, looking at its dead companion which I was holding in my hand.

Karl was on his knees, his gun to his shoulder, watching it eagerly until it should be within shot. "You have killed the duck," he said, "and the drake will not fly away."

He certainly did not fly away; he circled over our heads continually and continued his cries. Never have any groans of suffering pained me so much as that desolate appeal, as that lamentable reproach of this poor bird which was lost in space.

Occasionally he took flight under the menace of the gun which followed his movements and seemed ready to continue his flight alone, but as he could not make up his mind to this he returned to find his mate.

"Leave her on the ground," Karl said to me; "he will come within shot by and by." And he did indeed come near us, careless of danger, infatuated by his animal love, by his affection for his mate which I had just killed.

Karl fired, and it was as if somebody had cut the string which held the bird suspended. I saw something black descend, and I heard the noise of a fall among the rushes. And Pierrot brought it to me.

I put them—they were already cold—into the same gamebag, and I returned to Paris the same evening.

Love

Jesse Stuart (*American, 1907–*)

Yesterday when the bright sun blazed down on the wilted corn my father and I walked around the edge of the new ground to plan a fence. The cows kept coming through the chestnut oaks on the cliff and running over the young corn. They bit off the tips of the corn and trampled down the stubble.

My father walked in the cornbalk. Bob, our Collie, walked in front of my father. We heard a ground squirrel whistle down over the bluff among the dead treetops at the clearing's edge. "Whoop, take him, Bob," said my father. He lifted up a young stalk of corn, with wilted dried roots, where the ground squirrel had dug it up for the sweet grain of corn left on its tender roots. This has been a dry spring and the corn has kept well in the earth where the grain has sprouted. The ground squirrels love this corn. They dig up rows of it and eat the sweet grains. The young corn stalks are killed and we have to replant the corn.

I can see my father keep sicking Bob after the ground squirrel. He jumped over the corn rows. He started to run toward the ground squirrel. I, too, started running toward the clearing's edge where Bob was jumping and barking. The dust flew in tiny swirls behind our feet. There was a cloud of dust behind us.

"It's a big bull blacksnake," said my father. "Kill him, Bob! Kill him, Bob!"

Bob was jumping and snapping at the snake so as to make it strike and throw itself off guard. Bob had killed twenty-eight copperheads this spring. He knows how to kill a snake. He doesn't rush to do it. He takes his time and does the job well.

"Let's don't kill the snake," I said. "A blacksnake is a harmless snake. It kills poison snakes. It kills the copperhead. It catches more mice from the fields than a cat."

I could see the snake didn't want to fight the dog. The snake wanted to get away. Bob wouldn't let it. I wondered why it was crawling toward a heap of black loamy earth at the bench of the hill. I wondered why it had come from the chestnut oak sprouts and the matted greenbriars on the cliff. I looked as the snake lifted its pretty head in response to one of Bob's jumps. "It's not a bull blacksnake," I said. "It's a she-snake. Look at the white on her throat."

"A snake is an enemy to me," my father snapped. "I hate a snake. Kill it, Bob. Go in there and get that snake and quit playing with it!"

Bob obeyed my father. I hated to see him take this snake by the throat. She was so beautifully poised in the sunlight. Bob grabbed the white patch on her throat. He cracked her long body like an ox whip in the wind. He cracked it against the wind only. The blood spurted from her fine-curved throat. Something hit against my legs like pellets. Bob threw the snake down. I looked to see what had struck my legs. It was snake eggs. Bob had slung them from her body. She was going to the sand heap to lay her eggs, where the sun is the setting-hen that warms them and hatches them.

Bob grabbed her body there on the earth where the red blood was running down on the gray-piled loam. Her body was still writhing in pain. She acted like a greenweed held over a new-ground fire. Bob slung her viciously many times. He cracked her limp body against the wind. She was now limber as a shoestring in the wind. Bob threw her riddled body back on the sand. She quivered like a leaf in the lazy wind, then her riddled body lay perfectly still. The blood colored the loamy earth around the snake.

"Look at the eggs, won't you?" said my father. We counted thirty-seven eggs. I picked an egg up and held it in my hand. Only a minute ago there was life in it. It was an immature seed. It would not hatch. Mother sun could not incubate it on the warm earth. The egg I held in my hand was almost the size of a quail's egg. The shell on it was thin and tough and the egg appeared under the surface to be a watery egg.

"Well, Bob, I guess you see now why this snake couldn't fight," I said. "It is life. Weaker devour the stronger even among human beings. Dog kills snake. Snake kills birds. Birds kill the butterflies. Man conquers all. Man, too, kills for sport."

Bob was panting. He walked ahead of us back to the house. His tongue was out of his mouth. He was tired. He was hot under his shaggy coat of hair. His tongue nearly touched the dry dirt and white flecks of foam dripped from it. We walked toward the house. Neither my father nor I spoke. I still thought about the dead snake. The sun was going down over the chestnut ridge. A lark was singing. It was late for a lark to sing. The red evening clouds floated above the pine trees on our pasture hill. My father stood beside the path. His black hair was moved by the wind. His face was red in the blue wind of day. His eyes looked toward the sinking sun.

"And my father hates a snake," I thought.

I thought about the agony women know of giving birth. I thought about how they will fight to save their children. Then, I thought of the snake. I thought it was silly for me to think such thoughts.

This morning my father and I got up with the chickens. He says one has to get up with the chickens to do a day's work. We got the posthole digger, ax, spud, measuring pole and the mattock. We started for the clearing's edge. Bob didn't go along.

The dew was on the corn. My father walked behind with the posthole digger across his shoulder. I walked in front. The wind was blowing. It was a good morning wind to breathe and a wind that makes one feel like he can get under the edge of a hill and heave the whole hill upside down.

I walked out the corn row where we had come yesterday afternoon. I looked in front of me. I saw something. I saw it move. It was moving like a huge black rope winds around a windlass. "Steady," I says to my father. "Here is the bull blacksnake." He took one step up beside me and stood. His eyes grew wide apart.

"What do you know about this," he said.

"You have seen the bull blacksnake now," I said. "Take a good look at him! He is lying beside his dead mate. He has come to her. He, perhaps, was on her trail yesterday."

The male snake had trailed her to her doom. He had come in the night, under the roof of stars, as the moon shed rays of light on the quivering clouds of green. He had found his lover dead. He was coiled beside her, and she was dead.

The bull blacksnake lifted his head and followed us as we walked around the dead snake. He would have fought us to his death. He would have fought Bob to his death. "Take a stick," said my father, "and throw him over the hill so Bob won't find him. Did you ever see anything to beat that? I've heard they'd do that. But this is my first time to see it." I took a stick and threw him over the bank into the dewy sprouts on the cliff.

The Grave

Katherine Anne Porter (*American, 1890–*   )

The grandfather, dead for more than thirty years, had been twice disturbed in his long repose by the constancy and possessiveness of his widow. She removed his bones first to Louisiana and then to Texas as if she had set out to find her own burial place, knowing well she would never return to the places she had left. In Texas she set up a small cemetery in a corner of her first farm, and as the family connection grew, and oddments of relations came over from Kentucky to settle, it contained at last about twenty graves. After the grandmother's death, part of her land was to be sold for the benefit of certain of her children, and the cemetery happened to lie in the part set aside for sale. It was necessary to take up the bodies and bury them again in the family plot in the big new public cemetery, where the grandmother had been buried. At last her husband was to lie beside her for eternity, as she had planned.

The family cemetery had been a pleasant small neglected garden of tangled rose bushes and ragged cedar trees and cypress, the simple flat stones rising out of uncropped sweet-smelling wild grass. The graves were lying open and empty one burning day when Miranda and her brother Paul, who often went together to hunt rabbits and doves, propped their twenty-two Winchester rifles carefully against the rail fence, climbed over and explored among the graves. She was nine years old and he was twelve.

They peered into the pits all shaped alike with such purposeful accuracy, and looking at each other with pleased adventurous eyes, they said in solemn tones: "These were graves!" trying by words to shape a special, suitable emotion in their minds, but they felt nothing except an agreeable thrill of wonder: they were seeing a new sight, doing something they had not done before. In them both there was also a small disappointment at the entire commonplaceness of the actual spectacle. Even if it had once contained a coffin for years upon years, when the coffin was gone a grave was just a hole in the ground. Miranda leaped into the pit that had held her grandfather's bones. Scratching around aimlessly and pleasurably as any young animal, she scooped up a lump of earth and weighed it in her palm. It had a pleasantly sweet, corrupt smell, being mixed with cedar needles and small leaves, and as the crumbs fell apart, she saw a silver dove no larger than a hazel nut, with spread wings and a neat fan-shaped tail. The breast had a deep round hollow in it. Turning it up to the fierce sunlight, she saw that the inside of the hollow was cut in little whorls. She scrambled out, over the pile of loose earth that had fallen back into one end of the grave, calling to Paul that she had found something, he must guess what . . . His head appeared smiling over the rim of another grave. He waved a closed hand at her. "I've got something too!" They ran to compare treasures, making a game of it, so many guesses each, all wrong, and a final showdown with opened palms. Paul had found a thin wide gold ring carved with intricate flowers and leaves. Miranda was smitten at sight of the ring and wished to have it. Paul seemed more impressed by the dove. They made a trade, with some little bickering. After he had got the dove in his hand, Paul said, "Don't you know what this is? This is a screw head for a *coffin!* . . . I'll bet nobody else in the world has one like this!"

Miranda glanced at it without covetousness. She had the gold ring on her thumb; it fitted perfectly. "Maybe we ought to go now," she said, "maybe one of the niggers'll see us and tell somebody." They knew the land had been sold, the cemetery was no longer theirs, and they felt like trespassers. They climbed back over the fence, slung their rifles loosely under their arms—they had been shooting at targets with various kinds of firearms since they were seven years old—and set out to look for the rabbits and doves or whatever small game might happen along. On these expeditions Miranda always followed at Paul's heels along the path, obeying instructions about handling her gun when going through fences; learning how to stand it up properly so it would not slip and fire unexpectedly; how to wait her time for a shot and not just bang away in the air without looking, spoiling shots for Paul, who really could hit things if given a chance. Now and then, in her excitement at seeing birds whizz up suddenly before her face, or a rabbit leap across her very toes, she lost her head, and almost without sighting she flung her rifle up and pulled the trigger. She hardly ever hit any sort of mark. She had no proper sense of hunting at all. Her brother would be often completely disgusted with her. "You don't care whether you get your bird or not," he said. "That's no way to hunt." Miranda could not understand his indignation. She had seen him smash his hat and yell with fury when he had missed his aim. "What I like about shooting," said Miranda, with exasperating inconsequence, "is pulling the trigger and hearing the noise."

"Then, by golly," said Paul, "whyn't you go back to the range and shoot at bulls-eyes?"

"I'd just as soon," said Miranda, "only like this, we walk around more."

"Well, you just stay behind and stop spoiling my shots," said Paul, who, when he made a kill, wanted to be certain he had made it. Miranda, who alone brought down a bird once in twenty rounds, always claimed as her own any game they got when they fired at the same moment. It was tiresome and unfair and her brother was sick of it.

"Now, the first dove we see, or the first rabbit, is mine," he told her. "And the next will be yours. Remember that and don't get smarty."

"What about snakes?" asked Miranda idly. "Can I have the first snake?"

Waving her thumb gently and watching her gold ring glitter, Miranda lost interest in shooting. She was wearing her summer roughing outfit: dark blue overalls, a light blue shirt, a hired-man's straw hat, and thick brown sandals. Her brother had the same outfit except his was a sober hickory-nut color. Ordinarily Miranda preferred her overalls to any other dress, though it was making rather a scandal in the countryside, for the year was 1903, and in the back country the law of female decorum had teeth in it. Her father had been criticized for letting his girls dress like boys and go careering around astride barebacked horses. Big sister Maria, the really independent and fearless one, in spite of her rather affected ways, rode at a dead run with only a rope knotted around her horse's nose. It was said the motherless family was running down, with the Grandmother no longer there to hold it together. It was known that she had discriminated against her son Harry in her will, and that he was in straits about money. Some of his old neighbors reflected with vicious satisfaction that now he would probably not be so stiffnecked, nor have any more high-stepping horses either. Miranda knew this, though she could not say how. She had met along the road old women of the kind who smoked corn-cob pipes, who had treated her grandmother with most sincere respect. They slanted their gummy old eyes side-ways at the granddaughter and said, "Ain't you ashamed of yoself, Missy? It's aginst the Scriptures to dress like that. Whut yo Pappy thinkin about?" Miranda, with her powerful social sense, which was like a fine set of antennae radiating from every pore of her skin, would feel ashamed because she knew well it was rude and ill-bred to shock anybody, even bad-tempered old crones, though she had faith in her father's judgment and was perfectly comfortable in the clothes. Her father had said, "They're just what you need, and they'll save your dresses for school . . ." This sounded quite simple and natural to her. She had been brought up in rigorous economy. Wastefulness was vulgar. It was also a sin. These were truths; she had heard them repeated many times and never once disputed.

Now the ring, shining with the serene purity of fine gold on her rather grubby thumb, turned her feelings against her overalls and sockless feet, toes sticking through the thick brown leather straps. She wanted to go back to the farmhouse, take a good cold bath, dust herself with plenty of Maria's violet talcum powder—provided Maria was not present to object, of course—put on the thinnest, most becoming dress she owned, with a big sash, and sit in a wicker chair under the trees . . . These things were not all she wanted, of course; she had vague stirrings of desire for luxury and a grand way of living which could not take precise form in her imagination but were founded on family legend of past wealth and leisure. These immediate comforts were what she could have, and she wanted them at once. She lagged rather far behind Paul, and once she thought of just turning back without a word and going home. She stopped, thinking that Paul would never do that to her, and so she would have to tell him. When a rabbit leaped, she let Paul have it without dispute. He killed it with one shot.

When she came up with him, he was already kneeling, examining the wound, the rabbit trailing from his hands. "Right through the head," he said complacently, as if he had aimed for it. He took out his sharp, competent bowie knife and started to skin the body. He did it very cleanly and quickly. Uncle Jimbilly knew how to prepare the skins so that Miranda always had fur coats for her dolls, for though she never cared much for her dolls she liked seeing them in fur coats. The children knelt facing each other over the dead animal. Miranda watched admiringly while her brother stripped the skin away as if he were taking off a glove. The flayed flesh emerged dark scarlet, sleek, firm; Miranda with thumb and finger felt the long fine muscles with the silvery flat strips binding them to the joints. Brother lifted the oddly bloated belly. "Look," he said, in a low amazed voice. "It was going to have young ones."

Very carefully he slit the thin flesh from the center ribs to the flanks, and a scarlet bag appeared. He slit again and pulled the bag open, and there lay a bundle of tiny rabbits, each wrapped in a thin scarlet veil. The brother pulled these off and there they were, dark gray, their sleek wet down lying in minute even ripples, like a baby's head just washed, their unbelievably small delicate ears folded close, their little blind faces almost featureless.

Miranda said, "Oh, I want to *see,*" under her breath. She looked and looked—excited but not frightened, for she was accustomed to the sight of animals killed in hunting—filled with pity and astonishment and a kind of shocked delight in the wonderful little creatures for their own sakes, they were so pretty. She touched one of them ever so carefully, "Ah, there's blood running over them" she said and began to tremble without knowing why. Yet she wanted most deeply to see and to know. Having seen, she felt at once as if she had known all along. The very memory of her former ignorance faded, she had always known just this. No one had ever told her anything outright, she had been rather unobservant of the animal life around her because she was so accustomed to animals. They seemed simply disorderly and unaccountably rude in their habits, but altogether natural and not very interesting. Her brother had spoken as if he had known about everything all along. He may have seen all this before. He had never said a word to her, but she knew now a part at least of what he knew. She understood a little of the secret formless intuitions in her own mind and body, which had been clearing up, taking form, so gradually and so steadily she had not realized that she was learning what she had to know. Paul said cautiously, as if he were talking about something forbidden: "They were just about ready to be born." His voice dropped on the last word. "I know," said Miranda, "like kittens. I know, like babies." She was quietly and terribly agitated, standing again with her rifle under her arm, looking down at the bloody heap. "I don't want the skin," she said, "I won't have it." Paul buried the young rabbits again in their mother's body, wrapped the skin around her, carried her to a clump of sage bushes, and hid her away. He came out again at once and said to Miranda, with an eager friendliness, a confidential tone quite unusual in him, as if he were taking her into an important secret on equal terms: "Listen now. Now you listen to me, and don't ever forget. Don't you ever tell a living soul that you saw this. Don't tell a soul. Don't tell Dad because I'll get into trouble. He'll say I'm leading you into things you ought not to do. He's always saying that. So now don't you go and forget and blab out sometime the way you're always doing . . . Now, that's a secret. Don't you tell."

Miranda never told, she did not even wish to tell anybody. She thought about the whole worrisome affair with confused unhappiness for a few days. Then it sank quietly into her mind and was heaped over by accumulated thousands of impressions, for nearly twenty years. One day she was picking her path among the puddles and crushed refuse of a market street in a strange city of a strange country, when without warning, plain and clear in its true colors as if she looked through a frame upon a scene that had not stirred nor changed since the moment it happened, the episode of that far-off day leaped from its burial place before her mind's eye. She was so reasonlessly horrified she halted suddenly staring, the scene before her eyes dimmed by the vision back of them. An Indian vendor had held up before her a tray of dyed sugar sweets, in the shapes of all kinds of small creatures: birds, baby chicks, baby rabbits, lambs, baby pigs. They were in gay colors and smelled of vanilla, maybe. . . . It was a very hot day and the smell in the market, with its piles of raw flesh and wilting flowers, was like the mingled sweetness and corruption she had smelled that other day in the empty cemetery at home: the day she had remembered always until now vaguely as the time she and her brother had found treasure in the opened graves. Instantly upon this thought the dreadful vision faded, and she saw clearly her brother, whose childhood face she had forgotten, standing again in the blazing sunshine, again twelve years old, a pleased sober smile in his eyes, turning the silver dove over and over in his hands.

7

An Occurrence at Owl Creek Bridge

by Ambrose Bierce

Mr. Arcularis

by Conrad Aiken

The Reconciliation

by Lafcadio Hearn

AMBROSE BIERCE *Ambrose Bierce's ability to do many things well was both his gift and his bane as an artist. A restless man, Bierce fought in the Civil War, adventured, became an influential journalist in San Francisco, wrote short stories and impious epigrams in London, and finally disappeared (perhaps committing suicide) in Mexico.*

Because of his temperament, Bierce never accomplished an extended work; but he has written (besides the Devil's Dictionary, *for which he is best known), a handful of "gothic" tales which rival Poe at his best. "An Occurrence at Owl Creek Bridge" surely does. A delicately choreographed "surprise" story, it is both a tour de force and a poignantly reverberant fiction which verifies that startling phrase from Wallace Stevens's "Sunday Morning": "Death is the mother of beauty."*

CONRAD AIKEN *The most terrifying experience of Aiken's life must have been his discovery at age nine of his parents' double death. His father, a successful physician, first killed his wife, then himself. Though Conrad Aiken was himself to live until well past eighty, there is much in his copious poetry, fiction, and short stories to indicate that he never entirely outlived that terrible day of discovery.*

Eminently successful in a work like Ushant *(an autobiographical novel) and in occasional poems, Aiken was perhaps most consistently accomplished in certain of his short stories. Like Bierce's Farquhar, Mr. Arcularis's exacerbated vision of life's possibilities has come too late; yet it is precisely within the ever-widening chasm separating the vision from its apprehension that the wistful beauty of the story resides.*

LAFCADIO HEARN *Like Bierce, Lafcadio Hearn is one of the talented "eccentrics" of American Literature. He was born in the Ionian Islands, and several nationalities, including Greek, English, Gypsy, and Moorish commingled in his veins. After his fruitful if unorthodox career as writer and journalist in the United States,* Harper's Weekly *commissioned him to write a series of articles from Japan.*

Once in Japan, Hearn resigned his position at Harper's, *married the daughter of a Samurai family, and became a Buddhist. His final, distinctly ambivalent, view of his adopted country can be read in* Japan: An Attempt at Interpretation, *1904.*

An Occurrence at Owl Creek Bridge

Ambrose Bierce (*American, 1842–1914?*)

A man stood upon a railroad bridge in northern Alabama, looking down into the swift water twenty feet below. The man's hands were behind his back, the wrists bound with a cord. A rope loosely encircled his neck. It was attached to a stout cross-timber above his head, and the slack fell to the level of his knees. Some loose boards laid upon the sleepers supporting the metals of the railway supplied a footing for him and his executioners—two private soldiers of the Federal army, directed by a sergeant who in civil life may have been a deputy sheriff. At a short remove upon the same temporary platform was an officer in the uniform of his rank, armed. He was a captain. A sentinel at each end of the bridge stood with his rifle in the position known as "support," that is to say, vertical in front of the left shoulder, the hammer resting on the forearm thrown straight across the chest—a formal and unnatural position, enforcing an erect carriage of the body. It did not appear to be the duty of these two men to know what was occurring at the center of the bridge; they merely blockaded the two ends of the foot plank which traversed it.

Beyond one of the sentinels, nobody was in sight; the railroad ran straight away into a forest for a hundred yards, then, curving, was lost to view. Doubtless there was an outpost farther along. The other bank of the stream was open ground—a gentle acclivity topped with a stockade of vertical tree trunks, loopholed for rifles, with a single embrasure through which protruded the muzzle of a brass cannon commanding the bridge. Midway of the slope between bridge and fort were the spectators—a single company of infantry in line, at "parade rest," the butts of the rifles on the ground, the barrels inclining slightly backward against the right shoulder, the hands crossed upon the stock. A lieutenant stood at the right of the line, the point of his sword upon the ground, his left hand resting upon his right. Excepting the group of four at the center of the bridge, not a man moved. The company faced the bridge, staring stonily, motionless. The sentinels, facing the banks of the stream, might have been statues to adorn the bridge. The captain stood with folded arms, silent, observing the work of his subordinates, but making no sign. Death is a dignitary who when he comes announced is to be received with formal manifestations of respect, even by those most familiar with him. In the code of military etiquette silence and fixity are forms of deference.

The man who was engaged in being hanged was apparently about thirty-five years of age. He was a civilian, if one might judge from his habit, which was that of a planter. His features were good —a straight nose, firm mouth, broad forehead, from which his long, dark hair was combed straight back, falling behind his ears to the collar of his well-fitting frock coat. He wore a mustache and pointed beard, but no whiskers; his eyes were large and dark gray, and had a kindly expression which one would hardly have expected in one whose neck was in the hemp. Evidently this was no vulgar assassin. The liberal military code makes provision for hanging many kinds of persons, and gentlemen are not excluded.

The preparations being complete, the two private soldiers stepped aside and each drew away the plank upon which he had been standing. The sergeant turned to the captain, saluted, and placed himself immediately behind that officer, who in turn moved apart one pace. These movements left the condemned man and the sergeant standing on the two ends of the same plank, which spanned three of the crossties of the bridge. The end upon which the civilian stood almost, but not quite, reached a fourth. This plank had been held in place by the weight of the captain; it was now held by that of the sergeant. At a signal from the former, the latter would step aside, the plank would tilt, and the condemned man go down between two ties. The arrangement commended itself to his judgment as simple and effective. His face had not been covered nor his eyes bandaged. He looked a moment at his "unsteadfast footing," then let his gaze wander to the swirling water of the stream racing madly beneath his feet. A piece of dancing driftwood caught his attention and his eyes followed it down the current. How slowly it appeared to move! What a sluggish stream!

He closed his eyes in order to fix his last thoughts upon his wife and children. The water, touched to gold by the early sun, the brooding mists under the banks at some distance down the stream, the fort, the soldiers, the piece of drift—all had distracted him. And now he became conscious of a new disturbance. Striking through the thought of his dear ones was a sound which he could neither ignore nor understand, a sharp, distinct, metallic percussion like the stroke of a blacksmith's hammer upon the anvil; it had the same ringing quality. He wondered what it was, and whether immeasurably distant or near by—it seemed both. Its recurrence was regular, but as slow as the tolling of a death knell. He awaited each stroke with impatience and—he knew not why—apprehension. The intervals of silence grew progressively longer; the delays became maddening. With their greater infrequency the sounds increased in strength and sharpness. They hurt his ear like the thrust of a knife; he feared he would shriek. What he heard was the ticking of his watch.

He unclosed his eyes and saw again the water below him. "If I could free my hands," he thought, "I might throw off the noose and spring into the stream. By diving I could evade the bullets and, swimming vigorously, reach the bank, take to the woods, and get away home. My home, thank God, is as yet outside their lines; my wife and little ones are still beyond the invader's farthest advance."

As these thoughts, which have here to be set down in words, were flashed into the doomed man's brain rather than evolved from it, the captain nodded to the sergeant. The sergeant stepped aside.

II

Peyton Farquhar was a well-to-do planter of an old and highly respected Alabama family. Being a slave owner and like other slave owners a politician, he was naturally an original secessionist and ardently devoted to the Southern cause. Circumstances of an imperious nature, which it is unnecessary to relate here, had prevented him from taking service with the gallant army which had fought the disastrous campaigns ending with the fall of Corinth, and he chafed under the inglorious restraint, longing for the release of his energies, the larger life of the soldier, the opportunity for distinction. That opportunity, he felt, would come, as it comes to all in war time. Meanwhile he did what he could. No service was too humble for him to perform in aid of the South, no adventure too perilous for him to undertake if consistent with the character of a civilian who was at heart a soldier, and who in good faith and without too much qualification assented to at least a part of the frankly villainous dictum that all is fair in love and war.

One evening while Farquhar and his wife were sitting on a rustic bench near the entrance to his grounds, a gray-clad soldier rode up to the gate and asked for a drink of water. Mrs. Farquhar was only too happy to serve him with her own white hands. While she was fetching the water her husband approached the dusty horseman and inquired eagerly for news from the front.

"The Yanks are repairing the railroads," said the man, "and are getting ready for another advance. They have reached the Owl Creek bridge, put it in order, and built a stockade on the north bank. The commandant has issued an order, which is posted everywhere, declaring that any civilian caught interfering with the railroad, its bridges, tunnels, or trains will be summarily hanged. I saw the order."

"How far is it to the Owl Creek bridge?" Farquhar asked.

"About thirty miles."

"Is there no force on this side the creek?"

"Only a picket post half a mile out, on the railroad, and a single sentinel at this end of the bridge."

"Suppose a man—a civilian and student of hanging—should elude the picket post and perhaps get the better of the sentinel," said Farquhar, smiling, "what could he accomplish?"

The soldier reflected. "I was there a month ago," he replied. "I observed that the flood of last winter had lodged a great quantity of driftwood against the wooden pier at this end of the bridge. It is now dry and would burn like tow."

The lady had now brought the water, which the soldier drank. He thanked her ceremoniously, bowed to her husband, and rode away. An hour later, after nightfall, he repassed the plantation, going northward in the direction from which he had come. He was a Federal scout.

III

As Peyton Farquhar fell straight downward through the bridge he lost consciousness and was as one already dead. From this state he was awakened—ages later, it seemed to him—by the pain of a sharp pressure upon his throat, followed by a sense of suffocation. Keen, poignant agonies seemed to shoot from his neck downward through every fiber of his body and limbs. These pains appeared to flash along well-defined lines of ramification and to beat with an inconceivably rapid periodicity. They seemed like streams of pulsating fire heating him to an intolerable temperature. As to his head, he was conscious of nothing but a feeling of fullness—of congestion. These sensations were unaccompanied by thought. The intellectual part of his nature was already effaced; he had power only to feel, and feeling was torment. He was conscious of motion. Encompassed in a luminous cloud, of which he was now merely the fiery heart, without material substance, he swung through unthinkable arcs of oscillation, like a vast pendulum. Then all at once, with terrible suddenness, the light about him shot upward with the noise of a loud plash; a frightful roaring was in his ears, and all was cold and dark. The power of thought was restored; he knew that the rope had broken and he had fallen into the stream. There was no additional strangulation; the noose about his neck was already suffocating him and kept the water from his lungs. To die of hanging at the bottom of a river!—the idea seemed to him ludicrous. He opened his eyes in the darkness and saw above him a gleam of light, but how distant, how inaccessible! He was still sinking, for the light became fainter and fainter until it was a mere glimmer. Then it began to grow and brighten, and he knew that he was rising toward the surface—knew it with reluctance, for he was now very comfortable. "To be hanged and drowned," he thought, "that is not so bad; but I do not wish to be shot. No; I will not be shot; that is not fair."

He was not conscious of an effort, but a sharp pain in his wrist apprised him that he was trying to free his hands. He gave the struggle his attention, as an idler might observe the feat of a juggler, without interest in the outcome. What splendid effort!—what magnificent, what superhuman strength! Ah, that was a fine endeavor! Bravo! The cord fell away; his arms parted and floated upward, the hands dimly seen on each side in the growing light. He watched them with a new interest as first one and then the other pounced upon the noose at his neck. They tore it away and thrust it fiercely aside, its undulations resembling those of a water snake. "Put it back, put it back!" He thought he shouted these words to his hands, for the undoing of the noose had been succeeded by the direst pang that he had yet experienced. His neck ached horribly;

his brain was on fire; his heart, which had been fluttering faintly, gave a great leap, trying to force itself out at his mouth. His whole body was racked and wrenched with an insupportable anguish! But his disobedient hands gave no heed to the command. They beat the water vigorously with quick, downward strokes, forcing him to the surface. He felt his head emerge; his eyes were blinded by the sunlight; his chest expanded convulsively, and with a supreme and crowning agony his lungs engulfed a great draught of air, which instantly he expelled in a shriek!

He was now in full possession of his physical senses. They were, indeed, preternaturally keen and alert. Something in the awful disturbance of his organic system had so exalted and refined them that they made record of things never before perceived. He felt the ripples upon his face and heard their separate sounds as they struck. He looked at the forest on the bank of the stream, saw the individual trees, the leaves and the veining of each leaf—saw the very insects upon them: the locusts, the brilliant-bodied flies, the gray spiders stretching their webs from twig to twig. He noted the prismatic colors in all the dewdrops upon a million blades of grass. The humming of the gnats that danced above the eddies of the stream, the beating of the dragonflies' wings, the strokes of the water spiders' legs, like oars which had lifted their boat—all these made audible music. A fish slid along beneath his eyes and he heard the rush of its body parting the water.

He had come to the surface facing down the stream; in a moment the visible world seemed to wheel slowly round, himself the pivotal point, and he saw the bridge, the fort, the soldiers upon the bridge, the captain, the sergeant, the two privates, his executioners. They were in silhouette against the blue sky. They shouted and gesticulated, pointing at him. The captain had drawn his pistol, but did not fire; the others were unarmed. Their movements were grotesque and horrible, their forms gigantic.

Suddenly he heard a sharp report and something struck the water smartly within a few inches of his head, spattering his face with spray. He heard a second report, and saw one of the sentinels with his rifle at his shoulder, a light cloud of blue smoke rising from the muzzle. The man in the water saw the eye of the man on the bridge gazing into his own through the sights of the rifle. He observed that it was a gray eye and remembered having read that gray eyes were keenest, and that all famous marksmen had them. Nevertheless, this one had missed.

A counterswirl had caught Farquhar and turned him half round; he was again looking into the forest on the bank opposite the fort. The sound of a clear, high voice in a monotonous singsong now rang out behind him and came across the water with a distinctness that pierced and subdued all other sounds, even the beating of the ripples in his ears. Although no soldier, he had frequented camps enough to know the dread significance of that deliberate, drawling, aspirated chant; the lieutenant on shore was taking a part in the morning's work. How coldly and pitilessly—with what an even, calm intonation, presaging and enforcing tranquillity in the men—with what accurately measured intervals fell those cruel words:

"Attention, company! . . . Shoulder arms! . . .Ready! . . . Aim! . . . Fire!"

Farquhar dived—dived as deeply as he could. The water roared in his ears like the voice of Niagara, yet he heard the dulled thunder of the volley and, rising again toward the surface, met shining bits of metal, singularly flattened, oscillating slowly downward. Some of them touched him on the face and hands, then fell away, continuing their descent. One lodged between his collar and neck; it was uncomfortably warm and he snatched it out.

As he rose to the surface, gasping for breath, he saw that he had been a long time under water; he was perceptibly farther downstream—nearer to safety. The soldiers had almost finished reloading; the metal ramrods flashed all at once in the sunshine as they were drawn from the barrels, turned in the air, and thrust into their sockets. The two sentinels fired again, independently and ineffectually.

The hunted man saw all this over his shoulder; he was now swimming vigorously with the current. His brain was as energetic as his arms and legs; he thought with the rapidity of lightning.

"The officer," he reasoned, "will not make that martinet's error a second time. It is as easy to dodge a volley as a single shot. He has probably already given the command to fire at will. God help me, I cannot dodge them all!"

An appalling plash within two yards of him was followed by a loud, rushing sound, *diminuendo,* which seemed to travel back through the air to the fort and died in an explosion which stirred the very river to its deeps! A rising sheet of water, which curved over him, fell down upon him, blinded him, strangled him! The cannon had taken a hand in the game. As he shook his head free from the commotion of the smitten water, he heard the deflected shot humming through the air ahead, and in an instant it was cracking and smashing the branches in the forest beyond.

"They will not do that again," he thought; "the next time they will use a charge of grape. I must keep my eye upon the gun; the smoke will apprise me—the report arrives too late; it lags behind the missile. That is a good gun."

Suddenly he felt himself whirled round and round—spinning like a top. The water, the banks, the forests, the now distant bridge, fort, and men—all were commingled and blurred. Objects were represented by their colors only; circular horizontal streaks of color—that was all he saw. He had been caught in a vortex and was being whirled on with a velocity of advance and gyration which made him giddy and sick. In a few moments he was flung upon the gravel at the foot of the left bank of the stream—the southern bank—and behind a projecting point which concealed him from his enemies. The sudden arrest of his motion, the abrasion of one of his hands on the gravel, restored him, and he wept with delight. He dug his fingers into the sand, threw it over himself in handfuls, and audibly blessed it. It looked like diamonds, rubies, emeralds; he could think of nothing beautiful which it did not resemble. The trees upon the bank were giant garden plants; he noted a definite order in their arrangement, inhaled the fragrance of their blooms. A strange, roseate light shone through the spaces among their trunks and the wind made in their branches the music of æolian harps. He had no wish to perfect his escape—was content to remain in that enchanting spot until retaken.

A whiz and rattle of grapeshot among the branches high above his head roused him from his dream. The baffled cannoneer had fired him a random farewell. He sprang to his feet, rushed up the sloping bank, and plunged into the forest.

All that day he traveled, laying his course by the rounding sun. The forest seemed interminable; nowhere did he discover a break in it, not even a woodman's road. He had not known that he lived in so wild a region. There was something uncanny in the revelation.

By nightfall he was fatigued, footsore, famishing. The thought of his wife and children urged him on. At last he found a road which led him in what he knew to be the right direction. It was as wide and straight as a city street, yet it seemed untraveled. No fields bordered it, no dwelling anywhere. Not so much as the barking of a dog suggested human habitation. The black bodies of the trees formed a straight wall on both sides, terminating on the horizon in a point, like a diagram in a lesson in perspective. Overhead, as he looked up through this rift in the wood, shone great golden stars looking unfamiliar and grouped in strange constellations. He was sure they were arranged in some order which had a secret and malign significance. The wood on either side was full of singular noises, among which—once, twice, and again—he distinctly heard whispers in an unknown tongue.

His neck was in pain and lifting his hand to it he found it horribly swollen. He knew that it had a circle of black where the rope had bruised it. His eyes felt congested; he could no longer close them. His tongue was swollen with thirst; he relieved its fever by thrusting it forward from between his teeth into the cold air. How softly the turf had carpeted the untraveled avenue—he could no longer feel the roadway beneath his feet!

Doubtless, despite his suffering, he had fallen asleep while walking, for now he sees another scene—perhaps he has merely recovered from a delirium. He stands at the gate of his own home. All is as he left it, and all bright and beautiful in the morning sunshine. He must have traveled the entire night. As he pushes open the gate and passes up the wide white walk, he sees a flutter of female garments; his wife, looking fresh and cool and sweet, steps down from the veranda to meet him. At the bottom of the steps she stands waiting, with a smile of ineffable joy, an attitude of matchless grace and dignity. Ah, how beautiful she is! He springs forward with extended arms. As he is about to clasp her, he feels a stunning blow upon the back of the neck; a blinding white light blazes all about him with a sound like the shock of a cannon—then all is darkness and silence!

Peyton Farquhar was dead; his body, with a broken neck, swung gently from side to side beneath the timbers of the Owl Creek bridge.

Mr. Arcularis

Conrad Aiken *(American, 1889–1973)*

Mr. Arcularis stood at the window of his room in the hospital and looked down at the street. There had been a light shower, which had patterned the sidewalks with large drops, but now again the sun was out, blue sky was showing here and there between the swift white clouds, a cold wind was blowing the poplar trees. An itinerant band had stopped before the building and was playing, with violin, harp, and flute, the finale of "Cavalleria Rusticana." Leaning against the window-sill—for he felt extraordinarily weak after his operation—Mr. Arcularis suddenly, listening to the wretched music, felt like crying. He rested the palm of one hand against a cold window pane and stared down at the old man who was blowing the flute, and blinked his eyes. It seemed absurd that he should be so weak, so emotional, so like a child—and especially now that everything was over at last. In spite of all their predictions, in spite, too, of his own dreadful certainty that he was going to die, here he was, as fit as a fiddle—but what a fiddle it was, so out of tune!—with a long life before him. And to begin with, a voyage to England ordered by the doctor. What could be more delightful? Why should he feel sad about it and want to cry like a baby? In a few minutes Harry would arrive with his car to take him to the wharf; in an hour he would be on the sea, in two hours he would see the sunset behind him, where Boston had been, and his new life would be opening before him. It was many years since he had been abroad. June, the best of the year to come—England, France, the Rhine—how ridiculous that he should already be homesick!

There was a light footstep outside the door, a knock, the door opened, and Harry came in.

"Well, old man, I've come to get you. The old bus actually got here. Are you ready? Here, let me take your arm. You're tottering like an octogenarian!"

Mr. Arcularis submitted gratefully, laughing, and they made the journey slowly along the bleak corridor and down the stairs to the entrance hall. Miss Hoyle, his nurse, was there, and the Matron, and the charming little assistant with freckles who had helped to prepare him for the operation. Miss Hoyle put out her hand.

"Good-by, Mr. Arcularis," she said, "and *bon voyage*."

"Good-by, Miss Hoyle, and thank you for everything. You were very kind to me. And I fear I was a nuisance."

The girl with the freckles, too, gave him her hand, smiling. She was very pretty, and it would have been easy to fall in love with her. She reminded him of someone. Who was it? He tried in vain to remember while he said good-by to her and turned to the Matron.

"And not too many latitudes with the young ladies, Mr. Arcularis!" she was saying.

Mr. Arcularis was pleased, flattered, by all this attention to a middle-aged invalid, and felt a joke taking shape in his mind, and no sooner in his mind than on his tongue.

"Oh, no latitudes," he said, laughing. "I'll leave the latitudes to the ship!"

"Oh, come now," said the Matron, "we don't seem to have hurt him much, do we?"

"I think we'll have to operate on him again and *really* cure him," said Miss Hoyle.

He was going down the front steps, between the potted palmettoes, and they all laughed and waved. The wind was cold, very cold for June, and he was glad he had put on his coat. He shivered.

"Damned cold for June!" he said. "Why should it be so cold?"

"East wind," Harry said, arranging the rug over his knees. "Sorry it's an open car, but I believe in fresh air and all that sort of thing. I'll drive slowly. We've got plenty of time."

They coasted gently down the long hill towards Beacon Street, but the road was badly surfaced, and despite Harry's care Mr. Arcularis felt his pain again. He found that he could alleviate it a little by leaning to the right, against the arm-rest, and not breathing too deeply. But how glorious to be out again! How strange and vivid the world looked! The trees had innumerable green fresh leaves—they were all blowing and shifting and turning and flashing in the wind; drops of rainwater fell downward sparkling; the robins were singing their absurd, delicious little four-noted songs; even the street cars looked unusually bright and beautiful, just as they used to look when he was a child and had wanted above all things to be a motorman. He found himself smiling foolishly at everything, foolishly and weakly, and wanted to say something about it to Harry. It was no use, though—he had no strength, and the mere finding of words would be almost more than he could manage. And even if he should succeed in saying it, he would then most likely burst into tears. He shook his head slowly from side to side.

"Ain't it grand?" he said.

"I'll bet it looks good," said Harry.

"Words fail me."

"You wait till you get out to sea. You'll have a swell time."

"Oh, swell! . . . I hope not. I hope it'll be calm."

"Tut tut."

When they passed the Harvard Club Mr. Arcularis made a slow and somewhat painful effort to turn in his seat and look at it. It might be the last chance to see it for a long time. Why this sentimental longing to stare at it, though? There it was, with the great flag blowing in the wind, the Harvard seal now concealed by the swift folds and now revealed, and there were the windows in the library, where he had spent so many delightful hours reading—Plato, and Kipling, and the Lord knows what—and the balconies from which for so many years he had watched the finish of the Marathon. Old Talbot might be in there now, sleeping with a book on his knee, hoping forlornly to be interrupted by anyone, for anything.

"Good-by to the old club," he said.

"The bar will miss you," said Harry, smiling with friendly irony and looking straight ahead.

"But let there be no moaning," said Mr. Arcularis.

"What's *that* a quotation from?"

"'The Odyssey.'"

In spite of the cold, he was glad of the wind on his face, for it helped to dissipate the feeling of vagueness and dizziness that came over him in a sickening wave from time to time. All of a sudden everything would begin to swim and dissolve, the houses would lean their heads together, he had to close his eyes, and there would be a curious and dreadful humming noise, which at regular intervals rose to a crescendo and then drawlingly subsided again. It was disconcerting. Perhaps he still had a trace of fever. When he got on the ship he would have a glass of whisky. . . . From one of these spells he opened his eyes and found that they were on the ferry, crossing to East Boston. It must have been the ferry's engines that he had heard. From another spell he woke to find himself on the wharf, the car at a standstill beside a pile of yellow packing-cases.

"We're here because we're here because we're here," said Harry.

"Because we're here," added Mr. Arcularis.

He dozed in the car while Harry—and what a good friend Harry was!—attended to all the details. He went and came with tickets and passports and baggage checks and porters. And at last he unwrapped Mr. Arcularis from the rugs and led him up the steep gangplank to the deck, and thence by devious windings to a small cold stateroom with a solitary porthole like the eye of a cyclops.

"Here you are," he said, "and now I've got to go. Did you hear the whistle?"

"No."

"Well, you're half asleep. It's sounded the all-ashore. Good-by, old fellow, and take care of yourself. Bring me back a spray of edelweiss. And send me a picture post card from the Absolute."

"Will you have it finite or infinite?"

"Oh, infinite. But with your signature on it. Now you'd better turn in for a while and have a nap. Cheerio!"

Mr. Arcularis took his hand and pressed it hard, and once more felt like crying. Absurd! Had he become a child again?

"Good-by," he said.

He sat down in the little wicker chair, with his overcoat still on, closed his eyes, and listened to the humming of the air in the ventilator. Hurried footsteps ran up and down the corridor. The chair was not too comfortable, and his pain began to bother him again, so he moved, with his coat still on, to the narrow berth and fell asleep. When he woke up, it was dark, and the porthole had been partly opened. He groped for the switch and turned on the light. Then he rang for the steward.

"It's cold in here," he said. "Would you mind closing the port?"

The girl who sat opposite him at dinner was charming. Who was it she reminded him of? Why, of course, the girl at the hospital, the girl with the freckles. Her hair was beautiful, not quite red, not quite gold, nor had it been bobbed; arranged with a sort of graceful untidiness, it made him think of a Melozzo da Forli angel. Her face was freckled, she had a mouth which was both humorous and voluptuous. And she seemed to be alone.

He frowned at the bill of fare and ordered the thick soup.

"No hors d'œuvres?" asked the steward.

"I think not," said Mr. Arcularis. "They might kill me."

The steward permitted himself to be amused and deposited the menu card on the table against the water-bottle. His eyebrows were lifted. As he moved away, the girl followed him with her eyes and smiled.

"I'm afraid you shocked him," she said.

"Impossible," said Mr. Arcularis. "These stewards, they're dead souls. How could they be stewards otherwise? And they think they've seen and known everything. They suffer terribly from the *déjà vu*. Personally, I don't blame them."

"It must be a dreadful sort of life."

"It's because they're dead that they accept it."

"Do you think so?"

"I'm sure of it. I'm enough of a dead soul myself to know the signs!"

"Well, I don't know what you mean by that!"

"But nothing mysterious! I'm just out of hospital, after an operation. I was given up for dead. For six months I had given *myself* up for dead. If you've ever been seriously ill you know the feeling. You have a posthumous feeling—a mild, cynical tolerance for everything and everyone. What is there you haven't seen or done or understood? Nothing."

Mr. Arcularis waved his hands and smiled.

"I wish I could understand you," said the girl, "but I've never been ill in my life."

"Never?"

"Never."

"Good God!"

The torrent of the unexpressed and inexpressible paralyzed him and rendered him speechless. He stared at the girl, wondering who she was and then, realizing that he had perhaps stared too fixedly, averted his gaze, gave a little laugh, rolled a pill of bread between his fingers. After a second or two he allowed himself to look at her again and found her smiling.

"Never pay any attention to invalids," he said, "or they'll drag you to the hospital."

She examined him critically, with her head tilted a little to one side, but with friendliness.

"You don't *look* like an invalid," she said.

Mr. Arcularis thought her charming. His pain ceased to bother him, the disagreeable humming disappeared, or rather, it was dissociated from himself and became merely, as it should be, the sound of the ship's engines, and he began to think the voyage was going to be really delightful. The parson on his right passed him the salt.

"I fear you will need this in your soup," he said.

"Thank you. Is it as bad as that?"

The steward, overhearing, was immediately apologetic and solicitous. He explained that on the first day everything was at sixes and sevens. The girl looked up at him and asked him a question.

"Do you think we'll have a good voyage?" she said.

He was passing the hot rolls to the parson, removing the napkins from them with a deprecatory finger.

"Well, madam, I don't like to be a Jeremiah, but—"

"Oh, come," said the parson, "I hope we have no Jeremiahs."

"What do you mean?" said the girl.

Mr. Arcularis ate his soup with gusto—it was nice and hot.

"Well, maybe I shouldn't say it, but there's a corpse on board, going to Ireland; and I never yet knew a voyage with a corpse on board that we didn't have bad weather."

"Why, steward, you're just superstitious! What nonsense."

"That's a very ancient superstition," said Mr. Arcularis. "I've heard it many times. Maybe it's true. Maybe we'll be wrecked. And what does it matter, after all?" He was very bland.

"Then let's be wrecked," said the parson coldly.

Nevertheless, Mr. Arcularis felt a shudder go through him on hearing the steward's remark. A corpse in the hold—a coffin? Perhaps it was true. Perhaps some disaster would befall them. There might be fogs. There might be icebergs. He thought of all the wrecks of which he had read. There was the *Titanic,* which he had read about in the warm newspaper room at the Harvard Club—it had seemed dreadfully real, even there. That band, playing "Nearer My God to Thee" on the after-deck while the ship sank! It was one of the darkest of his memories. And the *Empress of Ireland*—all those poor people trapped in the smoking-room, with only one door between them and life, and that door locked for the night by the deck-steward, and the deck-steward nowhere to be found! He shivered, feeling a draft, and turned to the parson.

"How do these strange delusions arise?" he said.

The parson looked at him searchingly, appraisingly—from chin to forehead, from forehead to chin—and Mr. Arcularis, feeling uncomfortable, straightened his tie.

"From nothing but fear," said the parson. "Nothing on earth but fear."

"How strange!" said the girl.

Mr. Arcularis again looked at her—she had lowered her face—and again tried to think of whom she reminded him. It wasn't only the little freckle-faced girl at the hospital—both of them had reminded him of someone else. Someone far back in his life: remote, beautiful, lovely. But he couldn't think. The meal came to an end, they all rose, the ship's orchestra played a feeble fox-trot, and Mr. Arcularis, once more alone, went to the bar to have his whisky. The room was stuffy, and the ship's engines were both audible and palpable. The humming and throbbing oppressed him, the rhythm seemed to be the rhythm of his own pain, and after a short time he found his way, with slow steps, holding on to the walls in his moments of weakness and dizziness, to his forlorn and white little room. The port had been—thank God!—closed for the night: it was cold enough anyway. The white and blue ribbons fluttered from the ventilator, the bottle and glasses clicked and clucked as the ship swayed gently to the long, slow motion of the sea. It was all very peculiar—it was all like something he had experienced somewhere before. What was it? Where was it? . . . He untied his tie, looking at his face in the glass, and wondered, and from time to time put his hand to his side to hold in the pain. It wasn't at Portsmouth, in his childhood, nor at Salem, nor in the rose-garden at his Aunt Julia's, nor in the schoolroom at Cambridge. It was something very queer, very intimate, very precious. The jackstones, the Sunday-School cards which he had loved when he was a child . . . He fell asleep.

The sense of time was already hopelessly confused. One hour was like another, the sea looked always the same, morning was indistinguishable from afternoon—and was it Tuesday or Wednesday? Mr. Arcularis was sitting in the smoking-room, in his favorite corner, watching the parson teach Miss Dean to play chess. On the deck outside he could see the people passing and repassing in their restless round of the ship. The red jacket went by, then the black hat with the white feather, then the purple scarf, the brown tweed coat, the Bulgarian mustache, the monocle, the Scotch cap with fluttering ribbons, and in no time at all the red jacket again, dipping past the windows with its own peculiar rhythm, followed once more by the black hat and the purple scarf. How odd to reflect on the fixed little orbits of these things—as definite and profound, perhaps, as the orbits of the stars, and as important to God or the Absolute. There was a kind of tyranny in this fixedness, too—to think of it too much made one uncomfortable. He closed his eyes for a moment, to avoid seeing for the fortieth time the Bulgarian mustache and the pursuing monocle. The parson was explaining the movements of knights. Two forward and one to the side. Eight possible moves, always to the opposite color from that on which the piece stands. Two forward and one to the side: Miss Dean repeated the words several times with reflective emphasis. Here, too, was the terrifying fixed curve of the infinite, the creeping curve of logic which at last must become the final signpost at the edge of nothing. After that—the deluge. The great white light of annihilation. The bright flash of death. . . . Was it merely the sea which made these abstractions so insistent, so intrusive? The mere notion of *orbit* had somehow become extraordinarily naked; and to rid himself of the discomfort and also to forget a little the pain which bothered his side whenever he sat down, he walked slowly and carefully into the writing-room, and examined a pile of superannuated magazines and catalogues of travel. The bright colors amused him, the photographs of remote islands and mountains, savages in sampans or sarongs or both—it was all very far off and delightful, like something in a dream or a fever. But he found that he was too tired to read and was incapable of concentration. Dreams! Yes, that reminded him. That rather alarming business—sleep-walking!

Later in the evening—at what hour he didn't know—he was telling Miss Dean about it, as he had intended to do. They were sitting in deck-chairs on the sheltered side. The sea was black, and there was a cold wind. He wished they had chosen to sit in the lounge.

Miss Dean was extremely pretty—no, beautiful. She looked at him, too, in a very strange and lovely way, with something of inquiry, something of sympathy, something of affection. It seemed as if, between the question and the answer, they had sat thus for a very long time, exchanging an unspoken secret, simply looking at each other quietly and kindly. Had an hour or two passed? And was it at all necessary to speak?

"No," she said, "I never have."

She breathed into the low words a note of interrogation and gave him a slow smile.

"That's the funny part of it. I never had either until last night. Never in my life. I hardly ever even dream. And it really rather frightens me."

"Tell me about it, Mr. Arcularis."

"I dreamed at first that I was walking, alone, in a wide plain covered with snow. It was growing dark, I was very cold, my feet were frozen and numb, and I was lost. I came then to a signpost—at first it seemed to me there was nothing on it. Nothing but ice. Just before it grew finally dark, however, I made out on it the one word 'Polaris.'"

"The Pole Star."

"Yes—and you see, I didn't myself know that. I looked it up only this morning. I suppose I must have seen it somewhere? And of course it rhymes with my name."

"Why, so it does!"

"Anyway, it gave me—in the dream—an awful feeling of despair, and the dream changed. This time, I dreamed I was standing *outside* my stateroom in the little dark corridor, or *cul-de-sac,* and trying to find the door-handle to let myself in. I was in my pajamas, and again I was very cold. And at this point I woke up. . . . The extraordinary thing is that's exactly where I was!"

"Good heavens. How strange!"

"Yes. And now the question is, *where had I been*? I was frightened, when I came to—not unnaturally. For among other things I *did* have, quite definitely, the feeling that I *had been* somewhere. Somewhere where it was very cold. It doesn't sound very proper. Suppose I had been seen!"

"That might have been awkward," said Miss Dean.

"Awkward! It might indeed. It's very singular. I've never done such a thing before. It's this sort of thing that reminds one—rather wholesomely, perhaps, don't you think?"—and Mr. Arcularis gave a nervous little laugh—"how extraordinarily little we know about the workings of our own minds or souls. After all, what *do* we know?"

"Nothing—nothing—nothing—nothing," said Miss Dean slowly. "*Absolutely* nothing."

Their voices had dropped, and again they were silent; and again they looked at each other gently and sympathetically, as if for the exchange of something unspoken and perhaps unspeakable. Time ceased. The orbit—so it seemed to Mr. Arcularis—once more became pure, became absolute. And once more he found himself wondering who it was that Miss Dean—Clarice Dean—reminded him of. Long ago and far away. Like those pictures of the islands and mountains. The little freckle-faced girl at the hospital was merely, as it were, the stepping-stone, the signpost, or, as in algebra, the "equals" sign. But what was it they both "equalled"? The jackstones came again into his mind and his Aunt Julia's rose-garden—at sunset; but this was ridiculous. It couldn't be simply that they reminded him of his childhood! And yet why not?

They went into the lounge. The ship's orchestra, in the oval-shaped balcony among faded palms, was playing the finale of "Cavalleria Rusticana," playing it badly.

"Good God!" said Mr. Arcularis, "can't I ever escape from that damned sentimental tune? It's the last thing I heard in America, and the last thing I *want* to hear."

"But don't you like it?"

"As music? No! It moves me too much, but in the wrong way."

"What, exactly, do you mean?"

"Exactly? Nothing. When I heard it at the hospital—when was it?—it made me feel like crying. Three old Italians tootling it in the rain. I suppose, like most people, I'm afraid of my feelings."

"Are they so dangerous?"

"Now then, young woman! Are you pulling my leg?"

The stewards had rolled away the carpets, and the passengers were beginning to dance. Miss Dean accepted the invitation of a young officer, and Mr. Arcularis watched them with envy. Odd, that last exchange of remarks—very odd; in fact, everything was odd. Was it possible that they were falling in love? Was that what it was all about—all these concealed references and recollections? He had read of such things. But at his age! And with a girl of twenty-two!

After an amused look at his old friend Polaris from the open door on the sheltered side, he went to bed.

The rhythm of the ship's engines was positively a persecution. It gave one no rest, it followed one like the Hound of Heaven, it drove one out into space and across the Milky Way and then back home by way of Betelgeuse. It was cold there, too. Mr. Arcularis, making the round trip by way of Betelgeuse and Polaris, sparkled with frost. He felt like a Christmas tree. Icicles on his fingers and icicles on his toes. He tinkled and spangled in the void, hallooed to the waste echoes, rounded the buoy on the verge of the Unknown, and tacked glitteringly homeward. The wind whistled. He was barefooted. Snowflakes and tinsel blew past him. Next time, by George, he would go farther still—for altogether it was rather a lark. Forward into the untrodden! as somebody said. Some intrepid explorer of his own backyard, probably, some middle-aged professor with an umbrella: those were the fellows for courage! But give us time, thought Mr. Arcularis, give us time, and we will bring back with us the night-rime of the Obsolute. Or was it Absolete? If only there weren't this perpetual throbbing, this iteration of sound, like a pain, these circles and repetitions of light—the feeling as of everything coiling inward to a center of misery . . .

Suddenly it was dark, and he was lost. He was groping, he touched the cold, white, slippery woodwork with his fingernails, looking for an electric switch. The throbbing, of course, was the throbbing of the ship. But he was almost home—almost home. Another corner to round, a door to be opened, and there he would be. Safe and sound. Safe in his father's home.

It was at this point that he woke up: in the corridor that led to the dining salon. Such pure terror, such horror, seized him as he had never known. His heart felt as if it would stop beating. His back was towards the dining saloon; apparently he had just come from it. He was in his pajamas. The corridor was dim, all but two lights having been turned out for the night, and—thank God!—deserted. Not a soul, not a sound. He was perhaps fifty yards from his room. With luck he could get to it unseen. Holding tremulously to the rail that ran along the wall, a brown, greasy rail, he began to creep his way forward. He felt very weak, very dizzy, and his thoughts refused to concentrate. Vaguely he remembered Miss Dean—Clarice—and the freckled girl, as if they were one and the same person. But he wasn't in the hospital, he was on the ship. Of course. How absurd. The Great Circle. Here we are, old fellow . . . steady round the corner . . . hold hard to your umbrella . . .

In his room, with the door safely shut behind him, Mr. Arcularis broke into a cold sweat. He had no sooner got into his bunk, shivering, than he heard the night watchman pass.

"But where—" he thought, closing his eyes in agony—"have I been? . . ."

A dreadful idea had occurred to him.

"It's nothing serious—how could it be anything serious? Of course it's nothing serious," said Mr. Arcularis.

"No, it's nothing serious," said the ship's doctor urbanely.

"I knew you'd think so. But just the same—"

"Such a condition is the result of worry," said the doctor. "Are you worried—do you mind telling me—about something? Just try to think."

"Worried?"

Mr. Arcularis knitted his brows. *Was* there something? Some little mosquito of a cloud disappearing into the southwest, the northeast? Some little gnat-song of despair? But no, that was all over. All over.

"Nothing," he said, "nothing whatever."

"It's very strange," said the doctor.

"Strange! I should say so. I've come to sea for a rest, not for a nightmare! What about a bromide?"

"Well, I can give you a bromide, Mr. Arcularis—"

"Then, please, if you don't mind, give me a bromide."

He carried the little phial hopefully to his stateroom, and took a dose at once. He could see the sun through his porthole. It looked northern and pale and small, like a little peppermint, which was only natural enough, for the latitude was changing with every hour. But why was it that doctors were all alike? and all, for that matter, like his father, or that other fellow at the hospital? Smythe, his name was. Doctor Smythe. A nice, dry little fellow, and they said he was a writer. Wrote poetry, or something like that. Poor fellow—disappointed. Like everybody else. Crouched in there, in his cabin, night after night, writing blank verse or something—all about the stars and flowers and love and death; ice and the sea and the infinite; time and tide—well, every man to his own taste.

"But it's nothing serious," said Mr. Arcularis, later, to the parson. "How could it be?"

"Why, of course not, my dear fellow," said the parson, patting his back. "How could it be?"

"I know it isn't and yet I worry about it."

"It would be ridiculous to think it serious," said the parson.

Mr. Arcularis shivered: it was colder than ever. It was said that they were near icebergs. For a few hours in the morning there had been a fog, and the siren had blown—devastatingly—at three-minute intervals. Icebergs caused fog—he knew that.

"These things always come," said the parson, "from a sense of guilt. You feel guilty about something. I won't be so rude as to inquire what it is. But if you could rid yourself of the sense of guilt—"

And later still, when the sky was pink:

"But is it anything to worry about?" said Miss Dean. "Really?"

"No, I suppose not."

"Then don't worry. We aren't children any longer!"

"Aren't we? I wonder!"

They leaned, shoulders touching, on the deck-rail, and looked at the sea, which was multitudinously incarnadined. Mr. Arcularis scanned the horizon in vain for an iceberg.

"Anyway," he said, "the colder we are the less we feel!"

"I hope that's no reflection on *you*," said Miss Dean.

"Here . . . feel my hand," said Mr. Arcularis.

"Heaven knows it's cold!"

"It's been to Polaris and back! No wonder."

"Poor thing, poor thing!"

"Warm it."

"May I?"

"You can."

"I'll try."

Laughing, she took his hand between both of hers, one palm under and one palm over, and began rubbing it briskly. The decks were deserted, no one was near them, everyone was dressing for dinner. The sea grew darker, the wind blew colder.

"I wish I could remember who you are," he said.

"And you—who are you?"

"Myself."

"Then perhaps *I* am yourself."

"Don't be metaphysical!"

"But I *am* metaphysical!"

She laughed, withdrew, pulled the light coat about her shoulders.

The bugle blew the summons for dinner—"The Roast Beef of Old England"—and they walked together along the darkening deck toward the door, from which a shaft of soft light fell across the deck-rail. As they stopped over the brass door-sill Mr. Arcularis felt the throb of the engines again; he put his hand quickly to his side.

"Auf wiedersehen," he said. *"Tomorrow and tomorrow and tomorrow."*

Mr. Arcularis was finding it impossible, absolutely impossible, to keep warm. A cold fog surrounded the ship, had done so, it seemed, for days. The sun had all but disappeared, the transition from day to night was almost unnoticeable. The ship, too, seemed scarcely to be moving—it was as if anchored among walls of ice and rime. Monstrous, that merely because it was June, and supposed, therefore, to be warm, the ship's authorities should consider it unnecessary to turn on the heat! By day, he wore his heavy coat and sat shivering in the corner of the smoking-room. His teeth chattered, his hands were blue. By night, he heaped blankets on his bed, closed the porthole's black eye against the sea, and drew the yellow curtains across it, but in vain. Somehow, despite everything, the fog crept in, and the icy fingers touched his throat. The steward, questioned about it, merely said, "Icebergs." Of course—any fool knew that. But how long, in God's name, was it going to last? They surely ought to be past the Grand Banks by this time! And surely it wasn't necessary to sail to England by way of Greenland and Iceland!

Miss Dean—Clarice—was sympathetic.

"It's simply because," she said, "your vitality has been lowered by your illness. You can't expect to be your normal self so soon after an operation! When *was* your operation, by the way?"

Mr. Arcularis considered. Strange—he couldn't be quite sure. It was all a little vague—his sense of time had disappeared.

"Heaven knows!" he said. "Centuries ago. When I was a tadpole and you were a fish. I should think it must have been at about the time of the Battle of Teutoburg Forest. Or perhaps when I was a Neanderthal man with a club!"

"Are you sure it wasn't farther back still?"

What did she mean by that?

"Not at all. Obviously, we've been on this damned ship for ages—for eras—for æons. And even on this ship, you must remember, I've had plenty of time, in my nocturnal wanderings, to go several times to Orion and back. I'm thinking, by the way, of going farther still. There's a nice little star off to the left, as you round Betelgeuse, which looks as if it might be right at the edge. The last outpost of the finite. I think I'll have a look at it and bring you back a frozen rime-feather."

"It would melt when you got it back."

"Oh, no, it wouldn't—not on *this* ship!"

Clarice laughed.

"I wish I could go with you," she said.

"If only you would! If only—"

He broke off his sentence and looked hard at her—how lovely she was, and how desirable! No such woman had ever before come into his life; there had been no one with whom he had at once felt so profound a sympathy and understanding. It was a miracle, simply—a miracle. No need to put his arm around her or to kiss her—delightful as such small vulgarities would be. He had only to look at her, and to feel, gazing into those extraordinary eyes, that she knew him, had always known him. It was as if, indeed, she might be his own soul.

But as he looked thus at her, reflecting, he noticed that she was frowning.

"What is it?" he said.

She shook her head, slowly.

"I don't know."

"Tell me."

"Nothing. It just occurred to me that perhaps you weren't looking quite so well."

Mr. Arcularis was startled. He straightened himself up.

"What nonsense! Of course this pain bothers me—and I feel astonishingly weak—"

"It's more than that—much more than that. Something is worrying you horribly." She paused, and then with an air of challenging him, added, "Tell me, did you?"

Her eyes were suddenly asking him blazingly the question he had been afraid of. He flinched, caught his breath, looked away. But it was no use, as he knew: he would have to tell her. He had known all along that he would have to tell her.

"Clarice," he said—and his voice broke in spite of his effort to control it—"it's killing me, it's ghastly! Yes, I did."

His eyes filled with tears, he saw that her own had done so also. She put her hand on his arm.

"I knew," she said. "I knew. But tell me."

"It's happened twice again—*twice*—and each time I was farther away. The same dream of going round a star, the same terrible coldness and helplessness. That awful whistling curve . . ." He shuddered.

"And when you woke up—" she spoke quietly—"where were you when you woke up? Don't be afraid!"

"The first time I was at the farther end of the dining saloon. I had my hand on the door that leads into the pantry."

"I see. Yes. And the next time?"

Mr. Arcularis wanted to close his eyes in terror—he felt as if he were going mad. His lips moved before he could speak, and when at last he did speak it was in a voice so low as to be almost a whisper.

"I was at the bottom of the stairway that leads down from the pantry to the hold, past the refrigerating plant. It was dark, and I was crawling on my hands and knees . . . *Crawling on my hands and knees*! . . ."

"Oh!" she said, and again, "Oh!"

He began to tremble violently; he felt the hand on his arm trembling also. And then he watched a look of unmistakable horror come slowly into Clarice's eyes, and a look of understanding, as if she saw . . . She tightened her hold on his arm.

"Do you think . . ." she whispered.

They stared at each other.

"I know," he said. "And so do you . . . Twice more—three times—and I'll be looking down into an empty . . ."

It was then that they first embraced—then, at the edge of the infinite, at the last signpost of the finite. They clung together desperately, forlornly, weeping as they kissed each other, staring hard one moment and closing their eyes the next. Passionately, passionately, she kissed him, as if she were indeed trying to give him her warmth, her life.

"But what nonsense!" she cried, leaning back and holding his face between her hands, her hands which were wet with his tears. "What nonsense! It can't be!"

"It is," said Mr. Arcularis slowly.

"But how do you know? . . . How do you know where the—"

For the first time Mr. Arcularis smiled.

"Don't be afraid, darling—you mean the coffin?"

"How could you know where it is?"

"I don't need to," said Mr. Arcularis . . . "I'm already almost there."

Before they separated for the night, in the smoking-room, they had several whisky cocktails.

"We must make it gay!" Mr. Arcularis said. "Above all, we must make it gay. Perhaps even now it will turn out to be nothing but a nightmare from which both of us will wake! And even at the worst, at my present rate of travel, I ought to need two more nights! It's a long way, still, to that little star."

The parson passed them at the door.

"What! turning in so soon?" he said. "I was hoping for a game of chess."

"Yes, both turning in. But tomorrow?"

"Tomorrow, then, Miss Dean! And good-night!"

"Good-night."

They walked once round the deck, then leaned on the railing and stared into the fog. It was thicker and whiter than ever. The ship was moving barely perceptibly, the rhythm of the engines was slower, more subdued and remote, and at regular intervals, mournfully, came the long reverberating cry of the foghorn. The sea was calm, and lapped only very tenderly against the side of the ship, the sound coming up to them clearly, however, because of the profound stillness.

"'On such a night as this—'" quoted Mr. Arcularis grimly.

"'On such a night as this—'"

Their voices hung suspended in the night, time ceased for them, for an eternal instant they were happy. When at last they parted it was by tacit agreement on a note of the ridiculous.

"Be a good boy and take your bromide!" she said.

"Yes, mother, I'll take my medicine!"

In his stateroom, he mixed himself a strong potion of bromide, a very strong one, and got into bed. He would have no trouble in falling asleep: he felt more tired, more supremely exhausted, than he had ever been in his life; nor had bed ever seemed so delicious. And that long, magnificent, delirious swoop of dizziness . . . the Great Circle . . . the swift pathway to Arcturus . . .

It was all as before, but infinitely more rapid. Never had Mr. Arcularis achieved such phenomenal, such supernatural, speed. In no time at all he was beyond the moon, shot past the North Star as if it were standing still (which perhaps it was?), swooped in a long bright curve round the Pleiades, shouted his frosty greetings to Betelgeuse, and was off to the little blue star which pointed the way to the unknown. Forward into the untrodden! Courage, old man, and hold on to your umbrella! Have you got your garters on? Mind your hat! In no time at all we'll be back to Clarice with the frozen time-feather, the rime-feather, the snowflake of the Absolute, the Obsolete. If only we don't wake . . . if only we needn't wake . . . if only we don't wake in that—in that—time and space . . . somewhere or nowhere . . . cold and dark . . . "Cavalleria Rusticana" sobbing among the palms; if a lonely . . . if only . . . the coffers of the poor—not coffers, not coffers, not coffers. Oh, God, not coffers, but light, delight, supreme white and brightness, and above all whirling lightness, whirling lightness above all—and freezing—freezing—freezing . . .

At this point in the void the surgeon's last effort to save Mr. Arcularis's life had failed. He stood back from the operating table and made a tired gesture with a rubber-gloved hand.

"It's all over," he said. "As I expected."

He looked at Miss Hoyle, whose gaze was downward, at the basin she held. There was a moment's stillness, a pause, a brief flight of unexchanged comment, and then the ordered life of the hospital was resumed.

The Reconciliation

Lafcadio Hearn (*American, 1850–1904*)

There was a young samurai of Kyōto[1] who had been reduced to poverty by the ruin of his lord, and found himself obliged to leave his home, and to take service with the Governor of a distant province. Before quitting the capital, this samurai divorced his wife—a good and beautiful woman—under the belief that he could better obtain promotion by another alliance. He then married the daughter of a family of some distinction, and took her with him to the district whither he had been called.

But it was in the time of the thoughtlessness of youth, and the sharp experience of want, that the samurai could not understand the worth of the affection so lightly cast away. His second marriage did not prove a happy one; the character of his new wife was hard and selfish; and he soon found every cause to think with regret of Kyōto days. Then he discovered that he still loved his first wife—loved her more than he could ever love the second; and he began to feel how unjust and how thankless he had been. Gradually his repentance deepened into a remorse that left him no peace of mind. Memories of the woman he had wronged—her gentle speech, her smiles, her dainty, pretty ways, her faultless patience—continually haunted him. Sometimes in dreams he saw her at her loom, weaving as when she toiled night and day to help him during the years of their distress: more often he saw her kneeling alone in the desolate little room where he had left her, veiling her tears with

[1] The original story is to be found in the curious volume entitled *Konséki-Monogatari.*

her poor worn sleeve. Even in the hours of official duty, his thoughts would wander back to her: then he would ask himself how she was living, what she was doing. Something in his heart assured him that she could not accept another husband, and that she never would refuse to pardon him. And he secretly resolved to seek her out as soon as he could return to Kyōto—then to beg her forgiveness, to take her back, to do everything that a man could do to make atonement. But the years went by.

At last the Governor's official term expired, and the samurai was free. "Now I will go back to my dear one," he vowed to himself. "Ah, what a cruelty—what a folly to have divorced her!" He sent his second wife to her own people (she had given him no children); and hurrying to Kyōto, he went at once to seek his former companion—not allowing himself even the time to change his traveling garb.

When he reached the street where she used to live, it was late in the night—the night of the tenth day of the ninth month;—and the city was silent as a cemetery. But a bright moon made everything visible; and he found the house without difficulty. It had a deserted look: tall weeds were growing on the roof. He knocked at the sliding-doors, and no one answered. Then, finding that the doors had not been fastened from within, he pushed them open, and entered. The front room was matless and empty: a chilly wind was blowing through crevices in the planking; and the moon shone through a ragged break in the wall of the alcove. Other rooms presented a like forlorn condition. The house, to all seeming, was unoccupied. Nevertheless, the samurai determined to visit one other apartment at the farther end of the dwelling—a very small room that had been his wife's favorite resting-place. Approaching the sliding-screen that closed it, he was startled to perceive a glow within. He pushed the screen aside, and uttered a cry of joy; for he saw her there—sewing by the light of a paper-lamp. Her eyes at the same instant met his own; and with a happy smile she greeted him—asking only: "When did you come back to Kyōto? How did you find your way here to me, through all those black rooms?" The years had not changed her. Still she seemed as fair and young as in his fondest memory of her;—but sweeter than any memory there came to him the music of her voice, with its trembling of pleased wonder.

Then joyfully he took his place beside her, and told her all:—how deeply he repented his selfishness—how wretched he had been without her—how constantly he had regretted her—how long he had hoped and planned to make amends;—caressing her the while, and asking her forgiveness over and over again. She answered him, with loving gentleness, according to his heart's desire—entreating him to cease all self-reproach. It was wrong, she said, that he should have allowed himself to suffer on her account: she had always felt that she was not worthy to be his wife. She knew that he had separated from her, notwithstanding, only because of poverty; and while he lived with her, he had always been kind; and she had never ceased to pray for his happiness. But even if there had been a reason for speaking of amends, this honorable visit would be ample amends;—what greater happiness than thus to see him again, though it were only for a moment? "Only for a moment!" he answered, with a glad laugh—"say, rather, for the time of seven existences! My loved one, unless you forbid, I am coming back to live with you always—always—always! Nothing shall ever separate us again. Now I have means and friends: we need not fear poverty. To-morrow my goods will be brought here; and my servants will come to wait upon you; and we shall make this house beautiful. . . . To-night," he added, apologetically, "I came thus late—without even changing my dress—only because of the longing I had to see you, and to tell you this." She seemed greatly pleased by these words; and in her turn she told him about all that had happened in Kyōto since the time of his departure—excepting her own sorrows, of which she sweetly refused to speak. They chatted far into the night: then she conducted him to a warmer room, facing south—a room that had been their bridal chamber in former time. "Have you no one in the house to help you?" he asked, as she began to prepare the couch for him. "No," she answered, laughing cheerfully: "I could not afford a servant;—so I have been living all alone." "You will have plenty of servants to-morrow," he said—"good servants—and everything else that you need." They lay down to rest—not to sleep: they had too much to tell each other;—and they talked of the past and the present and the future, until the dawn was gray. Then, involuntarily, the samurai closed his eyes, and slept.

When he awoke, the daylight was streaming through the chinks of the sliding shutters; and he found himself, to his utter amazement lying upon the naked boards of a mouldering floor. . . . Had he only dreamed a dream? No: she was there;—she slept. . . . He bent above her—and looked—and shrieked—for the sleeper had no face!

. . . Before him, wrapped in its grave-sheet only, lay the corpse of a woman—a corpse so wasted that little remained save the bones, and the long black tangled hair.

Slowly—as he stood shuddering and sickening in the sun—the icy horror yielded to despair so intolerable, a pain so atrocious, that he clutched at the mocking shadow of a doubt. Feigning ignorance of the neighborhood, he ventured to ask his way to the house in which his wife had lived.

"There is no one in that house," said the person questioned. "It used to belong to the wife of a samurai who left the city several years ago. He divorced her in order to marry another woman before he went away; and she fretted a great deal, and so became sick. She had no relatives in Kyōto, and nobody to care for her; and she died in the autumn of the same year—on the tenth day of the ninth month. . . ."

8

My Kinsman, Major Molineux

by Nathaniel Hawthorne

The Sailor-Boy's Tale

by Isak Dinesen

NATHANIEL HAWTHORNE *Hawthorne once remarked that the disadvantage of being an American writer was the absence of a usable past; his entire literary career was a refutation of this. After graduating from Bowdoin College in Maine (where his classmates were Longfellow and Franklin Pierce), he sequestered himself in his mother's attic to study the legends of seventeenth century Puritanism, and to teach himself how to write. It was an arduous apprenticeship; he burned some of his first stories and tried to destroy all the copies of* Fanshawe, *a novel about his college days. In 1837, he published his* Twice-Told Tales *and demonstrated the successful merger of allegory and ambiguity that was to characterize his approach to fiction. Although detached and isolated, he lived in proximity to the Concord transcendentalists and, for nearly a year, at Brook Farm, a utopian community of intellectuals whose failure to manage the mundane he would later satirize in* The Blithedale Romance. *The first significant book on Hawthorne's art was written by Henry James in 1879.*

ISAK DINESON *Isak Dineson was Danish, and her early stories appeared in 1907 under the curious pseudonym of Osceola. Her father had been an adventurer who lived for three years among American Indians. In 1915, Dineson began her own adventure by marrying her Swedish cousin, Baron Blixen, emigrating to Kenya, and running a large coffee plantation for fifteen years, an experience she described in* Out of Africa, *1937.*

My Kinsman, Major Molineux

Nathaniel Hawthorne (*American, 1804–1864*)

After the kings of Great Britain had assumed the right of appointing the colonial governors, the measures of the latter seldom met with the ready and generous approbation which had been paid to those of their predecessors, under the original charters. The people looked with most jealous scrutiny to the exercise of power which did not emanate from themselves, and they usually rewarded their rulers with slender gratitude for the compliances by which, in softening their instructions from beyond the sea, they had incurred the reprehension of those who gave them. The annals of Massachusetts Bay will inform us, that of six governors in the space of about forty years from the surrender of the old charter, under James II, two were imprisoned by a popular insurrection; a third, as Hutchinson inclines to believe, was driven from the province by the whizzing of a musket-ball; a fourth, in the opinion of the same historian, was hastened to his grave by continual bickerings with the House of Representatives; and the remaining two, as well as their successors, till the Revolution, were favored with few and brief intervals of peaceful sway. The inferior members of the court party, in times of high political excitement, led scarcely a more desirable life. These remarks may serve as a preface to the following adventures, which chanced upon a summer night, not far from a hundred years ago. The reader, in order to avoid a long and dry detail of colonial affairs, is requested to dispense with an account of the train of circumstances that had caused much temporary inflammation of the popular mind.

It was near nine o'clock of a moonlight evening, when a boat crossed the ferry with a single passenger, who had obtained his conveyance at that unusual hour by the promise of an extra fare. While he stood on the landing-place, searching in either pocket for the means of fulfilling his agreement, the ferryman lifted a lantern, by the aid of which, and the newly risen moon, he took a very accurate survey of the stranger's figure. He was a youth of barely eighteen years, evidently country-bred, and now, as it should seem, upon his first visit to town. He was clad in a coarse gray coat, well worn, but in excellent repair; his under garments were durably constructed of leather, and fitted tight to a pair of serviceable and well-shaped limbs; his stockings of blue yarn were the incontrovertible work of a mother or a sister; and on his head was a three-cornered hat, which in its better days had perhaps sheltered the graver brow of the lad's father. Under his left arm was a heavy cudgel formed of an oak sapling, and retaining a part of the hardened root; and his equipment was completed by a wallet, not so abundantly stocked as to incommode the vigorous shoulders on which it hung. Brown, curly hair, well-shaped features, and bright, cheerful eyes were nature's gifts, and worth all that art could have done for his adornment.

The youth, one of whose names was Robin, finally drew from his pocket the half of a little province bill of five shillings, which, in the depreciation in that sort of currency, did but satisfy the ferryman's demand, with the surplus of a sexangular piece of parchment, valued at three pence. He then walked forward into the town, with as light a step as if his day's journey had not already exceeded thirty miles, and with as eager an eye as if he were entering London city, instead of the little metropolis of a New England colony. Before Robin had proceeded far, however, it occurred to him that he knew not whither to direct his steps; so he paused, and looked up and down the narrow street, scrutinizing the small and mean wooden buildings that were scattered on either side.

"This low hovel cannot be my kinsman's dwelling," thought he, "nor yonder old house, where the moonlight enters at the broken casement; and truly I see none hereabouts that might be worthy of him. It would have been wise to inquire my way of the ferryman, and doubtless he would have gone with me, and earned a shilling from the Major for his pains. But the next man I meet will do as well."

He resumed his walk, and was glad to perceive that the street now became wider, and the houses more respectable in their appearance. He soon discerned a figure moving on moderately in advance, and hastened his steps to overtake it. As Robin drew nigh, he saw that the passenger was a man in years, with a full periwig of gray hair, a wide-skirted coat of dark cloth, and silk stockings rolled above his knees. He carried a long and polished cane, which he struck down perpendicularly before him at every step; and at regular intervals he uttered two successive hems, of a peculiarly solemn and sepulchral intonation. Having made these observations, Robin laid hold of the skirt of the old man's coat, just when the light from the open door and windows of a barber's shop fell upon both their figures.

"Good evening to you, honored sir," said he, making a low bow, and still retaining his hold of the skirt. "I pray you tell me whereabouts is the dwelling of my kinsman, Major Molineux."

The youth's question was uttered very loudly; and one of the barbers, whose razor was descending on a well-soaped chin, and another who was dressing a Ramillies wig, left their occupations, and came to the door. The citizen, in the meantime, turned a long-favored countenance upon Robin, and answered him in a tone of excessive anger and annoyance. His two sepulchral hems, however, broke into the very centre of his rebuke, with most singular effect, like a thought of the cold grave obtruding among wrathful passions.

"Let go my garment, fellow! I tell you, I know not the man you speak of. What! I have authority, I have—hem, hem—authority; and if this be the respect you show for your betters, your feet shall be brought acquainted with the stocks by daylight, tomorrow morning!"

Robin released the old man's skirt, and hastened away, pursued by an ill-mannered roar of laughter from the barber's shop. He was at first considerably surprised by the result of his question, but, being a shrewd youth, soon thought himself able to account for the mystery.

"This is some country representative," was his conclusion, "who has never seen the inside of my kinsman's door, and lacks the breeding to answer a stranger civilly. The man is old, or verily—I might be tempted to turn back and smite him on the nose. Ah, Robin, Robin! even the barber's boys laugh at you for choosing such a guide! You will be wiser in time, friend Robin."

He now became entangled in a succession of crooked and narrow streets, which crossed each other, and meandered at no great distance from the water-side. The smell of tar was obvious to his nostrils, the masts of vessels pierced the moonlight above the tops of the buildings, and the numerous signs, which Robin paused to read, informed him that he was near the centre of business. But the streets were empty, the shops were closed, and lights were visible only in the second stories of a few dwelling-houses. At length, on the corner of a narrow lane, through which he was passing, he beheld the broad countenance of a British hero swinging before the door of an inn, whence proceeded the voices of many guests. The casement of one of the lower windows was thrown back, and a very thin curtain permitted Robin to distinguish a party at supper, round a well-furnished table. The fragrance of the good cheer steamed forth into the outer air, and the youth could not fail to recollect that the last remnant of his travelling stock of provision had yielded to his morning appetite, and that noon had found and left him dinnerless.

"Oh, that a parchment three-penny might give me a right to sit down at yonder table!" said Robin, with a sigh. "But the Major will make me welcome to the best of his victuals; so I will even step boldly in, and inquire my way to his dwelling."

He entered the tavern, and was guided by the murmur of voices and the fumes of tobacco to the public-room. It was a long and low apartment, with oaken walls, grown dark in the continual smoke, and a floor which was thickly sanded, but of no immaculate purity. A number of persons—the larger part of whom appeared to be mariners, or in some way connected with the sea—occupied the wooden benches, or leather-bottomed chairs, conversing on various matters, and occasionally lending their attention to some topic of general interest. Three or four little groups were draining as many bowls of punch, which the West India trade had long since made a familiar drink in the colony. Others, who had the appearance of men who lived by regular and laborious handicraft, preferred the insulated bliss of an unshared potation, and became more taciturn under its influence. Nearly all, in short, evinced a predilection for the Good Creature in some of its various shapes, for this is a vice to which, as Fast Day sermons of a hundred years ago will testify, we have a long hereditary claim. The only guests to whom Robin's sympathies inclined him were two or three sheepish countrymen, who were using the inn somewhat after the fashion of a Turkish caravansary; they had gotten themselves into the darkest corner of the room, and heedless of the Nicotian atmosphere, were supping on the bread of their own ovens, and the bacon cured in their own chimney-smoke. But though Robin felt a sort of brotherhood with these strangers, his eyes were attracted from them to a person who stood near the door, holding whispered conversation with a group of ill-dressed associates. His features were separately striking almost to grotesqueness, and the whole face left a deep impression on the memory. The forehead bulged out into a double prominence, with a vale between; the nose came boldly forth in an irregular curve, and its bridge was of more than a finger's breadth; the eyebrows were deep and shaggy, and the eyes glowed beneath them like fire in a cave.

While Robin deliberated of whom to inquire respecting his kinsman's dwelling, he was accosted by the innkeeper, a little man in a stained white apron, who had come to pay his professional welcome to the stranger. Being in the second generation from a French Protestant, he seemed to have inherited the courtesy of his parent nation; but no variety of circumstances was ever known to change his voice from the one shrill note in which he now addressed Robin.

"From the country, I presume, sir?" said he, with a profound bow. "Beg leave to congratulate you on your arrival, and trust you intend a long stay with us. Fine town here, sir, beautiful buildings, and much that may interest a stranger. May I hope for the honor of your commands in respect to supper?"

"The man sees a family likeness! the rogue has guessed that I am related to the Major!" thought Robin, who had hitherto experienced little superfluous civility.

All eyes were now turned on the country lad, standing at the door, in his worn three-cornered hat, gray coat, leather breeches, and blue yarn stockings, leaning on an oaken cudgel, and bearing a wallet on his back.

Robin replied to the courteous innkeeper, with such an assumption of confidence as befitted the Major's relative. "My honest friend," he said, "I shall make it a point to patronize your house on some occasion, when"—here he could not help lowering his voice —"when I may have more than a parchment three-pence in my pocket. My present business," continued he, speaking with lofty confidence, "is merely to inquire my way to the dwelling of my kinsman, Major Molineux."

There was a sudden and general movement in the room, which Robin interpreted as expressing the eagerness of each individual to become his guide. But the innkeeper turned his eyes to a written paper on the wall, which he read, or seemed to read, with occasional recurrences to the young man's figure.

"What have we here?" said he, breaking his speech into little dry fragments. "'Left the house of the subscriber, bounden servant, Hezekiah Mudge,—had on, when he went away, gray coat, leather breeches, master's third-best hat. One pound currency reward to whosoever shall lodge him in any jail of the providence.' Better trudge, boy; better trudge!"

Robin had begun to draw his hand towards the lighter end of the oak cudgel, but a strange hostility in every countenance induced him to relinquish his purpose of breaking the courteous innkeeper's head. As he turned to leave the room, he encountered a sneering glance from the bold-featured personage whom he had before noticed; and no sooner was he beyond the door, than he heard a general laugh, in which the innkeeper's voice might be distinguished, like the dropping of small stones into a kettle.

"Now, is it not strange," thought Robin, with his usual shrewdness,—"is it not strange that the confession of an empty pocket should outweigh the name of my kinsman, Major Molineux? Oh, if I had one of those grinning rascals in the woods, where I and my oak sapling grew up together, I would teach him that my arm is heavy though my purse be light!"

On turning the corner of the narrow lane, Robin found himself in a spacious street, with an unbroken line of lofty houses on each side, and a steepled building at the upper end, whence the ringing of a bell announced the hour of nine. The light of the moon, and the lamps from the numerous shop-windows, discovered people promenading on the pavement, and amongst them Robin had hoped to recognize his hitherto inscrutable relative. The result of his former inquiries made him unwilling to hazard another, in a scene of such publicity, and he determined to walk slowly and silently up the street, thrusting his face close to that of every elderly gentleman, in search of the Major's lineaments. In his progress, Robin encountered many gay and gallant figures. Embroidered garments of showy colors, enormous periwigs, gold-laced hats, and silver-hilted swords glided past him and dazzled his optics. Travelled youths, imitators of the European fine gentlemen of the period, trod jauntily along, half dancing to the fashionable tunes which they hummed, and making poor Robin ashamed of his quiet and natural gait. At length, after many pauses to examine the gorgeous display of goods in the shop-windows, and after suffering some rebukes for the impertinence of his scrutiny into people's faces, the Major's kinsman found himself near the steepled building, still unsuccessful in his search. As yet, however, he had seen only one side of the thronged street; so Robin crossed, and continued the same sort of inquisition down the opposite pavement, with stronger hopes than the philosopher seeking an honest man, but with no better fortune. He had arrived about midway towards the lower end, from which his course began, when he overheard the approach of someone who struck down a cane on the flag-stones at every step, uttering at regular intervals, two sepulchral hems.

"Mercy on us!" quoth Robin, recognizing the sound.

Turning a corner, which chanced to be close at his right hand, he hastened to pursue his researches in some other part of the town. His patience now was wearing low, and he seemed to feel more fatigue from his rambles since he crossed the ferry, than from his journey of several days on the other side. Hunger also pleaded loudly within him, and Robin began to balance the propriety of demanding, violently, and with lifted cudgel, the necessary guidance from the first solitary passenger whom he should meet. While a resolution to this effect was gaining strength, he entered a street of mean appearance, on either side of which a row of ill-built houses was straggling towards the harbor. The moonlight fell upon no passenger along the whole extent, but in the third domicile which Robin passed there was a half-opened door, and his keen glance detected a woman's garment within.

"My luck may be better here," said he to himself.

Accordingly, he approached the door, and beheld it shut closer as he did so; yet an open space remained, sufficing for the fair occupant to observe the stranger, without a corresponding display on her part. All that Robin could discern was a strip of scarlet petticoat, and the occasional sparkle of an eye, as if the moonbeams were trembling on some bright thing.

"Pretty mistress," for I may call her so with a good conscience, thought the shrewd youth, since I know nothing to the contrary, —"my sweet pretty mistress, will you be kind enough to tell me whereabouts I must seek the dwelling of my kinsman, Major Molineux?"

Robin's voice was plaintive and winning, and the female, seeing nothing to be shunned in the handsome country youth, thrust open the door, and came forth into the moonlight. She was a dainty little figure, with a white neck, round arms, and a slender waist, at the extremity of which her scarlet petticoat jutted out over a hoop, as if she were standing in a balloon. Moreover, her face was oval and pretty, her hair dark beneath the little cap, and her bright eyes possessed a sly freedom, which triumphed over those of Robin.

"Major Molineux dwells here," said this fair woman.

Now, her voice was the sweetest Robin had heard that night, yet he could not help doubting whether that sweet voice spoke Gospel truth. He looked up and down the mean street, and then surveyed the house before which they stood. It was a small, dark edifice of two stories, the second of which projected over the lower floor, and the front apartment had the aspect of a shop for petty commodities.

"Now, truly I am in luck," replied Robin, cunningly, "and so indeed is my kinsman, the Major, in having so pretty a housekeeper. But I prithee trouble him to step to the door; I will deliver him a message from his friends in the country, and then go back to my lodgings at the inn."

"Nay, the Major has been abed this hour or more," said the lady of the scarlet petticoat; "and it would be to little purpose to disturb him to-night, seeing his evening draught was of the strongest. But he is a kind-hearted man, and it would be as much as my life's worth to let a kinsman of his turn away from the door. You are the good old gentleman's very picture, and I could swear that was his rainy-weather hat. Also he has garments very much resembling those leather small-clothes. But come in, I pray, for I bid you hearty welcome in his name."

So saying, the fair and hospitable dame took our hero by the hand; and the touch was light, and the force was gentleness, and though Robin read in her eyes what he did not hear in her words, yet the slender-waisted woman in the scarlet petticoat proved stronger than the athletic country youth. She had drawn his half-willing footsteps nearly to the threshold, when the opening of a door in the neighborhood startled the Major's housekeeper, and, leaving the Major's kinsman, she vanished speedily into her own domicile. A heavy yawn preceded the appearance of a man, who, like the Moonshine of Pyramus and Thisbe, carried a lantern, needlessly aiding his sister luminary in the heavens. As he walked sleepily up the street, he turned his broad, dull face on Robin, and displayed a long staff, spiked at the end.

"Home, vagabond, home!" said the watchman, in accents that seemed to fall asleep as soon as they were uttered. "Home, or we'll set you in the stocks by peep of day!"

"This is the second hint of the kind," thought Robin. "I wish they would end my difficulties, by setting me there to-night."

Nevertheless, the youth felt an instinctive antipathy towards the guardian of midnight order, which at first prevented him from asking his usual question. But just when the man was about to vanish behind the corner, Robin resolved not to lose the opportunity, and shouted lustily after him,—

"I say, friend! will you guide me to the house of my kinsman, Major Molineux?"

The watchman made no reply, but turned the corner and was gone; yet Robin seemed to hear the sound of drowsy laughter stealing along the solitary street. At that moment, also, a pleasant titter saluted him from the open window above his head; he looked up, and caught the sparkle of a saucy eye; a round arm beckoned to him, and next he heard light footsteps descending the staircase within. But Robin, being of the household of a New England clergyman, was a good youth, as well as a shrewd one; so he resisted temptation, and fled away.

He now roamed desperately, and at random, through the town, almost ready to believe that a spell was on him, like that by which a wizard of his country had once kept three pursuers wandering, a whole winter night, within twenty paces of the cottage which they sought. The streets lay before him, strange and desolate, and the lights were extinguished in almost every house. Twice, however, little parties of men, among whom Robin distinguished individuals in outlandish attire, came hurrying along; but, though on both occasions, they paused to address him, such intercourse did not at all enlighten his perplexity. They did but utter a few words in some language of which Robin knew nothing, and perceiving his inability to answer, bestowed a curse upon him in plain English and hastened away. Finally, the lad determined to knock at the door of every mansion that might appear worthy to be occupied by his kinsman, trusting that perseverance would overcome the fatality that had hitherto thwarted him. Firm in this resolve, he was passing beneath the walls of a church, which formed the corner of two streets, when, as he turned into the shade of its steeple, he encountered a bulky stranger, muffled in a cloak. The man was proceeding with the speed of earnest business, but Robin planted himself full before him, holding the oak cudgel with both hands across his body as a bar to further passage.

."Halt, honest man, and answer me a question," said he, very resolutely. "Tell me, this instant, whereabouts is the dwelling of my kinsman, Major Molineux!"

"Keep your tongue between your teeth, fool, and let me pass!" said a deep, gruff voice, which Robin partly remembered. "Let me pass, or I'll strike you to the earth!"

"No, no, neighbor!" cried Robin, flourishing his cudgel, and then thrusting its larger end close to the man's muffled face. "No, no, I'm not the fool you take me for, nor do you pass till I have an answer to my question. Whereabouts is the dwelling of my kinsman, Major Molineux?"

The stranger, instead of attempting to force his passage, stepped back into the moonlight, unmuffled his face, and stared full into that of Robin.

"Watch here an hour, and Major Molineux will pass by," said he.

Robin gazed with dismay and astonishment on the unprecedented physiognomy of the speaker. The forehead with its double prominence, the broad hooked nose, the shaggy eyebrows, and fiery eyes were those which he had noticed at the inn, but the man's complexion had undergone a singular, or, more properly, a twofold change. One side of the face blazed an intense red, while the other was black as midnight, the division line being in the broad bridge of the nose; and a mouth which seemed to extend from ear to ear was black or red, in contrast to the color of the cheek. The effect was as if two individual devils, a fiend of fire and a fiend of darkness, had united themselves to form this infernal visage. The stranger grinned in Robin's face, muffled his party-colored features, and was out of sight in a moment.

"Strange things we travellers see!" ejaculated Robin.

He seated himself, however, upon the steps of the church-door, resolving to wait the appointed time for his kinsman. A few moments were consumed in philosophical speculations upon the species of man who had just left him; but having settled this point shrewdly, rationally, and satisfactorily, he was compelled to look elsewhere for his amusement. And first he threw his eyes along the street. It was of more respectable appearance than most of those into which he had wandered; and the moon, creating, like the imaginative power, a beautiful strangeness in familiar objects, gave something of romance to a scene that might not have possessed it in the light of day. The irregular and often quaint architecture of the houses, some of whose roofs were broken into numerous little peaks, while others ascended, steep and narrow, into a single point, and others again were square; the pure snow-white of some of their complexions, the aged darkness of others, and the thousand sparklings, reflected from bright substances in the walls of many; these matters engaged Robin's attention for a while, and then began to grow wearisome. Next he endeavored to define the forms of distant objects, starting away, with almost ghostly indistinctness, just as his eye appeared to grasp them; and finally he took a minute survey of an edifice which stood on the opposite side of the street, directly in front of the church-door, where he was stationed. It was a large, square mansion, distinguished from its neighbors by a balcony, which rested on tall pillars, and by an elaborate Gothic window, communicating therewith.

"Perhaps this is the very house I have been seeking," thought Robin.

Then he strove to speed away the time, by listening to a murmur which swept continually along the street, yet was scarcely audible, except to an unaccustomed ear like his; it was a low, dull, dreamy sound, compounded of many noises, each of which was at too great a distance to be separately heard. Robin marvelled at this snore of a sleeping town, and marvelled more whenever its continuity was broken by now and then a distant shout, apparently loud where it originated. But altogether it was a sleep-inspiring sound, and, to shake off its drowsy influence, Robin arose, and climbed a window-frame, that he might view the interior of the church. There the moonbeams came trembling in, and fell down upon the deserted pews, and extended along the quiet aisles. A fainter yet more awful radiance was hovering around the pulpit, and one solitary ray had dared to rest upon the open page of the great Bible. Had nature, in that deep hour, become a worshipper in the house which man had builded? Or was that heavenly light the visible sanctity of the place,—visible because no earthly and impure feet were within the walls? The scene made Robin's heart shiver with a sensation of loneliness stronger than he had ever felt in the remotest depths of his native woods; so he turned away and sat down again before the door. There were graves around the church, and now an uneasy thought obtruded into Robin's breast. What if the object of his search, which had been so often and so strangely thwarted, were all the time mouldering in his shroud? What if his kinsman should glide through yonder gate, and nod and smile to him in dimly passing by?

"Oh that any breathing thing were here with me!" said Robin.

Recalling his thoughts from this uncomfortable track, he sent them over forest, hill, and stream, and attempted to imagine how that evening of ambiguity and weariness had been spent by his father's household. He pictured them assembled at the door, beneath the tree, the great old tree, which had been spared for its huge twisted trunk and venerable shade, when a thousand leafy brethren fell. There, at the going down of the summer sun, it was his father's custom to perform domestic worship, that the neighbors might come and join with him like brothers of the family, and that the wayfaring man might pause to drink at that fountain, and keep his heart pure by freshening the memory of home. Robin distinguished the seat of every individual of the little audience; he saw the good man in the midst, holding the Scriptures in the golden light that fell from the western clouds; he beheld him close the book and all rise up to pray. He heard the old thanksgivings for daily mercies, the old supplications for their continuance, to which he had so often listened in weariness, but which were now among his dear remembrances. He perceived the slight inequality of his father's voice when he came to speak of the absent one; he noted how his mother turned her face to the broad and knotted trunk; how his elder brother scorned, because the beard was rough upon his upper lip, to permit his features to be moved; how the younger sister drew down a low hanging branch before her eyes; and how the little one of all, whose sports had hitherto broken the decorum of the scene, understood the prayer for her playmate, and burst into clamorous grief. Then he saw them go in at the door; and when Robin would have entered also, the latch tinkled into its place, and he was excluded from his home.

"Am I here, or there?" cried Robin, starting; for all at once, when his thoughts had become visible and audible in a dream, the long, wide, solitary street shone out before him.

He aroused himself, and endeavored to fix his attention steadily upon the large edifice which he had surveyed before. But still his mind kept vibrating between fancy and reality; by turns, the pillars of the balcony lengthened into the tall, bare stems of pines, dwindled down to human figures, settled again into their true shape and size, and then commenced a new succession of changes. For a single moment, when he deemed himself awake, he could have sworn that a visage—one which he seemed to remember, yet could not absolutely name as his kinsman's—was looking towards him from the Gothic window. A deeper sleep wrestled with and nearly overcame him, but fled at the sound of footsteps along the opposite pavement. Robin rubbed his eyes, discerned a man passing at the foot of the balcony, and addressed him in a loud, peevish, and lamentable cry.

"Hallo, friend! must I wait here all night for my kinsman, Major Molineux?"

The sleeping echoes awoke, and answered the voice; and the passenger, barely able to discern a figure sitting in the oblique shade of the steeple, traversed the street to obtain a nearer view. He was himself a gentleman in his prime, of open, intelligent, cheerful, and altogether prepossessing countenance. Perceiving a country youth, apparently homeless and without friends, he accosted him in a tone of real kindness, which had become strange to Robin's ears.

"Well, my good lad, why are you sitting here?" inquired he. "Can I be of service to you in any way?"

"I am afraid not, sir," replied Robin, despondingly; "yet I shall take it kindly, if you'll answer me a single question. I've been searching, half the night, for one Major Molineux; now, sir, is there really such a person in these parts, or am I dreaming?"

"Major Molineux! The name is not altogether strange to me," said the gentleman, smiling. "Have you any objection to telling me the nature of your business with him?"

Then Robin briefly related that his father was a clergyman, settled on a small salary, at a long distance back in the country, and that he and Major Molineux were brothers' children. The Major, having inherited riches, and acquired civil and military rank, had visited his cousin, in great pomp, a year or two before; had manifested much interest in Robin and an elder brother, and, being childless himself, had thrown out hints respecting the future establishment of one of them in life. The elder brother was destined to succeed to the farm which his father cultivated in the interval of sacred duties; it was therefore determined that Robin should profit by his kinsman's generous intentions, especially as he seemed to be rather the favorite, and was thought to possess other necessary endowments.

"For I have the name of being a shrewd youth," observed Robin, in this part of his story.

"I doubt not you deserve it," replied his new friend, good-naturedly; "but pray proceed."

"Well, sir, being nearly eighteen years old, and well grown, as you see," continued Robin, drawing himself up to his full height, "I thought it high time to begin in the world. So my mother and sister put me in handsome trim, and my father gave me half the remnant of his last year's salary, and five days ago I started for this place, to pay the Major a visit. But, would you believe it, sir! I crossed the ferry a little after dark, and have yet found nobody that would show me the way to his dwelling; only, an hour or two since, I was told to wait here, and Major Molineux would pass by."

"Can you describe the man who told you this?" inquired the gentleman.

"Oh, he was a very ill-favored fellow, sir," replied Robin, "with two great bumps on his forehead, a hook nose, fiery eyes; and, what struck me as the strangest, his face was of two different colors. Do you happen to know such a man, sir?"

"Not intimately," answered the stranger, "but I chanced to meet him a little time previous to your stopping me. I believe you may trust his word, and that the Major will very shortly pass through this street. In the meantime, as I have a singular curiosity to witness your meeting, I will sit down here upon the steps and bear you company."

He seated himself accordingly, and soon engaged his companion in animated discourse. It was but of brief continuance, however, for a noise of shouting, which had long been remotely audible, drew so much nearer that Robin inquired its cause.

"What may be the meaning of this uproar?" asked he. "Truly, if your town be always as noisy, I shall find little sleep while I am an inhabitant."

"Why, indeed, friend Robin, there do appear to be three or four riotous fellows abroad to-night," replied the gentleman. "You must not expect all the stillness of your native woods here in our streets. But the watch will shortly be at the heels of these lads and"—

"Ay, and set them in the stocks by peep of day," interrupted Robin, recollecting his own encounter with the drowsy lantern-bearer. "But, dear sir, if I may trust my ears, an army of watchmen would never make head against such a multitude of rioters. There were at least a thousand voices went up to make that one shout."

"May not a man have several voices, Robin, as well as two complexions?" said his friend.

"Perhaps a man may; but Heaven forbid that a woman should!" responded the shrewd youth, thinking of the seductive tones of the Major's housekeeper.

The sounds of a trumpet in some neighboring street now became so evident and continual, that Robin's curiosity was strongly excited. In addition to the shouts, he heard frequent bursts from many instruments of discord, and a wild and confused laughter filled up the intervals. Robin rose from the steps, and looked wistfully towards a point whither people seemed to be hastening.

"Surely some prodigious merry-making is going on," exclaimed he. "I have laughed very little since I left home, sir, and should be sorry to lose an opportunity. Shall we step round the corner by that darkish house, and take our share of the fun?"

"Sit down again, sit down, good Robin," replied the gentleman, laying his hand on the skirt of the gray coat. "You forget that we must wait here for your kinsman; and there is reason to believe that he will pass by, in the course of a very few moments."

The near approach of the uproar had now disturbed the neighborhood; windows flew open on all sides; and many heads, in the attire of the pillow, and confused by sleep suddenly broken, were protruded to the gaze of whoever had leisure to observe them. Eager voices hailed each other from house to house, all demanding the explanation, which not a soul could give. Half-dressed men hurried towards the unknown commotion, stumbling as they went over the stone steps that thrust themselves into the narrow foot-walk. The shouts, the laughter, and the tuneless bray, the antipodes of music, came onwards with increasing din, till scattered individuals, and then denser bodies, began to appear round a corner at the distance of a hundred yards.

"Will you recognize your kinsman, if he passes in this crowd?" inquired the gentleman.

"Indeed, I can't warrant it, sir; but I'll take my stand here, and keep a bright lookout," answered Robin, descending to the outer edge of the pavement.

A mighty stream of people now emptied into the street, and came rolling slowly towards the church. A single horseman wheeled the corner in the midst of them, and close behind him came a band of fearful wind-instruments, sending forth a fresher discord now that no intervening buildings kept it from the ear. Then a redder light disturbed the moonbeams, and a dense multitude of torches shone along the street, concealing, by their glare, whatever object they illuminated. The single horseman, clad in a military dress, and bearing a drawn sword, rode onward as the leader, and, by his fierce and variegated countenance, appeared like war personified; the red of one cheek was an emblem of fire and sword; the blackness of the other betokened the mourning that attends them. In his train were wild figures in the Indian dress, and many fantastic shapes without a model, giving the whole march a visionary air, as if a dream had broken forth from some feverish brain, and were sweeping visibly through the midnight streets. A mass of people, inactive, except as applauding spectators, hemmed the procession in; and several women ran along the sidewalk, piercing the confusion of heavier sounds with their shrill voices of mirth or terror.

"The double-faced fellow has his eye upon me," muttered Robin, with an indefinite but an uncomfortable idea that he was himself to bear a part in the pageantry.

The leader turned himself in the saddle, and fixed his glance full upon the country youth, as the steed went slowly by. When Robin had freed his eyes from those fiery ones, the musicians were passing before him, and the torches were close at hand; but the unsteady brightness of the latter formed a veil which he could not penetrate. The rattling of wheels over the stones sometimes found its way to his ear, and confused traces of a human form appeared at intervals, and then melted into the vivid light. A moment more, and the leader thundered a command to halt: the trumpets vomited a horrid breath, and then held their peace; the shouts and laughter of the people died away, and there remained only a universal hum, allied to silence. Right before Robin's eyes was an uncovered cart. There the torches blazed the brightest, there the moon shone out like day, and there, in tar-and-feathery dignity, sat his kinsman, Major Molineux!

He was an elderly man, of large and majestic person, and strong, square features, betokening a steady soul; but steady as it was, his enemies had found means to shake it. His face was pale as death, and far more ghastly; the broad forehead was contracted in his agony, so that his eyebrows formed one grizzled line; his eyes were red and wild, and the foam hung white upon his quivering lip. His whole frame was agitated by a quick and continual tremor, which his pride strove to quell, even in those circumstances of overwhelming humiliation. But perhaps the bitterest pang of all was when his eyes met those of Robin; for he evidently knew him on the instant, as the youth stood witnessing the foul disgrace of a head grown gray in honor. They stared at each other in silence, and Robin's knees shook, and his hair bristled, with a mixture of pity and terror. Soon, however, a bewildering excitement began to seize upon his mind; the preceding adventures of the night, the unexpected appearance of the crowd, the torches, the confused din and the hush that followed, the spectre of his kinsman reviled by that great multitude,—all this, and, more than all, a perception of tremendous ridicule in the whole scene, affected him with a sort of mental inebriety. At that moment a voice of sluggish merriment saluted Robin's ears; he turned instinctively, and just behind the corner of the church stood the lantern-bearer, rubbing his eyes, and drowsily enjoying the lad's amazement. Then he heard a peal of laughter like the ringing of silvery bells; a woman twitched his arm, a saucy eye met his, and he saw the lady of the scarlet petticoat. A sharp, dry cachinnation appealed to his memory, and standing on tiptoe in the crowd, with his white apron over his head, he beheld the courteous little innkeeper. And lastly, there sailed over the heads of the multitude a great, broad laugh, broken in the midst by two sepulchral hems; thus, "Haw, haw, haw,—hem, hem, —haw, haw, haw, haw!"

The sound proceeded from the balcony of the opposite edifice, and thither Robin turned his eyes. In front of the Gothic window stood the old citizen, wrapped in a wide gown, his gray periwig exchanged for a nightcap, which was thrust back from his forehead, and his silk stockings hanging about his legs. He supported himself on his polished cane in a fit of convulsive merriment, which manifested itself on his solemn old features like a funny inscription on a tombstone. Then Robin seemed to hear the voices of the barbers, of the guests of the inn, and of all who had made sport of him that night. The contagion was spreading among the multitude, when all at once, it seized upon Robin, and he sent forth a shout of laughter that echoed through the street,—every man shook his sides, every man emptied his lungs, but Robin's shout was the loudest there. The cloud-spirits peeped from their silvery islands, as the congregated mirth went roaring up the sky! The Man in the Moon heard the far bellow. "Oho," quoth he, "the old earth is frolicsome to-night!"

When there was a momentary calm in that tempestuous sea of sound, the leader gave the sign, the procession resumed its march. On they went, like fiends that throng in mockery around some dead potentate, mighty no more, but majestic still in his agony. On they went, in counterfeited pomp, in senseless uproar, in frenzied merriment, trampling all on an old man's heart. On swept the tumult, and left a silent street behind.

"Well, Robin, are you dreaming?" inquired the gentleman, laying his hand on the youth's shoulder.

Robin started, and withdrew his arm from the stone post to which he had instinctively clung, as the living stream rolled by him. His cheek was somewhat pale, and his eye not quite as lively as in the earlier part of the evening.

"Will you be kind enough to show me the way to the ferry?" said he, after a moment's pause.

"You have, then, adopted a new subject of inquiry?" observed his companion, with a smile.

"Why, yes, sir," replied Robin, rather dryly. "Thanks to you, and to my other friends, I have at last met my kinsman, and he will scarce desire to see my face again. I begin to grow weary of a town life, sir. Will you show me the way to the ferry?"

"No, my good friend Robin,—not tonight, at least," said the gentleman. "Some few days hence, if you wish it, I will speed you on your journey. Or, if you prefer to remain with us, perhaps, as you are a shrewd youth, you may rise in the world without the help of your kinsman, Major Molineux."

The Sailor-Boy's Tale

Isak Dinesen (*Danish, 1885–1962*)

The barque *Charlotte* was on her way from Marseille to Athens, in grey weather, on a high sea, after three days' heavy gale. A small sailor-boy, named Simon, stood on the wet, swinging deck, held on to a shroud, and looked up towards the drifting clouds, and to the upper top-gallant yard of the main-mast.

A bird, that had sought refuge upon the mast, had got her feet tangled in some loose tackle-yarn of the halliard, and high up there, struggled to get free. The boy on the deck could see her wings flapping and her head turning from side to side.

Through his own experience of life he had come to the conviction that in this world everyone must look after himself, and expect no help from others. But the mute, deadly fight kept him fascinated for more than an hour. He wondered what kind of bird it would be. These last days a number of birds had come to settle in the barque's rigging: swallows, quails, and a pair of peregrine falcons; he believed that this bird was a peregrine falcon. He remembered how, many years ago, in his own country and near his home, he had once seen a peregrine falcon quite close, sitting on a stone and flying straight up from it. Perhaps this was the same bird. He thought: "That bird is like me. Then she was there, and now she is here."

At that a fellow-feeling rose in him, a sense of common tragedy; he stood looking at the bird with his heart in his mouth. There were none of the sailors about to make fun of him; he began to think out how he might go up by the shrouds to help the falcon out. He brushed his hair back and pulled up his sleeves, gave the deck round him a great glance, and climbed up. He had to stop a couple of times in the swaying rigging.

It was indeed, he found when he got to the top of the mast, a peregrine falcon. As his head was on a level with hers, she gave up her struggle, and looked at him with a pair of angry, desperate yellow eyes. He had to take hold of her with one hand while he got his knife out, and cut off the tackle-yarn. He was scared as he looked down, but at the same time he felt that he had been ordered up by nobody, but that this was his own venture, and this gave him a proud, steadying sensation, as if the sea and the sky, the ship, the bird and himself were all one. Just as he had freed the falcon, she hacked him on the thumb, so that the blood ran, and he nearly let her go. He grew angry with her, and gave her a clout on the head, then he put her inside his jacket, and climbed down again.

When he reached the deck the mate and the cook were standing there, looking up; they roared to him to ask what he had had to do in the mast. He was so tired that the tears were in his eyes. He took the falcon out and showed her to them, and she kept still within his hands. They laughed and walked off. Simon set the falcon down, stood back and watched her. After a while he reflected that she might not be able to get up from the slippery deck, so he caught her once more, walked away with her and placed her upon a bolt of canvas. A little after she began to trim her feathers, made two or three sharp jerks forward, and then suddenly flew off. The boy could follow her flight above the troughs of the grey sea. He thought: "There flies my falcon."

When the *Charlotte* came home, Simon signed aboard another ship, and two years later he was a light hand on the schooner *Hebe* lying at Bodø, high up on the coast of Norway, to buy herrings.

To the great herring-markets of Bodø ships came together from all corners of the world; here were Swedish, Finnish and Russian boats, a forest of masts, and on shore a turbulent, irregular display of life, with many languages spoken, and mighty fists. On the shore booths had been set up, and the Lapps, small, yellow people, noiseless in their movements, with watchful eyes, whom Simon had never seen before, came down to sell bead-embroidered leather-goods. It was April, the sky and the sea were so clear that it was difficult to hold one's eyes up against them—salt, infinitely wide, and filled with bird-shrieks—as if someone were incessantly whetting invisible knives, on all sides, high up in Heaven.

Simon was amazed at the lightness of these April evenings. He knew no geography, and did not assign it to the latitude, but he took it as a sign of an unwonted good-will in the Universe, a favour. Simon had been small for his age all his life, but this last winter he had grown, and had become strong of limb. That good luck, he felt, must spring from the very same source as the sweetness of the weather, from a new benevolence in the world. He had been in need of such encouragement, for he was timid by nature; now he asked for no more. The rest he felt to be his own affair. He went about slowly, and proudly.

One evening he was ashore with land-leave, and walked up to the booth of a small Russian trader, a Jew who sold gold watches. All the sailors knew that his watches were made from bad metal, and would not go, still they bought them, and paraded them about. Simon looked at these watches for a long time, but did not buy. The old Jew had divers goods in his shop, and amongst others a case of oranges. Simon had tasted oranges on his journeys; he bought one and took it with him. He meant to go up on a hill, from where he could see the sea, and suck it there.

As he walked on, and had got to the outskirts of the place, he saw a little girl in a blue frock, standing at the other side of a fence and looking at him. She was thirteen or fourteen years old, as slim as an eel, but with a round, clear, freckled face, and a pair of long plaits. The two looked at one another.

"Who are you looking out for?" Simon asked, to say something. The girl's face broke into an ecstatic, presumptuous smile. "For the man I am going to marry, of course," she said. Something in her countenance made the boy confident and happy; he grinned a little at her. "That will perhaps be me," he said. "Ha, ha," said the girl, "he is a few years older than you, I can tell you." "Why," said Simon, "you are not grown up yourself." The little girl shook her head solemnly. "Nay," she said, "but when I grow up I will be exceedingly beautiful, and wear brown shoes with heels, and a hat." "Will you have an orange?" asked Simon, who could give her none of the things she had named. She looked at the orange and at him. "They are very good to eat," said he. "Why do you not eat it yourself then?" she asked. "I have eaten so many already," said he, "when I was in Athens. Here I had to pay a mark for it." "What is your name?" asked she. "My name is Simon," said he. "What is yours?" "Nora," said the girl. "What do you want for your orange now, Simon?"

When he heard his name in her mouth Simon grew bold. "Will you give me a kiss for the orange?" he asked. Nora looked at him gravely for a moment. "Yes," she said, "I should not mind giving you a kiss." He grew as warm as if he had been running quickly.

When she stretched out her hand for the orange he took hold of it. At that moment somebody in the house called out for her. "That is my father," said she, and tried to give him back the orange, but he would not take it. "Then come again tomorrow," she said quickly, "then I will give you a kiss." At that she slipped off. He stood and looked after her, and a little later went back to his ship.

Simon was not in the habit of making plans for the future, and now he did not know whether he would be going back to her or not.

The following evening he had to stay aboard, as the other sailors were going ashore, and he did not mind that either. He meant to sit on the deck with the ship's dog, Balthasar, and to practice upon a concertina that he had purchased some time ago. The pale evening was all round him, the sky was faintly roseate, the sea was quite calm, like milk-and-water, only in the wake of the boats going inshore it broke into streaks of vivid indigo. Simon sat and played; after a while his own music began to speak to him so strongly that he stopped, got up and looked upwards. Then he saw that the full moon was sitting high on the sky.

The sky was so light that she hardly seemed needed there; it was as if she had turned up by a caprice of her own. She was round, demure and presumptuous. At that he knew that he must go ashore, whatever it was to cost him. But he did not know how to get away since the others had taken the yawl with them. He stood on the deck for a long time, a small lonely figure of a sailor-boy on a boat, when he caught sight of a yawl coming in from a ship farther out, and hailed her. He found that it was the Russian crew from the boat named *Anna,* going ashore. When he could make himself understood to them, they took him with them; they first asked him for money for his fare, then laughing, gave it back to him. He thought: "These people will be believing that I am going in to town, wenching." And then he felt, with some pride, that they were right, although at the same time they were infinitely wrong, and knew nothing about anything.

When they came ashore they invited him to come in and drink in their company, and he would not refuse, because they had helped him. One of the Russians was a giant, as big as a bear; he told Simon that his name was Ivan. He got drunk at once, and then fell upon the boy with a bear-like affection, pawed him, smiled and laughed into his face, made him a present of a gold watch-chain, and kissed him on both cheeks. At that Simon reflected that he also ought to give Nora a present when they met again, and as soon as he could get away from the Russians he walked up to a booth that he knew of, and bought a small blue silk handkerchief, the same colour as her eyes.

It was Saturday evening, and there were many people amongst the houses; they came in long rows, some of them singing, all keen to have some fun that night. Simon, in the midst of this rich, bawling life under the clear moon, felt his head light with the flight from the ship and the strong drinks. He crammed the handkerchief in his pocket; it was silk, which he had never touched before, a present for his girl.

He could not remember the path up to Nora's house, lost his way, and came back to where he had started. Then he grew deadly afraid that he should be too late, and began to run. In a small passage between two wooden huts he ran straight into a big man, and found that it was Ivan once more. The Russian folded his arms round him and held him. "Good! Good!" he cried in high glee, "I have found you, my little chicken. I have looked for you everywhere, and poor Ivan has wept because he lost his friend." "Let me go, Ivan," cried Simon. "Oho," said Ivan, "I shall go with you and get you what you want. My heart and my money are all yours; I have been seventeen years old myself, a little lamb of God, and I want to be so again tonight." "Let me go," cried Simon, "I am in a hurry." Ivan held him so that it hurt, and patted him with his other hand. "I feel it, I feel it," he said. "Now trust me, my little friend. Nothing shall part you and me, I hear the others coming; we will have such a night together as you will remember when you are an old grandpapa."

Suddenly he crushed the boy to him, like a bear that carries off a sheep. The odious sensation of male bodily warmth and the bulk of a man close to him made the lean boy mad. He thought of Nora waiting, like a slender ship in the dim air, and of himself, here, in the hot embrace of a hairy animal. He struck Ivan with all his might. "I shall kill you, Ivan," he cried out, "if you do not let me go." "Oh, you will be thankful to me later on," said Ivan, and began to sing. Simon fumbled in his pocket for his knife, got it opened. He could not lift his hand, but he drove the knife, furiously, in under the big man's arm. Almost immediately he felt the blood spouting out, and running down in his sleeve. Ivan stopped short in the song, let go his hold of the boy and gave two long deep grunts. The next second he tumbled down to his knees. "Poor Ivan, poor Ivan," he groaned. He fell straight on his face. At that moment

Simon heard the other sailors coming along, singing, in the by-street.

He stood still for a minute, wiped his knife, and watched the blood spread into a dark pool underneath the big body. Then he ran. As he stopped for a second to choose his way, he heard the sailors behind him scream out over their dead comrade. He thought: "I must get down to the sea, where I can wash my hand." But at the same time he ran the other way. After a little while he found himself on the path that he had walked on the day before, and it seemed as familiar to him, as if he had walked it many hundred times in his life.

He slackened his pace to look round, and suddenly saw Nora standing on the other side of the fence; she was quite close to him when he caught sight of her in the moonlight. Wavering and out of breath he sank down on his knees. For a moment he could not speak. The little girl looked down at him. "Good evening, Simon," she said in her small coy voice. "I have waited for you a long time," and after a moment she added: "I have eaten your orange."

"Oh, Nora," cried the boy. "I have killed a man." She stared at him, but did not move. "Why did you kill a man?" she asked after a moment. "To get here," said Simon. "Because he tried to stop me. But he was my friend." Slowly he got on to his feet. "He loved me!" the boy cried out, and at that burst into tears. "Yes," said she slowly and thoughtfully. "Yes, because you must be here in time." "Can you hide me?" he asked. "For they are after me." "Nay," said Nora, "I cannot hide you. For my father is the parson here at Bodø, and he would be sure to hand you over to them, if he knew that you had killed a man." "Then," said Simon, "give me something to wipe my hands on." "What is the matter with your hands?" she asked, and took a little step forward. He stretched out his hands to her. "Is that your own blood?" she asked. "No," said he, "it is his." She took the step back again. "Do you hate me now?" he asked. "No, I do not hate you," said she. "But do put your hands at your back."

As he did so she came up close to him, at the other side of the fence, and clasped her arms round his neck. She pressed her young body to his, and kissed him tenderly. He felt her face, cool as the moonlight, upon his own, and when she released him, his head swam, and he did not know if the kiss had lasted a second or an hour. Nora stood up straight, her eyes wide open. "Now," she said slowly and proudly, "I promise you that I will never marry anybody, as long as I live." The boy kept standing with his hands on his back, as if she had tied them there. "And now," she said, "you must run, for they are coming." They looked at one another. "Do not forget Nora,"said she. He turned and ran.

He leapt over a fence, and when he was down amongst the houses he walked. He did not know at all where to go. As he came to a house, from where music and noise streamed out, he slowly went through the door. The room was full of people; they were dancing in here. A lamp hung from the ceiling, and shone down on them, the air was thick and brown with dust rising from the floor. There were some women in the room, but many of the men danced with each other, and gravely or laughingly stamped the floor. A moment after Simon had come in the crowd withdrew to the walls to clear the floor for two sailors, who were showing a dance from their own country.

Simon thought: "Now, very soon, the men from the boat will come round to look for their comrade's murderer, and from my hands they will know that I have done it." These five minutes during which he stood by the wall of the dancing-room, in the midst of the gay, sweating dancers, were of great significance to the boy. He himself felt it, as if during this time he grew up, and became like other people. He did not entreat his destiny, nor complain. Here he was, he had killed a man, and had kissed a girl. He did not demand any more from life, nor did life now demand more from him. He was Simon, a man like the men round him, and going to die, as all men are going to die.

He only became aware of what was going on outside him, when he saw a woman had come in, and was standing in the midst of the cleared floor, looking round her. She was a short, broad old woman, in the clothes of the Lapps, and she took her stand with such majesty and fierceness as if she owned the whole place. It was obvious that most of the people knew her, and were a little afraid of her, although a few laughed; the din of the dancing-room stopped when she spoke.

"Where is my son?" she asked in a high shrill voice, like a bird's. The next moment her eyes fell on Simon himself, and she steered through the crowd, which opened up before her, stretched out her old skinny, dark hand, and took him by the elbow. "Come home with me now," she said. "You need not dance here tonight. You may be dancing a high enough dance soon."

Simon drew back, for he thought that she was drunk. But as she looked him straight in the face with her yellow eyes, it seemed to him that he had met her before, and that he might do well in listening to her. The old woman pulled him with her across the floor, and he followed her without a word. "Do not birch your boy too badly, Sunniva," one of the men in the room cried to her. "He has done no harm, he only wanted to look at the dance."

At the same moment as they came out through the door there was an alarm in the street, a flock of people came running down it, and one of them as he turned into the house, knocked against Simon, looked at him and the old woman, and ran on.

While the two walked along the street, the old woman lifted up her skirt, and put the hem of it into the boy's hand. "Wipe your hand on my skirt," she said. They had not gone far before they came to a small wooden house, and stopped; the door to it was so low that they must bend to get through it. As the Lapp-woman went in before Simon, still holding on to his arm, the boy looked up for a moment. The night had grown misty; there was a wide ring round the moon.

The old woman's room was narrow and dark, with but one small window to it; a lantern stood on the floor and lighted it up dimly. It was all filled with reindeer skins and wolf skins, and with reindeer horns, such as the Lapps use to make their carved buttons and knife-handles, and the air in here was rank and stifling. As soon as they were in, the woman turned to Simon, took hold of his head, and with her crooked fingers parted his hair and combed it down in Lapp fashion. She clapped a Lapp cap on him and stood back to glance at him. "Sit down on my stool, now," she said. "But first take out your knife." She was so commanding in voice and manner that the boy could not but choose to do as she told him; he sat down on the stool, and he could not take his eyes off her face, which was flat and brown, and as if smeared with dirt in its net of fine wrinkles. As he sat there he heard many people come along outside, and stop by the house; then someone knocked at the door, waited a moment and knocked again. The old woman stood and listened, as still as a mouse.

"Nay," said the boy and got up. "This is no good, for it is me that they are after. It will be better for you to let me go out to them." "Give me your knife," she said. When he handed it to her, she stuck it straight into her thumb, so that the blood spouted out, and she let it drip all over her skirt. "Come in, then," she cried.

The door opened, and two Russian sailors came and stood in the opening; there were more people outside. "Has anybody come in here?" they asked. "We are after a man who has killed our mate, but he has run away from us. Have you seen or heard anybody this way?" The old Lapp-woman turned upon them, and her eyes shone like gold in the lamplight. "Have I seen or heard anyone?" she cried, "I have heard you shriek murder all over the town. You frightened me, and my poor silly boy there, so that I cut my thumb as I was ripping the skin-rug that I sew. The boy is too scared to help me, and the rug is all ruined. I shall make you pay me for that. If you are looking for a murderer, come in and search my house for me, and I shall know you when we meet again." She was so furious that she danced where she stood, and jerked her head like an angry bird of prey.

The Russian came in, looked round the room, and at her and her blood-stained hand and skirt. "Do not put a curse on us now, Sunniva," he said timidly. "We know that you can do many things when you like. Here is a mark to pay you for the blood you have spilled." She stretched out her hand, and he placed a piece of money in it. She spat on it. "Then go, and there shall be no bad blood between us," said Sunniva, and shut the door after them. She stuck her thumb in her mouth, and chuckled a little.

The boy got up from his stool, stood up before her and stared into her face. He felt as if he were swaying high up in the air, with but a small hold. "Why have you helped me?" he asked her. "Do you not know?" she answered. "Have you not recognised me yet? But you will remember the peregrine falcon which was caught in the tackle-yarn of your boat, the *Charlotte,* as she sailed in the Mediterranean. That day you climbed up by the shrouds of the top-gallant-mast to help her out, in a stiff wind, and with a high sea. That falcon was me. We Lapps often fly in such a manner, to see the world. When I first met you I was on my way to Africa, to see my younger sister and her children. She is a falcon too, when she chooses. By that time she was living at Takaunga, within an old ruined tower, which down there they call a minaret." She swarthed a corner of her skirt round her thumb, and bit at it, "We do not forget," she said. "I hacked your thumb, when you took hold of me; it is only fair that I should cut my thumb for you tonight."

She came close to him, and gently rubbed her two brown, claw-like fingers against his forehead. "So you are a boy," she said, "who will kill a man rather than be late to meet your sweetheart? We hold together, the females of this earth. I shall mark your forehead now, so that the girls will know of that, when they look at you, and they will like you for it." She played with the boy's hair, and twisted it round her finger.

"Listen now, my little bird," said she. "My great grandson's brother-in-law is lying with his boat by the landing-place at this moment; he is to take a consignment of skins out to a Danish boat. He will bring you back to your boat, in time, before your mates come. The *Hebe* is sailing tomorrow morning, is it not so? But when you are aboard, give him back my cap for me." She took up his knife, wiped it in her skirt and handed it to him. "Here is your knife," she said. "You will stick it into no more men; you will not need to, for from now you will sail the seas like a faithful seaman. We have enough trouble with our sons as it is."

The bewildered boy began to stammer his thanks to her. "Wait," said she, "I shall make you a cup of coffee, to bring back your wits, while I wash your jacket." She went and rattled an old copper kettle upon the fireplace. After a while she handed him a hot, strong, black drink in a cup without a handle to it. "You have drunk with Sunniva now," she said; "you have drunk down a little wisdom, so that in the future all your thoughts shall not fall like raindrops into the salt sea."

When we had finished and set down the cup, she led him to the door and opened it for him. He was so surprised to see that it was almost clear morning. The house was so high up that the boy could see the sea from it, and a milky mist about it. He gave her his hand to say good-bye.

She stared into his face. "We do not forget," she said. "And you, you knocked me on the head there, high up in the mast. I shall give you that blow back." With that she smacked him on the ear as hard as she could, so that his head swam. "Now we are quits," she said, gave him a great, mischievous, shining glance, and a little push down the doorstep, and nodded to him.

In this way the sailor-boy got back to his ship, which was to sail the next morning, and lived to tell the story.

9

Tennessee's Partner

by Bret Harte

The Bride Comes to Yellow Sky

by Stephen Crane

Bret Harte *Harte was a natural raconteur; his mode, the humorous "tall-tale," laconic and anecdotal. As a young man, after leaving school at the age of thirteen to work, he visited the gold mining camps in California, which later provided material for his most successful stories, "The Outcasts of Poker Flat," "The Luck of Roaring Camp," and "Tennessee's Partner."*

Stephen Crane *Crane lived to the age of only twenty-eight, but before he died he wrote* Maggie: A Girl of the Streets, The Red Badge of Courage, *1895,* The Black Riders *(a series of caustically pungent poems that he called pills), and a number of short stories—a remarkable body of work suggesting the appearance of a powerful new potential in American literature. His death by tuberculosis was precipitated by the reckless self-exposure and courage he displayed while covering the Spanish-American War as a journalist, and with that gambit he typified the eagerness of so many American writers to dare the edge of experience for the sake of new perception.*

Tennessee's Partner

Bret Harte (*American, 1836–1902*)

I do not think that we ever knew his real name. Our ignorance of it certainly never gave us any social inconvenience, for at Sandy Bar in 1854 most men were christened anew. Sometimes these appellatives were derived from some distinctiveness of dress, as in the case of "Dungaree Jack"; or from some peculiarity of habit, as shown in "Saleratus Bill," so called from an undue proportion of that chemical in his daily bread; or from some unlucky slip, as exhibited in "The Iron Pirate," a mild, inoffensive man, who earned that baleful title by his unfortunate mispronunciation of the term "iron pyrites." Perhaps this may have been the beginning of a rude heraldry; but I am constrained to think that it was because a man's real name in that day rested solely upon his own unsupported statement. "Call yourself Clifford, do you?" said Boston, addressing a timid newcomer with infinite scorn; "hell is full of such Cliffords!" He then introduced the unfortunate man, whose name happened to be really Clifford, as "Jaybird Charley"—an unhallowed inspiration of the moment that clung to him ever after.

But to return to Tennessee's Partner, whom we never knew by any other than this relative title. That he had ever existed as a separate and distinct individuality we only learned later. It seems that in 1853 he left Poker Flat to go to San Francisco, ostensibly to procure a wife. He never got any farther than Stockton. At that place he was attracted by a young person who waited upon the table at the hotel where he took his meals. One morning he said something to her which caused her to smile not unkindly, to somewhat coquettishly break a plate of toast over his upturned, serious, simple face, and to retreat to the kitchen. He followed her, and emerged a few moments later, covered with more toast and victory. That day week they were married by a justice of the peace, and returned to Poker Flat. I am aware that something more might be made of this episode, but I prefer to tell it as it was current at Sandy Bar—in the gulches and barrooms—where all sentiment was modified by a strong sense of humor.

Of their married felicity but little is known, perhaps for the reason that Tennessee, then living with his partner, one day took occasion to say something to the bride on his own account, at which, it is said, she smiled not unkindly and chastely retreated—this time as far as Marysville, where Tennessee followed her, and where they went to housekeeping without the aid of a justice of the peace. Tennessee's Partner took the loss of his wife simply and seriously, as was his fashion. But to everybody's surprise, when Tennessee one day returned from Marysville, without his partner's wife—she having smiled and retreated with somebody else—Tennessee's Partner was the first man to shake his hand and greet him with affection. The boys who had gathered in the canyon to see the shooting were naturally indignant. Their indignation might have found vent in sarcasm but for a certain look in Tennessee's Partner's eye that indicated a lack of humorous appreciation. In fact, he was a grave man, with a steady application to practical detail which was unpleasant in a difficulty.

Meanwhile a popular feeling against Tennessee had grown up on the Bar. He was known to be a gambler; he was suspected to be a thief. In these suspicions Tennessee's Partner was equally compromised; his continued intimacy with Tennessee after the affair above quoted could only be accounted for on the hypothesis of a copartnership of crime. At last Tennessee's guilt became flagrant. One day he overtook a stranger on his way to Red Dog. The stranger afterward related that Tennessee beguiled the time with interesting anecdote and reminiscence, but illogically concluded the interview in the following words: "And now, young man, I'll trouble you for your knife, your pistols, and your money. You see your weppings might get you into trouble at Red Dog, and your money's a temptation to the evilly disposed. I think you said your address was San Francisco. I shall endeavor to call." It may be stated here that Tennessee had a fine flow of humor, which no business preoccupation could wholly subdue.

This exploit was his last. Red Dog and Sandy Bar made common cause against the highwayman. Tennessee was hunted in very much the same fashion as his prototype, the grizzly. As the toils closed around him, he made a desperate dash through the Bar, emptying his revolver at the crowd before the Arcade Saloon, and so on up Grizzly Canyon; but at its farther extremity he was stopped by a small man on a gray horse. The men looked at each other a moment in silence. Both were fearless, both self-possessed and independent, and both types of a civilization that in the seventeenth century would have been called heroic, but in the nineteenth simply "reckless."

"What have you got there?—I call," said Tennessee quietly.

"Two bowers and an ace," said the stranger as quietly, showing two revolvers and a bowie knife.

"That takes me," returned Tennessee; and with this gambler's epigram, he threw away his useless pistol and rode back with his captor.

It was a warm night. The cool breeze which usually sprang up with the going down of the sun behind the chaparral-crested mountain was that evening withheld from Sandy Bar. The little canyon was stifling with heated resinous odors, and the decaying driftwood on the Bar sent forth faint sickening exhalations. The feverishness of day and its fierce passions still filled the camp. Lights moved restlessly along the bank of the river, striking no answering reflection from its tawny current. Against the blackness of the pines the windows of the old loft above the express office stood out staringly bright; and through their curtainless panes the loungers below could see the forms of those who were even then deciding the fate of Tennessee. And above all this, etched on the dark firmament, rose the Sierra, remote and passionless, crowned with remoter passionless stars.

The trial of Tennessee was conducted as fairly as was consistent with a judge and jury who felt themselves to some extent obliged to justify, in their verdict, the previous irregularities of arrest and indictment. The law of Sandy Bar was implacable, but not vengeful. The excitement and personal feeling of the chase were over; with Tennessee safe in their hands, they were ready to listen patiently to any defense, which they were already satisfied was insufficient. There being no doubt in their own minds, they were willing to give the prisoner the benefit of any that might exist. Secure in the hypothesis that he ought to be hanged on general principles, they indulged him with more latitude of defense than his reckless hardihood seemed to ask. The Judge appeared to be more anxious than the prisoner, who, otherwise unconcerned, evidently took a grim pleasure in the responsibility he had created. "I don't take any hand in this yer game." had been his invariable but good-humored reply to all questions. The Judge—who was also his captor—for a moment vaguely regretted that he had not shot him "on sight" that morning, but presently dismissed this human weakness as unworthy of the judicial mind. Nevertheless, when there was a tap at the door, and it was said that Tennessee's Partner was there on behalf of the prisoner, he was admitted at once without question. Perhaps the younger members of the jury, to whom the proceedings were becoming irksomely thoughtful, hailed him as a relief.

For he was not, certainly, an imposing figure. Short and stout, with a square face, sunburned into a preternatural redness, clad in a loose duck "jumper" and trousers streaked and splashed with red soil, his aspect under any circumstances would have been quaint, and was now even ridiculous. As he stooped to deposit at his feet a heavy carpetbag he was carrying, it became obvious, from partially developed legends and inscriptions, that the material with which his trousers had been patched had been originally intended for a less ambitious covering. Yet he advanced with great gravity, and after shaking the hand of each person in the room with labored cordiality, he wiped his serious perplexed face on a red bandana handkerchief, a shade lighter than his complexion, laid his powerful hand upon the table to steady himself, and thus addressed the Judge:

"I was passin' by," he began, by way of apology, "and I thought I'd just step in and see how things was gittin' on with Tennessee thar—my pardner. It's a hot night. I disremember any sich weather before on the Bar."

He paused a moment, but nobody volunteering any other meteorological recollection, he again had recourse to his pocket handkerchief, and for some moments mopped his face diligently.

"Have you anything to say on behalf of the prisoner?" said the Judge finally.

"Thet's it," said Tennessee's Partner, in a tone of relief. "I come yar as Tennessee's pardner—knowing him nigh on four year, off and on, wet and dry, in luck and out o' luck. His ways ain't aller my ways, but thar ain't any p'ints in that young man, thar ain't any liveliness as he's been up to, as I don't know. And you sez to me, sez you—confidential-like, and between man and man—sez you, 'Do you know anything in his behalf?' and I sez to you, sez I—confidential-like, as between man and man—'What should a man know of his pardner?'"

"Is this all you have to say?" asked the Judge impatiently, feeling, perhaps, that a dangerous sympathy of humor was beginning to humanize the court.

"Thet's so," continued Tennessee's Partner. "It ain't for me to say anything agin' him. And now, what's the case? Here's Tennessee wants money, wants it bad, and doesn't like to ask it of his old pardner. Well, what does Tennessee do? He lays for a stranger, and he fetches that stranger; and you lays for *him*, and you fetches *him*; and the honors is easy. And I put it to you, bein' a fa'r-minded man, and to you, gentlemen all, as fa'r-minded men, ef this isn't so."

"Prisoner," said the Judge, interrupting, "have you any questions to ask this man?"

"No! no!" continued Tennessee's Partner hastily. "I play this yer hand alone. To come down to the bedrock, it's just this: Tennessee thar has played it pretty rough and expensivelike on a stranger, and on this yer camp. And now, what's the fair thing? Some would say more, some would say less. Here's seventeen hundred dollars in coarse gold and a watch—it's about all my pile—and call it square!" And before a hand could be raised to prevent him, he had emptied the contents of the carpetbag upon the table.

For a moment his life was in jeopardy. One or two men sprang to their feet, several hands groped for hidden weapons, and a suggestion to "throw him from the window" was only overridden by a gesture from the Judge. Tennessee laughed. And apparently oblivious of the excitement, Tennessee's Partner improved the opportunity to mop his face again with his handkerchief.

When order was restored, and the man was made to understand by the use of forcible figures and rhetoric that Tennessee's offense could not be condoned by money, his face took a more serious and sanguinary hue, and those who were nearest to him noticed that his rough hand trembled slightly on the table. He hesitated a moment as he slowly returned the gold to the carpetbag, as if he had not yet entirely caught the elevated sense of justice which swayed the tribunal, and was perplexed with the belief that he had not offered enough. Then he turned to the Judge, and saying, "This yer is a lone hand, played alone, and without my pardner," he bowed to the jury and was about to withdraw, when the Judge called him back:

"If you have anything to say to Tennessee, you had better say it now."

For the first time that evening the eyes of the prisoner and his strange advocate met. Tennessee smiled, showed his white teeth, and saying, "Euchred, old man!" held out his hand. Tennessee's Partner took it in his own, and saying, "I just dropped in as I was passin' to see how things was gettin' on," let the hand passively fall, and adding that "it was a warm night," again mopped his face with his handkerchief, and without another word withdrew.

The two men never again met each other alive. For the unparalleled insult of a bribe offered to Judge Lynch—who, whether bigoted, weak, or narrow, was at least incorruptible—firmly fixed in the mind of that mythical personage any wavering determination of Tennessee's fate; and at the break of day he was marched, closely guarded, to meet it at the top of Marley's Hill.

How he met it, how cool he was, how he refused to say anything, how perfect were the arrangements of the committee, were all duly reported, with the addition of a warning moral and example to all future evildoers, in the *Red Dog Clarion* by its editor, who was present, and to whose vigorous English I cheerfully refer the reader. But the beauty of that midsummer morning, the blessed amity of earth and air and sky, the awakened life of the free woods and hills, the joyous renewal and promise of Nature, and above all, the infinite serenity that thrilled through each, was not reported, as not being a part of the social lesson. And yet, when the weak and foolish deed was done, and a life, with its possibilities and responsibilities, had passed out of the misshapen thing that dangled between earth and sky, the birds sang, the flowers bloomed, the sun shone, as cheerily as before; and possibly the *Red Dog Clarion* was right.

Tennessee's Partner was not in the group that surrounded the ominous tree. But as they turned to disperse, attention was drawn to the singular appearance of a motionless donkey cart halted at the side of the road. As they approached, they at once recognized the venerable Jenny and the two-wheeled cart as the property of Tennessee's Partner, used by him in carrying dirt from his claim; and a few paces distant the owner of the equipage himself, sitting under a buckeye tree, wiping the perspiration from his glowing face. In answer to an inquiry, he said he had come for the body of the "diseased," "if it was all the same to the committee." He didn't wish to "hurry anything;" he could "wait." He was not working that day; and when the gentlemen were done with the "diseased," he would take him. "Ef thar is any present," he added, in his simple, serious way, "as would care to jine in the fun'l, they kin come."

Perhaps it was from a sense of humor, which I have already intimated was a feature of Sandy Bar—perhaps it was from something even better than that, but two thirds of the loungers accepted the invitation at once.

It was noon when the body of Tennessee was delivered into the hands of his partner. As the cart drew up to the fatal tree, we noticed that it contained a rough oblong box—apparently made from a section of sluicing—and half filled with bark and the tassels of pine. The cart was further decorated with slips of willow and made fragrant with buckeye blossoms. When the body was deposited in the box, Tennessee's Partner drew over it a piece of tarred canvas, and gravely mounting the narrow seat in front, with his feet upon the shafts, urged the little donkey forward. The equipage moved slowly on, at that decorous pace which was habitual with Jenny even under less solemn circumstances. The men—half curiously, half jestingly, but all good-humoredly—strolled along beside the cart, some in advance, some a little in the rear of the homely catafalque. But whether from the narrowing of the road or some present sense of decorum, as the cart passed on, the company fell to the rear in couples, keeping step, and otherwise assuming the external show of a formal procession. Jack Folinsbee, who had at the outset played a funeral march in dumb show upon an imaginary trombone, desisted from a lack of sympathy and appreciation—not having, perhaps, your true humorist's capacity to be content with the enjoyment of his own fun.

The way led through Grizzly Canyon, by this time clothed in funereal drapery and shadows. The redwoods, burying their moccasined feet in the red soil, stood in Indian file along the track, trailing an uncouth benediction from their bending boughs upon the passing bier. A hare, surprised into helpless inactivity, sat upright and pulsating in the ferns by the roadside as the cortége went by. Squirrels hastened to gain a secure outlook from higher boughs; and the blue jays, spreading their wings, fluttered before them like outriders, until the outskirts of Sandy Bar were reached, and the solitary cabin of Tennessee's Partner.

Viewed under more favorable circumstances, it would not have been a cheerful place. The unpicturesque site, the rude and unlovely outlines, the unsavory details, which distinguish the nest-building of the California miner, were all here with the dreariness of decay superadded. A few paces from the cabin there was a rough enclosure, which, in the brief days of Tennessee's Partner's matrimonial felicity, had been used as a garden, but was now overgrown with fern. As we approached it, we were surprised to find that what we had taken for a recent attempt at cultivation was the broken soil about an open grave.

The cart was halted before the enclosure, and rejecting the offers of assistance with the same air of simple self-reliance he had displayed throughout, Tennessee's Partner lifted the rough coffin on his back, and deposited it unaided within the shallow grave. He then nailed down the board which served as a lid, and mounting the little mound of earth beside it, took off his hat and slowly mopped his face with his handkerchief. This the crowd felt was a preliminary to speech, and they disposed themselves variously on stumps and boulders, and sat expectant.

"When a man," began Tennessee's Partner slowly, "has been running free all day, what's the natural thing for him to do? Why, to come home. And if he ain't in a condition to go home, what can his best friend do? Why, bring him home. And here's Tennessee has been running free, and we brings him home from his wandering." He paused and picked up a fragment of quartz, rubbed it thoughtfully on his sleeve, and went on: "It ain't the first time that I've packed him on my back, as you see'd me now. It ain't the first time that I brought him to this yer cabin when he couldn't help himself; it ain't the first time that I and Jinny have waited for him on yon hill, and picked him up and so fetched him home, when he couldn't speak and didn't know me. And now that it's the last time, why"—he paused and rubbed the quartz gently on his sleeve—"you see it's sort of rough on his pardner. And now, gentlemen," he added abruptly, picking up his long-handled shovel, "the fun'l's over; and my thanks, and Tennessee's thanks, to you for your trouble."

Resisting any proffers of assistance, he began to fill in the grave, turning his back upon the crowd, that after a few moments' hesitation gradually withdrew. As they crossed the little ridge that hid Sandy Bar from view, some, looking back, thought they could see Tennessee's Partner, his work done, sitting upon the grave, his shovel between his knees, and his face buried in his red bandana handkerchief. But it was argued by others that you couldn't tell his face from his handkerchief at that distance, and this point remained undecided.

In the reaction that followed the feverish excitement of that day, Tennessee's Partner was not forgotten. A secret investigation had cleared him of any complicity in Tennessee's guilt, and left only a suspicion of his general sanity. Sandy Bar made a point of calling on him, and proffering various uncouth but well-meant kindnesses.

But from that day his rude health and great strength seemed visibly to decline; and when the rainy season fairly set in, and the tiny grass blades were beginning to peep from the rocky mound above Tennessee's grave, he took to his bed.

One night, when the pines beside the cabin were swaying in the storm and trailing their slender fingers over the roof, and the roar and rush of the swollen river were heard below, Tennessee's Partner lifted his head from the pillow, saying, "It is time to go for Tennessee; I must put Jinny in the cart;" and would have risen from his bed but for the restraint of his attendant. Struggling, he still pursued his singular fancy: "There, now, steady, Jinny, steady, old girl. How dark it is! Look out for the ruts, and look out for him, too, old gal. Sometimes, you know, when he's blind drunk, he drops down right in the trail. Keep on straight up to the pine on the top of the hill. Thar! I told you so!—thar he is—coming this way, too—all by himself, sober, and his face a-shining. Tennessee! Pardner!"

And so they met.

The Bride Comes to Yellow Sky

Stephen Crane (*American, 1871–1900*)

The great Pullman was whirling onward with such dignity of motion that a glance from the window seemed simply to prove that the plains of Texas were pouring eastward. Vast flats of green grass, dull-hued spaces of mesquit and cactus, little groups of frame houses, woods of light and tender trees, all were sweeping into the east, sweeping over the horizon, a precipice.

A newly married pair had boarded this coach at San Antonio. The man's face was reddened from many days in the wind and sun, and a direct result of his new black clothes was that his brick-coloured hands were constantly performing in a most conscious fashion. From time to time he looked down respectfully at his attire. He sat with a hand on each knee, like a man waiting in a barber's shop. The glances he devoted to other passengers were furtive and shy.

The bride was not pretty, nor was she very young. She wore a dress of blue cashmere, with small reservations of velvet here and there, and with steel buttons abounding. She continually twisted her head to regard her puff sleeves, very stiff, straight, and high. They embarrassed her. It was quite apparent that she had cooked, and that she expected to cook, dutifully. The blushes caused by the careless scrutiny of some passengers as she had entered the car were strange to see upon this plain, under-class countenance, which was drawn in placid, almost emotionless lines.

They were evidently very happy. "Ever been in a parlour-car before?" he asked, smiling with delight.

"No," she answered; "I never was. It's fine, ain't it?"

"Great! And then after a while we'll go forward to the diner, and get a big lay-out. Finest meal in the world. Charge a dollar."

"Oh, do they?" cried the bride. "Charge a dollar? Why, that's too much—for us—ain't it, Jack?"

"Not this trip, anyhow," he answered bravely. "We're going to go the whole thing."

Later he explained to her about the trains. "You see, it's a thousand miles from one end of Texas to the other; and this train runs right across it, and never stops but four times." He had the pride of an owner. He pointed out to her the dazzling fittings of the coach; and in truth her eyes opened wider as she contemplated the sea-green figured velvet, the shining brass, silver, and glass, the wood that gleamed as darkly brilliant as the surface of a pool of oil. At one end a bronze figure sturdily held a support for a separated chamber, and at convenient places on the ceiling were frescos in olive and silver.

To the minds of the pair, their surroundings reflected the glory of their marriage that morning in San Antonio; this was the environment of their new estate; and the man's face in particular beamed with an elation that made him appear ridiculous to the negro porter. This individual at times surveyed them from afar with an amused and superior grin. On other occasions he bullied them with skill in ways that did not make it exactly plain to them that they were being bullied. He subtly used all the manners of the most unconquerable kind of snobbery. He oppressed them; but of this oppression they had small knowledge, and they speedily forgot that infrequently a number of travellers covered them with stares of derisive enjoyment. Historically there was supposed to be something infinitely humorous in their situation.

"We are due in Yellow Sky at 3:42," he said, looking tenderly into her eyes.

"Oh, are we?" she said, as if she had not been aware of it. To evince surprise at her husband's statement was part of her wifely amiability. She took from a pocket a little silver watch; and as she held it before her, and stared at it with a frown of attention, the new husband's face shone.

"I bought it in San Anton' from a friend of mine," he told her gleefully.

"It's seventeen minutes past twelve," she said, looking up at him with a kind of shy and clumsy coquetry. A passenger, noting this play, grew excessively sardonic, and winked at himself in one of the numerous mirrors.

At last they went to the dining-car. Two rows of negro waiters, in glowing white suits, surveyed their entrance with the interest, and also the equanimity, of men who had been forewarned. The pair fell to the lot of a waiter who happened to feel pleasure in steering them through their meal. He viewed them with the manner of a fatherly pilot, his countenance radiant with benevolence. The patronage, entwined with the ordinary deference, was not plain to them. And yet, as they returned to their coach, they showed in their faces a sense of escape.

To the left, miles down a long purple slope, was a little ribbon of mist where moved the keening Rio Grande. The train was approaching it at an angle, and the apex was Yellow Sky. Presently it was apparent that, as the distance from Yellow Sky grew shorter, the husband became commensurately restless. His brick-red hands were more insistent in their prominence. Occasionally he was even rather absent-minded and far-away when the bride leaned forward and addressed him.

As a matter of truth, Jack Potter was beginning to find the shadow of a deed weigh upon him like a leaden slab. He, the town marshal of Yellow Sky, a man known, liked, and feared in his corner, a prominent person, had gone to San Antonio to meet a girl he believed he loved, and there, after the usual prayers, had actually induced her to marry him, without consulting Yellow Sky for any part of the transaction. He was now bringing his bride before an innocent and unsuspecting community.

Of course people in Yellow Sky married as it pleased them, in accordance with a general custom; but such was Potter's thought of his duty to his friends, or of their idea of his duty, or of an unspoken form which does not control men in these matters, that he felt he was heinous. He had committed an extraordinary crime. Face to face with this girl in San Antonio, and spurred by his sharp impulse, he had gone headlong over all the social hedges. At San Antonio he was like a man hidden in the dark. A knife to sever any friendly duty, any form, was easy to his hand in that remote city. But the hour of Yellow Sky—the hour of daylight—was approaching.

He knew full well that his marriage was an important thing to his town. It could only be exceeded by the burning of the new hotel. His friends could not forgive him. Frequently he had reflected on the advisability of telling them by telegraph, but a new cowardice had been upon him. He feared to do it. And now the train was hurrying him toward a scene of amazement, glee, and reproach. He glanced out of the window at the line of haze swinging slowly in toward the train.

Yellow Sky had a kind of brass band, which played painfully, to the delight of the populace. He laughed without heart as he thought of it. If the citizens could dream of his prospective arrival with his bride, they would parade the band at the station and escort them, amid cheers and laughing congratulations, to his adobe home.

He resolved that he would use all the devices of speed and plainscraft in making the journey from the station to his house. Once within that safe citadel, he could issue some sort of vocal bulletin, and then not go among the citizens until they had time to wear off a little of their enthusiasm.

The bride looked anxiously at him. "What's worrying you, Jack?"

He laughed again. "I'm not worrying, girl; I'm only thinking of Yellow Sky."

She flushed in comprehension.

A sense of mutual guilt invaded their minds and developed a finer tenderness. They looked at each other with eyes softly aglow. But Potter often laughed the same nervous laugh; the flush upon the bride's face seemed quite permanent.

The traitor to the feelings of Yellow Sky narrowly watched the speeding landscape. "We're nearly there," he said.

Presently the porter came and announced the proximity of Potter's home. He held a brush in his hand, and, with all his airy superiority gone, he brushed Potter's new clothes as the latter slowly turned this way and that way. Potter fumbled out a coin and gave it to the porter, as he had seen others do. It was a heavy and muscle-bound business, as that of a man shoeing his first horse.

The porter took their bag, and as the train began to slow they moved forward to the hooded platform of the car. Presently the two engines and their long string of coaches rushed into the station of Yellow Sky.

"They have to take water here," said Potter, from a constricted throat and in mournful cadence, as one announcing death. Before the train stopped his eye had swept the length of the platform, and he was glad and astonished to see there was none upon it but the station-agent, who, with a slightly hurried and anxious air, was walking toward the water-tanks. When the train had halted, the porter alighted first, and placed in position a little temporary step.

"Come on, girl," said Potter, hoarsely. As he helped her down they each laughed on a false note. He took the bag from the negro, and bade his wife cling to his arm. As they slunk rapidly away, his hang-dog glance perceived that they were unloading the two trunks, and also that the station-agent, far ahead near the baggage-car, had turned and was running toward him, making gestures. He laughed, and groaned as he laughed, when he noted the first effect of his marital bliss upon Yellow Sky. He gripped his wife's arm firmly to his side, and they fled. Behind them the porter stood, chuckling fatuously.

II

The California express on the Southern Railway was due at Yellow Sky in twenty-one minutes. There were six men at the bar of the Weary Gentleman saloon. One was a drummer who talked a great deal and rapidly; three were Texans who did not care to talk at that time; and two were Mexican sheep-herders, who did not talk as a general practice in the Weary Gentleman saloon. The barkeeper's dog lay on the board walk that crossed in front of the door. His head was on his paws, and he glanced drowsily here and there with the constant vigilance of a dog that is kicked on occasion. Across the sandy street were some vivid green grass-plots, so wonderful in appearance, amid the sands that burned near them in a blazing sun, that they caused a doubt in the mind. They exactly resembled the grass mats used to represent lawns on the stage. At the cooler end of the railway station, a man without a coat sat in a tilted chair and smoked his pipe. The fresh-cut bank of the Rio Grande circled near the town, and there could be seen beyond it a great plum-coloured plain of mesquit.

Save for the busy drummer and his companions in the saloon, Yellow Sky was dozing. The new-comer leaned gracefully upon the bar, and recited many tales with the confidence of a bard who has come upon a new field.

"—and at the moment that the old man fell downstairs with the bureau in his arms, the old woman was coming up with two scuttles of coal, and of course—"

The drummer's tale was interrupted by a young man who suddenly appeared in the open door. He cried: "Scratchy Wilson's drunk, and has turned loose with both hands." The two Mexicans at once set down their glasses and faded out of the rear entrance of the saloon.

The drummer, innocent and jocular, answered: "All right, old man. S'pose he has? Come in and have a drink, anyhow."

But the information had made such an obvious cleft in every skull in the room that the drummer was obliged to see its importance. All had become instantly solemn. "Say," said he, mystified, "what is this?" His three companions made the introductory gesture of eloquent speech; but the young man at the door forestalled them.

"It means, my friend," he answered, as he came into the saloon, "that for the next two hours this town won't be a health resort."

The barkeeper went to the door, and locked and barred it; reaching out of the window, he pulled in heavy wooden shutters, and barred them. Immediately a solemn, chapel-like gloom was upon the place. The drummer was looking from one to another.

"But say," he cried, "what is this, anyhow? You don't mean there is going to be a gun-fight?"

"Don't know whether there'll be a fight or not," answered one man, grimly; "but there'll be some shootin'—some good shootin'."

The young man who had warned them waved his hand. "Oh, there'll be a fight fast enough, if anyone wants it. Anybody can get a fight out there in the street. There's a fight just waiting."

The drummer seemed to be swayed between the interest of a foreigner and a perception of personal danger.

"What did you say his name was?" he asked.

"Scratchy Wilson," they answered in chorus.

"And will he kill anybody? What are you going to do? Does this happen often? Does he rampage around like this once a week or so? Can he break in that door?"

"No; he can't break down that door," replied the barkeeper. "He's tried it three times. But when he comes you'd better lay down on the floor, stranger. He's dead sure to shoot at it, and a bullet may come through."

Thereafter the drummer kept a strict eye upon the door. The time had not yet been called for him to hug the floor, but, as a minor precaution, he sidled near to the wall. "Will he kill anybody?" he said again.

The men laughed low and scornfully at the question.

"He's out to shoot, and he's out for trouble. Don't see any good in experimentin' with him."

"But what do you do in a case like this? What do you do?"

A man responded: "Why, he and Jack Potter—"

"But," in chorus the other men interrupted, "Jack Potter's in San Anton'."

"Well, who is he? What's he got to do with it?"

"Oh, he's the town marshal. He goes out and fights Scratchy when he gets on one of these tears.

"Wow!" said the drummer, mopping his brow. "Nice job he's got."

The voices had toned away to mere whisperings. The drummer wished to ask further questions, which were born of an increasing anxiety and bewilderment; but when he attempted them, the men merely looked at him in irritation and motioned him to remain silent. A tense waiting hush was upon them. In the deep shadows of the room their eyes shone as they listened for sounds from the street. One man made three gestures at the barkeeper; and the latter, moving like a ghost, handed him a glass and a bottle. The man poured a full glass of whisky, and set down the bottle noiselessly. He gulped the whisky in a swallow, and turned again toward the door in immovable silence. The drummer saw that the barkeeper, without a sound, had taken a Winchester from beneath the bar. Later he saw this individual beckoning to him, so he tiptoed across the room.

"You better come with me back of the bar."

"No, thanks," said the drummer, perspiring; "I'd rather be where I can make a break for the back door."

Whereupon the man of bottles made a kindly but peremptory gesture. The drummer obeyed it, and, finding himself seated on a box with his head below the level of the bar, balm was laid upon his soul at sight of various zinc and copper fittings that bore a resemblance to armour-plate. The barkeeper took a seat comfortably upon an adjacent box.

"You see," he whispered, "this here Scratchy Wilson is a wonder with a gun—a perfect wonder; and when he goes on the war-trail, we hunt our holes—naturally. He's about the last one of the old gang that used to hang out along the river here. He's a terror when he's drunk. When he's sober he's all right—kind of simple—wouldn't hurt a fly—nicest fellow in town. But when he's drunk—whoo!"

There were periods of stillness. "I wish Jack Potter was back from San Anton'," said the barkeeper. "He shot Wilson up once—in the leg—and he would sail in and pull out the kinks in this thing."

Presently they heard from a distance the sound of a shot, followed by three wild yowls. It instantly removed a bond from the men in the darkened saloon. There was a shuffling of feet. They looked at each other. "Here he comes," they said.

III

A man in a maroon-coloured flannel shirt, which had been purchased for purposes of decoration, and made principally by some Jewish women on the East Side of New York, rounded a corner and walked into the middle of the main street of Yellow Sky. In either hand the man held a long, heavy, blue-black revolver. Often he yelled, and these cries rang through a semblance of a deserted village, shrilly flying over the roofs in a volume that seemed to have no relation to the ordinary vocal strength of a man. It was as if the surrounding stillness formed the arch of a tomb over him. These cries of ferocious challenge rang against walls of silence. And his boots had red tops with gilded imprints, of the kind beloved in winter by little sledding boys on the hillsides of New England.

The man's face flamed in a rage begot of whisky. His eyes, rolling, and yet keen for ambush, hunted the still doorways and windows. He walked with the creeping movement of the midnight cat. As it occurred to him, he roared menacing information. The long revolvers in his hands were as easy as straws; they were moved with an electric swiftness. The little fingers of each hand played sometimes in a musician's way. Plain from the low collar of the shirt, the cords of his neck straightened and sank, straightened and sank, as passion moved him. The only sounds were his terrible invitations. The calm adobes preserved their demeanour at the passing of this small thing in the middle of the street.

There was no offer of fight—no offer of fight. The man called to the sky. There were no attractions. He bellowed and fumed and swayed his revolvers here and everywhere.

The dog of the barkeeper of the Weary Gentleman saloon had not appreciated the advance of events. He yet lay dozing in front of his master's door. At sight of the dog, the man paused and raised his revolver humorously. At sight of the man, the dog sprang up and walked diagonally away, with a sullen head, and growling. The man yelled, and the dog broke into a gallop. As it was about to enter an alley, there was a loud noise, a whistling, and something spat the ground directly before it. The dog screamed, and, wheeling in terror, galloped headlong in a new direction. Again there was a noise, a whistling, and sand was kicked viciously before it. Fear-stricken, the dog turned and flurried like an animal in a pen. The man stood laughing, his weapons at his hips.

Ultimately the man was attracted by the closed door of the

Weary Gentleman saloon. He went to it and, hammering with a revolver, demanded drink.

The door remaining imperturbable, he picked a bit of paper from the walk, and nailed it to the framework with a knife. He then turned his back contemptuously upon this popular resort and, walking to the opposite side of the street and spinning there on his heel quickly and lithely, fired at the bit of paper. He missed it by a half-inch. He swore at himself, and went away. Later he comfortably fusilladed the windows of his most intimate friend. The man was playing with this town; it was a toy for him.

But still there was no offer of fight. The name of Jack Potter, his ancient antagonist, entered his mind, and he concluded that it would be a glad thing if he should go to Potter's house, and by bombardment induce him to come out and fight. He moved in the direction of his desire, chanting Apache scalp-music.

When he arrived at it, Potter's house presented the same still front as had the other adobes. Taking up a strategic position, the man howled a challenge. But this house regarded him as might a great stone god. It gave no sign. After a decent wait, the man howled further challenges, mingling with them wonderful epithets.

Presently there came the spectacle of a man churning himself into deepest rage over the immobility of a house. He fumed at it as the winter wind attacks a prairie cabin in the North. To the distance there should have gone the sound of a tumult like the fighting of two hundred Mexicans. As necessity bade him, he paused for breath or to reload his revolvers.

IV

Potter and his bride walked sheepishly and with speed. Sometimes they laughed together shamefacedly and low.

"Next corner, dear," he said finally.

They put forth the efforts of a pair walking bowed against a strong wind. Potter was about to raise a finger to point the first appearance of the new home when, as they circled the corner, they came face to face with a man in a maroon-coloured shirt, who was feverishly pushing cartridges into a large revolver. Upon the instant the man dropped his revolver to the ground and, like lightning, whipped another from its holster. The second weapon was aimed at the bridegroom's chest.

There was a silence. Potter's mouth seemed to be merely a grave for his tongue. He exhibited an instinct to at once loosen his arm from the woman's grip, and he dropped the bag to the sand. As for the bride, her face had gone as yellow as old cloth. She was a slave to hideous rites, gazing at the apparitional snake.

The two men faced each other at a distance of three paces. He of the revolver smiled with a new and quiet ferocity.

"Tried to sneak up on me," he said. "Tried to sneak up on me!" His eyes grew more baleful. As Potter made a slight movement, the man thrust his revolver venomously forward. "No; don't you do it, Jack Potter. Don't you move a finger toward a gun just yet. Don't you move an eyelash. The time has come for me to settle with you, and I'm goin' to do it my own way, and loaf along with no interferin'. So if you don't want a gun bent on you, just mind what I tell you."

Potter looked at his enemy. "I ain't got a gun on me Scratchy," he said. "Honest, I ain't." He was stiffening and steadying, but yet somewhere at the back of his mind a vision of the Pullman floated: the sea-green figured velvet, the shining brass, silver, and glass, the wood that gleamed as darkly brilliant as the surface of a pool of oil—all the glory of the marriage, the environment of the new estate. "You know I fight when it comes to fighting, Scratchy Wilson; but I ain't got a gun on me. You'll have to do all the shootin' yourself."

His enemy's face went livid. He stepped forward, and lashed his weapon to and fro before Potter's chest. "Don't you tell me you ain't got no gun on you, you whelp. Don't tell me no lie like that. There ain't a man in Texas ever seen you without no gun. Don't take me for no kid." His eyes blazed with light, and his throat worked like a pump.

"I ain't takin' you for no kid," answered Potter. His heels had not moved an inch backward. "I'm takin' you for a damn fool. I tell you I ain't got a gun, and I ain't. If you're goin' to shoot me up, you better begin now; you'll never get a chance like this again."

So much enforced reasoning had told on Wilson's rage; he was calmer. "If you ain't got a gun, why ain't you got a gun?" he sneered. "Been to Sunday-school?"

"I ain't got a gun because I've just come from San Anton' with my wife. I'm married," said Potter. "And if I'd thought there was going to be any galoots like you prowling around when I brought my wife home, I'd had a gun, and don't you forget it."

"Married!" said Scratchy, not at all comprehending.

"Yes, married. I'm married," said Potter, distinctly.

"Married?" said Scratchy. Seemingly for the first time, he saw the drooping, drowning woman at the other man's side. "No!" he said. He was like a creature allowed a glimpse of another world. He moved a pace backward, and his arm, with the revolver, dropped to his side. "Is this the lady?" he asked.

"Yes; this is the lady," answered Potter.

There was another period of silence.

"Well," said Wilson at last, slowly, "I s'pose it's all off now."

"It's all off if you say so, Scratchy. You know I didn't make the trouble." Potter lifted his valise.

"Well, I 'low it's off, Jack," said Wilson. He was looking at the ground. "Married!" He was not a student of chivalry; it was merely that in the presence of this foreign condition he was a simple child of the earlier plains. He picked up his starboard revolver, and, placing both weapons in their holsters, he went away. His feet made funnel-shaped tracks in the heavy sand.

10

First Confession

by Frank O'Connor

Innocence

by Seán O'Faoláin

Frank O'Connor *Frank O'Connor was originally Michael O'Donovan of Cork, Ireland, the son of a charwoman and a frequently drunk soldier. O'Connor's formal education ended at age fourteen, when he went to work; two years later he joined the Irish Republican Army. After much fighting and at least two imprisonments, he became disillusioned and saddened at the continuing prospect of "Irishmen murdering Irishmen."*

Turning his impressive energies to his continuing self-education, O'Connor became first a librarian and then a director of the Abbey Theatre, all the time writing poems, essays, and particularly short stories. The story, O'Connor has remarked "is the nearest thing one can get to the quality of a pure lyric poem."

Seán O'Faoláin *Like his countryman O'Connor, Seán O'Faoláin was born in Cork and was active in the Irish rebellion. He subsequently attended the National University of Ireland and Harvard University. Although he had begun writing at a quite early age, at Harvard he began to write seriously.*

Best known for his short stories, O'Faoláin was also an accomplished novelist, critic, and biographer. "Innocence" comes from his volume called The Man Who Invented Sin, and Other Stories, *1949.*

First Confession

Frank O'Connor (*Irish, 1903–1966*)

It was a Saturday afternoon in early spring. A small boy whose face looked as though it had been but newly scrubbed was being led by the hand by his sister through a crowded street. The little boy showed a marked reluctance to proceed; he affected to be very interested in the shop-windows. Equally, his sister seemed to pay no attention to them. She tried to hurry him; he resisted. When she dragged him he began to bawl. The hatred with which she viewed him was almost diabolical, but when she spoke her words and tone were full of passionate sympathy.

"Ah, sha, God help us!" she intoned into his ear in a whine of commiseration.

"Leave me go!" he said, digging his heels into the pavement. "I don't want to go. I want to go home."

"But, sure, you can't go home, Jackie. You'll have to go. The parish priest will be up to the house with a stick."

"I don't care. I won't go."

"Oh, Sacred Heart, isn't it a terrible pity you weren't a good boy? Oh, Jackie, me heart bleeds for you! I don't know what they'll do to you at all, Jackie, me poor child. And all the trouble you caused your poor old nanny, and the way you wouldn't eat in the same room with her, and the time you kicked her on the shins, and the time you went for me with the bread knife under the table. I don't know will he ever listen to you at all, Jackie. I think meself he might sind you to the bishop. Oh, Jackie, how will you think of all your sins?"

Half stupefied with terror, Jackie allowed himself to be led through the sunny streets to the very gates of the church. It was an old one with two grim iron gates and a long, low, shapeless stone front. At the gates he stuck, but it was already too late. She dragged him behind her across the yard, and the commiserating whine with which she had tried to madden him gave place to a yelp of triumph.

"Now you're caught! Now, you're caught. And I hope he'll give you the pinitintial psalms! That'll cure you, you suppurating little caffler!"

Jackie gave himself up for lost. Within the old church there was no stained glass; it was cold and dark and desolate, and in the silence, the trees in the yard knocked hollowly at the tall windows. He allowed himself to be led through the vaulted silence, the intense and magical silence which seemed to have frozen within the ancient walls, buttressing them and shouldering the high wooden roof. In the street outside, yet seeming a million miles away, a ballad singer was drawling a ballad.

Nora sat in front of him beside the confession box. There were a few old women before her, and later a thin, sad-looking man with long hair came and sat beside Jackie. In the intense silence of the church that seemed to grow deeper from the plaintive moaning of the ballad singer, he could hear the buzz-buzz-buzz of a woman's voice in the box, and then the husky ba-ba-ba of the priest's. Lastly the soft thud of something that signalled the end of the confession, and out came the woman, head lowered, hands joined, looking neither to right nor left, and tiptoed up to the altar to say her penance.

It seemed only a matter of seconds till Nora rose and with a whispered injunction disappeared from his sight. He was all alone. Alone and next to be heard and the fear of damnation in his soul. He looked at the sadfaced man. He was gazing at the roof, his hands joined in prayer. A woman in a red blouse and black shawl had taken her place below him. She uncovered her head, fluffed her hair out roughly with her hand, brushed it sharply back, then, bowing, caught it in a knot and pinned it on her neck. Nora emerged. Jackie rose and looked at her with a hatred which was inappropriate to the occasion and the place. Her hands were joined on her stomach, her eyes modestly lowered, and her face had an expression of the most rapt and tender recollection. With death in his heart he crept into the compartment she left open and drew the door shut behind him.

He was in pitch darkness. He could see no priest nor anything else. And anything he had heard of confession got all muddled up in his mind. He knelt to the right-hand wall and said: "Bless me, father, for I have sinned. This is my first confession." Nothing happened. He repeated it louder. Still it gave no answer. He turned to the opposite wall, genuflected first, then again went on his knees and repeated the charm. This time he was certain he would receive a reply, but none came. He repeated the process with the remaining wall without effect. He had the feeling of someone with an unfamiliar machine, of pressing buttons at random. And finally the thought struck him that God knew. God knew about the bad confession he intended to make and had made him deaf and blind so that he could neither hear nor see the priest.

Then as his eyes grew accustomed to the blackness, he perceived something he had not noticed previously: a sort of shelf at about the height of his head. The purpose of this eluded him for a moment. Then he understood. It was for kneeling on.

He had always prided himself upon his powers of climbing, but this took it out of him. There was no foothold. He slipped twice before he succeeded in getting his knee on it, and the strain of drawing the rest of his body up was almost more than he was capable of. However, he did at last get his two knees on it, there was just room for those, but his legs hung down uncomfortably and the edge of the shelf bruised his shins. He joined his hands and pressed the last remaining button. "Bless me, father for I have sinned. This is my first confession."

At the same moment the slide was pushed back and a dim light streamed into the little box. There was an uncomfortable silence, and then an alarmed voice asked, "Who's there?" Jackie found it almost impossible to speak into the grille which was on a level with his knees, but he got a firm grip on the molding above it, bent his head down and sideways, and as though he were hanging by his feet like a monkey found himself looking almost upside down at the priest. But the priest was looking sideways at him, and Jackie, whose knees were being tortured by this new position, felt it was a queer way to hear confessions.

"'Tis me, father," he piped, and then, running all his words together in excitement, he rattled off, "Bless me, father, for I have sinned. This is my first confession."

"What?" exclaimed a deep and angry voice, and the sombre soutaned figure stood bolt upright, disappearing almost entirely from Jackie's view. "What does this mean? What are you doing there? Who are you?"

And with the shock Jackie felt his hands lose their grip and his legs their balance. He discovered himself tumbling into space, and, falling, he knocked his head against the door, which shot open and permitted him to thump right into the center of the aisle. Straight on this came a small, dark-haired priest with a biretta well forward on his head. At the same time Nora came skeltering madly down the church.

"Lord God!" she cried. "The snivelling little caffler! I knew he'd do it! I knew he'd disgrace me!"

Jackie received a clout over the ear which reminded him that for some strange reason he had not yet begun to cry and that people might possibly think he wasn't hurt at all. Nora slapped him again.

"What's this? What's this?" cried the priest. "Don't attempt to beat the child, you little vixen!"

"I can't do me pinance with him," cried Nora shrilly, cocking a shocked eye on the priest. "He have me driven mad. Stop your crying, you dirty scut! Stop it now or I'll make you cry at the other side of your ugly puss!"

"Run away out of this, you little jade!" growled the priest. He suddenly began to laugh, took out a pocket handkerchief, and wiped Jackie's nose. "You're not hurt, sure you're not. Show us the ould head. . . . Ah, 'tis nothing. 'Twill be better before you're twice married. . . . So you were coming to confession?"

"I was, father."

"A big fellow like you should have terrible sins. Is it your first?"

"'Tis, father."

"Oh, my, worse and worse! Here, sit down there and wait till I get rid of these ould ones and we'll have a long chat. Never mind that sister of yours."

With a feeling of importance that glowed through his tears Jackie waited. Nora stuck out her tongue at him, but he didn't even bother to reply. A great feeling of relief was welling up in him. The sense of oppression that had been weighing him down for a week, the knowledge that he was about to make a bad confession, disappeared. Bad confession, indeed! He had made friends, made friends with the priest, and the priest expected, even demanded terrible sins. Oh, women! Women! It was all women and girls and their silly talk. They had no real knowledge of the world!

And when the time came for him to make his confession he did not beat about the bush. He may have clenched his hands and lowered his eyes, but wouldn't anyone?

"Father," he said huskily, "I made it up to kill me grandmother."

There was a moment's pause. Jackie did not dare to look up, but he could feel the priest's eyes on him. The priest's voice also seemed a trifle husky.

"Your grandmother?" he asked, but he didn't after all sound very angry.

"Yes, father."

"Does she live with you?"

"She do, father."

"And why did you want to kill her?"

"Oh, God, father, she's a horrible woman!"

"Is she now?"

"She is, father."

"What way is she horrible?"

Jackie paused to think. It was hard to explain.

"She takes snuff, father."

"Oh, my!"

"And she goes round in her bare feet, father."

"Tut-tut-tut!"

"She's a horrible woman, father," said Jackie with sudden earnestness. "She takes porter. And she ates the potatoes off the table with her hands. And me mother do be out working most days, and since that one came 'tis she gives us our dinner and I can't ate the dinner." He found himself sniffling. "And she gives pinnies to Nora and she doesn't give no pinnies to me because she knows I can't stand her. And me father sides with her, father, and he bates me, and me heart is broken and wan night in bed I made it up the way I'd kill her."

Jackie began to sob again, rubbing his nose with his sleeve, as he remembered his wrongs.

"And what way were you going to kill her?" asked the priest smoothly.

"With a hatchet, father."

"When she was in bed?"

"No, father."

"How, so?"

"When she ates the potatoes and drinks the porter she falls asleep, father."

"And you'd hit her then?"

"Yes, father."

"Wouldn't a knife be better?"

"'Twould, father, only I'd be afraid of the blood."

"Oh, of course. I never thought of the blood."

"I'd be afraid of that, father. I was near hitting Nora with the bread knife one time she came after me under the table only I was afraid."

"You're a terrible child," said the priest with awe.

"I am, father," said Jackie noncommittally, sniffling back his tears.

"And what would you do with the body?"

"How, father?"

"Wouldn't someone see her and tell?"

"I was going to cut her up with a knife and take away the pieces and bury them. I could get an orange box for threepence and make a cart to take them away."

"My, my," said the priest. "You had it all well planned."

"Ah, I tried that," said Jackie with mounting confidence. "I borrowed a cart and practised it by meself one night after dark."

"And weren't you afraid?"

"Ah, no," said Jackie half-heartedly. "Only a bit."

"You have terrible courage," said the priest. "There's a lot of people I want to get rid of, but I'm not like you. I'd never have the courage. And hanging is an awful death."

"Is it?" asked Jackie, responding to the brightness of a new theme.

"Oh, an awful blooming death!"

"Did you ever see a fellow hanged?"

"Dozens of them, and they all died roaring."

"Jay!" said Jackie.

"They do be swinging out of them for hours and the poor fellows lepping and roaring, like bells in a belfry, and then they put lime on them to burn them up. Of course, they pretend they're dead but sure, they don't be dead at all."

"Jay!" said Jackie again.

"So if I were you I'd take my time and think about it. In my opinion 'tisn't worth it, not even to get rid of a grandmother. I asked dozens of fellows like you that killed their grandmothers about it, and they all said, no, 'twasn't worth it. . . ."

Nora was waiting in the yard. The sunlight struck down on her across the high wall and its brightness made his eyes dazzle. "Well?" she asked. "What did he give you?"

"Three Hail Marys."

"You mustn't have told him anything."

"I told him everything," said Jackie confidently.

"What did you tell him?"

"Things you don't know."

"Bah! He gave you three Hail Marys because you were a cry baby!"

Jackie didn't mind. He felt the world was very good. He began to whistle as well as the hindrance in his jaw permitted.

"What are you sucking?"

"Bull's eyes."

"Was it he gave them to you?"

"'Twas."

"Almighty God!" said Nora. "Some people have all the luck. I might as well be a sinner like you. There's no use in being good."

Innocence

Seán O'Faoláin (*Irish, 1900–*)

All this month the nuns have been preparing my little boy for his first Confession. In a few days he will go in a crocodile from the school to the parish church; enter the strange-looking cabinet in the corner of the aisle and see in the dusk of this secretive box an old priest's face behind a grille. He will acknowledge his wickedness to this pale, criss-crossed face. He will be a little frightened but he will enjoy it too, because he does not really believe any of it—for him it is a kind of game that the nuns and the priest are playing between them.

How could he believe it? The nuns tell him that the Infant Jesus is sad when he is wicked. But he is never wicked, so what can it matter? If they told him instead of the sorrow he causes the Weasel, or Two Toes, or the Robin in the Cow's Ear, all of which live in the fields below our house, he would believe it in just the same way. To be sure he tells lies, he is a terrible liar, and when he plays Rummy with me he cheats as often as he can, and when he is slow and I flurry him he flies into furious rages and his eyes swim with tears and he dashes the cards down and calls me A Pig. For this I love him so much that I hug him, because it is so transparent and innocent; and at night if I remember his tears I want to go into his room and hold his fat, sweaty hand that lies on the coverlet clutching some such treasure as an empty reel. How, then, can he believe that God could be angry with him because he tells lies or calls his daddy A Pig?

Yet, I hate to see him being prepared for his first Confession because one day he will really do something wicked, and I know the fear that will come over him on that day—and I cannot prevent it.

I have never forgotten the first time I knew that I had committed sin. I had been going to Confession for years, ever since I was seven, as he is now, telling the same things time after time just as he will do. 'Father, I told a lie . . . Father, I forgot to say my morning prayers . . . Father, I was disobedient to my parents . . . And that is all, Father.' It was always quite true: I had done these things; but, as with him, it was only true as a fable or a mock-battle is true since none of these things were any more sinful than childish lies and rages. Until, one dim, wintry afternoon, not long after Christmas, when I went as usual to Confession in an old, dark, windy church called Saint Augustine's, down a side-lane, away from the city's traffic, a place as cold and damp and smelly as a tomb. It has since been pulled down and if they had not pulled it down it must soon have fallen down. It was the sort of church where there was always a beggar or two sheltering from the weather in the porch or in the dusky part under the back gallery; and always some poor shawled woman sighing her prayers in a corner like the wind fluttering in the slates. The paint was always clean and fresh, but the floor and the benches and the woodwork were battered and worn by the generations. The priests dressed in the usual black Augustinian garment with a cowl and a leather cincture. Altogether, a stranger would have found it a gloomy place. But I was familiar with it ever since my mother brought me there to dedicate me to Saint Monica, the mother of Augustine, and I loved the bright candles before her picture, and the dark nooks under the galleries, and the painted tondos on the ceiling, and the stuffy confessional boxes with their heavy purple curtains, underneath which the heels of the penitents stuck out when they knelt to the grille.

There I was, glad to be out of the January cold, kneeling before Saint Monica, brilliant with the candles of her mendicants. I was reading down through the lists of sins in my penny prayer-book, heeding the ones I knew, passing over the ones I didn't know, when I suddenly stopped at the name of a sin that I had hitherto passed by as having nothing to do with me.

As I write down these words I again feel the terror that crept into me like a snake as I realized that I knew that sin. I knew it well. No criminal who feels the sudden grip of a policeman on his arm can have felt more fear than I did as I stared at the horrible words. . . .

I joined the long silent queue of penitents seated against the wall. I went, at last, into the dark confessional. I told my usual innocent litany. I whispered the sin.

Now, the old priest inside the confessional was a very aged man. He was so old and feeble that the community rarely allowed him to do anything but say Mass and hear Confessions. Whenever they let him preach he would ramble on and on for an hour; people would get up and go away; the sacristan would peep out in despair through the sacristy door; and in the end an altar-boy would be sent out to ring the great gong on the altar-steps to make him stop. I have seen the boy come out three times to the gong before the old man could be lured down from the pulpit.

When this old priest heard what I said to him he gave a groan that must have been heard in the farthest corner of the church. He leaned his face against the wire and called me his 'child,' as all priests in the confessional call every penitent. Then he began to question me about the details. I had not counted on this. I had thought that I would say my sin and be forgiven: for up to this every priest had merely told me that I was a very good little boy and asked me to pray for him as if I were a little angel whose prayers had a special efficacy, and then I would be dismissed jumping with joy.

To his questions I replied tremulously that it had happened 'more than once'—How soon we begin to evade the truth!—and, I said, 'Yes, Father, it was with another.' At this he let out another groan so that I wanted to beg him to be quiet or the people outside would hear him. Then he asked me a question that made my clasped hands sweat and shake on the ledge of the grille. He asked me if any harm had been done to me. At first I didn't know what he meant. Then horrible shapes of understanding came creeping towards me along the dark road of my ignorance, as, in some indistinct manner, I recognized that he was mistaking me for a girl! I cried out that nothing at all had happened, Father. Nothing! Nothing! Nothing! But he only sighed like the south wind and said:

'Ah, my poor child, you won't know for several months.'

I now had no desire but to escape. I was ready to tell him any story, any lie, if he would only stop his questions. What I did say I don't know but in some fashion I must have made the old man understand that I was a male sinner. For his next question, which utterly broke me, was:

'I see, I see. Well, tell me, my poor child. Was she married or unmarried?'

I need hardly say that as I remember this now I laugh at it for an absurd misadventure, and I have sometimes made my friends laugh at his questions and his groans, and at me with my two skinny heels sticking out under the curtains and knocking like castanets, and the next penitents wondering what on earth was going on inside the box. But, then, I was like a pup caught in a bramble bush, recanting and retracting and trying to get to the point where he would say the blessed words '*Absolvo te* . . .' and tell me what my penance would be.

What I said I cannot recall. All I remember distinctly is how I emerged under the eyes of the queue, walked up the aisle, as far away as I could get from the brightness of Saint Monica into the darkest corner under the gallery where the poorest of the poor crowd on Sundays. I saw everything through smoke. The scarlet eye of the sanctuary lamp—the only illumination apart from the candles before the shrine—stared at me. The shawled woman sighed at me. The wind under my bare knees crept away from me. A beggar in a corner, picking his nose and scratching himself, was Purity itself compared to me.

In the streets the building stood dark and wet against the after-Christmas pallor of the sky. High up over the city there was one tiny star. It was as bright and remote as lost innocence. The blank windows that held the winter sky were sullen. The wet cement walls were black. I walked around for hours. When I crept in home my mother demanded angrily where I had been all these hours and I told her lies that *were* lies, because I wanted to deceive her, and I knew that from this on I would always be deceiving everybody because I had something inside me that nobody must ever know. I was afraid of the dark night before me. And I still had to face another Confession when I would have to confess all these fresh lies that I had just told the old priest and my mother.

It's forty years ago, now: something long since put in its unimportant place. Yet, somehow, when I look across at this small kid clutching his penny prayer-book in his sweaty hands and wrinkling up his nose at the hard words—I cannot laugh. It does not even comfort me when I think of that second Confession, after I had carefully examined those lists of sins for the proper name of my sin. For, what I said to the next priest was: 'Father, I committed adultery.' With infinite tenderness he assured me that I was mistaken, and that I would not know anything about that sin for many years to come, indeed, that I would have to be married before I could commit it—and then asked me to pray for him, and said I was a very good little boy and sent me away jumping with joy. When I think of that and look at this small Adam he becomes like that indescribably remote and tender star, and I sigh like that old, dead priest, and it does not help to know that he is playing a fable of—'Father, I told lies . . . Father, I forgot to say my morning prayers. . . . Father, I called my daddy A Pig.'

11

A Painful Case

by James Joyce

A Red-Letter Day

by Elizabeth Taylor

JAMES JOYCE *One of the titanic figures of modern literature, Joyce was, as Frank Kermode put it, "an Irishman who had to escape from Ireland in order that his imagination might be able to cope with it." He left for Paris in 1902, returned to Dublin when his mother died, then left again for ever—at least bodily. The burden of Joyce's writing was ever Ireland; nor was it a "burden" that publishers were quite ready to accept.* Dubliners, *for example, from which "A Painful Case" is taken, was completed in 1905, but only published in 1914, the publisher fearing that its "obscenity" (Joyce used the adjective* bloody *in several stories) might cause serious legal problems. The vagaries connected with the reprintings of* Ulysses, *first published in 1922, are well-known.*

About Dubliners, *Joyce wrote to his reluctant publisher, "My intention was to write a chapter of the moral history of my country, and I chose Dublin for the scene because the city seemed to me the center of paralysis." The stories themselves are muted, so subtly etched that to a casual reader they might seem even listless. In fact, the modest fabric is infused everywhere with the weft of Joyce's extraordinary knowledge of the human predicament.*

The single indispensable book on the author is Richard Ellman's James Joyce, *1969.*

ELIZABETH TAYLOR *Arthur Mizener has called Elizabeth Taylor "the modern man's Jane Austen." This formulation is at least generally useful, for Miss Taylor, like Jane Austen, elegantly directs her reader to the violent emotions that quiver beneath an ostensibly tidy England. Throughout her fifteen-odd volumes of short stories and novels, Miss Taylor's subject matter has nearly always been "civilized"* society, *which with exquisite scalpel (and lambent wit), she has exposed for the sake of our imaginations.*

Her more recent works include a novel entitled The Wedding Group, *1968, and* The Devastating Boys, Stories, *1972.*

A Painful Case

James Joyce (*Irish, 1882–1941*)

Mr. James Duffy lived in Chapelizod because he wished to live as far as possible from the city of which he was a citizen and because he found all the other suburbs of Dublin mean, modern and pretentious. He lived in an old sombre house and from his windows he could look into the disused distillery or upwards along the shallow river on which Dublin is built. The lofty walls of his uncarpeted room were free from pictures. He had himself bought every article of furniture in the room: a black iron bedstead, an iron washstand, four cane chairs, a clothes-rack, a coal-scuttle, a fender and irons and a square table on which lay a double desk. A bookcase had been made in an alcove by means of shelves of white wood. The bed was clothed with white bedclothes and a black and scarlet rug covered the foot. A little hand-mirror hung above the washstand and during the day a white-shaded lamp stood as the sole ornament of the mantelpiece. The books on the white wooden shelves were arranged from below upwards according to bulk. A complete Wordsworth stood at one end of the lowest shelf and a copy of the *Maynooth Catechism,* sewn into the cloth cover of a notebook, stood at one end of the top shelf. Writing materials were always on the desk. In the desk lay a manuscript translation of Hauptmann's *Michael Kramer,* the stage directions of which were written in purple ink, and a little sheaf of papers held together by a brass pin. In these sheets a sentence was inscribed from time to time and, in an ironical moment, the headline of an advertisement for *Bile Beans* had been pasted on to the first sheet. On lifting the lid of the desk a faint fragrance escaped—the fragrance of new cedarwood pencils or of a bottle of gum or of an overripe apple which might have been left there and forgotten.

Mr. Duffy abhorred anything which betokened physical or mental disorder. A mediæval doctor would have called him saturnine. His face, which carried the entire tale of his years, was of the brown tint of Dublin streets. On his long and rather large head grew dry black hair and a tawny moustache did not quite cover an unamiable mouth. His cheekbones also gave his face a harsh character; but there was no harshness in the eyes which, looking at the world from under their tawny eyebrows, gave the impression of a man ever alert to greet a redeeming instinct in others but often disappointed. He lived at a little distance from his body, regarding his own acts with doubtful side-glances. He had an odd autobiographical habit which led him to compose in his mind from time to time a short sentence about himself containing a subject in the third person and a predicate in the past tense. He never gave alms to beggars and walked firmly, carrying a stout hazel.

He had been for many years cashier of a private bank in Baggot Street. Every morning he came in from Chapelizod by tram. At midday he went to Dan Burke's and took his lunch—a bottle of lager beer and a small trayful of arrowroot biscuits. At four o'clock he was set free. He dined in an eating-house in George's Street where he felt himself safe from the society of Dublin's gilded youth and where there was a certain plain honesty in the bill of fare. His evenings were spent either before his landlady's piano or roaming about the outskirts of the city. His liking for Mozart's music brought him sometimes to an opera or a concert: these were the only dissipations of his life.

He had neither companions nor friends, church nor creed. He lived his spiritual life without any communion with others, visiting his relatives at Christmas and escorting them to the cemetery when they died. He performed these two social duties for old dignity's sake but conceded nothing further to the conventions which regulate the civic life. He allowed himself to think that in certain circumstances he would rob his bank but, as these circumstances never arose, his life rolled out evenly—an adventureless tale.

One evening he found himself sitting beside two ladies in the Rotunda. The house, thinly peopled and silent, gave distressing prophecy of failure. The lady who sat next to him looked round at the deserted house once or twice and then said:

"What a pity there is such a poor house tonight! It's so hard on people to have to sing to empty benches."

He took the remark as an invitation to talk. He was surprised that she seemed so little awkward. While they talked he tried to fix her permanently in his memory. When he learned that the young girl beside her was her daughter he judged her to be a year or so younger than himself. Her face, which must have been handsome, had remained intelligent. It was an oval face with strongly marked features. The eyes were very dark blue and steady. Their gaze began with a defiant note but was confused by what seemed a deliberate swoon of the pupil into the iris, revealing for an instant a temperament of great sensibility. The pupil reasserted itself quickly, this half-disclosed nature fell again under the reign of prudence, and her astrakhan jacket, moulding a bosom of a certain fullness, struck the note of defiance more definitely.

He met her again a few weeks afterwards at a concert in Earlsfort Terrace and seized the moments when her daughter's attention was diverted to become intimate. She alluded once or twice to her husband but her tone was not such as to make the allusion a warning. Her name was Mrs. Sinico. Her husband's great-great-grandfather had come from Leghorn. Her husband was captain of a mercantile boat plying between Dublin and Holland; and they had one child.

Meeting her a third time by accident he found courage to make an appointment. She came. This was the first of many meetings; they met always in the evening and chose the most quiet quarters for their walks together. Mr. Duffy, however, had a distaste for underhand ways and, finding that they were compelled to meet stealthily, he forced her to ask him to her house. Captain Sinico encouraged his visits, thinking that his daughter's hand was in question. He had dismissed his wife so sincerely from his gallery of pleasures that he did not suspect that anyone else would take an interest in her. As the husband was often away and the daughter out giving music lessons Mr. Duffy had many opportunities of enjoying the lady's society. Neither he nor she had had any such adventure before and neither was conscious of any incongruity. Little by little he entangled his thoughts with hers. He lent her books, provided her with ideas, shared his intellectual life with her. She listened to all.

Sometimes in return for his theories she gave out some fact of her own life. With almost maternal solicitude she urged him to let his nature open to the full: she became his confessor. He told her that for some time he had assisted at the meetings of an Irish Socialist Party where he had felt himself a unique figure amidst a score of sober workmen in a garret lit by an inefficient oil-lamp. When the party had divided into three sections, each under its own leader and in its own garret, he had discontinued his attendances. The workmen's discussions, he said, were too timorous; the interest they took in the question of wages was inordinate. He felt that they were hard-featured realists and that they resented an exactitude which was the produce of a leisure not within their reach. No social revolution, he told her, would be likely to strike Dublin for some centuries.

She asked him why did he not write out his thoughts. For what, he asked her, with careful scorn. To compete with phrase-mongers, incapable of thinking consecutively for sixty seconds? To submit himself to the criticisms of an obtuse middle class which entrusted its morality to policemen and its fine arts to impresarios?

He went often to her little cottage outside Dublin; often they spent their evenings alone. Little by little, as their thoughts entangled, they spoke of subjects less remote. Her companionship was like a warm soil about an exotic. Many times she allowed the dark to fall upon them, refraining from lighting the lamp. The dark discreet room, their isolation, the music that still vibrated in their ears united them. This union exalted him, wore away the rough edges of his character, emotionalised his mental life. Sometimes he caught himself listening to the sound of his own voice. He thought that in her eyes he would ascend to an angelical stature; and, as he attached the fervent nature of his companion more and more closely to him, he heard the strange impersonal voice which he recognised as his own, insisting on the soul's incurable loneliness. We cannot give ourselves, it said: we are our own. The end of these discourses was that one night during which she had shown every sign of unusual excitement, Mrs. Sinico caught up his hand passionately and pressed it to her cheek.

Mr. Duffy was very much surprised. Her interpretation of his words disillusioned him. He did not visit her for a week; then he wrote to her asking her to meet him. As he did not wish their last interview to be troubled by the influence of their ruined confessional they met in a little cakeshop near the Parkgate. It was cold autumn weather but in spite of the cold they wandered up and down the roads of the Park for nearly three hours. They agreed to break off their intercourse: every bond, he said, is a bond to sorrow. When they came out of the Park they walked in silence towards the tram; but here she began to tremble so violently that, fearing another collapse on her part, he bade her good-bye quickly and left her. A few days later he received a parcel containing his books and music.

Four years passed. Mr. Duffy returned to his even way of life. His room still bore witness of the orderliness of his mind. Some new pieces of music encumbered the music-stand in the lower room and on his shelves stood two volumes by Nietzsche: *Thus Spake Zarathustra* and *The Gay Science*. He wrote seldom in the sheaf of papers which lay in his desk. One of his sentences, written two months after his last interview with Mrs. Sinico, read: Love between man and man is impossible because there must not be sexual intercourse and friendship between man and woman is impossible because there must be sexual intercourse. He kept away from concerts lest he should meet her. His father died; the junior partner of the bank retired. And still every morning he went into the city by train and every evening walked home from the city after having dined moderately in George's Street and read the evening paper for dessert.

One evening as he was about to put a morsel of corned beef and cabbage into his mouth his hand stopped. His eyes fixed themselves on a paragraph in the evening paper which he had propped against the water-carafe. He replaced the morsel of food on his plate and read the paragraph attentively. Then he drank a glass of water, pushed his plate to one side, doubled the paper down before him between his elbows and read the paragraph over and over again. The cabbage began to deposit a cold white grease on his plate. The girl came over to him to ask was his dinner not properly cooked. He said it was very good and ate a few mouthfuls of it with difficulty. Then he paid his bill and went out.

He walked along quickly through the November twilight, his stout hazel stick striking the ground regularly, the fringe of the buff *Mail* peeping out of a side-pocket of his tight reefer overcoat. On the lonely road which leads from the Parkgate to Chapelizod he slackened his pace. His stick struck the ground less emphatically and his breath, issuing irregularly, almost with a sighing sound, condensed in the wintry air. When he reached his house he went up at once to his bedroom and, taking the paper from his pocket, read the paragraph again by the failing light of the window. He read it not aloud, but moving his lips as a priest does when he reads the prayers *Secreto*. This was the paragraph:

DEATH OF A LADY AT SYDNEY PARADE

A Painful Case

Today at the City of Dublin Hospital the Deputy Coroner (in the absence of Mr. Leverett) held an inquest on the body of Mrs. Emily Sinico, aged forty-three years, who was killed at Sydney Parade Station yesterday evening. The evidence showed that the deceased lady, while attempting to cross the line, was knocked down by the engine of the ten o'clock slow train from Kingstown, thereby sustaining injuries of the head and right side which led to her death.

James Lennon, driver of the engine, stated that he had been in the employment of the railway company for fifteen years. On hearing the guard's whistle he set the train in motion and a second or two afterwards brought it to rest in response to loud cries. The train was going slowly.

P. Dunne, railway porter, stated that as the train was about to start he observed a woman attempting to cross the lines. He ran towards her and shouted, but, before he could reach her, she was caught by the buffer of the engine and fell to the ground.

A juror. "You saw the lady fall?"

Witness. "Yes."

Police Sergeant Croly deposed that when he arrived he found the deceased lying on the platform apparently dead. He had the body taken to the waiting-room pending the arrival of the ambulance.

Constable 57 corroborated.

Dr. Halpin, assistant house surgeon of the City of Dublin Hospital, stated that the deceased had two lower ribs fractured and had sustained severe contusions of the right shoulder. The right side of the head had been injured in the fall. The injuries were not sufficient to have caused death in a normal person. Death, in his opinion, had been probably due to shock and sudden failure of the heart's action.

Mr. H. B. Patterson Finlay, on behalf of the railway company, expressed his deep regret at the accident. The company had always taken every precaution to prevent people crossing the lines except by the bridges, both by placing notices in every station and by the use of patent spring gates at level crossings. The deceased had been in the habit of crossing the lines late at night from platform to platform and, in view of certain other circumstances of the case, he did not think the railway officials were to blame.

Captain Sinico, of Leoville, Sydney Parade, husband of the deceased, also gave evidence. He stated that the deceased was his wife. He was not in Dublin at the time of the accident as he had arrived only that morning from Rotterdam. They had been married for twenty-two years and had lived happily until about two years ago when his wife began to be rather intemperate in her habits.

Miss Mary Sinico said that of late her mother had been in the habit of going out at night to buy spirits. She, witness, had often tried to reason with her mother and had induced her to join a League. She was not at home until an hour after the accident. The jury returned a verdict in accordance with the medical evidence and exonerated Lennon from all blame.

The Deputy Coroner said it was a most painful case, and expressed great sympathy with Captain Sinico and his daughter. He urged on the railway company to take strong measures to prevent the possibility of similar accidents in the future. No blame attached to anyone.

Mr. Duffy raised his eyes from the paper and gazed out of his window on the cheerless evening landscape. The river lay quiet beside the empty distillery and from time to time a light appeared in some house on the Lucan road. What an end! The whole narrative of her death revolted him and it revolted him to think that he had ever spoken to her of what he held sacred. The threadbare phrases, the inane expressions of sympathy, the cautious words of a reporter won over to conceal the details of a commonplace vulgar death attacked his stomach. Not merely had she degraded herself; she had degraded him. He saw the squalid tract of her vice, miserable and malodorous. His soul's companion! He thought of the hobbling wretches whom he had seen carrying cans and bottles to be filled by the barman. Just God, what an end! Evidently she had been unfit to live, without any strength of purpose, an easy prey to habits, one of the wrecks on which civilisation has been reared. But that she could have sunk so low! Was it possible he had deceived himself so utterly about her? He remembered her outburst of that night and interpreted it in a harsher sense than he had ever done. He had no difficulty now in approving of the course he had taken.

As the light failed and his memory began to wander he thought her hand touched his. The shock which had first attacked his stomach was now attacking his nerves. He put on his overcoat and hat quickly and went out. The cold air met him on the threshold; it crept into the sleeves of his coat. When he came to the public-house at Chapelizod Bridge he went in and ordered a hot punch.

The proprietor served him obsequiously but did not venture to talk. There were five or six workingmen in the shop discussing the value of a gentleman's estate in County Kildare. They drank at intervals from their huge pint tumblers and smoked, spitting often on the floor and sometimes dragging the sawdust over their spits with their heavy boots. Mr. Duffy sat on his stool and gazed at them, without seeing or hearing them. After a while they went out and he called for another punch. He sat a long time over it. The shop was very quiet. The proprietor sprawled on the counter reading the *Herald* and yawning. Now and again a tram was heard swishing along the lonely road outside.

As he sat there, living over his life with her and evoking alternately the two images in which he now conceived her, he realised that she was dead, that she had ceased to exist, that she had become a memory. He began to feel ill at ease. He asked himself what else could he have done. He could not have carried on a comedy of deception with her; he could not have lived with her openly. He had done what seemed to him best. How was he to blame? Now that she was gone he understood how lonely her life must have been, sitting night after night alone in that room. His life would be lonely too until he, too, died, ceased to exist, became a memory—if anyone remembered him.

It was after nine o'clock when he left the shop. The night was cold and gloomy. He entered the Park by the first gate and walked along under the gaunt trees. He walked through the bleak alleys where they had walked four years before. She seemed to be near him in the darkness. At moments he seemed to feel her voice touch his ear, her hand touch his. He stood still to listen. Why had he withheld life from her? Why had he sentenced her to death? He felt his moral nature falling to pieces.

When he gained the crest of the Magazine Hill he halted and looked along the river towards Dublin, the lights of which burned redly and hospitably in the cold night. He looked down the slope and, at the base, in the shadow of the wall of the Park, he saw some human figures lying. Those venal and furtive loves filled him with despair. He gnawed the rectitude of his life; he felt that he had been outcast from life's feast. One human being had seemed to love him and he had denied her life and happiness; he had sentenced her to ignominy, a death of shame. He knew that the prostrate creatures down by the wall were watching him and wished him gone. No one wanted him; he was outcast from life's feast. He turned his eyes to the grey gleaming river, winding along towards Dublin. Beyond the river he saw a goods train winding out of Kingsbridge Station, like a worm with a fiery head winding through the darkness, obstinately and laboriously. It passed slowly out of sight; but still he heard in his ears the laborious drone of the engine reiterating the syllables of her name.

He turned back the way he had come, the rhythm of the engine pounding in his ears. He began to doubt the reality of what memory told him. He halted under a tree and allowed the rhythm to die away. He could not feel her near him in the darkness nor her voice touch his ear. He waited for some minutes listening. He could hear nothing: the night was perfectly silent. He listened again: perfectly silent. He felt that he was alone.

A Red-Letter Day

Elizabeth Taylor (*English, 1912–*)

The hedgerow was beaded with silver. In the English November fog, the leaves dripped with a deadly intensity, as if each falling drop were a drop of acid.

Through the mist, cabs came suddenly face to face with one another, passing and repassing between station and school. Backing into the hedges—twigs, withered berries striking the windows—the drivers leaned out to exchange remarks incomprehensible to their passengers, who felt oddly at their mercy. Town parents, especially, shrank from this malevolent landscape—the wastes of rotting cabbages, flint cottages with rakish privies, rubbish heaps, gray napkins drooping on clotheslines, soil like plum cake. Even turning in at the rather superior school gates, they were dismayed by the mossy stone and the smell of fungus. Then, as the building itself came into view, they could see Matron standing at the top of the steps, fantastically white, shaming Nature, her hands laid affectionately upon the shoulders of such boys as could not resist her. The weather was put in its place. The day would take its course. She had an air of professional bonhomie, as if she shared in the gaiety of the occasion. But, each term, Visiting Day to her was like Christmas Day to a clergyman, a great climax of work and preparation.

Tory was one of the last to get a cab. Having no man to exert authority for her, she must merely take her turn and stand on the slimy pavement waiting for a car to come back to the station empty. She stamped her feet, feeling the damp creeping through her shoes. When she left home, she had thought herself suitably dressed; even for such an early hour, her hat was surely plain enough? One after another, she had tried on every one she owned, and had come out, in the end, leaving hats all over the bed, so that it resembled a new grave with its mound of wreathed flowers. But the other mothers had hats of undreamed-of austerity, and the most sensible of Tory's shoes could not withstand the insidious damp.

One other woman was on her own. Tory eyed her with distaste. Her sons (for surely there were more than one; she looked as if she had what is often called a teeming womb, like a woman symbolizing maternity in a pageant), her many sons would never feel the lack of a father (as Tory's one boy was bound to), for she was large enough to be both father and mother to them. Yes, Tory thought, she would have them out on the lawn and bowl at them by the hour, would coach them in mathematics, oil their bats, dub their boots, tan their backsides. Tory was working herself up into a hatred of this woman, who seemed to be all that she herself was not, with only one love affair in her life, or, rather, one mating. She has probably eaten her husband now that her child-bearing days are over, Tory thought. He would never have dared to ask for a divorce, as mine did. The woman still carried her "mother's bag"—the vast thing that, full of diapers, bibs, bottles of orange juice, accompanies babies out to tea. Tory wondered what was in it now. Sensible things—a Bradshaw, ration books, a bag of biscuits, large, clean handkerchiefs, a tablet of soap, and aspirins?

A jolly manner. ("I love young people—I feed on them," Tory thought spitefully.) The furs on the woman's shoulders made her even larger; they clasped paws across her great, authoritative back, like hands across the ocean. Tory lifted her muffs to hide her smile.

Nervous dread made her feel fretful and vicious. In *her* life, all was frail, precarious—emotions fleeting, relationships fragmentary. Her life with her husband had suddenly loosened and dissolved; her love for her son was painful, shadowed by guilt—the guilt of having nothing solid to offer, of having grown up and forgotten, of adventuring still, away from her child, of not being able to resist those emotional adventures, the tenuous grasping after life. He was threatened by the very look of her, attracting those delicious secret glances, glimpses, and whispers, by the challenge she always felt, and the excitement—not deeply sexual, for she was merely flirtatious. But I am not, she thought, watching Mrs. Hay-Hardy (whose name she was soon to learn but did not yet know) rearranging her furs on her shoulders, I am not a great feather bed of oblivion. Between Edward and me there is no premise of love, none at all—nothing taken for granted, as between most sons and mothers, but all tentative and agonized. We are indeed amateurs, both of us; no tradition behind us, no gift for the job. All we achieve is too hard to come by. We try too piteously to please one another, and if we do, feel frightened by the miracle of it. I do indeed love him above all others. Above all others, but not exclusively . . .

Here a taxi swerved against the station curb and palpitated as she stepped forward quickly, triumphantly, before Mrs. Hay-Hardy could do so, and settled herself in the back seat.

"Could we share?" Mrs. Hay-Hardy asked, her voice confident, melodious, and one foot definitely on the running board. Tory smiled and moved over much farther than was necessary, as if such a teeming womb could scarcely be accommodated on the seat beside her.

Shifting her furs on her shoulders, settling herself, Mrs. Hay-Hardy glanced out through the filming windows, undaunted by the weather, which, she said, would clear, would lift. Oh, she was confident that it would lift by midday!

"One has to get up so early it seems midday now," Tory complained.

But Mrs. Hay-Hardy explained that she had not risen until six, so, naturally, it still seemed only eleven to her, as it was.

She will share the fare, down to the last penny, Tory thought. There will be a loud and forthright women's argument. She will count out coppers and make a fuss.

This did happen. At the top of the steps, Matron still waited, with the three Hay-Hardy boys grouped about her, and Edward, who blushed and whitened alternately with terrible excitement, a little to one side. Yes, he had grown, Tory thought, and his shorts were high above his roughened knees. He looked more than eleven, but his complexion was peachy and downy still, like a younger child's, and his long lashes threw shadows across his eyes. As an only son, he had not the same claim to Matron's attention as the Hay-Hardys, and she had chosen them to encircle. Sensing this, perhaps, Edward stood apart.

To meet this wonderful customer, this profitable womb, the headmaster's wife herself came into the hall. Her husband had sent her, instructing her with deft cynicism from behind his detective novel. He himself, of course, was one of those gods who rarely descend, except, like Zeus, in a very private capacity.

This is the moment I marked off on the calendar, Edward thought. Here it is. Every night, he and the other boys had thrown one of their pebbles out of the window to mark a day gone. The little stones had dropped back onto the gravel under the window, quite lost, untraceable—the days of their lives.

As smooth as minnows were Mrs. Lancaster's phrases of welcome; she had soothed so many mothers, mothered so many boys. Her words swam all one way, in unison, but her heart never moved. Matron, on the other hand, was always nervous; the results of her work were so much on the surface, so easily checked. The rest of the staff could hide their inefficiency or shift their responsibility. She could not. If Mrs. Hay-Hardy cried, as she did today, "Dear boy, your teeth!" to her first-born, it was Matron's work she criticized, and Matron flushed. And Mrs. Lancaster flushed for Matron, and Derrick Hay-Hardy flushed for his mother.

"Perhaps I am not a born mother," Tory thought, going down the steps with Edward. They would walk back to the town and have lunch at the Crown, she said to him. Edward pressed her arm as a taxi, bulging with Hay-Hardys, went away down the drive.

"Do you mean you wanted to go with them?" Tory asked. They will get there long before us, she thought. They will have eaten everything.

"No."

"Don't you like them?"

"No."

"But why?"

"They don't like me."

Unbearable news for any mother, for surely all the world loves one's child, one's only child. Doubt set in, a little, nagging toothache of doubt. You *are* happy? she wanted to ask. "I've looked forward so much to this," she said instead. "*So* much."

He stared ahead. All around the gateposts, drops of moisture fell from one leaf to another, and the stone griffins were hunched up in misery.

"But I imagined it being a different day," Tory added. "Quite different."

"It will be nice to get something different to eat," Edward said.

They walked down the road toward the Crown in silence, as if they could not make any progress until they had reached that point.

"You *are* warm enough at night?" Tory asked when at last they were sitting in the hotel dining room.

"Yes," he said absently, and then, bringing himself back to the earlier, distant politeness, added, "Stifling hot."

"Stifling? But surely you have plenty of fresh air?" She could feel her questions sliding off him.

"*I* do," he said reassuringly. "My bed's just under the window. Perishing. I have to keep my head under the bedclothes, or I get earache."

I am asking for all this, she thought. When the waiter brought her pink gin, she drank it quickly, conscious that Mrs. Hay-Hardy, across the hotel dining room, was pouring out a nice glass of water for herself, was so full of jokes that Tory felt she had perhaps brought a collection of them along with her in her shopping bag. Laughter ran around and around the Hay-Hardy's table, above the glasses of water. Edward turned once, and she glimpsed the faintest quiver under one eye, and an answering quiver on the middle Hay-Hardy's face.

She felt exasperated. Cold had settled in her; her mouth—her heart, too—felt stiff.

"What would you like to do after lunch?" she asked.

"We could look round the shops," Edward said, nibbling away at his bread, as if to keep hunger at arm's length.

The shops were in the market square. At the draper's, the hats were steadily coming around into fashion again. "I could astonish everyone with one of these," Tory thought, setting her own hat right by her reflection in the window. Bales of cotton apron print rose on both sides; a wax-faced boy wore a stiff suit, its price ticket dangling from his yellow, broken fingers, his painted blue eyes turned mildly upon the street. Edward gave him a look of contempt and went to the shop door. Breathing on the glass, peering in through a little space among suspended bibs and jabots and parlormaids' caps, he watched the cages flying overhead between cashier and counter.

The Hay-Hardys streamed by, heading for the open country.

Most minutely, Tory and Edward examined the windows of the draper's shop, the bicycle shop, the family grocer's. There was nothing to say. They were just reading the postcards in the news agent's window when Edward's best friend greeted them. His father, a clergyman, snatched off his hat and clapped it to his chest at the sight of Tory. When she turned back to the postcards, she could see how unsuitable they were—jokes about bloomers, about twins; a great seaside world of fat men in striped bathing suits; enormous women trotted down to the sea's edge while crabs humorously nipped their behinds; farcical situations arose over bathing machines; and little boys had trouble with their water. She blushed.

The afternoon seemed to give a little sigh, stirred itself, and shook down a spattering of rain over the pavements. Beyond the market square, the countryside, which had absorbed the Hay-Hardys, lowered at them.

"Is there anything you want?" Tory asked desperately, coveting the warm interiors of the shops.

"I could do with a new puncture outfit for my bike," Edward said.

They went back to the bicycle shop. My God, it's only three o'clock, Tory thought in despair as she glanced secretly under her glove at her watch.

The Museum Room at the Guildhall was not gay, but at least there were Roman remains, a few instruments of torture, and half of a mammoth's jawbone. Tory sat down on a seat among all the broken terra cotta and took out a cigarette.

"No smoking, please," the attendant said, coming out from behind a case of stuffed deer.

"Oh, please!" Tory begged. She sat primly on the chair, her feet together, and when she looked up at him, her violet eyes flashed with tears. Edward wandered away.

The attendant struck a match for her, and his hand, curving around it, trembled.

"It's the insurance," he apologized. "I'll have this later, if I may," he said when she offered him a cigarette, and he put it very carefully in his breast pocket, as if it were a lock of her hair.

"Do you have to stay here all day long with these dull little broken jugs and things?" she asked, looking about.

He forgave her at once for belittling his life's work, only pointing out his pride, the fine mosaic on the wall.

"But floors should be lying down," she said naïvely, without innocence.

Edward came tiptoeing back.

"You see that quite delightful floor hanging up there?" she said to him. "This gentleman will tell you all about it. . . . My son adores Greek mythology," she explained to the attendant.

"Your son!" he repeated, affecting gallant disbelief, his glance stripping ten or fifteen years from her. Then, "This happens to be a

Byzantine mosaic," he said, and looked reproachfully at it for not being what it could not be. Edward listened grudgingly. His mother had forced him into similar situations at other times—in the armory of the Tower of London and, once, at Kew. It was as if she kindled in men a flicker of interest and admiration that her son must keep fanned, for she would not. Boredom drew her away again, yet her charm must still hold sway. So now Edward listened crossly to the story of the Byzantine mosaic as, last holidays, he had minutely observed the chasing on Henry VIII's breastplate, and in utter exasperation, the holidays before, had watched curlews through field glasses ("Edward is so very keen on birds") for the whole of a hot day while Tory dozed elegantly in the heather.

Ordinary days perhaps are better, Edward thought. Sinking down through him were the lees of despair, which must at all costs be hidden from his mother. He glanced up at every clock they passed, and wondered about his friends. Alone with his mother, he felt unsafe, wounded and wounding, and, oppressed by responsibility, he saw himself in relation to the outside world. Thoughts of the future and even—as they stood in the church porch to shelter from another little gust of rain—of death seemed to brush against him, alight on him, and they disturbed him, as they would not do if he were at school, anonymous and safe.

Tory sat down on a seat and read a notice about missionaries, chafing her hands inside her muff, while all her bracelets jingled softly.

Flapping, black, in his cassock, a clergyman came hurrying through the graveyard, between the dripping umbrella trees. Edward stepped guiltily off the porch, as if he had been trespassing.

"Good afternoon," the vicar said.

"Good afternoon," Tory replied. She looked up from blowing the fur of her muff into divisions and her smile broke warmly, beautifully, over the dark afternoon.

Then, "The weather—" they both began ruefully, broke off, and hesitated, then laughed at one another.

It was wonderful; now they would soon be saying goodbye. It was over. The day they had longed for was almost over—the polite little tea among the chintz and the wheelback chairs of the Copper Kettle, Tory frosty and imperious with the waitresses, and, once, Edward beginning, "Father . . . ," at which she looked up sharply before she could gather together the careful indifference she always assumed at this name. Edward faltered, "He sent me a parcel." "How nice!" said Tory, laying ice all over his heart. She called the waitress. Her cup was cracked. She could not drink tea from riveted china, however prettily painted. The waitress went sulkily away. All around them sat other small boys with their parents. Tory's bracelets tinkled as she clasped her hands tightly together and leaned forward. "And how is your father's wife?" she asked brightly, indifferently.

They took a taxi back to the school. Sullenly, the day withdrew; as they turned in at the gates, they could see lights in the ground-floor windows. She thought of going back in the train, of a lonely evening. She would take a drink up to her bedroom and sip it while she did her hair, the gas fire roaring in its white ribs, Edward's photograph beside her bed.

The Hay-Hardys were unloading at the foot of the school steps; flushed from their country walk and all their laughter, they seemed to swarm and shout.

Edward got out of the taxi and stood looking up at Tory, his new puncture outfit clasped tightly in his hand. Uncertainly, awaiting a cue from her, he tried to begin his goodbye.

Warm, musky-scented, softly rustling with the sound of her bracelets, the touch of her fur, she leaned and kissed him. "So lovely, darling!" she murmured. She had no cue to give him. Mrs. Hay-Hardy had gone into the school to have a word with Matron, so Tory must find her own way of saying farewell.

They smiled gaily, as if they were greeting one another.

"See you soon," she said.

"Yes, see you soon."

"Goodbye, then darling."

"Goodbye," said Edward.

She slammed the door and, as the taxi moved off, leaned toward the window and waved. He stood there uncertainly, waving back, radiant with relief. Then, as she disappeared around the curve of the drive, he ran quickly up the steps to find his friends, and safety.

12

War

by Luigi Pirandello

Patriotism

by Yukio Mishima

LUIGI PIRANDELLO *Pirandello is most widely known as a dramatist of remarkable insight and, especially, of technical virtuosity.* Six Characters in Search of an Author, *1921, was in a sense the crystallization of Pirandello's seminal ideas on theater; and since that time the relationship of author to character, of theater to audience, of reality to dream has everywhere in drama been infused with his "new," or better, previously undiscerned perceptions of human complexity.*

His stories, while not technically adventurous, more clearly reflect his moral concerns and the Sicilian background of his early years. Pirandello was awarded the Nobel Prize in 1934.

YUKIO MISHIMA *Even if Mishima had not attempted to martyr himself by committing ritual suicide in the most dramatic manner possible (in the chambers of a "captured" high Japanese official), the controversy surrounding his work and his personality would not be put to rest.*

On the very day of his hara-kiri, *Mishima completed and delivered to his editor the final installment of the massive tetralogy,* The Sea of Fertility. *Thus it was that the last of his 230-odd works, including at least twenty novels, nearly 150 short stories, and fifty plays—was completed. All that remained, at age forty-five, was his incredible death: the actualization of what sometimes appeared as an obsession in his work from its very inception while he was yet in his teens.*

Whether Mishima's writings will ultimately be ranked with Kawabata's and with the author of Tale of Genjii *or whether the exceedingly romantic life and death will finally obscure the work—it is too early to discern.*

*War**

Luigi Pirandello (*Italian, 1867–1936*)

The passengers who had left Rome by the night express had had to stop until dawn at the small station of Fabriano in order to continue their journey by the small old-fashioned local joining the main line with Sulmona.

At dawn, in a stuffy and smoky second-class carriage in which five people had already spent the night, a bulky woman in deep mourning was hoisted in—almost like a shapeless bundle. Behind her, puffing and moaning, followed her husband—a tiny man, thin and weakly, his face death-white, his eyes small and bright and looking shy and uneasy.

Having at last taken a seat he politely thanked the passengers who had helped his wife and who had made room for her; then he turned round to the woman trying to pull down the collar of her coat, and politely inquired:

"Are you all right, dear?"

The wife, instead of answering, pulled up her collar again to her eyes, so as to hide her face.

"Nasty world," muttered the husband with a sad smile.

And he felt it his duty to explain to his traveling companions that the poor woman was to be pitied, for the war was taking away from her her only son, a boy of twenty to whom both had devoted their entire life, even breaking up their home at Sulmona to follow him to Rome, where he had to go as a student, then allowing him to volunteer for war with an assurance, however, that at least for six months he would not be sent to the front and now, all of a sudden,

* Translated by Michael Pettinati.

receiving a wire saying that he was due to leave in three days' time and asking them to go and see him off.

The woman under the big coat was twisting and wriggling, at times growling like a wild animal, feeling certain that all those explanations would not have aroused even a shadow of sympathy from those people who—most likely—were in the same plight as herself. One of them, who had been listening with particular attention, said:

"You should thank God that your son is only leaving now for the front. Mine was sent there the first day of the war. He has already come back twice wounded and been sent back again to the front."

"What about me? I have two sons and three nephews at the front," said another passenger.

"Maybe, but in our case it is our *only* son," ventured the husband.

"What difference can it make? You may spoil your only son with excessive attentions, but you cannot love him more than you would all your other children if you had any. Paternal love is not like bread that can be broken into pieces and split amongst the children in equal shares. A father gives *all* his love to each one of his children without discrimination, whether it be one or ten, and if I am suffering now for my two sons, I am not suffering half for each of them but double . . ."

"True . . . true . . ." sighed the embarrassed husband, "but suppose (of course we all hope it will never be your case) a father has two sons at the front and he loses one of them, there is still one left to console him . . . while . . ."

"Yes," answered the other, getting cross, "a son left to console him but also a son left for whom he must survive, while in the case of the father of an only son if the son dies the father can die too and put an end to his distress. Which of the two positions is the worse? Don't you see how my case would be worse than yours?"

"Nonsense," interrupted another traveler, a fat, red-faced man with bloodshot eyes of the palest gray.

He was panting. From his bulging eyes seemed to spurt inner violence of an uncontrolled vitality which his weakened body could hardly contain.

"Nonsense," he repeated, trying to cover his mouth with his hand so as to hide the two missing front teeth. "Nonsense. Do we give life to our children for our own benefit?"

The other travelers stared at him in distress. The one who had had his son at the front since the first day of the war sighed: "You are right. Our children do not belong to us, they belong to the Country. . . ."

"Bosh," retorted the fat traveler. "Do we think of the Country when we give life to our children? Our sons are born because . . . well, because they must be born and when they come to life they take our own life with them. This is the truth. We belong to them but they never belong to us. And when they reach twenty they are exactly what we were at their age. We too had a father and mother, but there were so many other things as well . . . girls, cigarettes, illusions, new ties . . . and the Country, of course, whose call we would have answered—when we were twenty—even if father and mother had said no. Now at our age, the love of our Country is still great, of course, but stronger than it is the love for our children. Is there any one of us here who wouldn't gladly take his son's place at the front if he could?"

There was a silence all round, everybody nodding as to approve.

"Why then," continued the fat man, "shouldn't we consider the feelings of our children when they are twenty? Isn't it natural that at their age they should consider the love for their Country (I am speaking of decent boys, of course) even greater than the love for us? Isn't it natural that it should be so, as after all they must look upon us as upon old boys who cannot move any more and must stay at home? If Country exists, if Country is a natural necessity, like bread, of which each of us must eat in order not to die of hunger, somebody must go to defend it. And our sons go, when they are twenty, and they don't want tears, because if they die, they die inflamed and happy (I am speaking, of course, of decent boys). Now, if one dies young and happy, without having the ugly sides of life, the boredom of it, the pettiness, the bitterness of disillusion . . . what more can we ask for him? Everyone should stop crying; everyone should laugh, as I do . . . or at least thank God—as I do—because my son, before dying, sent me a message saying that he was dying satisfied at having ended his life in the best way he could have wished. That is why, as you see, I do not even wear mourning. . . ."

He shook his light fawn coat as to show it; his livid lip over his missing teeth was trembling, his eyes were watery and motionless, and soon after he ended with a shrill laugh which might well have been a sob.

"Quite so . . . quite so . . ." agreed the others.

The woman who, bundled in a corner under her coat, had been sitting and listening had—for the last three months—tried to find in the words of her husband and her friends something to console her in her deep sorrow, something that might show her how a mother should resign herself to send her son not even to death but to a probably dangerous life. Yet not a word had she found amongst the many which had been said . . . and her grief had been greater in seeing that nobody—as she thought—could share her feelings.

But now the words of the traveler amazed and almost stunned her. She suddenly realized that it wasn't the others who were wrong and could not understand her but herself who could not rise up to the same height of those fathers and mothers willing to resign themselves, without crying, not only to the departure of their sons but even to their death.

She lifted her head, she bent over from her corner trying to listen with great attention to the details which the fat man was giving to his companions about the way his son had fallen as a hero, for his King and his Country, happy and without regrets. It seemed to her that she had stumbled into a world she had never dreamt of, a world so far unknown to her and she was so pleased to hear everyone joining in congratulating that brave father who could so stoically speak of his child's death.

Then suddenly, just as if she had heard nothing of what had been said and almost as if waking up from a dream, she turned to the old man, asking him:

"Then . . . is your son really dead?"

Everybody stared at her. The old man, too, turned to look at her, fixing his great, bulging, horribly watery light gray eyes, deep in her face. For some little time he tried to answer, but words failed him. He looked and looked at her, almost as if only then—at that silly, incongruous question—he had suddenly realized at last that his son was really dead—gone for ever—for ever. His face contracted, became horribly distorted, then he snatched in haste a handkerchief from his pocket and, to the amazement of everyone, broke into harrowing, heart-rending, uncontrollable sobs.

*Patriotism**

Yukio Mishima (*Japanese, 1925–1970*)

On the twenty-eighth of February, 1936 (on the third day, that is, of the February 26 Incident), Lieutenant Shinji Takeyama of the Konoe Transport Battalion—profoundly disturbed by the knowledge that his closest colleagues had been with the mutineers from the beginning, and indignant at the imminent prospect of Imperial troops attacking Imperial troops—took his officer's sword and ceremonially disemboweled himself in the eight-mat room of his private residence in the sixth block of Aoba-chō, in Yotsuya Ward. His wife, Reiko, followed him, stabbing herself to death. The lieutenant's farewell note consisted of one sentence: "Long live the Imperial Forces." His wife's, after apologies for her unfilial conduct in thus preceding her parents to the grave, concluded: "The day which, for a soldier's wife, had to come, has come. . . ." The last moments of this heroic and dedicated couple were such as to make the gods themselves weep. The lieutenant's age, it should be noted, was thirty-one, his wife's twenty-three; and it was not half a year since the celebration of their marriage.

II

Those who saw the bride and bridegroom in the commemorative photograph—perhaps no less than those actually present at the lieutenant's wedding—had exclaimed in wonder at the bearing of

* Translated by Geoffrey W. Sargent

this handsome couple. The lieutenant, majestic in military uniform, stood protectively beside his bride, his right hand resting upon his sword, his officer's cap held at his left side. His expression was severe, and his dark brows and wide-gazing eyes well conveyed the clear integrity of youth. For the beauty of the bride in her white over-robe no comparisons were adequate. In the eyes, round beneath soft brows, in the slender, finely shaped nose, and in the full lips, there was both sensuousness and refinement. One hand, emerging shyly from a sleeve of the over-robe, held a fan, and the tips of the fingers, clustering delicately, were like the bud of a moonflower.

After the suicide, people would take out this photograph and examine it, and sadly reflect that too often there was a curse on these seemingly flawless unions. Perhaps it was no more than imagination, but looking at the picture after the tragedy it almost seemed as if the two young people before the gold-lacquered screen were gazing, each with equal clarity, at the deaths which lay before them.

Thanks to the good offices of their go-between, Lieutenant General Ozeki, they had been able to set themselves up in a new home at Aoba-chō in Yotsuya. "New home" is perhaps misleading. It was an old three-room rented house backing onto a small garden. As neither the six- nor the four-and-a-half-mat room downstairs was favored by the sun, they used the upstairs eight-mat room as both bedroom and guest room. There was no maid, so Reiko was left alone to guard the house in her husband's absence.

The honeymoon trip was dispensed with on the grounds that these were times of national emergency. The two of them had spent the first night of their marriage at this house. Before going to bed, Shinji, sitting erect on the floor with his sword laid before him, had bestowed upon his wife a soldierly lecture. A woman who had become the wife of a soldier should know and resolutely accept that her husband's death might come at any moment. It could be tomorrow. It could be the day after. But, no matter when it came—he asked—was she steadfast in her resolve to accept it? Reiko rose to her feet, pulled open a drawer of the cabinet, and took out what was the most prized of her new possessions, the dagger her mother had given her. Returning to her place, she laid the dagger without a word on the mat before her, just as her husband had laid his sword. A silent understanding was achieved at once, and the lieutenant never again sought to test his wife's resolve.

In the first few months of her marriage Reiko's beauty grew daily more radiant, shining serene like the moon after rain.

As both were possessed of young, vigorous bodies, their relationship was passionate. Nor was this merely a matter of the night. On more than one occasion, returning home straight from maneuvers, and begrudging even the time it took to remove his mud-splashed uniform, the lieutenant had pushed his wife to the floor almost as soon as he had entered the house. Reiko was equally ardent in her response. For a little more or a little less than a month, from the first night of their marriage Reiko knew happiness, and the lieutenant, seeing this, was happy too.

Reiko's body was white and pure, and her swelling breasts conveyed a firm and chaste refusal; but, upon consent, those breasts were lavish with their intimate, welcoming warmth. Even in bed these two were frighteningly and awesomely serious. In the very midst of wild, intoxicating passions, their hearts were sober and serious.

By day the lieutenant would think of his wife in the brief rest periods between training; and all day long, at home, Reiko would recall the image of her husband. Even when apart, however, they had only to look at the wedding photograph for their happiness to be once more confirmed. Reiko felt not the slightest surprise that a man who had been a complete stranger until a few months ago should now have become the sun about which her whole world revolved.

All these things had a moral basis, and were in accordance with the Education Rescript's injunction that "husband and wife should be harmonious." Not once did Reiko contradict her husband, nor did the lieutenant ever find reason to scold his wife. On the god shelf below the stairway, alongside the tablet from the Great Ise Shrine, were set photographs of their Imperial Majesties, and regularly every morning, before leaving for duty, the lieutenant would stand with his wife at this hallowed place and together they would bow their heads low. The offering water was renewed each morning, and the sacred sprig of *sasaki* was always green and fresh. Their lives were lived beneath the solemn protection of the gods and were filled with an intense happiness which set every fiber in their bodies trembling.

III

Although Lord Privy Seal Saitō's house was in their neighborhood, neither of them heard any noise of gunfire on the morning of February 26. It was a bugle, sounding muster in the dim, snowy dawn, when the ten-minute tragedy had already ended, which first disrupted the lieutenant's slumbers. Leaping at once from his bed, and without speaking a word, the lieutenant donned his uniform, buckled on the sword held ready for him by his wife, and hurried swiftly out into the snow-covered streets of the still darkened morning. He did not return until the evening of the twenty-eighth.

Later, from the radio news, Reiko learned the full extent of this sudden eruption of violence. Her life throughout the subsequent two days was lived alone, in complete tranquillity, and behind locked doors.

In the lieutenant's face, as he hurried silently out into the snowy morning, Reiko had read the determination to die. If her husband did not return, her own decision was made: she too would die. Quietly she attended to the disposition of her personal possessions. She chose her sets of visiting kimonos as keepsakes for friends of her schooldays, and she wrote a name and address on the stiff paper wrapping in which each was folded. Constantly admonished by her husband never to think of the morrow, Reiko had not even kept a diary and was now denied the pleasure of assiduously rereading her record of the happiness of the past few months and consigning each page to the fire as she did so. Ranged across the top of the radio were a small china dog, a rabbit, a squirrel, a bear, and a fox. There were also a small vase and a water pitcher. These comprised Reiko's one and only collection. But it would hardly do, she imagined, to give such things as keepsakes. Nor again would it be quite proper to ask specifically for them to be included in the coffin. It seemed to Reiko, as these thoughts passed through her mind, that the expressions on the small animals' faces grew even more lost and forlorn.

Reiko took the squirrel in her hand and looked at it. And then, her thoughts turning to a realm far beyond these childlike affections, she gazed up into the distance at the great sunlike principle which her husband embodied. She was ready, and happy, to be hurtled along to her destruction in that gleaming sun chariot—but now, for these few moments of solitude, she allowed herself to luxuriate in this innocent attachment to trifles. The time when she had genuinely loved these things, however, was long past. Now she merely loved the memory of having once loved them, and their place in her heart had been filled by more intense passions, by a more frenzied happiness. . . . For Reiko had never, even to herself, thought of those soaring joys of the flesh as a mere pleasure. The February cold, and the icy touch of the china squirrel, had numbed Reiko's slender fingers; yet, even so, in her lower limbs, beneath the ordered repetition of the pattern which crossed the skirt of her trim *meisen* kimono, she could feel now, as she thought of the lieutenant's powerful arms reaching out toward her, a hot moistness of the flesh which defied the snows.

She was not in the least afraid of the death hovering in her mind. Waiting alone at home, Reiko firmly believed that everything her husband was feeling or thinking now, his anguish and distress, was leading her—just as surely as the power in his flesh—to a welcome death. She felt as if her body could melt away with ease and be transformed to the merest fraction of her husband's thought.

Listening to the frequent announcements on the radio, she heard the names of several of her husband's colleagues mentioned among those of the insurgents. This was news of death. She followed the developments closely, wondering anxiously, as the situation became daily more irrevocable, why no Imperial ordinance was sent down, and watching what had at first been taken as a movement to restore the nation's honor come gradually to be branded with the infamous name of mutiny. There was no communication from the regiment. At any moment, it seemed, fighting might commence in the city streets, where the remains of the snow still lay.

Toward sundown on the twenty-eighth Reiko was startled by a furious pounding on the front door. She hurried downstairs. As she pulled with fumbling fingers at the bolt, the shape dimly outlined beyond the frosted-glass panel made no sound, but she knew it was her husband. Reiko had never known the bolt on the sliding door to be so stiff. Still it resisted. The door just would not open.

In a moment, almost before she knew she had succeeded, the lieutenant was standing before her on the cement floor inside the porch, muffled in a khaki greatcoat, his top boots heavy with slush from the street. Closing the door behind him, he returned the bolt once more to its socket. With what significance, Reiko did not understand.

"Welcome home."

Reiko bowed deeply, but her husband made no response. As he had already unfastened his sword and was about to remove his greatcoat, Reiko moved around behind to assist. The coat, which was cold and damp and had lost the odor of horse dung it normally exuded when exposed to the sun, weighed heavily upon her arm. Draping it across a hanger, and cradling the sword and leather belt in her sleeves, she waited while her husband removed his top boots and then followed behind him into the "living room." This was the six-mat room downstairs.

Seen in the clear light from the lamp, her husband's face, covered with a heavy growth of bristle, was almost unrecognizably wasted and thin. The cheeks were hollow, their luster and resilience gone. In his normal good spirits he would have changed into old clothes as soon as he was home and have pressed her to get supper at once, but now he sat before the table still in his uniform, his head drooping dejectedly. Reiko refrained from asking whether she should prepare the supper.

After an interval the lieutenant spoke.

"I knew nothing. They hadn't asked me to join. Perhaps out of consideration, because I was newly married. Kanō, and Homma too, and Yamaguchi."

Reiko recalled momentarily the faces of high-spirited young officers, friends of her husband, who had come to the house occasionally as guests.

"There may be an Imperial ordinance sent down tomorrow. They'll be posted as rebels, I imagine. I shall be in command of a unit with orders to attack them. . . . I can't do it. It's impossible to do a thing like that."

He spoke again.

"They've taken me off guard duty, and I have permission to return home for one night. Tomorrow morning, without question, I must leave to join the attack. I can't do it, Reiko."

Reiko sat erect with lowered eyes. She understood clearly that her husband had spoken of his death. The lieutenant was resolved. Each word, being rooted in death, emerged sharply and with powerful significance against this dark, unmovable background. Although the lieutenant was speaking of his dilemma, already there was no room in his mind for vacillation.

However, there was a clarity, like the clarity of a stream fed from melting snows, in the silence which rested between them. Sitting in his own home after the long two-day ordeal, and looking across at the face of his beautiful wife, the lieutenant was for the first time experiencing true peace of mind. For he had at once known, though she said nothing, that his wife divined the resolve which lay beneath his words.

"Well, then . . ." The lieutenant's eyes opened wide. Despite his exhaustion they were strong and clear, and now for the first time they looked straight into the eyes of his wife. "Tonight I shall cut my stomach."

Reiko did not flinch.

Her round eyes showed tension, as taut as the clang of a bell.

"I am ready," she said. "I ask permission to accompany you."

The lieutenant felt almost mesmerized by the strength in those eyes. His words flowed swiftly and easily, like the utterances of a man in delirium, and it was beyond his understanding how permission in a matter of such weight could be expressed so casually.

"Good. We'll go together. But I want you as a witness, first, for my own suicide. Agreed?"

When this was said a sudden release of abundant happiness welled up in both their hearts. Reiko was deeply affected by the greatness of her husband's trust in her. It was vital for the lieutenant, whatever else might happen, that there should be no irregularity in his death. For that reason there had to be a witness. The fact that he had chosen his wife for this was the first mark of his trust. The second, and even greater mark, was that though he had pledged that they should die together he did not intend to kill his wife first—he had deferred her death to a time when he would no longer be there to verify it. If the lieutenant had been a suspicious husband, he would doubtless, as in the usual suicide pact, have chosen to kill his wife first.

When Reiko said, "I ask permission to accompany you," the lieutenant felt these words to be the final fruit of the education which he had himself given his wife, starting on the first night of their marriage, and which had schooled her, when the moment came, to say what had to be said without a shadow of hesitation. This flattered the lieutenant's opinion of himself as a self-reliant man. He was not so romantic or conceited as to imagine that the words were spoken spontaneously, out of love for her husband.

With happiness welling almost too abundantly in their hearts, they could not help smiling at each other. Reiko felt as if she had returned to her wedding night.

Before her eyes was neither pain nor death. She seemed to see only a free and limitless expanse opening out into vast distances.

"The water is hot. Will you take your bath now?"

"Ah yes, of course."

"And supper . . .?"

The words were delivered in such level, domestic tones that the lieutenant came near to thinking, for the fraction of a second, that everything had been a hallucination.

"I don't think we'll need supper. But perhaps you could warm some sake?"

"As you wish."

As Reiko rose and took a *tanzen* gown from the cabinet for after the bath, she purposely directed her husband's attention to the opened drawer. The lieutenant rose, crossed to the cabinet, and looked inside. From the ordered array of paper wrappings he read, one by one, the addresses of the keepsakes. There was no grief in the lieutenant's response to this demonstration of heroic resolve. His heart was filled with tenderness. Like a husband who is proudly shown the childish purchases of a young wife, the lieutenant, overwhelmed by affection, lovingly embraced his wife from behind and implanted a kiss upon her neck.

Reiko felt the roughness of the lieutenant's unshaven skin against her neck. This sensation, more than being just a thing of this world, was for Reiko almost the world itself, but now—with the feeling that it was soon to be lost forever—it had freshness beyond all her experience. Each moment had its own vital strength, and the senses in every corner of her body were reawakened. Accepting her husband's caresses from behind, Reiko raised herself on the tips of her toes, letting the vitality seep through her entire body.

"First the bath, and then, after some sake . . . lay out the bedding upstairs, will you?"

The lieutenant whispered the words into his wife's ear. Reiko silently nodded.

Flinging off his uniform, the lieutenant went to the bath. To faint background noises of slopping water Reiko tended the charcoal brazier in the living room and began the preparations for warming the sake.

Taking the *tanzen,* a sash, and some underclothes, she went to the bathroom to ask how the water was. In the midst of a coiling cloud of steam the lieutenant was sitting cross-legged on the floor, shaving, and she could dimly discern the rippling movements of the muscles on his damp, powerful back as they responded to the movement of his arms.

There was nothing to suggest a time of any special significance. Reiko, going busily about her tasks, was preparing side dishes from odds and ends in stock. Her hands did not tremble. If anything, she managed even more efficiently and smoothly than usual. From time to time, it is true, there was a strange throbbing deep within her breast. Like distant lightning, it had a moment of sharp intensity and then vanished without trace. Apart from that, nothing was in any way out of the ordinary.

The lieutenant, shaving in the bathroom, felt his warmed body miraculously healed at last of the desperate tiredness of the days of indecision and filled—in spite of the death which lay ahead—with pleasurable anticipation. The sound of his wife going about her work came to him faintly. A healthy physical craving, submerged for two days, reasserted itself.

The lieutenant was confident there had been no impurity in that joy they had experienced when resolving upon death. They had both sensed at that moment—though not, of course, in any clear and conscious way—that those permissible pleasures which they shared in private were once more beneath the protection of Righteousness and Divine Power, and of a complete and unassailable morality. On looking into each other's eyes and discovering there an honorable death, they had felt themselves safe once more behind steel walls which none could destroy, encased in an impenetrable armor of Beauty and Truth. Thus, so far from seeing any inconsistency or conflict between the urges of his flesh and the sincerity of his patriotism, the lieutenant was even able to regard the two as parts of the same thing.

Thrusting his face close to the dark, cracked, misted wall mirror, the lieutenant shaved himself with great care. This would be his death face. There must be no unsightly blemishes. The clean-shaven face gleamed once more with a youthful luster, seeming to brighten the darkness of the mirror. There was a certain elegance, he even felt, in the association of death with this radiantly healthy face.

Just as it looked now, this would become his death face! Already, in fact, it had half departed from the lieutenant's personal possession and had become the bust above a dead soldier's memorial. As an experiment he closed his eyes tight. Everything was wrapped in blackness, and he was no longer a living, seeing creature.

Returning from the bath, the traces of the shave glowing faintly blue beneath his smooth cheeks, he seated himself beside the now well-kindled charcoal brazier. Busy though Reiko was, he noticed, she had found time lightly to touch up her face. Her cheeks were gay and her lips moist. There was no shadow of sadness to be seen. Truly, the lieutenant felt, as he saw this mark of his young wife's passionate nature, he had chosen the wife he ought to have chosen.

As soon as the lieutenant had drained his sake cup he offered it to Reiko. Reiko had never before tasted sake, but she accepted without hesitation and sipped timidly.

"Come here," the lieutenant said.

Reiko moved to her husband's side and was embraced as she leaned backward across his lap. Her breast was in violent commotion, as if sadness, joy, and the potent sake were mingling and reacting within her. The lieutenant looked down into his wife's face. It was the last face he would see in this world, the last face he would see of his wife. The lieutenant scrutinized the face minutely, with the eyes of a traveler bidding farewell to splendid vistas which he will never revisit. It was a face he could not tire of looking at—the features regular yet not cold, the lips lightly closed with a soft strength. The lieutenant kissed those lips, unthinkingly. And suddenly, though there was not the slightest distortion of the face into the unsightliness of sobbing, he noticed that tears were welling slowly from beneath the long lashes of the closed eyes and brimming over into a glistening stream.

When, a little later, the lieutenant urged that they should move to the upstairs bedroom, his wife replied that she would follow after taking a bath. Climbing the stairs alone to the bedroom, where the air was already warmed by the gas heater, the lieutenant lay down on the bedding with arms outstretched and legs apart. Even the time at which he lay waiting for his wife to join him was no later and no earlier than usual.

He folded his hands beneath his head and gazed at the dark boards of the ceiling in the dimness beyond the range of the standard lamp. Was it death he was now waiting for? Or a wild ecstasy of the senses? The two seemed to overlap, almost as if the object of this bodily desire was death itself. But, however that might be, it was certain that never before had the lieutenant tasted such total freedom.

There was the sound of a car outside the window. He could hear the screech of its tires skidding in the snow piled at the side of the street. The sound of its horn re-echoed from near-by walls. . . . Listening to these noises he had the feeling that this house rose like a solitary island in the ocean of a society going as restlessly about its business as ever. All around, vastly and untidily, stretched the country for which he grieved. He was to give his life for it. But would that great country, with which he was prepared to remonstrate to the extent of destroying himself, take the slightest heed of his death? He did not know; and it did not matter. His was a battlefield without glory, a battlefield where none could display deeds of valor: it was the front line of the spirit.

Reiko's footsteps sounded on the stairway. The steep stairs in this old house creaked badly. There were fond memories in that creaking, and many a time, while waiting in bed, the lieutenant had listened to its welcome sound. At the thought that he would hear it no more he listened with intense concentration, striving for every corner of every moment of this precious time to be filled with the sound of those soft footfalls on the creaking stairway. The moments seemed transformed to jewels, sparkling with inner light.

Reiko wore a Nagoya sash about the waist of her *yukata,* but as the lieutenant reached toward it, its redness sobered by the dimness of the light, Reiko's hand moved to his assistance and the sash fell away, slithering swiftly to the floor. As she stood before him, still in her *yukata,* the lieutenant inserted his hands through the side slits beneath each sleeve, intending to embrace her as she was; but at the touch of his finger tips upon the warm naked flesh, and as the armpits closed gently about his hands, his whole body was suddenly aflame.

In a few moments the two lay naked before the glowing gas heater.

Neither spoke the thought, but their hearts, their bodies, and their pounding breasts blazed with the knowledge that this was the very last time. It was as if the words "The Last Time" were spelled out, in invisible brushstrokes, across every inch of their bodies.

The lieutenant drew his wife close and kissed her vehemently. As their tongues explored each other's mouths, reaching out into the smooth, moist interior, they felt as if the still unknown agonies of death had tempered their senses to the keenness of red-hot steel. The agonies they could not yet feel, the distant pains of death, had refined their awareness of pleasure.

"This is the last time I shall see your body," said the lieutenant. "Let me look at it closely." And, tilting the shade on the lampstand to one side, he directed the rays along the full length of Reiko's outstretched form.

Reiko lay still with her eyes closed. The light from the low lamp clearly revealed the majestic sweep of her white flesh. The lieutenant, not without a touch of egocentricity, rejoiced that he would never see this beauty crumble in death.

At his leisure, the lieutenant allowed the unforgettable spectacle to engrave itself upon his mind. With one hand he fondled the hair, with the other he softly stroked the magnificent face, implanting kisses here and there where his eyes lingered. The quiet coldness of the high, tapering forehead, the closed eyes with their long lashes beneath faintly etched brows, the set of the finely shaped nose, the gleam of teeth glimpsed between full, regular lips, the soft cheeks and the small, wise chin . . . these things conjured up in the lieutenant's mind the vision of a truly radiant death face, and again and again he pressed his lips tight against the white throat—where Reiko's own hand was soon to strike—and the throat reddened faintly beneath his kisses. Returning to the mouth he laid his lips against it with the gentlest of pressures, and moved them rhythmically over Reiko's with the light rolling motion of a small boat. If he closed his eyes, the world became a rocking cradle.

Wherever the lieutenant's eyes moved his lips faithfully followed. The high, swelling breasts, surmounted by nipples like the buds of a wild cherry, hardened as the lieutenant's lips closed about them. The arms flowed smoothly downward from each side of the breast, tapering toward the wrists, yet losing nothing of their roundness or symmetry, and at their tips were those delicate fingers which had held the fan at the wedding ceremony. One by one, as the lieutenant kissed them, the fingers withdrew behind their neighbor as if in shame. . . . The natural hollow curving between the bosom and the stomach carried in its lines a suggestion not only of softness but of resilient strength, and while it gave forewarning of the rich curves spreading outward from here to the hips it had, in itself, an appearance only of restraint and proper discipline. The whiteness and richness of the stomach and hips was like milk brimming in a great bowl, and the sharply shadowed dip of the navel could have been the fresh impress of a raindrop, fallen there that very moment. Where the shadows gathered more thickly, hair clustered, gentle and sensitive, and as the agitation mounted in the now no longer passive body there hung over this region a scent like the smoldering of fragrant blossoms, growing steadily more pervasive.

At length, in a tremulous voice, Reiko spoke.

"Show me. . . . Let me look too, for the last time."

Never before had he heard from his wife's lips so strong and unequivocal a request. It was as if something which her modesty had wished to keep hidden to the end had suddenly burst its bonds of constraint. The lieutenant obediently lay back and surrendered himself to his wife. Lithely she raised her white, trembling body, and—burning with an innocent desire to return to her husband what he had done for her—placed two white fingers on the lieutenant's eyes, which gazed fixedly up at her, and gently stroked them shut.

Suddenly overwhelmed by tenderness, her cheeks flushed by a dizzying uprush of emotion, Reiko threw her arms about the lieutenant's close cropped head. The bristly hairs rubbed painfully against her breast, the prominent nose was cold as it dug into her flesh, and his breath was hot. Relaxing her embrace, she gazed down at her husband's masculine face. The severe brows, the closed eyes, the splendid bridge of the nose, the shapely lips drawn firmly together . . . the blue, cleanshaven cheeks reflecting the light and gleaming smoothly. Reiko kissed each of these. She kissed the broad nape of the neck, the strong, erect shoulders, the powerful chest with its twin circles like shields and its russet nipples. In the armpits, deeply shadowed by the ample flesh of the shoulders and chest, a sweet and melancholy odor emanated from the growth of hair, and in the sweetness of this odor was contained, somehow, the essence of young death. The lieutenant's naked skin glowed like a field of barley, and everywhere the muscles showed in sharp relief, converging on the lower abdomen about the small, unassuming navel. Gazing at the youthful, firm stomach, modestly covered by a vigorous growth of hair, Reiko thought of it as it was soon to be, cruelly cut by the sword, and she laid her head upon it, sobbing in pity, and bathed it with kisses.

At the touch of his wife's tears upon his stomach the lieutenant felt ready to endure with courage the cruelest agonies of his suicide.

What ecstasies they experienced after these tender exchanges may well be imagined. The lieutenant raised himself and enfolded his wife in a powerful embrace, her body now limp with exhaustion after her grief and tears. Passionately they held their faces close, rubbing cheek against cheek. Reiko's body was trembling. Their breasts, moist with sweat, were tightly joined, and every inch of the young and beautiful bodies had become so much one with the other that it seemed impossible there should ever again be a separation. Reiko cried out. From the heights they plunged into the abyss, and from the abyss they took wing and soared once more to dizzying heights. The lieutenant panted like the regimental standard-bearer on a route march. . . . As one cycle ended, almost immediately a new wave of passion would be generated, and together —with no trace of fatigue—they would climb again in a single breathless movement to the very summit.

IV

When the lieutenant at last turned away, it was not from weariness. For one thing, he was anxious not to undermine the considerable strength he would need in carrying out his suicide. For another, he would have been sorry to mar the sweetness of these last memories by overindulgence.

Since the lieutenant had clearly desisted, Reiko too, with her usual compliance, followed his example. The two lay naked on their backs, with fingers interlaced, staring fixedly at the dark ceiling. The room was warm from the heater, and even when the sweat had ceased to pour from their bodies they felt no cold. Outside, in the hushed night, the sounds of passing traffic had ceased. Even the noises of the trains and streetcars around Yotsuya station did not penetrate this far. After echoing through the region bounded by the moat, they were lost in the heavily wooded park fronting the broad driveway before Akasaka Palace. It was hard to believe in the tension gripping this whole quarter, where the two factions of the bitterly divided Imperial Army now confronted each other, poised for battle.

Savoring the warmth glowing within themselves, they lay still and recalled the ecstasies they had just known. Each moment of the experience was relived. They remembered the taste of kisses which had never wearied, the touch of naked flesh, episode after episode of dizzying bliss. But already, from the dark boards of the ceiling, the face of death was peering down. These joys had been final, and their bodies would never know them again. Not that joy of this intensity—and the same thought had occurred to them both —was ever likely to be re-experienced, even if they should live on to old age.

The feel of their fingers intertwined—this too would soon be lost. Even the wood-grain patterns they now gazed at on the dark ceiling boards would be taken from them. They could feel death edging in, nearer and nearer. There could be no hesitation now. They must have the courage to reach out to death themselves, and to seize it.

"Well, let's make our preparations," said the lieutenant. The note of determination in the words was unmistakable, but at the same time Reiko had never heard her husband's voice so warm and tender.

After they had risen, a variety of tasks awaited them.

The lieutenant, who had never once before helped with the bedding, now cheerfully slid back the door of the closet, lifted the mattress across the room by himself, and stowed it away inside.

Reiko turned off the gas heater and put away the lamp standard. During the lieutenant's absence she had arranged this room carefully, sweeping and dusting it to a fresh cleanness, and now—if one overlooked the rosewood table drawn into one corner—the eight-mat room gave all the appearance of a reception room ready to welcome an important guest.

"We've seen some drinking here, haven't we? With Kanō and Homma and Noguchi . . ."

"Yes, they were great drinkers, all of them."

"We'll be meeting them before long, in the other world. They'll tease us, I imagine, when they find I've brought you with me."

Descending the stairs, the lieutenant turned to look back into this calm, clean room, now brightly illuminated by the ceiling lamp. There floated across his mind the faces of the young officers who had drunk there, and laughed, and innocently bragged. He had never dreamed then that he would one day cut open his stomach in this room.

In the two rooms downstairs husband and wife busied themselves smoothly and serenely with their respective preparations. The lieutenant went to the toilet, and then to the bathroom to wash. Meanwhile Reiko folded away her husband's padded robe, placed his uniform tunic, his trousers, and a newly cut bleached loincloth in the bathroom, and set out sheets of paper on the living-room table for the farewell notes. Then she removed the lid from the writing box and began rubbing ink from the ink tablet. She had already decided upon the wording of her own note.

Reiko's fingers pressed hard upon the cold gilt letters of the ink tablet, and the water in the shallow well at once darkened, as if a black cloud had spread across it. She stopped thinking that this repeated action, this pressure from her fingers, this rise and fall of faint sound, was all and solely for death. It was a routine domestic task, a simple paring away of time until death should finally stand before her. But somehow, in the increasingly smooth motion of the tablet rubbing on the stone, and in the scent from the thickening ink, there was unspeakable darkness.

Neat in his uniform, which he now wore next to his skin, the lieutenant emerged from the bathroom. Without a word he seated himself at the table, bolt upright, took a brush in his hand, and stared undecidedly at the paper before him.

Reiko took a white silk kimono with her and entered the bathroom. When she reappeared in the living room, clad in the white kimono and with her face lightly made up, the farewell note lay completed on the table beneath the lamp. The thick black brushstrokes said simply:

"Long Live the Imperial Forces—Army Lieutenant Takeyama Shinji."

While Reiko sat opposite him writing her own note, the lieutenant gazed in silence, intensely serious, at the controlled movement of his wife's pale fingers as they manipulated the brush.

With their respective notes in their hands—the lieutenant's sword strapped to his side, Reiko's small dagger thrust into the sash of her white kimono—the two of them stood before the god shelf and silently prayed. Then they put out all the downstairs lights. As he mounted the stairs the lieutenant turned his head and gazed back at the striking, white-clad figure of his wife, climbing behind him, with lowered eyes, from the darkness beneath.

The farewell notes were laid side by side in the alcove of the upstairs room. They wondered whether they ought not to remove the hanging scroll, but since it had been written by their go-between, Lieutenant General Ozeki, and consisted, moreover, of two Chinese characters signifying "Sincerity," they left it where it was. Even if it were to become stained with splashes of blood, they felt that the lieutenant general would understand.

The lieutenant, sitting erect with his back to the alcove, laid his sword on the floor before him.

Reiko sat facing him, a mat's width away. With the rest of her so severely white the touch of rouge on her lips seemed remarkably seductive.

Across the dividing mat they gazed intently into each other's eyes. The lieutenant's sword lay before his knees. Seeing it, Reiko recalled their first night and was overwhelmed with sadness. The lieutenant spoke, in a hoarse voice:

"As I have no second to help me I shall cut deep. It may look unpleasant, but please do not panic. Death of any sort is a fearful thing to watch. You must not be discouraged by what you see. Is that all right?"

"Yes."

Reiko nodded deeply.

Looking at the slender white figure of his wife the lieutenant experienced a bizarre excitement. What he was about to perform was an act in his public capacity as a soldier, something he had never previously shown his wife. It called for a resolution equal to the courage to enter battle; it was a death of no less degree and quality than death in the front line. It was his conduct on the battlefield that he was now to display.

Momentarily the thought led the lieutenant to a strange fantasy. A lonely death on the battlefield, a death beneath the eyes of his beautiful wife . . . in the sensation that he was now to die in these two dimensions, realizing an impossible union of them both, there was sweetness beyond words. This must be the very pinnacle of good fortune, he thought. To have every moment of his death observed by those beautiful eyes—it was like being borne to death on a gentle, fragrant breeze. There was some special favor here. He did not understand precisely what it was, but it was a domain unknown to others: a dispensation granted to no one else had been permitted to himself. In the radiant, bridelike figure of his white-robed wife the lieutenant seemed to see a vision of all those things he had loved and for which he was to lay down his life—the Imperial Household, the Nation, the Army Flag. All these, no less than the wife who sat before him, were presences observing him closely with clear and never-faltering eyes.

Reiko too was gazing intently at her husband, so soon to die, and she thought that never in this world had she seen anything so beautiful. The lieutenant always looked well in uniform, but now, as he contemplated death with severe brows and firmly closed lips, he revealed what was perhaps masculine beauty at its most superb.

"It's time to go," the lieutenant said at last.

Reiko bent her body low to the mat in a deep bow. She could not raise her face. She did not wish to spoil her make-up with tears, but the tears could not be held back.

When at length she looked up she saw hazily through the tears that her husband had wound a white bandage around the blade of his now unsheathed sword, leaving five or six inches of naked steel showing at the point.

Resting the sword in its cloth wrapping on the mat before him, the lieutenant rose from his knees, resettled himself cross-legged, and unfastened the hooks of his uniform collar. His eyes no longer saw his wife. Slowly, one by one, he undid the flat brass buttons. The dusky brown chest was revealed, and then the stomach. He unclasped his belt and undid the buttons of his trousers. The pure whiteness of the thickly coiled loincloth showed itself. The lieutenant pushed the cloth down with both hands, further to ease his stomach, and then reached for the white-bandaged blade of his sword. With his left hand he massaged his abdomen, glancing downward as he did so.

To reassure himself on the sharpness of his sword's cutting edge the lieutenant folded back the left trouser flap, exposing a little of his thigh, and lightly drew the blade across the skin. Blood welled up in the wound at once, and several streaks of red trickled downward, glistening in the strong light.

It was the first time Reiko had ever seen her husband's blood, and she felt a violent throbbing in her chest. She looked at her husband's face. The lieutenant was looking at the blood with calm appraisal. For a moment—though thinking at the same time that it was hollow comfort—Reiko experienced a sense of relief.

The lieutenant's eyes fixed his wife with an intense, hawk-like stare. Moving the sword around to his front, he raised himself slightly on his hips and let the upper half of his body lean over the sword point. That he was mustering his whole strength was apparent from the angry tension of the uniform at his shoulders. The lieutenant aimed to strike deep into the left of his stomach. His sharp cry pierced the silence of the room.

Despite the effort he had himself put into the blow, the lieutenant had the impression that someone else had struck the side of his stomach agonizingly with a thick rod of iron. For a second or so his head reeled and he had no idea what had happened. The five or six inches of naked point had vanished completely into his flesh, and the white bandage, gripped in his clenched fist, pressed directly against his stomach.

He returned to consciousness. The blade had certainly pierced the wall of the stomach, he thought. His breathing was difficult, his chest thumped violently, and in some far deep region, which he could hardly believe was a part of himself, a fearful and excruciating pain came welling up as if the ground had split open to disgorge a boiling stream of molten rock. The pain came suddenly nearer, with terrifying speed. The lieutenant bit his lower lip and stifled an instinctive moan.

Was this *seppuku*?—he was thinking. It was a sensation of utter chaos, as if the sky had fallen on his head and the world was reeling drunkenly. His will power and courage, which had seemed so robust before he made the incision, had now dwindled to something like a single hairlike thread of steel, and he was assailed by the uneasy feeling that he must advance along this thread, clinging to it with desperation. His clenched fist had grown moist. Looking down, he saw that both his hand and the cloth about the blade were drenched in blood. His loincloth too was dyed a deep red. It struck him as incredible that, amidst this terrible agony, things which could be seen could still be seen, and existing things existed still.

The moment the lieutenant thrust the sword into his left side and she saw the deathly pallor fall across his face, like an abruptly lowered curtain, Reiko had to struggle to prevent herself from rushing to his side. Whatever happened, she must watch. She must be a witness. That was the duty her husband had laid upon her. Opposite her, a mat's space away, she could clearly see her husband biting his lip to stifle the pain. The pain was there, with absolute certainty, before her eyes. And Reiko had no means of rescuing him from it.

The sweat glistened on her husband's forehead. The lieutenant closed his eyes, and then opened them again, as if experimenting. The eyes had lost their luster, and seemed innocent and empty like the eyes of a small animal.

The agony before Reiko's eyes burned as strong as the summer sun, utterly remote from the grief which seemed to be tearing herself apart within. The pain grew steadily in stature, stretching upward. Reiko felt that her husband had already become a man in a separate world, a man whose whole being had been resolved into pain, a prisoner in a cage of pain where no hand could reach out to him. But Reiko felt no pain at all. Her grief was not pain. As she thought about this, Reiko began to feel as if someone had raised a cruel wall of glass high between herself and her husband.

Ever since her marriage her husband's existence had been her own existence, and every breath of his had been a breath drawn by herself. But now, while her husband's existence in pain was a vivid reality, Reiko could find in this grief of hers no certain proof at all of her own existence.

With only his right hand on the sword the lieutenant began to cut sideways across his stomach. But as the blade became entangled with the entrails it was pushed constantly outward by their soft resilience; and the lieutenant realized that it would be necessary, as he cut, to use both hands to keep the point pressed deep into his stomach. He pulled the blade across. It did not cut as easily as he had expected. He directed the strength of his whole body into his right hand and pulled again. There was a cut of three or four inches.

The pain spread slowly outward from the inner depths until the whole stomach reverberated. It was like the wild clanging of a bell. Or like a thousand bells which jangled simultaneously at every breath he breathed and every throb of his pulse, rocking his whole being. The lieutenant could no longer stop himself from moaning. But by now the blade had cut its way through to below the navel, and when he noticed this he felt a sense of satisfaction, and a renewal of courage.

The volume of blood had steadily increased, and now it spurted from the wound as if propelled by the beat of the pulse. The mat before the lieutenant was drenched red with splattered blood, and more blood overflowed onto it from pools which gathered in the folds of the lieutenant's khaki trousers. A spot, like a bird, came flying across to Reiko and settled on the lap of her white silk kimono.

By the time the lieutenant had at last drawn the sword across to the right side of his stomach, the blade was already cutting shallow and had revealed its naked tip, slippery with blood and grease. But, suddenly stricken by a fit of vomiting, the lieutenant cried out hoarsely. The vomiting made the fierce pain fiercer still, and the stomach, which had thus far remained firm and compact, now abruptly heaved, opening wide its wound, and the entrails burst through, as if the wound too were vomiting. Seemingly ignorant of their master's suffering, the entrails gave an impression of robust health and almost disagreeable vitality as they slipped smoothly out and spilled over into the crotch. The lieutenant's head drooped, his shoulders heaved, his eyes opened to narrow slits, and a thin trickle of saliva dribbled from his mouth. The gold markings on his epaulettes caught the light and glinted.

Blood was scattered everywhere. The lieutenant was soaked in it to his knees, and he sat now in a crumpled and listless posture, one hand on the floor. A raw smell filled the room. The lieutenant, his head drooping, retched repeatedly, and the movement showed vividly in his shoulders. The blade of the sword, now pushed back by the entrails and exposed to its tip, was still in the lieutenant's right hand.

It would be difficult to imagine a more heroic sight than that of the lieutenant at this moment, as he mustered his strength and flung back his head. The movement was performed with sudden violence, and the back of his head struck with a sharp crack against the alcove pillar. Reiko had been sitting until now with her face lowered, gazing in fascination at the tide of blood advancing toward her knees, but the sound took her by surprise and she looked up.

The lieutenant's face was not the face of a living man. The eyes were hollow, the skin parched, the once so lustrous cheeks and lips the color of dried mud. The right hand alone was moving. Laboriously gripping the sword, it hovered shakily in the air like the hand of a marionette and strove to direct the point at the base of the lieutenant's throat. Reiko watched her husband make this last, most heart-rending, futile exertion. Glistening with blood and grease, the point was thrust at the throat again and again. And each time it missed its aim. The strength to guide it was no longer there. The straying point struck the collar and the collar badges. Although its hooks had been unfastened, the stiff military collar had closed together again and was protecting the throat.

Reiko could bear the sight no longer. She tried to go to her husband's help, but she could not stand. She moved through the blood on her knees, and her white skirts grew deep red. Moving to the rear of her husband, she helped no more than by loosening the collar. The quivering blade at last contacted the naked flesh of the throat. At that moment Reiko's impression was that she herself had propelled her husband forward; but that was not the case. It was a movement planned by the lieutenant himself, his last exertion of strength. Abruptly he threw his body at the blade, and the blade pierced his neck, emerging at the nape. There was a tremendous spurt of blood and the lieutenant lay still, cold blue-tinged steel protruding from his neck at the back.

V

Slowly, her socks slippery with blood, Reiko descended the stairway. The upstairs room was now completely still.

Switching on the ground-floor lights, she checked the gas jet and the main gas plug and poured water over the smoldering, half-buried charcoal in the brazier. She stood before the upright mirror in the four-and-a-half-mat room and held up her skirts. The bloodstains made it seem as if a bold, vivid pattern was printed across the lower half of her white kimono. When she sat down before the mirror, she was conscious of the dampness and coldness of her husband's blood in the region of her thighs, and she shivered. Then, for a long while, she lingered over her toilet preparations. She applied the rouge generously to her cheeks, and her lips too she painted heavily. This was no longer make-up to please her husband. It was make-up for the world which she would leave behind, and there was a touch of the magnificent and the spectacular in her brushwork. When she rose, the mat before the mirror was wet with blood. Reiko was not concerned about this.

Returning from the toilet, Reiko stood finally on the cement floor of the porchway. When her husband had bolted the door here last night it had been in preparation for death. For a while she stood immersed in the consideration of a simple problem. Should she now leave the bolt drawn? If she were to lock the door, it could be that the neighbors might not notice their suicide for several days. Reiko did not relish the thought of their two corpses putrefying before discovery. After all, it seemed, it would be best to leave it open. . . . She released the bolt, and also drew open the frosted-glass door a fraction. . . . At once a chill wind blew in. There was no sign of anyone in the midnight streets, and stars glittered ice-cold through the trees in the large house opposite.

Leaving the door as it was, Reiko mounted the stairs. She had walked here and there for some time and her socks were no longer slippery. About halfway up, her nostrils were already assailed by a peculiar smell.

The lieutenant was lying on his face in a sea of blood. The point protruding from his neck seemed to have grown even more prominent than before. Reiko walked heedlessly across the blood. Sitting beside the lieutenant's corpse, she stared intently at the face, which lay on one cheek on the mat. The eyes were opened wide, as if the lieutenant's attention had been attracted by something. She raised the head, folding it in her sleeve, wiped the blood from the lips, and bestowed a last kiss.

Then she rose and took from the closet a new white blanket and a waist cord. To prevent any derangement of her skirts, she wrapped the blanket about her waist and bound it there firmly with the cord.

Reiko sat herself on a spot about one foot distant from the lieutenant's body. Drawing the dagger from her sash, she examined its dully gleaming blade intently, and held it to her tongue. The taste of the polished steel was slightly sweet.

Reiko did not linger. When she thought how the pain which had previously opened such a gulf between herself and her dying husband was now to become a part of her own experience, she saw before her only the joy of herself entering a realm her husband had already made his own. In her husband's agonized face there had been something inexplicable which she was seeing for the first time. Now she would solve that riddle. Reiko sensed that at last she too would be able to taste the true bitterness and sweetness of that great moral principle in which her husband believed. What had until now been tasted only faintly through her husband's example she was about to savor directly with her own tongue.

Reiko rested the point of the blade against the base of her throat. She thrust hard. The wound was only shallow. Her head blazed, and her hands shook uncontrollably. She gave the blade a strong pull sideways. A warm substance flooded into her mouth, and everything before her eyes reddened, in a vision of spouting blood. She gathered her strength and plunged the point of the blade deep into her throat.

13

In Dreams Begin Responsibilities

by Delmore Schwartz

King of the Bingo Game

by Ralph Ellison

DELMORE SCHWARTZ *Although Delmore Schwartz published poems, stories, essays, and plays during his lifetime, he is perhaps remembered less for the occasional brilliance of his writing, than for the dazzling brilliance of his personality. Volatile, immensely charming, and troubled from the first by what he called the "wound of consciousness," Schwartz during the last two decades of his life became increasingly disturbed, isolating himself from friends and colleagues.*

In the years since his pathetic death, apparently of a heart attack in a seedy Times Square hotel, Schwartz has come to stand for the frail poetic genius who does battle with, and is finally broken by, what the mass of people are constrained to accept as "life." In his Dream Songs, *John Berryman wrote movingly of this aspect of Schwartz. And more recently, Saul Bellow has created in* Humboldt's Gift *what many critics saw as a fictionalized life of the poet. For Schwartz is above all a poet—even in his fiction, as is apparent in the elegiac strains of "In Dreams Begin Responsibilities."*

RALPH ELLISON *In 1952, when Ralph Ellison was thirty-eight, his* Invisible Man *appeared. Though his first novel, a great many readers recognized at once that it was a work of genius. In the decades since its publication,* Invisible Man *has even grown in stature. Yet to this date, Ellison, an extremely painstaking writer, has published but one other volume, a collection of essays called* Shadow and Act, *in 1964.*

"King of the Bingo Game," written before Invisible Man, *is a deceptively rich, and finally poignant, story of a black man's attempts against overwhelming odds to become visible, noticed,* human. *He does not succeed. Or, more accurately, he* does *in a sense succeed—at the expense of his life.*

In Dreams Begin Responsibilities

Delmore Schwartz (*American, 1913–1966*)

I think it is the year 1909. I feel as if I were in a moving-picture theater, the long arm of light crossing the darkness and spinning, my eyes fixed upon the screen. It is a silent picture, as if an old Biograph one, in which the actors are dressed in ridiculously old-fashioned clothes, and one flash succeeds another with sudden jumps, and the actors, too, seem to jump about, walking too fast. The shots are full of rays and dots, as if it had been raining when the picture was photographed. The light is bad.

It is Sunday afternoon, June 12th, 1909, and my father is walking down the quiet streets of Brooklyn on his way to visit my mother. His clothes are newly pressed, and his tie is too tight in his high collar. He jingles the coins in his pocket, thinking of the witty things he will say. I feel as if I had by now relaxed entirely in the soft darkness of the theater; the organist peals out the obvious approximate emotions on which the audience rocks unknowingly. I am anonymous. I have forgotten myself: it is always so when one goes to a movie, it is, as they say, a drug.

My father walks from street to street of trees, lawns and houses, once in a while coming to an avenue on which a streetcar skates and yaws, progressing slowly. The motorman, who has a handlebar mustache, helps a young lady wearing a hat like a feathered bowl onto the car. He leisurely makes change and rings his bell as the passengers mount the car. It is obviously Sunday, for everyone is wearing Sunday clothes and the streetcar's noises emphasize the quiet of the holiday. (Brooklyn is said to be the city of churches.) The shops are closed and their shades drawn but for an occasional stationery store or drugstore with great green balls in the window.

My father has chosen to take this long walk because he likes to walk and think. He thinks about himself in the future and so arrives at the place he is to visit in a mild state of exaltation. He pays no attention to the houses he is passing, in which the Sunday dinner is being eaten, nor to the many trees which line each street, now coming to their full green and the time when they will enclose the whole street in leafy shadow. An occasional carriage passes, the horses' hooves falling like stones in the quiet afternoon, and once in a while an automobile, looking like an enormous upholstered sofa, puffs and passes.

My father thinks of my mother, of how lady-like she is, and of the pride which will be his when he introduces her to his family. They are not yet engaged and he is not yet sure that he loves my mother, so that, once in a while, he becomes panicky about the bond already established. But then he reassures himself by thinking of the big men he admires who are married: William Randolph Hearst and William Howard Taft, who has just become the President of the United States.

My father arrives at my mother's house. He has come too early and so is suddenly embarrassed. My aunt, my mother's younger sister, answers the loud bell with her napkin in her hand, for the family is still at dinner. As my father enters, my grandfather rises from the table and shakes hands with him. My mother has run upstairs to tidy herself. My grandmother asks my father if he has had dinner and tells him that my mother will be down soon. My grandfather opens the conversation by remarking about the mild June weather. My father sits uncomfortably near the table, holding his hat in his hand. My grandmother tells my aunt to take my father's hat. My uncle, twelve years old, runs into the house, his hair tousled. He shouts a greeting to my father, who has often given him nickels, and then runs upstairs, as my grandmother shouts after him. It is evident that the respect in which my father is held in this house is tempered by a good deal of mirth. He is impressive, but also very awkward.

II

Finally my mother comes downstairs and my father, being at the moment engaged in conversation with my grandfather, is made uneasy by her entrance, for he does not know whether to greet my mother or to continue the conversation. He gets up from his chair clumsily and says "Hello" gruffly. My grandfather watches this, examining their congruence, such as it is, with a critical eye, and meanwhile rubbing his bearded cheek roughly, as he always does when he reasons. He is worried; he is afraid that my father will not make a good husband for his oldest daughter. At this point something happens to the film, just as my father says something funny to my mother: I am awakened to myself and my unhappiness just as my interest has become most intense. The audience begins to clap impatiently. Then the trouble is attended to, but the film has been returned to a portion just shown, and once more I see my grandfather rubbing his bearded cheek, pondering my father's character. It is difficult to get back into the picture once more and forget myself, but as my mother giggles at my father's words, the darkness drowns me.

My father and mother depart from the house, my father shaking hands with my grandfather once more, out of some unknown uneasiness. I stir uneasily also, slouched in the hard chair of the theater. Where is the older uncle, my mother's older brother? He is studying in his bedroom upstairs, studying for his final examinations at the College of the City of New York, having been dead of double pneumonia for the last twenty-one years. My mother and father walk down the same quiet streets once more. My mother is holding my father's arm and telling him of the novel she has been reading and my father utters judgments of the characters as the plot is made clear to him. This is a habit which he very much enjoys, for he feels the utmost superiority and confidence when he is approving or condemning the behavior of other people. At times he feels moved to utter a brief "Ugh," whenever the story becomes what he would call sugary. This tribute is the assertion of his manliness. My mother feels satisfied by the interest she has awakened; and she is showing my father how intelligent she is and how interesting.

They reach the avenue, and the streetcar leisurely arrives. They are going to Coney Island this afternoon, although my mother really considers such pleasures inferior. She has made up her mind to indulge only in a walk on the boardwalk and a pleasant dinner, avoiding the riotous amusements as being beneath the dignity of so dignified a couple.

My father tells my mother how much money he has made in the week just past, exaggerating an amount which need not have been exaggerated. But my father has always felt that actualities somehow fall short, no matter how fine they are. Suddenly I begin to weep. The determined old lady who sits next to me in the theater is annoyed and looks at me with an angry face, and being intimidated, I stop. I drag out my handkerchief and dry my face, licking the drop which has fallen near my lips. Meanwhile I have missed something, for here are my father and mother alighting from the streetcar at the last stop, Coney Island.

III

They walk toward the boardwalk and my mother commands my father to inhale the pungent air from the sea. They both breathe in deeply, both of them laughing as they do so. They have in common a great interest in health, although my father is strong and husky, and my mother is frail. They are both full of theories about what is good to eat and not good to eat, and sometimes have heated discussions about it, the whole matter ending in my father's announcement, made with a scornful bluster, that you have to die sooner or later anyway. On the boardwalk's flagpole, the American flag is pulsing in an intermittent wind from the sea.

My father and mother go to the rail of the boardwalk and look down on the beach where a good many bathers are casually walking about. A few are in the surf. A peanut whistle pierces the air with its pleasant and active whine, and my father goes to buy peanuts. My mother remains at the rail and stares at the ocean. The ocean seems merry to her; it pointedly sparkles and again and again the pony waves are released. She notices the children digging in the wet sand, and the bathing costumes of the girls who are her own age. My father returns with the peanuts. Overhead the sun's lightning strikes and strikes, but neither of them are at all aware of it. The boardwalk is full of people dressed in their Sunday clothes and casually strolling. The tide does not reach as far as the boardwalk, and the strollers would feel no danger if it did. My father and mother lean on the rail of the boardwalk and absently stare at the ocean. The ocean is becoming rough; the waves come in slowly, tugging strength from far back. The moment before they somersault, the moment when they arch their backs so beautifully, showing white veins in the green and black, that moment is intolerable. They finally crack, dashing fiercely upon the sand, actually driving, full force downward, against it, bouncing upward and forward, and at last petering out into a small stream of bubbles which slides up the beach and then is recalled. The sun overhead does not disturb my father and my mother. They gaze idly at the ocean scarcely interested in its harshness. But I stare at the terrible sun which breaks up sight, and the fatal merciless passionate ocean. I forget my parents. I stare fascinated, and finally, shocked by their indifference, I burst out weeping once more. The old lady next to me pats my shoulder and says: "There, there, young man, all of this is only a movie, only a movie," but I look up once more at the terrifying sun and the terrifying ocean, and being unable to control my tears I get up and go to the men's room, stumbling over the feet of the other people seated in my row.

IV

When I return, feeling as if I had just awakened in the morning sick for lack of sleep, several hours have apparently passed and my parents are riding on the merry-go-round. My father is on a black horse, my mother on a white one, and they seem to be making an eternal circuit for the single purpose of snatching the nickel rings which are attached to an arm of one of the posts. A hand-organ is playing; it is inseparable from the ceaseless circling of the merry-go-round.

For a moment it seems that they will never get off the carousel, for it will never stop, and I feel as if I were looking down from the fiftieth story of a building. But at length they do get off; even the hand-organ has ceased for a moment. There is a sudden and sweet stillness, as if the achievement of so much motion. My mother has acquired only two rings, my father, however, ten of them, although it was my mother who really wanted them.

They walk on along the boardwalk as the afternoon descends by imperceptible degrees into the incredible violet of dusk. Everything fades into a relaxed glow, even the ceaseless murmuring from the beach. They look for a place to have dinner. My father suggests the best restaurant on the boardwalk and my mother demurs, according to her principles of economy and housewifeliness.

However they do go to the best place, asking for a table near the window so that they can look out upon the boardwalk and the mo-bile ocean. My father feels omnipotent as he places a quarter in the waiter's hand in asking for a table. The place is crowded and here too there is music, this time from a kind of string trio. My father orders with a fine confidence.

As their dinner goes on, my father tells of his plans for the future and my mother shows with expressive face how interested she is, and how impressed. My father becomes exultant, lifted up by the waltz that is being played and his own future begins to intoxicate him. My father tells my mother that he is going to expand his business, for there is a great deal of money to be made. He wants to settle down. After all, he is twenty-nine, he has lived by himself since his thirteenth year, he is making more and more money, and he is envious of his friends when he visits them in the security of their homes, surrounded, it seems, by the calm domestic pleasures, and by delightful children, and then as the waltz reaches the moment when the dancers all swing madly, then, then with awful daring, then he asks my mother to marry him, although awkwardly enough and puzzled as to how he had arrived at the question, and she, to make the whole business worse, begins to cry, and my father looks nervously about, not knowing at all what to do now, and my mother says: "It's all I've wanted from the first moment I saw you," sobbing, and he finds all of this very difficult, scarcely to his taste, scarcely as he thought it would be, on his long walks over Brooklyn Bridge in the revery of a fine cigar, and it was then, at that point, that I stood up in the theater and shouted: "Don't do it! It's not too late to change your minds, both of you. Nothing good will come of it, only remorse, hatred, scandal, and two children whose characters are monstrous." The whole audience turned to look at me, annoyed, the usher came hurrying down the aisle flashing his searchlight, and the old lady next to me tugged me down into my seat, saying: "Be quiet. You'll be put out, and you paid thirty-five cents to come in." And so I shut my eyes because I could not bear to see what was happening. I sat there quietly.

V

But after a while I begin to take brief glimpses and at length I watch again with thirsty interest, like a child who tries to maintain his sulk when he is offered a bribe of candy. My parents are now having their picture taken in a photographer's booth along the boardwalk. The place is shadowed in the mauve light which is apparently necessary. The camera is set to the side on its tripod and looks like a Martian man. The photographer is instructing my parents in how to pose. My father has his arm over my mother's shoulder, and both of them smile emphatically. The photographer brings my mother a bouquet of flowers to hold in her hand, but she holds it at the wrong angle. Then the photographer covers himself with the black cloth which drapes the camera and all that one sees of him is one protruding arm and his hand with which he holds tightly to the rubber ball which he squeezes when the picture is taken. But he is not satisfied with their appearance. He feels that somehow there is something wrong in their pose. Again and again he comes out from his hiding place with new directions. Each suggestion merely makes matters worse. My father is becoming impatient. They try a seated pose. The photographer explains that he has his pride, he wants to make beautiful pictures, he is not merely interested in all of this for the money. My father says: "Hurry up, will you? We haven't got all night." But the photographer only scurries about apologetically, issuing new directions. The photographer charms me, and I approve of him with all my heart, for I know exactly how he feels, and as he criticizes each revised pose according to some obscure idea of rightness, I become quite hopeful. But then my father says angrily: "Come on, you've had enough time, we're not going to wait any longer." And the photographer, sighing unhappily, goes back into the black covering, and holds out his hand, saying: "One, two, three, Now!" and the picture is taken, with my father's smile turned to a grimace and my mother's bright and false. It takes a few minutes for the picture to be developed and as my parents sit in the curious light they become depressed.

VI

They have passed a fortune-teller's booth and my mother wishes to go in, but my father does not. They begin to argue about it. My mother becomes stubborn, my father once more impatient. What my father would like to do now is walk off and leave my mother there, but he knows that that would never do. My mother refuses to budge. She is near tears, but she feels an uncontrollable desire to hear what the palm-reader will say. My father consents angrily and they both go into the booth which is, in a way, like the photographer's, since it is draped in black cloth and its light is colored and shadowed. The place is too warm, and my father keeps saying that this is all nonsense, pointing to the crystal ball on the table. The fortune-teller, a short, fat woman garbed in robes supposedly exotic, comes into the room and greets them, speaking with an accent, but suddenly my father feels that the whole thing is intolerable; he tugs at my mother's arm but my mother refuses to budge. And then, in terrible anger, my father lets go of my mother's arm and strides out, leaving my mother stunned. She makes a movement as if to go after him, but the fortune-teller holds her and begs her not to do so, and I in my seat in the darkness am shocked and horrified. I feel as if I were walking a tight-rope one hundred feet over a circus audience and suddenly the rope is showing signs of breaking, and I get up from my seat and begin to shout once more the first words I can think of to communicate my terrible fear, and once more the usher comes hurrying down the aisle flashing his searchlight, and the old lady pleads with me, and the shocked audience has turned to stare at me, and I keep shouting: "What are they doing? Don't they know what they are doing? Why doesn't my mother go after my father and beg him not to be angry? If she does not do that, what will she do? Doesn't my father know what he is doing?" But the usher has seized my arm, and is dragging me away, and as he does so, he says: "What are *you* doing? Don't you know you can't do things like this, you can't do whatever you want to do, even if other people aren't about? You will be sorry if you do not do what you should do. You can't carry on like this, it is not right, you will find that out soon enough, everything you do matters too much," and as he said that, dragging me through the lobby of the theatre, into the cold light, I woke up into the bleak winter morning of my twenty-first birthday, the window-sill shining with its lip of snow, and the morning already begun.

King of the Bingo Game

Ralph Ellison (*American, 1914–*)

The woman in front of him was eating roasted peanuts that smelled so good that he could barely contain his hunger. He could not even sleep and wished they'd hurry and begin the bingo game. There, on his right, two fellows were drinking wine out of a bottle wrapped in a paper bag, and he could hear soft gurgling in the dark. His stomach gave a low, gnawing growl. "If this was down South," he thought, "all I'd have to do is lean over and say, 'Lady, gimme a few of those peanuts, please ma'm,' and she'd pass me the bag and never think nothing of it." Or he could ask the fellows for a drink in the same way. Folks down South stuck together that way; they didn't even have to know you. But up here it was different. Ask somebody for something, and they'd think you were crazy. Well, I ain't crazy. I'm just broke, 'cause I got no birth certificate to get a job, and Laura 'bout to die 'cause we got no money for a doctor. But I ain't crazy. And yet a pinpoint of doubt was focused in his mind as he glanced toward the screen and saw the hero stealthily entering a dark room and sending the beam of a flashlight along a wall of bookcases. This is where he finds the trapdoor, he remembered. The man would pass abruptly through the wall and find the girl tied to a bed, her legs and arms spread wide, and her clothing torn to rags. He laughed softly to himself. He had seen the picture three times, and this was one of the best scenes.

On his right the fellow whispered wide-eyed to his companion, "Man, look a-yonder!"

"Damn!"

"Wouldn't I like to have her tied up like that . . ."

"Hey! That fool's letting her loose!"

"Aw, man, he loves her."

"Love or no love!"

The man moved impatiently beside him, and he tried to involve himself in the scene. But Laura was on his mind. Tiring quickly of watching the picture he looked back to where the white beam filtered from the projection room above the balcony. It started small and grew large, specks of dust dancing in its whiteness as it reached the screen. It was strange how the beam always landed right on the screen and didn't mess up and fall somewhere else. But they had it all fixed. Everything was fixed. Now suppose when they showed that girl with her dress torn the girl started taking off the rest of her clothes, and when the guy came in he didn't untie her but kept her there and went to taking off his own clothes? *That* would be something to see. If a picture got out of hand like that those guys up there would go nuts. Yeah, and there'd be so many folks in here you couldn't find a seat for nine months! A strange sensation played over his skin. He shuddered. Yesterday he'd seen a bedbug on a woman's neck as they walked out into the bright street. But exploring his thigh through a hole in his pocket he found only goose pimples and old scars.

The bottle gurgled again. He closed his eyes. Now a dreamy music was accompanying the film and train whistles were sounding in the distance, and he was a boy again walking along a railroad trestle down South, and seeing the train coming, and running back as fast as he could go, and hearing the whistle blowing, and getting off the trestle to solid ground just in time, with the earth trembling beneath his feet, and feeling relieved as he ran down the cinder-strewn embankment onto the highway, and looking back and seeing with terror that the train had left the track and was following him right down the middle of the street, and all the white people laughing as he ran screaming . . .

"Wake up there, buddy! What the hell do you mean hollering like that! Can't you see we trying to enjoy this here picture?"

He stared at the man with gratitude.

"I'm sorry, old man," he said. "I musta been dreaming."

"Well, here, have a drink. And don't be making no noise like that, damn!"

His hands trembled as he tilted his head. It was not wine, but whiskey. Cold rye whiskey. He took a deep swoller, decided it was better not to take another, and handed the bottle back to its owner.

"Thanks, old man," he said.

Now he felt the cold whiskey breaking a warm path straight through the middle of him, growing hotter and sharper as it moved.

He had not eaten all day, and it made him light-headed. The smell of the peanuts stabbed him like a knife, and he got up and found a seat in the middle aisle. But no sooner did he sit than he saw a row of intense-faced young girls, and got up again, thinking, "You chicks musta been Lindy-hopping somewhere." He found a seat several rows ahead as the lights came on, and he saw the screen disappear behind a heavy red and gold curtain; then the curtain rising, and the man with the microphone and a uniformed attendant coming on the stage.

He felt for his bingo cards, smiling. The guy at the door wouldn't like it if he knew about his having *five* cards. Well, not everyone played the bingo game; and even with five cards he didn't have much of a chance. For Laura, though, he had to have faith. He studied the cards, each with its different numerals, punching the free center hole in each and spreading them neatly across his lap; and when the lights faded he sat slouched in his seat so that he could look from his cards to the bingo wheel with but a quick shifting of his eyes.

Ahead, at the end of the darkness, the man with the microphone was pressing a button attached to a long cord and spinning the bingo wheel and calling out the number each time the wheel came to rest. And each time the voice rang out his finger raced over the cards for the number. With five cards he had to move fast. He became nervous; there were too many cards, and the man went too fast with his grating voice. Perhaps he should just select one and throw the others away. But he was afraid. He became warm. Wonder how much Laura's doctor would cost? Damn that, watch the cards! And with despair he heard the man call three in a row which he missed on all five cards. This way he'd never win . . .

When he saw the row of holes punched across the third card, he sat paralyzed and heard the man call three more numbers before he stumbled forward, screaming,

"Bingo! Bingo!"

"Let that fool up there," someone called.

"Get up there, man!"

He stumbled down the aisle and up the steps to the stage into a light so sharp and bright that for a moment it blinded him, and he felt that he had moved into the spell of some strange, mysterious power. Yet it was as familiar as the sun, and he knew it was the perfectly familiar bingo.

The man with the microphone was saying something to the audience as he held out his card. A cold light flashed from the man's finger as the card left his hand. His knees trembled. The man stepped closer, checking the card against the numbers chalked on the board. Suppose he had made a mistake? The pomade on the man's hair made him feel faint, and he backed away. But the man was checking the card over the microphone now, and he had to stay. He stood tense, listening.

"Under the O, forty-four," the man chanted. "Under the I, seven. Under the G, three. Under the B, ninety-six. Under the N, thirteen!"

His breath came easier as the man smiled at the audience.

"Yessir, ladies and gentlemen, he's one of the chosen people!"

The audience rippled with laughter and applause.

"Step right up to the front of the stage."

He moved slowly forward, wishing that the light was not so bright.

"To win tonight's jackpot of $36.90 the wheel must stop between the double zero, understand?"

He nodded, knowing the ritual from the many days and nights he had watched the winners march across the stage to press the button that controlled the spinning wheel and receive the prizes. And now he followed the instructions as though he'd crossed the slippery stage a million prize-winning times.

The man was making some kind of a joke, and he nodded vacantly. So tense had he become that he felt a sudden desire to cry and shook it away. He felt vaguely that his whole life was determined by the bingo wheel; not only that which would happen now that he was at last before it, but all that had gone before, since his birth, and his mother's birth and the birth of his father. It had always been there, even though he had not been aware of it, handing out the unlucky cards and numbers of his days. The feeling persisted, and he started quickly away. I better get down from here before I make a fool of myself, he thought.

"Here, boy," the man called. "You haven't started yet."

Someone laughed as he went hesitantly back.

"Are you all reet?"

He grinned at the man's jive talk, but no words would come, and he knew it was not a convincing grin. For suddenly he knew that he stood on the slippery brink of some terrible embarrassment.

"Where are you from, boy?" the man asked.

"Down South."

"He's from down South, ladies and gentlemen," the man said. "Where from? Speak right into the mike."

"Rocky Mont," he said. "Rock' Mont, North Car'lina."

"So you decided to come down off that mountain to the U.S.," the man laughed. He felt that the man was making a fool of him, but then something cold was placed in his hand, and the lights were no longer behind him.

Standing before the wheel he felt alone, but that was somehow right, and he remembered his plan. He would give the wheel a short quick twirl. Just a touch of the button. He had watched it many times, and always it came close to double zero when it was short and quick. He steeled himself; the fear had left, and he felt a profound sense of promise, as though he were about to be repaid for all the things he'd suffered all his life. Trembling, he pressed the button. There was a whirl of lights, and in a second he realized with finality that though he wanted to, he could not stop. It was as though he held a high-powered line in his naked hand. His nerves tightened. As the wheel increased its speed it seemed to draw him more and more into its power, as though it held his fate; and with it came a deep need to submit, to whirl, to lose himself in its swirl of color. He could not stop it now, he knew. So let it be.

The button rested snugly in his palm where the man had placed it. And now he became aware of the man beside him, advising him through the microphone, while behind the shadowy audience hummed with noisy voices. He shifted his feet. There was still that feeling of helplessness within him, making part of him desire to turn back, even now that the jackpot was right in his hand. He squeezed the button until his fist ached. Then, like the sudden shriek of a subway whistle, a doubt tore through his head. Suppose he did not spin the wheel long enough? What could he do, and how could he tell? And then he knew, even as he wondered, that as long as he pressed the button, he could control the jackpot. He and only he could determine whether or not it was to be his. Not even the man with the microphone could do anything about it now. He felt drunk. Then, as though he had come down from a high hill into a valley of people, he heard the audience yelling.

"Come down from there, you jerk!"

"Let somebody else have a chance . . ."

"Ole Jack thinks he done found the end of the rainbow . . ."

The last voice was not unfriendly, and he turned and smiled dreamily into the yelling mouths. Then he turned his back squarely on them.

"Don't take too long, boy," a voice said.

He nodded. They were yelling behind him. Those folks did not understand what had happened to him. They had been playing the bingo game day in and night out for years, trying to win rent money or hamburger change. But not one of those wise guys had discovered this wonderful thing. He watched the wheel whirling past the numbers and experienced a burst of exaltation: This is God! This is the really truly God! He said it aloud, "This is God!"

He said it with such absolute conviction that he feared he would fall fainting into the footlights. But the crowd yelled so loud that they could not hear. Those fools, he thought. I'm here trying to tell them the most wonderful secret in the world, and they're yelling like they gone crazy. A hand fell upon his shoulder.

"You'll have to make a choice now, boy. You've taken too long."

He brushed the hand violently away.

"Leave me alone, man. I know what I'm doing!"

The man looked surprised and held on to the microphone for support. And because he did not wish to hurt the man's feelings he smiled, realizing with a sudden pang that there was no way of explaining to the man just why he had to stand there pressing the button forever.

"Come here," he called tiredly.

The man approached, rolling the heavy microphone across the stage.

"Anybody can play this bingo game, right?" he said.

"Sure, but . . ."

He smiled, feeling inclined to be patient with this slick looking white man with his blue sport shirt and his sharp gabardine suit.

"That's what I thought," he said. "Anybody can win the jackpot as long as they get the lucky number, right?"

"That's the rule, but after all . . ."

"That's what I thought," he said. "And the big prize goes to the man who knows how to win it?"

The man nodded speechlessly.

"Well then, go on over there and watch me win like I want to. I ain't going to hurt nobody," he said, "and I'll show you how to win. I mean to show the whole world how it's got to be done."

And because he understood, he smiled again to let the man know that he held nothing against him for being white and impatient. Then he refused to see the man any longer and stood pressing the button, the voices of the crowd reaching him like sounds in distant streets. Let them yell. All the Negroes down there were just ashamed because he was black like them. He smiled inwardly, knowing how it was. Most of the time he was ashamed of what Negroes did himself. Well, let them be ashamed for something this time. Like him. He was like a long thin black wire that was being stretched and wound upon the bingo wheel; wound until he wanted to scream; wound, but this time himself controlling the winding and the sadness and the shame, and because he did, Laura would be all right. Suddenly the lights flickered. He staggered backwards. Had something gone wrong? All this noise. Didn't they know that although he controlled the wheel, it also controlled him, and unless he pressed the button forever and forever and ever it would stop, leaving him high and dry, dry and high on this hard high slippery hill and Laura dead? There was only one chance; he had to do whatever the wheel demanded. And gripping the button in despair, he discovered with surprise that it imparted a nervous energy. His spine tingled. He felt a certain power.

Now he faced the raging crowd with defiance, its screams penetrating his eardrums like trumpets shrieking from a jukebox. The vague faces glowing in the bingo lights gave him a sense of himself that he had never known before. He was running the show, by God! They had to react to him, for he was their luck. This is *me*, he thought. Let the bastards yell. Then someone was laughing inside him, and he realized that somehow he had forgotten his own name. It was a sad, lost feeling to lose your name, and a crazy thing to do. That name had been given him by the white man who had owned his grandfather a long lost time ago down South. But maybe those wise guys knew his name.

"Who am I?" he screamed.

"Hurry up and bingo, you jerk!"

They didn't know either, he thought sadly. They didn't even know their own names, they were all poor nameless bastards. Well, he didn't need that old name; he was reborn. For as long as he pressed the button he was The-man-who-pressed-the-button-who-held-the-prize-who-was-the-King-of-Bingo. That was the way it was, and he'd have to press the button even if nobody understood, even though Laura did not understand.

"Live!" he shouted.

The audience quieted like the dying of a huge fan.

"Live, Laura, baby. I got holt of it now, sugar. Live!"

He screamed it, tears streaming down his face. "I got nobody but YOU!"

The screams tore from his very guts. He felt as though the rush of blood to his head would burst out in baseball seams of small red droplets, like a head beaten by police clubs. Bending over he saw a trickle of blood splashing the toe of his shoe. With his free hand he searched his head. It was his nose. God, suppose something has gone wrong? He felt that the whole audience had somehow entered him and was stamping its feet in his stomach, and he was unable to throw them out. They wanted the prize, that was it. They wanted the secret for themselves. But they'd never get it; he would keep the bingo wheel whirling forever, and Laura would be safe in the wheel. But would she? It had to be, because if she were not safe the wheel would cease to turn; it could not go on. He had to get away, *vomit* all, and his mind formed an image of himself running with Laura in his arms down the tracks of the subway just ahead of an A train, running desperately *vomit* with people screaming for him to come out but knowing no way of leaving the tracks because to stop would bring the train crushing down upon him and to attempt to leave across the other tracks would mean to run into a hot third rail as high as his waist which threw blue sparks that blinded his eyes until he could hardly see.

He heard singing and the audience was clapping its hands.

> Shoot the liquor to him, Jim, boy!
> Clap-clap-clap
> Well a-calla the cop
> He's blowing his top!
> Shoot the liquor to him, Jim, boy!

Bitter anger grew within him at the singing. They think I'm crazy. Well let 'em laugh. I'll do what I got to do.

He was standing in an attitude of intense listening when he saw that they were watching something on the stage behind him. He felt weak. But when he turned he saw no one. If only his thumb did not ache so. Now they were applauding. And for a moment he thought that the wheel had stopped. But that was impossible, his thumb still pressed the button. Then he saw them. Two men in uniform beckoned from the end of the stage. They were coming toward him, walking in step, slowly, like a tap-dance team returning for a third encore. But their shoulders shot forward, and he backed away, looking wildly about. There was nothing to fight them with. He had only the long black cord which led to a plug somewhere back stage, and he couldn't use that because it operated the bingo wheel. He backed slowly, fixing the men with his eyes as his lips stretched over his teeth in a tight, fixed grin; moved toward the end of the stage and realizing that he couldn't go much further, for suddenly the cord became taut and he couldn't afford to break the cord. But he had to do something. The audience was howling. Suddenly he stopped dead, seeing the men halt, their legs lifted as in an interrupted step of a slow-motion dance. There was nothing to do but run in the other direction and he dashed forward, slipping and sliding. The men fell back, surprised. He struck out violently going past.

"Grab him!"

He ran, but all too quickly the cord tightened, resistingly, and he turned and ran back again. This time he slipped them, and discovered by running in a circle before the wheel he could keep the cord from tightening. But this way he had to flail his arms to keep the men away. Why couldn't they leave a man alone? He ran, circling.

"Ring down the curtain," someone yelled. But they couldn't do that. If they did the wheel flashing from the projection room would be cut off. But they had him before he could tell them so, trying to pry open his fist, and he was wrestling and trying to bring his knees into the fight and holding on to the button, for it was his life. And now he was down, seeing a foot coming down, crushing his wrist cruelly, down, as he saw the wheel whirling serenely above.

"I can't give it up," he screamed. Then quietly, in a confidential tone, "Boys, I really can't give it up."

It landed hard against his head. And in the blank moment they had it away from him, completely now. He fought them trying to pull him up from the stage as he watched the wheel spin slowly to a stop. Without surprise he saw it rest at double-zero.

"You see," he pointed bitterly.

"Sure, boy, sure, it's O. K.," one of the men said smiling.

And seeing the man bow his head to someone he could not see, he felt very, very happy; he would receive what all the winners received.

But as he warmed in the justice of the man's tight smile he did not see the man's slow wink, nor see the bow-legged man behind him step clear of the swiftly descending curtain and set himself for a blow. He only felt the dull pain exploding in his skull, and he knew even as it slipped out of him that his luck had run out on the stage.

14

Bright and Morning Star

by Richard Wright

Red Leaves

by William Faulkner

RICHARD WRIGHT *Wright's grandparents were slaves, and he was born in Natchez, Mississippi. Largely self-educated, he described the deprivations of his childhood in* Black Boy, *1945. During the depression, he was involved in left-wing activities in Chicago and joined the Communist party. His most important book was* Native Son, *1940, the naturalistic study of Bigger Thomas, a black man convicted of a murder he had accidentally committed.*

WILLIAM FAULKNER *Faulkner's family lived for generations in one small section of north Mississippi, and almost all of his prodigious output was devoted to exploring his Southern heritage. No American writer since Henry James had been as experimental, had found so complex a voice or as rich a prose texture, had so dared to innovate a form that profoundly affected the dimensions of fiction. Faulkner's imagined Yoknapatawpha County became a mythic fable that he revisited in novel after novel, often using the same characters, and including a vast range of sensibility. From 1931 to 1935, Faulkner wrote a series of masterpieces:* The Sound and the Fury, Light In August, As I Lay Dying, *and* Absalom, Absalom—*but by the end of World War II none of his work was in print. Malcolm Cowley edited a Faulkner anthology for Viking, and the resurgence of critical interest which ensued culminated in the award of the Nobel Prize in 1949.*

Bright and Morning Star

Richard Wright (*American, 1908–1960*)

She stood with her black face some six inches from the moist windowpane and wondered when on earth would it ever stop raining. It might keep up like this all week, she thought. She heard rain droning upon the roof and high up in the wet sky her eyes followed the silent rush of a bright shaft of yellow that swung from the airplane beacon in far off Memphis. Momently she could see it cutting through the rainy dark; it would hover a second like a gleaming sword above her head, then vanish. She sighed, troubling, Johnny-Boys been trampin in this slop all day wid no decent shoes on his feet. . . . Through the window she could see the rich black earth sprawling outside in the night. There was more rain than the clay could soak up; pools stood everywhere. She yawned and mumbled: "Rains good n bad. It kin make seeds bus up thu the ground, er it kin bog things down lika watah-soaked coffin." Her hands were folded loosely over her stomach and the hot air of the kitchen traced a filmy vein of sweat on her forehead. From the cook stove came the soft singing of burning wood and now and then a throaty bubble rose from a pot of simmering greens.

"Shucks, Johnny-Boy coulda let somebody else do all tha runnin in the rain. Theres others bettah fixed fer it than he is. But, naw! Johnny-Boy ain the one t trust nobody t do nothin. Hes gotta do it *all* hissef. . . ."

She glanced at a pile of damp clothes in a zinc tub. Waal, Ah bettah git t work. She turned, lifted a smoothing iron with a thick pad of cloth, touched a spit-wet finger to it with a quick, jerking motion: *smiiitz!* Yeah; its hot! Stooping, she took a blue work-shirt from the tub and shook it out. With a deft twist of her shoulders she caught the iron in her right hand; the fingers of her left hand took a piece of wax from a tin box and a frying sizzle came as she smeared the bottom. She was thinking of nothing now; her hands followed a life-long ritual of toil. Spreading a sleeve, she ran the hot iron to and fro until the wet cloth became stiff. She was deep in the midst of her work when a song rose up out of the far off days of her childhood and broke through half-parted lips:

> Hes the Lily of the Valley, the Bright n
>   Mawnin Star
> Hes the Fairest of Ten Thousan t ma soul . . .

A gust of wind dashed rain against the window. Johnny-Boy oughta c mon home n eat his suppah. Aw, Lawd! Itd be fine ef Sug could eat wid us tonight! Itd be like ol times! Mabbe aftah all it wont be long fo he comes back. Tha lettah Ah got from im last week said *Don give up hope*. . . . Yeah; we gotta live in hope. Then both of her sons, Sug and Johnny-Boy, would be back with her.

With an involuntary nervous gesture, she stopped and stood still, listening. But the only sound was the lulling fall of rain. Shucks, ain no usa me ackin this way, she thought. Ever time they gits ready to hol them meetings Ah gits jumpity. Ah been a lil scared ever since Sug went t jail. She heard the clock ticking and looked. Johnny-Boys a *hour* late! He sho must be havin a time doin all tha trampin, trampin thu the mud. . . . But her fear was a quiet one; it was more like an intense brooding than a fear; it was a sort of hugging of hated facts so closely that she could feel their grain, like letting cold water run over her hand from a faucet on a winter morning.

She ironed again, faster now, as if she felt the more she engaged her body in work the less she would think. But how could she forget Johnny-Boy out there on those wet fields rounding up white and black Communists for a meeting tomorrow? And that was just what Sug had been doing when the sheriff had caught him, beat him, and tried to make him tell who and where his comrades were. Po Sug! They sho musta beat the boy somethin awful! But, thank Gawd, he didnt talk! He ain no weaklin, Sug ain! Hes been lion-hearted all his life long.

That had happened a year ago. And now each time those meetings came around the old terror surged back. While shoving the iron a cluster of toiling days returned; days of washing and ironing to feed Johnny-Boy and Sug so they could do party work; days of carrying a hundred pounds of white folks' clothes upon her head across fields sometimes wet and sometimes dry. But in those days a hundred pounds was nothing to carry carefully balanced upon her head while stepping by instinct over the corn and cotton rows. The only time it had seemed heavy was when she had heard of Sug's arrest. She had been coming home one morning with a bundle upon her head, her hands swinging idly by her sides, walking slowly with her eyes in front of her, when Bob, Johnny-Boy's pal, had called from across the fields and had come and told her that the sheriff had got Sug. That morning the bundle had become heavier than she could ever remember.

And with each passing week now, though she spoke of it to no one, things were becoming heavier. The tubs of water and the smoothing iron and the bundles of clothes were becoming harder to lift, with her back aching so; and her work was taking longer, all because Sug was gone and she didn't know just when Johnny-Boy would be taken too. To ease the ache of anxiety that was swelling her heart, she hummed, then sang softly:

He walks wid me, He talks wid me
He tells me Ahm His own. . . .

Guiltily, she stopped and smiled. Looks like Ah just cant seem t fergit them ol songs, no mattah how hard Ah tries. . . . She had learned them when she was a little girl living and working on a farm. Every Monday morning from the corn and cotton fields the slow strains had floated from her mother's lips, lonely and haunting; and later, as the years had filled with gall, she had learned their deep meaning. Long hours of scrubbing floors for a few cents a day had taught her who Jesus was, what a great boon it was to cling to Him, to be like Him and suffer without a mumbling word. She had poured the yearning of her life into the songs, feeling buoyed with a faith beyond this world. The figure of the Man nailed in agony to the Cross, His burial in a cold grave, His transfigured Resurrection, His being breath and clay, God and Man—all had focused her feelings upon an imagery which had swept her life into a wondrous vision.

But as she had grown older, a cold white mountain, the white folks and their laws, had swum into her vision and shattered her songs and their spell of peace. To her that white mountain was temptation, something to lure her from her Lord, a part of the world God had made in order that she might endure it and come through all the stronger, just as Christ had risen with greater glory from the tomb. The days crowded with trouble had enhanced her faith and she had grown to love hardship with a bitter pride; she had obeyed the laws of the white folks with a soft smile of secret knowing.

After her mother had been snatched up to heaven in a chariot of fire, the years had brought her a rough workingman and two black babies, Sug and Johnny-Boy, all three of whom she had wrapped in the charm and magic of her vision. Then she was tested by no less than God; her man died, a trial which she bore with the strength shed by the grace of her vision; finally even the memory of her man faded into the vision itself, leaving her with two black boys growing tall, slowly into manhood.

Then one day grief had come to her heart when Johnny-Boy and Sug had walked forth demanding their lives. She had sought to fill their eyes with her vision, but they would have none of it. And she had wept when they began to boast of the strength shed by a new and terrible vision.

But she had loved them, even as she loved them now; bleeding, her heart had followed them. She could have done no less, being an old woman in a strange world. And day by day her sons had ripped from her startled eyes her old vision, and image by image had given her a new one, different, but great and strong enough to fling her into the light of another grace. The wrongs and sufferings of black men had taken the place of Him nailed to the Cross; the meager beginnings of the party had become another Resurrection; and the hate of those who would destroy her new faith had quickened in her a hunger to feel how deeply her new strength went.

"Lawd, Johnny-Boy," she would sometimes say, "Ah jus wan them white folks to try to make me tell *who* is *in* the party n who *ain!* Ah just wan em t try, Ahll show em somethin they never thought a black woman could have!"

But sometimes like tonight, while lost in the forgetfulness of work, the past and the present would become mixed in her; while toiling under a strange star for a new freedom the old songs would slip from her lips with their beguiling sweetness.

The iron was getting cold. She put more wood into the fire, stood again at the window and watched the yellow blade of light cut through the wet darkness. Johnny-Boy ain here yit . . . Then, before she was aware of it, she was still, listening for sounds. Under the drone of rain she heard the slosh of feet in mud. Tha ain Johnny-Boy. She knew his long, heavy footsteps in a million. She heard feet come on the porch. Some woman. . . . She heard bare knuckles knock three times, then once. Thas some of them comrades! She unbarred the door, cracked it a few inches, and flinched from the cold rush of damp wind.

"Whos tha?"

"Its me!"

"Who?"

"Me, Reva!"

She flung the door open.

"Lawd, chile, c mon in!"

She stepped to one side and a thin, blond-haired white girl ran through the door; as she slid the bolt she heard the girl gasping and shaking her wet clothes. Somethings wrong! Reva wouldna walked a mile t mah house in all this slop fer nothin! That gals stuck onto Johnny-Boy. Ah wondah ef anythin happened t im?

"Git on inter the kitchen, Reva, where its warm."

"Lawd, Ah sho is wet!"

"How yuh reckon yuhd be, in all tha rain?"

"Johnny-Boy ain here *yit*?" asked Reva.

"Naw! N ain no usa yuh worryin bout im. Jus yuh git them shoes off! Yuh wanna ketch yo deatha col?" She stood looking absently. Yeah; its somethin about the party er Johnny-Boy thas gone wrong. Lawd, Ah wondah ef her pa knows how she feels bout Johnny-Boy? "Honey, yuh hadn't oughta come out in sloppy weather like this."

"Ah had t come, An Sue."

She led Reva to the kitchen.

"Git them shoes off n git close t the stove so yuhll git dry!"

"An Sue, Ah got somethin t tell yuh . . ."

The words made her hold her breath. Ah bet its somethin bout Johnny-Boy!

"Whut, honey?"

"The sheriff wuz by our house tonight. He come t see pa."

"Yeah?"

"He done got word from somewheres bout tha meetin tomorrow."

"Is it Johnny-Boy, Reva?"

"Aw, naw, An Sue! Ah ain hearda word bout im. Ain yuh seen im tonight?"

"He ain come home t eat yit."

"Where kin he be?"

"Lawd knows, chile."

Somebody's gotta tell them comrades that meetings off," said Reva. "The sheriffs got men watchin our house. Ah had t slip out t git here widout em followin me."

"Reva?"

"Hunh?"

"Ahma ol woman n Ah wans yuh t tell me the truth."

"Whut, An Sue?"

"Yuh ain tryin t fool me, is yuh?"

"*Fool* yuh?"

"Bout Johnny-Boy?"

"Lawd, naw, An Sue!"

"Ef theres anythin wrong jus tell me, chile. Ah kin stan it."

She stood by the ironing board, her hands as usual folded loosely over her stomach, watching Reva pull off her water-clogged shoes. She was feeling that Johnny-Boy was already lost to her; she was feeling the pain that would come when she knew it for certain; and she was feeling that she would have to be brave and bear it. She was like a person caught in a swift current of water and knew where the water was sweeping her and did not want to go on but had to go on to the end.

"It ain nothin bout Johnny-Boy, An Sue," said Reva. "But we gotta do somethin er we'll all git inter trouble."

"How the sheriff know about tha meetin?"

"Thas what pa wants t know."

"Somebody done turned Judas."

"Sho looks like it."

"Ah bet it wuz some of them new ones," she said.

"Its hard t tell," said Reva.

"Listen, Reva, yuh oughta stay here n git dry, but yuh bettah git back n tell yo pa Johnny-Boy ain here n Ah don know when hes gonna show up. *Some*bodys gotta tell them comrades t stay erway from yo pas house."

She stood with her back to the window, looking at Reva's wide, blue eyes. Po critter! Gotta go back thu all tha slop! Though she felt sorry for Reva, not once did she think that it would not have to be done. Being a woman, Reva was not suspect; she would *have* to go. It was just as natural for Reva to go back through the cold rain as it was for her to iron night and day, or for Sug to be in jail. Right now, Johnny-Boy was out there on those dark fields trying to get home. Lawd, don let em git im tonight! In spite of herself her feelings became torn. She loved her son and, loving him, she loved what he was trying to do. Johnny-Boy was happiest when he was working for the party, and her love for him was for his happiness. She frowned, trying hard to fit something together in her feelings: for her to try to stop Johnny-Boy was to admit that all the toil of years meant nothing; and to let him go meant that sometime or other he would be caught, like Sug. In facing it this way she felt a little stunned, as though she had come suddenly upon a blank wall in the dark. But outside in the rain were people, white and black, whom she had known all her life. Those people depended upon Johnny-Boy, loved him and looked to him as a man and leader. Yeah; hes gotta keep on; he cant stop now. . . .She looked at Reva; she was crying and pulling her shoes back on with reluctant fingers.

"What yuh carryin on tha way fer, chile?"

"Yuh done los Sug, now yuh sendin Johnny-Boy . . ."

"Ah got t, honey."

She was glad she could say that. Reva believed in black folks and not for anything in the world would she falter before her. In Reva's trust and acceptance of her she had found her first feelings of humanity; Reva's love was her refuge from shame and degradation. If in the early days of her life the white mountain had driven her back from the earth, then in her last days Reva's love was drawing her toward it, like the beacon that swung through the night outside. She heard Reva sobbing.

"Hush, honey!"

"Mah brothers in jail too! Ma cries every day . . ."

"Ah know, honey."

She helped Reva with her coat; her fingers felt the scant flesh of the girl's shoulders. She don git ernuff t eat, she thought. She slipped her arms around Reva's waist and held her close for a moment.

"Now, yuh stop that cryin."

"A-a-ah-c-c-cant hep it. . . ."

"Everythingll be awright; Johnny-Boyll be back."

"Yuh think so?"

"Sho, chile. Cos he will."

Neither of them spoke again until they stood in the doorway. Outside they could hear water rushing through the ruts of the street.

"Be sho n send Johnny-Boy t tell the folks t stay erway from pas house," said Reva.

"Ahll tell im. Don yuh worry."

"Good-bye!"

"Good-bye!"

Leaning against the door jamb, she shook her head slowly and watched Reva vanish through the falling rain.

II

She was back at her board, ironing, when she heard feet sucking in the mud of the back yard; feet she knew from long years of listening were Johnny-Boy's. But tonight, with all the rain and fear, his coming was like a leaving, was almost more than she could bear. Tears welled to her eyes and she blinked them away. She felt that he was coming so that she could give him up; to see him now was to say good-bye. But it was a good-bye she knew she could never say; they were not that way toward each other. All day long they could sit in the same room and not speak; she was his mother and he was her son. Most of the time a nod or a grunt would carry all the meaning that she wanted to convey to him, or he to her. She did not even turn her head when she heard him come stomping into the kitchen. She heard him pull up a chair, sit, sigh, and draw off his muddy shoes; they fell to the floor with heavy thuds. Soon the kitchen was full of the scent of his drying socks and his burning pipe. Tha boys hongry! She paused and looked at him over her shoulder; he was puffing at his pipe with his head tilted back and his feet propped up on the edge of the stove; his eyelids drooped and his wet clothes steamed from the heat of the fire. Lawd, tha boy gits mo like his pa every day he lives, she mused, her lips breaking in a slow, faint smile. Hols tha pipe in his mouth just like his pa usta hol his. Wondah how they woulda got erlong ef his pa hada lived? They oughta liked each other, they so mucha like. She wished there could have been other children besides Sug, so Johnny-Boy would not have to be so much alone. A man needs a woman by his side. . . . She thought of Reva; she liked Reva; the brightest glow her heart had ever known was when she had learned that Reva loved Johnny-Boy. But beyond Reva were cold white faces. Ef theys caught it means *death*. . . . She jerked around when she heard Johnny-Boy's pipe clatter to the floor. She saw him pick it up, smile sheepishly at her, and wag his head.

"Gawd, Ahm sleepy," he mumbled.

She got a pillow from her room and gave it to him.

"Here," she said.

"Hunh," he said, putting the pillow between his head and the back of the chair.

They were silent again. Yes, she would have to tell him to go back out into the cold rain and slop; maybe to get caught; maybe for the last time; she didn't know. But she would let him eat and get dry before telling him that the sheriff knew of the meeting to be held at Lem's tomorrow. And she would make him take a big dose of soda before he went out; soda always helped to stave off a cold. She looked at the clock. It was eleven. Theres time yit. Spreading a newspaper on the apron of the stove, she placed a heaping plate of greens upon it, a knife, a fork, a cup of coffee, a slab of cornbread, and a dish of peach cobbler.

"Yo suppahs ready," she said.

"Yeah," he said.

He did not move. She ironed again. Presently, she heard him eating. When she could no longer hear his knife tinkling against the edge of the plate, she knew he was through. It was almost twelve now. She would let him rest a little while longer before she told him. Till one er'clock, mabbe. Hes so tired. . . . She finished her ironing, put away the board, and stacked the clothes in her dresser drawer. She poured herself a cup of black coffee, drew up a chair, sat down and drank.

"Yuh almos dry," she said, not looking around.

"Yeah," he said, turning sharply to her.

The tone of voice in which she had spoken had let him know that more was coming. She drained her cup and waited a moment longer.

"Reva wuz here."

"Yeah?"

"She lef bout a hour ergo."

"Whut she say?"

"She said ol man Lem hada visit from the sheriff today."

"Bout the meetin?"

She saw him stare at the coals glowing red through the crevices of the stove and run his fingers nervously through his hair. She knew he was wondering how the sheriff had found out. In the silence he would ask a wordless question and in the silence she would answer wordlessly. Johnny-Boys too trustin, she thought. Hes trying t make the party big n hes takin in folks fastern he kin git t know em. You cant trust ever white man yuh meet. . . .

"Yuh know, Johnny-Boy, yuh been takin in a lotta them white folks lately . . ."

"Aw, ma!"

"But Johnny-Boy . . ."

"Please, dont talk t me bout tha now, ma."

"Yuh ain t ol t lissen n learn, son," she said.

"Ah know whut yuh gonna say, ma. N yuh wrong. Yuh cant judge folks just by how yuh feel bout em n by how long yuh done knowed em. Ef we start that we wouldnt have *no*body in the party. When folks pledge they word t be with us, then we gotta take em in. Wes too weak t be choosy."

He rose abruptly, rammed his hands into his pockets, and stood facing the window; she looked at his back in a long silence. She knew his faith; it was deep. He had always said that black men could not fight the rich bosses alone; a man could not fight with every hand against him. But he believes so hard hes blind, she thought. At odd times they had had these arguments before; always she would be pitting her feelings against the hard necessity of his thinking, and always she would lose. She shook her head. Po Johnny-Boy; he don know . . .

"But ain nona our folks tol, Johnny-Boy," she said.

"How yuh know?" he asked. His voice came low and with a tinge of anger. He still faced the window and now and then the yellow blade of light flicked across the sharp outline of his black face.

"Cause Ah know em," she said.

"*Any*body mighta tol," he said.

"It wuznt nona *our* folks," she said again.

She saw his hand sweep in a swift arc of disgust.

"*Our* folks! Ma, who in Gawds name is *our* folks?"

"The folks we wuz born n raised wid, son. The folks we *know!*"

"We cant make the party grow tha way, ma."

"It mighta been Booker," she said.

"Yuh don know."

". . . er Blattberg . . ."

"Fer Chrissakes!"

". . . er any of the fo-five others whut joined las week."

"Ma, yuh jus don wan me t go out tonight," he said.

"Yo ol ma wans yuh t be careful, son."

"Ma, when yuh start doubtin folks in the party, then there ain no end."

"Son, Ah knows ever black man n woman in this parta the county," she said, standing too. "Ah watched em grow up; Ah even heped birth n nurse some of em; Ah knows em *all* from way back. There ain none of em that *coulda* tol! The folks Ah know jus don open they dos n ast death t walk in! Son, it wuz some of them *white* folks! Yuh just mark mah word n wait n see!"

"Why is it gotta be *white* folks?" he asked. "Ef they tol, then theys jus Judases, thas all."

"Son, look at whuts befo yuh."

He shook his head and sighed.

"Ma, Ah done tol yuh a hundred times. Ah cant see white n Ah cant see black," he said. "Ah sees rich men n Ah sees po men."

She picked up his dirty dishes and piled them in a pan. Out of the corners of her eyes she saw him sit and pull on his wet shoes. Hes goin! When she put the last dish away he was standing fully dressed, warming his hands over the stove. Jus a few mo minutes now n hell be gone, like Sug, mabbe. Her throat tightened. This black mans fight takes *ever*thin! Looks like Gawd put us in this world jus t beat us down!

"Keep this, ma," he said.

She saw a crumpled wad of money in his outstretched fingers.

"Naw, yuh keep it. Yuh might need it."

"It ain mine, ma. It berlongs t the party."

"But, Johnny-Boy, yuh might hafta go erway!"

"Ah kin make out."

"Don fergit yosef too much, son."

"Ef Ah don come back theyll need it."

He was looking at her face and she was looking at the money.

"Yuh keep tha," she said slowly. "Ahll give em the money."

"From where?"

"Ah got some."

"Where yuh git it from?"

She sighed.

"Ah been savin a dollah a week fer Sug ever since hes been in jail."

"Lawd, ma!"

She saw the look of puzzled love and wonder in his eyes. Clumsily, he put the money back into his pocket.

"Ahm gone," he said.

"Here; drink this glass of soda watah."

She watched him drink, then put the glass away.

"Waal," he said.

"Take the stuff outta yo pockets!"

She lifted the lid of the stove and he dumped all the papers from his pocket into the fire. She followed him to the door and made him turn round.

"Lawd, yuh tryin to maka revolution n yuh cant even keep yo coat buttoned." Her nimble fingers fastened his collar high around his throat. "There!"

He pulled the brim of his hat low over his eyes. She opened the door and with the suddenness of the cold gust of wind that struck her face, he was gone. She watched the black fields and the rain take him, her eyes burning. When the last faint footstep could no longer be heard, she closed the door, went to her bed, lay down, and pulled the cover over her while fully dressed. Her feelings coursed with the rhythm of the rain: Hes gone! Lawd, Ah *knows* hes gone! Her blood felt cold.

III

She was floating in a grey void somewhere between sleeping and dreaming and then suddenly she was wide awake, hearing and feeling in the same instant the thunder of the door crashing in and a cold wind filling the room. It was pitch black and she stared, resting on her elbows, her mouth open, not breathing, her ears full of the sound of tramping feet and booming voices. She knew at once: They lookin fer im! Then, filled with her will, she was on her feet, rigid, waiting, listening.

"The lamps burnin!"

"Yuh see her?"

"Naw!"

"Look in the kitchen!"

"Gee, this place smells like niggers!"

"Say, somebodys here er been here!"

"Yeah; theres fire in the stove!"

"Mabbe hes been here n gone?"

"Boy, look at these jars of jam!"

"Niggers make good jam!"

"Git some bread!"

"Heres some cornbread!"

"Say, lemme git some!"

"Take it easy! Theres plenty here!"

"Ahma take some of this stuff home!"

"Look, heres a pota greens!"

"N some hot cawffee!"

"Say, yuh guys! C mon! Cut it out! We didn't come here fer a feas!"

She walked slowly down the hall. They lookin fer im, but they ain got im yit! She stopped in the doorway, her gnarled, black hands as always folded over her stomach, but tight now, so tightly the veins bulged. The kitchen was crowded with white men in glistening raincoats. Though the lamp burned, their flashlights still glowed in red fists. Across her floor she saw the muddy tracks of their boots.

"Yuh white folks git outta mah house!"

There was a quick silence; every face turned toward her. She saw a sudden movement, but did not know what it meant until something hot and wet slammed her squarely in the face. She gasped, but did not move. Calmly, she wiped the warm, greasy liquor of greens from her eyes with her left hand. One of the white men had thrown a handful of greens out of the pot at her.

"How they taste, ol bitch?"

"Ah ast yuh t git outta mah house!"

She saw the sheriff detach himself from the crowd and walk toward her.

"Now, Anty . . ."

"White man, don yuh *Anty* me!"

"Yuh ain got the right sperit!"

"Sperit hell! Yuh git these men outta mah house!"

"Yuh ack like yuh don like it!"

"Naw, Ah don like it, n yuh knows dam waal Ah don!"

"What yuh gonna do about it?"

"Ahm telling yuh t git outta mah house!"

"Gittin sassy?"

"Ef telling yuh t git outa mah house is sass, then Ahm sassy!"

Her words came in a tense whisper; but beyond, back of them, she was watching, thinking, judging the men.

"Listen, Anty," the sheriff's voice came soft and low. "Ahm here t hep yuh. How come yuh wanna ack this way?"

"Yuh ain never heped yo *own* sef since yuh been born," she flared. "How kin the likes of yuh hep me?"

One of the white men came forward and stood directly in front of her.

"Lissen, nigger woman, yuh talkin t *white* men!"

"Ah don care who Ahm talkin t!"

"Yuhll wish some day yuh did!"

"Not t the likes of yuh!"

"Yuh need somebody t teach yuh how t be a good nigger!"

"*Yuh* cant teach it t me!"

"Yuh gonna change yo tune."

"Not longs mah bloods warm!"

"Don git smart now!"

"Yuh git outta mah house!"

"Spose we don go?" the sheriff asked.

They were crowded round her. She had not moved since she had taken her place in the doorway. She was thinking only of Johnny-Boy as she stood there giving and taking words; and she knew that they, too, were thinking of Johnny-Boy. She knew they wanted him, and her heart was daring them to take him from her.

"Spose we don go?" the sheriff asked again.

"Twenty of yuh runnin over one ol woman! Now, ain yuh white men glad yuh so brave?"

The sheriff grabbed her arm.

"C mon, now! Yuh don did ernuff sass fer one night. Wheres tha nigger son of yos?"

"Don yuh wished yuh knowed?"

"Yuh wanna git slapped?"

"Ah ain never seen one of yo kind that wuznt too low fer . . ."

The sheriff slapped her straight across her face with his open palm. She fell back against a wall and sank to her knees.

"Is tha whut white men do t nigger women?"

She rose slowly and stood again, not even touching the place that ached from his blow, her hands folded over her stomach.

"Ah ain never seen one of yo kind tha wuznt too low fer . . ."

He slapped her again; she reeled backward several feet and fell on her side.

"Is tha whut we too low t do?"

She stood before him again, dry-eyed, as though she had not been struck. Her lips were numb and her chin was wet with blood.

"Aw, let her go! Its the nigger we wan!" said one.

"Wheres that nigger son of yos?" the sheriff asked.

"Find im," she said.

"By Gawd, ef we hafta find im well kill im!"

"He wont be the only nigger yuh ever killed," she said.

She was consumed with a bitter pride. There was nothing on this earth, she felt then, that they could not do to her but that she could take. She stood on a narrow plot of ground from which she would die before she was pushed. And then it was, while standing there feeling warm blood seeping down her throat, that she gave up Johnny-Boy, gave him up to the white folks. She gave him up because they had come tramping into her heart demanding him, thinking they could get him by beating her, thinking they could scare her into making her tell where he was. She gave him up because she wanted them to know that they could not get what they wanted by bluffing and killing.

"Wheres this meetin gonna be?" the sheriff asked.

"Don yuh wish yuh knowed?"

"Aint there gonna be a meetin?"

"How come yuh astin me?"

"There *is* gonna be a meetin," said the sheriff.

"Is it?"

"Ah gotta great mind t choke it outta yuh!"

"Yuh so smart," she said.

"We ain playing wid yuh!"

"Did Ah say yuh wuz?"

"Tha nigger son of yos is erroun here somewheres n Ah aim to find im," said the sheriff. "Ef yuh tell us where he is n ef he talks, mabbie hell git off easy. But ef we hafta find im, well kill im! Ef we hafta find im, then yuh git a sheet t put over im in the mawnin, see? Git yuh a sheet, cause hes gonna be dead!"

"He wont be the only nigger yuh ever killed," she said again.

The sheriff walked past her. The others followed. Yuh didnt git whut yuh wanted! she thought exultingly. N yuh ain gonna *never* git it! Hotly, something arched in her to make them feel the intensity of her pride and freedom; her heart groped to turn the bitter hours of her life into words of a kind that would make them feel that she had taken all they had done to her in stride and could still take more. Her faith surged so strongly in her she was all but blinded. She walked behind them to the door, knotting and twisting her fingers. She saw them step to the muddy ground. Each whirl of the yellow beacon revealed glimpses of slanting rain. Her lips moved, then she shouted:

"Yuh didnt git whut yuh wanted! N yuh ain gonna nevah git it!"

The sheriff stopped and turned; his voice came low and hard.

"Now, by Gawd, thas ernuff outta yuh!"

"Ah know when Ah done said ernuff!"

"Aw, naw, yuh don!" he said. "Yuh don know when yuh done said ernuff, but Ahma teach yuh ternight!"

He was up the steps and across the porch with one bound. She backed into the hall, her eyes full on his face.

"Tell me when yuh gonna stop talkin!" he said, swinging his fist.

The blow caught her high on the cheek; her eyes went blank; she fell flat on her face. She felt the hard heel of his wet shoes coming into her temple and stomach.

"Lemme hear yuh talk some mo!"

She wanted to, but could not; pain numbed and choked her. She lay still and somewhere out of the grey void of unconsciousness she heard someone say: *Aw fer chrissakes leave her erlone, its the nigger we wan. . . .*

IV

She never knew how long she had lain huddled in the dark hallway. Her first returning feeling was of a nameless fear crowding the inside of her, then a deep pain spreading from her temple downward over her body. Her ears were filled with the drone of rain and she shuddered from the cold wind blowing through the door. She opened her eyes and at first saw nothing. As if she were imagining it, she knew she was half lying and half sitting in a corner against a wall. With difficulty she twisted her neck and what she saw made her hold her breath—a vast white blur was suspended directly above her. For a moment she could not tell if her fear was from the blur or if the blur was from her fear. Gradually the blur resolved itself into a huge white face that slowly filled her vision. She was stone still, conscious really of the effort to breathe, feeling somehow that she existed only by the mercy of that white face. She had seen it before; its fear had gripped her many times; it had for her the fear of all the white faces she had ever seen in her life. *Sue . . .* As from a great distance, she heard her name being called. She was regaining consciousness now, but the fear was coming with her. She looked into the face of a white man, wanting to scream out for him to go; yet accepting his presence because she felt she had to. Though some remote part of her mind was active, her limbs were powerless. It was as if an invisible knife had split her in two, leaving one half of her lying there helpless, while the other half shrank in dread from a forgotten but familiar enemy. *Sue its me Sue its me* . . . Then all at once the voice came clearly.

"Sue, its me! Its Booker!"

And she heard an answering voice speaking inside of her. Yeah, its Booker . . . The one whut just joined . . . She roused herself, struggling for full consciousness; and as she did so she transferred to the person of Booker the nameless fear she felt. It seemed that

Booker towered above her as a challenge to her right to exist upon the earth.

"Yuh awright?"

She did not answer; she started violently to her feet and fell.

"Sue, yuh hurt!"

"Yeah," she breathed.

"Where they hit yuh?"

"Its mah head," she whispered.

She was speaking even though she did not want to; the fear that had hold of her compelled her.

"They beat yuh?"

"Yeah."

"Them bastards! Them Gawddam bastards!"

She heard him saying it over and over; then she felt herself being lifted.

"Naw!" she gasped.

"Ahma take yuh t the kitchen!"

"Put me down!"

"But yuh cant stay here like this!"

She shrank in his arms and pushed her hands against his body; when she was in the kitchen she freed herself, sank into a chair, and held tightly to its back. She looked wonderingly at Booker. There was nothing about him that should frighten her so, but even that did not ease her tension. She saw him go to the water bucket, wet his handkerchief, wring it, and offer it to her. Distrustfully, she stared at the damp cloth.

"Here; put this on yo fohead . . ."

"Naw!"

"C mon; itll make yuh feel bettah!"

She hesitated in confusion. What right had she to be afraid when someone was acting as kindly as this toward her? Reluctantly, she leaned forward and pressed the damp cloth to her head. It helped. With each passing minute she was catching hold of herself, yet wondering why she felt as she did.

"Whut happened?"

"Ah don know."

"Yuh feel bettah?"

"Yeah."

"Who all wuz here?"

"Ah don know," she said again.

"Yo head still hurt?"

"Yeah."

"Gee, Ahm sorry."

"Ahm awright," she sighed and buried her face in her hands.

She felt him touch her shoulder.

"Sue, Ah got some bad news fer yuh . . ."

She knew; she stiffened and grew cold. It had happened; she stared dry-eyed, with compressed lips.

"Its mah Johnny-Boy," she said.

"Yeah; Ahm awful sorry t hafta tell yuh this way. But Ah thought yuh oughta know . . ."

Her tension eased and a vacant place opened up inside of her. A voice whispered, Jesus, hep me!

"W-w-where is he?"

"They got im out t Foleys Woods tryin t make him tell who the others is."

"He ain gonna tell," she said. "They jus as waal kill im, cause he ain gonna nevah tell."

"Ah hope he don," said Booker. "But he didnt have a chance t tell the others. They grabbed im jus as he got t the woods."

Then all the horror of it flashed upon her; she saw flung out over the rainy countryside an array of shacks where white and black comrades were sleeping; in the morning they would be rising and going to Lem's; then they would be caught. And that meant terror, prison, and death. The comrades would have to be told; she would have to tell them; she could not entrust Johnny-Boy's work to another, and especially not to Booker as long as she felt toward him as she did. Gripping the bottom of the chair with both hands, she tried to rise; the room blurred and she swayed. She found herself resting in Booker's arms.

"Lemme go!"

"Sue, yuh too weak t walk!"

"Ah gotta tell em!" she said.

"Set down, Sue! Yuh hurt! Yuh sick!"

When seated, she looked at him helplessly.

"Sue, lissen! Johnny-Boys caught. Ahm here. Yuh tell me who they is n Ahll tell em."

She stared at the floor and did not answer. Yes; she was too weak to go. There was no way for her to tramp all those miles through the rain tonight. But should she tell Booker? If only she had somebody like Reva to talk to! She did not want to decide alone; she must make no mistake about this. She felt Booker's fingers pressing on her arm and it was as though the white mountain was pushing her to the edge of a sheer height; she again exclaimed inwardly. Jesus, hep me! Booker's white face was at her side, waiting. Would she be doing right to tell him? Suppose she did not tell and then the comrades were caught? She could not ever forgive herself for doing a thing like that. But maybe she was wrong; maybe her fear was what Johnny-Boy had always called "jus foolishness." She remembered his saying, Ma, we cant make the party grow ef we start doubtin everbody. . . .

"Tell me who they is, Sue, n Ahll tell em. Ah jus joined n Ah don know who they is."

"Ah don know who they is," she said.

"Yuh *gotta* tell me who they is, Sue!"

"Ah tol yuh Ah don know!"

"Yuh *do* know! C mon! Set up n talk!"

"Naw!"

"Yuh wan em all t git *killed*?"

She shook her head and swallowed. Lawd, Ah don believe in this man!

"Lissen, Ahll call the names n yuh tell me which ones is in the party n which ones ain, see?"

"Naw!"

"Please, Sue!"

"Ah don know," she said.

"Sue, yuh ain doin right by em. Johnny-Boy wouldnt wan yuh t be this way. Hes out there holdin up his end. Les hol up ours . . ."

"Lawd, Ah don know . . ."

"Is yuh scared a me cause Ahm *white*? Johnny-Boy ain like tha. Don let all the work we done go fer nothin."

She gave up and bowed her head in her hands.

"Is it Johnson? Tell me, Sue?"

"Yeah," she whispered in horror; a mounting horror of feeling herself being undone.

"Is it Green?"

"Yeah."

"Murphy?"

"Lawd, Ah don know!"

"Yuh gotta tell me, Sue!"

"Mistah Booker, please leave me erlone . . ."

"Is it Murphy?"

She answered yes to the names of Johnny-Boy's comrades; she answered until he asked her no more. Then she thought, How he know the sheriffs men is watchin Lems house? She stood up and held onto her chair, feeling something sure and firm within her.

"How yuh know bout Lem?"

"Why . . . How Ah know?"

"Whut yuh doin here this tima night? How yuh know the sheriff got Johnny-Boy?"

"Sue, don yuh believe in me?"

She did not, but she could not answer. She stared at him until her lips hung open; she was searching deep within herself for certainty.

"You meet Reva?" she asked.

"Reva?"

"Yeah; Lems gal?"

"Oh, yeah. Sho, Ah met Reva."

"She tell yuh?"

She asked the question more of herself than of him; she longed to believe.

"Yeah," he said softly. "Ah reckon Ah oughta be goin t tell em now."

"Who?" she asked. "Tell *who*?"

The muscles of her body were stiff as she waited for his answer; she felt as though life depended upon it.

"The comrades," he said.

"Yeah," she sighed.

She did not know when he left; she was not looking or listening. She just suddenly saw the room empty and from her the thing that had made her fearful was gone.

V

For a space of time that seemed to her as long as she had been upon the earth, she sat huddled over the cold stove. One minute she would say to herself. They both gone now; Johnny-Boy n Sug. . . . Mabbe Ahll never see em ergin. Then a surge of guilt would blot out her longing. "Lawd, Ah shouldna tol!" she mumbled. "But no man kin be so lowdown as to do a thing like that . . ." Several times she had an impulse to try to tell the comrades herself; she was feeling a little better now. But what good would that do? She had told Booker the names. He jus couldnt be a Judas to po folks like us . . ." He *couldnt!*

"An Sue!"

Thas Reva! Her heart leaped with an anxious gladness. She rose without answering and limped down the dark hallway. Through the open door, against the background of rain, she saw Reva's face lit now and then to whiteness by the whirling beams of the beacon. She was about to call, but a thought checked her. Jesus, hep me! Ah gotta tell her bout Johnny-Boy . . . Lawd, Ah cant!

"An Sue, yuh there?"

"C'mon in, chile!"

She caught Reva and held her close for a moment without speaking.

"Lawd, Ahm sho glad yuh here," she said at last.

"Ah thought somethin had happened t yuh," said Reva, pulling away. "Ah saw the do open . . . Pa told me to come back n stay wid yuh tonight . . ." Reva paused and started, "W-w-whuts the mattah?"

She was so full of having Reva with her that she did not understand what the question meant.

"Hunh?"

"Yo neck . . ."

"Aw, it aint nothin, chile. C mon in the kitchen."

"But theres blood on yo neck!"

"The sheriff wuz here . . ."

"Them fools! Whut they wanna bother yuh fer? Ah could kill em! So hep me Gawd, Ah could!"

"It ain nothin," she said.

She was wondering how to tell Reva about Johnny-Boy and Booker. Ahll wait a lil while longer, she thought. Now that Reva was here, her fear did not seem as awful as before.

"C mon, lemme fix yo head, An Sue. Yuh hurt."

They went to the kitchen. She sat silent while Reva dressed her scalp. She was feeling better now; in just a little while she would tell Reva. She felt the girl's finger pressing gently upon her head.

"Tha hurt?"

"A lil, chile."

"Yuh po thing."

"It ain nothin."

"Did Johnny-Boy come?"

She hesitated.

"Yeah."

"He done gone t tell the others?"

Reva's voice sounded so clear and confident that it mocked her. Lawd, Ah cant tell this chile . . .

"Yuh tol im, didnt yuh, An Sue?"

"Y-y-yeah . . ."

"Gee! Thas good! Ah tol pa he didnt hafta worry ef Johnny-Boy got the news. Mabbe thingsll come out awright."

"Ah hope . . ."

She could not go on; she had gone as far as she could. For the first time that night she began to cry.

"Hush, An Sue! Yuh awways been brave. Itll be awright!"

"Ain nothin awright, chile. The worls jus too much fer us, Ah reckon."

"Ef yuh cry that way itll make me cry."

She forced herself to stop. Naw; Ah cant carry on this way in fronta Reva . . . Right now she had a deep need for Reva to believe in her. She watched the girl get pine-knots from behind the stove, rekindle the fire, and put on the coffee pot.

"Yuh wan some cawffee?" Reva asked.

"Naw, honey."

"Aw, c mon, An Sue."

"Jusa lil, honey."

"Thas the way to be. Oh, say, Ah fergot," said Reva, measuring out spoonsful of coffee. "Pa tol me t tell yuh t watch out fer tha Booker man. Hes a stool."

She showed not one sign of outward movement or expression, but as the words fell from Reva's lips she went limp inside.

"Pa tol me soon as Ah got back home. He got word from town . . ."

She stopped listening. She felt as though she had been slapped to the extreme outer edge of life, onto a cold darkness. She knew now what she had felt when she had looked up out of her fog of pain and had seen Booker. It was the image of all the white folks, and the fear that went with them, that she had seen and felt during her lifetime. And again, for the second time that night, something she had felt had come true. All she could say to herself was, Ah didnt like im! Gawd knows, Ah didnt! Ah tol Johnny-Boy it wuz some of them white folks . . .

"Here; drink yo cawffee . . ."

She took the cup; her fingers trembled and the steaming liquid spilt onto her dress and leg.

"Ahm sorry, An Sue!"

Her leg was scalded, but the pain did not bother her.

"Its awright," she said.

"Wait; lemme put some lard on tha burn!"

"It don hurt."

"Yuh worried bout somethin."

"Naw, honey."

"Lemme fix yuh so mo cawffee."

"Ah don wan nothin now, Reva."

"Waal, buck up. Don be tha way . . ."

They were silent. She heard Reva drinking. No; she would not tell Reva; Reva was all she had left. But she had to do something, some way, somehow. She was undone too much as it was; and to tell Reva about Booker or Johnny-Boy was more than she was equal to; it would be too coldly shameful. She wanted to be alone and fight this thing out with herself.

"Go t bed, honey. Yuh tired."

"Naw; Ahm awright, An Sue."

She heard the bottom of Reva's empty cup clank against the top of the stove. Ah *got* t make her go t bed! Yes; Booker would tell the names of the comrades to the sheriff. If she could only stop him some way! That was the answer, the point, the star that grew bright in the morning of new hope. Soon, maybe half an hour from now, Booker would reach Foleys Woods. Hes boun t go the long way, cause he don know no short cut, she thought. Ah could wade the creek n beat im there. . . . But what would she do after that?

"Reva, honey, go t bed. Ahm awright. Yuh need res."

"Ah ain sleepy, An Sue."

"Ah knows whuts bes fer yuh, chile. Yuh tired n wet."

"Ah wanna stay up wid yuh."

She forced a smile and said:

"Ah don think they gonna hurt Johnny-Boy . . ."

"Fer *real,* An Sue?"

"Sho, honey."

"But Ah wanna wait up wid yuh."

"Thas mah job, honey. Thas whut a mas fer, t wait up fer her chullun."

"Good night, An Sue."

"Good night, honey."

She watched Reva pull up and leave the kitchen; presently she heard the shucks in the mattress whispering, and she knew that Reva had gone to bed. She was alone. Through the cracks of the stove she saw the fire dying to grey ashes; the room was growing cold again. The yellow beacon contined to flit past the window and the rain still drummed. Yes; she was alone; she had done this awful thing alone; she must find some way out, alone. Like touching a festering sore, she put her finger upon that moment when she had shouted her defiance to the sheriff, when she had shouted to feel her strength. She had lost Sug to save others; she had let Johnny-Boy go to save others; and then in a moment of weakness that came from too much strength she had lost all. If she had not shouted to the sheriff, she would have been strong enough to have resisted Booker; she would have been able to tell the comrades herself. Something tightened in her as she remembered and understood the fit of fear she had felt on coming to herself in the dark hallway. A part of her life she thought she had done away with forever had had hold of her then. She had thought the soft, warm past was over; she had thought that it did not mean much when now she sang: *"Hes the Lily of the Valley, the Bright n Mawnin Star"* . . . The days when she had sung that song were the days when she had not hoped for anything on this earth, the days when the cold mountain had driven her into the arms of Jesus. She had thought that Sug and Johnny-Boy had taught her to forget Him, to fix her hope upon the fight of black men for freedom. Through the gradual years she had believed and worked with them, had felt strength shed from the grace of their terrible vision. That grace had been upon her when she had let the sheriff slap her down; it had been upon her when she had risen time and again from the floor and faced him. But she had trapped herself with her own hunger; to water the long, dry thirst of her faith; her pride had made a bargain which her flesh could not keep. Her having told the names of Johnny-Boy's comrades was but an incident in a deeper horror. She stood up and looked at the floor while call and countercall, loyalty and counter-loyalty struggled in her soul. Mired she was between two abandoned worlds, living, but dying without the strength of the grace that either gave. The clearer she felt it the fuller did something well up from the depths of her for release; the more urgent did she feel the need to fling into her black sky another star, another hope, one more terrible vision to give her the strength to live and act. Softly and restlessly she walked about the kitchen, feeling herself naked against the night, the rain, the world; and shamed whenever the thought of Reva's love crossed her mind. She lifted her empty hands and looked at her writhing fingers. Lawd, whut kin Ah do now? She could still wade the creek and get to Foleys Woods before Booker. And then what? How could she manage to see Johnny-Boy or Booker? Again she heard the sheriff's threatening voice: Git yuh a sheet, cause hes gonna be dead! The sheet! Thas it, the *sheet!* Her whole being leaped with will; the long years of her life bent toward a moment of focus, a point. Ah kin go wid mah sheet! Ahll be doin whut he said! Lawd Gawd in Heaven, Ahma go lika nigger woman wid mah windin sheet t git mah dead son! But then what? She stood straight and smiled grimly; she had in her heart the whole meaning of her life; her entire personality was poised on the brink of a total act. Ah know! Ah *know!* She thought of Johnny-Boy's gun in the dresser drawer. Ahll hide the gun in the sheet n go aftah Johnny-Boys body. . . . She tiptoed to her room, eased out the dresser drawer, and got a sheet. Reva was sleeping; the darkness was filled with her quiet breathing. She groped in the drawer and found the gun. She wound the gun in the sheet and held them both under her apron. Then she stole to the bedside and watched Reva. Lawd, hep her! But mabbe shes bettah off. This had t happen sometime . . . She n Johnny-Boy couldna been together in this here South . . . N Ah couldnt tell her about Booker. Itll come out awright n she wont nevah know. Reva's trust would never be shaken. She caught her breath as the shucks in the mattress rustled dryly; then all was quiet and she breathed easily again. She tiptoed to the door, down the hall, and stood on the porch. Above her the yellow beacon whirled through the rain. She went over muddy ground, mounted a slope, stopped and looked back at her house. The lamp glowed in her window, and the yellow beacon that swung every few seconds seemed to feed it with light. She turned and started across the fields, holding the gun and sheet tightly, thinking, Po Reva . . . Po critter . . . Shes fas ersleep . . .

VI

For the most part she walked with her eyes half shut, her lips tightly compressed, leaning her body against the wind and the driving rain, feeling the pistol in the sheet sagging cold and heavy in her fingers. Already she was getting wet; it seemed that her feet found every puddle of water that stood between the corn rows.

She came to the edge of the creek and paused, wondering at what point was it low. Taking the sheet from under her apron, she wrapped the gun in it so that her finger could be upon the trigger. Ahll cross here, she thought. At first she did not feel the water; her feet were already wet. But the water grew cold as it came up to her knees; she gasped when it reached her waist. Lawd, this creeks high! When she had passed the middle, she knew that she was out of danger. She came out of the water, climbed a grassy hill, walked on, turned a bend and saw the lights of autos gleaming ahead. Yeah; theys still there! She hurried with her head down. Wondah did Ah beat im here? Lawd, Ah *hope* so! A vivid image of Booker's white face hovered a moment before her eyes and a surging will rose up in her so hard and strong that it vanished. She was among the autos now. From nearby came the hoarse voices of the men.

"Hey, yuh!"

She stopped, nervously clutching the sheet. Two white men with shotguns came toward her.

"Whut in hell yuh doin out here?"

She did not answer.

"Didnt yuh hear somebody speak t yuh?"

"Ahm comin aftah mah son," she said humbly.

"Yo *son*?"

"Yessuh."

"What yo son doin out here?"

"The sheriffs got im."

"Holy Scott! Jim, its the niggers ma!"

"Whut yuh got there?" asked one.

"A sheet."

"A *sheet*?"

"Yessuh."

"Fer whut?"

"The sheriff tol me t bring a sheet t git his body."

"Waal, waal . . ."

"Now, ain tha somethin?"

The white men looked at each other.

"These niggers sho love one ernother," said one.

"N tha ain no lie," said the other.

"Take me t the sheriff," she begged.

"Yuh ain givin us *orders,* is yuh?"

"Nawsuh."

"Well take yuh when wes good n ready."

"Yessuh."

"So yuh wan his body?"

"Yessuh."

"Waal, he ain dead yit."

"They gonna kill im," she said.

"Ef he talks they wont."

"He ain gonna talk," she said.

"How yuh know?"

"Cause he ain."

"We got ways of makin niggers talk."

"Yuh ain got no way fer im."

"Yuh thinka lot of that black Red, don yuh?"

"Hes mah son."

"Why don yuh teach im some sense?"

"Hes mah son," she said again.

"Lissen, ol nigger woman, yuh stand there wid yo hair white. Yuh got bettah sense than t believe tha niggers kin make a revolution . . ."

"A black republic," said the other one, laughing.

"Take me t the sheriff," she begged.

"Yuh his ma," said one. "Yuh kin make im talk n tell whose in this thing wid im."

"He ain gonna talk" she said.

"Don yuh wan im t live?"

She did not answer.

"C mon, les take her t Bradley."

They grabbed her arms and she clutched hard at the sheet and gun; they led her toward the crowd in the woods. Her feelings were simple; Booker would not tell; she was there with the gun to see to that. The louder became the voices of the men the deeper became her feeling of wanting to right the mistake she had made; of wanting to fight her way back to solid ground. She would stall for time until Booker showed up. Oh, ef theyll only lemme git close t Johnny-Boy! As they led her near the crowd she saw white faces turning and looking at her and heard a rising clamor of voices.

"Whose tha?"

"A nigger woman!"

"Whut she doin out here?"

"This is his ma!" called one of the men.

"Whut she wans?"

"She brought a sheet t cover his body!"

"He ain dead yit!"

"They tryin t make im talk!"

"But he will be dead soon ef he don open up!"

"Say, look! The niggers ma brought a sheet t cover up his body!"

"Now, ain that sweet?"

"Mabbe she wans t hol a prayer meetin!"

"Did she git a preacher?"

"Say, go git Bradley!"

"O.K.!"

The crowd grew quiet. They looked at her curiously; she felt their cold eyes trying to detect some weakness in her. Humbly, she stood with the sheet covering the gun. She had already accepted all that they could do to her.

The sheriff came.

"So yuh brought yuh sheet, hunh?"

"Yessuh," she whispered.

"Looks like them slaps we gave yuh learned yuh some sense, didnt they?"

She did not answer.

"Yuh don need tha sheet. Yo son ain dead yit," he said, reaching toward her.

She backed away, her eyes wide.

"Naw!"

"Now, lissen, Anty!" he said. "There ain no use in yuh ackin a fool! Go in there n tell tha nigger son of yos t tell us whos in this wid im, see? Ah promise we wont kill im ef he talks. We'll let im git outta town."

"There ain nothin Ah kin tell im," she said.

"Yuh wan us t kill im?"

She did not answer. She saw someone lean toward the sheriff and whisper.

"Bring her erlong," the sheriff said.

They led her to a muddy clearing. The rain streamed down through the ghostly glare of the flashlights. As the men formed a semi-circle she saw Johnny-Boy lying in a trough of mud. He was tied with rope; he lay hunched and one side of his face rested in a pool of black water. His eyes were staring questioningly at her.

"Speak t im," said the sheriff.

If she could only tell him why she was here! But that was impossible; she was close to what she wanted and she stared straight before her with compressed lips.

"Say, nigger!" called the sheriff, kicking Johnny-Boy. "Heres yo ma!"

Johnny-Boy did not move or speak. The sheriff faced her again.

"Lissen, Anty," he said. "Yuh got mo say wid im than anybody. Tell im t talk n hava chance. Whut he wanna pertect the other niggers n white folks fer?"

She slid her finger about the trigger of the gun and looked stonily at the mud.

"Go t him," said the sheriff.

She did not move. Her heart was crying out to answer the amazed question in Johnny-Boy's eyes. But there was no way now.

"Waal, yuhre astin fer it. By Gawd, we gotta way to *make* yuh talk t im," he said, turning away. "Say, Tim, git one of them logs n turn that nigger upside-down n put his legs on it!"

A murmur of assent ran through the crowd. She bit her lips; she knew what that meant.

"Yuh wan yo nigger son crippled?" she heard the sheriff ask.

She did not answer. She saw them roll the log up; they lifted Johnny-Boy and laid him on his face and stomach, then they pulled his legs over the log. His kneecaps rested on the sheer top of the log's back and the toes of his shoes pointed groundward. So absorbed was she in watching that she felt that it was she who was being lifted and made ready for torture.

"Git a crowbar!" said the sheriff.

A tall, lank man got a crowbar from a nearby auto and stood over the log. His jaws worked slowly on a wad of tobacco.

"Now, its up t yuh, Anty," the sheriff said. "Tell the man whut t do!"

She looked into the rain. The sheriff turned.

"Mebbe she think wes playin. Ef she don say nothin, then break em at the kneecaps!"

"O.K., Sheriff!"

She stood waiting for Booker. Her legs felt weak; she wondered if she would be able to wait much longer. Over and over she said to herself, Ef he came now Ahd kill em both!

"She ain sayin nothin, Sheriff!"

"Waal, Gawddammit, let im have it!"

The crowbar came down and Johnny-Boy's body lunged in the mud and water. There was a scream. She swayed, holding tight to the gun and sheet.

"Hol im! Git the other leg!"

The crowbar fell again. There was another scream.

"Yuh break em?" asked the sheriff.

The tall man lifted Johnny-Boy's legs and let them drop limply again, dropping rearward from the kneecaps. Johnny-Boy's body lay still. His head had rolled to one side and she could not see his face.

"Jus lika broke sparrow wing," said the man, laughing softly.

Then Johnny-Boy's face turned to her; he screamed.

"Go way, ma! Go way!"

It was the first time she had heard his voice since she had come out of the woods; she all but lost control of herself. She started violently forward, but the sheriff's arm checked her.

"Aw, naw! Yuh had yo chance!" He turned to Johnny-Boy. "She kin go ef yuh talk."

"Mistah, he ain gonna talk," she said.

"Go way, ma!" said Johnny-Boy.

"Shoot im! Don make im suffah so," she begged.

"He'll either talk or he'll never hear yuh ergin," the sheriff said. "Theres other things we kin do t im."

She said nothing.

"Whut yuh come here fer, ma?" Johnny-Boy sobbed.

"Ahm gonna split his eardrums," the sheriff said. "Ef yuh got anythin to say t im yuh bettah say it *now!*"

She closed her eyes. She heard the sheriff's feet sucking in mud. Ah could save im! She opened her eyes; there were shouts of eagerness from the crowd as it pushed in closer.

"Bus em, Sheriff!"

"Fix im so he cant hear!"

"He knows how t do it, too!"

"He busted a Jew boy tha way once!"

She saw the sheriff stoop over Johnny-Boy, place his flat palm over one ear and strike his fist against it with all his might. He placed his palm over the other ear and struck again. Johnny-Boy moaned, his head rolling from side to side, his eyes showing white amazement in a world without sound.

"Yuh wouldnt talk t im when yuh had the chance," said the sheriff. "Try n talk now."

She felt warm tears on her cheeks. She longed to shoot Johnny-Boy and let him go. But if she did that they would take the gun from her, and Booker would tell who the others were. Lawd, hep me! The men were talking loudly now, as though the main business was over. It seemed ages that she stood there watching Johnny-Boy roll and whimper in his world of silence.

"Say, Sheriff, heres somebody lookin fer yuh!"

"Who is it?"

"Ah don know!"

"Bring em in!"

She stiffened and looked around wildly, holding the gun tight. Is tha Booker? Then she held still, feeling that her excitement might betray her. Mabbe Ah kin shoot em both! Mabbe Ah kin shoot *twice!* The sheriff stood in front of her, waiting. The crowd parted and she saw Booker hurrying forward.

"Ah know em all, Sheriff!" he called.

He came full into the muddy clearing where Johnny-Boy lay.

"Yuh mean yuh got the names?"

"Sho! The ol nigger . . ."

She saw his lips hang open and silent when he saw her. She stepped forward and raised the sheet.

"Whut . . ."

She fired, once; then, without pausing, she turned, hearing them yell. She aimed at Johnny-Boy, but they had their arms around her, bearing her to the ground, clawing at the sheet in her hand. She glimpsed Booker lying sprawled in the mud, on his face, his hands stretched out before him; then a cluster of yelling men blotted him out. She lay without struggling, looking upward through the rain at the white faces above her. And she was suddenly at peace; they were not a white mountain now; they were not pushing her any longer to the edge of life. Its awright . . .

"She shot Booker!"

"She hada gun in the sheet!"

"She shot im right thu the head!"

"Whut she shoot im fer?"

"Kill the bitch!"

"Ah *thought* somethin wuz wrong bout her!"

"Ah wuz fer givin it t her from the firs!"

"Thas whut yuh git fer treatin a nigger nice!"

"Say, Bookers dead!"

She stopped looking into the white faces, stopped listening. She waited, giving up her life before they took it from her; she had done what she wanted. Ef only Johnny-Boy . . . She looked at him; he lay looking at her with tired eyes. Ef she could only tell im! But he lay already buried in a grave of silence.

"Whut yuh kill im fer, hunh?"

It was the sheriff's voice; she did not answer.

"Mabbe she wuz shootin at yuh, Sheriff?"

"Whut yuh kill im fer?"

She felt the sheriff's foot come into her side; she closed her eyes.

"Yuh black bitch!"

"Let her have it!"

"Yuh reckon she foun out bout Booker?"

"She mighta."

"Jesus Chris, whut yuh dummies *waitin* on!"

"Yeah; kill her!"

"Kill em *both!*"

"Let her know her nigger sons dead firs!"

She turned her head toward Johnny-Boy; he lay looking puzzled in a world beyond the reach of voices. At leas he cant hear, she thought.

"C'mon, let im have it!"

She listened to hear what Johnny-Boy could not. They came, two of them, one right behind the other; so close together that they sounded like one shot. She did not look at Johnny-Boy now; she looked at the white faces of the men, hard and wet in the glare of the flashlights.

"Yuh hear tha, nigger woman?"

"Did tha surprise im? Hes in hell now wonderin what hit im!"

"C mon! Give it t her, Sheriff!"

"Lemme shoot her, Sheriff! It wuz mah pal she shot!"

"Awright, Pete! Thas fair ernuff!"

She gave up as much of her life as she could before they took it from her. But the sound of the shot and the streak of fire that tore its way through her chest forced her to live again, intensely. She had not moved, save for the slight jarring impact of the bullet. She felt the heat of her own blood warming her cold, wet back. She yearned suddenly to talk. "Yuh didnt git whut yuh wanted! N yuh ain gonna nevah git it! Yuh didnt kill me; Ah come here by mahsef . . ." She felt rain falling into her wide-open, dimming eyes and heard faint voices. Her lips moved soundlessly. *Yuh didnt git yuh didnt yuh didnt* . . . Focused and pointed she was, buried in the depths of her star, swallowed in its peace and strength; and not feeling her flesh growing cold, cold as the rain that fell from the invisible sky upon the doomed living and the dead that never dies.

Red Leaves

William Faulkner (*American, 1897–1962*)

The two Indians crossed the plantation toward the slave quarters. Neat with whitewash, of baked soft brick, the two rows of houses in which lived the slaves belonging to the clan, faced one another across the mild shade of the lane marked and scored with naked feet and with a few homemade toys mute in the dust. There was no sign of life.

"I know what we will find," the first Indian said.

"What we will not find," the second said. Although it was noon, the lane was vacant, the doors of the cabins empty and quiet; no cooking smoke rose from any of the chinked and plastered chimneys.

"Yes. It happened like this when the father of him who is now the Man, died."

"You mean, of him who was the Man."

"Yao."

The first Indian's name was Three Basket. He was perhaps sixty. They were both squat men, a little solid, burgherlike; paunchy, with big heads, big, broad, dust-colored faces of a certain blurred serenity like carved heads on a ruined wall in Siam or Sumatra, looming out of a mist. The sun had done it, the violent sun, the violent shade. Their hair looked like sedge grass on burnt-over land. Clamped through one ear Three Basket wore an enameled snuffbox.

"I have said all the time that this is not the good way. In the old days there were no quarters, no Negroes. A man's time was his own then. He had time. Now he must spend most of it finding work for them who prefer sweating to do."

"They are like horses and dogs."

"They are like nothing in this sensible world. Nothing contents them save sweat. They are worse than the white people."

"It is not as though the Man himself had to find work for them to do."

"You said it. I do not like slavery. It is not the good way. In the old days, there was the good way. But not now."

"You do not remember the old way either."

"I have listened to them who do. And I have tried this way. Man was not made to sweat."

"That's so. See what it has done to their flesh."

"Yes. Black. It has a bitter taste, too."

"You have eaten of it?"

"Once. I was young then, and more hardy in the appetite than now. Now it is different with me."

"Yes. They are too valuable to eat now."

"There is a bitter taste to the flesh which I do not like."

"They are too valuable to eat, anyway, when the white men will give horses for them."

They entered the lane. The mute, meager toys—the fetish-shaped objects made of wood and rags and feathers—lay in the dust about the patinaed doorsteps, among bones and broken gourd dishes. But there was no sound from any cabin, no face in any door; had not been since yesterday, when Issetibbeha died. But they already knew what they would find.

It was in the central cabin, a house a little larger than the others, where at certain phases of the moon the Negroes would gather to begin their ceremonies before removing after nightfall to the creek bottom, where they kept the drums. In this room they kept the minor accessories, the cryptic ornaments, the ceremonial records which consisted of sticks daubed with red clay in symbols. It had a hearth in the center of the floor, beneath a hole in the roof, with a few cold wood ashes and a suspended iron pot. The window shutters were closed; when the two Indians entered, after the abashless sunlight they could distinguish nothing with the eyes save a movement, shadow, out of which eyeballs rolled, so that the place appeared to be full of Negroes. The two Indians stood in the doorway.

"Yao," Basket said. "I said this is not the good way."

"I don't think I want to be here," the second said.

"That is black man's fear which you smell. It does not smell as ours does."

"I don't think I want to be here."

"Your fear has an odor too."

"Maybe it is Issetibbeha which we smell."

"Yao. He knows. He knows what we will find here. He knew when he died what we should find here today." Out of the rank twilight of the room the eyes, the smell, of Negroes rolled about them. "I am Three Basket, whom you know," Basket said into the room. "We are come from the Man. He whom we seek is gone?" The Negroes said nothing. The smell of them, of their bodies, seemed to ebb and flux in the still hot air. They seemed to be musing as one upon something remote, inscrutable. They were like a single octopus. They were like the roots of a huge tree uncovered, the earth broken momentarily upon the writhen, thick, fetid tangle of its lightless and outraged life. "Come," Basket said. "You know our errand. Is he whom we seek gone?"

"They are thinking something," the second said. "I do not want to be here."

"They are knowing something," Basket said.

"They are hiding him, you think?"

"No. He is gone. He has been gone since last night. It happened like this before, when the grandfather of him who is now the Man died. It took us three days to catch him. For three days Doom lay above the ground, saying 'I see my horse and my dog. But I do not see my slave. What have you done with him that you will not permit me to lie quiet?'"

"They do not like to die."

"Yao. They cling. It makes trouble for us, always. A people without honor and without decorum. Always a trouble."

"I do not like it here."

"Nor do I. But then, they are savages; they cannot be expected to regard usage. That is why I say that this way is a bad way."

"Yao. They cling. They would even rather work in the sun than to enter the earth with a chief. But he is gone."

The Negroes had said nothing, made no sound. The white eyeballs rolled, wild, subdued; the smell was rank, violent. "Yes, they fear," the second said. "What shall we do now?"

"Let us go and talk with the Man."

"Will Moketubbe listen?"

"What can he do? He will not like to. But he is the Man now."

"Yao. He is the Man. He can wear the shoes with the red heels all the time now." They turned and went out. There was no door in the door frame. There were no doors in any of the cabins.

"He did that anyway," Basket said.

"Behind Issetibbeha's back. But now they are his shoes, since he is the Man."

"Yao. Issetibbeha did not like it. I have heard. I know that he said to Moketubbe: 'When you are the Man, the shoes will be yours. But until then, they are my shoes.' But now Moketubbe is the Man; he can wear them."

"Yao," the second said. "He is the Man now. He used to wear the shoes behind Issetibbeha's back, and it was not known if Issetibbeha knew this or not. And then Issetibbeha became dead, who was not old, and the shoes are Moketubbe's since he is the Man now. What do you think of that?"

"I don't think about it," Basket said. "Do you?"

"No," the second said.

"Good," Basket said. "You are wise."

II

The house sat on a knoll, surrounded by oak trees. The front of it was one story in height, composed of the deck house of a steamboat which had gone ashore and which Doom, Issetibbeha's father, had dismantled with his slaves and hauled on cypress rollers twelve miles home overland. It took them five months. His house consisted at the time of one brick wall. He set the steamboat broadside on to the wall, where now the chipped and flaked gilding of the rococo cornices arched in faint splendor above the gilt lettering of the stateroom names above the jalousied doors.

Doom had been born merely a subchief, a Mingo, one of three children on the mother's side of the family. He made a journey—he was a young man then and New Orleans was a European city—from north Mississippi to New Orleans by keel boat, where he met the Chevalier Sœur Blonde de Vitry, a man whose social position, on its face, was as equivocal as Doom's own. In New Orleans, among the gamblers and cutthroats of the river front, Doom, under the tutelage of his patron, passed as the chief, the Man, the hereditary owner of that land which belonged to the male side of the family; it was the Chevalier de Vitry who spoke of him as *l'Homme* or *de l'Homme,* and hence Doom.

They were seen everywhere together—the Indian, the squat man with a bold, inscrutable, underbred face, and the Parisian, the expatriate, the friend, it was said, of Carondelet and the intimate of General Wilkinson. Then they disappeared the two of them, vanishing from their old equivocal haunts and leaving behind them the legend of the sums which Doom was believed to have won, and some tale about a young woman, daughter of a fairly well-to-do West Indian family, the son and brother of whom sought Doom with a pistol about his old haunts for some time after his disappearance.

Six months later the young woman herself disappeared, boarding the Saint Louis packet, which put in one night at a wood landing on the north Mississippi side, where the woman, accompanied by a Negro maid, got off. Four Indians met her with a horse and wagon, and they traveled for three days, slowly, since she was already big with child, to the plantation, where she found that Doom was now chief. He never told her how he accomplished it, save that his uncle and his cousin had died suddenly. Before that time the house had consisted of a brick wall built by shiftless slaves, against which was propped a thatched lean-to divided into rooms and littered with bones and refuse, set in the center of ten thousand acres of matchless parklike forest where deer grazed like domestic cattle. Doom and the woman were married there a short time before Issetibbeha was born, by a combination itinerant minister and slave trader who arrived on a mule, to the saddle of which was lashed a cotton umbrella and a three-gallon demijohn of whiskey. After that, Doom began to acquire more slaves and to cultivate some of his land, as the white people did. But he never had enough for them to do. In utter idleness the majority of them led lives transplanted whole out of African jungles, save on the occasions when, entertaining guests, Doom coursed them with dogs.

When Doom died, Issetibbeha, his son, was nineteen. He became proprietor of the land and of the quintupled herd of blacks for which he had no use at all. Though the title of Man rested with him, there was a hierarchy of cousins and uncles who ruled the clan and who finally gathered in squatting conclave over the Negro question, squatting profoundly beneath the golden names above the doors of the steamboat.

"We cannot eat them," one said.

"Why not?"

"There are too many of them."

"That's true," a third said. "Once we started, we should have to eat them all. And that much flesh diet is not good for man."

"Perhaps they will be like deer flesh. That cannot hurt you."

"We might kill a few of them and not eat them," Issetibbeha said.

They looked at him for a while. "What for?" one said.

"That is true," a second said. "We cannot do that. They are too valuable; remember all the bother they have caused us, finding things for them to do. We must do as the white men do."

"How is that?" Issetibbeha said.

"Raise more Negroes by clearing more land to make corn to feed them, then sell them. We will clear the land and plant it with food and raise Negroes and sell them to the white men for money."

"But what will we do with this money?" a third said.

They thought for a while.

"We will see," the first said. They squatted, profound, grave.

"It means work," the third said.

"Let the Negroes do it," the first said.

"Yao. Let them. To sweat is bad. It is damp. It opens the pores."

"And then the night air enters."

"Yao. Let the Negroes do it. They appear to like sweating."

So they cleared the land with the Negroes and planted it in grain. Up to that time the slaves had lived in a huge pen with a lean-to roof over one corner, like a pen for pigs. But now they began to build quarters, cabins, putting the young Negroes in the cabins in pairs to mate; five years later Issetibbeha sold forty head to a Memphis trader, and he took the money and went abroad upon it, his maternal uncle from New Orleans conducting the trip. At that time the Chevalier Sœur Blonde de Vitry was an old man in Paris, in a toupee and a corset and a careful, toothless old face fixed in a grimace quizzical and profoundly tragic. He borrowed three hundred dollars from Issetibbeha and in return he introduced him into certain circles; a year later Issetibbeha returned home with a gilt bed, a pair of girandoles by whose light it was said that Pompadour arranged her hair while Louis smirked at his mirrored face across her powdered shoulder, and a pair of slippers with red heels. They were too small for him, since he had not worn shoes at all until he reached New Orleans on his way abroad.

He brought the slippers home in tissue paper and kept them in the remaining pocket of a pair of saddlebags filled with cedar shavings, save when he took them out on occasion for his son, Moketubbe, to play with. At three years of age Moketubbe had a broad, flat, Mongolian face that appeared to exist in a complete and unfathomable lethargy, until confronted by the slippers.

Moketubbe's mother was a comely girl whom Issetibbeha had seen one day working in her shift in a melon patch. He stopped and watched her for a while—the broad, solid thighs, the sound back, the serene face. He was on his way to the creek to fish that day, but he didn't go any farther; perhaps while he stood there watching the unaware girl he may have remembered his own mother, the city woman, the fugitive with her fans and laces and her Negro blood, and all the tawdry shabbiness of that sorry affair. Within the year Moketubbe was born; even at three he could not get his feet into the slippers. Watching him in the still, hot afternoons as he struggled with the slippers with a certain monstrous repudiation of fact, Issetibbeha laughed quietly to himself. He laughed at Moketubbe's antics with the shoes for several years, because Moketubbe did not give up trying to put them on until he was sixteen. Then he quit. Or Issetibbeha thought he had. But he had merely quit trying in Issetibbeha's presence. Issetibbeha's newest wife told him that Moketubbe had stolen and hidden the shoes. Issetibbeha quit laughing then, and he sent the woman away, so that he was alone. "Yao," he said. "I too like being alive, it seems." He sent for Moketubbe. "I give them to you," he said.

Moketubbe was twenty-five then, unmarried. Issetibbeha was not tall, but he was taller by six inches than his son and almost a hundred pounds lighter. Moketubbe was already diseased with flesh, with a pale, broad, inert face and dropsical hands and feet. "They are yours now," Issetibbeha said, watching him. Moketubbe had looked at him once when he entered, a glance brief, discreet, veiled.

"Thanks," he said.

Issetibbeha looked at him. He could never tell if Moketubbe saw anything, looked at anything. "Why will it not be the same if I give the slippers to you?"

"Thanks," Moketubbe said. Issetibbeha was using snuff at the time; a white man had shown him how to put the powder into his lip and scour it against his teeth with a twig of gum or of alphea.

"Well," he said, "a man cannot live forever." He looked at his son, then his gaze went blank in turn, unseeing, and he mused for an instant. You could not tell what he was thinking, save that he said half aloud: "Yao. But Doom's uncle had no shoes with red heels." He looked at his son again, fat, inert. "Beneath all that, a man might think of doing anything and it not be known until too late." He sat in a splint chair hammocked with deer thongs. "He cannot even get them on; he and I are both frustrated by the same gross meat which he wears. He cannot even get them on. But is that my fault?"

He lived for five years longer, then he died. He was sick one night, and though the doctor came in a skunkskin vest and burned sticks, Issetibbeha died before noon.

That was yesterday; the grave was dug, and for twelve hours now the People had been coming in wagons and carriages and on horseback and afoot, to eat the baked dog and the succotash and the yams cooked in ashes and to attend the funeral.

III

"It will be three days," Basket said, as he and the other Indian returned to the house. "It will be three days and the food will not be enough; I have seen it before."

The second Indian's name was Louis Berry. "He will smell too, in this weather."

"Yao. They are nothing but a trouble and a care."

"Maybe it will not take three days."

"They run far. Yao. We will smell this Man before he enters the earth. You watch and see if I am not right."

They approached the house.

"He can wear the shoes now," Berry said. "He can wear them now in man's sight."

"He cannot wear them for a while yet," Basket said. Berry looked at him. "He will lead the hunt."

"Moketubbe?" Berry said. "Do you think he will? A man to whom even talking is travail?"

"What else can he do? It is his own father who will soon begin to smell."

"That is true," Berry said. "There is even yet a price he must pay for the shoes. Yao. He has truly bought them. What do you think?"

"What do you think?"

"What do you think?"

"I think nothing."

"Nor do I. Issetibbeha will not need the shoes now. Let Moketubbe have them; Issetibbeha will not care."

"Yao. Man must die."

"Yao. Let him; there is still the Man."

The bark roof of the porch was supported by peeled cypress poles, high above the texas of the steamboat, shading an unfloored banquette where on the trodden earth mules and horses were tethered in bad weather. On the forward end of the steamboat's deck sat an old man and two women. One of the women was dressing a fowl, the other was shelling corn. The old man was talking. He was barefoot, in a long linen frock coat and a beaver hat.

"This world is going to the dogs," he said. "It is being ruined by white men. We got along fine for years and years, before the white men foisted their Negroes upon us. In the old days the old men sat in the shade and ate stewed deer's flesh and corn and smoked tobacco and talked of honor and grave affairs; now what do we do? Even the old wear themselves into the grave taking care of them that like sweating." When Basket and Berry crossed the deck he ceased and looked up at them. His eyes were querulous, bleared; his face was myriad with tiny wrinkles. "He is fled also," he said.

"Yes," Berry said, "he is gone."

"I knew it. I told them so. It will take three weeks, like when Doom died. You watch and see."

"It was three days, not three weeks," Berry said.

"Were you there?"

"No," Berry said. "But I have heard."

"Well, I was there," the old man said. "For three whole weeks, through the swamps and the briers—" They went on and left him talking.

What had been the saloon of the steamboat was now a shell, rotting slowly; the polished mahogany, the carving glinting momentarily and fading through the mold in figures cabalistic and profound; the gutted windows were like cataracted eyes. It contained a few sacks of seed or grain, and the fore part of the running gear of a barouche, to the axle of which two C-springs rusted in graceful curves, supporting nothing. In one corner a fox cub ran steadily and soundlessly up and down a willow cage; three scrawny gamecocks moved in the dust, and the place was pocked and marked with their dried droppings.

They passed through the brick wall and entered a big room of chinked logs. It contained the hinder part of the barouche, and the dismantled body lying on its side, the window slatted over with willow withes, through which protruded the heads, the still, beady, outraged eyes and frayed combs of still more game chickens. It was floored with packed clay; in one corner leaned a crude plow and two hand-hewn boat paddles. From the ceiling, suspended by four deer thongs, hung the gilt bed which Issetibbeha had fetched from Paris. It had neither mattress nor springs, the frame crisscrossed now by a neat hammocking of thongs.

Issetibbeha had tried to have his newest wife, the young one, sleep in the bed. He was congenitally short of breath himself, and he passed the nights half reclining in his splint chair. He would see her to bed and, later, wakeful, sleeping as he did but three or four hours a night, he would sit in the darkness and simulate slumber and listen to her sneak infinitesimally from the gilt and ribboned bed, to lie on a quilt pallet on the floor until just before daylight. Then she would enter the bed quietly again and in turn simulate slumber, while in the darkness beside her Issetibbeha quietly laughed and laughed.

The girandoles were lashed by thongs to two sticks propped in a corner where a ten-gallon whiskey keg lay also. There was a clay hearth; facing it, in the splint chair, Moketubbe sat. He was maybe an inch better than five feet tall, and he weighed two hundred and fifty pounds. He wore a broadcloth coat and no shirt, his round, smooth copper balloon of belly swelling above the bottom piece of a suit of linen underwear. On his feet were the slippers with the red heels. Behind his chair stood a stripling with a punkah-like fan made of fringed paper. Moketubbe sat motionless, with his broad, yellow face with its closed eyes and flat nostrils, his flipper-like arms extended. On his face was an expression profound, tragic, and inert. He did not open his eyes when Basket and Berry came in.

"He has worn them since daylight?" Basket said.

"Since daylight," the stripling said. The fan did not cease. "You can see."

"Yao," Basket said. "We can see." Moketubbe did not move. He looked like an effigy, like a Malay god in frock coat, drawers, naked chest, the trivial scarlet-heeled shoes.

"I wouldn't disturb him, if I were you," the stripling said.

"Not if I were you," Basket said. He and Berry squatted. The stripling moved the fan steadily. "O Man," Basket said, "listen." Moketubbe did not move. "He is gone," Basket said.

"I told you so," the stripling said. "I knew he would flee. I told you."

"Yao." Basket said. "You are not the first to tell us afterward what we should have known before. Why is it that some of you wise men took no steps yesterday to prevent this?"

"He does not wish to die," Berry said.

"Why should he not wish it?" Basket said.

"Because he must die some day is no reason," the stripling said. "That would not convince me either, old man."

"Hold your tongue," Berry said.

"For twenty years," Basket said, "while others of his race sweat in the fields, he served the Man in the shade. Why should he not wish to die, since he did not wish to sweat?"

"And it will be quick," Berry said. "It will not take long."

"Catch him and tell him that," the stripling said.

"Hush," Berry said. They squatted, watching Moketubbe's face. He might have been dead himself. It was as though he were cased so in flesh that even breathing took place too deep within him to show.

"Listen, O Man," Basket said. "Issetibbeha is dead. He waits. His dog and his horse we have. But his slave has fled. The one who held the pot for him, who ate of his food, from his dish, is fled. Issetibbeha waits."

"Yao," Berry said.

"This is not the first time," Basket said. "This happened when Doom, thy grandfather, lay waiting at the door of the earth. He lay waiting three days, saying, 'Where is my Negro?' And Issetibbeha, thy father, answered, 'I will find him. Rest; I will bring him to you so that you may begin the journey.'"

"Yao," Berry said.

Moketubbe had not moved, had not opened his eyes.

"For three days Issetibbeha hunted in the bottom," Basket said. "He did not even return home for food, until the Negro was with him; then he said to Doom, his father, 'Here is thy dog, thy horse, thy Negro; rest.' Issetibbeha, who is dead since yesterday, said it. And now Issetibbeha's Negro is fled. His horse and his dog wait with him, but his Negro is fled."

"Yao," Berry said.

Moketubbe had not moved. His eyes were closed; upon his supine monstrous shape there was a colossal inertia, something profoundly immobile, beyond and impervious to flesh. They watched his face, squatting.

"When thy father was newly the Man, this happened," Basket said. "And it was Issetibbeha who brought back the slave to where his father waited to enter the earth." Moketubbe's face had not moved, his eyes had not moved. After a while Basket said, "Remove the shoes."

The stripling removed the shoes. Moketubbe began to pant, his bare chest moving deep, as though he were rising from beyond his unfathomed flesh back into life, like up from the water, the sea. But his eyes had not opened yet.

Berry said, "He will lead the hunt."

"Yao," Basket said. "He is the Man. He will lead the hunt."

IV

All that day the Negro, Issetibbeha's body servant, hidden in the barn, watched Issetibbeha's dying. He was forty, a Guinea man. He had a flat nose, a close, small head; the inside corners of his eyes showed red a little, and his prominent gums were a pale bluish red above his square, broad teeth. He had been taken at fourteen by a trader off Kamerun, before his teeth had been filed. He had been Issetibbeha's body servant for twenty-three years.

On the day before, the day on which Issetibbeha lay sick, he returned to the quarters at dusk. In that unhurried hour the smoke of the cooking fires blew slowly across the street from door to door, carrying into the opposite one the smell of the identical meat and bread. The women tended them; the men were gathered at the head of the lane, watching him as he came down the slope from the house, putting his naked feet down carefully in a strange dusk. To the waiting men his eyeballs were a little luminous.

"Issetibbeha is not dead yet," the headman said.

"Not dead," the body servant said. "Who not dead?"

In the dusk they had faces like his, the different ages, the thoughts sealed inscrutable behind faces like the death masks of apes. The smell of the fires, the cooking, blew sharp and slow across the strange dusk, as from another world, above the lane and the pickaninnies naked in the dust.

"If he lives past sundown, he will live until daybreak," one said.

"Who says?"

"Talk says."

"Yao. Talk says. We know but one thing." They looked at the body servant as he stood among them, his eyeballs a little luminous. He was breathing slow and deep. His chest was bare; he was sweating a little. "He knows. He knows it."

"Let us let the drums talk."

"Yao. Let the drums tell it."

The drums began after dark. They kept them hidden in the creek bottom. They were made of hollowed cypress knees, and the Negroes kept them hidden; why, none knew. They were buried in the mud on the bank of a slough; a lad of fourteen guarded them. He was undersized, and a mute; he squatted in the mud there all day, clouded over with mosquitoes, naked save for the mud with which he coated himself against the mosquitoes, and about his neck a fiber bag containing a pig's rib to which black shreds of flesh still adhered, and two scaly barks on a wire. He slobbered onto his clutched knees, drooling; now and then Indians came noiselessly out of the bushes behind him and stood there and contemplated him for a while and went away, and he never knew it.

From the loft of the stable where he lay hidden until dark and after, the Negro could hear the drums. They were three miles away, but he could hear them as though they were in the barn itself below him, thudding and thudding. It was as though he could see the fire too, and the black limbs turning into and out of the flames in copper gleams. Only there would be no fire. There would be no more light there than where he lay in the dusty loft, with the whispering arpeggios of rat feet along the warm and immemorial ax-squared rafters. The only fire there would be the smudge against mosquitoes where the women were nursing children crouched, their heavy, sluggish breasts nippled full and smooth into the mouths of men children; contemplative, oblivious of the drumming, since a fire would signify life.

There was a fire in the steamboat, where Issetibbeha lay dying among his wives, beneath the lashed girandoles and the suspended bed. He could see the smoke, and just before sunset he saw the doctor come out, in a waistcoat made of skunk skins, and set fire to two clay-daubed sticks at the bows of the boat deck. "So he is not dead yet," the Negro said into the whispering gloom of the loft, answering himself; he could hear the two voices, himself and himself:

"Who not dead?"

"You are dead."

"Yao, I am dead," he said quietly. He wished to be where the drums were. He imagined himself springing out of the bushes, leaping among the drums on his bare, lean, greasy, invisible limbs. But he could not do that, because man leaped past life, into where death was; he dashed into death and did not die because when death took a man, it took him just this side of the end of living. It was when death overran him from behind, still in life. The thin whisper of rat feet died in fainting gusts along the rafters. Once he had eaten rat. He was a boy then, but just come to America. They had lived ninety days in a three-foot-high 'tween deck in tropic latitudes, hearing from topside the drunken New England captain intoning aloud from a book which he did not recognize for ten years afterward to be the Bible. Squatting in the stable so, he had watched the rat, civilized, by association with man reft of its inherent cunning of limb and eye; he had caught it without difficulty, with scarce a movement of his hand, and he ate it slowly, wondering how any of the rats had escaped so long. At that time he was still wearing the single white garment which the trader, a deacon in the Unitarian church, had given him, and he spoke then only his native tongue.

He was naked now, save for a pair of dungaree pants bought by Indians from white men, and an amulet slung on a thong about his hips. The amulet consisted of one half of a mother-of-pearl lorgnon which Issetibbeha had brought back from Paris, and the skull of a cottonmouth moccasin. He had killed the snake himself and eaten it, save the poison head. He lay in the loft, watching the house, the steamboat, listening to the drums, thinking of himself among the drums.

He lay there all night. The next morning he saw the doctor come out, in his skunk vest, and get on his mule and ride away, and he became quite still and watched the final dust from beneath the mule's delicate feet die away, and then he found that he was still breathing and it seemed strange to him that he still breathed air, still needed air. Then he lay and watched quietly, waiting to move, his eyeballs a little luminous, but with a quiet light, and his breathing light and regular, and saw Louis Berry come out and look at the sky. It was good light then, and already five Indians squatted in their Sunday clothes along the steamboat deck; by noon there were twenty-five there. That afternoon they dug the trench in which the meat would be baked, and the yams; by that time there were almost a hundred guests—decorous, quiet, patient in their stiff European finery—and he watched Berry lead Issetibbeha's mare from the stable and tie her to a tree, and then he watched Berry emerge from the house with the old hound which lay beside Issetibbeha's chair. He tied the hound to the tree too, and it sat there, looking gravely about at the faces. Then it began to howl. It was still howling at sundown, when the Negro climbed down the back wall of the barn and entered the spring branch, where it was already dusk. He began to run then. He could hear the hound howling behind him, and near the spring, already running, he passed another Negro. The two men, the one motionless and the other running, looked for an instant at each other as though across an actual boundary between two different worlds. He ran on into full darkness, mouth closed, fists doubled, his broad nostrils bellowing steadily.

He ran on in the darkness. He knew the country well, because he had hunted it often with Issetibbeha, following on his mule the course of the fox or the cat beside Issetibbeha's mare; he knew it as well as did the men who would pursue him. He saw them for the first time shortly before sunset of the second day. He had run thirty miles then, up the creek bottom, before doubling back; lying in a pawpaw thicket he saw the pursuit for the first time. There were two of them, in shirts and straw hats, carrying their neatly rolled trousers under their arms, and they had no weapons. They were middle-aged, paunchy, and they could not have moved very fast anyway; it would be twelve hours before they could return to where he lay watching them. "So I will have until midnight to rest," he said. He was near enough to the plantation to smell the cooking fires, and he thought how he ought to be hungry, since he had not eaten in thirty hours. "But it is more important to rest," he told himself. He continued to tell himself that, lying in the pawpaw thicket, because the effort of resting, the need and the haste to rest, made his heart thud the same as the running had done. It was as though he had forgot how to rest, as though the six hours were not long enough to do it in, to remember again how to do it.

As soon as dark came he moved again. He had thought to keep going steadily and quietly through the night, since there was nowhere for him to go, but as soon as he moved he began to run at top speed, breasting his panting chest, his broad-flaring nostrils through the choked and whipping darkness. He ran for an hour, lost by then, without direction, when suddenly he stopped, and after a time his thudding heart unraveled from the sound of the drums. By the sound they were not two miles away; he followed the sound until he could smell the smudge fire and taste the acrid smoke. When he stood among them the drums did not cease; only the headman came to him where he stood in the drifting smudge, panting, his nostrils flaring and pulsing, the hushed glare of his ceaseless eyeballs in his mud-daubed face as though they were worked from lungs.

"We have expected thee," the headman said. "Go, now."

"Go?"

"Eat, and go. The dead may not consort with the living; thou knowest that."

"Yao. I know that." They did not look at one another. The drums had not ceased.

"Wilt thou eat?" the headman said.

"I am not hungry. I caught a rabbit this afternoon, and ate while I lay hidden."

"Take some cooked meat with thee, then."

He accepted the cooked meat, wrapped in leaves, and entered the creek bottom again; after a while the sound of the drums ceased. He walked steadily until daybreak. "I have twelve hours," he said. "Maybe more, since the trail was followed by night." He squatted and ate the meat and wiped his hands on his thighs. Then he rose and removed the dungaree pants and squatted again beside a slough and coated himself with mud—face, arms, body and legs—and squatted again, clasping his knees, his head bowed. When it was light enough to see, he moved back into the swamp and squatted again and went to sleep so. He did not dream at all. It was well that he moved, for, waking suddenly in broad daylight and the high sun, he saw the two Indians. They still carried their neatly rolled trousers; they stood opposite the place where he lay hidden, paunchy, thick, soft-looking, a little ludicrous in their straw hats and shirt tails.

"This is wearying work," one said.

"I'd rather be at home in the shade myself," the other said. "But there is the Man waiting at the door to the earth."

"Yao." They looked quietly about; stooping, one of them removed from his shirt tail a clot of cockleburs. "Damn that Negro," he said.

"Yao. When have they ever been anything but a trial and a care to us?"

In the early afternoon, from the top of a tree, the Negro looked down into the plantation. He could see Issetibbeha's body in a hammock between the two trees where the horse and the dog were tethered, and the concourse about the steamboat was filled with wagons and horses and mules, with carts and saddlehorses, while in bright clumps the women and the smaller children and the old men squatted about the long trench where the smoke from the barbecuing meat blew slow and thick. The men and the big boys would all be down there in the creek bottom behind him, on the trail, their Sunday clothes rolled carefully up and wedged into tree crotches. There was a clump of men near the door to the house, to the saloon of the steamboat, though, and he watched them, and after a while he saw them bring Moketubbe out in a litter made of buckskin and persimmon poles; high hidden in his leafed nook the

Negro, the quarry, looked quietly down upon his irrevocable doom with an expression as profound as Moketubbe's own. "Yao," he said quietly. "He will go then. That man whose body has been dead for fifteen years, he will go also."

In the middle of the afternoon he came face to face with an Indian. They were both on a footlog across a slough—the Negro gaunt, lean, hard, tireless and desperate; the Indian thick, soft-looking, the apparent embodiment of the ultimate and the supreme reluctance and inertia. The Indian made no move, no sound; he stood on the log and watched the Negro plunge into the slough and swim ashore and crash away into the undergrowth.

Just before sunset he lay behind a down log. Up the log in slow procession moved a line of ants. He caught them and ate them slowly, with a kind of detachment, like that of a dinner guest eating salted nuts from a dish. They too had a salt taste, engendering a salivary reaction out of all proportion. He ate them slowly, watching the unbroken line move up the log and into oblivious doom with a steady and terrific undeviation. He had eaten nothing else all day; in his caked mud mask his eyes rolled in reddened rims. At sunset, creeping along the creek bank toward where he had spotted a frog, a cottonmouth moccasin slashed him suddenly across the forearm with a thick, sluggish blow. It struck clumsily, leaving two long slashes across his arm like two razor slashes, and half sprawled with its own momentum and rage, it appeared for the moment utterly helpless with its own awkwardness and choleric anger. "Olé, Grandfather," the Negro said. He touched its head and watched it slash him again across his arm, and again, with thick, raking, awkward blows. "It's that I do not wish to die," he said. Then he said it again—"It's that I do not wish to die"—in a quiet tone, of slow and low amaze, as though it were something that, until the words had said themselves, he found that he had not known, or had not known the depth and extent of his desire.

V

Moketubbe took the slippers with him. He could not wear them very long while in motion, not even in the litter where he was slung reclining, so they rested upon a square of fawnskin upon his lap—the cracked, frail slippers a little shapeless now, with their scaled patent-leather surface and buckleless tongues and scarlet heels, lying upon the supine, obese shape just barely alive, carried through swamp and brier by swinging relays of men who bore steadily all day long the crime and its object, on the business of the slain. To Moketubbe it must have been as though, himself immortal, he were being carried rapidly through hell by doomed spirits which, alive, had contemplated his disaster, and, dead, were oblivious partners to his damnation.

After resting for a while, the litter propped in the center of the squatting circle and Moketubbe motionless in it, with closed eyes and his face at once peaceful for the instant and filled with inescapable foreknowledge, he could wear the slippers for a while. The stripling put them on him, forcing his big, tender, dropsical feet into them; whereupon into his face came again that expression, tragic, passive, and profoundly attentive, which dyspeptics wear. Then they went on. He made no move, no sound, inert in the rhythmic litter out of some reserve of inertia, or maybe of some kingly virtue such as courage or fortitude. After a time they set the litter down and looked at him, at the yellow face like that of an idol, beaded over with sweat. Then Three Basket or Louis Berry would say: "Take them off. Honor has been served." They would remove the shoes. Moketubbe's face would not alter, but only then would his breathing become perceptible, going in and out of his pale lips with a faint ah-ah-ah sound, and they would squat again while the couriers and the runners came up.

"Not yet?"

"Not yet. He is going east. By sunset he will reach Mouth of Tippah. Then he will turn back. We may take him tomorrow."

"Let us hope so. It will not be too soon."

"Yao. It has been three days now."

"When Doom died, it took only three days."

"But that was an old man. This one is young."

"Yao. A good race. If he is taken tomorrow, I will win a horse."

"May you win it."

"Yao. This work is not pleasant."

That was the day on which the food gave out at the plantation. The guests returned home and came back the next day with more food, enough for a week longer. On that day Issetibbeha began to smell; they could smell him for a long way up and down the bottom when it got hot toward noon and the wind blew. But they didn't capture the Negro on that day, nor on the next. It was about dusk on the sixth day when the couriers came up to the litter; they had found blood. "He has injured himself."

"Not bad, I hope," Basket said. "We cannot send with Issetibbeha one who will be of no service to him."

"Nor whom Issetibbeha himself will have to nurse and care for," Berry said.

"We do not know," the courier said. "He has hidden himself. He has crept back into the swamp. We have left pickets."

They trotted with the litter now. The place where the Negro had crept into the swamp was an hour away. In the hurry and excitement they had forgotten that Moketubbe still wore the slippers; when they reached the place Moketubbe had fainted. They removed the slippers and brought him to.

With dark, they formed a circle about the swamp. They squatted, clouded over with gnats and mosquitoes; the evening star burned low and close down the west, and the constellations began to wheel overhead. "We will give him time," they said. "Tomorrow is just another name for today."

"Yao. Let him have time." Then they ceased, and gazed as one into the darkness where the swamp lay. After a while the noise ceased, and soon the courier came out of the darkness.

"He tried to break out."

"But you turned him back?"

"He turned back. We feared for a moment, the three of us. We could smell him creeping in the darkness, and we could smell something else, which we did not know. That was why we feared, until he told us. He said to slay him there, since it would be dark and he would not have to see the face when it came. But it was not that which we smelled; he told us what it was. A snake had struck him. That was two days ago. The arm swelled, and it smelled bad. But it was not that which we smelled then, because the swelling had gone down and his arm was no larger than that of a child. He showed us. We felt the arm, all of us did; it was no larger than that of a child. He said to give him a hatchet so he could chop the arm off. But tomorrow is today also."

"Yao. Tomorrow is today."

"We feared for a while. Then he went back into the swamp."

"That is good."

"Yao. We feared. Shall I tell the Man?"

"I will see," Basket said. He went away. The courier squatted, telling again about the Negro. Basket returned. "The Man says that it is good. Return to your post."

The courier crept away. They squatted about the litter; now and then they slept. Some time after midnight the Negro waked them.

He began to shout and talk to himself, his voice coming sharp and sudden out of the darkness, then he fell silent. Dawn came; a white crane flapped slowly across the jonquil sky. Basket was awake. "Let us go now," he said. "It is today."

Two Indians entered the swamp, their movements noisy. Before they reached the Negro they stopped, because he began to sing. They could see him, naked and mud-caked, sitting on a log, singing. They squatted silently a short distance away, until he finished. He was chanting something in his own language, his face lifted to the rising sun. His voice was clear, fully, with a quality wild and sad. "Let him have time," the Indians said, squatting, patient, waiting. He ceased and they approached. He looked back and up at them through the cracked mud mask. His eyes were bloodshot, his lips cracked upon his square short teeth. The mask of mud appeared to be loose on his face, as if he might have lost flesh since he put it there; he held his left arm close to his breast. From the elbow down it was caked and shapeless with black mud. They could smell him, a rank smell. He watched them quietly until one touched him on the arm. "Come," the Indian said. "You ran well. Do not be ashamed."

VI

As they neared the plantation in the tainted bright morning, the Negro's eyes began to roll a little, like those of a horse. The smoke from the cooking pit blew low along the earth and upon the squatting and waiting guests about the yard and upon the steamboat deck, in their bright, stiff, harsh finery; the women, the children, the old men. They had sent couriers along the bottom, and another on ahead, and Issetibbeha's body had already been removed to where the grave waited, along with the horse and the dog, though they could still smell him in death about the house where he had lived in life. The guests were beginning to move toward the grave when the bearers of Moketubbe's litter mounted the slope.

The Negro was the tallest there, his high, close, mud-caked head looming above them all. He was breathing hard, as though the desperate effort of the six suspended and desperate days had capitulated upon him at once; although they walked slowly, his naked scarred chest rose and fell above the close-clutched left arm. He looked this way and that continuously, as if he were not seeing, as though sight never quite caught up with the looking. His mouth was open a little upon his big white teeth; he began to pant. The already moving guests halted, pausing, looking back, some with pieces of meat in their hands, as the Negro looked about at their faces with his wild, restrained, unceasing eyes.

"Will you eat first?" Basket said. He had to say it twice.

"Yes," the Negro said. "That's it. I want to eat."

The throng had begun to press back toward the center; the word passed to the outermost: "He will eat first."

They reached the steamboat. "Sit down," Basket said. The Negro sat on the edge of the deck. He was still panting, his chest rising and falling, his head ceaseless with its white eyeballs, turning from side to side. It was as if the inability to see came from within, from hopelessness, not from absence of vision. They brought food and watched quietly as he tried to eat it. He put the food into his mouth and chewed it, but chewing, the half-masticated matter began to emerge from the corners of his mouth and to drool down his chin, onto his chest, and after a while he stopped chewing and sat there, naked, covered with dried mud, the plate on his knees, and his mouth filled with a mass of chewed food, open, his eyes wide and unceasing, panting and panting. They watched him, patient, implacable, waiting.

"Come," Basket said at last.

"It's water I want," the Negro said. "I want water."

The well was a little way down the slope toward the quarters. The slope lay dappled with the shadows of noon, of that peaceful hour when, Issetibbeha napping in his chair and waiting for the noon meal and the long afternoon to sleep in, the Negro, the body servant, would be free. He would sit in the kitchen door then, talking with the women that prepared the food. Beyond the kitchen the lane between the quarters would be quiet, peaceful, with the women talking to one another across the lane and the smoke of the dinner fires blowing upon the pickaninnies like ebony toys in the dust.

"Come," Basket said.

The Negro walked among them, taller than any. The guests were moving on toward where Issetibbeha and the horse and the dog waited. The Negro walked with his high ceaseless head, his panting chest. "Come," Basket said. "You wanted water."

"Yes," the Negro said. "Yes." He looked back at the house, then down to the quarters, where today no fire burned, no face showed in any door, no pickaninny in the dust, panting. "It struck me here, raking me across this arm; once, twice, three times. I said, 'Olé, Grandfather.'"

"Come now," Basket said. The Negro was still going through the motion of walking, his knee action high, his head high, as though he were on a treadmill. His eyeballs had a wild, restrained glare, like those of a horse. "You wanted water," Basket said. "Here it is."

There was a gourd in the well. They dipped it full and gave it to the Negro, and they watched him try to drink. His eyes had not ceased rolling as he tilted the gourd slowly against his caked face. They could watch his throat working and the bright water cascading from either side of the gourd, down his chin and breast. Then the water stopped. "Come," Basket said.

"Wait," the Negro said. He dipped the gourd again and tilted it against his face, beneath his ceaseless eyes. Again they watched his throat working and the unswallowed water sheathing broken and myriad down his chin, channeling his caked chest. They waited, patient, grave, decorous, implacable; clansman and guest and kin. Then the water ceased, though still the empty gourd tilted higher and higher, and still his black throat aped the vain motion of his frustrated swallowing. A piece of water-loosened mud carried away from his chest and broke at his muddy feet, and in the empty gourd they could hear his breath: ah-ah-ah-

"Come," Basket said, taking the gourd from the Negro and hanging it back in the well.

15

Notes of a Native Son

by James Baldwin

91 Revere Street

by Robert Lowell

James Baldwin *Baldwin's accession in the 1950s and early 1960s to the eminence of "foremost black American writer" coincided with the burgeoning civil rights movement, and Baldwin proved in his own way to be a superlatively articulate spokesman for the "Negro cause." Unlike other black intellectuals, Baldwin usually kept out of the public arenas, restricting himself to whatever impact he might make as a writer.*

In fiction, in his dramas, such as Blues for Mister Charlie *and* The Amen Corner, *but especially in his polemical essays like* The Fire Next Time, Notes of a Native Son, *and* Nobody Knows My Name, *Baldwin has trenchantly exposed nuances of the race issue that many white Americans had not previously understood—or chosen to understand.*

Robert Lowell *Robert Lowell is of course best known as a poet, and in the estimation of many, "the most important living American poet," as the phrase goes. Although his poetic concerns, his intensity, and his poetic texture have varied considerably since his first volume in 1944, it can surely be argued that he has continued (from varying perspectives) his exploration of his own identity and relationship to the past.*

Lowell was born in Boston, and his past on his mother's side reaches back to Edward Winslow, who arrived on the Mayflower and became governor of the Plymouth Colony. On his father's side, the illustrious relatives include James Russell Lowell and Amy Lowell.

Converted to Catholicism as an undergraduate, Lowell wrote about the burdens of his life (and of Life) in the furiously wrenched and convoluted verses of Lord Weary's Castle. *But his most widely influential book,* Life Studies, *appeared twelve years later in 1959, and signaled the beginning of what has been called the "confessional mode" in modern poetry. "91 Revere Street" is excerpted from this volume.*

Notes of a Native Son

James Baldwin (*American, 1924–*   )

On the 29th of July, in 1943, my father died. On the same day, a few hours later, his last child was born. Over a month before this, while all our energies were concentrated in waiting for these events, there had been, in Detroit, one of the bloodiest race riots of the century. A few hours after my father's funeral, while he lay in state in the undertaker's chapel, a race riot broke out in Harlem. On the morning of the 3rd of August, we drove my father to the graveyard through a wilderness of smashed plate glass.

The day of my father's funeral had also been my nineteenth birthday. As we drove him to the graveyard, the spoils of injustice, anarchy, discontent, and hatred were all around us. It seemed to me that God himself had devised, to mark my father's end, the most sustained and brutally dissonant of codas. And it seemed to me, too, that the violence which rose all about us as my father left the world had been devised as a corrective for the pride of his eldest son. I had declined to believe in that apocalypse which had been central to my father's vision; very well, life seemed to be saying, here is something that will certainly pass for an apocalypse until the real thing comes along. I had inclined to be contemptuous of my father for the conditions of his life, for the conditions of our lives. When his life had ended I began to wonder about that life and also, in a new way, to be apprehensive about my own.

I had not known my father very well. We had got on badly, partly because we shared, in our different fashions, the vice of stubborn pride. When he was dead I realized that I had hardly ever spoken to him. When he had been dead a long time I began to wish I had. It seems to be typical of life in America, where opportunities, real and fancied, are thicker than anywhere else on the globe, that the second generation has no time to talk to the first. No one, including my father, seems to have known exactly how old he was, but his mother had been born during slavery. He was of the first generation of free men. He, along with thousands of other Negroes, came North after 1919 and I was part of that generation which had never seen the landscape of what Negroes sometimes call the Old Country.

He had been born in New Orleans and had been a quite young man there during the time that Louis Armstrong, a boy, was running errands for the dives and honky-tonks of what was always presented to me as one of the most wicked of cities—to this day, whenever I think of New Orleans, I also helplessly think of Sodom and Gomorrah. My father never mentioned Louis Armstrong, except to forbid us to play his records; but there was a picture of him on our wall for a long time. One of my father's strong-willed female relatives had placed it there and forbade my father to take it down. He never did, but he eventually maneuvered her out of the house and when, some years later, she was in trouble and near death, he refused to do anything to help her.

He was, I think, very handsome. I gather this from photographs and from my own memories of him, dressed in his Sunday best and on his way to preach a sermon somewhere, when I was little. Handsome, proud, and ingrown, "like a toe-nail," somebody said. But he looked to me, as I grew older, like pictures I had seen of African tribal chieftains: he really should have been naked, with war-paint on and barbaric mementos, standing among spears. He could be chilling in the pulpit and indescribably cruel in his personal life and he was certainly the most bitter man I have ever met; yet it must be said that there was something else in him, buried in him, which lent him his tremendous power and, even, a rather crushing charm. It had something to do with his blackness, I think—he was very black—with his blackness and his beauty, and with the fact that he knew that he was black but did not know that he was beautiful. He claimed to be proud of his blackness but it had also been the cause of much humiliation and it had fixed bleak boundaries to his life. He was not a young man when we were growing up and he had already suffered many kinds of ruin; in his outrageously demanding and protective way he loved his children, who were black like him and menaced, like him; and all these things sometimes showed in his face when he tried, never to my knowledge with any success, to establish contact with any of us. When he took one of his children on his knee to play, the child always became fretful and began to cry; when he tried to help one of us with our homework the absolutely unabating tension which emanated from him caused our minds and our tongues to become paralyzed, so that he, scarcely knowing why, flew into a rage and the child, not knowing why, was punished. If it ever entered his head to bring a surprise home for his children, it was, almost unfailingly, the wrong surprise and even the big watermelons he often brought home on his back in the summertime led to the most appalling scenes. I do not remember, in all those years, that one of his children was ever glad to see him come home. From what I was able to gather of his early life, it seemed that this inability to establish contact with other people had always marked him and had been one of the things which had driven him out of New Orleans. There was something in him, therefore, groping and tentative, which was never expressed and which was buried with him. One saw it most clearly when he was facing new people and hoping to impress them. But he never did, not for long. We went from church to smaller and more improbable church, he found himself in less and less demand as a minister, and by the time he died none of his friends had come to see him for a long time. He had lived and died in an intolerable bitterness of spirit and it frightened me, as we drove him to the graveyard through those unquiet, ruined streets, to see how powerful and overflowing this bitterness could be and to realize that this bitterness now was mine.

When he died I had been away from home for a little over a year. In that year I had had time to become aware of the meaning of all my father's bitter warnings, had discovered the secret of his proudly pursed lips and rigid carriage: I had discovered the weight of white people in the world. I saw that this had been for my ancestors and now would be for me an awful thing to live with and that the bitterness which had helped to kill my father could also kill me.

He had been ill a long time—in the mind, as we now realized, reliving instances of his fantastic intransigence in the new light of his affliction and endeavoring to feel a sorrow for him which never, quite, came true. We had not known that he was being eaten up by paranoia, and the discovery that his cruelty, to our bodies and our minds, had been one of the symptoms of his illness was not, then, enough to enable us to forgive him. The younger children felt, quite simply, relief that he would not be coming home anymore. My mother's observation that it was he, after all, who had kept them alive all these years meant nothing because the problems of keeping children alive are not real for children. The older children felt, with my father gone, that they could invite their friends to the house without fear that their friends would be insulted or, as had sometimes happened with me, being told that their friends were in league with the devil and intended to rob our family of everything we owned. (I didn't fail to wonder, and it made me hate him, what on earth we owned that anybody else would want.)

His illness was beyond all hope of healing before anyone realized that he was ill. He had always been so strange and had lived, like a prophet, in such unimaginably close communion with the Lord that his long silences which were punctuated by moans and hallelujahs and snatches of old songs while he sat at the living-room window never seemed odd to us. It was not until he refused to eat because, he said, his family was trying to poison him that my mother was forced to accept as a fact what had, until then, been only an unwilling suspicion. When he was committed, it was discovered that he had tuberculosis and, as it turned out, the disease of his mind allowed the disease of his body to destroy him. For the doctors could not force him to eat, either, and, though he was fed intravenously, it was clear from the beginning that there was no hope for him.

In my mind's eye I could see him, sitting at the window, locked up in his terrors; hating and fearing every living soul including his children who had betrayed him, too, by reaching towards the world which had despised him. There were nine of us. I began to wonder what it could have felt like for such a man to have had nine children whom he could barely feed. He used to make little jokes about our poverty, which never, of course, seemed very funny to us; they could not have seemed very funny to him, either, or else our all too feeble response to them would never have caused such rages. He spent great energy and achieved, to our chagrin, no small amount of success in keeping us away from the people who surrounded us, people who had all-night rent parties to which we listened when we should have been sleeping, people who cursed and drank and flashed razor blades on Lenox Avenue. He could not understand why, if they had so much energy to spare, they could not use it to make their lives better. He treated almost everybody on our block with a most uncharitable asperity and neither they, nor, of course, their children were slow to reciprocate.

The only white people who came to our house were welfare workers and bill collectors. It was almost always my mother who dealt with them, for my father's temper, which was at the mercy of his pride, was never to be trusted. It was clear that he felt their very presence in his home to be a violation: this was conveyed by his carriage, almost ludicrously stiff, and by his voice, harsh and vindictively polite. When I was around nine or ten I wrote a play which was directed by a young, white schoolteacher, a woman, who then took an interest in me, and gave me books to read and, in order to corroborate my theatrical bent, decided to take me to see what she somewhat tactlessly referred to as "real" plays. Theater-going was forbidden in our house, but, with the really cruel intuitiveness of a child, I suspected that the color of this woman's skin would carry the day for me. When, at school, she suggested taking me to the theater, I did not, as I might have done if she had been a Negro, find a way of discouraging her, but agreed that she should pick me up at my house one evening. I then, very cleverly, left all the rest to my mother, who suggested to my father, as I knew she would, that it would not be very nice to let such a kind woman make the trip for nothing. Also, since it was a schoolteacher, I imagine that my mother countered the idea of sin with the idea of "education," which word, even with my father, carried a kind of bitter weight.

Before the teacher came my father took me aside to ask *why* she was coming, what *interest* she could possibly have in our house, in a boy like me. I said I didn't know but I, too, suggested that it had something to do with education. And I understood that my father was waiting for me to say something—I didn't quite know what; perhaps that I wanted his protection against this teacher and her "education." I said none of these things and the teacher came and we went out. It was clear, during the brief interview in our living room, that my father was agreeing very much against his will and that he would have refused permission if he had dared. The fact that he did not dare caused me to despise him: I had no way of knowing that he was facing in that living room a wholly unprecedented and frightening situation.

Later, when my father had been laid off from his job, this woman became very important to us. She was really a very sweet and generous woman and went to a great deal of trouble to be of help to us, particularly during one awful winter. My mother called her by the highest name she knew: she said she was a "christian." My father could scarcely disagree but during the four or five years of our relatively close association he never trusted her and was always trying to surprise in her open, Midwestern face the genuine, cunningly hidden, and hideous motivation. In later years, particularly when it began to be clear that this "education" of mine was going to lead me to perdition, he became more explicit and warned me that my white friends in high school were not really my friends and that I would see, when I was older, how white people would do anything to keep a Negro down. Some of them could be nice, he admitted, but none of them were to be trusted and most of them were not even nice. The best thing was to have as little to do with them as possible. I did not feel this way and I was certain, in my innocence, that I never would.

But the year which preceded my father's death had made a great change in my life. I had been living in New Jersey, working in defense plants, working and living among southerners, white and black. I knew about the south, of course, and about how southerners treated Negroes and how they expected them to behave, but it had never entered my mind that anyone would look at me and expect *me* to behave that way. I learned in New Jersey that to be a Negro meant, precisely, that one was never looked at but was simply at the mercy of the reflexes the color of one's skin caused in other people. I acted in New Jersey as I had always acted, that is as though I thought a great deal of myself—I had to *act* that way—with results that were, simply, unbelievable. I had scarcely arrived before I had earned the enmity, which was extraordinarily ingenious, of all my superiors and nearly all my co-workers. In the beginning, to make matters worse, I simply did not know what was happening. I did not know what I had done, and I shortly began to wonder what *anyone* could possibly do, to bring about such unanimous, active, and unbearably vocal hostility. I knew about jim-crow but I had never experienced it. I went to the same self-service restaurant three times and stood with all the Princeton boys before the counter, waiting for a hamburger and coffee; it was always an extraordinarily long time before anything was set before me; but it was not until the fourth visit that I learned that, in fact, nothing had ever been set before me: I had simply picked something up. Negroes were not served there, I was told, and they had been waiting for me to realize that I was always the only Negro present. Once I was told this, I determined to go there all the time. But now they were ready for me and, though some dreadful scenes were subsequently enacted in that restaurant, I never ate there again.

It was the same story all over New Jersey, in bars, bowling alleys, diners, places to live. I was always being forced to leave, silently, or with mutual imprecations. I very shortly became notorious and children giggled behind me when I passed and their elders whispered or shouted—they really believed that I was mad.

And it did begin to work on my mind, of course; I began to be afraid to go anywhere and to compensate for this I went places to which I really should not have gone and where, God knows, I had no desire to be. My reputation in town naturally enhanced my reputation at work and my working day became one long series of acrobatics designed to keep me out of trouble. I cannot say that these acrobatics succeeded. It began to seem that the machinery of the organization I worked for was turning over, day and night, with but one aim: to eject me. I was fired once, and contrived, with the aid of a friend from New York, to get back on the payroll; was fired again, and bounced back again. It took a while to fire me for the third time, but the third time took. There were no loopholes anywhere. There was not even any way of getting back inside the gates.

That year in New Jersey lives in my mind as though it were the year during which, having an unsuspected predilection for it, I first contracted some dread, chronic disease, the unfailing symptom of which is a kind of blind fever, a pounding in the skull and fire in the bowels. Once this disease is contracted, one can never be really carefree again, for the fever, without an instant's warning, can recur at any moment. It can wreck more important things than race relations. There is not a Negro alive who does not have this rage in his blood—one has the choice, merely, of living with it consciously or surrendering to it. As for me, this fever has recurred in me, and does, and will until the day I die.

My last night in New Jersey, a white friend from New York took me to the nearest big town, Trenton, to go to the movies and have a few drinks. As it turned out, he also saved me from, at the very least, a violent whipping. Almost every detail of that night stands out very clearly in my memory. I even remember the name of the movie we saw because its title impressed me as being so patly ironical. It was a movie about the German occupation of France, starring Maureen O'Hara and Charles Laughton and called *This Land Is Mine*. I remember the name of the diner we walked into when the movie ended: it was the "American Diner." When we walked in the counterman asked what we wanted and I remember answering with the casual sharpness which had become my habit: "We want a hamburger and a cup of coffee, what do you think we want?" I do not know why, after a year of such rebuffs, I so completely failed to anticipate his answer, which was, of course, "We don't serve Negroes here." This reply failed to discompose me, at least for the moment. I made some sardonic comment about the name of the diner and we walked out into the streets.

This was the time of what was called the "brown-out," when the lights in all American cities were very dim. When we re-entered the streets something happened to me which had the force of an optical illusion, or a nightmare. The streets were very crowded and I was facing north. People were moving in every direction but it seemed to me, in that instant, that all of the people I could see, and many more than that, were moving toward me, against me, and that everyone was white. I remember how their faces gleamed. And I felt, like a physical sensation, a *click* at the nape of my neck as though some interior string connecting my head to my body had been cut. I began to walk. I heard my friend call after me, but I ignored him. Heaven only knows what was going on in his mind, but he had the good sense not to touch me—I don't know what would have happened if he had—and to keep me in sight. I don't know what was going on in my mind, either; I certainly had no conscious plan. I wanted to do something to crush these white faces, which were crushing me. I walked for perhaps a block or two until I came to an enormous, glittering, and fashionable restaurant in which I knew not even the intercession of the Virgin would cause me to be served. I pushed through the doors and took the first vacant seat I saw, at a table for two, and waited.

I do not know how long I waited and I rather wonder, until today, what I could possibly have looked like. Whatever I looked like, I frightened the waitress who shortly appeared, and the moment she appeared all of my fury flowed towards her. I hated her for her white face, and for her great, astounded, frightened eyes. I felt that if she found a black man so frightening I would make her fright worth-while.

She did not ask me what I wanted, but repeated, as though she had learned it somewhere, "We don't serve Negroes here." She did not say it with the blunt, derisive hostility to which I had grown so accustomed, but, rather, with a note of apology in her voice, and fear. This made me colder and more murderous than ever. I felt I had to do something with my hands. I wanted her to come close enough for me to get her neck between my hands.

So I pretended not to have understood her, hoping to draw her closer. And she did step a very short step closer, with her pencil poised incongruously over her pad, and repeated the formula: ". . . don't serve Negroes here."

Somehow, with the repetition of that phrase, which was already ringing in my head like a thousand bells of a nightmare, I realized that she would never come any closer and that I would have to strike from a distance. There was nothing on the table but an ordinary watermug half full of water, and I picked this up and hurled it with all my strength at her. She ducked and it missed her and shattered against the mirror behind the bar. And, with that sound, my frozen blood abruptly thawed, I returned from wherever I had been, I *saw*, for the first time, the restaurant, the people with their mouths open, already, as it seemed to me, rising as one man, and I realized what I had done, and where I was, and I was frightened. I rose and began running for the door. A round, potbellied man grabbed me by the nape of the neck just as I reached the doors and began to beat me about the face. I kicked him and got loose and ran into the streets. My friend whispered, "*Run!*" and I ran.

My friend stayed outside the restaurant long enough to misdirect my pursuers and the police, who arrived, he told me, at once. I do not know what I said to him when he came to my room that night. I could not have said much. I felt, in the oddest, most awful way, that I had somehow betrayed him. I lived it over and over and over again, the way one relives an automobile accident after it has happened and one finds oneself alone and safe. I could not get over two facts, both equally difficult for the imagination to grasp, and one was that I could have been murdered. But the other was that I had been ready to commit murder. I saw nothing very clearly but I did see this: that my life, my *real* life, was in danger, and not from anything other people might do but from the hatred I carried in my own heart.

II

I had returned home around the second week in June—in great haste because it seemed that my father's death and my mother's confinement were both but a matter of hours. In the case of my mother, it soon became clear that she had simply made a miscalculation. This had always been her tendency and I don't believe that a single one of us arrived in the world, or has since arrived anywhere else, on time. But none of us dawdled so intolerably about the business of being born as did my baby sister. We sometimes amused ourselves, during those endless, stifling weeks, by picturing the baby sitting within in the safe, warm dark, bitterly regretting the necessity of becoming a part of our chaos and stubbornly putting it off as long as possible. I understood her perfectly and congratulated her on showing such good sense so soon. Death, however, sat as purposefully at my father's bedside as life stirred within my mother's womb and it was harder to understand why he so lingered in that long shadow. It seemed that he had bent, and for a long time, too, all of his energies toward dying. Now death was ready for him but my father held back.

All of Harlem, indeed, seemed to be infected by waiting. I had never before known it to be so violently still. Racial tensions throughout this country were exacerbated during the early years of the war, partly because the labor market brought together hundreds of thousands of ill-prepared people and partly because Negro soldiers, regardless of where they were born, received their military training in the south. What happened in defense plants and army camps had repercussions, naturally, in every Negro ghetto. The situation in Harlem had grown bad enough for clergymen, policemen, educators, politicians, and social workers to assert in one breath that there was no "crime wave" and to offer, in the very next breath, suggestions as to how to combat it. These suggestions always seemed to involve playgrounds, despite the fact that racial skirmishes were occurring in the playgrounds, too. Playground or not, crime wave or not, the Harlem police force had been augmented in March, and the unrest grew—perhaps, in fact, partly as a result of the ghetto's instinctive hatred of policemen. Perhaps the most revealing news item, out of the steady parade of reports of muggings, stabbings, shootings, assaults, gang wars, and accusations of police brutality, is the item concerning six Negro girls who set upon a white girl in the subway because, as they all too accurately put it, she was stepping on their toes. Indeed she was, all over the nation.

I had never before been so aware of policemen, on foot, on horseback, on corners, everywhere, always two by two. Nor had I ever been so aware of small knots of people. They were on stoops and on corners and in doorways, and what was striking about them, I think, was that they did not seem to be talking. Never, when I passed these groups, did the usual sound of a curse or a laugh ring out and neither did there seem to be any hum of gossip. There was certainly, on the other hand, occurring between them communication extraordinarily intense. Another thing that was striking was the unexpected diversity of the people who made up these groups. Usually, for example, one would see a group of sharpies standing on the street corner, jiving the passing chicks; or a group of older men, usually, for some reason, in the vicinity of a barber shop, discussing baseball scores, or the numbers, or making rather chilling observations about women they had known. Women, in a general way, tended to be seen less often together—unless they were church women, or very young girls, or prostitutes met together for an unprofessional instant. But that summer I saw the strangest combinations: large, respectable, churchly matrons standing on the stoops or the corners with their hair tied up, together with a girl in sleazy satin whose face bore the marks of gin and the razor, or heavy-set, abrupt, no-nonsense older men, in company with the most disreputable and fanatical "race" men, or these same "race" men with the sharpies, or these sharpies with the churchly women. Seventh Day Adventists and Methodists and Spiritualists seemed to be hobnobbing with Holyrollers and they were all, alike, entangled with the most flagrant disbelievers; something heavy in their stance seemed to indicate that they had all, incredibly, seen a common vision, and on each face there seemed to be the same strange, bitter shadow.

The churchly women and the matter-of-fact, no-nonsense men had children in the Army. The sleazy girls they talked to had lovers there, the sharpies and the "race" men had friends and brothers there. It would have demanded an unquestioning patriotism, happily as uncommon in this country as it is undesirable, for these people not to have been disturbed by the bitter letters they received, by the newspaper stories they read, not to have been enraged by the posters, then to be found all over New York, which described the Japanese as "yellow-bellied Japs." It was only the "race" men, to be sure, who spoke ceaselessly of being revenged—how this vengeance was to be exacted was not clear—for the indignities and dangers suffered by Negro boys in uniform; but everybody felt a directionless, hopeless bitterness, as well as that panic which can scarcely be suppressed when one knows that a human being one loves is beyond one's reach, and in danger. This helplessness and this gnawing uneasiness does something, at length, to even the toughest mind. Perhaps the best way to sum all this up is to say that the people I knew felt, mainly, a peculiar kind of relief when they knew that their boys were being shipped out of the south, to do battle overseas. It was, perhaps, like feeling that the most dangerous part of a dangerous journey had been passed and that now, even if death should come, it would come with honor and without the complicity of their countrymen. Such a death would be, in short, a fact with which one could hope to live.

It was on the 28th of July, which I believe was a Wednesday, that I visited my father for the first time during his illness and for the last time in his life. The moment I saw him I knew why I had put off this visit so long. I had told my mother that I did not want to see him because I hated him. But this was not true. It was only that I *had* hated him and I wanted to hold on to this hatred. I did not want to look on him as a ruin: it was not a ruin I had hated. I imagine that one of the reasons people cling to their hates so stubbornly is because they sense, once hate is gone, that they will be forced to deal with pain.

We traveled out to him, his older sister and myself, to what seemed to be the very end of a very Long Island. It was hot and dusty and we wrangled, my aunt and I, all the way out, over the fact that I had recently begun to smoke and, as she said, to give myself airs. But I knew that she wrangled with me because she could not bear to face the fact of her brother's dying. Neither could I endure the reality of her despair, her unstated bafflement as to what had happened to her brother's life, and her own. So we wrangled and I smoked and from time to time she fell into a heavy reverie. Covertly, I watched her face, which was the face of an old woman; it had fallen in, the eyes were sunken and lightless; soon she would be dying, too.

In my childhood—it had not been so long ago—I had thought her beautiful. She had been quick-witted and quick-moving and very generous with all the children and each of her visits had been an event. At one time one of my brothers and myself had thought of running away to live with her. Now she could no longer produce out of her handbag some unexpected and yet familiar delight. She made me feel pity and revulsion and fear. It was awful to realize that she no longer caused me to feel affection. The closer we came to the hospital the more querulous she became and at the same time, naturally, grew more dependent on me. Between pity and guilt and fear I began to feel that there was another me trapped in my skull like a jack-in-the-box who might escape my control at any moment and fill the air with screaming.

She began to cry the moment we entered the room and she saw him lying there, all shriveled and still, like a little black monkey. The great, gleaming apparatus which fed him and would have compelled him to be still even if he had been able to move brought to mind, not beneficence, but torture; the tubes entering his arm made me think of pictures I had seen when a child, of Gulliver, tied down by the pygmies on that island. My aunt wept and wept, there was a whistling sound in my father's throat; nothing was said; he could not speak. I wanted to take his hand, to say something. But

I do not know what I could have said, even if he could have heard me. He was not really in that room with us, he had at last really embarked on his journey; and though my aunt told me that he said he was going to meet Jesus, I did not hear anything except that whistling in his throat. The doctor came back and we left, into that unbearable train again, and home. In the morning came the telegram saying that he was dead. Then the house was suddenly full of relatives, friends, hysteria, and confusion and I quickly left my mother and the children to the care of those impressive women, who, in Negro communities at least, automatically appear at times of bereavement armed with lotions, proverbs, and patience, and an ability to cook. I went downtown. By the time I returned, later the same day, my mother had been carried to the hospital and the baby had been born.

III

For my father's funeral I had nothing black to wear and this posed a nagging problem all day long. It was one of those problems, simple, or impossible of solution, to which the mind insanely clings in order to avoid the mind's real trouble. I spent most of that day at the downtown apartment of a girl I knew, celebrating my birthday with whiskey and wondering what to wear that night. When planning a birthday celebration one naturally does not expect that it will be up against competition from a funeral and this girl had anticipated taking me out that night, for a big dinner and a night club afterwards. Sometime during the course of that long day we decided that we would go out anyway, when my father's funeral service was over. I imagine *I* decided it, since, as the funeral hour approached, it became clearer and clearer to me that I would not know what to do with myself when it was over. The girl, stifling her very lively concern as to the possible effects of the whiskey on one of my father's chief mourners, concentrated on being conciliatory and practically helpful. She found a black shirt for me somewhere and ironed it and, dressed in the darkest pants and jacket I owned, and slightly drunk, I made my way to my father's funeral.

The chapel was full, but not packed, and very quiet. There were, mainly, my father's relatives, and his children, and here and there I saw faces I had not seen since childhood, the faces of my father's one-time friends. They were very dark and solemn now, seeming somehow to suggest that they had known all along that something like this would happen. Chief among the mourners was my aunt, who had quarreled with my father all his life; by which I do not mean to suggest that her mourning was insincere or that she had not loved him. I suppose that she was one of the few people in the world who had, and their incessant quarreling proved precisely the strength of the tie that bound them. The only other person in the world, as far as I knew, whose relationship to my father rivaled my aunt's in depth was my mother, who was not there.

It seemed to me, of course, that it was a very long funeral. But it was, if anything, a rather shorter funeral than most, nor, since there were no overwhelming, uncontrollable expressions of grief, could it be called—if I dare to use the word—successful. The minister who preached my father's funeral sermon was one of the few my father had still been seeing as he neared his end. He presented to us in his sermon a man whom none of us had ever seen—a man thoughtful, patient, and forbearing, a Christian inspiration to all who knew him, and a model for his children. And no doubt the children, in their disturbed and guilty state, were almost ready to believe this; he had been remote enough to be anything and, anyway, the shock of the incontrovertible, that it was really our father lying up there in that casket, prepared the mind for anything. His sister moaned and this grief-stricken moaning was taken as corroboration. The other faces held a dark, non-committal thoughtfulness. This was not the man they had known, but they had scarcely expected to be confronted with *him;* this was, in a sense deeper than questions of fact, the man they had not known, and the man they had not known may have been the real one. The real man, whoever he had been, had suffered and now he was dead: this was all that was sure and all that mattered now. Every man in the chapel hoped that when his hour came he, too, would be eulogized, which is to say forgiven, and that all of his lapses, greeds, errors, and strayings from the truth would be invested with coherence and looked upon with charity. This was perhaps the last thing human beings could give each other and it was what they demanded, after all, of the Lord. Only the Lord saw the midnight tears, only He was present when one of His children, moaning and wringing hands, paced up and down the room. When one slapped one's child in anger the recoil in the heart reverberated through heaven and became part of the pain of the universe. And when the children were hungry and sullen and distrustful and one watched them, daily, growing wilder, and further away, and running headlong into danger, it was the Lord who knew what the charged heart endured as the strap was laid to the backside; the Lord alone who knew what one *would* have said if one had had, like the Lord, the gift of the living word. It was the Lord who knew of the impossibility every parent in that room faced: how to prepare the child for the day when the child would be despised and how to *create* in the child—by what means?—a stronger antidote to this poison than one had found for oneself. The avenues, side streets, bars, billiard halls, hospitals, police stations, and even the playgrounds of Harlem—not to mention the houses of correction, the jails, and the morgue—testified to the potency of the poison while remaining silent as to the efficacy of whatever antidote, irresistibly raising the question of whether or not such an antidote existed; raising, which was worse, the question of whether or not an antidote was desirable; perhaps poison should be fought with poison. With these several schisms in the mind and with more terrors in the heart than could be named, it was better not to judge the man who had gone down under an impossible burden. It was better to remember: *Thou knowest this man's fall; but thou knowest not his wrassling.*

While the preacher talked and I watched the children—years of changing their diapers, scrubbing them, slapping them, taking them to school, and scolding them had had the perhaps inevitable result of making me love them, though I am not sure I knew this then—my mind was busily breaking out with a rash of disconnected impressions. Snatches of popular songs, indecent jokes, bits of books I had read, movie sequences, faces, voices, political issues—I thought I was going mad; all these impressions suspended, as it were, in the solution of the faint nausea produced in me by the heat and liquor. For a moment I had the impression that my alcoholic breath, inefficiently disguised with chewing gum, filled the entire chapel. Then someone began singing one of my father's favorite songs and, abruptly, I was with him, sitting on his knee, in the hot, enormous, crowded church which was the first church we attended. It was the Abyssinia Baptist Church on 138th Street. We had not gone there long. With this image, a host of others came. I had forgotten, in the rage of my growing up, how proud my father had been of me when I was little. Apparently, I had had a voice and my father had liked to show me off before the members of the church. I had forgotten what he had looked like when he was pleased but now I remembered that he had always been grinning with pleasure when my solos ended. I even remembered certain expressions on his face when he teased my mother—had he loved her? I would never know. And when had it all begun to change? For now it seemed that he had not always been cruel. I remembered being taken for a haircut and scraping my knee on the footrest of the barber's chair and I remembered my father's face as he soothed my crying and applied the stinging iodine. Then I remembered our fights, fights which had been of the worst possible kind because my technique had been silence.

I remembered the one time in all our life together when we had really spoken to each other.

It was on a Sunday and it must have been shortly before I left home. We were walking, just the two of us, in our usual silence, to or from church. I was in high school and had been doing a lot of writing and I was, at about this time, the editor of the high school magazine. But I had also been a Young Minister and had been preaching from the pulpit. Lately, I had been taking fewer engagements and preached as rarely as possible. It was said in the church, quite truthfully, that I was "cooling off."

My father asked me abruptly, "You'd rather write than preach, wouldn't you?"

I was astonished at his question—because it was a real question. I answered, "Yes."

That was all we said. It was awful to remember that that was all we had *ever* said.

The casket now was opened and the mourners were being led up the aisle to look for the last time on the deceased. The assumption was that the family was too overcome with grief to be allowed to make this journey alone and I watched while my aunt was led to the casket and, muffled in black, and shaking, led back to her seat. I disapproved of forcing the children to look on their dead father, considering that the shock of his death, or, more truthfully, the shock of death as a reality, was already a little more than a child could bear, but my judgment in this matter had been overruled and there they were, bewildered and frightened and very small, being led, one by one, to the casket. But there is also something very gallant about children at such moments. It has something to do with their silence and gravity and with the fact that one cannot help them. Their legs, somehow, seem *exposed,* so that it is at once incredible and terribly clear that their legs are all they have to hold them up.

I had not wanted to go to the casket myself and I certainly had not wished to be led there, but there was no way of avoiding either of these forms. One of the deacons led me up and I looked on my father's face. I cannot say that it looked like him at all. His blackness had been equivocated by powder and there was no suggestion in that casket of what his power had or could have been. He was simply an old man dead, and it was hard to believe that he had ever given anyone either joy or pain. Yet, his life filled that room. Further up the avenue his wife was holding his newborn child. Life and death so close together, and love and hatred, and right and wrong, said something to me which I did not want to hear concerning man, concerning the life of man.

After the funeral, while I was downtown desperately celebrating my birthday, a Negro soldier, in the lobby of the Hotel Braddock, got into a fight with a white policeman over a Negro girl. Negro girls, white policemen, in or out of uniform, and Negro males—in or out of uniform—were part of the furniture of the lobby of the Hotel Braddock and this was certainly not the first time such an incident had occurred. It was destined, however, to receive an unprecedented publicity, for the fight between the policeman and the soldier ended with the shooting of the soldier. Rumor, flowing immediately to the streets outside, stated that the soldier had been shot in the back, an instantaneous and revealing invention, and that the soldier had died protecting a Negro woman. The facts were somewhat different—for example, the soldier had not been shot in the back, and was not dead, and the girl seems to have been as dubious a symbol of womanhood as her white counterpart in Georgia usually is, but no one was interested in the facts. They preferred the invention because this invention expressed and corroborated their hates and fears so perfectly. It is just as well to remember that people are always doing this. Perhaps many of those legends, including Christianity, to which the world clings began their conquest of the world with just some such concerted surrender to distortion. The effect, in Harlem, of this particular legend was like the effect of a lit match in a tin of gasoline. The mob gathered before the doors of the Hotel Braddock simply began to swell and to spread in every direction, and Harlem exploded.

The mob did not cross the ghetto lines. It would have been easy, for example, to have gone over Morningside Park on the west side or to have crossed the Grand Central railroad tracks at 125th Street on the east side, to wreak havoc in white neighborhoods. The mob seems to have been mainly interested in something more potent and real than the white face, that is, in white power, and the principal damage done during the riot of the summer of 1943 was to white business establishments in Harlem. It might have been a far bloodier story, of course, if, at the hour the riot began, these establishments had still been open. From the Hotel Braddock the mob fanned out, east and west along 125th Street, and for the entire length of Lenox, Seventh, and Eighth avenues. Along each of these avenues, and along each major side street—116th, 125th, 135th, and so on—bars, stores, pawnshops, restaurants, even little luncheonettes had been smashed open and entered and looted—looted, it might be added, with more haste than efficiency. The shelves really looked as though a bomb had struck them. Cans of beans and soup and dog food, along with toilet paper, corn flakes, sardines and milk tumbled every which way, and abandoned cash registers and cases of beer leaned crazily out of the splintered windows and were strewn along the avenues. Sheets, blankets, and clothing of every description formed a kind of path, as though people had dropped them while running. I truly had not realized that Harlem *had* so many stores until I saw them all smashed open; the first time the word *wealth* ever entered my mind in relation to Harlem was when I saw it scattered in the streets. But one's first, incongruous impression of plenty was countered immediately by an impression of waste. None of this was doing anybody any good. It would have been better to have left the plate glass as it had been and the goods lying in the stores.

It would have been better, but it would also have been intolerable, for Harlem had needed something to smash. To smash something is the ghetto's chronic need. Most of the time it is the members of the ghetto who smash each other, and themselves. But as long as the ghetto walls are standing there will always come a moment when these outlets do not work. That summer, for example, it was not enough to get into a fight on Lenox Avenue, or curse out one's cronies in the barber shops. If ever, indeed, the violence which fills Harlem's churches, pool halls, and bars erupts outward in a more direct fashion, Harlem and its citizens are likely to vanish in an apocalyptic flood. That this is not likely to happen is due to a great many reasons, most hidden and powerful among them the Negro's real relation to the white American. This relation prohibits, simply, anything as uncomplicated and satisfactory as pure hatred. In order really to hate white people, one has to blot so much out of the mind—and the heart—that this hatred itself becomes an exhausting and self-destructive pose. But this does not mean, on the other hand, that love comes easily: the white world is too powerful, too complacent, too ready with gratuitous humiliation, and, above all, too ignorant and too innocent for that. One is absolutely forced to make perpetual qualifications and one's own reactions are always canceling each other out. It is this, really, which has driven so many people mad, both white and black. One is always in the position of having to decide between amputation and gangrene. Amputation is swift but time may prove that the amputation was not necessary—or one may delay the amputation too long. Gangrene is slow, but it is impossible to be sure that one is reading one's symptoms right. The idea of going through life as a cripple is more than one can bear, and equally unbearable is the risk of swelling up slowly, in agony, with poison. And the trouble, finally, is that the risks are real even if the choices do not exist.

"But as for me and my house," my father had said, "we will serve the Lord." I wondered, as we drove him to his resting place, what this line had meant for him. I had heard him preach it many times. I had preached it once myself, proudly giving it an interpretation different from my father's. Now the whole thing came back to me, as though my father and I were on our way to Sunday school and I were memorizing the golden text: *And if it seem evil unto you to serve the Lord, choose you this day whom you will serve; whether the gods which your fathers served that were on the other side of the flood, or the gods of the Amorites, in whose land ye dwell: but as for me and my house, we will serve the Lord.* I suspected in these familiar lines a meaning which had never been there for me before. All of my father's texts and songs, which I had decided were meaningless, were arranged before me at his death like empty bottles, waiting to hold the meaning which life would give them for me. This was his legacy: nothing is ever escaped. That bleakly memorable morning I hated the unbelievable streets and the Negroes and whites who had, equally, made them that way. But I knew that it was folly, as my father would have said, this bitterness was folly. It was necessary to hold on to the things that mattered. The dead man mattered, the new life mattered; blackness and whiteness did not matter; to believe that they did was to acquiesce in one's own destruction. Hatred, which could destroy so much, never failed to destroy the man who hated and this was an immutable law.

It began to seem that one would have to hold in the mind forever two ideas which seemed to be in opposition. The first idea was acceptance, the acceptance, totally without rancor, of life as it is, and men as they are: in the light of this idea, it goes without saying that injustice is a commonplace. But this did not mean that one could be complacent, for the second idea was of equal power: that one must never, in one's own life, accept these injustices as commonplace but must fight them with all one's strength. This fight begins, however, in the heart and it now had been laid to my charge to keep my own heart free of hatred and despair. This intimation made my heart heavy and, now that my father was irrecoverable, I wished that he had been beside me so that I could have searched his face for the answers which only the future would give me now.

91 Revere Street

Robert Lowell (*American, 1917–*)

In 1924 people still lived in cities. Late that summer, we bought the 91 Revere Street house, looking out on an unbuttoned part of Beacon Hill bounded by the North End slums, though reassuringly only four blocks away from my Grandfather Winslow's brown-pillared house at 18 Chestnut Street. In the decades preceding and following the First World War, old Yankee families had upset expectation by regaining this section of the Hill from the vanguards of the lace-curtain Irish. This was bracing news for my parents in that topsy-turvy era when the Republican Party and what were called "people of the right sort" were no longer dominant in city elections. Still, even in the palmy, laissez-faire '20s, Revere Street refused to be a straightforward, immutable residential fact. From one end to the other, houses kept being sanded down, repainted, or abandoned to the flaking of decay. Houses, changing hands, changed their language and nationality. A few doors to our south the householders spoke "Beacon Hill British" or the flat *nay nay* of the Boston Brahmin. The parents of the children a few doors north spoke mostly in Italian.

My mother felt a horrified giddiness about the adventure of our address. She once said, "We are barely perched on the outer rim of the hub of decency." We were less than fifty yards from Louisburg Square, the cynosure of old historic Boston's plain-spoken, cold roast elite—the Hub of the Hub of the Universe. Fifty yards!

As a naval ensign, Father had done postgraduate work at Harvard. He had also done postgraduate work at M.I.T., preferred the purely scientific college, and condescended to both. In 1924, however, his tone began to change; he now began to speak warmly of

Harvard as his second alma mater. We went to football games at the Harvard Stadium, and one had the feeling that our lives were now being lived in the brutal, fashionable expectancy of the stadium: we had so many downs, so many minutes, and so many yards to go for a winning touchdown. It was just such a winning financial and social advance that my parents promised themselves would follow Father's resignation from the Navy and his acceptance of a sensible job offered him at the Cambridge branch of Lever Brothers' Soap.

The advance was never to come. Father resigned from the service in 1927, but he never had a civilian *career;* he instead had merely twenty-two years of the civilian *life*. Almost immediately he bought a larger and more stylish house; he sold his ascetic, stove-black Hudson and bought a plump brown Buick; later the Buick was exchanged for a high-toned, as-good-as-new Packard with a custom-designed royal blue and mahogany body. Without drama, his earnings more or less decreased from year to year.

But so long as we were on Revere Street, Father tried to come to terms with it and must have often wondered whether he on the whole liked or disliked the neighborhood's lack of side. He was still at this time rather truculently democratic in what might be described as an upper middle-class, naval, and Masonic fashion. He was a mumbler. His opinions were almost morbidly hesitant, but he considered himself a matter-of-fact man of science and had an unspoiled faith in the superior efficiency of northern nations. He modeled his allegiances and humor on the cockney imperialism of Rudyard Kipling's swearing Tommies, who did their job. Autochthonous Boston snobs, such as the Winslows or members of Mother's reading club, were alarmed by the brassy callousness of our naval visitors, who labeled the Italians they met on Revere Street as "grade-A" and "grade-B wops." The Revere Street "grade-B's" were Sicilian Catholics and peddled crummy second-hand furniture on Cambridge Street, not far from the site of Great-great-Grandfather Charles Lowell's disused West Church, praised in an old family folder as "a haven from the Sodom and Gomorrah of Trinitarian orthodoxy and the tyranny of the letter." Revere Street "grade-A's," good North Italians, sold fancy groceries and Colonial heirlooms in their shops near the Public Garden. Still other Italians were Father's familiars; they sold him bootleg Scotch and *vino rosso* in teacups.

The outside of our Revere Street house was a flat red brick surface unvaried by the slightest suggestion of purple panes, delicate bay, or triangular window-cornice—a sheer wall formed by the seamless conjunction of four inseparable façades, all of the same commercial and purgatorial design. Though placed in the heart of Old Boston, it was ageless and artless, an epitome of those "leveler" qualities Mother found most grueling about naval service. 91 Revere Street was mass-produced, *regulation-issue,* and yet struck Boston society as stupidly out of the ordinary, like those white elephants—a mother-of-pearl scout knife or a tea-kettle barometer—which my father used to pick up on sale at an Army-Navy store.

The walls of Father's minute Revere Street den-parlor were bare and white. His bookshelves were bare and white. The den's one adornment was a ten-tube home-assembled battery radio set, whose loud-speaker had the shape and color of a Mexican sombrero. The radio's specialty was getting programs from Australia and New Zealand in the early hours of the morning.

My father's favorite piece of den furniture was his oak and "rhinoceros hide" armchair. It was ostentatiously a masculine, or rather a bachelor's, chair. It had a notched, adjustable back; it was black, cracked, hacked, scratched, splintered, gouged, initialed, gunpowder-charred and tumbler-ringed. It looked like pale tobacco leaves laid on dark tobacco leaves. I doubt if Father, a considerate man, was responsible for any of the marring. The chair dated from his plebe days at the Naval Academy, and had been bought from a shady, shadowy, roaring character, midshipman "Beauty" Burford. Father loved each disfigured inch.

My father had been born two months after his own father's death. At each stage of his life, he was to be forlornly fatherless. He was a deep boy brought up entirely by a mild widowed mother and an intense widowed grandmother. When he was fourteen and a half, he became a deep young midshipman. By the time he graduated from Annapolis, he had a high sense of abstract form, which he beclouded with his humor. He had reached, perhaps, his final mental possibilities. He was deep—not with profundity, but with the dumb depth of one who trusted in statistics and was dubious of personal experience. In his forties, Father's soul went underground: as a civilian he kept his high sense of form, his humor, his accuracy, but this accuracy was henceforth unimportant, recreational, *hors de combat.* His debunking grew myopic; his shyness grew evasive; he argued with a fumbling languor. In the twenty-two years Father lived after he resigned from the Navy, he never again deserted Boston and never became Bostonian. He survived to drift from job to job, to be displaced, to be grimly and literally that old cliché, a fish out of water. He gasped and wheezed with impotent optimism, took on new ideals with each new job, never ingeniously enjoyed his leisure, never even hid his head in the sand.

Mother hated the Navy, hated naval society, naval pay, and the trip-hammer rote of settling and unsettling a house every other year when Father was transferred to a new station or ship. She had been married nine or ten years and still suspected that her husband was savorless, unmasterful, merely considerate. Unmasterful—Father's specialized efficiency lacked utterly the flattering bossiness she so counted on from her father, my Grandfather Winslow. It was not Father's absence on sea-duty that mattered; it was the eroding necessity of moving *with* him, of keeping in step. When he was far away on the Pacific, she had her friends, her parents, a house to herself—Boston! Fully conscious of her uniqueness and normality she basked in the refreshing stimulation of dreams in which she imagined Father as suitably sublimed. She used to describe such a sublime man to me over tea and English muffins. He was Siegfried carried lifeless through the shining air by Brünnhilde to Valhalla, and accompanied by the throb of my Great Aunt Sarah playing his leitmotif in the released manner taught her by the Abbé Liszt. Or Mother's hero dove through the grottoes of the Rhine and slaughtered the homicidal and vulgar dragon coiled about the golden hoard. Mother seemed almost light-headed when she retold the romance of Sarah Bernhardt in *L'Aiglon,* the Eaglet, the weakling! She would speak the word *weakling* with such amused vehemence that I formed a grandiose and false image of L'Aiglon's father, the *big* Napoleon: he was a strong man who scratched under his paunchy little white vest a torso all hair, muscle, and manliness. Instead of the dreams, Mother now had the insipid fatigue of keeping house. Instead of the *Eagle,* she had a twentieth-century naval commander interested in steam, radio, and "the fellows." To avoid naval yards, steam, and "the fellows," Mother had impulsively bought the squalid, impractical Revere Street house. Her marriage daily forced her to squander her subconsciously hoarded energies.

"Weelawaugh, we-ee-eeelawaugh, weelawaugh," shrilled Mother's high voice. *"But-and, but-and, but-and!"* Father's low mumble would drone in answer. Though I couldn't be sure that I had caught the meaning of the words, I followed the sounds as though they were a movie. I felt drenched in my parents' passions.

91 Revere Street was the setting for those arthritic spiritual pains that troubled us for the two years my mother spent in trying to argue my father into resigning from the Navy. When the majestic, hollow boredom of the second year's autumn dwindled to the mean boredom of a second winter, I grew less willing to open my mouth. I bored my parents, they bored me.

"Weelawaugh, we-ee-eelawaugh, weelawaugh!" "But-and, but-and, but-and!"

During the week ends I was at home much of the time. All day I used to look forward to the nights when my bedroom walls would once again vibrate, when I would awake with rapture to the rhythm of my parents arguing, arguing one another to exhaustion. Sometimes, without bathrobe or slippers, I would wriggle out into the cold hall on my belly and ambuscade myself behind the banister. I could often hear actual words. "Yes, yes, yes," Father would mumble. He was "backsliding" and "living in the fool's paradise of habitual retarding and retarded do-nothing inertia." Mother had violently set her heart on the resignation. She was hysterical even in her calm, but like a patient and forbearing strategist, she tried to pretend her neutrality. One night she said with murderous coolness, "Bobby and I are leaving for Papá's." This was an ultimatum to force Father to sign a deed placing the Revere Street house in Mother's name.

I writhed with disappointment on the nights when Mother and Father only lowed harmoniously together like cows, as they criticized Helen Bailey or Admiral De Stahl. Once I heard my mother say, "A *man* must make up his *own* mind. Oh Bob, if you are going to resign, do it *now* so I can at least plan for your son's *survival* and education on a single continent."

About this time I was being sent for my *survival* to Dr. Dane, a Quaker chiropractor with an office on Marlborough Street. Dr. Dane wore an old-fashioned light tan druggist's smock; he smelled like a healthy old-fashioned drugstore. His laboratory was free of intimidating technical equipment, and had only the conservative lay roughness and toughness that was so familiar and disarming to us in my Grandfather Winslow's country study or bedroom. Dr. Dane's rosy hands wrenched my shoulders with tremendous éclat and made me feel a hero; I felt unspeakable joy whenever an awry muscle fell back into serenity. My mother, who had no curiosity or imagination for cranky occultism, trusted Dr. Dane's clean, undrugged manliness—so like home. She believed that chiropractic had cured me of my undiagnosed asthma, which had defeated the expensive specialists.

"A penny for your thoughts, Schopenhauer," my mother would say.

"I am thinking about pennies," I'd answer.

"When *I* was a child I used to love telling Mamá everything I had done," Mother would say.

"But you're not a child," I would answer.

I used to enjoy dawdling and humming "Anchors Aweigh" up Revere Street after a day at school. "Anchors Aweigh," the official Navy song, had originally been the song composed for my father's class. And yet my mind always blanked and seemed to fill with a clammy hollowness when Mother asked prying questions. Like other tongue-tied, difficult children, I dreamed I was a master of cool, stoical repartee. "What have you been doing, Bobby?" Mother would ask. "I haven't," I'd answer. At home I thus saved myself from emotional exhaustion.

At school, however, I was extreme only in my conventional mediocrity, my colorless, distracted manner, which came from restless dreams of being admired. My closest friend was Eric Burckhard, the son of a professor of architecture at Harvard. The Burckhards came from Zurich and were very German, not like Ludendorff, but in the kindly, comical, nineteenth-century manner of Jo's German husband in *Little Men,* or in the manner of the crusading *sturm und drang* liberal scholars in second-year German novels. "Eric's mother and father are *both* called Dr. Burckhard," my mother once said, and indeed there was something endearingly repellent about Mrs. Burckhard with her doctor's degree, her long, unstylish skirts, and her dramatic, dulling blond braids. Strangely the Burckhards' sober continental bourgeois house was without golden mean—everything was either hilariously old Swiss or madly modern. The Frau Doctor Burckhard used to serve midmorning hot chocolate with rosettes of whipped cream, and receive her friends in a long, uncarpeted hall-drawing room with lethal ferns and a yellow beeswaxed hardwood floor shining under a central skylight. On the wall there were large expert photographs of what at a distance appeared to be Mont Blanc—they were in reality views of Frank Lloyd Wright's Japanese hotel.

I admired the Burckhards and felt at home in their house, and these feelings were only intensified when I discovered that my mother was always ill at ease with them. The heartiness, the enlightenment, and the bright, ferny greenhouse atmosphere were too much for her.

Eric and I were too young to care for books or athletics. Neither of our houses had absorbing toys or an elevator to go up and down in. We were inseparable, but I cannot imagine what we talked about. I loved Eric because he was more popular than I and yet absolutely *sui generis* at the Brimmer School. He had a chalk-white face and limp, fine, white-blond hair. He was frail, elbowy, started talking with an enthusiastic Mont Blanc chirp and would flush with bewilderment if interrupted. All the other boys at Brimmer wore little tweed golf suits with knickerbockers, but Eric always arrived in a black suit coat, a Byronic collar, and cuffless gray flannel trousers that almost hid his shoes. The long trousers were replaced on warm days by gray flannel shorts, such as were worn by children still in kindergarten. Eric's unenviable and freakish costumes were too old or too young. He accepted the whims of his parents with a buoyant tranquillity that I found unnatural.

My first and terminating quarrel with Eric was my fault. Eventually almost our whole class at Brimmer had whooping cough, but Eric's seizure was like his long trousers—untimely: he was sick a month too early. For a whole month he was in quarantine and forced to play by himself in a removed corner of the Public Garden. He was certainly conspicuous as he skip-roped with his Swiss nurse under the out-of-the-way Ether Memorial Fountain far from the pond and the swan boats. His parents had decided that this was an excellent opportunity for Eric to brush up on his German, and so the absoluteness of his quarantine was monstrously exaggerated by the fact that child and nurse spoke no English but only a guttural, British-sounding, Swiss German. Round and round and round the Fountain, he played intensely, frailly, obediently, until I began to tease him. Though motioned away by him, I came close. I had attracted some of the most popular Brimmer School boys. For the first time I had gotten favorable attention from several little girls. I came close. I shouted. Was Eric afraid of girls? I imitated his German. *Ein, zwei, drei, BEER.* I imitated Eric's coughing. "He is afraid he will give you whooping cough if he talks or lets you come nearer," the nurse said in her musical Swiss-English voice. I came nearer. Eric flushed, grew white, bent double with coughing. He began to cry, and had to be led away from the Public Garden. For a whole week I routed Eric from the Garden daily, and for two or three days I was a center of interest. "Come see the Lake Geneva spider monkey!" I would shout. I don't know why I couldn't stop. Eric never told his father, I think, but when he recovered we no longer spoke. The breach was so unspoken and intense that our classmates were actually horrified. They even devised a solemn ritual for our reconciliation. We crossed our hearts, mixed spit, mixed blood. The reconciliation was hollow.

My parents' confidences and quarrels stopped each night at ten or eleven o'clock, when my father would hang up his tuxedo, put on his commander's uniform, and take a trolley back to the naval yard at Charlestown. He had just broken in a new car. Like a chauffer, he watched this car, a Hudson, with an informed vigilance, always giving its engine hair-trigger little tinkerings of adjustment or friendship, always fearful lest the black body, unbeautiful as his boiled shirts, should lose its outline and gloss. He drove with flawless, almost instrumental, monotony. Mother, nevertheless, was forever encouraging him to walk or take taxis. She would tell him that his legs were growing vestigial from disuse and remind him of the time a jack had slipped and he had broken his leg while shifting a tire. "Alone and at night," she would say, "an amateur driver is unsafe in a car." Father sighed and obeyed—only, putting on a martyred and penny-saving face, he would keep his self-respect by taking the trolley rather than a taxi. Each night he shifted back into his uniform, but his departures from Revere Street were so furtive that several months passed before I realized what was happening—we had *two* houses! Our second house was the residence in the Naval Yard assigned to the third in command. It was large, had its own flagpole, and screen porches on three levels—yet it was something to be ashamed of. Whatever pomp or distinction its possession might have had for us was destroyed by an eccentric humiliation inflicted on Father by his superior, Admiral De Stahl, the commandant at Charlestown. De Stahl had not been consulted about our buying the 91 Revere Street house. He was outraged, stormed about "flaunting private fortunes in the face of naval tradition," and ordered my father to sleep on bounds at the Yard in the house provided for that purpose.

On our first Revere Street Christmas Eve, the telephone rang in the middle of dinner; it was Admiral De Stahl demanding Father's instant return to the Navy Yard. Soon Father was back in his uniform. In taking leave of my mother and grandparents he was, as was usual with him under pressure, a little evasive and magniloquent. "A woman works from sun to sun," he said, "but a sailor's watch is never done." He compared a naval officer's hours with a doctor's, hinted at surprise maneuvers, and explained away the uncommunicative arrogance of Admiral De Stahl: "The Old Man has to be hush-hush." Later that night, I lay in bed and tried to imagine that my father was leading his engineering force on a surprise maneuver through arctic wastes. A forlorn hope! "Hush-hush, hush-hush," whispered the snowflakes as big as street lamps as they broke on Father—broke and buried. Outside, I heard real people singing carols, shuffling snow off their shoes, opening and shutting doors. I worried at the meaning of a sentence I had heard quoted from the *Boston Evening Transcript:* "On this Christmas Eve, as usual, the whole of Beacon Hill can be expected to become a single old-fashioned open house—the names of mine host the Hill and her guests will read like the contents of the Social Register." I imagined Beacon Hill changed to the snow queen's palace, as vast as the North Pole. My father pressed a cold finger to his lip: "hush-hush," and led his surprise squad of sailors around an altar, but the altar was a tremendous cash register, whose roughened nickel surface was cheaply decorated with trowels, pyramids, and Arabic swirls. A great drawer helplessly chopped back and forth, unable to shut because choked with greenbacks. "Hush-hush!" My father's engineers wound about me with their eyepatches, orange sashes, and curtain-ring earrings, like the Gilbert and Sullivan pirates' chorus. . . . Outside on the streets of Beacon Hill, it was night, it was dismal, it was raining. Something disturbing had befallen the familiar and honorable Salvation Army band; its big drum and accordion were now accompanied by drunken voices howling: *The Old Gray Mare, she ain't what she used to be, when Mary went to milk the cow.* A sound of a bosun's whistle. Women laughing. Someone repeatedly rang our doorbell. I heard my mother talking on the telephone. "Your inebriated sailors have littered my doorstep with the dregs of Scollay Square." There was a gloating panic in her voice that showed she enjoyed the drama of talking to Admiral De Stahl. "Sir," she shrilled, "you have compelled my husband to leave me alone and defenseless on Christmas Eve!" She ran into my bedroom. She hugged me. She said, "Oh Bobby, it's such a comfort to have a man in the house." "I am not a man," I said, "I am a boy."